Nora Roberts is the number one *New York Times* bestselling author of more than 190 novels. With more than 300 million copies of her books in print, and over 150 *New York Times* best-sellers to date, Nora Roberts is indisputably the most celebrated women's fiction writer today.

Become a fan on Facebook at
Nora Roberts and J. D. Robb
and be the first to hear all the latest from Piatkus
about Nora Roberts and J. D. Robb

www.noraroberts.com
www.nora-roberts.co.uk
www.jd-robb.co.uk

By Nora Roberts

Romantic Suspense

Homeport
The Reef
River's End
Carolina Moon
The Villa
Midnight Bayou
Three Fates
Birthright
Northern Lights
Blue Smoke
Montana Sky
Angels Fall
High Noon
Divine Evil
Tribute
Sanctuary
Black Hills
The Search
Chasing Fire

By Nora Roberts

Trilogies and Quartets

The Born In Trilogy:
Born in Fire
Born in Ice
Born in Shame

The Sign of Seven Trilogy:
Blood Brothers
The Hollow
The Pagan Stone

The Bride Quartet:
Vision in White
Bed of Roses
Savour the Moment
Happy Ever After

Chesapeake Bay Quartet:
Sea Swept
Rising Tides
Inner Harbour
Chesapeake Blue

The Key Trilogy:
Key of Light
Key of Knowledge
Key of Valour

In the Garden Trilogy:
Blue Dahlia
Black Rose
Red Lily

The Irish Trilogy:
Jewels of the Sun
Tears of the Moon
Heart of the Sea

The Circle Trilogy:
Morrigan's Cross
Dance of the Gods
Valley of Silence

Three Sisters Island Trilogy:
Dance upon the Air
Heaven and Earth
Face the Fire

The Dream Trilogy:
Daring to Dream
Holding the Dream
Finding the Dream

Nora Roberts also writes the In Death series
using the pseudonym J. D. Robb

Naked in Death
Glory in Death
Immortal in Death
Rapture in Death
Ceremony in Death
Vengeance in Death
Holiday in Death
Conspiracy in Death
Loyalty in Death
Witness in Death
Judgement in Death
Betrayal in Death
Seduction in Death
Reunion in Death
Purity in Death
Portrait in Death
Imitation in Death
Divided in Death
Visions in Death
Survivor in Death
Origin in Death
Memory in Death
Born in Death
Innocent in Death
Creation in Death
Strangers in Death
Salvation in Death
Promises in Death
Kindred in Death
Fantasy in Death
Indulgence in Death
Treachery in Death

NORA ROBERTS OMNIBUS

The Reef
Midnight Bayou

piatkus

PIATKUS

This omnibus edition first published in Great Britain in 2011 by Piatkus
Copyright © Nora Roberts 2011

Previously published separately:
The Reef first published in Great Britain in 1999 by Piatkus Books Ltd
Reprinted 2002 (twice), 2003, 2004, 2005, 2006 (three times), 2007,
2008 (twice), 2009 (twice)
Published in paperback in 2009 by Piatkus
Reprinted 2009, 2010
Copyright © Nora Roberts 1998

Midnight Bayou first published in paperback in Great Britain in 2002
by Piatkus Books
Reprinted 2006, 2007 (twice)
Published in paperback in 2009 by Piatkus
Reprinted 2010 (twice)
Copyright © Nora Roberts 2001

The moral right of the author has been asserted.

A CIP catalogue record for this book
is available from the British Library.

ISBN 978-0-7499-5650-9

Typeset in Bembo by Phoenix Photosetting, Chatham, Kent
Printed and bound in Great Britain by CPI Mackays, Chatham ME5 8TD

Piatkus
An imprint of
Little, Brown Book Group
100 Victoria Embankment
London EC4Y 0DY

An Hachette UK Company
www.hachette.co.uk
www.piatkus.co.uk

The Reef

To Ruth Langan and Marianne Willman,
for the past, the present, and the future

Part One

Past

The present contains nothing more than the past, and what is found in the effect was already in the cause.
—*Henri Bergson*

Prologue

JAMES LASSITER WAS forty years old, a well-built, ruggedly hand-some man in the prime of his life, in the best of health.

In an hour, he'd be dead.

From the deck of the boat, he could see nothing but the clear silky ripple of blue, the luminous greens and deeper browns of the great reef shimmering like islands below the surface of the Coral Sea. Far to the west, the foamy froth and surge of sea surf rose up and crashed against the false shore of coral.

From his stance at the port side, he could watch the shapes and shadows of fish, darting like living arrows through the world he'd been born to share with them.

The coast of Australia was lost in the distance, and there was only the vastness.

The day was perfect, the jewel-clear shimmer of the water, dashed by white facets of light tossed down by the gold flash of sun. The teasing hint of a breeze carried no taste of rain.

Beneath his feet, the deck swayed gently, a cradle on the quiet sea. Wavelets lapped musically against the hull. Below, far below, was treasure waiting to be discovered.

They were mining the wreck of the *Sea Star*, a British merchant ship that had met its doom on the Great Barrier Reef two centuries before. For more than a year, breaking for bad weather, equipment failure and other inconveniences, they had worked, often like dogs, to reap the riches the *Star* had left behind.

There were riches yet, James knew. But his thoughts traveled beyond the *Sea Star*, north of that spectacular and dangerous reef to the balmy waters of the West Indies. To another wreck, to another treasure.

To Angelique's Curse.

He wondered now if it was the richly jeweled amulet that was cursed, or the woman, the witch Angelique, whose power – it was reputed – remained strong in the rubies and diamonds and gold. Legend was that she had worn it, a gift from the husband it was said she murdered, on the day she was burned at the stake.

The idea fascinated him, the woman, the necklace, the legend. The search for it, which he would begin shortly, was taking on a personal twist. James didn't simply want the riches, the glory. He wanted Angelique's Curse, and the legend it carried.

He had been weaned on the hunt, on tales of wrecked ships and the bounty the sea hoarded from them. All of his life, he had dived, and he had dreamed. The dreams had cost him a wife, and given him a son.

James turned from the rail to study the boy. Matthew was nearly sixteen now. He had grown tall, but had yet to fill out. There was potential there, James mused, in the thin frame and ropey muscle. They shared the same dark, unmanageable hair, though the boy refused to have his cut short so that even now as Matthew checked the diving gear, it fell forward to curtain his face.

The face was rawboned, James thought. It had fined down in the last year or two and had lost the childish roundness. An angel face, a waitress had called it once, and had embarrassed the boy into hot cheeks and grimaces.

It had more of the devil in it now, and those blue eyes he'd passed to Matthew were more often hot than cool. The Lassiter temper, the Lassiter luck, James thought with a shake of his head. Tough legacies for a half-grown boy.

One day, he thought, one day soon, he would be able to give his son all the things a father hoped for. The key to it all lay quietly waiting in the tropical seas of the West Indies.

A necklace of rubies and diamonds beyond price, heavy with history, dark with legend, tainted with blood.

Angelique's Curse.

James's mouth twisted into a thin smile. When he had it, the bad luck that had dogged the Lassiters would change. He only had to be patient.

'Hurry up with those tanks, Matthew. The day's wasting.'

Matthew looked up, tossed his hair out of his eyes. The sun was rising behind his father's back, sending light shimmering around him. He looked, Matthew thought, like a king preparing for battle. As always, love and admiration welled up and startled him with its intensity.

'I replaced your pressure gauge. I want to take a look at the old one.'

'You look out for your old man.' James hooked his arm around Matthew's throat for a playful tussle. 'Going to bring you up a fortune today.'

'Let me go down with you. Let me take the morning shift instead of him.'

James suppressed a sigh. Matthew hadn't learned the wisdom of controlling his emotions. Particularly his dislikes. 'You know how the teams work. You and Buck'll dive this afternoon. VanDyke and I take the morning.'

'I don't want you to dive with him.' Matthew shook off his father's friendly arm. 'I heard the two of you arguing last night. He hates you. I could hear it in his voice.'

A mutual feeling, James thought, but winked. 'Partners often disagree. The bottom line here is that VanDyke's putting up most of the money. Let him have his fun, Matthew. For him treasure-hunting's just a hobby for a bored, rich businessman.'

'He can't dive worth shit.' And that, in Matthew's opinion, was the measure of a man.

'He's good enough. Just doesn't have much style at forty feet down.' Tired of the argument, James began to don his wetsuit. 'Buck take a look at the compressor?'

'Yeah, he got the kinks out. Dad—'

'Leave it, Matthew.'

'Just this one day,' Matthew said stubbornly. 'I don't trust that prissy-faced bastard.'

'Your language continues to deteriorate.' Silas VanDyke, elegant and pale despite the hard sun, smiled as he exited the cabin

5

at Matthew's back. It amused him nearly as much as it annoyed him to see the boy sneer. 'Your uncle requires your assistance below, young Matthew.'

'I want to dive with my father today.'

'I'm afraid that would inconvenience me. As you see, I'm already wearing my wetsuit.'

'Matthew.' There was impatient command in James's voice. 'Go see what Buck needs.'

'Yes, sir.' Eyes defiant, he went below decks.

'The boy has a poor attitude and worse manners, Lassiter.'

'The boy hates your guts,' James said cheerfully. 'I'd say he has good instincts.'

'This expedition is coming to an end,' VanDyke shot back. 'And so is my patience and my largesse. Without me, you'll run out of money in a week.'

'Maybe.' James zipped his suit. 'Maybe not.'

'I want the amulet, Lassiter. You know it's down there, and I believe you know where. I want it. I've bought it. I've bought you.'

'You've bought my time, and you've bought my skill. You haven't bought me. Rules of salvage, VanDyke. The man who finds Angelique's Curse owns Angelique's Curse.' And it wouldn't be found, he was sure, on the *Sea Star*. He lifted a hand to VanDyke's chest. 'Now keep out of my face.'

Control, the kind he wielded in board rooms, kept VanDyke from lashing out. He had always won his rounds with patience, with money, and with power. Success in business, he knew, was a simple matter of who maintained control.

'You'll regret trying to double-cross me.' He spoke mildly now, with the faintest hint of a smile curving his lips. 'I promise you.'

'Hell, Silas, I'm enjoying it.' With a quiet chuckle, James stepped inside the cabin. 'You guys reading girlie magazines, or what? Let's get going here.'

Moving quickly, VanDyke dealt with the tanks. It was, very simply, business. When the Lassiters came back on deck, he was hitching on his own gear.

The three of them, VanDyke thought, were pathetically beneath him. Obviously they had forgotten who he was, what he was. He was a VanDyke, a man who had been given or earned or taken whatever he wanted. One who intended to continue to do so, as long as there was profit. Did they think he cared that they tightened their little triangle and excluded him? It was past time he dismissed them and brought in a fresh team.

Buck, he mused, pudgy, already balding, a foolish foil to his handsome brother. Loyal as a mongrel puppy and just as intelligent.

Matthew, young and eager, brash, defiant. A hateful little worm VanDyke would be pleased to squash.

And James, of course, he mused as the three Lassiters stood together, sharing idle conversation. Tough and more canny than VanDyke had supposed. More than the simple tool he had expected. The man thought he had outwitted Silas VanDyke.

James Lassiter thought he would find and own Angelique's Curse, the amulet of power, of legend. Worn by a witch, coveted by many. And that made him a fool. VanDyke had invested in it, time, money, and effort, and Silas VanDyke never made poor investments.

'There's going to be good hunting today.' James strapped on his tanks. 'I can smell it. Silas?'

'Right with you.'

James secured his weight belt, adjusted his mask and rolled into the water.

'Dad, wait—'

But James just saluted and disappeared under the surface.

The world was silent and stunning. The drenching blue was broken by fingers of sunlight that stabbed through the surface and shimmered clear white. Caves and castles of coral spread out to form secret worlds.

A reef shark, eyes bored and black, gave a twist of its body and slid through the water and away.

More at home here than in the air, James dived deep with VanDyke at his heels. The wreck was already well exposed, trenches dug around it and mined of treasure. Coral claimed the shattered bow and turned the wood into a fantasy of color and shape that seemed studded with amethyst, emerald, ruby.

This was the living treasure, the miracle of art created by seawater and sun.

It was, as always, a pleasure to see it.

When they began to work, James's sense of well-being increased. The Lassiter luck was behind him, he thought dreamily. He would soon be rich, famous. He smiled to himself. After all, he'd stumbled onto the clue, he'd spent days and hours researching and piecing the trail of the amulet together.

7

He could even feel a little sorry for that asshole VanDyke, since it would be the Lassiters who brought her up, from other waters, on their own expedition.

He caught himself reaching out to stroke a spine of coral as though it were a cat.

He shook his head, but couldn't clear it. The alarm bell sounded in one part of his brain, far off and dim. But he was an experienced diver and recognized the signs. He'd had a brush or two with nitrogen narcosis before. Never at such a shallow depth, he thought dimly. They were well shy of a hundred feet.

Regardless, he tapped his tanks. VanDyke was already watching him, eyes cool and assessing behind his mask. James signaled to surface. When VanDyke pulled him back, signaled toward the wreck, he was only mildly confused. Up, he signaled again, and again VanDyke restrained him.

He didn't panic. James wasn't a man to panic easily. He knew he'd been sabotaged, though his mind was too muddled to calculate how. VanDyke was an amateur in this world, he reminded himself, didn't realize the extent of the danger. So he would have to show him. His eyes narrowed with purpose. He swung out, barely missing a grip on VanDyke's airhose.

The underwater struggle was slow, determined, eerily silent. Fish scattered like colorful silks, then gathered again to watch the drama of predator and prey. James could feel himself slipping, the dizziness, disorientation as the nitrogen pumped into him. He fought it, managed to kick another ten feet toward the surface.

Then wondered why he'd ever wanted to leave. He began to laugh, the bubbles bursting out and speeding high as the rapture claimed him. He embraced VanDyke in a kind of slow whirling dance, to share his delight. It was so beautiful here in the gilded blue light with gems and jewels of a thousand impossible colors waiting, just waiting to be plucked.

He'd been born to dive the depths.

Soon, James Lassiter's merriment would slide toward unconsciousness. And a quiet, comforting death.

VanDyke reached out as James began to flounder. The lack of coordination was only one more symptom. One of the last. VanDyke's sweeping grab pulled the airhose free. James blinked in bemusement as he drowned.

Chapter One

TREASURE. GOLD DOUBLOONS and pieces of eight. With luck, they could be plucked from the seabed as easily as peaches from a tree. Or so, Tate thought as she dived, her father said.

She knew it took a great deal more than luck, as ten years of searching had already proven. It took money and time and exhausting effort. It took skill and months of research and equipment.

But as she swam toward her father through the crystal blue Caribbean, she was more than willing to play the game.

It wasn't a hardship to spend the summer of her twentieth year diving off the coast of St. Kitts, skimming through gloriously warm water among brilliantly hued fish and sculptures of rainbow coral. Each dive was its own anticipation. What might lie beneath that white sand, hidden among the fans and sea grass, buried under the cleverly twisted formations of coral?

It wasn't the treasure, she knew. It was the hunt.

And occasionally, you did get lucky.

She remembered very well the first time she had lifted a silver spoon from its bed of silt. The shock and the thrill of holding that blackened cup in her fingers, wondering who had used it to scoop up broth. A captain perhaps of some rich galleon. Or the captain's lady.

And the time her mother had been cheerfully hacking away at a hunk of conglomerate, the chunk of material formed by centuries of chemical reactions under the sea. The sound of her squeal, then the bray of delighted laughter when Marla Beaumont had unearthed a gold ring.

The occasional luck allowed the Beaumonts to spend several months a year hunting for more. For more luck, and more treasure.

As they swam side by side, Raymond Beaumont tapped his daughter's arm, pointed. Together they watched a sea turtle paddle lazily.

The laugh in her father's eyes said everything. He had worked hard all of his life, and was now reaping the rewards. For Tate, a moment like this was as good as gold.

They swam together, bonded by a love of the sea, the silence, the colors. A school of sergeant majors streaked by, their black and gold stripes gleaming. For no more than the joy of it, Tate did a slow roll and watched the sunlight strike the surface overhead. The freedom of it had a laugh gurgling out in a spray of bubbles that startled a curious grouper.

She dived deeper, following her father's strong kicks. The sand could hold secrets. Any mound could be a plank of worm-eaten wood from a Spanish galleon. That dark patch could blanket a pirate's cache of silver. She reminded herself to pay attention, not to the sea fans or hunks of coral, but to the signs of sunken treasure.

They were here in the balmy waters of the West Indies, searching for every treasure hunter's dream. A virgin wreck reputed to hold a king's treasure. This, their first dive, was to acquaint themselves with the territory they had so meticulously researched through books, maps and charts. They would test the currents, gauge the tides. And maybe – just maybe – get lucky.

Aiming toward a hillock of sand, she began to fan briskly. Her father had taught her this simple method of excavating sand when Tate had delighted him by her boundless interest in his new hobby of scuba diving.

10

Over the years, he'd taught her many other things. A respect for the sea and what lived there. And what lay there, hidden. Her fondest hope was to one day discover something, for him.

She glanced toward him now, watched the way he examined a low ridge of coral. However much he dreamed of treasure made by man, Raymond Beaumont loved the treasures made by the sea.

Finding nothing in the hillock, Tate moved off in pursuit of a pretty striped shell. Out of the corner of her eyes, she caught the blur of a dark shape coming toward her, swift and silent. Tate's first and frozen thought was shark, and her heart stumbled. She turned, as she had been taught, one hand reaching for her diver's knife, and prepared to defend herself and her father.

The shape became a diver. Sleek and fast as a shark, perhaps, but a man. Her breath whooshed out in a stream of bubbles before she remembered to regulate it. The diver signaled to her, then to the man swimming in his wake.

Tate found herself face mask to face mask with a recklessly grinning face, eyes as blue as the sea around them. Dark hair streamed in the current. She could see he was laughing at her, undoubtedly having guessed her reaction to the unexpected company. He held his hands up, a gesture of peace, until she sheathed her knife. Then he winked and sent a fluid salute toward Ray.

As silent greetings were exchanged, Tate studied the newcomers. Their equipment was good, and included those necessary items of the treasure seeker. The goody bag, the knife, the wrist compass and diver's watch. The first man was young, lean in his black wetsuit. His gesturing hands were wide-palmed, long-fingered, and carried the nicks and scars of a veteran hunter.

The second man was bald, thick in the middle, but as agile as a fish in his undersea movements. Tate could see he was reaching some sort of tacit agreement with her father. She wanted to protest. This was their spot. After all, they'd been there first.

But she could do no more than frown as her father curled his fingers into an 'okay' sign. The four of them spread out to explore.

Tate went back to another mound to fan. Her father's research indicated that four ships of the Spanish fleet had gone down north of Nevis and St. Kitts during the hurricane of July 11, 1733. Two, the *San Cristobal* and the *Vaca*, had been discovered and salvaged years earlier, broken on the reefs near Dieppe Bay. This left, undiscovered and untouched, the *Santa Marguerite* and the *Isabella*.

Documents and manifests boasted that these ships carried much more than cargoes of sugar from the islands. There were jewels and porcelain and more than ten million pesos of gold and silver. In addition, if true to the custom of the day, there would be the hoards secreted by the passengers and seamen.

Both wrecks would be very rich indeed. More than that, discovery would be one of the major finds of the century.

Finding nothing, Tate moved on, bearing north. The competition from the other divers caused her to keep her eyes and her instincts sharp. A school of gem-bright fish speared around her in a perfect vee, a slice of color within color. Delighted, she swam through their bubbles.

Competition or not, she would always enjoy the small things. She explored tirelessly, fanning sand and studying fish with equal enthusiasm.

It looked like a rock at first glance. Still, training had her swimming toward it. She was no more than a yard away when something streaked by her. She saw with faint irritation that scarred, long-fingered hand reach down and close over the rock.

Jerk, she thought, and was about to turn away when she saw him work it free. Not a rock at all, but the crusted handle of a sword that he drew from the scabbard of the sea. Grinning around his mouthpiece, he hefted it.

He had the nerve to salute her with it, cutting a swatch through the water. As he headed up, Tate went after him. They broke the surface in tandem.

She spit out her mouthpiece. 'I saw it first.'

'I don't think so.' Still grinning, he levered up his face mask. 'Anyway, you were slow, and I wasn't. Finders keepers.'

'Rules of salvage,' she said, struggling for calm. 'You were in my space.'

'The way I see it, you were in mine. Better luck next time.'

'Tate, honey.' From the deck of the *Adventure*, Marla Beaumont waved her hands and called out. 'Lunch is ready. Invite your friend and come aboard.'

'Don't mind if I do.' In a few powerful strokes, he was at the stern of the *Adventure*. The sword hit the deck with a clatter, his flippers followed.

Cursing the poor beginning to what had promised to be a wonderful summer, Tate headed in. Ignoring his gallantly offered hand, she hauled herself in just as her father and the other diver broke the surface.

'Nice meeting you.' He dragged a hand through his dripping hair and smiled charmingly at Marla. 'Matthew Lassiter.'

'Marla Beaumont. Welcome aboard.' Tate's mother beamed at Matthew from under the wide brim of her flowered sunhat. She was a striking woman, with porcelain skin and a willowy frame beneath loose and flowing shirt and slacks. She tipped down her dark glasses in greeting.

'I see you've met my daughter, Tate, and my husband, Ray.'

'In a manner of speaking.' Matthew unhooked his weight belt, set it and his mask aside. 'Nice rig here.'

'Oh yes, thank you.' Marla looked proudly around the deck. She wasn't a fan of housework, but there was nothing she liked better than keeping the *Adventure* spit and polished. 'And that's your boat there.' She gestured off the bow. 'The *Sea Devil*.'

Tate snorted at the name. It was certainly apt, she thought, for the man, and the boat. Unlike the *Adventure*, the *Sea Devil* didn't gleam. The old fishing boat badly needed painting. At a distance, it looked like little more than a tub floating on the brilliant platter of the sea.

'Nothing fancy,' Matthew was saying, 'but she runs.' He walked over to offer a hand to the other divers.

'Good eye, boy.' Buck Lassiter slapped Matthew on the back. 'This boy was born with the knack,' he said to Ray in a voice as rough as broken glass, then belatedly held out a hand. 'Buck Lassiter, my nephew, Matthew.'

Ignoring the introductions making their way around the deck, Tate stowed her equipment, then tugged out of her wetsuit. While the others admired the sword, she ducked into the deckhouse and cut through to her cabin.

It wasn't anything unusual, she supposed as she found an oversized T-shirt. Her parents were always making friends with strangers, inviting them onboard, fixing them meals. Her father had simply never developed the wary and suspicious manner of a veteran treasure hunter. Instead her parents shimmered with Southern hospitality.

Normally she found the trait endearing. She only wished they would be a little choosy.

She heard her father offer cheerful congratulations to Matthew on his find, and gritted her teeth.

Damn it, she'd seen it first.

Sulking, Matthew decided as he offered the sword to Ray for examination. A peculiarly female trait. And there was no doubt the little redhead was female. Her copper-toned hair might be cut short as a boy's, but she'd certainly filled out that excuse for a bikini just fine.

Pretty enough, too, he mused. Her face might have been all angles, with cheekbones sharp enough to slice a man's exploring finger, but she had big, delicious green eyes. Eyes, he recalled, that had shot prickly little darts at him in the water, and out.

That only made annoying her more interesting.

Since they were going to be diving in the same pool for a while, he might as well enjoy himself.

He was sitting cross-legged on the forward sundeck when Tate came back out. She gave him a quick glance, having nearly talked herself out of the sulks. His skin was bronzed, and against his chest winked a silver piece of eight hanging from a chain. She wanted to ask him about it, to hear where he'd found it, and how.

But he was smirking at her. Manners, pride and curiosity collided with a wall that kept her unnaturally silent as conversation flowed around her.

Matthew bit into one of Marla's generous ham sandwiches.

'Terrific, Mrs. Beaumont. A lot better than the swill Buck and I are used to.'

'You have some more of this potato salad.' Flattered, she heaped a mound on his paper plate. 'And it's Marla, dear. Tate, you come on and get yourself some lunch.'

'Tate.' Matthew squinted against the sun as he studied her. 'Unusual name.'

'Marla's maiden name.' Ray slipped an arm over his wife's shoulders. He sat in wet bathing trunks, enjoying the warmth and company. His silvered hair danced in the light breeze. 'Tate here's been diving since she was pint-sized. Couldn't ask for a better partner. Marla loves the sea, loves to sail, but she barely swims a stroke.'

With a chuckle, Marla refilled tall glasses of iced tea. 'I like looking at the water. Being in it's something different altogether.' She sat back placidly with her drink. 'Once it gets past my knees, I just panic. I always wonder if I drowned in a former life. So for this one, I'm happy tending the boat.'

'And a fine one she is.' Buck had already assessed the *Adventure*. A tidy thirty-eight footer, teak decking, fancy brightwork. He'd guess she carried two staterooms, a full galley. Without his prescription face mask, he could still make out the massive windows of the pilothouse. He'd liked to have taken his fingers for a walk through the engine and control station.

A look around later was in order, after he had his glasses. Even without them, he calculated that the diamond on Marla's finger was a good five carats, and the gold circle on her right hand was antique.

He smelled money.

'So, Ray . . .' Casually, he tipped back his glass. 'Matthew and me, we've been diving around here for the past few weeks. Haven't seen you.'

'First dive today. We sailed down from North Carolina, started out the day Tate finished her spring semester.'

College girl. Matthew took a hard swallow of cold tea. Jesus. He deliberately turned his gaze away from her legs and concentrated on his lunch. All bets were definitely off, he decided. He was nearly twenty-five and didn't mess with snotty college kids.

'We're going to spend the summer here,' Ray went on. 'Possibly longer. Last winter, we dived off the coast of Mexico a few weeks. Couple of good wrecks there, but mostly played out. We managed to bring up a thing or two though. Some nice pottery, some clay pipes.'

'And those lovely perfume bottles,' Marla put in.

'Been at it awhile, then,' Buck prompted.

'Ten years.' Ray's eyes shone. 'Fifteen since the first time I went down.' He leaned forward, hunter to hunter. 'Friend of mine talked me into scuba lessons. After I'd certified, I went with him to Diamond Shoals. Only took one dive to hook me.'

'Now he spends every free minute diving, planning a dive or talking about the last dive.' Marla let out her lusty laugh. Her eyes, the same rich green as her daughter's, danced. 'So I learned how to handle a boat.'

'Me, I've been hunting more than forty years.' Buck scooped up the last of his potato salad. He hadn't eaten so well in more than a month. 'In the blood. My father was the same. We salvaged off the coast of Florida, before the government got so tight-assed. Me, my father and my brother. The Lassiters.'

'Yes, of course.' Ray slapped a hand on his knee. 'I've read about you. Your father was Big Matt Lassiter. Found the *El Diablo* off Conch Key in 'sixty-four.'

''Sixty-three,' Buck corrected, with a grin. 'Found it, and the fortune she held. The kind of gold a man dreams of, jewels, ingots of silver. I held in my hand a gold chain with a figure of a dragon. A fucking gold dragon,' he said, then stopped, flushed. 'Beg pardon, ma'am.'

'No need.' Fascinated with the image, Marla urged another sandwich on him. 'What was it like?'

'Like nothing you can imagine.' At ease again, Buck chomped into ham. 'There were rubies for its eyes, emeralds in its tail.' Bitterly, he looked down at his hands now and found them empty. 'It was worth five fortunes.'

Caught up in the wonder, Ray stared. 'Yes. I've seen pictures of it. Diablo's Dragon. You brought it up. Extraordinary.'

'The state closed in,' Buck continued. 'Kept us in court for years. Claimed the three-mile limit started at the end of the reef, not at shore. Bastards bled us dry before it was done. In the end they took, and we lost. No better than pirates,' he said and finished off his drink.

'How terrible for you,' Marla murmured. 'To have done all that, discovered all that, only to have it taken.'

'Broke the old man's heart. Never did dive again.' Buck moved his shoulders. 'Well, there are other wrecks. Other treasures.' Buck judged his man, and gambled. 'Like the *Santa Marguerite*, the *Isabella*.'

'Yes, they're here.' Ray met Buck's eye steadily. 'I'm sure of it.'

'Could be.' Matthew picked up the sword, turned it over in his hands. 'Or it could be that both of them were swept out to sea. There's no record of survivors. Only two ships crashed on the reef.'

Ray lifted a finger. 'Ah, but witnesses of the day claim they saw the *Isabella* and the *Santa Marguerite* go down. Survivors from the other ships saw the waves rise and scuttle them.'

Matthew lifted his gaze to Ray's, nodded. 'Maybe.'

'Matthew's a cynic,' Buck commented. 'Keeps me level. I'm going to tell you something, Ray.' He leaned forward, pale blue eyes keen. 'I've been doing research of my own. Five years on and off. Three years ago, the boy and I spent better than six months combing these waters – mostly the two-mile stretch between St. Kitts and Nevis and the peninsula area. We found this, we found that, but we didn't find those two ships. But I know they're here.'

'Well, now.' Ray tugged on his bottom lip, a gesture that Tate knew meant he was considering. 'I think you were looking in the wrong spot, Buck. Not that I want to say I'd know more about it. The ships took off from Nevis, but from what I've been able to piece together, the two lost wrecks made it farther north, just past the tip of St. Kitts before they broke.'

Buck's lips curved. 'I figure the same. It's a big sea, Ray.' He flicked a glance toward Matthew and was rewarded with a careless shrug. 'I've got forty years' experience, and the boy's been diving since he could walk. What I don't have is financial backing.'

As a man who had worked his way up to CEO of a top brokerage firm before his early retirement, Ray knew a deal when it was placed on the table. 'You're looking for a partnership, Buck. We'd have to talk about that. Discuss terms, percentages.' Rising, Ray flashed a smile. 'Why don't we step into my office?'

'Well, then.' Marla smiled as her husband and Buck stepped into the deckhouse. 'I think I'm going to sit in the shade and nap over my book. You children entertain yourselves.' She moved off under a striped awning and settled down with her iced tea and a paperback novel.

'I guess I'll go over and clean up my booty.' Matthew reached for a large plastic bag. 'Mind if I borrow this?' Without waiting for a response, he loaded his gear into it, then hefted his tanks. 'Want to give me a hand?'

'No.'

He only lifted a brow. 'I figured you might want to see how this cleans up.' He gestured with the sword, waited to see if her curiosity would overpower her irritation. He didn't wait long.

With a mutter, she snatched the plastic bag and took it down the ladder to the swim step and over the side with her.

The *Sea Devil* looked worse close up. Tate judged its sway in the current expertly and hauled herself over the rail. She caught a faint whiff of fish.

Gear was carefully stowed and secured. But the deck needed washing as much as it needed painting. The windows on the tiny wheelhouse where a hammock swung were smudged and smeared with salt and smoke. A couple of overturned buckets, and a second hammock, served as seats.

'It's not the *Queen Mary*.' Matthew stored his tanks. 'But it's not the *Titanic* either. She ain't pretty, but she's seaworthy.'

He took the bag from her and stored his wetsuit in a large plastic garbage can. 'Want a drink?'

Tate took another slow look around. 'Got anything sterilized?'

He flipped open the lid of an ice chest, fished out a Pepsi. Tate caught it on the fly and sat down on a bucket. 'You're living on board.'

'That's right.' He went into the wheelhouse. When she heard him rattling around, she reached over to stroke the sword he'd laid across the other bucket.

Had it graced the belt of some Spanish captain with lace at his cuffs and recklessness in his soul? Had he killed buccaneers with it, or worn it for style? Perhaps he had gripped it in a white-knuckled hand as the wind and the waves had battered his ship.

And no one since then had felt its weight.

She looked up, saw Matthew standing at the wheelhouse door watching her. Furiously embarrassed, Tate snatched her hand back, took a casual drink from her Pepsi.

'We have a sword at home,' she said evenly. 'Sixteenth century.' She didn't add that they had only the hilt, and that it was broken.

'Good for you.' He took the sword, settled with it on the deck. He was already regretting the impulsive invitation. It didn't do much good for him to keep repeating to himself that she was too young. Not with her T-shirt wet and molded against her, and those creamy, just sun-kissed legs looking longer than they had a right to. And that voice – half whiskey, half prim lemonade – didn't belong to a child, but to a woman. Or it should have.

She frowned, watching him patiently working on the corrosion. She hadn't expected those scarred, rough-looking hands to be patient.

'Why do you want partners?'

He didn't look up. 'Didn't say I did.'

'But your uncle—'

'That's Buck.' Matthew lifted a shoulder. 'He handles the business.'

She propped her elbows on her knees, her chin in the heels of her hands. 'What do you handle?'

He glanced up then, and his eyes, restless despite the patience of his hands, clashed with hers. 'The hunt.'

She understood that, exactly, and smiled at him with an eagerness that ignored the sword between them. 'It's wonderful, isn't it? Thinking about what could be there, and that you might be the one to find it. Where did you find the coin?' At his baffled look, she grinned and reached out to touch the disk of silver at his chest. 'The piece of eight.'

'My first real salvage dive,' he told her, wishing she didn't look so appealingly fresh and friendly. 'California. We lived there for a while. What are you doing diving for treasure instead of driving some college boy nuts?'

Tate tossed her head and tried her hand at sophistication. 'Boys are easy,' she drawled, and slid down to sit on the deck across from him. 'I like challenges.'

The quick twist in his gut warned him. 'Careful, little girl,' he murmured.

'I'm twenty,' she said with all the frigid pride of burgeoning womanhood. Or she would be, she amended, by summer's end. 'Why are you out here diving for treasure instead of working for a living?'

Now he grinned. 'Because I'm good. If you'd been better, you'd have this, and I wouldn't.'

Rather than dignify that with a response, she took another sip of Pepsi. 'Why isn't your father along? Has he given up diving?'

'In a manner of speaking. He's dead.'

'Oh. I'm sorry.'

'Nine years ago,' Matthew continued, and kept cleaning the sword. 'We were doing some hunting off of Australia.'

'A diving accident?'

19

'No. He was too good to have an accident.' He picked up the can she'd set down, took a swallow. 'He was murdered.'

It took Tate a moment. Matthew had spoken so matter-of-factly that the word 'murder' didn't register. 'My God, how—'

'I don't know, for sure.' Nor did he know why he had told her. 'He went down alive; we brought him up dead. Hand me that rag.'

'But—'

'That was the end of it,' he said and reached for the rag himself. 'No use dwelling on the past.'

She had an urge to lay a hand on his scarred one, but judged, correctly, that he'd snap it off at the wrist. 'An odd statement from a treasure hunter.'

'Babe, it's what it brings you now that counts. And this ain't bad.'

Distracted, she looked back down at the hilt. As Matthew rubbed, she began to see the gleam. 'Silver,' she murmured. 'It's silver. A mark of rank. I knew it.'

'It's a nice piece.'

Forgetting everything but the find, she leaned closer, let her finger-tip skim along the gleam. 'I think it's eighteenth-century.'

His eyes smiled. 'Do you?'

'I'm majoring in marine archeology.' She gave her bangs an impatient push. 'It could have belonged to the captain.'

'Or any other officer,' Matthew said dryly. 'But it'll keep me in beer and shrimp for a while.'

Stunned, she jerked back. 'You're going to sell it? You're just going to sell it? For money?'

'I'm not going to sell it for clamshells.'

'But don't you want to know where it came from, who it came from?'

'Not particularly.' He turned the cleaned portion of the hilt toward the sun, watched it glint in the light. 'There's an antique dealer on St. Bart's who'll give me a square deal.'

'That's horrible. That's . . .' She searched for the worst insult she could imagine. 'Ignorant.' In a flash, she was on her feet. 'To just sell it that way. For all you know, it may have belonged to the captain of the *Isabella* or the *Santa Marguerite*. That would be a historic find. It could belong in a museum.'

Amateurs, Matthew thought in disgust. 'It belongs where I put it.' He rose fluidly. 'I found it.'

Her heart stuttered at the thought of it wasting away in some dusty antique shop, or worse, being bought by some careless tourist who would hang it on the wall of his den.

'I'll give you a hundred dollars for it.'

His grin flashed. 'Red, I could get more than that by melting down the hilt.'

She paled at the thought. 'You wouldn't do that. You couldn't.' When he only cocked his head, she bit her lip. The stereo system she envisioned gracing her college dorm room would have to wait. 'Two hundred then. It's all I have saved.'

'I'll take my chances on St. Bart's.'

Color flooded back into her cheeks. 'You're nothing but an opportunist.'

'You're right. And you're an idealist.' He smiled as she stood in front of him, hands fisted, eyes fired. Over her shoulder, he caught movement on the deck of the *Adventure*. 'And for better or worse, Red, it looks like we're partners.'

'Over my dead body.'

He took her by the shoulders. For one startled minute, she thought he meant to heave her overboard. But he simply turned her until she faced her own boat.

Her heart sank as she watched her father and Buck Lassiter shake hands.

Chapter Two

A BRILLIANT SUNSET poured gold and pink across the sky and melted into the sea. The glory was followed by the finger-snap twilight so usual in the tropics. Over the calm water came the scratchy sound of a portable radio aboard the *Sea Devil* that did little justice to the bouncy reggae beat. The air might have been redolent with the scent of sautéing fish, but Tate's mood was foul.

'I don't see why we need partners.' Tate propped her elbows on the narrow table in the galley and frowned at her mother's back.

'Your father took a real shine to Buck.' Marla sprinkled crushed rosemary into the pan. 'It's good for him to have a man near his own age to pal around with.'

'He has us,' Tate grumbled.

'Of course he has.' Marla smiled over her shoulder. 'But men need men, honey. They've just got to spit and belch now and again.'

Tate snorted at the idea of her impeccably mannered father doing either. 'The point is we don't know anything about them. I mean, they just showed up in our space.' She was still smarting over the sword. 'Dad spent months researching these wrecks. Why should we trust the Lassiters?'

'Because they're Lassiters,' Ray said as he swung into the galley. Bending over, he planted a noisy kiss on the top of Tate's head. 'Our girl's got a suspicious nature, Marla.' He winked at his wife, then because it was his turn for galley duty, began to set the table. 'That's a good thing, to a point. It's not smart to believe everything you see, everything you hear. But sometimes you've got to go with the gut. Mine tells me the Lassiters are just what we need to round out this little adventure.'

'How?' Tate propped her chin on her fist. 'Matthew Lassiter is arrogant and shortsighted and–'

'Young.' Ray finished with a twinkle in his eye. 'Marla, that smells wonderful.' He slipped his arms around her waist and nuzzled the back of her neck. She smelled of suntan lotion and Chanel.

'Then let's sit down and see how it tastes.'

But Tate wasn't willing to let the matter drop. 'Dad, do you know what he plans to do with that sword? He's just going to sell it to some dealer.'

Ray sat and pursed his lips. 'Most salvagers sell their booty, honey. That's how they make a living.'

'Well, that's fine.' Tate took the platter her mother offered automatically and chose her portion. 'But it should be dated and assessed first. He doesn't even care what it is or who it belonged to. To him it's just something to trade for a case of beer.'

'That's a shame.' Marla sighed as Ray poured dinner wine into her glass. 'And I know how you feel, honey. The Tates have always been defenders of history.'

'And the Beaumonts,' her husband put in. 'It's the Southern way. You have a point, Tate.' Ray gestured with his fork. 'And I sympathize. But I also understand Matthew's side of it. The quick turnaround, the quick profit for his efforts. If his grandfather had taken that route, he'd have died a rich man. Instead, he chose to share his discovery and ended up with nothing.'

'There's a middle ground,' Tate insisted.

'Not for some. But I believe Buck and I found it. If we find the *Isabella* or the *Santa Marguerite*, we'll apply for a lease, if we're not outside the limit. Regardless, we'll share what we salvage with the government of St. Kitts and Nevis, a term he agreed to reluctantly.' Ray lifted his glass, eyed the wine. 'He agreed to it because we have something he needs.'

'What do we have?' Tate wanted to know.

'We have a strong enough financial base to continue this operation for some time with or without results. We can afford the time, as we agreed you could defer the upcoming fall semester. And if it becomes an issue, we can afford the equipment needed for an extensive salvage operation.'

'So, they're using us.' Exasperated, Tate pushed her plate aside. 'That's my point, Dad.'

'In a partnership, one-half must have use of the other.'

Far from convinced, Tate rose to pour herself a glass of fresh lemonade. In theory, she wasn't against partnership. From an early age, she'd been taught the value of teamwork. It was this specific team she worried over. 'And what are they bringing into this partnership?'

'In the first place, they're professionals. We're amateurs.' Ray waved a hand as Tate started to protest. 'However much I like to dream otherwise, I've never discovered a wreck, only explored those found and salvaged by others. Oh, we've been lucky a few times.' He picked up Marla's hand, ran a thumb around the gold ring she wore. 'Brought up trinkets others have overlooked. Since my first dive, I've dreamed of finding an undiscovered ship.'

'And you will,' Marla claimed with undiluted faith.

'This could be the one.' Tate dragged a hand through her hair. As much as she loved her parents, their lack of practicality baffled her. 'Dad, all the research you've done, the archives, the manifests, the letters. The way you worked on the records of the storm, the tides, everything. You've put so much work into this.'

'I have,' he agreed. 'And because of that, I'm very interested that a great deal of Buck's research aligns with mine. I can learn so much from him. Do you know he worked for three years in the North Atlantic, in depths of five hundred feet and more? Frigid water, dark water. He's salvaged in mud, in coral, in the feeding area of shark. Imagine it.'

Tate could see he was, the way his eyes unfocused, how his lips curved with dreams. With a sigh, she set a hand on his shoulder. 'Dad, just because he's had more experience—'

'A lifetime more.' Ray reached back, patted her hand. 'That's what he brings to us. Experience, perseverance, the mind of a hunter. And something as basic as manpower. Two teams, Tate, are more efficient than one.' He paused. 'Tate, it's important to me that you understand my decision. If you can't accept it, I'll tell Buck the deals's off.'

And that would cost him, Tate thought, miserably. Pride, because he'd already given his word. Hope, because he was counting on the success of this new team.

'I understand it,' she said, tucking her personal distaste aside. 'And I can accept it. Just one more question.'

'Ask away,' Ray invited.

'How can we be sure that when their team goes down, they won't keep whatever they find to themselves?'

'Because we're splitting the partnership.' He stood to clear the table. 'I'll dive with Buck. You'll dive with Matthew.'

'Isn't that a nice idea?' Marla chuckled to herself at her daughter's horrified expression. 'Who wants a piece of cake?'

Dawn spread over the water in bronze and rose streaks that mirrored the sky. The air was pure as silver and deliciously warm. In the distance, the high bluffs of St. Kitts awoke to the light in misty greens and browns. Farther south, the volcano cone that dominated the little island of Nevis was shrouded in clouds. Sugar-white beaches were deserted.

A trio of pelicans skimmed by, then dived with three quick, nearly soundless plops, shooting the water high in a cascade of individual drops. They rose again, skimmed again, dived again, in comical unity. Wavelets lapped lazily against the hull.

Slowly, beautifully, the light strengthened, and the water was sapphire.

Tate's mood wasn't lifted by the scenery as she suited up. She checked her diver's watch, her wrist compass, the gauges on her tanks. While her father and Buck shared coffee and conversation on the foredeck, she strapped her diver's knife onto her calf.

Beside her, Matthew mirrored the routine.

'I'm not any happier about this than you are,' he muttered. He hefted her tanks, helped her secure them.

'That brightens my mood.'

They attached weight belts, eyeing each other with mutual distrust. 'Just try to keep up, and stay out of my way. We'll be fine.'

'Really.' She spat into her mask, rubbed, rinsed. 'Why don't you stay out of my way?' She plastered a smile on her face as Buck and her father sauntered over.

'Set?' Ray asked her, checking her tank harnesses himself. He glanced at the bright-orange plastic bottle that served as a marker. It bobbed quietly on calm seas. 'Remember your direction.'

'North by northwest – just like Cary Grant.' Tate pecked his cheek, sniffed his aftershave. 'Don't worry.'

He didn't worry, Ray told himself. Of course he didn't. It was just rare that his little girl went down without him. 'Have fun.'

Buck hooked his thumbs in the waistband of his shorts. His legs were stubby trunks knobbed by prominent knees. Covering his bald pate was an oil-smeared Dodgers fielder's cap. His eyes were masked by tinted prescription glasses.

Tate thought he looked like an overweight, poorly dressed gnome. For some reason, she found it appealing. 'I'll keep an eye on your nephew, Buck.'

He grinned at that, his laugh like gravel hitting stone. 'You do that, girl. And good hunting.'

With a nod, Tate executed a smooth back roll from the rail, and headed down. She waited, as a responsible partner, for Matthew's dive. The moment she saw him enter the water, she turned and swam toward the bottom.

Sea fans the color of lilacs waved gracefully in the current. Fish, startled by the intrusion, darted away, a colorful stream of life and motion. If she had been with her father, she might have lingered to enjoy the moment, that always-stunning transition between being a creature of the air, and one of the sea.

She might have taken the time to gather a few pretty shells for her mother, or remained still long enough to coax a fish to glide over and inspect the newcomer.

But with Matthew closing the distance between them, Tate was struck less by the wonder of it than by a keen sense of competition.

Let's see him try to keep up, she decided, and kicking hard, skimmed westward. The water cooled on descent, but remained comfortable. It was a pity, she thought, that they were far from the more interesting reefs and coral gardens, but there was enough to please the senses – the water itself, the sway of fans, a flashing fish.

She kept her eyes peeled for lumps or discolorations in the sand. Damned if she'd miss something and let him surface in triumph again.

She reached for a broken piece of coral, examined it, discarded it. Matthew swam by her, taking the lead. Though Tate reminded herself the change of lead was basic diving procedure, she fretted until she could once more take the point.

They communicated only when strictly necessary. After agreeing to spread out, they kept each other in view. As much, Tate thought, in suspicion as safety.

For an hour, they combed the area where they had found the sword. Tate's first sense of anticipation began to wane when they discovered nothing more. Once she fanned away at sand, her heart thumping as she caught a glint. Her visions of some ancient shoe buckle or plate faded when she uncovered a twentieth-century can of Coke.

Discouraged, she swam farther north. Here, suddenly, a vast undersea garden of brightly patterned shells and coral with darting fish feeding. Lovely branched coral, too fragile to survive the wave action of shallow water, speared and spread in ruby and emerald and mustard yellow. It was home to dozens of creatures that hid in it, fed on it, or indeed fed it.

Pleasure slid through her as she watched a volute with its pumpkin-colored shell creep its laborious way along a rock. A clown fish darted through the purple-tipped tentacles of a sea anemone, immune to their stinging. A trio of regal angelfish glided along, a formation in search of breakfast.

Like a kid in a candy store, Matthew thought, as he watched her. She was holding her position with slow movements, her eyes darting as she tried to take in everything at once.

He'd liked to have dismissed her as foolish, but he appreciated the sea's theater. Both the drama and comedy continued around them – the sunny yellow wrasses busily cleaning the demanding queen trigger-fish, devoted as ladies-in-waiting. There, quick and lethal, the ambushing moray darted from his cave to clamp his jaws over the unwary grouper.

She didn't flinch from her up-close seat of instant death, but studied it. And he had to admit she was a good diver. Strong, skilled, sensible. She didn't like working with him, but she held up her end.

He knew that most amateurs became discouraged if they didn't stumble across some stray coin or artifact within an hour. But she was systematic and apparently tireless. Two other traits he appreciated in a diving partner.

If they were going to be stuck with each other, at least for a couple of months, he might as well make the best of it.

In what he considered a gesture of truce, he swam over, tapped her shoulder. She glanced over, her eyes bland behind her mask.

Matthew pointed behind them and watched those eyes brighten with appreciation when she spotted the school of tiny silver-tipped minnows. In a glinting wave, they veered as a mass barely six inches from Tate's outstretched hand, and vanished.

She was still grinning when she saw the barracuda.

It was perhaps a yard off, hovering motionless with its toothy grin and staring eyes. This time she pointed. When Matthew noted that she was amused rather than afraid, he resumed his search.

Tate glanced back occasionally to be certain their movements didn't attract their audience. But the barracuda remained placidly at a distance. Sometime later when she looked back, he was gone.

She saw the conglomerate just as Matthew's hand closed over it. Disgusted, and certain only her inattention had kept her from finding it first, she swam another few yards to the north.

It irritated her the way he seemed to work in her pocket. If she didn't keep her eye on him, he was practically at her shoulder. In a gesture of dismissal, she kicked away, damned if she'd let him think his misshapen hunk of rock interested her, however promising its pebbly surface.

And that's when she found the coin.

The small spread of darkened sand drew her closer. She fanned more from habit than enthusiasm, imagining she'd probably unearth someone's pocket change or a rusted tin can tossed from a passing boat. But the blackened disk was barely an inch under the silt. She knew the moment she plucked it up that she was holding a legend.

Pieces of eight, she thought, giddy with discovery. A pirate's chant, a buccaneer's booty.

Realizing she was holding her breath, a dangerous mistake, she began to breathe slowly as she rubbed at the discoloration with her thumb. There was the dull sheen of silver at the corner of the irregularly shaped coin.

With a cautious glance over her shoulder to be certain Matthew was occupied, she tucked it into the sleeve of her wetsuit. Smug now, she began to search for more signs.

When a check of her gauge and her watch indicated their time was up, she noted her position, and turned toward her partner. He nodded, jerked a thumb. They began to swim east, ascending slowly.

His goody bag was laden with conglomerate, which he pointed out to her before gesturing to her own empty one. She

28

gave him the equivalent of a shrug and broke the surface just ahead of him.

'Bad luck, Red.'

She suffered his superior smile as they headed in. 'Maybe.' Gripping the ladder of the *Adventure*, she tossed her flippers up to where her father waited. 'Maybe not.'

'How'd it go?' Once his daughter was on deck, Ray relieved her of her weight belt and tanks. Noting her empty bag, he struggled to mask disappointment. 'Nothing worth bringing up, huh?'

'I wouldn't say that,' Matthew commented. He handed Buck his full bag before unzipping his suit. Water dripped from his hair, pooled at his feet. 'Might be something worthwhile once we chip away at it.'

'The boy's got a sixth sense about these things.' Buck set the bag on a bench. His fingers were already itching to start hammering at the conglomerate.

'I'll work on it,' Marla offered. She was wearing her flowered sunhat and a sundress of canary yellow that set off her flame-colored hair. 'I just want to get some videos first. Tate, you and Matthew have a nice cold drink and something to eat. I know these two want to go down and try their luck.'

'Sure.' Tate pushed her wet hair back from her face. 'Oh, and speaking of luck.' She pulled the wrists of her wetsuit. A half dozen coins fell jingling to the deck. 'I had a little myself.'

'Sonofabitch.' Matthew crouched down. He knew by the weight and the shape what she'd found. While the others erupted with excitement, he rubbed a coin between his fingers and looked up coolly into Tate's self-satisfied smile.

He didn't begrudge her the find. But he sure as hell hated that she'd managed to make him look like a fool.

'Where'd you find them?'

'A couple of yards north of where you were harvesting your rocks.' She decided the way annoyance narrowed his eyes almost made up for the sword. 'You were so busy I didn't want to interrupt you.'

'Yeah. I bet.'

'Spanish.' Ray stared down at the coin nestled in his palm. 'Seventeen thirty-three. This could be it. The date's right.'

'Could be from the other ships,' Matthew responded. 'Time, current, storms – they spread things out.'

'They could just as easily be from the *Isabella* or *Santa Marguerite*.' There was a fever in Buck's eyes. 'Ray and me, we'll

29

concentrate on the area where you found these.' He rose from his crouched position, held out a coin to Tate. 'These'll go in the kitty. But I figure you ought to keep one, for yourself. That sit right with you, Matthew?'

'Sure.' He shrugged his shoulders before turning to the ice chest. 'No big deal.'

'It is to me,' Tate murmured as she accepted the coin from Buck. 'It's the first time I've ever found coins. Pieces of eight.' She laughed and leaned forward to give Buck an impulsive kiss. 'What a feeling.'

His ruddy cheeks darkened. Women had always remained a mystery to him and mostly at a distance. 'You hold on to it – that feeling. Sometimes it's a long stretch before you have it again.' He slapped Ray on the back. 'Let's suit up, partner.'

Within thirty minutes, the second team was under way. Marla had spread out a drop cloth and was busily chipping away at the conglomerate. Tate postponed lunch to clean the silver coins.

Nearby, Matthew sat on the deck and polished off his second BLT. 'I tell you, Marla, I might just shanghai you. You sure have a way of putting food together.'

'Anybody can make a sandwich.' Her hammer rang in counterpoint to her molasses-drenched voice. 'You'll have to have dinner with us, Matthew. Then you'll see what cooking's all about.'

He was sure he heard Tate's teeth gnash. 'Love to. I can run over to St. Kitts for you if you need any supplies.'

'That's very sweet.' She'd changed into work shorts and an oversized shirt, and was sweating. Somehow she still managed to look like a Southern belle planning a tea party. 'I could use a little fresh milk to make biscuits.'

'Biscuits? Marla, for homemade biscuits, I'd swim back from the island with the whole cow.'

He was rewarded by her quick, infectious laughter. 'Just a gallon will do me. Oh, not this minute,' she said, waving him back when he started to rise. 'Plenty of time. You enjoy your lunch and the sunshine.'

'Stop trying to charm my mother,' Tate said under her breath.

Matthew scooted closer. 'I like your mother. You've got her hair,' he murmured. 'Her eyes, too.' He picked up another section of sandwich, bit in. 'Too bad you don't take after her otherwise.'

30

'I also have her delicate bone structure,' Tate said with a clench-toothed smile.

Matthew took his time with his study. 'Yeah, I guess you do.'

Suddenly uncomfortable, she shifted back an inch. 'You're crowding me,' she complained. 'Just like you do on a dive.'

'Here, take a bite.' He held out the sandwich, nearly plowing it into her mouth so that she had little choice but to accept. 'I've decided you're my good-luck charm.'

Rather than choke, she swallowed. 'I beg your pardon?'

'There's a nice Southern flow to the way you say that,' he observed. 'Just a hint of ice under the honey. My good-luck charm,' he repeated. 'Because you were around when I found the sword.'

'You were around when I found it.'

'Whatever. There are a couple of things I don't turn my back on. A man with greed in his eyes, a woman with fire in hers.' He offered Tate more of the sandwich. 'And luck. Good or bad.'

'I'd think it would be smarter to walk away from bad luck.'

'Facing it's better. Usually quicker. Lassiters have had a long run of the bad.' With a shrug, he finished the sandwich himself. 'Seems to me you've brought me some of the good.'

'I'm the one who found the coins.'

'Maybe I'm bringing you some, too.'

'I've got something,' Marla sang out. 'Come and see.'

Matthew rose, and after a moment's hesitation, held out a hand. With matching wariness, Tate took it and let him haul her to her feet.

'Nails,' Marla said, gesturing with one hand as she dabbed a handkerchief over her damp face with the other. 'They look old. And this . . .' She picked up a small disk from amid the rubble. 'Looks like some sort of button. Copper or bronze perhaps.'

With a grunt, Matthew crouched down. There were two iron spikes, a pile of pottery shards, a broken piece of metal that might have been a buckle or pin of some sort. But it was the nails that interested him most.

Marla was right. They were old. He picked one up, turned it in his fingers, imagining it once being hammered into planks that were doomed to storms and seaworms.

'Brass,' Tate announced with delight as she worked off the corrosion with solvent and a rag. 'It is a button. It's got some etching on it, a flower. A little rose. It was probably on a dress of a female passenger.'

31

The thought made her sad. The woman, unlike the button, hadn't survived.

'Maybe.' Matthew spared the button a glance. 'Odds are we hit a bounce site.'

Tate reached for her own sunglasses to cut the glare. 'What's a bounce site?'

'Just what it sounds like. We probably found the spot where a ship hit while it was being driven in by waves. The wreck's somewhere else.' He lifted his gaze, scanned the sea to the horizon. 'Somewhere else,' he repeated.

But Tate shook her head. 'You're not going to discourage me after this. We haven't come up empty-handed, Matthew. One full dive and we have all this. Coins and nails–'

'Broken pottery and a brass button.' Matthew tossed the nail he held back into the pile. 'Chump change, Red. Even for an amateur.'

She reached out and took hold of the coin that dangled around his neck. 'Where there's some, there's more. My father believes we have a chance at a major find. So do I.'

She was ready to quiver with anger, he noted. Her chin thrust up, sharp as the spikes at their feet, eyes hard and hot.

Christ, why did she have to be a college girl?

He moved his shoulder, and deliberately gave her a light, insulting pat on the cheek. 'Well, it'll keep us entertained. But it's more often true that where there's some, that's all.' He brushed off his hands and rose. 'I'll clean this up for you, Marla.'

'You're a real upbeat kind of guy, Lassiter.' Tate tugged off her T-shirt. For some reason, the way he'd looked at her, just for an instant, had heated her skin. 'I'm going for a swim.' Moving to the rail, she dove off the side.

'She's her father's daughter,' Marla said with a quiet smile. 'Always sure hard work, perseverance and a good heart will pay off. Life's harder on them than it is for those of us who know those things aren't always enough.' She patted Matthew's arm. 'I'll tidy up here, Matthew. I have my own little system. You go on and get me that milk.'

Chapter Three

TATE FOUND PESSIMISM cowardly. It seemed to her that it was simply an excuse never to face disappointment.

It was even worse when pessimism won out.

After two weeks of dawn-to-dusk double-team diving, they found nothing but a few more scraps of corroded metal. She told herself she wasn't discouraged and hunted on her shift with more care and more enthusiasm than was warranted.

At night, she took to poring over her father's charts, the copies he'd made from his research. The more cavalier Matthew became, the more determined she was to prove him wrong. She wanted the wreck now, passionately. If only to beat him.

She had to admit the weeks weren't a total loss. The weather was beautiful, the diving spectacular. The time she spent on the island when her mother insisted on a break was filled with souvenir shopping, exploring, picnics on the beach. She hunted through cemeteries and old churches, hoping she might find another clue to the secret of the wrecks of 1733.

But most of all, she enjoyed watching her father with Buck. They were an odd pair – one squat and round and cue-ball bald, the other aristocratically lean with a mane of silvering blond hair.

Her father spoke with the slow, sweet drawl of coastal Carolina while Buck's conversation was peppershot with oaths delivered with Yankee quickness. Yet they merged together like old friends reunited.

Often when they surfaced after a dive, they were laughing like boys fresh from some misdemeanor. And one always seemed to have a tale to tell on the other.

It was illuminating for Tate to watch the friendship bloom and grow so rapidly. On land, her father's companions were businessmen, a suit-and-tie brigade of success, moderate wealth and staunch Southern heritage.

Here she watched him bronzing in the sun with Buck, sharing a beer and dreams of fortune.

Marla would snap their picture or pull out her ubiquitous video camera and call them two old salts.

As Tate prepared for her morning dive, she watched them arguing baseball over coffee and croissants.

'What Buck knows about baseball you could swallow in one gulp,' Matthew commented. 'He's been boning up so he can fight with Ray.'

Tate sat down to pull on her flippers. 'I think it's nice.'

'Didn't say it wasn't.'

'You never say anything's nice.'

He sat beside her. 'Okay, it's nice. Hanging with your father's been good for Buck. He's had a rough time the last few years. I haven't seen him enjoy himself so much since . . . for a long time.'

Tate let out a long sigh. It was difficult to work up any annoyance with straight sincerity. 'I know you care about him.'

'Sure I do. He's always been there for me. I'd do anything for Buck.' Matthew pressed a securing hand to his mask. 'Hell, I'm diving with you, aren't I?' With that, he rolled into the water.

Instead of being insulted, she grinned, and rolled in after him.

They followed the marker down. They had been moving the search steadily northward. Each time they tried new territory, Tate felt that quickening surge of anticipation. Each time they went down, she told herself today could be the day.

34

The water was pleasantly cool on the exposed skin of her hands and face. She enjoyed the way it streamed through her hair on her descent.

The fish had grown used to them. It wasn't unusual for a curious grouper or angelfish to peer into her mask. She'd gotten into the habit of bringing a plastic bag of crackers or bread crumbs with her, and took a few minutes at the start of every dive to feed them, and have them swirl around her.

Invariably the barracuda they'd dubbed 'Smiley' came to call, always keeping his distance, always watching. As a mascot, he wasn't particularly lively, but he was loyal.

She and Matthew developed an easy routine. They worked in sight of each other, rarely crossing the invisible line both recognized as separating their territories. Still, they shared their glimpses of sea life. A hand signal, a tap on the tank to point out a school of fish, a burrowing ray.

He was, Tate decided, easier to tolerate in the silence of the sea than above it. Now and again that silence was broken by the blurred roar of a tourist boat above them. Tate had even heard the eerie echo of music from a blasting portable radio with Tina Turner's raw-throated voice wanting to know what love had to do with it.

Singing in her head, Tate aimed for an odd formation of coral. She startled a grouper, who gave her one baleful glance before gliding off. Amused, she glanced over her shoulder. Matthew was swimming west, but was still in her line of vision. She flipped north toward the pretty soft reds and browns of the formation.

Tate was on top of it before she realized it wasn't coral, but rocks. Bubbles burst from her mouthpiece. If she had been above the water rather than below, she might have babbled.

Ballast rocks. Surely they had to be ballast rocks. From her studies she knew the color meant galleon. Schooners had used the brittle gray egg rock. The ballast of a galleon, she thought with a dreamy sense of unreality. That had been lost, forgotten. And now found.

One of the lost wrecks of 1733 was here. And she had found it.

She let out a shout that did nothing more than spray bubbles that blurred her vision. Remembering herself, she slipped her knife from its sheath and rapped sharply on her tank.

Turning a circle, she saw the shadow of her partner yards away. She thought he was signaling, and impatient, rapped again.

Come here, damn it.

She rapped a third time, putting as much insistence as she could manage into the one-toned signal. With satisfaction, and the beginnings of smugness, she watched him cut through the water toward her.

Be as irritated as you like, hot shot, she thought. And prepared to be humbled.

She could see the moment he recognized the stones, the slight hesitation in rhythm, then the quickening of pace. Unable to help herself, she grinned at him and attempted a watery pirouette.

Behind his face mask his eyes were blue as cobalt, intense, with a recklessness that had her heart thudding hard in response. He circled the pile once, apparently satisfied. When he took her hand, Tate gave his fingers a quick, friendly squeeze. She expected they would surface, announce her discovery, but he tugged her back in the direction from where he'd come.

She pulled back, shaking her head, jerking her thumb up. Matthew pointed west. Tate rolled her eyes, gestured back toward the ballast pile and started to kick toward the surface.

Matthew grabbed her ankle, shocking her with the familiar way his hands worked up her leg as he drew her back down. She considered swinging at him, but he had her arm again and was towing her.

It left her no choice but to go along, and to imagine all the vicious things she would say to him once she could speak.

Then she saw and her mouth fell open in reaction. She readjusted her mouthpiece, remembered to breathe and stared at the cannons.

They were corroded, covered with sea life and half buried in the sand. But they were there, the great guns that had once graced the Spanish fleet, defended it against pirates and enemies of the king. She could have wept for the joy of it.

Instead, she grabbed Matthew in a clumsy hug and spun him around in what passed for a victory dance. Water swirled around them, and a school of silver fish cut around them like blades. Their face masks bumped, and she bubbled out a giggle, still holding on to him as they kicked toward the surface forty feet above.

The moment they broke through, she pushed back her face mask, let her mouthpiece drop. 'Matthew, you saw it. It's really there.'

'Seems to be.'

'We're the first to find it. After more than two hundred and fifty years, we're the first.'

His grin flashed, his legs tangling with hers as they trod water. 'A virgin wreck. And it's all ours, Red.'

'I can't believe it. It's nothing like the other times. Someone else had always been there first, and we just puttered around what they'd overlooked or left behind. But this . . .' She tossed back her head and laughed. 'Oh God. It feels wonderful. Enormous.'

With another laugh, she threw her arms around him, nearly sinking them both, and pressed her lips to his in an innocent kiss of delight.

Her lips were wet and cool and curved. The shock of them against his blanked his mind for a full three heartbeats. He wasn't fully aware that he tugged her lips apart with his teeth, slipped his tongue into her mouth to taste, that he changed the kiss from innocent to hungry.

He felt her breath hitch, and her lips soften. Then heard her low, catchy sigh.

Mistake. The word flashed like neon in his brain. But she was pouring herself into the kiss now, in a surrender as irresistible as it was unexpected.

She tasted salt and sea and man, and wondered if anyone had ever sampled such potent flavors all at once. Sun-showered golden light, diamonds of it dancing on the water; the water cool and soft and seductive. She thought her heart had stopped, but it didn't seem to matter. Nothing mattered in this strange and lovely world but the taste and feel of his mouth.

Then she was cut loose and floundering, the door to that fascinating world slamming shut in her face. She kicked instinctively to keep her head above water and blinked at Matthew with huge, dreamy eyes.

'We're wasting time.' He snapped it at her and cursed himself. When she pressed her lips together as if to recapture the kiss, he bit back a groan and cursed her.

'What?'

'Snap out of it. Somebody your age has been kissed before.'

The hard edge of his voice and the insult beneath it cut away the mists. 'Of course I have. It was just a gesture of congratulations.' That shouldn't have left this hollow sensation in the pit of her stomach.

'Well, save it. We've got to tell the others and put out markers.'

'Fine.' She headed toward the boat with a quick, efficient crawl. 'I don't see what you're so mad about.'

'You wouldn't,' Matthew muttered and started after her.

Determined not to let him spoil the most exciting day of her life, Tate clambered onto the boat.

Marla was sitting under the awning giving herself a manicure. One hand was already tipped with bright-salmon pink. She looked over with a smile. 'You're early, honey. We didn't expect you up for another hour or so.'

'Where are Dad and Buck?'

'In the pilothouse, studying that old map again.' Marla's smile began to crumble at the edges. 'Something's wrong. Matthew.' She scrambled out of her chair, panic darting out of her eyes. Her secret, never-voiced fear of sharks clawed at her throat. 'Is he hurt? What happened?'

'He's fine.' Tate unhooked her weight belt. 'He's right behind me.' She heard his flippers hit the deck, but didn't turn to offer him a hand up. Instead she took a deep breath. 'Nothing's wrong, Mom. Nothing at all. Everything's great. We found it.'

Marla had hurried over to the rail to make certain of Matthew's safety. Her heartbeat began to level again when she saw him whole and unharmed. 'Found what, honey?'

'The wreck.' Tate passed a hand over her face, stunned to see her fingers were trembling. There was a roaring in her ears, a flutter in her chest. 'One of them. We found it.'

'Christ Jesus.' Buck stood at the door to the deckhouse. His normally ruddy face was pale, the eyes behind his lenses stunned. 'Which one?' he said in a strained voice. 'Which one did you find, boy?'

'Can't say.' Matthew shrugged off his tanks. His pulse was scrambling fast, but he knew it had as much to do with the fact he'd nearly devoured Tate as it did with the possibilities of treasure. 'But she's down there, Buck. We found ballast, galleon ballast, and cannon.' He looked beyond Buck to where Ray stood, goggling. 'The other spot was a bounce site, like I figured. But this site has real possibilities.'

'What –' Ray had to clear his throat. 'What was the position, Tate?'

She opened her mouth, closed it again when she realized she'd been too enthralled to mark it. A flush bloomed on her cheeks.

Matthew glanced at her, offered a thin, superior smile before giving Ray the coordinates. 'We'll need to put out marker buoys. You guys want to suit up, I'll show you what we have.' Then he grinned. 'I'd say we're going to put that nice new airlift of yours to use, Ray.'

'Yeah.' Ray looked at Buck. His dazed expression began to clear. 'I'd say you're right.' With a whoop he grabbed Buck. The two men hugged, rocking like drunks.

They needed a plan. It was Tate who, after the noisy celebration that night, offered the voice of reason. A system was required in order to salvage the wreck, and preserve it. Their claim had to be staked legally, and concretely. And the artifacts had to be precisely catalogued.

They needed a good underwater camera to record the sight and the position of artifacts they uncovered, several good note-books to use for cataloguing. Slates and graphite pencils for sketching underwater.

'Used to be,' Buck began as he helped himself to another beer, 'a man found a wreck, and all it held was his – long as he could hold off pirates and claim jumpers. You had to be cagey, know how to keep your mouth shut, and be willing to fight for what was yours.'

His words slurred a bit as he gestured with his bottle. 'Now there's rules and regulations, and every bloody body wants a piece of what you find with your own work and God-given luck. And there's plenty who're more worried about some planks of worm-eaten timber than about a mother lode of silver.'

'The historical integrity of a wreck's important, Buck.' Ray cruised on his own beer, and the possibilities. 'It's historical value, our responsibility to the past, and the future.'

'Shit.' Buck lighted one of the ten cigarettes he permitted himself a day. 'Time was we blew her to kingdom come if that's what it took to get to the mother lode. Not saying it was smart.'

He chuffed out smoke, and his eyes grew dim with memory. 'But it sure as hell was fun.'

'We haven't any right to destroy something to get to something else,' Tate murmured.

Buck glanced over at Tate, grinned. 'Wait, girl, till you get a taste of gold fever. It does something to you. You see that glint come out of the sand. It's shiny and bright, not like silver. Could be a coin, a chain, a medallion, some trinket a long-dead man gave his long-dead woman. There it is, in your hand, true as the day it was made. And all you can think about is more.'

Curious, she tilted her head. 'Is that why you keep going down? If you found all the treasure the *Isabella* and *Santa Marguerite* held – if you found it all and were rich, would you still go down for more?'

'I'll go down till I die. It's all I know. All I need to. Your father was like that,' he added, gesturing to Matthew. 'Whether he struck the mother lode or came back with nothing but a cannonball, he had to go down again. Dying stopped him. That was all that could.' His voice roughened as he looked down at his beer again. 'He wanted the *Isabella*. Spent the last months he lived figuring how and where and when. Now we'll harvest her for him. Angelique's Curse.'

'What?' Ray's brows drew together. 'Angelique's Curse?'

'Killed my brother,' Buck said blearily. 'Damn witch's spell.'

Recognizing the signs, Matthew leaned forward, plucked the nearly empty beer from his uncle's fingers. 'A man killed him, Buck. A flesh-and-blood man. No curse, no spell.' Rising, he hauled Buck to his feet. 'He gets maudlin when he drinks too much,' he explained. 'Next he'll be talking about Blackbeard's ghost.'

'Saw it,' Buck mumbled around a foolish smile. His glasses slid down his nose so that he peered myopically over them. 'Thought I did. Off the coast of Okracoke. Remember that, Matthew?'

'Sure, I remember. We've got a long day ahead of us. Better get back to the boat.'

'Want some help?' Ray rose, was surprised, and a little chagrined to discover he wasn't entirely steady on his feet.

'I can manage. I'll just pour him into the inflatable, row him across. Thanks for dinner, Marla. Never in my life tasted fried chicken to match yours. Be ready at dawn, kid,' he told Tate. 'And for a taste of real work.'

'I'll be ready.' Despite the fact he hadn't asked for help, she went to Buck's other side, draped his arm over her shoulders. 'Come on, Buck, time for bed.'

'You're a sweet kid.' With drunken affection, he gave her a clumsy squeeze. 'Ain't she, Matthew?'

'She's a regular sugar cube. I'm going down the ladder first, Buck. If you fall in, I might let you drown.'

'That'll be the day.' Buck chuckled, shifting his weight onto Tate as Matthew swung over the side. 'That boy'd fight off a school of sharks for me. Lassiters stick together.'

'I know.' Carefully, rocking a bit under his weight, Tate managed to maneuver Buck over the rail. 'Hold on, now.' The absurdity had her giggling as he swayed over the ladder and Matthew cursed from below. 'Hold on, Buck.'

'Don't you worry, girl. There isn't a boat been made I can't board.'

'Goddamn it, you're going to capsize us. Buck, you idiot.' As the dinghy pitched dangerously, Matthew shoved Buck down. Water sloshed in, soaking both of them.

'I'll bail her out, Matthew.' With a good-natured chuckle, Buck began to scoop water out of the bottom with his hands.

'Just sit still.' Matthew took the oars out of the locks, glanced up to see the Beaumonts grinning over the side. 'I should have made him swim for it.'

''Night, Ray.' Buck waved cheerfully as Matthew rowed. 'There'll be gold doubloons tomorrow. Gold and silver and bright, shiny jewels. A new wreck, Matthew,' he mumbled as his chin dropped to his chest. 'Always knew we'd find it. Was the Beaumonts brought us the luck.'

'Yeah.' After securing the oars and the line, Matthew eyed his uncle dubiously. 'Can you make the ladder, Buck?'

'Sure, I can make the ladder. Got the sea legs I was born with, don't I?' Those legs wobbled, as did the small raft as he weaved toward the side of the *Sea Devil*.

Through more luck than design, he gripped a rung and hauled himself up before he could turn the inflatable over. Soaked to the knees, Matthew joined him on deck. Buck was weaving and waving enthusiastically to the Beaumonts.

'Ahoy the *Adventure*. All's well.'

'Let's see if you say that in the morning,' Matthew muttered and half carried Buck to the closet-sized wheelhouse.

'Those are good people, Matthew. First I was thinking we'd just use their equipment, string them along, then take us the lion's share. Be easy for you and me to go down at night, lay off some of the best salvage. Don't think they'd know the difference.'

'Probably not,' Matthew agreed, as he stripped the wet pants off his uncle. 'I gave it some thought myself. Amateurs usually deserve to be fleeced.'

'And we've fleeced a few,' Buck said merrily. 'Just can't do it to old Ray, though. Got a friend there. Haven't had a friend like that since your dad died. There's his pretty wife, pretty daughter. Nope.' He shook his head with some regret. 'Can't pirate from people you like.'

Matthew acknowledged this with a grunt and eyed the hammock strung between the cabin's forward and aft walls. He hoped to God he wouldn't have to heft Buck into it. 'You've got to get into your bunk.'

'Yep. Going to play straight with Ray.' Like a bear climbing into his cave, Buck heaved himself up. The hammock swayed dangerously before he settled. 'Should tell them about Angelique's Curse. Thinking about it, but never told nobody but you.'

'Don't worry about it.'

'Maybe if I don't tell them, they won't be jinxed by it. Don't want to see anything happen to them.'

'They'll be fine.' Matthew unzipped his jeans, peeled them off.

'Remember that picture I showed you? All that gold, the rubies, the diamonds. Doesn't seem like something so beautiful could be evil.'

'Because it can't.' Matthew stripped off his shirt, tossed it after his jeans. He slipped Buck's glasses off his nose, set them aside. 'Get some sleep, Buck.'

'More than two hundred years since they burned that witch and people still die. Like James.'

Matthew's jaw set, and his eyes went cold. 'It wasn't a necklace that killed my father. It was a man. It was Silas VanDyke.'

'VanDyke.' Buck repeated the name in a voice slurred with sleep. 'Never prove it.'

'It's enough to know it.'

'It's the curse. The witch's curse. But we'll beat her, Matthew. You and me'll beat her.' Buck began to snore.

Curse be damned, Matthew thought. He'd find the amulet all right. He'd follow in his father's footsteps until he had it. And when he did, he'd take his revenge on the bastard who had murdered James Lassiter.

In his underwear, he stepped out of the cabin into the balmy, starsplattered night. The moon hung, a silver coin struck in half. He settled under it in his own hammock, far enough away that his uncle's habitual snoring was only a low hum.

There was a necklace, a chain of heavy gold links and a pendant etched with names of doomed lovers and studded with rubies and diamonds. He'd seen the pictures, read the sketchy documentation his father had unearthed.

He knew the legend as well as a man might know fairy tales recited to him as a child at bedtime. A woman burned at the stake, condemned for witchcraft and murder. Her final promise that any who profited from her death would pay in kind.

The doom and despair that had followed the path of the necklace for two centuries. The greed and lust that had caused men to kill for it and women to plot.

He might even believe the legend, but it meant only that the greed and the lust had caused the doom and despair. A priceless jewel needed no curse to drive men to murder.

That he was sure of. That he knew, too well. Angelique's Curse had been the motive behind his father's death.

But it was a man who had planned it, executed it.

Silas VanDyke. Matthew could conjure up his face if he needed to, the voice, the build, even the smell. No matter how many years passed, he forgot nothing.

And he knew, as he had known as a helpless, grief-ravaged teenager, that one day he would find the amulet, and use it against VanDyke.

For revenge.

It was odd, that with such dark and violent thoughts hovering in his mind as he drifted to sleep, he would dream of Tate.

Swimming in impossibly clear waters, free of weight, of equipment, slick and agile as a fish. Deeper and deeper, to where the sun could no longer penetrate. The fans waved and

43

toothy clumps of colors gleamed like jewels and carried bright fish in their pockets.

Still deeper, to where the colors – reds and oranges and yellows – faded to cool, cool blue. Yet there was no pressure, no need to equalize, no fears. Only a bursting sense of freedom that mellowed into complete and utter contentment.

He could stay here forever, in this soundless world, with nothing on his back, neither tanks nor worries.

There. There below him, a child's fairy-tale image of a sunken ship. The masts, the hull, the tattered flags waving in the current. It lay tilted in the bed of sand, impossibly whole and impossibly clear. He could see the cannons, still aimed against ancient enemies. And the wheel waiting for its captain ghost to steer it.

Delighted, he swam toward it, through swirls of fish, past an octopus that curled its tentacles and ballooned away, under the shadow of a gaint ray that danced overhead.

He circled the deck of the Spanish galleon, read the proud lettering that christened her the *Isabella*. The crow's nest creaked above him, like a tree in the wind.

Then he saw her. Like a mermaid, she hovered just out of reach, smiling a siren's smile, gesturing with lovely, graceful hands. Her hair was long, not a flaming cap, but long, silken ropes of fire waving and swirling over her shoulders and naked breasts. Her skin was like a pearl, white and gleaming.

Her eyes were the same, green and amused.

As if a tide had swept him, he was helpless to do anything but go to her.

Her arms went around him, satin chains. Her lips parted for his and were sweet as honey. When he touched her, it was as if he'd waited all his life for that alone. The feel of her skin sliding under his hand, the quiver of muscle as he aroused her. The drum of pulse under flesh.

The taste of her sigh was in his mouth. Then the slick and glorious heat enveloped as he slid inside her, as her legs wrapped around him and her body bowed back to take him deeper.

It was all dreamy movements, endless sensation. They drifted, rolling through the water in a soundless mating that left him weak and stunned and blissfully happy. He felt himself spill into her.

Then she kissed him, softly, deeply and with incredible sweetness. When he saw her face again, she was smiling. He reached for her, but she shook her head and danced away. He gave chase, and they frolicked like children, darting around the sunken ship.

She led him to a chest, laughing as she tossed back the lid and revealed the mountain of gold. Coins spilled as she dipped her hand in. The glint was like sunlight, and scattered with it were jewels of great size. Diamonds as big as his fist, emeralds larger than her eyes, pools of sapphires and rubies. Their color was dazzling against the cool gray of the world around them.

He dragged his hand through the chest, spilled a shower of starshaped diamonds over her hair and made her laugh.

Then he found the amulet, the heavy gold chain, the blood and tears that studded the pendant. He could feel heat from it, as if it lived. Never in his life had he seen anything so beautiful, so compelling.

He held it up, looked at Tate's delighted face through the circle of the chain, then slipped it over her head. She laughed, kissed him, then cupped the pendant in her hand.

Suddenly fire exploded from it, a spear of violent heat and light that slammed him back like a blow. He watched in horror as the fire grew, in size and intensity, covering her in a sheath of flame. All he could see were her eyes, anguished and terrified.

He couldn't reach her. Though he fought and he struggled, the water that had been so calm and peaceful was a whirlwind of movement and sound. A tornado of sand funneled up, blinding him. He heard the lightning crack of the mast splitting, the seaquake roar that burst through the bed of sand and silt to tear through the hull of the ship like cannon fire.

Through it he heard screams – hers, his own.

Then it was gone, the flames, the sea, the wreck, the amulet. Tate. The sky was overhead, with its half disk of moon and splatter of stars. The sea was calm and ink-black, barely whispering against the boat.

He was alone on the deck of the *Sea Devil*, dripping sweat and gasping for breath.

Chapter Four

TATE TOOK TWO dozen pictures of ballast and cannon as she and Matthew explored. He humored her by posing at the mouth of a corroded gun, or manned the camera himself to take shots of her among the rocks and patient fish. Together, they attached a crusted cannonball to a flotation and sent it up to the second team.

Then, after a tug on the line, the work began.

Maneuvering an airlift well requires skill, patience and teamwork. It was a simple tool, hardly more than a pipe, four inches in diameter and about ten feet long with an airhose. Pressurized air ran into the pipe, rising and creating suction that would vacuum water, sand and solid objects. It was as essential to a treasure hunter as a hammer to a carpenter. Used too quickly, or with too much power, it could destroy. Used too carelessly, the pipe would become clogged with conglomerate, shells, coral.

While Matthew ran the airlift, Tate examined and collected its fallout that spewed from the top of the pipe. It was hard and tedious work on both sides. Sand and light debris swirled, obscuring vision in a dirty cloud downcurrent. It took a sharp eye and endless patience to search through the fallout, load the bits and pieces and chunks into buckets to be hauled to the surface.

Matthew continued to make test holes with a steady, almost soothing rhythm. Stingrays basked in the fallout, apparently enjoying the massage of sand and small rock. Tate allowed herself to dream, imagining a slew of glinting gold bursting out of the pipe, like a jackpot in a slot machine.

Fantasies aside, she gathered fused nails, bits of conglomerate and the shards of broken pottery. They were every bit as fascinating to her as gold bullion. Her college studies in the past year had accented her love of history and the fragments of culture buried in the shifting sea.

Her long-term ambitions and goals were very clear. She would study, earn her degree, absorbing all the knowledge she could hold through books, lectures, and most of all, by doing. One day, she would join the ranks of scientists who sailed the oceans, plumbed the depths to discover and analyze the relics of doomed ships.

Her name would make an impact, and her finds from doubloons to iron spikes would matter.

Eventually, there would be a museum carrying the Beaumont name filled with artifacts.

Now and again as she worked, she would catch herself falling behind because she'd paused to wonder over a broken cup. What had it held the last time someone sipped from it?

When she nicked her finger on a sharp edge, she took it philosophically. The thin drip of blood washed away in the swirl.

Matthew signaled her through the cloud. In the hole, perhaps a foot deep, she saw the iron spikes crossed like swords. Caught between their calcified tips was a platter of pewter.

Forty feet of water didn't prevent Tate from expressing her glee. She caught his hand and squeezed it, then blew him a kiss. Efficiently, she unhooked her camera from her belt and documented the find. Records, she knew, were essential to scientific discoveries. She might have spent some time examining it, gloating over it unscientifically, but Matthew was already moving off to dig another hole.

There was more. Each time they transferred the airlift, they would uncover another discovery. A clump of spoons cemented in coral, a bowl that even with a third of it missing caused Tate's heart to slam against her ribs.

Time and fatigue ceased to exist. An audience of thousands watched the progress, small fish scanning the disturbed area for exposed worms. If one got lucky, dozens of others would rush in to search for food in a colorful flood of motion.

At his usual distance, the barracuda remained like a statue, looking on in grinning approval.

Matthew ran the lift like an artist, Tate thought. Probing here, then shifting with a delicacy that seemed to remove sand a grain at a time. He brushed away silt clouds with a wave of the pipe. If the wall of sand was parted by an object, he would back off the pipe, work carefully to prevent damage.

She saw with dazzled eyes a fragile piece of porcelain, a bowl with elegant rosebuds rimming its cup.

He would have left it for the time being, knowing that something that fragile when cemented to coral or some other object could be snapped off at the slightest touch.

But her eyes were so big with wonder, so bright with delight. He wanted to give her the bowl, see her face when she held it. Signaling her back, Matthew began the tedious and time-consuming process of whispering the sand clear. When he was satisfied, he handed her the pipe. Reaching below the bowl to the coral that had claimed it, Matthew worked it free.

It cost him some skin, but when he offered it to her, the nicks and scratches were forgotten. Her eyes glowed, then filled so unexpectedly both of them stared. Disconcerted, Matthew took the pipe back, jerked a thumb to the surface. He cracked the valve on the airlift, released a torrent of bubbles. Together, they swam up in the spray.

She didn't speak, couldn't. Grateful they were hampered by the airlift and her last bucket of conglomerate, she reached the side of the *Adventure*. Her father beamed over the side.

'You've been keeping us busy.' He'd pitched his voice over the roar of the compressor, winced when Buck shut it off. 'We've got dozens of artifacts, Tate.' He hauled up the bucket she held out. 'Spoons, forks, buckets, copper coins, buttons . . .' He trailed off when she held up the bowl. 'My God. Porcelain. Unbroken. Marla.' His voice cracked on the name. 'Marla, come over here and look at this.'

Reverently, Ray took the bowl from Tate. By the time she and Matthew had gotten aboard, Marla was sitting on deck, surrounded by debris, the flowered bowl in her lap, her video camera beside her.

'Pretty piece,' Buck commented. However casual the words, his voice betrayed his excitement.

'Tate liked it.' Matthew glanced toward her. She was standing in her wetsuit, the tears that had threatened forty feet below flowing freely.

'There are so many things,' she managed. 'Dad, you can't imagine. Under the sand. All these years under the sand. Then you find them. Something like this.' After rubbing the heels of her hands over her face, she crouched by her mother, dared to skim a gentle fingertip over the rim of the bowl. 'Not a chip. It survived a hurricane and more than two hundred and fifty years, and it's perfect.'

She rose. Her fingers felt numb as she tugged at the zipper of her wetsuit. 'There was a platter, pewter. It's caught between two iron spikes like a sculpture. You only had to close your eyes to see it heaped with food and set on a table. Nothing I've been studying comes close to doing it, to seeing it.'

'I figure we hit the galley area,' Matthew put in. 'Plenty of wooden utensils, wine jugs, broken dishes.' Grateful, he accepted the cold juice Ray offered him. 'I dug a lot of test holes, about a thirty-foot area. The two of you might want to move a few degrees north of that.'

'Let's get started.' Buck was already suiting up. Casually, Matthew walked over to pour more juice.

'Saw a shark cruising,' he said in an undertone. It was well known among the partners that Marla paled and panicked at the thought of sharks. 'Wasn't interested in us, but it wouldn't hurt to take a couple of bangsticks down.'

Ray glanced toward his wife, who was reverently documenting the latest treasures on video. 'Better safe than sorry,' he agreed. 'Tate,' he called out. 'Want to reload the camera for me?'

Twenty minutes later, the compressor was pumping again. Tate worked at the big drop-leaf table in the deckhouse with her mother, cataloguing every item they'd brought up from the wreck.

'It's the *Santa Marguerite*.' Tate fingered a spoon before setting it in the proper pile. 'We found the ordinance mark on one of the cannons. We found our Spanish galleon, Mom.'

'Your father's dream.'

'And yours?'

'And mine,' Marla agreed with a slow smile. 'Used to be I just went along for the ride. It was such a nice, interesting hobby, I thought. It gave us such adventurous vacations, and was certainly a change from our mundane jobs.'

Tate looked up, a pucker of a frown between her brows. 'I never knew you thought your job was mundane.'

'Oh, being a legal secretary is fine except when you start asking yourself why you didn't have the gumption to be the lawyer.' She moved her shoulders. 'The way I was raised, Tate, honey, a woman didn't move in a man's world except to quietly pick up behind him. Your grandma was a very old-fashioned woman. I was expected to work in an acceptable job until I found a suitable husband.' She laughed and set aside a pewter cup with a missing handle. 'I just got lucky on the husband part. Very lucky.'

This, too, was a new discovery. 'Did you want to be a lawyer?'

'Never occurred to me,' Marla admitted. 'Until I was heading on toward forty. A dangerous time for a woman. I can't say I looked back when your father decided to retire. I did the same, and I thought I was more than content to drift with him, playing at treasure-hunting. Now seeing these things, she picked up a silver coin, 'makes me realize we're doing something important. Valuable in its way. I never thought to make a mark again.'

'Again.'

Marla looked up with a smile. 'I made my mark when I had you. This is wonderful, and it's exciting. But you'll always be treasure enough for your father and me.'

'You've always made me feel like I can do anything. Be anything.'

'You can.' Marla glanced over. 'Matthew, come join us.'

'I don't want to interrupt.' He felt out of his depth, and clumsy, stepping into the family unit.

'Don't be silly.' Marla was already on her feet. 'I bet you'd like some coffee. I've got fresh in the galley. Tate and I are organizing our treasure trove.'

Matthew scanned the scatter of artifacts over the table. 'I think we're going to need more room.'

Marla laughed as she stepped back in with the coffee. 'Oh, I like an optimistic man.'

'Realistic,' Tate corrected and patted the seat on the settee in invitation. 'My diving partner is far from optimistic.'

Not certain if he was amused or insulted, Matthew sat beside her and sampled his coffee. 'I wouldn't say that.'

'I would.' Tate dived into the bowl of pretzels her mother set out. 'Buck's the dreamer. You like the life – sun, sea, sand.' Nibbling, she leaned back. 'No real responsibilities, no real ties. You don't expect to find some crusted chest filled with gold doubloons, but you know how to make do with the occasional trinket. Enough to keep you in shrimp and beer.'

'Tate.' Marla shook her head, muffled a laugh. 'Don't be rude.'

'No, she's hitting it.' Matthew bit into a pretzel. 'Let her finish.'

'You're not afraid of hard work because there's always plenty of time for lying in a hammock, snoozing. There's the excitement of the dive, of the discovery, and always the turnover value rather than the intrinsic value of some small booty.' She handed him a silver spoon. 'You're a realist, Matthew. So when you say we'll need more room, I believe you.'

'Fine.' He realized no matter how he weighed it, he was insulted. He tossed the spoon with a clatter back onto the pile. 'I figure we can use the *Sea Devil* for storage.' When she angled her chin, peered down her nose, he sneered at her. 'Buck and I can bunk here, on deck. We can use the *Adventure* for our work station. We dive from here, we clean the conglomerate and artifacts here, then transport them to the *Sea Devil*.'

'That seems very sensible,' Marla agreed. 'After all, we have two boats, we might as well make full use of both of them.'

'All right. If Dad and Buck agree, so will I. In the meantime, Matthew, why don't you help me bring in another load from on deck?'

'Fine. Thanks for the coffee, Marla.'

'Oh, you're welcome, sweetie.'

'I'm going to have to run to St. Kitts later,' Tate began as they started out. 'To have the film developed. Want to come with me?'

'Maybe.'

She caught the edge to his voice and smothered a smile. 'Matthew.' To stop his progress, she touched a hand to his arm. 'Do you know why I think we work so well together down there?'

'No.' He turned. Her skin was still an impossible alabaster even after weeks at sea. He could smell the cream she used to

51

protect it, and the perfume that was salt and sea air that clung to her hair. 'But you're going to tell me.'

'I think it's because you're realistic, and I'm idealistic. You're reckless, I'm cautious. Contradicting traits inside ourselves and against each other. Somehow we make a balance.'

'You really like to analyze things, don't you, Red?'

'I guess I do.' Hoping he was unaware of how much courage it took, she shifted closer. 'I've been analyzing why you were so angry after you kissed me.'

'I wasn't angry,' he corrected evenly. 'And you kissed me.'

'I started it.' Determined to finish it, she kept her eyes on his. 'You changed it, then you got mad because it surprised you. What you felt surprised you. It surprised me, too.' Lifting her hands, she spread them on his chest. 'I wonder if we'd be surprised now.'

He wanted, more than anything he could remember, he wanted to swoop down and plunder that fresh and eager mouth. The hunger to taste it came in swift, sharp waves, and made his hands rough as they snagged her wrists.

'You're moving into dark water, Tate.'

'Not alone.' She wasn't afraid any longer, she realized. Why, she wasn't even nervous. 'I know what I'm doing.'

'No, you don't.' He shoved her back, arm's-length, hardly realizing his hands were still cuffed around her wrists. 'You figure there aren't any consequences, but there are. If you don't watch your step, you'll pay them.'

A shiver worked up her spine, deliciously. 'I'm not afraid to be with you. I want to be with you.'

The muscles in his stomach twisted. 'Easy to say, with your mother in the galley. Then again, maybe you're more clever than you look.' Furious, he tossed her hands down and strode away.

The implication brought a bright bloom to her cheeks. She had been teasing him, she realized. Taunting him. To see if she could, needing to know if he felt even half of this draw toward her that she felt toward him. Ashamed, contrite, she hurried after him.

'Matthew, I'm sorry. Really I–'

But he was over the side with a splash and swimming toward the *Sea Devil*. Tate let out a huff of breath. Damn it, the least he could do was listen when she apologized. She dived in after him.

When she dragged herself onto the deck, he was popping the top on a beer.

'Go home, little girl, before I toss you overboard.'

'I said I was sorry.' She dragged wet hair out of her eyes. 'That was unfair and stupid, and I apologize.'

'Fine.' The quick swim and cold beer weren't doing much to scratch the itch. Hoping to ignore her, he swung into his hammock. 'Go home.'

'I don't want you to be mad.' Determined to make amends, she marched to the hammock. 'I was only trying to . . . I was just testing.'

He set the open beer on the deck. 'Testing,' he repeated, then lunged before she could draw in the breath to gasp. He hauled her onto the hammock atop him. It swung wildly as she clawed at the sides to keep from upending. Her eyes popped wide with shock when his hands clamped intimately over her bottom.

'Matthew!'

He gave her a quick, not altogether loving tap, then shoved her off. She landed in a heap on the butt he'd just explored.

'I'd say we're even now,' he stated, and reached for his beer.

Her first impulse was to spring to attack. Only the absolute certainty that the result would be either humiliating or disastrous prevented her. Mixed with that was the lowering thought that she'd deserved just what she'd gotten.

'All right.' With calm and dignity, she rose. 'We're even.'

He'd expected her to lash at him. At the very least to blubber. The fact that she stood beside him, cool, composed, touched off a glint of admiration in his eyes. 'You're okay, Red.'

'Friends again?' she asked and offered a hand.

'Partners, anyway.'

Crisis avoided, she thought. At least temporarily. 'So, do you want to take a break? Maybe do some snorkeling?'

'Maybe. Couple of masks and snorkels in the wheelhouse.'

'I'll get them.' But she came back with a sketchbook. 'What's this?'

'A silk tie. What does it look like?'

Overlooking the sarcasm, she sat on the edge of the hammock. 'Did you do this sketch of the *Santa Marguerite?*'

'Yeah.'

'It's pretty good.'

'I'm a regular Picasso.'

'I said "pretty good." It would have been great to see her like this. Are these figures measurements?'

He sighed again, thinking of amateurs. 'If you want to try to figure out how much area the wreck covers, you've got to do some calculations. We hit the galley today.' He swung his legs over until he was sitting beside her. 'Officers' cabins, passengers' cabins.' He laid a fingertip on the sketch at varying points. 'Cargo hold. Best way is to imagine a gull's-eye view.' To demonstrate, he flipped a page and began to sketch out a rough grid. 'This is the sea floor. Here's where we found the ballast.'

'So the cannon is over here.'

'Right.' In quick deft moves, he penciled them in. 'Now we dug test holes from here to here. We want to move more midship for the mother lode.'

Her shoulder bumped his as she studied the sketch. 'But we want to excavate the whole thing, right?'

He glanced up briefly, then continued to draw. 'That could take months, years.'

'Well, yes, but the ship itself is as important as what it holds. We have to excavate and preserve all of it.'

From his viewpoint, the ship itself was wood and worthless. But he could humor her. 'We'll be in hurricane season before too much longer. We could be lucky, but we concentrate on finding the mother lode. Then you can afford to take as much time as you want on the rest.'

For himself, he'd take his share and split. With gold jingling in his pocket, he could afford the time to build that boat, to finish his father's research on the *Isabella*.

To find Angelique's Curse and VanDyke.

'I guess that makes sense.' She glanced up, startled by the hard, distant gleam in his eye. 'What are you thinking about?' It was foolish, of course, but she thought it looked like murder.

He shook himself back. Here and now, he thought, was what mattered most. 'Nothing. Sure it makes sense,' he continued. 'Before long, word's going to get out that we've found a new wreck. We'll have company.'

'Reporters?'

He snorted. 'They're the least of it. Poachers.'

'But we have a legal claim,' Tate began, and broke off when he laughed at her.

'Legal don't mean jack, Red, especially when you've got the Lassiter luck to deal with. We'll have to start sleeping as well as working in shifts,' he went on. 'If we start to bring up gold, Red, hunters will smell it from Australia to the Red Sea. Believe me.'

'I do.' And because she did, she hopped down to fetch the snorkeling equipment. 'Let's check on Dad and Buck. Then I want to get that film developed.'

By the time Tate was ready to go ashore, she had a list of errands in addition to the film. 'I should have known Mom would give me a grocery list.'

Matthew hopped into the *Adventure's* little tender with her, cranked the engine. 'No big deal.'

Tate merely adjusted her sunglasses. 'You didn't see the list. Look!' She gestured west where a school of dolphin leapt before the lowering sun. 'I swam with one once. We were in the Coral Sea and a school of them followed the boat. I was twelve.' She smiled and watched them flash toward the horizon. 'It was incredible. They have such kind eyes.'

Tate rose as Matthew cut speed. She timed the distance to the pier, braced her legs and secured the line.

Once the boat was secure, they started across the strip of beach.

'Matthew, if we hit the mother lode, and you were rich, what would you do?'

'Spend it. Enjoy it.'

'On what? How?'

'Stuff.' He moved his shoulders, but he knew by now generalities wouldn't satisfy her. 'A boat. I'm going to build my own as soon as I have the time and means. Maybe I'd buy a place on an island like this.'

They moved by guests of the nearby hotel as they baked lazily in the lowering sun. Staff with flowered shirts and white shorts strolled across the sand with trays of tropical drinks.

'I've never been rich,' he said half to himself. 'It couldn't be too hard to get used to it, to live like this. Fancy hotels, fancy clothes, being able to pay to do nothing.'

'But you'd still dive?'

'Sure.'

'So would I.' Unconsciously she took his hand as they walked through the hotel's fragrant gardens. 'The Red Sea, the Great

Barrier Reef, the North Atlantic, the Sea of Japan. There're so many places to see. Once I finish college, I'm going to see them all.'

'Marine archeology, right?'

'That's right.'

He skimmed a glance over her. Her bright cap of hair was tousled by the salt and wind. She wore baggy cotton slacks, a skimpy T-shirt and square, black-framed sunglasses.

'You don't look much like a scientist.'

'Science takes brains and imagination, not looks or fashion sense.'

'Good thing about the fashion sense.'

Unoffended, she shrugged. In spite of her mother's occasional despair, Tate never gave clothes or style a thought. 'What's the difference, as long as you've got a good wetsuit? I don't need a wardrobe to excavate and that's what I'm going to spend my life doing. Imagine getting paid to go on treasure hunts, to examine and study artifacts.' She shook her head at the wonder of it. 'There's so much to learn.'

'I never thought a whole lot of school myself.' Of course, they had moved around so much, he'd never had a choice. 'I'm more a fan of on-the-job training.'

'I'm certainly getting that.'

They took a cab into town where Tate could drop off her film. To her pleasure, Matthew didn't seem to mind when she wanted to poke around the shops, dallying over trinkets. She sighed for a while over a small gold locket with a single pearl dripping from its base. Clothes were for keeping out the weather, but baubles were a nice, harmless weakness.

'I didn't think you went in for stuff like that,' he commented, leaning on the counter beside her. 'You don't really wear any bangles.'

'I had this little ruby ring Mom and Dad gave me for Christmas when I was sixteen. I lost it on a dive. It really broke my heart, so I stopped wearing jewelry in the water.' She tore her eyes away from the delicate locket and tugged on his silver piece. 'Maybe I'll take that coin Buck gave me and wear it as a charm.'

'Works for me. You want to get a drink or something?'

She touched her tongue to her top lip. 'Ice cream.'

'Ice cream.' He thought it over. 'Let's go.'

Sharing cones, they strolled along the sidewalk, explored narrow streets. He charmed her by plucking a creamy white hibiscus from a bush, tucking it carelessly behind her ear. While they shopped for Marla's essentials, he had her gurgling with laughter over the story of Buck and Blackbeard's ghost.

'We were off Ocracoke, on Buck's birthday. His fiftieth. The idea of half a century behind him had Buck so depressed he'd finished off half a bottle of whiskey. I helped him work on the other half.'

'I bet.' Tate chose a bunch of ripening bananas and added it to her basket.

'He was going on about all these might have's – you know what I mean. We might have found that wreck if we'd looked another month. If we'd gotten there first, we might have hit the mother lode. If the weather had held, we might have struck it rich. Between the whiskey and the boredom, I passed out on deck. That melon's not ripe. This one.'

He switched fruit, chose the grapes himself. 'Anyway, the next thing I know, the engines are roaring and the boat's lurching off southeast at a good twelve knots. Buck's at the wheel, screaming about pirates. Scared the shit out of me. I jumped up, tripped, knocked my head on the rail so hard I saw stars. Nearly went overboard when he swung to starboard. He's yelling for me and I'm cursing him, fighting to stay upright as he circles the boat. His eyes are about six inches out from his face and white. You know he can't see more than three feet in front of him without his glasses. But he's pointing out to sea and shouting all this pirate cant. "Avast, ahoy, shiver me timbers." '

Tate's laughter turned heads. 'He did not say "shiver me timbers." '

'Hell, he didn't. He nearly capsized us doing a jig and singing "yo, ho, ho." ' The memory of it had a grin tugging at his mouth. 'I almost had to knock him out to get the wheel away from him. "The ghost, Matthew. Blackbeard's ghost. Don't you see it?" I told him he wasn't going to be seeing anything either after I poked his eyes out. He tells me it's there, right there, ten degrees off the forward bow. There's not a damn thing there but a little mist. But to Buck, it was Blackbeard's severed head, smoke curling from the beard. He claimed it was a sign, and if we dived there the next day, we'd find Blackbeard's treasure, the one everyone else figured was buried on land.'

Tate paid for the groceries, Matthew hefted the bags. 'And you went down the next morning,' she said, 'because he asked you to.'

'That and because if I hadn't, I'd never have heard the end of it. We didn't find a damn thing, but he sure got over turning fifty.'

It was nearly dusk when they got back to the beach. Matthew stowed the bags and turned to see Tate had rolled up her pants legs so she could stand in the surf.

Light gilded her hair, her skin. Suddenly he was painfully reminded of his dream and how she had looked aglow in the water. How she had tasted.

'It's so beautiful here,' she murmured. 'It's like nothing else exists. How can there be anything wrong with the world when there are spots like this? When there are days like this?'

She was sure he was unaware that this had been the most romantic day of her life. Such simple things like a flower for her hair, a hand to hold as she walked along the beach.

'Maybe we shouldn't leave here, ever.' With a laugh in her voice, she turned. 'Maybe we should just stay and . . .'

She trailed off, her throat closing at the look in his eyes. They were so dark, so intense, so suddenly focused on her. Only her.

She didn't think, didn't hesitate, but walked to him. Her hands slid up his chest, linked behind his head. His eyes stayed on hers, a dozen frantic pulse beats, then he dragged her against him and flashed fire in her blood.

Yes, she'd been kissed before. But she knew the difference between boy and man. It was a man who held her, drew from her. It was a man she wanted. Eager and quick, she pressed against him, racing her lips over his face in frenzied kisses until they found his again on a sob of pleasure.

She was so slim, so willing, so avid to accept any demand. She flowed like water under each pass of his hands, and her mouth clung greedily to his. Each hum and whimper of desire that sounded in her throat cut through him, a blade of fire that ruptured new needs.

'Tate.' His voice was rough, nearly desperate. 'We can't do this.'

'We can. We are.' God, she couldn't breathe. 'Kiss me again. Hurry.'

His mouth crushed down on hers. The taste of her seemed to explode inside him. Everything about it was painful, nearly agonizing, as heat would be after cold.

'This is crazy,' he murmured against her mouth. 'I'm out of my mind.'

'Me, too. Oh, I want you, Matthew. I want you.'

And that struck him hard. He jerked back, gripped unsteady hands on her shoulders. 'Listen, Tate . . . What the hell are you smiling at?'

'You want me, too.' She lifted a hand, laid it gently against his cheek and almost unmanned him. 'For a while I thought you didn't. And it hurt because I want you so much. I didn't even like you at first, and wanted you anyway.'

'Jesus.' To gain control of himself, he let his brow rest on hers. 'I thought you said you were the careful one.'

'Not about you.' Full of love and trust, she nuzzled into him. Heart to heart. 'Never about you. When you kissed me the first time, I knew you were what I'd been waiting for.'

He had no compass, no direction, but he knew it was essential to reverse course. 'Tate, we have to take this slow. You're not ready for what I'm thinking of. Believe me.'

'You want to make love with me.' Her chin came up. Her eyes, all at once, were a woman's, and just as mysterious. 'I'm not a child, Matthew.'

'Then I'm not ready. And I'm not willing to do something that would hurt your parents. They've been straight with me and Buck.'

Pride, she thought. Pride, loyalty and integrity. Was it any wonder she loved him? Her lips curved. 'All right. We'll take it slow. But it's between us, Matthew. What we decide, and what we want.' She leaned forward, touched her lips to his. 'I can wait.'

Chapter Five

STORMS SWEPT IN and made diving impossible for the next two days. When the first wave of impatience passed, Tate settled down on the boatdeck of the *Adventure* to clean and catalogue the pieces of the *Santa Marguerite* her father and Buck had brought up on the last dive.

Rain drummed on the tarp stretched overhead. The islands had vanished in the mist, leaving only restless seas and angry skies. Their world had whittled down to water, and each other.

In the deckhouse, a marathon poker game was in progress. Voices, a laugh, a curse, drifted out to her over the monotonous patter of rain. Tate cleaned the corrosion from a crudely made silver cross, and knew she'd never been happier in her life.

With a mug of coffee in each hand, Matthew ducked under the tarp. 'Want some help?'

'Sure.' Just looking at him had her heart cartwheeling into her throat. 'Is the poker game breaking up?'

'No, but my luck is.' He sat beside her, offered a mug. 'Buck just blew down my full house with a straight flush.'

'I can never keep straight what beats what. I'm better at gin.' She held up the cross. 'Maybe the ship's cook wore this, Matthew. It would have banged against his chest when he beat batter for biscuits.'

'Yeah.' He fingered the silver. It was an ugly piece, more likely fashioned by a blacksmith than a jeweler. Neither did it have weight. Matthew dismissed it as little value. 'What else you got here?'

'These rigging hasps. See, they've still got traces of rope in them. Imagine.' She handled the black metal reverently. 'How they would have fought to save the ship. The wind would have been screaming, the sails in tatters.'

She looked beyond into the mist and saw what had been. 'Men clinging to lines and masts as the ship heeled. Passengers terrified. Mothers holding their children while the ship pitched and heeled. And we're finding what's left of them.'

She set the fitting down and lifted a clay pipe with both hands. 'A seaman kept this tucked in his pocket, stood on deck after his watch to light it and enjoy a quiet smoke. And this tankard would have been filled with ale.'

'Too bad it's missing the handle.' He plucked it up, turned it over. He didn't want to admit her vision had moved him. 'Devaluates it.'

'You can't just think about the money.'

He grinned. 'Sure I can, Red. You take the drama, I'll take the dough.'

'But–' He cut off her objection with a quick, sneaky kiss.

'You look so cute when you're indignant.'

'Really?' She was young enough, and in love enough, to be flattered. Picking up her coffee, she sipped, watching him over the rim. 'I don't believe you're nearly as mercenary as you pretend.'

'Believe it. History's fine if you can make something from it. Otherwise, it's just dead guys.' He glanced up, barely noticing her frown. 'Rain's slowing down. We'll dive tomorrow.'

'Restless?'

'Some. The trouble is hanging out here, having your mother put a plate under my nose every time I blink. I could get used to it.' He lifted a hand, ran it over her hair. 'It's a different world. You're a different world.'

'Not so different, Matthew,' she murmured and turned her lips to his. 'Maybe just different enough.'

61

His fingers tensed, relaxed slowly. She hadn't seen enough of the world, his world, he thought, to know the difference. If he were a good man, a kind one, he knew he wouldn't be touching her now, tempting them both toward a step that could only be a mistake.

'Tate—' He was riding the wire between pushing her away or bringing her closer, when Buck stuck his head under the tarp.

'Hey, Matthew, you—' Buck's jaw dropped open as they broke apart. His unshaven cheeks bloomed with color. 'Ah, 'scuze me. Ah, Matthew . . .' While Buck searched for what to say, Tate calmly picked up her pen and catalogued the clay pipe.

'Hi, Buck.' Tate sent him a bright, easy smile while the two men eyed each other uncertainly. 'I heard you were having a run of luck at the poker table.'

'Yeah. Yeah, I, ah . . .' He jammed his hands into his pockets, shifted his feet. 'Rain's slacking off,' he announced. 'Me and Matthew, we'll load this stuff up, store it on the *Sea Devil*.'

'I'm just finishing cataloguing.' Meticulously, Tate capped the pen. 'I'll give you a hand.'

'No, no, we'll do her.' Buck dragged his hand out of his pocket long enough to shove his glasses back up his nose. 'Me and Matthew, we've got to do some tinkering with the engine over there anyhow. Your mama said something about you being on kitchen duty tonight.'

'She's right,' Tate said with a sigh. 'I guess I'll get started.' She unfolded her legs and rose before tucking her notebook under her arm. 'I'll see you at dinner.'

The men said little as they wrapped and loaded the booty. Matthew's suggestion that they might need to rent a room or a garage for storage was met by a grunt and a shrug. Buck waited until they were putting toward the *Sea Devil* before he exploded.

'Have you lost your mind, boy?'

Matthew jogged the wheel slightly. 'I don't need you crawling up my back, Buck.'

'If I got to crawl up your back to get to your brain, then that's what I'll do.' He rose smoothly when Matthew cut the engine. 'Haven't you got more sense than to mess around with that young thing?'

'I haven't been messing around with her,' Matthew said between his teeth. He secured the bow line. 'Not like you mean.'

'Thank God for that.' Agilely, Buck shouldered the first tarp, hooked his foot on the ladder. 'You got no business playing games with Tate, boy. She ain't a loose one.'

'I know what she is.' Matthew hauled the second tarp. 'And I know what she isn't.'

'Then you remember it.' Buck carried his tarp into the wheelhouse, unrolled it carefully on the counter. 'The Beaumonts are good, decent people, Matthew.'

'And I'm not.'

Surprised at the bitterness in the tone, Buck looked up as Matthew set down his tarp. 'Never said you weren't good or decent, boy. But we ain't like them. Never have been. Maybe you figure it's okay to dally around with her before we move on, but a girl like that expects things.'

He took out a cigarette, lighted it, peering at his nephew through the smoke. 'You going to tell me you're thinking about giving them to her.'

Matthew pulled out a beer, swallowed long to wash some of the anger out of his throat. 'No, I'm not going to tell you that. But I'm not going to hurt her, either.'

Wouldn't mean to, Buck thought. 'Change your course, boy. There's plenty of females out there if you've got an itch.' He saw the fury flash into Matthew's eyes and met it equably. 'I'm telling you 'cause I'm the one who's got to. A man hooks up with the wrong woman, it can ruin both of them.'

Struggling for calm, Matthew set the half-drained bottle of beer aside. 'Like my mother and father.'

'That's true enough,' Buck said, but his voice had gentled. 'They set sparks off each other, sure. Got themselves tangled before either of them thought it through. Left them both pretty scraped up.'

'I don't think she did a hell of a lot of bleeding,' Matthew shot back. 'She left him, didn't she? And me. Never came back. Never looked back as far as I can tell.'

'She couldn't take the life. Ask me, most women can't. No use blaming them for it.'

But Matthew could. 'I'm not my father. Tate's not my mother. That's the bottom line.'

'I'll give you the bottom line.' Eyes heavy with concern, Buck crushed out his cigarette. 'That girl over there's having herself some fun and excitement for a few months. You're a

63

good-looking man, so it's natural you'd be part of that fun and excitement. But when it's over, she'll go back to college, get herself a fancy job, a fancy husband. That leaves you high and dry. If you forget that, and take advantage of the stars in her eyes, both of you'll be the worse for it.'

'It wouldn't occur to you that I might be good enough for her.'

'You're good enough for anybody,' Buck corrected. 'Better'n most. But being right for somebody's different.'

'So speaks the voice of experience.'

'Maybe I don't know a goddamn thing about women. But I know you.' Hoping to calm the waters, he laid a hand on Matthew's rigid shoulder. 'We got a chance at the big time here, Matthew. Men like us look all our lives, only a few of us find it. We found it. All we have to do is take it. You can make something out of yourself with your share. Once you do, there'll be plenty of time for women.'

'Sure.' Matthew picked up his beer, tipped it back. 'No sweat.'

'There you go.' Relieved, Buck gave his shoulder a slap. 'Let's take a look at the engine.'

'I'll be right there.'

Alone, Matthew stared at the bottle in his hand until he'd willed back the clawing urge to smash it into jagged pieces. There was nothing Buck had told him that he hadn't already told himself. And less kindly.

He was a third-generation treasure hunter with a legacy of bad luck that had dogged him like a bloodhound all of his life. He'd lived by his wits, and the occasional flip side of that luck. He had no ties but to Buck, no property other than what he could strap on his back.

He was a drifter, nothing more, nothing less. The prospect of fortune forty feet beneath his feet would make the drifting more comfortable, but it wouldn't change it.

Buck was right. Matthew Lassiter of no fixed address and less than four hundred dollars tucked into a cigar box had no right picturing himself with Tate Beaumont.

Tate had other ideas. It was frustrating to discover over the next few days that the only time she found herself alone with Matthew was underwater. There communication and physical contact were hampered.

64

She would change that, she promised herself as she searched the fallout from the airlift. And she would change it today. After all, it was her twentieth birthday.

Carefully, she picked among the nails, the spikes, the shells, eyes peeled for the valuables that scattered. Ship fittings, a sextant, a small, hinged brass box, a silver coin embedded in a hunk of coral. A wooden crucifix, an octant and a lovely china cup sliced delicately in two.

All this she gathered, ignoring the pings of debris against her back, the occasional nick on her hand.

A glint of gold shot by her. Tate's heart careened in her chest as she scanned the cloud for the telltale flash of it. The small, quick gleam had her darting forward, dipping toward the sand and sending the burrowing rays rising in a swirling cloud.

Her mind was screaming treasure, doubloons, jewels of great price and age. But when her hand closed around the piece of gold, her eyes began to swim.

It wasn't a coin, or jewelry long buried beneath the waves. Not a priceless artifact, but priceless nonetheless. She lifted the gold locket with the single pearl dripping from its point.

When Tate turned back, she saw that Matthew was pointing the airlift pipe away and watching her. He sketched letters in the water with his finger. H. B. D. Happy birthday. With a gurgle of laughter, she swam toward him. Undaunted by tanks and hoses, she took his hand, pressed it to her cheek.

He let it lie there a moment, then waved her away. His signal an obvious 'Stop loafing.'

Once more the airlift sucked at sand. Ignoring the fallout, Tate carefully secured the necklace by looping it around her wrist. She went back to work with love soaring in her heart.

Matthew concentrated on the offshore end of the ballast mound. Patiently, he cut into the sand, creating an ever-widening circle with sloping sides. He was a foot down, then two, while Tate worked busily to pick through the fallout. A school of triggerfish darted by. Matthew glanced up and saw through the murky cloud that the barracuda was grinning at him.

On impulse, he shifted his position. He wouldn't have considered himself superstitious. As a man of the sea he followed signs and lived by lore. The toothy fish hovered in nearly the same spot day after day. It wouldn't hurt to use the mascot as a marker.

Curious, Tate looked over as Matthew hauled the airlift several feet north where he was already forming a new hole. Tate let her attention drift and watched a kaleidoscope of fish whirl through the clouded water hunting for the seaworms displaced by the cut of the pipe.

Something clinked against her tank. Efficiently, she turned back to resume her chores. The first glint of gold barely registered. She stared through the roiling water at the bed of sand. The flashes of brightness were scattered around her like flowers that had just bloomed. Stupefied, she reached down and plucked up a doubloon. The long-dead Spanish king stared back at her.

The coin dropped from her numbed fingers. In a sudden fever, she began to harvest them, pushing them into her wetsuit, jamming them into her lobster bag and ignoring the solid objects that drifted down in the thick column of fallout. The conglomerate rained, but she was oblivious to it, facedown, scanning the seafloor like a miner panning for gold.

Five coins, then ten. Twenty and more. Her breath rushed out in a shriek of laughter. She couldn't seem to get enough air. When she looked up, she saw Matthew grinning at her, his eyes dark and wild. Behind her mask, her face was bone white.

They'd hit the mother lode.

He gestured to her. As if in a dream, she swam over and her trembling hand reached for his. Sand trickled down into the test hole, but she saw the sparkle of crystal from a perfectly preserved goblet, the sheen of coins and medallions. And everywhere the calcified shapes of artifacts. And there the blackened streak of sand that every hunter knew meant a river of silver.

Behind them the ballast pile loomed. And beneath, the shining prize of the galleon *Santa Marguerite* and all her treasure.

There was a roaring in Tate's ears as she reached down and closed her hand over a thick gold chain. Slowly she drew it up. From it dangled a heavy cross crusted by sea life. And by emeralds.

Her vision blurred as she held it out to Matthew. With sudden formality she carefully lifted the chain over his head. The simple generosity of the gesture touched him. He wished he could have held her, told her. All he could do was point a finger up. He cracked the valve on the airlift and followed her to the surface.

She couldn't speak. Even now it took all of her effort just to draw air in and out of her lungs. She was trembling like a leaf when she hoisted herself aboard. Strong arms lifted her.

'Honey, you okay?' Buck's face, lined with worry, loomed over her, 'Ray, Ray, come on out here. Something wrong with Tate.'

'Nothing wrong,' she managed and sucked in air.

'Just lie still.' Fretting like a mother hen, he eased off her face mask and nearly shuddered with relief when he heard Matthew clattering over the side. 'What happened down there?' he demanded without turning around.

'Not much.' Matthew let his weight belt fall.

'Not much, my ass. Girl's white as a sheet. Ray, get us some brandy here.'

But Ray and Marla were already rushing out. Voices buzzed in Tate's head. Hands were poking and probing for injury. She got her breath back on a giggle, then couldn't stop.

'I'm all right.' She had to press both hands over her mouth to hold back a fresh stream of hysterical laughter. 'I'm fine. We're both fine, aren't we, Matthew?'

'Fine and dandy,' he agreed. 'We just had a little excitement.'

'Come on, honey, let's get you out of that suit.' With some impatience, Marla shot a glance at Matthew. 'Just what kind of excitement? Tate's shaking.'

'I can explain.' Tate snorted behind her hands. 'I gotta get up. Would you let me up?' Tears began to stream from her eyes as she fought to control the laughter. Brushing away restraining hands, she got unsteadily to her feet. Trembling with breathless giggles, she upended her goody bag, tugged open her suit.

Coins rained gold onto the deck.

'Fuck me,' Buck croaked and sat down heavily.

'We found the mother lode.' Tate threw back her head and screamed at the sun. 'We found the mother lode.'

She threw her arms around her father, whirled him into a dance, only to break off and swing her mother. She planted a big smacking kiss on Buck's bald head as he continued to sit and stare at the coins at his feet.

With their voices babbling around her, Tate turned a circle and launched herself into Matthew's arms. By the time he'd managed to regain his balance, her mouth was clinging to his.

His hands went to her shoulders. He knew he should push her away, keep the kiss a product of the moment's excitement.

But a current of helplessness swamped him, and his hands slid to her back, crossed, embraced.

So it was she who drew away, her eyes still glowing, her face flushed now and eager. 'I thought I was going to faint. When I looked down and saw the coins, all the blood drained out of my head. The only other time I've ever felt like that is when you kissed me.'

'We're not a bad team.' He ran a hand over her hair.

'We're a great team.' She clamped a hand over his and dragged him to where Buck and Ray were already suiting up. 'You should have seen it, Dad. Matthew moved the airlift like it was a divining rod.'

Happily recounting every minute of the discovery, she helped Buck and her father with their tanks. Only Matthew noticed that Marla remained silent, and the warmth in her eyes had been cooled by concern.

'I'm going down to take pictures,' Tate announced, hooking on fresh tanks. 'We have to document everything. Before we're done, we'll have the cover of *National Geographic*.'

'Don't go pulling them in yet.' Buck sat on the side, rinsed his mask. 'We gotta keep this quiet.' He looked around as if expecting a dozen boats to come speeding in on the claim. 'Finds like this are one in a million, and there're plenty who'd do whatever it took to get a piece.'

Tate only grinned. 'Eat your heart out, Jacques Cousteau,' she said, and rolled into the water.

'Get some champagne chilling,' Ray called to his wife. 'We'll have a double celebration tonight. Tate's earned herself a hell of a birthday party.' He flashed a smile at Buck. 'Ready, partner?'

'Ready and willing, hoss.' After lowering the airlift, they disappeared beneath the surface.

Matthew fueled the compressor, murmuring a thanks when Marla brought him a tall frosted glass of lemonade.

'An exciting day,' she commented.

'Yeah. You don't get many like this.'

'No. Twenty years ago today I thought this is the happiest I can ever be.' She sat on a deck chair, tilted her sunhat to shade her eyes. 'But over the years I've had a lot of happy moments. Tate's been a joy to her father and me right from the first. She's bright, eager, generous.'

'And you want me to keep my distance,' Matthew concluded.

'I'm not sure.' Marla sighed, tapped her finger against her own glass. 'I'm not blind, Matthew. I've seen the signs between the two of you. It's natural enough. You're healthy attractive people, working and living in close quarters.'

He took off the cross, ran a thumb over the glint of grass-green stones. Like Tate's eyes, he thought, and set the chain aside. 'Nothing's happened.'

'I appreciate your telling me that. But you see, if I haven't given Tate the foundation to know how to make her own decisions, then I've failed as a parent. I don't believe I have.' She smiled a little. 'That doesn't stop me from worrying. She has so much ahead of her. I can't help wanting her to have all of it, and at the right time. I suppose what I'm asking you to do is be careful with her. If she's in love with you—'

'We haven't talked about that,' Matthew said quickly.

Under other circumstances, Marla might have smiled at the panic in his voice. 'If she's in love with you,' Marla repeated, 'it will block everything else. Tate thinks with her heart. Oh, she thinks she's practical, sensible. And she is. Until her emotions are stirred. So be careful with her.'

Now she did smile, and rose. 'I'm going to fix you some lunch.' Laying a hand on his arm, she lifted to her toes and kissed his cheek. 'Sit in the sun, honey, and enjoy your moment of triumph.'

Chapter Six

IN A MATTER of days, the seabed was riddled with holes. The *Santa Marguerite* gave up her stores generously. Between the airlift, and the simple tools of coal shovel and bare hands the team mined both the spectacular and the ordinary. A wooden worm-eaten bowl, a dazzling gold chain, pipe bowls and spoons, a sumptuous cross crusted with pearls. All were lifted from the sandy vault where they had rested for centuries, and hauled into the light in buckets.

Now and again a pleasure boat would cruise by and hail the *Adventure*. If Tate was onboard, she would lean on the rail and chat. There was no disguising the murky cloud from the airlift that stained the surface. Word of the underwater excavation was spreading. They were careful to downplay their progress. But each day, they worked harder and faster as the prospect of rival treasure hunters arriving increased.

'A legal claim don't mean squat to some of these pirates,' Buck told her. He zipped his thick torso into his wetsuit. 'You gotta be alert, and you gotta be tough.' He winked at her as he passed her his glasses. 'And cagey. We'll dig out that mother lode, Tate, and we'll play her out.'

'I know we will.' She handed him his face mask. 'We've already found more than I ever imagined.'

'You start imagining bigger.' He grinned, spat into his mask. 'It's good having a couple of young ones like you and Matthew along. Figure you could work twenty hours out of twenty-four if you had to. You're a good diver, girl. And a good hunter.'

'Thanks, Buck.'

'Don't know many females who can handle it.'

Her brow shot up as he rinsed out his mask. 'Really?'

'Now don't go shooting that equal stuff at me. Just stating a fact. Plenty of girls like to dive all right, but when it comes to pulling their weight on a dig, they ain't got what it takes. You do.'

She thought it through, then smiled at him. 'I'll take that as a compliment.'

'Should. Best damn team I ever worked with.' He settled into position, slapped a hand on Ray's shoulder. 'Since I hunted with my old man and my brother. 'Course once we get it all up, I'm going to have to kill hoss here.' Buck grinned as he lowered his mask into place. 'Figure on beating him to death with his own flippers.'

'I'm on to you, Buck.' Ray slipped over the side. 'I've already decided to smother you with a boat cushion. The treasure's mine.' He let out a wild, evil laugh. 'Mine, do you hear? All mine.' Rolling his eyes madly, Ray plugged in his mouthpiece and did a surface dive.

'I'm after you, hoss. Going to run him through with a coal shovel,' Buck promised and splashed into the water.

'They're crazy,' Tate decided. 'Like a couple of bad little boys playing hooky.' She turned to grin at Matthew. 'I've never seen Dad have so much fun.'

'Buck's not this loose unless he's got a quart of whiskey in him.'

'It's not just the treasure.' She held out a hand so that he would join her at the rail.

'No, I guess it's not.' Looking out over the water, Matthew linked his fingers with hers. 'But it helps.'

She leaned her head on his shoulder and chuckled. 'It doesn't hurt. But they'd have clicked without it. So would we.' She

71

turned her head so that her lips could graze his jaw. 'We'd have found each other, Matthew. We were supposed to.'

'Like we were supposed to find the *Marguerite*.'

'No.' She turned into his arms. 'Like this.'

Her lips were warm and soft. Irresistible. He could feel himself sinking into them, slowly, weightlessly, until he was steeped in the seduction that was Tate. She seemed to surround him, tastes and scents and flavors so unique he would have recognized them, recognized her, if he'd been deaf, dumb and blind.

There had never been another woman who could twist his system into such shivering, slippery knots with one quiet kiss. He wanted her so desperately it terrified him.

And when she drew away, her eyes dreamy, her lips curved, he knew she had no notion of his need, his desperation or his terror.

'What's wrong?' Tate lifted a hand to his cheek. 'You look so serious.'

'No. Nothing.' Pull yourself together, Lassiter. She's not ready for what's running through your mind. With an effort, he smiled. 'I was just thinking it's too bad.'

'What is?'

'That after Buck takes care of Ray, I'll have to get rid of you.'

'Oh.' Willing to play, she tilted her head. 'And just how do you propose to do that?'

'I figured I'd just strangle you.' He circled her throat with his hand. 'Then toss you overboard. We're going to keep Marla, though. Chain her to the stove. A man's gotta eat.'

'Very practical of you. Of course, that only works if I don't get you first.' She wiggled her brows, then dug her fingers into his ribs.

Helpless laughter buckled his knees. He made a weak grab, but she was darting away. By the time he'd gotten his breath back, she was around the starboard side of the deckhouse.

'Want to play rough?' He charged the port side to cut her off. He'd nearly made the bow when he saw her, and the bucket. Before he could dodge, she'd heaved the load of cool seawater.

While he choked and dripped, she held her sides. But when he'd blinked the stinging water out of his eyes, she saw their intent. With a shriek, she went into full retreat.

Her only mistake was in dropping the bucket.

72

Marla came out of the deckhouse, where she'd been cleaning cob coins, and ran headlong into Tate.

'Goodness. Is there a war?'

'Mom.' Giddy with laughter, Tate ducked behind her mother just as Matthew rounded the cabin, armed with a freshly loaded bucket.

He skidded to a halt. 'You'd better stand aside, Marla. This could get messy.'

Choking with laughter, Tate wrapped her arms around her mother's waist, using her ruthlessly as a shield. 'She's not going anywhere.'

'Now, children.' Marla patted Tate's hand. 'Behave.'

'She started it,' Matthew claimed. He couldn't wipe the grin off his face. It had been years since he had felt this free, this foolish. 'Come on, coward. Stand clear and take your medicine.'

'No way.' Smug, Tate sneered at him. 'You lose, Lassiter. You wouldn't use that with my mother between us.'

He narrowed his eyes, frowned down at the bucket. When he looked back up, Tate was fluttering her lashes at him. 'Sorry, Marla,' he said, and drenched them both.

Female shrieks rang in his ears as he raced to the side for more ammunition.

It was a messy battle, ripe with ambush and retaliation. Since Marla threw herself into the war with an enthusiasm Matthew hadn't anticipated, he found himself outgunned and outmaneuvered.

He did the manly thing. He dived overboard.

'Good aim, Mom,' Tate managed before she collapsed weakly against the rail.

'Well.' Marla fluffed a hand over her tangled hair. 'I did what had to be done.' She'd lost her hat somewhere during combat, and her crisp blouse and shorts were limp and running with water. Still, she was all gracious Southern hospitality as she peered over to where Matthew was warily treading water. 'You give up, Yankee?'

'Yes, ma'am. I know when I'm licked.'

'Then haul yourself aboard, honey. I was about to fix up some nice beer-battered shrimp when I was interrupted.'

He swam toward the ladder, but shot Tate a cautious look. 'Truce?'

'Truce,' she agreed and held out a hand. When their hands locked, she slitted her eyes. 'Don't even think about it, Lassiter.'

He had. The idea of toppling her into the water had its merits. But it wasn't nearly as much fun since she was on to him. Revenge could wait. He dropped lightly on deck, slicked his hair out of his eyes.

'That cooled us off, anyway.'

'I never thought you'd blast Mom.'

He grinned, settled on a boat cushion. 'Sometimes the innocent have to suffer. She's terrific, you know. You're lucky.'

'Yeah.' Tate settled beside him, stretched out her legs. She couldn't remember ever being more content. 'You've never mentioned your own mother.'

'I don't remember her much. She took off when I was a kid.'

'Took off?'

'Lost interest,' he said with a shrug. 'We were based in Florida then, and my father and Buck were doing some boat building and repair on the side. Things were pretty lean. I remember them fighting a lot. One day she sent me over to the neighbors. Said she had errands to run and didn't want me underfoot. She never came back.'

'That's terrible. I'm so sorry.'

'We got by.' And after so many years, the hurt had healed over with only the occasional unexpected throb. 'After my father died, I found divorce papers and a letter from a lawyer dated a couple of years after she'd left. She didn't want custody or visitation rights. She just wanted her freedom. She got it.'

'You haven't seen her?' It was incomprehensible to Tate that a mother, any mother, could walk so carelessly away from a child she had carried and held and watched grow. 'Never once since then?'

'Nope. She had her life, we had ours. We moved around a lot. Up the coast, California, the islands. We did okay. Better than okay, now and then. We got work doing straight salvage up in Maine, and my father hooked up with VanDyke.'

'Who's that?'

'Silas VanDyke. The man who murdered him.'

'But–' She sat up, her face pale and tense. 'If you know who . . .'

'I know,' Matthew said quietly. 'They were partners for about a year. Well, maybe not partners so much as my father worked for him. VanDyke picked up diving as a hobby, and got interested in treasure-hunting along the way, I guess. He's one of these business tycoons who figures he can buy anything he wants. That's the way he looked at treasure. Something to buy. He was looking for a necklace. An amulet. He thought he'd traced it to a ship that went down on the Great Barrier Reef. He wasn't much of a diver, but he had money, pots of money.'

'So, he hired your father?' Tate prompted.

'The Lassiters still had a rep back then. He was the best and VanDyke wanted the best. My father trained him, taught him everything, and got caught up in the legend. Angelique's Curse.'

'What does that mean?' she demanded. 'Buck was talking about that.'

'It's the necklace.' Matthew rose to go to the ice chest, fished out two cans of Pepsi. 'Supposedly it belonged to a witch who was executed in the fifteen hundreds somewhere in France. Gold, rubies, diamonds. Priceless. But it's the power it's said to hold that caught VanDyke's interest. He even claimed he had some sort of family connection way back to the witch.'

He sat again, passed her a chilled can. 'Bullshit, of course, but men kill for less.'

'What kind of power?'

'Magic,' he said with a sneer. 'There's a spell on it. Whoever has it, and can control it, will have untold riches and power – whatever their heart desires. If it controls them, they lose whatever's most precious to them. Like I said,' he added, swallowing deep. 'Bullshit. But VanDyke's big on control.'

'It's fascinating.' And she made up her mind to do some research on the legend at the first opportunity. 'I've never heard the story before.'

'There's not a lot of documentation. Bits and pieces. The necklace bounced around, wreaking havoc supposedly and gaining a rep.'

'Like the Hope Diamond?'

'Yeah, if you go for that stuff.' He eyed her. 'You would.'

'It's interesting,' she said with some dignity. 'Did VanDyke find it?'

'No. He thought my father had. Got the idea in his head that my father was holding back on him. He was right.' Matthew took a long, cold drink. 'Buck told me that my father had found some papers that made him think the necklace had been sold to this rich Spanish merchant or aristocrat or something. He spent a lot of time researching, really got into it. He decided it was on the *Isabella*, but kept it between him and Buck.'

'Because he didn't trust VanDyke.'

'He should have trusted him less.' The memory glinted like a sword in Matthew's eyes. 'I heard them going at it the night before that last dive. VanDyke accused him of hiding the necklace. He still figured it was on the wreck they were digging. My father just laughed at him. Told him he was crazy. The next day, he was dead.'

'You never told me how he died.'

'He drowned. They said it was bad tanks, that the equipment hadn't been properly rigged. That was a fucking lie. I was in charge of the equipment. There was nothing wrong with it when I checked it that morning. VanDyke sabotaged it. And when my father was eighty feet down, he was taking in too much nitrogen.'

'Nitrogen narcosis. Rapture of the deep,' Tate murmured.

'Yeah. VanDyke claimed he tried to get him up when he realized something was wrong, but my father fought him off. There was a struggle, he said. VanDyke's story is he started up for help, but my father kept pulling him back. I went down right away once the bastard came up with the story, but he was already dead.'

'It could have been an accident, Matthew. A terrible accident.'

'It wasn't an accident. And it wasn't Angelique's Curse the way Buck likes to think. It was murder. I saw that bastard's face when I brought my father up.' His tensed fingers crushed the can in his hand. 'He was smiling.'

'Oh, Matthew.' To comfort, she cuddled against him. 'How horrible for you.'

'One day I'll find the *Isabella*, and I'll find the necklace. VanDyke will come looking for me. I'll be waiting.'

She shivered. 'Don't. Don't think about it.'

'I don't very often.' Wanting to change the mood, he draped an arm over her shoulders. 'Like I said, the past is past. And it's too nice a day to think about it. Maybe we should take some time off later in the week. Rent some skis or try some parasailing.'

'Parasailing.' She looked up at the sky, relieved that his voice was casual again. 'Have you ever done it?'

'Sure. The next best thing to being under the water is being over it.'

'I'm game if you are. But if we're going to talk the rest of this crew into a day off, we'd better get to work. Get your hammer, Lassiter. It's back to the chain gang.'

They'd barely begun to work on conglomerate, when they heard a shout over the port side. Tate brushed off her hands and strolled over.

'Matthew,' she said in a thin voice. 'Come here. Mom.' She cleared her throat. 'Mom! Come out. Bring the camera. Oh, God. Hurry.'

'For heaven's sake, Tate, I'm frying shrimp.' Exasperated, Marla came on deck with the video camera swinging from her arm. 'I don't have time to take movies.'

Tate, with her hand vised on Matthew's, turned and grinned idiotically. 'I think you'll want to take one of this.'

Marla scooted to Tate's other side, and the three of them looked over the rail.

Both Buck and Ray bobbed in the water, faces beaming maniacally. Each gripped the side of a bucket that shimmered and dripped with gold doubloons.

'Jesus Christ,' Matthew breathed. 'Is that thing full?'

'To the brim,' Ray called out. 'And we've filled two more below.'

'You ain't seen nothing like it, boy. We're rich as kings.' Water trickled down Buck's face, from his eyes. 'There are thousands of them, thousands, just lying there. You gonna haul this up, or you want us to pitch them to you one at a time?'

Ray howled with laughter, and the two men batted each other on the head. Coins spilled out of the bucket, like loose fish.

'Wait, wait, I have to get you in frame.' Marla fumbled, cursed, laughed. 'Oh hell, I can't find the record button.'

'I'll do it.' Tate snatched the camera, bobbled it. 'Hold it steady, guys, and smile.'

'They're going to drown each other.' Matthew gripped the rope and drew the bucket up. 'Christ, it's heavy. Give me a hand here.'

Marla grunted, nearly upended over the rail, but hauled the rope with him while Tate gleefully recorded the scene. 'I'm

77

going to go down with the underwater camera.' Awed, she plunged her hand into the coins when Matthew set the bucket on deck. 'God, who'd have imagined it? I'm up to my elbow in doubloons.'

'Told you to imagine big, girl,' Buck shouted. 'Marla, you get out your fanciest dress 'cause we're going dancing tonight.'

'That's my wife, pal.'

'Not after I kill you, hoss. Going to get another bucket.'

'Not if I get there first.'

Tate sprang up and raced for her wetsuit. 'I'm going down with the underwater camera. I want to get this on film, give them a hand.'

'I'll be right with you. Marla.' Matthew snapped his fingers in front of Marla's glazed eyes. 'Marla, I think your shrimp's burning.'

'Oh. Oh, my lord.' Still clutching a handful of doubloons, she dashed to the galley.

'Do you know what this means?' Tate demanded as she fought her way into her wetsuit.

'That we're stinking rich.' Matthew snatched her off her feet and whirled her around.

'Think of the equipment we can buy. Sonar, magnetometers, a bigger boat.' She gave him a sloppy kiss before wriggling away. 'Two bigger boats. I'll get a computer for listing artifacts.'

'Maybe we should get a submersible while we're at it.'

'Good. Put that down. One submersible with robotics so we can mine the abyss on our next expedition.'

He hooked on his weight belt. 'What about fancy clothes, cars, jewelry?'

'Not a priority, but I'll keep it in mind. Mom! We're going down to give Dad and Buck a hand.'

'See if you can catch me some more shrimp.' Marla poked her head out, held out a platter filled with blackened blobs. 'These aren't fit to eat.'

'Marla, I'm going to buy you a trawler of shrimp, another of beer.' On impulse, Matthew caught her face in his hands and kissed her full on the mouth. 'I love you.'

'Might try telling me that,' Tate mumbled under her breath, then jumped off the side. She went in feet first, then tucked neatly and began to swim. Following the line, she kicked through the murky cloud, and into the clear.

There Ray and Buck hovered at the bottom, a second bucket of gold beside them as they plucked through the pay dirt. She snapped a picture as Buck handed her father a blackened brick that was an ingot of silver.

Fish swam around them, a living carousel, as they mined the sand. Medallions, more coins, oblong bricks of discolored silver. Ray found a dagger, its handle and blade crusted with sea life. Feigning a dueling stance, he jabbed it playfully at Buck, who hefted an ingot and mimed a defense.

Beside Tate, Matthew shook his head, circled his finger around his ear.

Yes, she thought, they were crazy. And wasn't it great?

She swam clear to take her pictures from different angles. She wanted a good composition of the little pyramid of ingots, another of the odd sculpture of coins and medals fused together beside the glinting bucket.

National Geographic, she thought gleefully, here I come. The Beaumont Museum just found its cornerstone.

She accepted the dagger her father offered. With her diver's knife she scraped delicately at the handle. Her eyes rounded at the glint of a ruby. Like a buccaneer she tucked it into her weight belt.

Through signals, Buck indicated that he and Matthew would haul up the next load. Ray pantomimed opening a bottle of champagne, drinking. This met with unanimous agreement. Giving the 'okay' sign, Buck and Matthew kicked toward the surface with a bucket between them.

Tate gestured for her father to stand with one flipper poised on the pile of ingots and snapped pictures as he happily hammed it up for her. She was bubbling with laughter when she let the camera drop by its strap.

And then she noticed the stillness.

It was odd, she thought absently. All the fish were gone. Even Smiley seemed to have whisked himself away. Nothing stirred in the water, and the silence was suddenly and eerily heavy.

She glanced up through the murk and saw the shadow of Matthew and Buck as they carried their rich burden to the surface.

And then she saw the nightmare.

It came so fast, so quiet, that her mind rejected it. First there was nothing but the figures of the men swimming through the cloudy water, the sun fighting through it in thin misty streams. Then the shadow bulleted out of nowhere.

Someone screamed. Later her father would tell her the sound had come from her, and had alerted him. But by that time she was already clawing her way up.

The shark was longer than a man, perhaps ten feet. In her horror, she could see that its jaw was already open for the kill. She saw the moment they understood the danger and screamed again because she knew it was too late.

The men broke apart, as if propelled. Gold poured down through the water like dazzling rain. With terror digging talons into her throat, Tate watched the shark take Buck in his vicious mouth, shake him like a dog shakes a rat. The force of the attack ripped off his mask and mouthpiece as the shark tore him through the blood-smeared water. Somehow her knife was in her hand.

The shark dived, still thrashing as Matthew plunged his blade into its flesh, aiming for and missing the brain. The desperate jab left a gash, but the fish, frenzied on blood, held on to its prey and rammed his attacker.

Lips peeled back from his teeth, Matthew stabbed and hacked. Buck was dead. He knew Buck was dead. And his only thought was to kill. The shark's black, glasslike eye fixed on him, rolled back white. Buck's body drifted free in the swirling blood as the fish sought fresh prey and mindless revenge.

Matthew braced himself, prepared to kill or die. And Tate burst through the hideous murk like a warrior angel, an ancient dagger in one hand, a diver's knife in the other.

He thought his fear had reached his limit. But it doubled then, almost paralyzed him, as the shark turned toward the movement and charged her. Blind with terror, he kicked forward through the curtain of blood, rammed hard against the wounded shark to impede its progress. With a strength born of hot panic, Matthew plunged his knife into its back to the hilt.

And prayed as he had never known he could.

Grimly, he held on while the shark rolled and thrashed. He saw that while his blade had found its mark, so had hers. She'd ripped open its belly.

Matthew let the carcass go and saw that Ray was struggling toward them with his knife freed in one hand while he hauled Buck's limp body. Knowing what the bloody water could bring, Matthew dragged Tate toward the surface.

'Get in the boat,' he ordered. But her face was chalk white, her eyes beginning to roll back. He slapped her once, twice, until she focused. 'Get in the fucking boat. Haul anchor. Do it.'

She nodded, breath sobbing, and struck out in awkward strokes as he dived again. Her hands kept slipping on the ladder, and she'd forgotten to pull off her flippers. She couldn't find the air to call out. Her mother had turned on the radio, and Madonna was slyly claiming to be just like a virgin.

Her tanks clattered on deck, and the noise had Marla strolling over from the starboard side. In an instant, she was crouched beside Tate.

'Mama. Shark.' Tate rolled over to her hands and knees and choked up water. 'Buck. Oh God.'

'You're all right?' Marla's voice was high and thin. 'Oh, baby, are you all right?'

'It's Buck. Hospital. He needs a hospital. Pull up the anchor. Hurry.'

'Ray, Tate. Your father?'

'He's all right. Hurry. Radio the island.'

As Marla raced off, Tate pushed herself up; she dragged off her belt, turning her eyes away from the blood on her hands. She stood, swayed, bit her lip hard to keep from passing out. As she ran to the side, she dragged off her tanks.

'He's alive.' Ray grabbed for the ladder. Between them, he and Matthew supported Buck's body. 'Help us get him onboard.' His eyes, full of horror and pain, met hers. 'Hold on to yourself, baby.'

As they lifted Buck's unconscious form into the boat, she saw why he had warned her. The shark had taken his leg below the knee.

Bile rose to her throat. Grimly, she swallowed it, gritting her teeth until the nausea and dizziness passed. She heard her mother gasp, but when she turned, her movements slow and sluggish, Marla was moving forward briskly.

'We need blankets, Tate. And towels. Plenty of towels. Hurry. And the first-aid kit. Ray, I radioed ahead. They're expecting us at Frigate Bay. You'd better take the wheel.' She pulled off her blouse beneath which she wore a pretty white lace bra. Without a wince she used the crisp cotton to staunch the blood at the stub of Buck's leg.

'Good girl,' she murmured when Tate ran back with arm-loads of towels. 'Matthew, pack these around the wound. Hold them firmly against it. Matthew.' Her voice was dead calm and with enough steel to have his head jerking up. 'He needs lots of pressure on that leg, understand me. We're not having him bleed to death.'

'He's not dead,' Matthew said dully as she took his hands and pressed them to the towels she'd packed against the wound. There was already a sickening pool of blood welling on the deck.

'No, he's not dead. And he's not going to be. We'll need a tourniquet.' Her eyes stung as she noticed Buck was still wearing his left flipper, but her hands were quick and efficient. They never trembled as she fixed the tourniquet above the gory stump of his right leg.

'We need to keep him warm,' she said calmly. 'We'll have him to the hospital in a few minutes. In just a few minutes.'

Tate covered Buck with a blanket, then knelt on the bloody deck to take his hand. Then she reached for Matthew's and linked the three of them.

She held on as the boat flew through the water toward land.

Chapter Seven

MATTHEW SAT ON the floor in the hospital corridor and tried to keep his mind blank. If he let down his guard, for even an instant, he was back in the bloody swirl of water, staring into the doll's eyes of the shark, seeing those wicked rows of teeth slice into Buck.

He knew he would see it hundreds, thousands of times in his sleep – the blinding scream of bubbles, the thrashing of man and fish, the blade of his own knife plunging and hacking.

Each time the scene rolled through his brain, what had taken only minutes stretched hideously into hours, each movement slowed into horrible clarity. He could see it all, from the first bump when Buck had shoved him out of the shark's attack path and through to the rush and noise of the Emergency Room.

Slowly, he lifted his hand, flexed it. He remembered how Buck's fingers had tightened on it, gripped hard on that race to the island. He'd known then that Buck was alive. And that was somehow worse, because he couldn't convince himself that Buck would stay that way.

It seemed that the sea delighted in taking the people he cared for most.

Angelique's Curse, he thought on a wave of guilt and grief. Maybe Buck had been right. The fucking necklace was down there, just lying in wait for a victim. The search for it had taken two people he'd loved.

It wasn't going to get another.

He opened his hand, rubbed it hard over his face like a man waking from a long sleep. He thought he must be going a little crazy, thinking this way. A man had killed his father, and a shark had killed Buck. It was a pitiful defense against his own failure to save them that had him blaming an amulet he'd never even seen.

However bloody that ancient necklace and the lore surrounding it might be, Matthew knew he couldn't point the guilt at anyone or anything but himself. If he'd been quicker, Buck would still be whole. If he'd been smarter, his father would still be alive.

As he was alive. As he was whole. He would have to carry that weight for the rest of his life.

For a moment, he rested his brow on his knees, fought to clear his head again. He knew the Beaumonts were just down the hall in the waiting room. They'd offered him comfort, support, unity. And he'd had to escape. Their quiet compassion had all but destroyed him.

He already knew that if Buck had even a slim chance of survival, it wasn't due to him, but to Marla's quick, calm and unflinching handling of a crisis. It was she who had taken control, even down to remembering to grab clothes from the boat.

He hadn't even been able to fill out the hospital forms, but had only stared at them until she'd taken the clipboard from him, gently asked the questions and filled in the blanks herself.

It was frightening to discover that he was, essentially, useless.

'Matthew.' Tate crouched in front of him, took his hands and wrapped them around a cup of coffee. 'Come in and sit down.'

He shook his head. Because the coffee was in his hands he lifted it and sipped. He could see that her face was still pale and glossy with shock, her eyes red. But the hand she rested on his updrawn knee was steady.

In one terrifying mental blip, he saw her hurtling through the water toward the jaws of the shark.

'Go away, Tate.'

84

Instead, she sat beside him, draped an arm around his shoulders. 'He's going to make it, Matthew. I know it.'

'What, are you a fortune teller now, on top of everything else?'

His voice was cold and sharp. Though it wounded, she leaned her head on his shoulder. 'It's important to believe it. It helps to believe it.'

She was wrong. It hurt to believe it. Because it did, he jerked away from her, got to his feet. 'I'm going for a walk.'

'I'll go with you.'

'I don't want you.' He whirled on her, letting all the fear, the guilt, the grief explode into fury. 'I don't want you anywhere near me.'

Her stomach quaked, her eyes stung, but she held her ground. 'I'm not leaving you alone, Matthew. You'd better get used to it.'

'I don't want you,' he repeated, and stunned her by putting a hand just under her throat and pushing her against the wall. 'I don't need you. Now, why don't you go get your nice, pretty family and take off?'

'Because Buck matters to us.' Though she managed to swallow the tears, they roughened her voice. 'So do you.'

'You don't even know us.' Something was screaming inside him to get out. To keep it hidden even from himself, he pushed her. His face, inches from hers, was hard, cold, merciless. 'You're just out for a lark, taking a few months in the sun to play at treasure-hunting. You got lucky. You don't know what it's like to go month after month, year after year and have nothing to show for it. To die and have nothing.'

Her breath was hitching now no matter how she fought to control it. 'He's not going to die.'

'He's already dead.' The fury died from his eyes like a light switched off and left them blank and flat. 'He was dead the minute he pushed me out of the way. The goddamn idiot pushed me out of the way.'

There it was, the worst of it, out, ringing on the sterilized hospital air. He turned from it, covered his face, but couldn't escape it.

'He pushed me out of the way, got in front of me. What the hell was he thinking of? What were you thinking of?' Matthew demanded, spinning back to her with all the helpless anger rolling back into him like a riptide. 'Coming at us that way. Don't you know anything? When a shark's got blood it'll attack anything. You should have headed for the boat. With that much

85

blood in the water, we were lucky it didn't draw a dozen sharks in to feed. What the hell were you thinking of?'

'You.' She said it quietly and stayed where she was, backed against the wall. 'I guess both Buck and I were thinking about you. I couldn't have handled it if anything had happened to you, Matthew. I couldn't have lived with it. I love you.'

Undone, he stared at her. There had been no one, in his whole life, who had said those three words to him. 'Then you're stupid,' he managed, and pulled unsteady fingers through his hair.

'Maybe.' Her lips were trembling. Even when she pressed them hard together, they vibrated with the power of her roiling emotions. 'I guess you were pretty stupid, too. You didn't leave Buck. You thought he was dead and you could have gotten away while the shark had him. You didn't. Why didn't you head for the boat, Matthew?'

He only shook his head. When she stepped forward to put her arms around him, he buried his face in her hair. 'Tate.'

'It's all right,' she murmured, running soothing strokes up his rigid back. 'It's going to be all right. Just hold on to me.'

'I'm bad luck.'

'That's foolish. You're just tired now, and worried. Come in and sit down. We'll all wait together.'

She stayed beside him. The hours passed in that dream state so common to hospitals. People came and went. There was the soft flap of crepesoled shoes on tile as nurses passed the doorway, the smell of overbrewed coffee, the sharp tang of antiseptic that never quite masked the underlying odor of sickness. Occasionally there was the faint swish as the elevator doors opened and closed.

Then softly, gently, rain began to patter on the windows.

Tate dozed with her head pillowed on Matthew's shoulder. She was awake and aware the instant his body tensed. Instinctively, she reached for his hand as she looked toward the doctor.

He came in quietly, a surprisingly young man with lines of fatigue around his eyes and mouth. His skin, the color of polished ebony, looked like folded black silk.

'Mr. Lassiter.' Despite the obvious weariness, his voice was as musical as the evening rain.

'Yes.' Braced for condolences, Matthew pushed himself to his feet.

'I am Doctor Farrge. Your uncle has come through the surgery. Please sit.'

'What do you mean, come through?'

'He has survived the operation.' Farrge sat on the edge of the coffee table, waited for Matthew to settle. 'His condition is critical. You know he lost a great deal of blood. More than three liters. If he had lost even a fraction more, if it had taken you even ten minutes longer to get him here, there would have been no chance. However, his heart is very strong. We're optimistic.'

Hope was too painful. Matthew simply nodded. 'Are you telling me he's going to live?'

'Every hour his chances improve.'

'And those chances are?'

Farrge took a moment to measure his man. With some, kindness didn't comfort. 'He has perhaps a forty percent chance of surviving the night. If he does, I would upgrade that. Further treatment will be necessary, of course, when he is stabilized and stronger. When this time comes I can recommend to you several specialists who have good reputations in treating patients with amputated limbs.'

'Is he conscious?' Marla asked quietly.

'No. He will be in recovery for some time, then in our Critical Care Unit. I would not expect him to be alert for several hours. I would suggest that you leave a number where you can be reached at the nurses' station. We'll contact you if there is any change.'

'I'm staying,' Matthew said simply. 'I want to see him.'

'Once he is in CCU, you'll be able to see him. But only for a short period.'

'We'll get a hotel.' Ray rose, laid a hand on Matthew's shoulder. 'We'll take shifts here.'

'I'm not leaving.'

'Matthew.' Ray squeezed gently. 'We need to work as a team.' He glanced at his daughter, read what was in her eyes. 'Marla and I will find us some rooms, make the arrangements. We'll come back and relieve you and Tate in a few hours.'

There were so many tubes snaking out from the still figure in the bed. Machines beeped and hummed. Outside the thin curtain Matthew could hear the quiet murmurings of the nurses, their brisk steps as they went about the business of tending lives.

But in this room, narrow and dim, he was alone with Buck. He forced himself to look down at the sheet, at the odd way it lay. He would have to get used to it, he thought. They would both have to get used to it.

If Buck lived.

He barely looked alive now, his face slack, his body so strangely tidy in the bed. Buck was a tosser, Matthew remembered, a man who tugged and kicked at sheets, one who snored violently enough to scrape the paint from the walls.

But he was as still and silent now as a man in a coffin.

Matthew took the broad, scarred hand in his, a gesture he knew would have embarrassed both of them had Buck been conscious. He held it, studying the face he'd thought he knew as well as his own.

Had he ever noticed how thick Buck's eyebrows were, or how the gray peppered them? And when had the lines around his eyes begun to crisscross that way? Wasn't it strange that his forehead, which rose into that egg-shaped skull, was so smooth? Like a girl's.

Jesus, Matthew thought, and squeezed his eyes tight. His leg was gone.

Fighting off panic, Matthew leaned down. He was nearly comforted by the sound of Buck's breathing.

'That was a damn stupid thing to do. You made a mistake getting in front of me that way. Maybe you figured on wrestling with that shark, but I guess you're not as quick as you used to be. Now you probably figure I owe you. Well, you've got to live to collect.'

He tightened his grip. 'You hear that, Buck? You've got to live to collect. Think about that. You kick off on me, you lose, and me and the Beaumonts will just split your share of the *Marguerite* on top of it. Your first big strike, Buck, and if you don't pull out of this, you won't get to spend the first coin.'

A nurse parted the curtain, a gentle reminder that the time was up.

'It'd be a real shame if you didn't get to enjoy some of that fame and fortune you've always wanted, Buck. You keep that in mind. They're tossing me out of here, but I'll be back.'

In the corridor, Tate paced, as much from nerves as the need to keep herself awake. The moment she saw Matthew come through the doors, she hurried over.

'Did he wake up at all?'

'No.'

Taking his hand, Tate struggled with her own fears. 'The doctor said he wouldn't. I suppose we were all hoping otherwise. Mom and Dad are going to take a shift now.' When he started to shake his head, she squeezed his fingers impatiently. 'Matthew, listen to me. We're all a part of this. And I think he's going to need all of us, so we may as well start now. You and I are going to the hotel. We're going to get a meal, and we're going to sleep for a few hours.'

As she spoke, she drew him down the corridor. After sending her parents a bolstering smile, she steered Matthew toward the elevators.

'We're all going to lean on each other, Matthew. That's the way it works.'

'There has to be something I can do.'

'You're doing it,' she said gently. 'We'll be back soon. You just need to rest a little. So do I.'

He looked at her then. Her skin was so pale it seemed he could pass his hand through it. Smudges of exhaustion bruised her eyes. He hadn't been thinking of her, he realized. Nor had he considered that she might have needed to lean on him.

'You need sleep.'

'I could use a couple of hours.' Keeping her hand on his, she stepped into the elevator car, pushed the button for the lobby. 'Then we'll come back. You can sit with Buck again until he wakes up.'

'Yeah.' Matthew stared blankly at the descending numbers. 'Until he wakes up.'

Outside, the wind kicked at the rain, swept through palm fronds. The cab bumped along the narrow, deserted streets, its tires sluicing at puddles. It was like driving through someone else's dream – the dark, the huddle of unfamiliar buildings shifting in the glare of headlights, the monotonous squeak of the wipers across the windshield.

Matthew fished Caribbean bills from his wallet as Tate climbed out. In seconds, the rain plastered her hair to her head.

'Dad gave me the room keys,' she began. 'It's not the Ritz.' She tried another smile as they entered the tiny lobby crowded with wicker chairs and leafy plants. 'But it's close to the hospital. We're on the second floor.'

They took the steps with Tate jingling the keys nervously in her hand. 'This is your room. Dad said we were right next door.' She looked down at the keys, studied the number.

'Matthew, can I come in with you? I don't want to be by myself.' She shifted her gaze to his. 'I know it's stupid, but–'

'It's okay. Come on.' He took the key from her, unlocked the door.

There was a bed with a spread of brightly colored orange and red flowers, a small dresser. The lamp's shade was askew. Marla had brought him a kit from the boat, and had left it neatly at the foot of the bed. Matthew switched on the lamp. Its glow was yellowed by the crooked shade. Rain beat against the window in angry fists.

'It's not much,' Tate murmured. Compelled, she reached out to straighten the lampshade, as if the little homemaker's gesture would make the room less sad.

'Not what you're used to, I guess.' Matthew strode into the adjoining bath and came out with a thin towel the size of a place mat. 'Dry your hair.'

'Thanks. I know you need to sleep. I should probably leave you alone.'

He sat on the side of the bed, concentrated on removing his shoes. 'You can sleep in here if you want. You don't have to worry about anything.'

'I wouldn't be worried.'

'You should.' On a sigh, he rose and, taking the towel, rubbed it briskly over her hair himself. 'But you don't have to. Take off your shoes, and stretch out.'

'You'll lie down with me?'

He glanced over as she sat and fumbled tiredly with the laces of her sneakers. He knew he could have her – one touch, one word. He could lose himself and all of this misery in her. She would be soft, and willing, and sweet.

And he would hate himself.

Saying nothing, he turned down the spread. He stretched out on the sheet, held out a hand to her. Without hesitation, she lay down beside him, curled her body to his, pillowed her head on his shoulder.

There was one keen slice of need low in his gut. It mellowed to a dull ache as she settled her palm on his chest. He turned his face into her rain-scented hair and found a baffling mix of comfort and pain.

Safe, lulled by trust, she let her eyes close. 'It's going to be all right. I know it's going to be all right. I love you, Matthew.'

She slipped into sleep as easily as a child. Matthew listened to the rain and waited for dawn.

The shark shot through the water, a sleek gray bullet armed with ready teeth and a lust for blood. The water was red and roiling, choking her as she struggled to escape. She was screaming, gasping for air she couldn't find. Those jaws opened, hideously wide. Then closed over her with a pain too excruciating to name.

She came awake with a scream locked in her throat. Curling into a ball, she fought her way out of the nightmare. She was in Matthew's room, she reminded herself. She was safe. He was safe.

And she was alone.

Lifting her head, she saw the murky sunlight just easing in the window. Panic came first that he had somehow gotten word that Buck had died, and had gone back to the hospital without her. Then she realized what she thought was rain was the shower.

The storm was over, and Matthew was here.

She let out a long breath, pushed at her disheveled hair. She could be grateful he hadn't been with her when she'd had the nightmare. He was already carrying so much weight, she thought. She wouldn't add to it. She would be brave and strong, and give him whatever support he needed.

When the bathroom door opened, Tate had a smile ready. Despite her worries, her heart did a quick tumble at the sight of him, damp from his shower, bare chested, his jeans carelessly unfastened.

'You're awake.' Matthew hooked his thumbs into his front pockets and tried not to think about how she looked sitting with her arms wrapped around her knees in the middle of the bed. 'I thought you might sleep awhile longer.'

'No, I'm fine.' Suddenly awkward, she moistened her lips. 'The rain stopped.'

'I noticed.' Just as he noticed how big and soft and aware her eyes had become. 'I'm going to head back to the hospital.'

'We're going back to the hospital,' she corrected. 'I'll go shower and change.' She was already climbing off the bed, picking up her key. 'Mom said there was a coffee shop next door. I'll meet you there in ten minutes.'

'Tate.' He hesitated when she stopped at the door, turned back. What could he say? How could he say it? 'Nothing. Ten minutes.'

They were back at the hospital in thirty. Both Ray and Marla rose from the bench outside of CCU, where they had taken up the watch.

They looked, Matthew thought, rumpled. It had always impressed him that no matter what the circumstances, the Beaumonts were so neatly groomed. Now, their clothes were wrinkled and limp. Ray's face was shadowed by a night's growth of beard. In all the weeks they'd worked together, he'd never seen Ray unshaven. For reasons Matthew couldn't pinpoint, he focused on that one small fact. Ray hadn't shaved.

'They won't tell us much,' Ray began. 'Only that he had a restful night.'

'They let us go in for a few minutes every hour.' Marla took Matthew's hand, gave it a squeeze. 'Did you get some rest, honey?'

'Yeah.' Matthew cleared his throat. She hadn't brushed her hair, he thought foolishly. Ray hadn't shaved, and Marla hadn't brushed her hair. 'I want to tell both of you how much I appreciate—'

'Don't insult us.' Marla deliberately laced a scold into her voice. 'Matthew Lassiter, you use that polite tone with that polite phrase on strangers when you feel obligated. Not with friends who love you.'

He'd never known anyone else who could shame and touch him at the same time. 'What I meant was I'm glad you're here.'

'I think his color's better.' Ray put an arm around his wife, gave her a quick, warm hug. 'Don't you, Marla?'

'Yes, I do. And the nurse said Doctor Farrge would be looking in on him shortly.'

'Matthew and I will take over now. I want the two of you to go get some breakfast, and a little more sleep.'

Ray studied his daughter's face, judged her fit, and nodded. 'We'll do just that. You call the hotel if there's any change. Otherwise, we'll be back by noon.'

When they were alone, Tate took Matthew's hand. 'Let's go see him.'

Maybe his color was better, Matthew thought a few moments later when he stood over his uncle's bed. Buck's face was still drawn, but that horrible gray wash had faded.

'His chances go up every hour,' Tate reminded him, and slipped her hand over Buck's. 'He made it through surgery, Matthew, and he made it through the night.'

The dim glow of hope was more painful than despair. 'He's tough. See that scar there.' With a fingertip, Matthew traced a jagged pucker along Buck's right forearm. 'Barracuda. Yucatán. I was running the airlift, and Buck and the fish ran into each other in the fallout cloud. Went and got himself stitched up. Was back in the water within an hour. He's got a beaut on his hip where—'

'Matthew.' Tate's voice was shaky. 'Matthew, he squeezed my hand.'

'What?'

'He squeezed my hand. Look. Look at his fingers.'

They flexed on Tate's, a slow curl. Matthew's skin went cold, then hot as he looked at his uncle's face. Buck's eyelids fluttered.

'I think he's coming around.'

A tear leaked out of the corner of Tate's eye as she gave Buck's hand an answering squeeze. 'Talk to him, Matthew.'

'Buck.' With his heart skidding in his chest, Matthew leaned closer. 'Goddamn it, Buck, I know you hear me. I'm not going to waste my time·talking to myself.'

Buck's eyelids fluttered again. 'Shit.'

'Shit.' Tate began to weep quietly. 'Did you hear that, Matthew? He said "shit." '

'He would.' Matthew grabbed Buck's hand as his throat burned. 'Come on, you candy ass. Wake up.'

'I'm 'wake. Jesus.' Buck opened his eyes, saw blurs. Shapes swam and shivered. He had the sensation of floating, found it not altogether unpleasant. His vision cleared enough for him to make out Matthew's face. 'What the hell. Thought I was dead.'

'That makes two of us.'

'He didn't get you, did he?' Buck's voice slurred as he struggled to get the words around his tongue. 'That bastard didn't get you?'

'No.' Guilt crashed down on Matthew like cold, honed steel. 'No, he didn't get me. It was a tiger, about a ten-footer,' he said, understanding that Buck would want to know. 'We killed him, Tate and me. He's fish bait now.'

'Good.' Buck closed his eyes again. 'Fucking hate sharks.'

'I'll go tell the nurse,' Tate said quietly.

'Fucking hate them,' Buck repeated. 'Ugly bastards. Probably a rogue, but make sure we got bats and bangsticks.'

He opened his eyes again. Gradually the machines and the tubes came into focus. His brow puckered. 'Not the boat.'

Matthew's heart began to thud in his throat. 'No. You're in the hospital.'

'Hate hospitals. Goddamn doctors. Boy, you know I hate hospitals.'

'I know.' Matthew concentrated on soothing the panic he saw in Buck's eyes. He'd worry about his own reaction later. 'Had to bring you in, Buck. The fish hurt you.'

'A couple of stitches . . .'

Matthew could see the instant Buck began to remember. 'Take it easy, Buck. You've got to take it easy.'

'Got hold of me.' The sensations rushed back, one tumbled over another like nasty children in a street brawl. Fear, pain, horror and a skittering dread that triumphed over the rest.

He remembered the agony, the helplessness of being shaken and torn, choking on his own blood, blinded by it. That last clear memory of staring into those black, hate-filled eyes as they rolled up white with cold pleasure.

'Son of a bitch got hold of me.' Buck's voice jerked as he fought against Matthew to sit up. 'How bad? How bad he get me, boy?'

'Calm down. You've got to calm down.' Struggling to keep his hands gentle, Matthew pinned Buck to the bed. It was pitifully easy. 'If you act like this, they'll knock you out again.'

'Tell me.' Panic darting in his eyes, Buck took a fistful of Matthew's shirt. The grip was so weak, Matthew could have shaken it off with a shrug. But he didn't have the heart. 'You tell me what that bastard did to me.'

Of all the things that had been between them, there had never been lies. Matthew covered Buck's hands with his, looked him square in the eyes.

'He took your leg, Buck. The fucker took your leg.'

Chapter Eight

'YOU'RE NOT GOING to blame yourself.'

Tate stopped her restless pacing to sit beside Matthew on the bench outside CCU. It had been a full day since Buck had regained consciousness. The better the outlook for his recovery, the deeper Matthew sank into depression.

'I don't see anyone else around here to blame.'

'Things sometimes happen that aren't anyone's fault. Matthew . . .' Patience, she warned herself. The snap of her temper wouldn't help him. 'What happened was horrible, tragic. You couldn't stop it. You can't change it now. All you can do, all we can do, is see him through it.'

'He lost his goddamn leg, Tate. And every time he looks at me, we both know it should have been me.'

'Well, it wasn't you.' The thought that it could have been haunted her relentlessly. 'And thinking it should have been is stupid.' Weary of reasoning, drained from the struggle to stay strong and supportive, she dragged a hand through her hair. 'He's afraid now, and he's angry and depressed. But he isn't blaming you.'

'Isn't he?' Matthew looked up. Grief now warred with bitterness in his eyes.

'No, he's not. Because he isn't as shallow and self-important as you.' She sprang up from the bench. 'I'm going in to see him. You can sit here and wallow in self-pity by yourself.'

Head high, she sailed across the corridor and through the doors to Critical Care. The moment she was out of Matthew's sight, she stopped, took time to compose herself. After fixing on a sunny smile, she nudged Buck's curtain aside.

His eyes opened when she came in. Behind his thick lenses, his eyes were dull.

'Hey.' As if he'd greeted her with a wink and a wave, she marched over to kiss his cheek. 'I hear they're moving you down to a regular room in a day or two. One with a TV and better-looking nurses.'

'Said they might.' He winced as pain in his phantom leg plagued him. 'Thought you and the boy'd gone back to the boat.'

'No, Matthew's right outside. Do you want him?'

Buck shook his head. He began to pleat the sheet between his fingers. 'Ray was in before.'

'Yes, I know.'

'Said there was some specialist in Chicago I'm supposed to go to once they let me out of here.'

'Yeah. He's supposed to be brilliant.'

'Not smart enough to put my leg back on.'

'They'll give you an even better one.' She knew her voice was over-bright, but couldn't control it. 'Did you ever see that show, Buck? The one with the bionic man. I loved it when I was a kid. You'll be "Bionic Buck." '

The corner of his mouth twitched briefly. 'Yeah, sure, that's me. Bionic Buck, king of the cripples.'

'I'm not going to stay if you talk that way.'

He shrugged a shoulder. He was too tired to argue. Almost too tired to feel sorry for himself. 'Better if you didn't. You should get back to the boat. Got to get that booty up before somebody else does.'

'You shouldn't worry about that. We've got our claim.'

'You don't know nothing,' he snapped at her. 'That's the trouble with amateurs. Word's out by now. It's out all right, after this especially. Shark attacks are always news, especially in tourist waters. They'll be coming.' His fingers began to drum a quick

96

tattoo on the mattress. 'You locked up what we got already, didn't you? Someplace nice and tight?'

'I–' She hadn't given the treasure a thought in two days. Doubted anyone had. 'Sure.' She had to swallow on the lie. 'Sure, Buck, don't worry.'

'Got to go down, get the rest up quick. Did I tell Ray?' His eyes fluttered and he forced them open again. 'Did I tell him? Fucking medication makes my head foggy. Got to get it up. All that gold. Like blood to sharks.' He laughed as his head lolled back on the pillow. 'Like blood to sharks. Ain't that a kick in the ass? Got the treasure. Only cost me my goddamn leg. Get it up, lock it away, girl. You do that.'

'Okay, Buck.' Gently, she stroked his brow. 'I'm going to take care of it. Rest now.'

'Don't go down alone.'

'No, of course not,' she murmured and slipped his glasses off.

'Angelique's Curse. She don't want anyone to win. Be careful.'

'I will. Just rest.'

When she was sure he was asleep, she went out quietly. Matthew was no longer on the bench, nor in the corridor. A check of her watch told her that her parents would be there in less than an hour.

She hesitated, then walked decisively to the elevators. She'd take care of things herself.

She felt at home the moment she stepped aboard the *Adventure*. Someone, her mother she imagined, had washed down the decks. There was no trace of blood, and the equipment was once again tidily stowed away.

Rather than try to remember what they had left aboard before Buck's accident, she ducked into the deckhouse for her notebook.

The moment she did, she knew something was wrong.

Everything was tidy. The cushions were plumped, the table gleaming. The galley beyond the living area was spotless. But there was no notebook on the table. There were no artifacts carefully set there, or on the counter for cleaning and cataloguing.

After the first shiver of alarm had passed, she told herself her parents had probably done just what she had come to do. They had gathered up the booty and taken it to the hotel. Or out to the *Sea Devil*.

The boat was more logical, she decided. They would keep it all together. Wouldn't they?

She looked back to shore, wondering if she should go and find them. But here, alone, Buck's urgency began to claw at her. She would go out to the *Sea Devil* and check for herself. It was a short trip, one she could easily handle alone.

Calmer now that she had a goal, she went to the bridge, weighed anchor. An hour, she thought. No more for a quick round-trip. Then she could reassure Buck that everything was taken care of.

As she cruised out to open sea, her tension dissolved. Life always seemed so simple with a deck under her feet. Overhead, gulls swooped and scolded, and the sea, the sheer blue stretch of it, beckoned. With the wind on her face and the wheel under her hands, she wondered if she would have found this fascinating world if she'd had different parents. Would the lure have been there if she had been raised conventionally, without tales of the sea and treasures as her bedtime stories?

Just then, with the sea shimmering around her, she was sure she would. Destiny, she thought, was a patient master. It waited.

She had found hers, earlier than some, she supposed. Already she could see her life with Matthew unfolding before her. Together they would sail the world, unlocking secrets from the sea's vault. Partners, she mused, in every way.

In time, he would come to learn that the value of what they did went beyond the flash of gold. They would build a museum, and bring the thrill and the pulse of history to hundreds of people.

One day they would have children, make a family, and she would write a book about their adventures. He'd come to understand that there was nothing they couldn't do, nothing they couldn't be, with each other.

Like destiny, Tate would be patient.

She was smiling over her daydreams when she caught sight of the *Sea Devil*. The smile faded into puzzlement. Anchored off its port was a gleaming white yacht.

It was a stunner, a hundred feet of luxury and shine. She could see people on deck. A uniformed man carrying a tray of glasses, a woman sunbathing lazily, and apparently naked, a seaman polishing the brightwork on the foredeck. Glass that ribboned the deckhouse and bridge tossed back the sun.

Under different circumstances, she would have admired it, the lovely, somehow feminine lines, the celebration ripple of the brightly striped umbrellas and awnings, but the telltale murk on the surface of the water had already caught her eye.

Someone was below, running an airlift.

Almost shaking with fury, Tate cut her speed, maneuvered the *Adventure* to starboard of the *Sea Devil*. With quick efficiency, she moored her boat.

Now she could smell it, the unmistakable rotten-egg scent that was perfume to treasure hunters. The gases released from a wreck. Without hesitation, she darted from the bridge. Taking time only to pry off her sneakers, she dived over the side and swam to the *Sea Devil*.

Shaking her wet hair out of her eyes, she hauled herself on deck. The tarps she and Matthew had used to cover the booty from the *Santa Marguerite* were in place. But it took only one swift glance to see that much of what they had recovered was missing.

It was the same in the cabin. The emerald cross, the bucket that had been filled with silver coins, the fragile porcelain, the pewter she and her mother had carefully cleaned. Gone. Teeth gritted, she looked back toward the yacht.

Armed with temper and a sense of righteousness, she dived back in the water. She was snarling by the time she climbed the ladder onto the glossy mahogany deck of the yacht.

A blonde, wearing sunglasses, a headset and a thong bottom lounged in a padded chaise.

Tate marched to her, rapped her sharply on the shoulder. 'Who's in charge here?'

'*Qu'est-ce que c'est?*' After a huge yawn, the blonde tipped down the oversized glasses and studied Tate over them with bored blue eyes. '*Qui le diable es-tu?*'

'Who in hell are you?' Tate shot back in angry, fluent French. 'And what do you think you're doing with my wreck?'

The blonde moved a creamy shoulder and slipped off her headphones. 'American,' she decided in poor and irritated English. 'You Americans are so tedious. *Allez.* Go away. You're dripping on me.'

'I'm going to do more than drip on you in a minute, Fifi.'

'Yvette.' With an amused cat smile, she took a long brown cigarette from the pack at her elbow and struck the flame on a slim, gold lighter. 'Ah, what a noise.' She stretched, the movement as feline as her smile. 'All the day and half the night.'

Tate set her teeth. The noise Yvette complained about was the compressor busily running the airlift. 'We have a claim on the *Santa Marguerite*, and you have no right to work her.'

'Marguerite? *C'est qui, cette* Marguerite?' She blew out a fragrant stream of smoke. 'I am the only woman here.' Lifting a brow, she scanned Tate from head to toe. 'The only,' she repeated. Her gaze drifted beyond Tate, and warmed. '*Mon cher*, we have company.'

'So I see.'

Tate turned and saw a slim man in crisp buff-colored shirt and slacks, a tie of muted pastel stripes knotted handsomely at his neck. He wore a panama at a rakish angle over pewter-colored hair. Gold winked against his tanned skin at his wrist and neck. His face, as smooth as a boy's, glowed with health and good cheer. It was strikingly handsome with its long, narrow nose, neatly arched silver brows and thin, curved mouth. His eyes, a translucent blue, were bright with interest.

Tate's first impression was of money and manners. He smiled and offered a hand so charmingly that she nearly accepted before she remembered why she was there.

'Is this your boat?'

'Yes, indeed. Welcome aboard the *Triumphant*. It isn't often we have visits from water nymphs. André,' he called out, his voice cultured and vaguely European. 'Bring a towel for the lady. She's quite wet.'

'I don't want a damn towel. I want you to get your divers up here. That's my wreck.'

'Really? How odd. Won't you sit down, Miss . . .'

'No, I won't sit down, you thieving pirate.'

He blinked, and his smile never wavered. 'It seems you've mistaken me for someone else. I'm sure we can clear up this little misunderstanding in a civilized manner. Ah.' He took the towel from a uniformed steward. 'We need champagne, André. Three glasses.'

'It's going to get real uncivilized,' Tate warned. 'If you don't cut off that compressor.'

'It does make conversation difficult.' He nodded to his steward, then sat. 'Please, do sit down.'

The longer he talked in that calm, lovely voice, smiled that easy, charming smile, the more she felt like a clumsy fool. As a sop to her dignity, she sat stiffly on a deck chair. She would, she determined, be cool, logical and as mannered as he.

'You've taken property off my boats,' Tate began.

He lifted a brow, turning his head so that he could study the *Sea Devil*. 'That unfortunate thing is yours?'

'It belongs to my partners,' Tate muttered. Beside the *Triumphant*, the *Sea Devil* resembled a secondhand garbage scow. 'A number of items are missing from the *Sea Devil* and the *Adventure*. And—'

'My dear girl.' He folded his hands, smiled benignly. A square-cut diamond the size of a Scrabble tile winked on his pinkie. 'Do I look as though I need to steal?'

She said nothing as the steward uncorked a bottle of champagne with a rich, echoing pop. Her voice was as honeyed as the breeze. 'Not everyone steals because they need to. Some people simply enjoy it.'

Now his eyes rounded with delight. 'Astute, as well as attractive. Impressive attributes for one so young.'

Yvette mumbled something uncomplimentary in French, but he only chuckled and patted her hand. '*Ma belle*, do cover yourself. You're embarrassing our guest.'

While Yvette pouted and fastened a scrap of electric blue over her magnificent breasts, he offered Tate a flute of champagne. She had her hand around the stem before she realized she'd been maneuvered.

'Listen—'

'I'd be happy to,' he agreed. He sighed as the compressor fell silent. 'Ah, that is better. Now, you were saying you're missing some property?'

'You're well aware of it. Artifacts from the *Santa Marguerite*. We've been excavating for weeks. We have a legitimate claim.'

He studied her face with obvious interest. It was always a pleasure for him to observe someone so animated and bold, particularly when he had already won. He pitied those who didn't appreciate the true challenge of the business deal, and the true triumph of winning. 'There may be some confusion about that. The claim.' He pursed his lips, then sampled his champagne. 'We are in free water here. The government often disputes such things, which is why I contacted them several months ago to apprise them of my plans to dig here.' He drank again. 'It's unfortunate you weren't informed. Of course, when I

101

arrived I did notice that someone had been poking about. But then, there was no one here.'

Several months ago, my ass, Tate thought, but forced herself to speak calmly. 'We had an accident. One of our team is in the hospital.'

'Oh, how unfortunate. Treasure-hunting can be a dangerous business. It's been a hobby of mine for some years now. I've been quite lucky all in all.'

'The *Sea Devil* was left here,' Tate continued. 'Our markers were here. The rules of salvage–'

'I'm willing to overlook the impropriety.'

Her mouth fell open. '*You're* willing?' The hell with calm. 'You jump our claim, you steal artifacts and records from our boats–'

'I don't know anything about this property you're missing,' he interrupted. His voice firmed, as it would with a difficult underling. 'I suggest you contact the authorities on St. Kitts or Nevis about that.'

'You can be sure I will.'

'Sensible.' He plucked the champagne from its silver bucket, poured more into his glass, into Yvette's. 'Don't you care for Taittinger's?'

Tate set the flute down with a snap. 'You're not going to get away with this. We found the *Marguerite*, we worked her. One of our team nearly died. You're not going to sail in and take what's ours.'

'Ownership in such matters is a foggy area.' He paused a moment to study the wine in his glass. And ownership, of course, was what life was all about. 'You can of course dispute it, but I'm afraid you'll be disappointed with the outcome. I have a reputation for winning.' He beamed at her and stroked a fingertip down Yvette's gleaming arm. 'Now,' he said and rose. 'Perhaps you'd like a tour. I'm very proud of the *Triumphant*. She has some very unique features.'

'I don't give a damn if you've done the head in solid gold.' Her own control surprised her as she rose and stared him down. 'Fancy boats and a European flair don't negate piracy.'

'Sir.' The steward cleared his throat politely. 'You're wanted forward.'

'I'll be along in a moment, André.'

'Yes, Mr. VanDyke.'

'VanDyke,' Tate repeated, and her stomach trembled. 'Silas VanDyke.'

'My reputation precedes me.' He seemed only more pleased that she knew of him. 'How remiss of me not to have introduced myself, Miss . . .'

'Beaumont. It's Tate Beaumont. I know who you are, Mr. VanDyke, and I know what you've done.'

'That's flattering.' He lifted his glass, toasting her before finishing off the frothy wine. 'But then, I've done many things.'

'Matthew told me about you. Matthew Lassiter.'

'Oh, yes, Matthew. I'm sure he has spoken, none too kindly, of me. And since he has, you're probably aware that there is one particular item that interests me.'

'Angelique's Curse.' Her palms might have been damp, but Tate lifted her chin. 'Since you've already killed for it, stealing shouldn't be an obstacle.'

'Ah, young Matthew's been filling your head with nonsense,' he said pleasantly. 'It's understandable that the boy had to blame someone for his father's accident, particularly when his own negligence might have caused it.'

'Matthew isn't negligent,' she snapped back.

'He was young, and hardly to blame. I might have offered to help them financially at the time, but I'm afraid he was unreachable.' He moved his shoulders gently. 'And as I said, Miss Beaumont, treasure-hunting is a dangerous business. Accidents happen. I can make one thing very clear for all of us, however. If the amulet is on the *Marguerite*, it's mine. As is anything else she holds.' The light in his eyes was brighter now, chillingly gracious. 'And I always take, and treasure, what's mine. Isn't that true, *ma belle*?'

Yvette ran a hand down one gleaming thigh. 'Always true.'

'You don't have it yet, do you?' Tate walked to the rail. 'And we'll see who holds the rights to the *Santa Marguerite*.'

'I'm sure we will.' VanDyke turned the empty flute in his hands. 'Oh, and Miss Beaumont, be sure to give the Lassiters my regards, and my regrets.'

Tate heard him chuckling as she dived into the water.

'Silas.' Yvette lighted another cigarette and snuggled down in her chaise. 'What was that annoying American babbling about?'

'Did you find her annoying?' With a pleased smile, Silas watched Tate swim strongly back to the *Adventure*. 'I didn't. I

103

found her fascinating – young, foolishly bold and rather sweetly naive. In my circles, I rarely come across such qualities.'

'So.' Yvette blew out smoke, sulked. 'You think she's attractive with her skinny body and hair like a boy.'

Because his mood was mellow, VanDyke sat on the edge of the chaise and prepared to placate. 'Hardly more than a child. It's women who interest me.' He touched his lips to Yvette's pouty ones. 'You who fascinate me,' he murmured, reaching behind to tug loose the knot of her brief top. 'That's why you're here, *ma chère amie.*'

And would be, he thought as he cupped one of her perfect breasts in his hand. Until she began to bore him.

Leaving Yvette's feathers smoothed, VanDyke rose. With a smile, he watched Tate pilot the *Adventure* toward St. Kitts.

There was something to be said for youth, he thought. It was something even his money, and his business skills couldn't buy. He had a feeling it would take a long, long time for someone as fresh as Tate Beaumont to grow tedious.

He strolled forward, a hum on his lips. There, his divers had spread the latest haul over a tarp. His heart began to sing. What was there, corroded, calcified or gleaming, was his. Success. Profit for investment. It was only more thrilling that it had belonged to the Lassiters.

No one spoke as VanDyke knelt and began to pick through the booty with his jeweled and manicured fingers. It was so satisfying for him to know that he had brought up treasure while the brother of James Lassiter had been fighting for his life.

It only enhanced the legend, didn't it? he mused as he lifted a cob coin, turned it in his hand. Angelique's Curse would strike them down, strike all down who searched for it. But him.

Because he'd been willing to wait, to bide his time, to use his resources. Time and again, his business sense had told him to forget it, to cut his losses, which had been considerable to date. Yet the amulet remained, always in the back of his mind.

If he didn't find it, own it, he would have failed. Failure was simply unacceptable. Even in a hobby. He could justify the time and the money. He had more than enough of both. And he hadn't forgotten that James Lassiter had laughed at him, had tried to outwit him on a deal.

If Angelique's Curse haunted him, there was a reason for it. It belonged to him.

He glanced up. His divers waited. The crew looked on in silence, ready to obey any order. Such things, VanDyke thought with contentment, money could buy.

'Continue the excavation.' He rose, brushed fussily at the knees of his sharply creased slacks. 'I want armed guards, five on deck, five at the wreck. Deal discreetly, but firmly, with any interference.' Satisfied, he flicked a glance out to sea. 'Don't harm the girl should she return. She interests me. Piper.' With a crook of his finger, he gestured to his marine archeologist.

VanDyke moved briskly through the forward doors and into his office, with Piper on his heels like a loyal hound.

Like the rest of the yacht, VanDyke's floating office was stylish and efficient. The walls were paneled in glossy rosewood, the floor gleamed with its polish of hot wax. The desk, securely anchored, was a nineteenth-century antique that had once graced the home of a British lord.

Rather than typical seafaring decor, he preferred the feel of a manor house, complete with a Gainsborough and heavy brocade drapes. Due to the tropical weather, the small marble fireplace housed a thriving bromeliad rather than crackling logs. The chairs were buttery leather in tones of burgundy and hunter green. Antiques and priceless artifacts were displayed with taste that just edged toward opulence.

With a practical nod to the twentieth century, the office was fully outfitted with the finest electronic equipment.

Never one to shrug away work, VanDyke had crowded his desk with charts and logs and copies of the documents and manifests that guided him on his search for treasure. Hobby or business, knowledge was control.

VanDyke sat behind his desk, waited a few beats. Piper wouldn't sit until he was told. That small and vital twist of power pleased. Prepared to be benign, VanDyke gestured to a chair.

'You've finished transferring the notebooks I gave you onto disk?'

'Yes, sir.' Piper's thick-lensed glasses magnified the dog-like devotion in his brown eyes. He had a brilliant mind that VanDyke respected. And an addiction to cocaine and gambling VanDyke detested and used.

'You found no mention of the amulet?'

'No, sir.' Piper folded his always-nervous hands, pulled them apart. 'Whoever was in charge of the cataloguing did a first-class job, though. Everything, down to the last iron spike, is listed, dated. The photographs are excellent, and the notes and sketches detailing the work are clear and concise.'

They hadn't found the amulet, he mused. He had known it, of course, in his heart, in his gut. But he preferred tangible details.

'That's something. Keep whatever might be of use and destroy the rest.' Considering, VanDyke tugged at his earlobe. 'I'll want a full accounting of today's haul by ten tomorrow morning. I realize that will keep you busy most of the night.' He unlocked a drawer, took out a small vial of white powder. Necessity overcame disgust as he saw the desperate gratitude on Piper's face. 'Use this sensibly, Piper, and privately.'

'Yes, Mr. VanDyke.' The vial disappeared into Piper's baggy pocket. 'You'll have everything by morning.'

'I know I can count on you, Piper. That's all for now.'

Alone, VanDyke leaned back. His eyes scanned the papers on his desk as he sighed. It was possible that the Lassiters had simply lucked onto a virgin wreck, and it had nothing to do with the amulet. Years of indulging in his hobby, and the search, had given him a true appreciation for luck.

If that was the case, he would simply take what they'd found and add to his own fortune.

But if the amulet was on the *Santa Marguerite*, it would soon be his. He would excavate every inch of her and the surrounding sea until he was sure.

James had found something, he mused, tapping his steepled fingers to his lips. Something he had refused to share. And oh, how that grated still. After all this time, the search around Australia and New Zealand had gone cold. There was a piece of documentation missing. VanDyke was sure of it.

James had known something, but had he had the time or the inclination to share that something with his fool of a brother, or the son he left behind?

Perhaps not. Perhaps he had died clutching the secret to himself. He detested not being sure, detested knowing he might have miscalculated. The fury of that, the slim chance that he had mistaken his man had VanDyke balling his pampered hands into fists.

His eyes darkened with temper, his handsome mouth thinned and trembled while he fought back the tantrum as a man might fight a wild beast snapping at his throat. He recognized the signs – the thundering heartbeat, the pounding of blood in his head, behind his eyes, the roaring in his ears.

The violent moods were coming on him more often, as they had when he'd been a boy and had been denied some wish.

But that had been before he'd learned to use his strength of will, before he'd groomed his power to manipulate and win. The vicious, furious waves of black rage rolled over him, taunted him to drum his heels, to scream, to break something. Anything. Oh, how he despised being thwarted, how he loathed losing the upper hand.

Still, he would not give in to weak and useless emotions, he ordered himself. He would, under all circumstances, stay in control, stay cool and clearheaded. Losing the grip on emotions made a man vulnerable, caused him to make foolish mistakes. It was vital to remember it.

And to remember how his mother had lost that battle, and had lived her last years drooling on her silk blouses in a locked room.

His body shivered once with the final effort to battle back rage. He took a long, steadying breath, straightened his tie, massaged his tensed hands.

It was possible, he thought with utter calm now, that he had been a bit impatient with James Lassiter. It wasn't a mistake he would make with the others. Years of search had only strengthened him, added wisdom and knowledge. Made him more aware of the value of the prize, the power of its possession.

It waited for him just as he waited for it, he reminded himself, and saw that his hands were again perfectly steady. Neither he nor Angelique's Curse would tolerate any interlopers. But, interlopers could be used before they were discarded.

Time would tell, VanDyke thought and closed his eyes. There was no sea, no ocean, no pond where the Lassiters could sail without him being aware.

One day, they would lead him to Angelique's Curse and the one fortune that continued to allude him.

Chapter Nine

OUT OF BREATH and pale with fury, Tate rushed into the hospital. She spotted her parents and Matthew in a huddle at the end of the corridor and barely prevented herself from calling out. She headed for them at a jog that had her mother turning and staring.

'Tate, for goodness sake, you look as though you've been swimming in your clothes.'

'I have. We have trouble. There was a boat. They're excavating. There was nothing I could do to stop them.'

'Slow down,' Ray ordered and put both hands on her shoulders. 'Where have you been?'

'I went out to the site. There's a boat there, a hell of a boat, luxury yacht, fully loaded. First-class excavation equipment. They're working the *Marguerite*. Saw the airlift cloud.' She paused half a second to catch her breath. 'We have to get out there. They've been aboard the *Adventure* and the *Sea Devil*. My catalogues are gone, and a lot of the artifacts are missing. I know he took them. He'll deny it, but I know.'

'Who?'

Tate shifted her gaze from her father and looked at Matthew. 'VanDyke. It's Silas VanDyke.'

Before she could speak again, Matthew gripped her arm, whirled her to face him. 'How do you know?'

'His steward called him by name.' The fear she'd experienced onboard the *Triumphant* was nothing compared to seeing murder leap into the eyes of the man she loved. 'He knew you. He knew what happened to Buck. He said – Matthew.' Alarm trembled in her voice as he strode down the hall. 'Wait.' She managed to catch him, brace herself in front of him. 'What are you going to do?'

'What I should have done a long time ago.' His eyes were cold and flat and frightening. 'I'm going to kill him.'

'Get a hold of yourself.' Though Ray's voice was calm, he had Matthew's arm in a surprisingly strong grip. Tate recognized the tone and breathed a small sigh of relief. Little or nothing got past her father in this mood. Not even murderous rage. 'We have to be careful, and we have to be sensible,' he continued. 'There's a lot at stake.'

'That bastard isn't going to walk away this time.'

'We'll go out. Marla, you and Tate wait here. Matthew and I will straighten this out.'

'I'm not waiting here.'

'Neither of us is waiting here.' Marla ranged herself with her daughter. 'This is a team operation, Ray. If one goes, we all go.'

'I don't have time for family debates.' Matthew shook himself free. 'I'm going now. You can hang here and see if you can control your women.'

'You ignorant–'

'Tate.' Marla took a deep breath to control her own temper. 'Let's consider the circumstances.' She aimed a look at Matthew that could have melted steel. When she spoke again, the southern honey in her voice was frozen over ice. 'You're right about one thing, Matthew, we're wasting time.' With this, she sailed to the elevator, jabbed the down button.

'Idiot,' was all Tate said.

When they were aboard the *Adventure*, Tate joined her mother at the rail. Ray and Matthew were at the bridge, piloting the boat and, she imagined, discussing strategy. The insult of it burned in her blood.

More frightened than she wanted to admit, Marla turned to her daughter. 'What was your impression of this man? This VanDyke?'

'He's slick.' It was the first word to come to Tate's mind. 'With a nasty layer under the shine. Smart, too. He knew there was nothing I could do, and he enjoyed that.'

'Did he frighten you?'

'He offered me champagne and a tour of the boat. Genial host to welcomed guest. He was reasonable, entirely too reasonable.' Tate flexed her hand on the rail. 'Yes, he frightened me. I could see him as a Roman emperor, nibbling on sugared grapes while the lions tore the Christians to shreds. He'd enjoy the show.'

Marla suppressed a shudder. Her daughter was whole and safe and here, she reminded herself. But she kept a hand over Tate's as reassurance. 'Do you believe he killed Matthew's father?'

'Matthew believes it. There.' She lifted a hand to point. 'There's the boat.'

On the bridge, Matthew studied the *Triumphant*. It was new, he noted, more luxurious than the rig they had used in Australia. As far as he could see, the decks were deserted.

'I'm going over, Ray.'

'Let's take this one step at a time.'

'VanDyke's already taken too many steps.'

'We'll hail them first.' Ray maneuvered the boat between the *Triumphant* and the *Sea Devil*, cut the engines.

'Get the women in the cabins, keep them there.' Matthew picked up a diving knife.

'And what are you going to do?' Ray demanded. 'Clamp that between your teeth and swing over on a rope? Use your head.' Hoping the scathing tone worked, he left the bridge. On deck, he glanced at his wife and daughter before going to the rail.

'Ahoy the *Triumphant*,' he called out.

'There was a woman,' Tate supplied. The hair on her arms and neck began to tingle as Matthew joined them. 'Crew-seamen and stewards. Divers.'

Now, the *Triumphant* looked like a ghost ship, silent but for the flap of awnings and lap of the water on its hull.

'I'm going over,' Matthew said again. As he readied to dive into the water, VanDyke strolled out on deck.

'Good afternoon.' His beautiful voice carried over the water. 'Gorgeous day for a sail, isn't it?'

'Silas VanDyke?'

Like a pose, VanDyke leaned on the rail, ankles crossed, arms folded.

'Yes, indeed. And what can I do for you?'

'I'm Raymond Beaumont.'

'Ah, of course.' In a gallant gesture, he tipped the brim of his panama. 'I've met your charming daughter. Lovely to see you again, Tate. And you must be Mrs. Beaumont.' He bowed slightly in Marla's direction. 'I see where Tate gets her fresh and intriguing beauty. And it's young Matthew Lassiter, isn't it? How interesting to meet you here.'

'I knew you were a murderer, VanDyke,' Matthew called out. 'But I didn't know you'd sink to piracy.'

'You haven't changed.' VanDyke's teeth flashed. 'I'm glad. It would be a shame to have all those rough edges polished away. I'd invite you all onboard, but we're rather busy at the moment. Perhaps we can arrange a little dinner party for later in the week.'

Before Matthew could speak, Ray clamped a hand on his arm, fingers vising. 'We have first claim on the *Santa Marguerite*. We discovered her, and we've been working her for several weeks. The necessary paperwork was filed with the government of St. Kitts.'

'I'm afraid we disagree.' Gracefully, Silas took a slim silver case from his pocket, chose a cigarette. 'You're welcome to check with the authorities if you find it necessary. Of course, we are beyond the legal limit. And when I arrived, there was no one here. Just that unfortunate, and empty, boat.'

'My partner was seriously injured a few days ago. We had to postpone the excavation.'

'Ah.' VanDyke lighted his cigarette, took a contemplative drag. 'I heard about poor Buck's accident. How difficult for him, for you all. My sympathies. However, the fact remains that I'm here, and you're not.'

'You took property from our boats,' Tate shouted out.

'That's a ridiculous accusation, and one you'll have a great deal of difficulty proving. Of course, you're welcome to try.' He paused to study and admire a pair of pelicans in their dance from sky to sea and back again. 'Treasure-hunting is a frustrating business, isn't it?' he said conversationally. 'And often heartbreaking. Do give my best regards to your uncle, Matthew. I hope this bad luck that runs in your family ends with you.'

111

'Fuck this.' Even as Matthew vaulted to the rail, Tate sprang to stop him. He'd barely shaken her off when Ray shoved him back.

'Top deck,' he murmured. 'Forward and aft.'

Two men had stepped into view, each with rifles shouldered and aimed.

'I believe in guarding my possessions,' VanDyke explained. 'A man in my position learns that security isn't merely a luxury, but a vital business tool. Raymond, I'm sure you're a sensible man, sensible enough to keep young Matthew from getting himself hurt over a few trinkets.' Well satisfied with the situation, he took another drag on his cigarette as the pelicans plopped gleefully into the water between them. 'And I would be devastated if a stray bullet happened to strike you, or either of those precious jewels beside you.' His smile spread. 'Matthew would be the first to tell you that accidents, tragic accidents, happen.'

Matthew's fingers were bone white on the rail. Everything inside him screamed to take his chances, to dive in. 'Get them inside.'

'If he shoots you, what happens to Buck?'

Matthew shook his head, riding on the rush of blood to his head. 'I only need ten seconds. Ten goddamn seconds.' And a knife across VanDyke's throat.

'What happens to Buck?' Ray insisted.

'You're not going to ask me to walk away from this.'

'No, I'm telling you.' Fear and fury helped Ray muscle Matthew back from the rail. 'This isn't worth your life. And it sure as hell isn't worth the lives of my wife and daughter. Take the wheel, Matthew. We're heading back to St. Kitts.'

Even the thought of retreat made him ill. If he'd been alone . . . But he wasn't. Saying nothing, he turned on his heels and headed for the bridge.

'Very wise, Raymond,' VanDyke commented with a glint of admiration in his voice. 'Very wise. The boy is a tad reckless, I'm afraid, not as mature and sensible as men like us. It was a pleasure to meet you all. Mrs. Beaumont, Tate.' He tipped the brim of his hat again. 'Good sailing.'

'Oh, Ray.' As the boat circled around, Marla crossed to her husband on jellied knees. 'They would have killed us.'

Feeling unmanned, helpless, Ray stroked her hair and watched the dashing figure of VanDyke grow smaller with distance. 'We'll go to the authorities,' he said quietly.

Tate left them, rushed to the bridge. There Matthew gripped the wheel, the course set.

'There was nothing we could do,' she began. Something about his stance warned her against touching him in any way. When he said nothing, she stepped closer, but kept her hands locked together. 'He would have had them shoot you, Matthew. He wanted to. We'll report him as soon as we dock.'

'And what the fuck do you think that will do?' There was something mixed with the bitterness in his voice. Something she didn't recognize as shame. 'Money talks.'

'We went through all the proper channels,' she insisted. 'The records–'

He cut her off with one flaming look. 'Don't be stupid. There won't be any records. There won't be anything he doesn't want there to be. He'll take the wreck. He'll strip her, take it all. And I let him. I stood there, just the way I did nine years ago, and I did nothing.'

'There was nothing you could do.' Ignoring her own instincts, she laid a hand on his back. 'Matthew . . .'

'Leave me alone.'

'But, Matthew–'

'Leave me the hell alone.'

Hurt and helpless, she did what he asked.

That evening, she sat alone in her room. She imagined this was what was meant by being shell-shocked. The day had been a series of hard slaps, ending with her father's shaken announcement that there was no record of their claim. None of the paperwork they had so meticulously filed existed, and the clerk Ray had worked with personally denied ever having seen him before.

There was no longer any doubt that Silas VanDyke had won. Again.

Everything they had done, all the work, the suffering Buck had endured was for nothing. For the first time in her life, she was faced with the fact that being right, and doing right, didn't always matter.

She thought of all the beautiful things she had held in her hands. The emerald cross, the porcelain, the bits and pieces of history she had lifted out of its blanket of sand and brought into the light.

She would never touch them again, or study them, see them winking behind glass at a museum. There would be no discreet

113

card heralding them as pieces of the Beaumont-Lassiter collection. She would not see her father's name in *National Geographic*, or pore over photographs she'd taken herself on those glossy pages.

They'd lost.

And it shamed her to realize how much she had wanted those flashes of glory. She'd imagined herself going back to college, impressing her professors, sailing through to her degree on a wave of triumph.

Or simply sailing off with Matthew, riding on the current of their victory on the way to the next.

Now there was nothing but bitter failure.

Too restless to stay in her room, she headed out. She would walk on the beach, she decided. Try to clear her head and plan the future.

It was there she found him, standing with his face to the sea. He'd chosen the spot where they had once come onto the island. Where she had looked, seen him look, and had known she loved him.

Her heart squeezed with sorrow for him, then settled. For she was sure now what to do.

She walked to his side and stood, letting the breeze ruffle her hair. 'I'm so sorry, Matthew.'

'It's nothing new. Bad luck's my usual kind.'

'This had to do with cheating and stealing. Not with luck.'

'It always has to do with luck. If I'd had better, I'd have gotten to VanDyke alone.'

'And done what? Rammed his boat, boarded it, fought off his armed crew single-handedly?'

It didn't matter now how foolish she made it sound. 'I'd have done something.'

'Gotten yourself shot,' she agreed. 'A lot of good that would have done any of us. Buck needs you, Matthew. I need you.'

He hunched his shoulders. A poor defense, he thought. Being needed didn't suit him. 'I'll see to Buck.'

'We'll see to him. There are other wrecks, Matthew. Waiting. When he's better, we'll find them.' Needing to let hope surge, she took his hands. 'He can even dive again if he wants to. I talked to Doctor Farrge. They're doing amazing things with prostheses. We can take him to Chicago next week. The specialist there will have him up and around in no time.'

'Right.' As soon as he figured out how to pay for a trip to Chicago, a specialist, therapy.

'When he gets the go-ahead, we'll go someplace warm where he can recuperate. That'll give us time to research another wreck. The *Isabella*, if it's still what he wants. What you want.'

'You can't spend time researching wrecks in college.'

'I'm not going back to college.'

'What the hell are you talking about?'

'I'm not going back.' Delighted with her decision, she threw her arms around his neck. 'I don't know why I thought I needed to. I can learn everything I have to learn by doing. What difference does a degree make?'

'That's stupid talk, Tate.' He reached up to pry her arms loose, but she pressed against him.

'No, it's not. It's absolutely logical. I'll stay with you and Buck in Chicago until we decide where to go next. Then we'll go.' She touched her lips to his. 'Anywhere. As long as we're together. Can't you see it, Matthew, sailing wherever we want, whenever we want, on the *Sea Devil.*'

'Yeah.' The fact that he could, all too well, made his limbs weak.

'Mom and Dad will join us when we find another wreck. And we will find one, better than the *Marguerite.* VanDyke won't beat us, Matthew, unless we let him.'

'He already has.'

'No.' With her eyes closed, she laid her cheek against his. 'Because we're here, we're together. And we have everything ahead of us. He wants the amulet, but he doesn't have it. And I know, I just know he never will. Whether we find it or not, Matthew, we have more than he ever can.'

'You're dreaming.'

'What if I am?' She drew back and was smiling again. 'Isn't that what hunting for treasure's all about? Now we can dream together. I don't care if we never find another wreck. Let VanDyke take it all, every last doubloon. You're what I want.'

She meant it. The certainty of that made him giddy with need, terrified with guilt. He had only to snap his fingers and she would go with him wherever he asked. She would leave everything she had, or could have, behind.

And before long she would hate him nearly as much as he hated himself.

'Seems to me you're not giving a lot of thought to what I want.' His voice was cool as he tipped up her chin and gave her a careless kiss.

'I don't know what you mean.'

'Listen, Red, things went to hell here. I put in a lot of work and had to watch it slip right through my fingers. That sucks, but it's not even the worst of it. I'm already saddled with a cripple. What makes you think I want to take you on as well?'

The cut was so quick, so sharp, she barely felt it. 'You don't mean that. You're still upset.'

'Upset doesn't cover it. If you and your by-the-book family hadn't gotten in the way, I wouldn't be standing here empty-handed. Ray just had to go through channels. How the hell do you think VanDyke got on to us?'

Color leeched from her cheeks. 'You can't blame him.'

'Hell I can't.' He tucked his hands into his pockets. 'Me and Buck, we ran a different kind of operation. But you had the dough. Now we've got nothing. All I have left after months of work is a gimpy uncle.'

'That's a horrible thing to say.'

'Plain fact,' he corrected and ignored the coating of disgust in his throat. 'I'll get him set up somewhere. I owe him that. But you and me, Red, that's a different can of worms. Passing the time for a few weeks, a little entertainment on the side to break the monotony is one thing. And it's been fun. But you hanging around my neck now that the deal's in the toilet – that cramps my style.'

She felt as if someone had hollowed her out in one vicious scoop. He was looking at her with a faint grin on his mouth, cool amusement in his eyes. 'You're in love with me,' she insisted.

'You're dreaming again. Hey, you want to weave a little romantic fantasy with me in the starring role, fine. But don't expect to sail off into the sunset.'

It had to be worse, he decided. He had to be worse. Words alone wouldn't shake her loose, wouldn't save her from him. Even as his own actions revolted him, he cupped his hands over her hips, drew her intimately close.

'I didn't mind playing the game, honey. Hell, I enjoyed every minute of it. As lousy as things turned out, why don't we try to cheer each other up. End things with a real bang.'

He clamped his mouth over hers, hard. He wanted nothing soft or sweet in the kiss. It was greedy, demanding and just a

116

little mean. Even as she started to struggle, he slipped a hand under her blouse, closed it over her breast.

'Don't.' This was wrong, she thought frantically. It wasn't supposed to be like this. It couldn't be like this. 'You're hurting me.'

'Come on, baby.' Christ, her skin was like satin. He wanted to stroke it, savor it, seduce it. Instead he bruised it, knowing whatever marks he left there would fade much sooner than the ones he was leaving on himself. 'You know we both want it.'

'No.' Sobbing, she shoved and clawed herself free. In defense, she hugged her arms tight. 'Don't touch me.'

'Just a tease after all.' He forced himself to meet her haunted eyes. 'All talk, no action, Tate?'

She could barely see him for the tears spilling out of her eyes. 'You don't care about me at all.'

'Sure I do.' He heaved a sigh. 'What's it going to take to get you in the sack? You want poetry? I can dig some up. Too shy to do it on the beach? Fine. I've got a room your old man's paying for.'

'None of us meant anything to you.'

'Hey. I pulled my weight.'

'I loved you. We all cared.'

Already past tense, he thought. It wasn't so hard to kill love. 'Big fucking deal. Partnership's dissolved. You and your parents go back to your nice, tidy lives. I go on with mine. Now, do you want to go bounce on the mattress a while, or do I go find somebody else?'

Part of her mind wondered that she could still stand, still speak, when he had torn out her heart. 'I never want to see you again. I want you to stay away from me and my parents. I don't want them to have to know what a bastard you are.'

'No problem. Run on home, kid. I got places to go.'

She told herself she wouldn't, that she would walk, head high. But after a few steps, she did just that. She fled, with her tattered heart bleeding.

When she was gone, Matthew sat down in the sand, laid his aching head on his knees. He figured he'd just completed the first heroic act of his life, by saving hers.

And he decided as the ache pulsed through him, that he wasn't cut out to be a hero.

Chapter Ten

'I CAN'T IMAGINE where Matthew could be.' Marla spoke in undertones, fretting as she paced the hospital corridor. 'It's not like him to miss his visit to Buck. And especially today, when they're transferring Buck to a regular room.'

Tate shrugged. Even that hurt, she discovered. She'd spent a sleepless night mourning a broken heart, giving it every tear inside her. Still, in the end, she had salvaged her pride and now braced against it.

'He probably found a more interesting way to spend his day.'

'Well, it's not like him.' Marla glanced over when Ray stepped out of Buck's room.

'He's settling in.' The bolstering smile did little to erase the concern in Ray's eyes. 'He's a little tired, doesn't really feel up to visitors. Matthew come in yet?'

'No.' Marla looked down the hall as if she could will the elevator doors to open up, and Matthew to stroll out. 'Ray, did you tell him about Silas VanDyke, the treasure?'

'I didn't have the heart.' Wearily Ray sat down. The last ten minutes with Buck had sapped him. 'I think it's just beginning to sink in about his leg. He's angry and bitter. Nothing I said seemed to help. How could I tell him everything we'd worked for is gone?'

'It can wait.' Knowing there was little else they could do, Marla sat down beside him. 'Don't start blaming yourself, Ray.'

'I keep going over that moment in my mind,' he murmured. 'One instant we were flying. We were kings. Midases turning everything we touched into gold. Then there was horror and fear. Could I have done something, Marla, moved faster? I don't know. It all happened in a heartbeat. Angelique's Curse.' Ray lifted his hands, let them fall. 'That's what Buck keeps saying.'

'It was an accident,' Marla insisted, though a shiver raced through her. 'It has nothing to do with curses or legends. You know that, Ray.'

'I know Buck's lost his leg, and the dream that was just at our fingertips turned into a nightmare. There's nothing we can do about it. That's the worst of it. There's nothing we can do.'

'You need rest.' Briskly, Marla rose, took his hands. 'We all do. We're going back to the hotel and putting all of this aside for a few hours. In the morning, we'll do whatever needs to be done.'

'Maybe you're right.'

'You two go ahead.' Tate tucked her hands in her pockets. The idea of sitting in her room for the rest of the afternoon was far from appealing. 'I think I'll go for a walk, maybe sit on the beach awhile.'

'That's a good idea.' Marla slipped an arm around Tate's shoulders as they walked to the elevators. 'Get yourself some sun. We'll all feel better for a little break.'

'Sure.' Tate managed a smile as they stepped into the elevator. But she knew nothing was going to make her feel better for a long, long time.

As the Beaumonts went their separate ways, Matthew sat down in Dr. Farrge's office. Already that day he'd put into play several of the decisions he'd made during the night. Decisions, he felt, that were necessary for everyone.

'I need you to contact that doctor you told me about, the one in Chicago,' Matthew began. 'I have to know if he'll take care of Buck.'

'I can do that for you, Mr. Lassiter.'

'I'd appreciate it. And I need an accounting of what I owe here plus what it's going to cost to transfer him.'

'Your uncle is without medical insurance?'

'That's right.' Matthew braced his shoulders against the fresh weight. It was always humiliating to owe more than you could pay. He doubted a professional treasure hunter was a prime candidate for a loan. 'I'll give you what I've got. I'll have more tomorrow.' From the sale of the *Sea Devil* and most of the equipment. 'I'll need some sort of payment schedule for the rest. I've made some calls myself. I've got a line on a couple of jobs. I'm good for it.'

Farrge sat back, rubbed a finger along the side of his nose. 'I'm sure we can make arrangements. In your country there are programs—'

'Buck's not going on welfare,' Matthew interrupted, a bite of fury in his voice. 'Not as long as I can work. Just figure up the bottom line. I'll deal with it.'

'As you wish. Mr. Lassiter, it's fortunate that your uncle is a strong man. I have no doubt that he will recover physically. He could, in fact, dive again. If he chooses. But his emotional and mental recovery will be slower even than the physical. He'll need your support. You will need help to—'

'I'll deal with it,' Matthew repeated and rose. At the moment, he didn't think he could stand hearing about psychiatrists and social workers. 'The way I figure it, you saved his life. I owe you for that. Now I've got to take it from here.'

'It's a great deal to shoulder alone, Mr. Lassiter.'

'That's the breaks, isn't it?' Matthew said with cool dispassion. 'For better or worse, mostly worse, I'm all he's got.'

That was his personal bottom line, Matthew thought as he headed down to Buck's floor. He was the only family Buck had left. And Lassiters, whatever their failings, paid their debts.

Oh, maybe they skipped out on a bar bill now and again when times were lean. And he'd been known to fleece a tourist or two by inflating the price and history of a clay pipe or broken jug. If some idiot paid through the nose for some chipped wine jar just because a stranger claimed it was from Jean Lafitte's personal stash, they deserved what they got.

But there were matters of honor that couldn't be shaken. Whatever it took, Buck was his responsibility.

The treasure was gone, he thought, giving himself a moment in the corridor before going in to Buck. The *Sea Devil* was history. All he had left were clothes, his wetsuit, flippers, mask, and his tanks.

He'd hustled the sales. Hustling was something that came easily, he thought with a thin smile. The money in his pocket would get them to Chicago.

After that . . . Well, after that, they'd see.

He pushed open Buck's door, relieved to find his uncle alone.

'Wondered if you'd show.' Buck scowled and fought back the bitter tears that stung his eyes. 'Least you could do is be around when they go poking and prodding and wheeling me all over hell and back in this place.'

'Nice room.' Matthew glanced toward the curtain that separated Buck from the patient in the next bed.

'It's crap. I'm not staying here.'

'Not for long. We're taking a trip to Chicago.'

'What the hell is there in Chicago for me?'

'A doctor who's going to fix you up with a new leg.'

'New leg my ass.' The leg was gone, and only the nagging pain was left to remind him he'd once stood like a man. 'Piece of plastic with hinges.'

'We could always strap a peg on you instead.' Matthew pulled a folding chair to the bedside and sat. He couldn't remember the last time he'd really slept. If he could get through the next couple of hours, he promised himself he'd zero out for another eight. 'I thought the Beaumonts might be around.'

'Ray was in.' Buck frowned, tugged on his sheet. 'Sent him away. Don't need his damn long face in here. Where's that damn nurse?' Buck fumbled for his call button. 'Always around when you don't want 'em. Sticking needles in you. I want my pills,' he barked the minute the nurse stepped in. 'I'm in pain here.'

'After your meal, Mr. Lassiter,' she said patiently. 'Your dinner will be here in a few moments.'

'I don't want any of that goddamn slop.'

The more she tried to placate him, the louder he shouted, until she stalked off with blood in her eye.

'Nice way to make friends, Buck,' Matthew commented. 'You know, if I were you, I'd be a little more careful with a woman who could come back at me with a six-inch needle.'

'You're not me, are you? You got two legs.'

'Yeah.' Guilt ate a ragged hole in his gut. 'I got two legs.'

'Lot of good the treasure's gonna do me now,' Buck muttered. 'Finally got all the money a man could ever want, and it can't make me whole again. What am I gonna do? Buy some big fucking boat and spin around it in a wheelchair? Angelique's Curse is what it is. Goddamn witch gives with one hand and takes the best away with the other.'

'We didn't find the amulet.'

'It's down there. It's down there all right.' Buck's eyes began to glimmer with bitterness and hate. 'It didn't even have the goodness to kill me. Better if it had. Nothing but a cripple. A rich cripple.'

'You can be a cripple if you want,' Matthew said wearily. 'That part's up to you. But you're not going to be rich. VanDyke's taken care of that.'

'What the hell are you talking about?' The color fury had pumped into Buck's cheeks drained away like water. 'What about VanDyke?'

Do it now, Matthew ordered himself. All at once. 'He jumped our claim. And he's taken it all.'

'It's our wreck. Me and Ray, we even registered it.'

'Funny thing about that. The only paperwork anybody can find is VanDyke's. All he had to do was bribe a couple of clerks.'

To lose it all now was unthinkable. Without his share of the treasure he'd not only be a cripple, he'd be a helpless one. 'You gotta stop him.'

'How?' Matthew shot up, pressed his hands against Buck's shoulders to keep him in bed. 'He's got a full crew, armed. They're working around the clock. I'll guarantee he's already transported what he's brought up, and what he took off the *Sea Devil* and the *Adventure*.'

'You're just gonna let him get away with it?' Fueled by desperation, Buck gripped Matthew by the shirtfront. 'You're just gonna turn around and walk away from what's ours? It cost me my leg.'

'I know what it cost you. And yeah, I'm walking away. I'm not going to die for a wreck.'

'Never thought you'd turn coward.' Buck released him, turned his head away. 'If I wasn't laid up here . . .'

If you weren't laid up here, Matthew thought, I wouldn't have to walk away. 'It looks like you'd better work at getting up

122

and out of here so you can handle it your way. Meantime, I'm in charge and we're going to Chicago.'

'How the hell are we going to get there? We've got nothing.' Unconsciously, he reached down to where his leg should have been. 'Less than nothing.'

'The *Sea Devil*, the equipment and some odds and ends brought in a few thousand.'

Glassily pale, Buck turned back. 'You sold the boat? What right did you have to sell the boat? The *Sea Devil* belonged to me, boy.'

'It was half mine,' Matthew said with a shrug. 'When I sold my share, yours went with it. I'm doing what I have to do.'

'Running away,' Buck said and turned his head again. 'Selling out.'

'That's right. Now I'm going to go book us a flight to Chicago.'

'I ain't going to Chicago.'

'You're going to go where I tell you. That's the way it is.'

'Well, I'm telling you to go to hell.'

'As long as we go by way of Chicago,' Matthew said and walked out.

The bottom line, Matthew learned, was a great deal steeper than he had imagined. Swallowing his pride left his throat raw. He soothed it with a cold beer while he waited for Ray in the hotel lounge.

His life, he decided, was about as bad as it could get. Funny, a few months before, he'd had basically nothing. A boat that had seen better days, a little cash in a tin box, no urgent plans, no urgent problems. Looking back, he supposed he'd been happy enough.

Then, suddenly, he'd had so much. A woman who loved him, the prospect of fame and fortune. Success, the kind he'd never really believed in, had been briefly his. Revenge, which he'd dreamed of for nine years, had been almost within his grasp.

Now he'd lost it all, the woman, the prospects, even the bits of nothing he'd once considered more than enough. It was so much harder to lose once you'd won.

'Matthew.'

He looked up at the clap on his shoulder. Ray slid onto the stool beside him. 'Thanks for coming down.'

'Glad to. I'll have a beer,' he told the bartender. 'Another for you, Matthew?'

'Yeah, why not?' It was only the beginning of what Matthew planned for one long night of stinking drunkenness.

'We've been missing each other the last few days,' Ray began, then tapped his bottle against Matthew's fresh one. 'Kept figuring we'd run into you at the hospital. Though we haven't been there as much as we'd like. Buck's not feeling up for company much.'

'No.' Matthew tipped the bottle back, let the chilled beer run down his throat. 'He won't even talk to me.'

'I'm sorry, Matthew. He's wrong taking it out on you this way. There was nothing you could have done.'

'I don't know which he's taking harder. The leg or the *Marguerite*.' Matthew moved a shoulder. 'I guess it doesn't matter.'

'He'll dive again,' Ray stated and stroked a fingertip down the condensation on the bottle. 'Doctor Farrge told me his physical recovery is ahead of schedule.'

'That's one of the things I needed to talk to you about.' There was no way to put it off any longer, Matthew reminded himself. He would have preferred getting roaring drunk first, but that little pleasure would have to wait. 'I've got the go-ahead to take him to Chicago. Tomorrow.'

'Tomorrow?' Torn between pleasure and alarm, Ray set his beer down with a clack. 'That's so quick. I had no idea arrangements were already made.'

'Farrge says there's no reason to delay it. He's strong enough to make the trip, and the sooner he gets hooked up with this specialist, the better.'

'That's great, Matthew. Really. You'll keep in touch, won't you? Let us know about his progress. Marla and I will take a trip up ourselves as soon as you think he's up to it.'

'You're . . . you're the best friend he ever had,' Matthew said carefully. 'It would mean a lot if you come to see him when you can manage it. I know he's hard to deal with right now, but—'

'Don't worry about that.' Ray spoke quietly. 'A man lucky enough to make that kind of a friend, he doesn't toss it away because times are rough. We'll come, Matthew. Tate's decided to start college in September after all. But I'm sure she'd like to go up with us on her first break.'

'She's going back to college in September,' Matthew murmured.

'Yes, Marla and I are pleased she's decided not to defer after all. She's so down about this whole business right now that I can't think of anything better for her than getting back into routine. I know she's not sleeping well. Tate's so young to have to face all we've had to face these last few days. Concentrating on her studies is the best thing for her.'

'Yeah. You're right.'

'I don't want to pry, Matthew. But I get the feeling you and Tate have had some sort of disagreement.'

'No big deal.' Matthew signaled for another beer. 'She'll land on her feet.'

'I don't doubt it. Tate's a strong-willed and sensible girl.' Ray frowned down at the circles of damp his bottle left on the bar. Rings within rings, he thought. 'Matthew, I'm not blind. I realize the two of you were becoming involved.'

'We had a few laughs,' Matthew interrupted. 'Nothing serious.' He looked at Ray, and answered the unspoken question. 'Nothing serious,' he repeated.

Relieved, Ray nodded. 'I'd hoped I could trust both of you to be responsible. I know she's not a child anymore, but a father still worries.'

'And you wouldn't want her to hook up with someone like me.'

Ray glanced over, met the cool derision in Matthew's eyes with some surprise. 'No, Matthew. I'd be sorry, at this point in her life, to see her hooked up seriously with anyone. With the right motivation, Tate would throw everything she'd hoped to accomplish to the winds. I'm grateful she's not doing that.'

'Fine. Terrific.'

Ray let out a long breath. Something he hadn't even considered had just jumped out and slapped him in the face. 'If she knew you were in love with her, she wouldn't be going back to North Carolina.'

'I don't know what you're talking about. I told you we had a few laughs.' But the compassion in Ray's eyes had him turning away, dropping his face in his hands. 'Shit. What was I supposed to do? Tell her to pack it up and come with me?'

'You could have,' Ray said quietly.

125

'I've got nothing for her but bad times and worse luck. Once I get Buck to Chicago, I'm taking a job on a salvage boat off Nova Scotia. Lousy conditions, but decent pay.'

'Matthew—'

But he shook his head. 'The thing is, Ray, it's not going to be enough, money-wise. Especially at first. I can pretty well square things here. Back in the States with the fancy doctor and the fancy treatment, it's going to be another story. Farrge worked it so they'd cut us a break. Buck's kind of an experiment,' he added with a sneer. 'And they're talking about social security and Medicaid or Medicare or some such shit. Even with that . . .' He swallowed more beer along with his pride. 'I need money, Ray. There's nobody else I can ask for it, and I gotta say it doesn't go down real good to have to ask you.'

'Buck's my partner, Matthew. And my friend.'

'Was your partner,' Matthew corrected. 'Anyway, I need ten thousand.'

'All right.'

The mild tone slashed like a blade across the throat of his pride. 'Don't agree so fast. Goddamn it.'

'Would it really help if I made you beg for it? If I outlined terms and conditions?'

'I don't know.' Matthew gripped the bottle, fighting furiously the need to hurl it, hear it shatter. Like that pride. 'It's going to take me some time to pay it back. I'm going to pay it back,' he said between his teeth before Ray could speak. 'I need enough to set Buck up for the operation, for the therapy and the prosthesis. And he's going to need a place to live after. But I've got work, and when that job peters out, I'll get another one.'

'I know you're good for the money, Matthew, just as you know I don't care about being paid back.'

'I care.'

'Yes, I understand that. I'll write you a check on the condition that you keep me apprised of Buck's progress.'

'I'll take the check. On the condition that you keep this between the two of us. Just the two of us, Ray. All of it.'

'In other words you don't want Buck to know. And you don't want Tate to know.'

'That's right.'

'You're hoeing a hard row for yourself, Matthew.'

'Maybe, but that's the way I want it.'

'All right, then.' If it was all he could do, he would do it as he was asked. 'I'll leave the check at the front desk for you.'

'Thanks, Ray.' Matthew offered a hand. 'For everything. Mostly it was a hell of a summer.'

'Mostly it was. There'll be other summers, Matthew. Other wrecks. The time might come when we'll dive for one together again. The *Isabella*'s still down there.'

'With Angelique's Curse.' Matthew shook his head. 'No thanks. She costs too much, Ray. The way I'm feeling right now, I'd just as soon leave her for the fish.'

'Time will tell. Take care of yourself, Matthew.'

'Yeah. Tell . . . tell Marla I'll miss her cooking.'

'She'll miss you. We all will. And Tate? Anything you want me to tell her?'

There was too much to tell her. And nothing to tell her. Matthew only shook his head.

Alone at the bar, Matthew shoved his beer aside. 'Whiskey,' he told the bartender. 'And bring the bottle.'

It was his last night on the island. He couldn't think of one good reason to spend it sober.

Part Two

Present

The now, the here, through which all future plunges to the past.
—James Joyce

Chapter Eleven

THERE WERE TWENTY-SEVEN crew members aboard the *Nomad*. Tate was delighted to be one of them. It had taken her five years of intense year-round work and study to earn her master's degree in the field of marine archeology. Friends and family had often worried, told her to slow down. But that degree had been the one goal she felt she could control.

She had it. And in the three years since, had put it to use. Now through her association with the Poseidon Institute and her assignment with SeaSearch aboard the *Nomad*, she was taking the next step to earning her doctorate, and her reputation.

Best of all, she was doing what she loved.

This expedition was for science as well as profit. To Tate's mind that was the proper and only logical rank of priority.

The crew quarters were a bit on the spare side, but the labs and equipment were state of the art. The old cargo vessel had been meticulously refitted for deep-sea exploration and excavation. Perhaps it was slow and unhandsome as ships went, she mused, but she'd learned long ago that an attractive outer layer meant nothing compared to what was within.

One summer of naive dreams had taught her that, and more.

The *Nomad* had a great deal within. She was manned by the top scientists and technicians in the field of ocean research.

And she was one of them.

The day was as fine as anyone could ask for. The waters of the Pacific gleamed like a blue jewel. And beneath it, fathoms deep where the light never reached and man could never venture, lay the side-wheeler *Justine*, and her treasure trove.

In her deck chair, Tate settled her laptop on her knees to complete a letter to her parents.

> *We'll find her. The equipment on this ship is as sophisticated as any I've seen. Dart and Bowers can't wait to put their robot to use. We've dubbed it 'Chauncy.' I'm not sure why. But we're putting a lot of faith in the little guy. Until we find the* Justine *and begin to excavate, my duties are light. Everybody pitches in, but there's a lot of free time just now. And the food, Mom, is incredible. We're expecting an airdrop today. I've managed to charm a few recipes from the cook though you'll have to cut them down from the bulk necessary to feed almost thirty people.*
>
> *After nearly a month at sea, there have been squabbles. Family-like, we snipe and fight and make up. There are even a couple of romances. I think I told you about Lorraine Ross, the chemist who shares a cabin with me. The assistant cook, George, has a major crush on her. It's kind of sweet. Other flirtations are more to pass the time, I think, and will fade away once the real work begins.*
>
> *So far the weather's been with us. I wonder how it is back home. I imagine the azaleas will bloom within a few weeks, and the magnolias. I miss seeing them, and I miss seeing you. I know you'll be leaving for your trip to Jamaica soon, so I hope this letter reaches you before you ship out. Maybe we can mesh schedules in the fall. If things go well, my dissertation will be complete. It would be fun to do a little diving back home.*
>
> *Meanwhile I should get back. Hayden's bound to be poring over the charts again, and I'm sure he could use a little help. We don't have a mail drop until the end of the week, so this won't go out until then. Write back, okay? Letters are like gold out here. I love you.*
>
> *Tate*

She hadn't mentioned the tedium, Tate thought as she took the laptop back to the cabin she shared with Lorraine. Or the personal loneliness that could strike without warning when you were surrounded by mile after mile of water. She knew a great many of the crew were beginning to lose hope. The time, the money, the energy that was tied up in this expedition were extensive. If they failed, they would lose their backers, their share of the trove, and perhaps most important, their chance to make history.

Once inside the narrow cabin, Tate automatically scooped up the shirts and shorts and socks scattered over the floor. Lorraine might have been a brilliant scientist, but outside of the lab she was as disorganized as a teenager. Tate piled the clothes on Lorraine's unmade bunk, her nose twitching at the musky perfume that haunted the air.

Lorraine, Tate concluded, was determined to drive poor George insane.

It still amazed and amused her that she and Lorraine had managed to become friends. Certainly no two women were more different. Where Tate was neat and precise, Lorraine was careless and messy. Tate was driven, Lorraine was unapologetically lazy. Over the years since college, Tate had experienced one serious relationship that had ended amicably while Lorraine had gone through two nasty divorces and innumerable volatile affairs.

Her roommate was a tiny, fairylike woman with a curvy body and a halo of golden hair. She wouldn't so much as turn on a Bunsen burner unless she was wearing full makeup and the proper accessories.

Tate was long, lean and had only recently let her straight red hair grow to her shoulders. She rarely bothered with cosmetics and was forced to agree with Lorraine's statement that she was fashion-impaired.

She didn't think to glance in the full-length mirror Lorraine had hung on the door of the head before she left the cabin.

Turning left, she proceeded to the metal stairs that would take her to the next deck. The clattering and wheezing above made her smile.

'Hey, Dart.'

'Hey.' Dart came to a red-faced halt at the base of the stairs. Unlike his name, he was anything but slim and sharp. Pudgy, with all his edges softly rounded, he resembled an overweight

St. Bernard. His thin, sandy-brown hair flopped into his guile-less brown eyes. When he smiled, he added another chin to the two he habitually carried. 'How's it going?'

'Slow. I was going up to see if Hayden wanted some help.'

'I think he's up there, buried in his books.' Dart flipped his hair back again. 'Bowers just relieved me at Ground Zero, but I'm going back in a couple minutes.'

Tate's interest peaked. 'Something interesting on screen?'

'Not the *Justine*. But Litz is up there having multi-orgasms.' Dart referred to the marine biologist with a shrug. 'Lots of interesting critters when you get down below a couple thousand feet. Bunch of crabs really got him off.'

'That's his job,' Tate pointed out, though she sympathized. No one was fond of the cold, demanding Frank Litz.

'Doesn't make him less of a creep. See you.'

'Yeah.' Tate made her way forward to Dr. Hayden Deel's workroom. Two computers were humming. A long table bolted to the floor was covered with open books, notes, copies of logs and manifests, charts held down with more books.

Hunkered over them and peering through black horn-rims, Hayden ran fresh calculations. Tate knew he was a brilliant scientist. She had read his papers, applauded his lectures, studied his documentaries. It was a bonus, she thought, that he was simply a nice man.

She knew he was roughly forty. His dark-brown hair was sprinkled with gray and tended to curl. Behind the lenses, his eyes were the color of honey, and usually distracted. There were character-building lines that fanned from his eyes and scored his brow. He was tall, broad-shouldered and just a little clumsy. As usual, his shirt was wrinkled.

Tate thought he looked a bit like Clark Kent approaching middle age.

'Hayden?'

He grunted. As that was more than she'd expected, Tate took a seat directly across from him, folded her arms on the table and waited until he'd finished muttering to himself.

'Hayden?' she said again.

'Huh? What?' Blinking like an owl, he looked up. His face became quietly charming when he smiled. 'Hi. Didn't hear you come in. I'm recalculating the drift. I think we're off, Tate.'

'Oh, by much?'

'It doesn't take much out here. I decided to start from the beginning.' As if preparing for one of his well-attended lectures, he tapped papers together, folded his hands over them.

'The side-wheeler *Justine* left San Francisco on the morning of June eighth, 1857, en route to Ecuador. She held one hundred and ninety-eight passengers, sixty-one crew. In addition to the passengers' personal belongings, she carried twenty million dollars in gold. Bars and coins.'

'It was a rich time in California,' Tate murmured. She'd read the manifests. Even for a woman who had spent most of her life studying and diving for treasure, it had boggled her.

'She took this route,' Hayden continued, tapping keys on the computer so that the graphics mirrored the doomed ship's journey south through the Pacific. 'She went into port at Guadalajara, discharging some passengers, taking on others. She pulled out on June nineteenth, with two hundred and two passengers.'

He pushed through copies of old newspaper clippings. '"She was a bright ship,"' he quoted, ' '"and the mood was celebrational. The weather was calm and hot, the sky clear as glass."'

'Too calm,' Tate said, well able to imagine the mood, the hope. Elegantly dressed men and women parading the decks. Children laughing, perhaps watching the sea for a glimpse of a leaping dolphin or sounding whale.

'One of the survivors noted the brilliant, almost impossibly beautiful sunset on the night of June twenty-first,' Hayden continued. 'The air was still and very heavy. Hot. Most put it down to their nearness to the equator.'

'But the captain would have known then.'

'Would have, or should have.' Hayden moved his shoulders. 'Neither he nor the log survived. But by midnight on the evening of that beautiful sunset, the winds came – and the waves. Their route and speed put them here.' He took the computer-generated *Justine* south and west. 'We have to assume he would have headed for land, Costa Rica by most accounts, hoping he could ride it out. But with fifty-foot swells battering his ship, there wasn't much of a chance.'

'All that night and all the next day, they fought the storm,' Tate added. 'Terrified passengers, crying children. You'd hardly be able to tell day from night, or hear your own prayers. If you

135

were brave, or frightened enough to look, all you would see would be wall after wall of water.'

'By the night of the twenty-second, the *Justine* was breaking apart,' Hayden continued. 'There was no hope of saving her, or of reaching land in her. They put the women, the children, and the injured in the lifeboats.'

'Husbands kissing their wives goodbye,' Tate said softly. 'Fathers holding their children for the last time. And all of them knowing it would take a miracle for any of them to survive.'

'Only fifteen did.' Hayden scratched his cheek. 'One lifeboat outwitted the hurricane. If they hadn't, we wouldn't even have these small clues as to where to find her.' He glanced up, noticed with alarm that Tate's eyes were wet. 'It was a long time ago, Tate.'

'I know.' Embarrassed, she blinked back the tears. 'It's just so easy to see it, to imagine what they went through, what they felt.'

'For you it is.' He reached over and gave her hand an awkward pat. 'That's what makes you such a fine scientist. We all know how to calculate facts and theories. Too many of us lack imagination.'

He wished he had a handkerchief to offer her. Or better yet, the nerve to brush away the single tear that had escaped to trail down her cheek. Instead, Hayden cleared his throat and went back to his calculations.

'I'm going to suggest we move ten degrees south, southwest.'

'Oh, why?'

Delighted she'd asked, he began to show her.

Tate rose, moved behind him to view his screens and his hastily scribbled notes over his shoulder. Occasionally, she laid her hand on it or leaned closer to get a better look or ask a question.

Each time she did, Hayden's heart would stutter. He called himself a fool, even a middle-aged fool, but it didn't stop the hitch.

He could smell her – soap and skin. Each time she laughed in that low, carelessly sexy way, his mind would cloud. He loved everything about her, her mind, her heart, and when he let himself fantasize, her wonderfully willowy body. Her voice was like honey poured over brown sugar.

'Did you hear that?'

How could he hear anything but her voice when he was all but swimming in it. 'What?'

'That.' She pointed overhead, toward the sound of engines. Planes, she realized, and grinned. 'It must be the food drop. Come on, Hayden. Let's go up top, get some sun and watch them.'

'Well, I haven't quite finished my—'

'Come on.' Laughing, she grabbed his hand and pulled him to his feet. 'You're like a mole in here. Just a few minutes on deck.'

He went with her, of course, feeling very much like a mole chasing a butterfly. She had the loveliest legs. He knew he shouldn't stare at them, but they were the most incredible shade of alabaster. And there was that enchanting little freckle just above the back of her right knee.

He'd like to press his mouth just there. The thought of doing it, of perhaps being invited to do it, made his head swim.

He cursed himself for being an idiot, reminding himself he was thirteen years her senior. He had a responsibility to her and to the expedition.

She was onboard the *Nomad* due to his agreement with the recommendation that had come straight from Trident through its Poseidon arm. He'd been delighted to agree. After all, she'd been his best and brightest student.

Wasn't it wonderful the way the sun gilded the flame of her hair?

'Here comes another one!' Tate shouted and cheered along with the other crew who had gathered as the next package splashed off the stern.

'We'll eat like kings tonight.' Lorraine, her lush little body stuffed into a snug halter and shorts, leaned over the rail. Below, crew were manning a dinghy. 'Don't leave anything behind, boys. I put in a request for some Fume Blanc, Tate.' She winked, then turned to flutter her gilded lashes at Hayden. 'Doc, where have you two been hiding out?'

'Hayden's running new figures.' Tate leaned over the rail to shout encouragement as the dinghy putted out to retrieve the supplies. 'I hope they remembered the chocolate.'

'You only eat sweets because you're repressed.'

'You're just jealous because M&M's go straight to your thighs.'

Lorraine pursed her lips. 'My thighs are terrific.' She ran a fingertip along one, slanted Hayden a sly look. 'Aren't they, doc?'

'Leave Hayden alone,' Tate began, then squealed when she was grabbed from behind.

'Break time.' Bowers, tough and sinewy, scooped her up. While others applauded, he dashed to one of the ropes they'd rigged. 'We're going swimming, babycakes.'

'I'll kill you, Bowers.' She knew their robotics and computer expert loved nothing better than to play. Still laughing, she struggled weakly. 'This time I mean it.'

'She's nuts about me.' With one muscled arm, he snagged the rope. 'Better hold on, honey child.'

She looked down as his eyes rolled in his glossy ebony face. He bared his teeth, made her giggle helplessly. 'How come you always pick on me?'

''Cause we look so fine together. Grab hold. Me Tarzan, you Jane.'

Tate gripped the rope, sucked in her breath. With Bowers's wild Tarzan yell ringing in her ears, she pushed off with him into space. She screamed, because it felt good. The wide, wide sea tilted beneath her, and as the rope arched, she let go. The air whisked over her, the water rushed up. She heard Bowers cackling like a loon an instant before she hit.

It was bracingly cool. She let it bathe her before kicking her way to the surface.

'Only an 8.4 from the Japanese judge, Beaumont, but they're picky devils.' Bowers winked at her, then shaded his eyes. 'Oh Christ almighty, here comes Dart. Everybody out of the pool.'

From the rail, Hayden watched Tate and his associates play like children freshly released to recess. It made him feel old, and more than a little stodgy.

'Come on, doc.' Lorraine gave him her quick, flirtatious smile. 'Why don't we take a dip?'

'I'm a lousy swimmer.'

'So, wear a flotation, or better yet, use Dart as a raft.'

That made him smile. At the moment, Dart was bobbing around in the Pacific like a bloated cork. 'I think I'll just watch.'

Keeping her smile in place, Lorraine shrugged her bare shoulders. 'Suit yourself.'

More than three thousand miles away from where Tate frolicked in the crystal Pacific, Matthew shivered in the frigid waters of the North Atlantic.

The fact that he headed the salvage team was a small point of pride. He'd worked his way up in Fricke Salvage over the years, taking on all and any assignments that paid. Now he was in charge of the underwater dig and hauled in ten percent of the net profits.

And he hated every minute of it.

There wasn't a nastier cut to the pride of a hunter than crewing a big, ugly boat on straight metal salvage. There was no gold, no treasure to be discovered on the *Reliant*. The World War II vessel was crusted with the icy mud of the North Atlantic, its value solely in its metal.

Often when his fingers felt like icicles and the exposed skin around his mouth was blue with cold, Matthew dreamed about the days when he'd dived for pleasure as well as profit.

In warm, mirrorlike water in the company of jeweled fish. He remembered what it had felt like to see that flash of gold, or a blackened disk of silver.

But treasure-hunting was a gamble, and he was a man with debts to pay. Doctors, lawyers, rehab centers. Jesus, the more he worked, the more he owed. Ten years before, if anyone had suggested his life would turn out to be a cycle of work and bills to be paid, he would have laughed in their faces.

Instead, he'd discovered that life was laughing in his.

Through the murk, he signaled to his team. It was time to start the slow rise to the surface. The damned ugly *Reliant* lay on its side, already half hacked away by the crew. Matthew poured salt on his own wounds by studying it as he stopped at the first rest point.

To think he'd once dreamed of galleons and man o' wars. Privateers bursting at the seams with bullion. Worse, he'd had one only to lose it. And everything else.

Now he was little better than a junkyard dog, harvesting and guarding scraps. Here, the sea was a cave, dark, hostile, almost colorless, cold as fish blood. A man never felt quite human here – not free and weightless as a diver felt in the live waters, but distant and alien where there was little to see that wasn't eating or being eaten.

A careless movement sent an icy spurt of water down the neck of his suit, reminding him that like it or not, human he was.

He kicked to the next point, knowing better than to hurry. However cold the water, however tedious the dive, biology and physics were kings here. Once, five years before, he'd watched a careless diver collapse on deck and die painfully from the bends because he'd hurried the rest stops. It wasn't an experience Matthew intended to have.

Once he'd boarded, Matthew reached for the hot coffee a galley mate offered. When his teeth stopped chattering, he gave his orders to the next team. And he damn well intended to tell Fricke that the men were getting a bonus on this trip.

It pleased him that Fricke, the miserly bastard, was just enough afraid of him to dip a little deeper into his tight pockets.

'Mail came in.' The mate, a scrawny French Canadian who went only by LaRue, shouldered Matthew's tanks. 'Put yours in your cabin.' He grinned, showing a gleaming gold front tooth. 'One letter, many bills. Me, I get six letters from six sweethearts. I feel so bad, maybe I give one to you. Marcella, she not so pretty, but she fuck you blind, deaf and dumb, eh?'

Matthew peeled off the hood of his wetsuit. The chill Atlantic air breathed frigidly on his ears. 'I'll pick my own women.'

'Then why don't you? You need you a good bounce or two, Matthew. LaRue, he can spot these things.'

Matthew brooded out toward the cold, gray sea. 'Women are a little scarce out here.'

'You come with me to Quebec, Matthew. I show you where to get a good drink and a good lay.'

'Get your mind off sex, LaRue. At this rate, we're going to be out here another month.'

'If my mind's all I can get on sex, then it's going to stay there,' LaRue called out as Matthew stalked away. Chuckling to himself, he took out his precious tobacco pouch to roll one of his favored fat, foul-smelling cigarettes. The boy needed guidance, the wisdom of an older man, and a good fuck.

What Matthew wanted were warm clothes and another shot of coffee. He found the first in his cabin. After he'd tugged on a sweater and jeans, he poked through the envelopes braced under a rock on the small table that served as his desk.

Bills, of course. Medical, the rent on Buck's apartment in Florida, the lawyer Matthew had hired to square things when

140

Buck had wrecked a bar in Fort Lauderdale, the last statement from the last rehabilitation center he'd hauled Buck into in hopes of drying out his uncle.

They wouldn't break him, he mused. But they sure as hell weren't going to leave him a lot to play with. The single letter gave him some pleasure.

Ray and Marla, he thought as he sat down with the rest of his coffee to enjoy it. They never failed. Once a month, rain or shine, wherever he happened to be, they'd get a letter to him.

Not once in eight years had they let him down.

As usual it was a chatty letter of several pages. Marla's looping, feminine handwriting was offset by Ray's quick scrawl in notes and messages in the margins. Nearly five years earlier, they'd moved to the Outer Banks of North Carolina and built a cottage on the sound side of Hatteras Island. Marla would pepper the letters with descriptions of Ray's puttering around the house, her luck, good or bad, with her garden. Woven through were details of their adventures at sea. Their trips to Greece, Mexico, the Red Sea, their impulsive dives along the coast of the Carolinas.

And of course, they wrote of Tate.

Matthew knew she was nearing thirty, working on her Ph.D., joining varying expeditions. Yet he still saw her as she'd been that long-ago summer. Young and fresh and full of promise. Over the years when he thought of her, it was with a vaguely pleasant nostalgic tug. In his mind, she and those days they'd spent together had taken on a burnished golden hue. Almost too perfect for reality.

He'd long ago stopped dreaming of her.

There were debts to be paid, and plans, still in the dim future, to be settled.

Matthew savored each word on each page. The expected invitation for him to visit touched a chord, making him both wistful and bitter. Three years before, he'd browbeaten Buck into making the trip. The four-day visit had been anything but a success.

Still, he could remember how quietly at home he felt, looking at the serene waters of the sound through the fan of pines and bay trees, smelling Marla's cooking, listening to Ray talk of the next wreck and the next shot at gold. Until Buck had managed to hitch a ride over to Ocracoke on the ferry and get himself stinking drunk.

There wasn't any point in going back, Matthew thought. Humiliating himself, putting the Beaumonts in that miserable position. The letters were enough.

When he shuffled the last page to the front, Ray's crablike handwriting shot Tate, and that summer in the West Indies, into sharp and painful focus.

Matthew, I've got some concerns I haven't shared with Marla. I will, but I wanted to get your thoughts first. You know Tate is in the Pacific, working for SeaSearch. She's thrilled with the assignment. We all were. But a few days ago, I was researching some stocks for an old client. I had an impulse to invest in SeaSearch myself, a kind of personal tribute to Tate's success. I discovered that the company is an arm of Trident, which in turn is a part of The VanDyke Corporation. Our VanDyke. Obviously this concerns me. I don't know if Tate is aware. I strongly doubt it. There's probably no need for me to worry. I can't imagine Silas VanDyke would take a personal interest in one of his marine archeologists. It's doubtful he even remembers her, or would care. And yet, I'm uncomfortable knowing she's so far away and even remotely associated with him. I haven't decided if I should contact Tate and let her know what I've learned, or leave well enough alone. I'd very much like your thoughts on this.

Matthew, I'd like them in person, if you can find a way to come to Hatteras. There's something more I want very much to discuss with you. I made an incredible find only a few weeks ago – something I've been searching for, for nearly eight years. I want to show it to you. When I do, I hope you'll share my excitement. Matthew, I'm going back for the Isabella. *I need you and Buck with me. Please, come to Hatteras and take a look at what I've put together before you reject the idea.*

She's ours, Matthew. She's always been ours. It's time for us to claim her.

Fondly,
Ray

Jesus. Matthew skipped back to the beginning of the page and read it a second time. Ray Beaumont didn't believe in dropping his bombshells lightly. In a couple of quick paragraphs he had set off charges that exploded from Tate to VanDyke to the *Isabella*.

Go back? Suddenly, fiercely angry, Matthew slapped the letter down on the table. Damned if he'd go back and dredge up his most complete and horrendous failure. He was making his life, wasn't he? Such as it was. He didn't need old ghosts tempting him back toward that glint of gold.

He wasn't a hunter anymore, he thought as he lunged out of the chair to pace the small cabin. He neither wanted nor needed to be. Some men could live on dreams. He had once – and didn't intend to do so again.

It was money he needed, he fumed, money and time. When both were in his pocket, he would finish what was begun half a lifetime ago over his father's body. He would find VanDyke, and he would kill him.

And as for Tate, she wasn't his problem. He'd done her a good turn once, Matthew remembered, and scowled down at the letter on the table. The best turn of her life. If she'd screwed it up by getting hooked into one of VanDyke's schemes, it was on her head. She was a grown woman now, wasn't she? With a potload of education and fancy degrees. Goddamn it, she owed him every bit of it, and no one had the right to make him feel responsible for her now.

But he could see her, as she'd been then, awed by a simple silver coin, glowing in his arms, courageously attacking a shark with a diver's knife.

He swore again, viciously. Then again, quietly. Leaving the letter and the mug where they were, he headed out to the radio room. He needed to make some calls.

Tate entered the room the crew had dubbed 'Ground Zero.' It was crammed with computers, keyboards, monitors. The sonar dial glowed green as the needle swept. Remotes for the cameras that took stereophotos were easily at hand.

At the moment, however, the area was more of a rec room for adolescents than a scientific lab.

Dart was in a corner with Bowers, relieving tedium by trouncing the computer at a game of Mortal Combat.

It was late, nearly midnight, and she'd have been better off in her cabin, getting a good night's sleep or working on her dissertation. But she was restless, and Lorraine had been edgy. The cabin had seemed too small for both of them.

Taking a handful of Dart's candy, she settled down to watch the monitor that showed the sweep of the seafloor.

It was so dark, she mused. Cold. Tiny luminescent fish hunted food. They moved slowly, surrounded by points of phosphorescence that resembled stars. The soft, even sediments of the sea plane were featureless. Yet there was life. She saw a seaworm, hardly more than a primitive stomach, glide by the camera's range. The huge eyes of a cystosoma made her smile.

It was, in its own way, a kind of fairy land, she thought. Hardly the wasteland a number of oceanographers had once thought. And certainly not the dumping ground certain industries chose to regard it as. It was colorless, true, but those magically transparent, pulsing fish and animals turned it into an eerie wonder.

Tate was comforted by it, the continuity, the antiquity. The monitor lulled her like an old late-night movie until she was nearly dozing in the chair.

Then she was blinking, her subconscious struggling to transmit to her eyes what she was viewing.

Coral crabs. They would colonize any handy structure. And they were busily doing so. It was wood, she realized, leaning forward. It was the hull of a ship, encrusted with life of the deep sea.

'Bowers.'

'Just a minute, Tate, I gotta finish ragging on this boy.'

'Bowers, now!'

'What's the hurry?' Forehead furrowed, he swiveled back to her. 'Nobody's going anywhere. Holy hell.' Staring at the monitor, he slipped his chair forward, hitting the necessary controls to stop the camera's sweep.

But for the beep of the equipment, the room was silent as the three of them stared at the screen.

'It could be her.' Tate's voice was thin with excitement.

'Could be,' Bowers replied and got to work. 'Handle the digitals, Dart. Tate, signal the bridge for full stop.'

They didn't speak again for several moments. While the tapes ran, Bowers zoomed in closer and sent the camera on a slow sweep.

The wreck was teaming with life. Tate imagined that Litz and the other biologists on board would soon be singing hosannahs. With her lips pressed together, she held her breath. Then let it out on an explosive puff.

144

'Oh Christ, look! Do you see it?'

Dart's answer was a nervous giggle. 'It's the wheel. Look at that honey lying there, just waiting for us to come along and find her. She's a side-wheeler, Bowers. It's the goddamn beautiful *Justine*.'

Bowers halted the camera. 'Children,' he said and got shakily to his feet. 'At a moment like this, I believe I should say something profound.' He laid a hand on his heart. 'We've done did it.'

With one wild hoot, he grabbed Tate and did a fast boogie. Laughter and excitement had tears rushing to her eyes.

'Let's wake up the ship,' she decided and dashed off.

She raced to her own cabin first to rouse a cranky Lorraine. 'Get down to Ground Zero, now.'

'What? Are we sinking? Go away, Tate. I'm busy being seduced by Harrison Ford.'

'He'll wait. Get down there.' To ensure obedience, Tate ripped the sheet off Lorraine's curled, naked body. 'But for God's sake put a robe on first.'

Leaving Lorraine swearing at her, she dashed down the corridor to Hayden's cabin. 'Hayden?' Struggling with giggles, she pounded on his door. 'Come on, Hayden, red alert, all hands on deck, get the lead out.'

'What is it?' His eyes owlishly wide without his glasses, his hair sticking straight up and a blanket held modestly around his waist, he blinked at Tate. 'Is somebody hurt?'

'No, everybody's wonderful.' In that moment, she was sure he was quite simply the sweetest man she had ever met. Following impulse, she threw her arms around him, nearly knocking him down, and kissed him. 'Oh, Hayden, I can't wait to—'

The first shock of his mouth closing hungrily over hers had her going still. She knew desire when she tasted it on a man's lips, knew need when she felt it trembling in a man's arms.

For both of them, she relaxed, lifting a hand gently to his cheek until the kiss played out.

'Hayden—'

'I'm sorry.' Appalled, he stepped stiffly back. 'You caught me off guard, Tate. I shouldn't have done that.'

'It's all right.' She smiled, laid both hands on his shoulders. 'Really it's all right, Hayden. I'd say we caught each other off guard, and it was nice.'

'As associates,' he began, terrified he might stammer. 'As your superior, I had no right to make an advance.'

She suppressed a sigh. 'Hayden, it was only a kiss. And I kissed you first. I don't think you're going to fire me over it.'

'No, of course not. I only meant—'

'You meant you wanted to kiss me, you did, and it was nice.' Patiently, she took his hand. 'Let's not go crazy over it. Especially since we've got a lot more to go crazy over. You want to know why I beat on your door, dragged you out of bed and threw myself at you?'

'Well, I . . .' He pushed at glasses he wasn't wearing and poked himself in the nose. 'Yes.'

'Hayden, we found the *Justine*. Now hold onto yourself,' she warned, 'because I'm going to kiss you again.'

Chapter Twelve

THE DROID DID the work. And that was the problem. A week into the excavation of the *Justine*, Tate found herself struggling with a vague sense of dissatisfaction.

It was everything they'd hoped for. The wreck was rich. There were gold coins, gold bars – some of them a full sixty pounds. Artifacts were transferred to the surface in abundance. The droid worked busily, digging, lifting, shifting booty with Bowers and Dart working the controls at Ground Zero.

Now and again Tate took a break from her own work to watch the monitor and observe how the machine would haul a heavy load in its mechanical arms, or snag a sea sponge delicately with its pincers for the biologists to study.

The expedition was a complete success.

Tate was suffering through a profound sense of envy for an ugly metal robot.

At her station in a forward cabin, she photographed, examined and catalogued the bits and pieces of mid-nineteenth-century life. A cameo brooch, bits of crockery, spoons, a pewter inkwell, a child's worm-eaten wooden top. And, of course, the coins.

Both silver and gold were stacked on her worktable. They glittered, thanks to Lorraine's work in the lab, as though they were freshly minted.

Tate picked up a five-dollar gold piece, a beautiful little disk dated 1857, the year the *Justine* sank. How many hands had it passed through? she wondered. Perhaps only a few. It might have been tucked into a lady's purse or a gentleman's pocket. Maybe it had paid for a bottle of wine or a Cuban cigar. A new hat. Or maybe it had never been used, only held in anticipation of some small treat it could buy at the end of the journey.

Now it was in her hand, part of so many lost treasures.

'Pretty, isn't it?' Lorraine came in. She carried a tray of artifacts newly decalcified and cleaned in her lab.

'Yeah.' Tate replaced the coin, logged it in her computer. 'There's enough work here for a year.'

'You sound real happy about it.' Curious, Lorraine tilted her head. 'Scientists are supposed to be pleased when they have themselves steady field work.'

'I am pleased.' Tate meticulously logged the brooch, set it aside in a tray. 'Why wouldn't I be? I'm involved in one of the most exciting finds of my career, part of a team of top scientists. I have the very best equipment, better-than-average working and living conditions.' She picked up the child's toy. 'I'd be crazy not to be pleased.'

'So why don't you tell me why you're crazy?'

Lips pursed, Tate gave the toy a quick spin. 'You've never dived. It's hard to explain to someone who's never gone down, never seen it.'

Lorraine sat down, tipped her feet up on the edge of the table. A tattoo of a unicorn rode colorfully over the inside of her ankle. 'I've got some time. Why don't you try?'

'This isn't hunting for treasure,' she began, her voice sharp with annoyance fully self-directed. 'It's computers and machines and robotics, and it's marvelous in its way. We'd never have found the *Justine* or been able to study her without the equipment, obviously.'

A fresh wave of restlessness had her pushing back from her work-table, pacing to the porthole that was her miserly view of the sea. 'It couldn't be excavated or studied without it. The pressure and temperature at that depth make diving impossible. It's basic biology, basic physics. I know it. But damn it, Lorraine,

148

I want to go down. I want to touch it. I want to fan away the sand and find some piece of yesterday. Bowers's droid's having all the fun.'

'Yeah, he's always bragging about it.'

'I know it sounds stupid.' Because it did, Tate was able to smile as she turned back. 'But diving a wreck, being there, is an incredible high. And this is all so sterile. I didn't know I'd feel this way, but every time I come in here to work, I remember what it was like. My first dive, my first wreck, working the airlift, hauling up conglomerate. All the fish, the coral, the mud and sand. The work, Lorraine, the physical strain of it. You feel like you're part of it.' She spread her arms, let them fall. 'This seems so removed, so cold and intrusive somehow.'

'So scientific?' Lorraine put in.

'Science without participation, for me, anyway. I remember when I found my first coin, a silver piece of eight. We had a virgin wreck in the West Indies.' She sighed, sat again. 'I was twenty. It was a very eventful summer for me. We found a Spanish galleon, and lost it. I fell in love and had my heart broken. I've never been that involved with anything or anyone again. I haven't wanted to be.'

'Because of the ship or the man?'

'Both. In a few weeks, I experienced absolute joy and absolute grief. A difficult ride at twenty. I went back to college that fall with my goals very well defined. I would get my degree and be the very best in my field. I would do exactly what I'm doing now and keep a logical, professional distance. And here I am, eight years later, wondering if I've made some terrible mistake.'

Lorraine cocked a brow. 'You don't like your work?'

'I love my work. I'm just having a hard time letting machines do the best part of it for me. Keeping me at that logical, professional distance.'

'It doesn't sound like a crisis to me, Tate. It just sounds like you need to strap on your tanks and have a little fun.' She studied the nails she'd recently manicured. 'If that's the way you define fun. When's the last time you took a vacation?'

'Oh, let's see . . .' Tate leaned back, closed her eyes. 'That would have been about eight years ago, unless we count a couple of quick weekends and Christmases at home.'

'We don't,' Lorraine said definitely. 'Doctor Lorraine's prescription is very simple. What you've got here is a case of the blues. Take a month off when we're done here, go someplace with lots of palm trees and spend lots of time with fish.'

Lorraine developed a sudden avid interest in her manicure and peered at the coral-pink enamel. 'If you wanted company, Hayden would jump at the chance to go with you.'

'Hayden?'

'To use a technical term, the man's nuts about you.'

'Hayden?'

'Yes, Hayden.' Lorraine jerked back so that her feet slapped on the floor. 'Christ, Tate, pay attention. He's been mooning over you for weeks.'

'Hay–' Tate began before she caught herself. 'We're friends, Lorraine, associates.' Then she remembered the way he'd kissed her the night they'd found the *Justine*. 'Well, hell.'

'He's a terrific man.'

'Of course he is.' Baffled, Tate dragged a hand through her hair. 'I just never thought about him that way.'

'He's thinking about you that way.'

'It's not a good idea,' Tate murmured. 'It's not a good idea to get involved with someone you're working with. I know.'

'Your choice,' Lorraine said carelessly. 'I just thought it was time somebody gave the guy a break and let you know. I'm also supposed to let you know that some reps from SeaSearch and Poseidon are coming to examine and transport some of the loot. And they're bringing a film crew.'

'A film crew.' Automatically, Tate filed the problem of Hayden in the back of her mind. 'I thought we were doing our own video records.'

'They'll use ours as well. We're going to be a cable document-ary, so don't forget your mascara and lipstick.'

'When are they due?'

'They're on their way.'

Hardly realizing it, Tate picked up the wooden top, cupped it possessively in her hands. 'They're not moving anything I haven't finished studying and cataloguing.'

'You be sure to tell them that, champ.' Lorraine headed for the door. 'But remember, we're just the hired help.'

The hired help, Tate thought and set the top carefully aside. Maybe that was the crux of it. Somehow she'd gone from being an independent woman looking for adventure to a competent drone who worked for a faceless corporation.

It made her work possible, she reminded herself. Scientists were always beggars. And yet . . .

There were a lot of 'and yets' in her life, she realized. She was going to have to take some time and decide which ones mattered.

Matthew decided he had lost his mind. He'd quit his job. A job he'd hated, but one that had paid the bills and left enough to spare to keep a couple of small dreams from dying. Without the job, the boat he'd been building bit by bit over the years would never be completed, his uncle would be forced to live on subsidies and he would be lucky to be able to afford a decent meal in six months' time.

Not only had he quit his job, but he'd been maneuvered into taking LaRue along with him. The man had simply packed up and shipped out with him with no encouragement at all. As Matthew saw it, he was now stuck with two dependents, two men who spent most of their time arguing with each other and pointing out his flaws.

So here he sat, outside a trailer in southern Florida wondering when he had gone mad.

It was the letter from the Beaumonts that had started it. The mention of Tate, of VanDyke, and of course, the *Isabella*. It had brought back too many memories, too many failures and too much hope. Before he'd let himself think through the consequences, he'd been packing his gear.

Now that his bridges were burning at his back, Matthew had plenty of time to think. What the hell was he going to do with Buck? The man's drinking was out of hand again.

Big surprise, Matthew thought. Every year, he came back to Florida and spent his month on shore struggling to get his uncle dry. And every year he went back to sea, hampered with guilt, regrets and the grief that he would never be able to make a difference.

Even now, he could hear Buck's voice lifted in drunken bitterness. Despite the rain that was falling in steady, sodden sheets, Matthew remained outside under the rusted, leaking awning.

'What is this slop?' Buck demanded, clattering into the tiny kitchen.

LaRue didn't bother to glance up from the book he was reading. 'It is bouillabaisse. A family recipe.'

'Slop,' Buck said again. 'French slop.' Unshaven, wearing the clothes he'd slept in, Buck slammed open a cabinet door in search of a bottle. 'I don't want it smelling up my house.'

In answer, LaRue turned a page.

'Where the fuck's my whiskey?' Buck stabbed his hand into the cupboard, knocking over and scattering the meager supplies. 'I had a bottle in here, goddamn it.'

'Me, I prefer a good Beaujolais,' LaRue commented. 'At room temperature.' He heard the screen door open and marked his place in his Faulkner novel. The evening show was about to begin.

'You been stealing my whiskey, you fucking Canuk?'

As LaRue's tooth gleamed in a snarl, Matthew stepped in. 'There isn't any whiskey. I got rid of it.'

Hampered more by his morning's drinking than by his prosthesis, Buck turned on him. 'You got no right to take my bottle.'

Who was this man, Matthew thought, this stranger? If Buck was somewhere in that bloated, unshaven face, in those red-rimmed, bleary eyes, he could no longer see him. 'Right or not,' he said calmly, 'I got rid of it. Try the coffee.'

In response, Buck grabbed the pot from the stove and hurled it against the wall.

'So don't try the coffee.' Because he was tempted to ball them into fists, Matthew tucked his hands into his pockets. 'You want to drink, you're going to have to do it somewhere else. I'm not going to watch you kill yourself.'

'What I do's my business,' Buck muttered, crunching over broken glass and slopped coffee.

'Not while I'm around.'

'You're never around, are you?' Buck nearly skidded on the wet tile, righted himself. His face went pink with humiliation. Every step he took was a reminder. 'You blow in here when you please, and blow out the same way. You got no business, boy, telling me what to do in my own house.'

'It's my house,' Matthew said softly. 'You're just dying in it.'

He could have dodged the blow. He took Buck's fist on his jaw philosophically. In some perverse part of his brain, he was pleased to note that his uncle could still pack a punch.

While Buck stared at him, Matthew wiped the blood from his mouth with the back of his hand. 'I'm going out,' he said and left.

'Go away, walk away.' Buck shambled to the door to shout after him over the drumming rain. 'Walking away's what you're best at. Why don't you keep walking? Nobody here needs you. Nobody needs you.'

LaRue waited until Buck lumbered back toward the bedroom, then rose to turn down the heat on his stew. He took his jacket, and Matthew's, and slipped out of the trailer.

They had only been in Florida three days, but LaRue knew just where Matthew would go. Adjusting the brim of his cap so that the rain sluiced off in front of his face, he made his way down to the marina.

It was nearly deserted, and the lock was off the door of the concrete garage that Matthew rented by the month. He found Matthew inside, sitting in the bow of a nearly finished boat.

It was a double hull, almost as wide as it was long. LaRue's first glimpse of it after they'd arrived had impressed him. It was a pretty thing, not dainty by any means, but sturdy and tough. The way LaRue preferred his boats, and his women.

Matthew had designed the deck section to lie across the top of the hulls so that it would stay clear in rough seas. Each bow had an inward curve that would create a cushioning effect and lead to not only a smoother ride, but a faster one. There was plenty of storage area and seating. But the genius of the design in LaRue's opinion was the sixty square feet of open deck forward.

Treasure room, LaRue thought.

All it lacked were the finishing touches. The paint and brightwork, the bridge equipment, navigational devices. And, LaRue thought, a suitable name.

He climbed up, impressed again by the sharp, cutting look of the bows. It would take the water, he mused. It would fly.

'So, when you finish this thing, eh?'

'I've got the time now, don't I?' Matthew envisioned the rails. Brass and teak. 'All I need's the money.'

'Me, I got plenty of money.' Thoughtfully, LaRue took out a leather pouch and began the slow and, to him, pleasurable process of rolling a cigarette. 'What do I spend it on but women? And they don't cost so much as most men think. So maybe I give you the money to finish it, and you give me part of the boat.'

Matthew let out a sour laugh. 'What part do you want?'

LaRue leaned into the backrest, carefully sealing the cigarette paper around the tobacco. 'A boat a man builds is a good place

153

to come when he wants to brood. Tell me this, Matthew, why did you let him hit you?'

'Why not?'

'Seems to me he'd be better if you hit him.'

'Right. That would be great. It would do a lot of good for me to knock down a—'

'Cripple?' LaRue finished mildly. 'No, you never let him forget he's not what he was.'

Furious, surprised into hurt, Matthew lunged to his feet. 'Where the hell do you come off saying that? What the hell do you know about it? I've done everything I can for him.'

'You've done.' LaRue struck a match, let it flare on the edge of the neatly rolled cigarette. 'You pay for the roof over his head, the food in his belly, the whiskey he kills himself with. All it costs him is his pride.'

'What the hell am I supposed to do, toss him out into the street?'

LaRue shrugged. 'You don't ask him to be a man, so he's not a man.'

'Butt out.'

'I think you like your guilt, Matthew. It keeps you from doing what you want, and maybe failing at it.' He only grinned when Matthew hauled him up by the shirtfront. 'See, me, you treat like a man.' He cocked up his chin, not entirely sure it wouldn't be broken in the next ten seconds. 'You can hit me. I'll hit you back. When we're finished, we'll make a deal for the boat.'

'What the hell are you doing here?' In disgust, Matthew shoved him back. 'I don't need company, I don't need another partner.'

'You do, yes. And I like you, Matthew.' LaRue sat again, neatly tapping the ash from his cigarette into his palm. 'And I figure this. You're going to go back for that ship you once told me about. Maybe you'll go after this VanDyke you hate so much. Maybe you'll even go back for the woman you want. I'm going, because I don't mind being rich. I like to see a good fight, and me, I have a soft spot for romance.'

'You're an asshole, LaRue. Christ knows why I ever told you about that shit.' He lifted his hands and rubbed them over his face. 'I must have been drunk.'

'No, you never let yourself get drunk. You were talking to yourself, *mon ami*. I was just there.'

'Maybe I'll go back for the wreck. And maybe, if I get lucky, I'll cross paths with VanDyke again. But there's no woman anymore.'

154

'There's always a woman. If not one, another.' LaRue shrugged his bony shoulders. 'Me, I don't understand why men lose their minds over a woman. One leaves, another comes along. But an enemy, that's worth working for. And money, well, it's easier to be rich than poor. So we finish your boat, eh, and go looking for fortune and revenge.'

Wary, Matthew eyed LaRue. 'The equipment I want isn't cheap.'

'Nothing worthwhile is cheap.'

'We may never find the wreck. Even if we do, mining her is going to be hard, dangerous work.'

'Danger is what makes life interesting. You've forgotten that, Matthew.'

'Maybe,' he murmured. He began to feel something stir again. It was the blood he'd let settle and cool over the years. He held out a hand. 'We finish the boat.'

★

It was three days later when Buck made his way into the garage. He'd gotten a bottle somewhere, Matthew deduced. The sour stench of whiskey surrounded him.

'Where the hell you think you're going to take this tub?'

Matthew continued to lovingly sand the teak for the rail. 'Hatteras to start. I'm hooking up with the Beaumonts.'

'Shit, amateurs.' A little rocky on his feet, Buck walked to the stern. 'What the hell did you build a catamaran for?'

'Because I wanted to.'

'Single hull's always been good enough for me. Good enough for your father, too.'

'It's not your boat. It's not his boat. It's mine.'

That stung. 'What kind of color is this you're painting her. Damn sissy blue.'

'Caribbean blue,' Matthew corrected. 'I like it.'

'Probably sink the first time you hit weather.' Buck sniffed and stopped himself from caressing one of the hulls. 'I guess all you and Ray are good for now is pleasure sailing.'

Experimentally, Matthew ran the pad of his thumb over the teak. It was satin smooth. 'We're going after the *Isabella*.'

Silence sparked like naked wires crossed. Matthew hefted the sanded rail over his shoulder and turned. Buck had a hand on the boat now, braced as he swayed like a man already at sea.

'The hell you are.'

'Ray's decided to go. He found something he wants to show me. As soon as I can get things done here, I'm heading up. Regardless of what Ray's come up with, I'm going after her. It's long past time I did.'

'Are you out of your mind, boy? Do you know what she cost us? Cost me?'

Matthew set the rail aside for varnishing. 'I've got a pretty good idea.'

'You had a treasure, didn't you? You let her go. You let that bastard VanDyke dance off with it. You lost it for me when I was half dead. Now you think you're going back and leaving me here to rot?'

'I'm going. What you do is your business.'

Panicked, Buck slammed the heel of his hand into Matthew's chest. 'Who's going to see to what I need here? You go off like this, the money'll be gone in a month. You owe me, boy. I saved your worthless life. I lost my leg for you. I lost everything for you.'

The guilt still came, waves of it a strong man could drown in. But this time, Matthew shook his head. He wasn't going under again. 'I'm finished owing you, Buck. Eight years I've worked my ass off so you could drink yourself into a coma and make me pay for every breath I took. I'm done. I'm going after something I'd convinced myself I couldn't have. And I'm going to get her.'

'They'll kill you. The *Isabella* and Angelique's Curse. And if they don't, VanDyke will. Then where will I be?'

'Just where you are now. Standing on two legs. One of them I paid for.'

He didn't take the punch this time. Instead he caught Buck's fist in his hand an inch before it struck his face. Without thinking he shoved back so that Buck stumbled into the stern of the boat.

'Try that again, and I'll take you down, old man or not.' Matthew planted his feet, prepared to face-off if Buck lunged again. 'In ten days, I'm leaving for Hatteras with LaRue. You can pull yourself together, or you can go fuck yourself. It's your choice. Now get the hell out. I've got work to do.'

With a shaking hand, Buck wiped his mouth. His phantom leg began to throb, a nasty, grinning ghost that never quite gave up the haunting. Sick at heart, he hurried off to find a bottle.

Alone, Matthew hefted another section of rail and went to work like a man possessed.

Chapter Thirteen

As FAR AS Silas VanDyke was concerned, Manzanillo was the only place to spend the first breaths of spring. His cliff house on the western Mexican coast afforded him the most spectacular view of the restless Pacific. There was nothing more relaxing than standing by his wall of windows and watching the waves crash and spew.

Power never failed to fascinate him.

As an Aquarian, he considered water his element. He loved the sight of it, the smell of it, the sound of it. Though he traveled extensively for both business and pleasure, he could never be away from his element for long.

All of his homes had been bought or built near some body of water. His villa in Capri, his plantation in Fiji, his bungalow on Martinique. Even his brownstone in New York afforded him a view of the Hudson. But he had a particular fondness for his hideaway in Mexico.

Not that this particular trip was one of leisure. VanDyke's work ethic was as disciplined as the rest of him. Rewards were earned – and he had earned his. He believed in labor, the exercise of the body as well as the mind. It was true that he had inherited a great deal of his wealth, but he had not whiled away his time or whittled away his resources. No, he had built on them doggedly and shrewdly until he had easily tripled the legacy passed to him.

He considered himself discreet and dignified. No publicity-seeking Trump, VanDyke pursued his personal and business affairs quietly and with a subtle flare that kept his name out of the press and tabloid news.

Unless he put it there. Publicity, of the proper type, could shade a business deal and tip the scales when necessary.

He had never married, though he admired women greatly. Marriage was a contract, and the negating of that contract was too often messy, too often public. Heirs were often a result of that contract, and heirs could be used against a man.

Instead, he chose his companions with care, treated them with the same respect and courtesy as he would treat any employee. And when a woman ceased to entertain him, she was generously dispatched.

Few complained.

The little Italian socialite he had recently grown weary of had been a bit of a problem. The icy diamonds he'd offered as a parting gift hadn't cooled her hot temper. She'd actually threatened him. With some regret, he'd arranged for her to be taught a lesson. But he'd given strict orders that there were to be no visible scars.

After all, she'd had a lovely face and body that had given him a great deal of pleasure.

It seemed to him that violence, well-skilled violence, was a tool no successful man could afford to ignore. In the last few years, he had used it often, and he thought, quite well.

The oddest thing was that it gave him so much more pleasure than he had expected. A kind of cheap, emotional profit, he decided. Privately, he could admit that by paying for it, he often soothed those black tempers that raged over him.

So many men he knew, men who, like him, controlled great wealth and managed responsibilities, lost their edge by accepting certain failures, making too many concessions. Or they simply burned themselves out by fighting to stay on top. Frustrations, he thought, unreleased, festered. A wise man took his relief and always, always, counted the profit.

Now he had business to attend to, business to entertain him. At the moment, his priority was the *Nomad*, its crew, and its brilliant find.

As he'd ordered, the reports were on his desk. He'd hand-picked the team for his expedition, from the scientists to the technicians and down to the galley staff. It pleased him to know that once again, his instincts had been on target. They hadn't failed him. When the expedition was complete, VanDyke would see to it that each and every member of the *Nomad* team received a bonus.

He admired scientists tremendously, their logic and discipline, their vision. He was more than satisfied with Frank Litz, both as a biologist and as a spy. The man kept him up to date on the personal dynamics and intimacies of the *Nomad's* crew.

Yes, he thought Litz a happy find, particularly after the dis-appointment of Piper. The young archeologist had had poten-tial, VanDyke mused. But that one little flaw had made him sloppy.

Addictions led to a lack of order. Why, he himself had given up smoking years before simply to make a point. Inner strength equaled power over personal environment. A pity Piper had lacked inner strength. In the end, VanDyke had har-bored no regrets in offering him the uncut cocaine that had killed him.

In truth, it had been rather thrilling. The ultimate termina-tion of an employee.

Settling back, he studied the reports from Litz and his team of marine biologists on the ecosystem, the plants and animals that had colonized the wreck of the *Justine*. Sponges, gold coral, worms. Nothing was beneath VanDyke's interest.

What was there could be harvested and used.

With the same respect and interest, he studied the reports of the geologists, the chemist, those of the representatives he had sent to observe the operation and its results.

Like a child with a treat, he saved the archeologist's report for last. It was meticulously organized, thorough and clear as new glass. No detail was omitted, down to the last shard of crockery. Each artifact was described, dated and photographed, each item catalogued according to the date and time it was discovered. There was a cross-reference with the chemist's report as to how the article was treated, tested, cleaned.

A father's pride swept through VanDyke as he read the carefully typed pages. He was glowingly pleased with Tate Beaumont, considered her a protégée.

She would make a fine replacement for the unfortunate Piper.

Perhaps it had been impulse that had urged him to have her education monitored over the years. But the impulse had more than paid off. The way she had faced him onboard the *Triumphant* with fury and intelligence firing her eyes. Oh, he admired that. Courage was a valuable asset, when tempered with a well-ordered mind.

Tate Beaumont possessed both.

Professionally, she had more than exceeded his early expectations of her. She'd graduated third in her class, publishing her first paper in her sophomore year. Her postgraduate work had simply been brilliant. She would earn her doctorate years before the majority of her contemporaries.

He was thrilled with her.

So thrilled he had opened several doors for her along the way. Doors that even with her skills and tenacity might have been difficult for her to unlatch. Her opportunity to research in a two-man sub off Turkey in depths of six hundred feet had come through him. Though like an indulgent uncle, he had taken no credit. Yet.

Her personal life earned his admiration as well. Initially, he'd been disappointed that she hadn't remained attached to Matthew Lassiter. A continued connection would have been one more method of keeping tabs on Matthew. Yet he'd been pleased that she'd shown the obvious good taste to shrug off a man so clearly beneath her.

She'd concentrated on her studies, her goals, as he would have expected from his own daughter, had he a daughter. Twice she had explored relationships. The first no more than the rebellion of youth, in VanDyke's opinion. The young man she'd attached herself to in the initial weeks after her return to college had been little more than an experiment, he was sure. But she'd soon shaken herself loose from the muscle-bound empty-headed jock.

A woman like Tate required intellect, style, breeding.

Indeed, after graduation she had been drawn into a liaison with a fellow postgraduate student who shared many of her

160

interests. That had lasted just under ten months, and had caused VanDyke some concern. But that, too, had ended when he'd arranged to have the man offered a position at his oceanographic institute in Greenland.

To fully realize her potential, he felt Tate needed to limit her distractions, as he had over the years. Marriage and family would only tilt her priorities.

He was delighted that she was now working for him. He intended to keep her on the fringes for the present. In time, if she continued to prove worthy, he would draw her into the core.

A women of her intelligence and ambitions would recognize the debt she owed him, and would understand the value of what he could continue to offer.

One day they would meet again, work side by side.

He was a patient man and could wait for her. As he waited for Angelique's Curse. His instincts told him that when the time was finally right, one would lead him to the other.

Then he would have everything.

VanDyke glanced over as his fax began to hum. Rising, he poured himself a large tumbler of freshly squeezed orange juice. If he hadn't had such a full schedule that day, he would have added just a dollop of champagne. Such small luxuries could wait.

He lifted a brow as he picked up the fax. It was his latest report on the Lassiters. So, he mused, Matthew had jumped ship and gone back to his uncle. Perhaps he would stick the drunken fool in another rehab center. It continued to surprise him that Matthew didn't simply leave the old man to wallow in his own vomit and disappear.

Family loyalty, he thought, shaking his head. It was something VanDyke knew existed, but had never experienced. If his own father hadn't conveniently died at fifty, VanDyke would have implemented his plans for a takeover. Fortunately, he had no siblings to rival with, and his mother had faded quietly away in an exclusive mental hospital when he'd been barely thirteen.

He had only himself, VanDyke thought, sipping the chilled juice. And his fortune. It was well worth using a small part of it to keep an eye on Matthew Lassiter.

Family loyalty, he thought again with a small smile. If it ran true, Matthew's father had found a way to pass his secret to his

161

son. Sooner or later, Matthew would be compelled to hunt for Angelique's Curse. And VanDyke, patient as a spider, would be waiting.

Rough weather hit the *Nomad* and halted excavation for forty-eight hours. High seas had half the crew down for the count despite seasick pills and patches. Tate and her cast-iron constitution rode out the storm with a Thermos of coffee at her worktable.

She'd left the cabin to a moaning, green-faced Lorraine.

The rock and roll of the boat didn't stop her from cataloguing the newest additions to the trove.

'I thought I'd find you here.'

She looked up, let her fingers pause on her keyboard and smiled at Hayden. 'I thought you were lying down.' She tilted her head. 'You're a little pale yet, but you've lost that interesting green tinge.' Her smile widened wickedly. 'Want a cookie?'

'Feeling smug?' Warily, he kept his eyes averted from the plate of cookies on the table. 'I hear Bowers is having a great time finding new ways to describe pork to Dart.'

'Hmm. Bowers and I, and a few of the others, enjoyed quite a hardy breakfast this morning.' She laughed. 'Rest easy, Hayden, I won't describe it to you. Have a seat?'

'It's embarrassing for the team leader to lose his dignity this way.' Grateful, he lowered himself into a folding chair. 'Too much time in the classroom, not enough in the field, I guess.'

'You're doing okay.' Happy to have company, she turned away from the monitor. 'The entire film crew's down. I hate to be pleased with anyone's misfortune, but it's a relief not to have them hovering for a couple days.'

'A documentary will pump up interest in this kind of expedition,' he pointed out. 'We can use the exposure, and the grants.'

'I know. It isn't often you have the benefit of a privately funded expedition, or one that pays off so successfully. Look at this, Hayden.' She lifted a gold watch, complete with chain and fob. 'Beautiful, isn't it? The detail of etching on the cover. You can practically smell the roses.'

Lovingly, she rubbed a thumb over the delicately etched spring of buds before carefully opening the clasp.

' "To David, my beloved husband, who makes time stop for me. Elizabeth. 2/4/49." '

Her heart sighed over it. 'There was a David and Elizabeth MacGowan on the manifest,' she told Hayden in a voice that had thickened. 'And their three children. She and her eldest daughter survived. She lost a son, another daughter, and her beloved David. Time stopped for them, and never started again.'

She closed the watch gently. 'He'd have been wearing this when the ship went down,' she murmured. 'He'd have kept it with him. He might have even opened it, read the inscription one last time after he said goodbye to her and their children. They never saw each other again. For a hundred and fifty years, this token of how much she loved him has been waiting for someone to find it. And remember them.'

'It's humbling,' Hayden said after a moment, 'when the student outstrips the teacher. You have more than I ever did,' he added when Tate glanced up in surprise. 'I would see a watch, the style, the manufacturer. I would note the inscription down, pleased to have a date to corroborate my calculation of its era. I might give David and Elizabeth a passing thought, certainly I would have looked for them in the manifest. But I wouldn't see them. I wouldn't feel them.'

'It isn't scientific.'

'Archeology is meant to study culture. Too often we forget that people make culture. The best of us don't. The best of us make it matter.' He laid a hand over hers. 'The way you do.'

'I don't know what to do when it makes me sad.' She turned her hand over so that their fingers linked. 'If I could, I'd take this and I'd find their great-great-grandchildren so I could say – look, this is part of David and Elizabeth. This is who they were.' Feeling foolish, she set the watch aside. 'But it doesn't belong to me. It doesn't even belong to them now. It belongs to SeaSearch.'

'Without SeaSearch, it would never have been found.'

'I understand that. I do.' Needing to clarify her own feelings, she leaned closer. 'What we're doing here is important, Hayden. The way we're doing it is innovative and efficient. Over and above the fortune we're bringing up, there's knowledge, discovery, theory. We're making the *Justine*, and the people who died with her, real and vital again.'

'But?'

'That's where I stumble. Where will David's watch go, Hayden? And the dozens and dozens of other personal treasures people carried with them? We have no control over it, because no matter how important our work, we're employees. We're dots, Hayden, in some huge conglomerate. SeaSearch to Poseidon, Poseidon to Trident, and on.'

His lips curved. 'Most of us spend our working lives as dots, Tate.'

'Are you content with that?'

'I suppose I am. I'm able to do the work I love, teach, lecture, publish. Without those conglomerates, with their slices of social conscience, or eye for a tax write-off, I'd never be able to take time for this kind of hands-on field work and still eat on a semi-regular basis.'

It was true, of course. It made perfect sense. And yet . . . 'But is it enough, Hayden? Should it be enough? How much are we missing by being up here? Not risking anything, or experiencing the hunt. Not having some claim or control over what we do, and what we discover. Aren't we in danger of losing the passion that pulled us into this in the first place?'

'You aren't.' His heart began to accept what his head had told him all along. She would never be for him. She was an exotic flower to his simple, plodding drone. 'You'll never lose it, because it's what defines you.'

In a symbolic farewell to a foolish dream, he lifted her hand and pressed his lips to her knuckles.

'Hayden . . .'

He could read the concern, the regret and, painfully, the sympathy in her eyes. 'Don't worry. Just a token of admiration from colleague to colleague. I have a suspicion we're not going to be working together much longer.'

'I haven't decided,' she said quickly.

'I think you have.'

'I have responsibilities here. And I owe you, Hayden, for recommending me for this position.'

'Your name was already on the list,' he corrected. 'I merely agreed with the choice.'

'But I thought–' Her brow creased.

'You've earned a reputation, Tate.'

'I appreciate that, Hayden, but … Already on the list, you said. Whose list?'

'Trident's. The brass there was impressed with your record. Actually, I got the feeling there was some definite pressure to put you on, from one of the moneymen. Not that I wasn't happy to go along with the recommendation.'

'I see.' For reasons she couldn't name, her throat felt dry. 'Who would that be, the moneyman?'

'Like you said, I'm just a dot.' He shrugged his shoulders as he rose. 'Anyway, should you decide to resign before the expedition is finished, I'd be sorry to lose you, but it's your choice.'

'You're getting ahead of me.' It made her nervous to realize she'd been singled out somehow, but she smiled at Hayden. 'But thanks.'

When he left her, she rubbed her hands over her mouth. Where had this spooky feeling come from? she wondered. Why hadn't she known about a list, or that her name had been on it?

Turning to her monitor, she clattered keys, eyes narrowed on the screen. Trident, Hayden had said. So she would bypass Poseidon and SeaSearch for the moment. To find where the power was at any level, you looked for the money.

'Hey, friends and neighbors.' Bowers strolled in, gnawing on a chicken leg. 'Lunch is up, in more ways than one.' He wiggled his brows at Tate and waited for her to chuckle.

'Give me a hand here, Bowers.'

'Sure, sweet thing. My hand is your hand.'

'Just work your magic on the computer. I want to find out who the big backers are in Trident.'

'Going to write thank-you notes?' Setting his lunch aside, he wiped his hands on his shirtfront and started in.

'Hmm … a lot of layers here,' he murmured after a moment. 'Good thing I'm the best. You're hooked up to the main here, so the data we need's in there somewhere. Always is. You want board of directors, or what?'

'No,' she said slowly. 'Forget that. Ownership of the *Nomad*, Bowers, under the corporation. Who owns the ship?'

'Ownership shouldn't be tough to find. Not with your friendly technology. SeaSearch owns it, baby. Hold on … donated. God, I love philanthropists. Some cat named VanDyke.'

Tate stared at the screen. 'Silas VanDyke.'

'He's a big wheel and a big deal. You musta heard of him. Finances a lot of expeditions. We ought to give the man a big, sloppy kiss.' His grin faded when he looked down at Tate's face. 'What's up?'

165

'I am.' She gritted her teeth against the fury. 'That son of a bitch put me on here. That … Well, I'm taking myself off.'

'Off?' Baffled, Bowers stared at her. 'Off what?'

'He thought he could use me.' Almost blind with temper, she stared at the artifacts carefully arranged on her worktable. David and Elizabeth's watch. 'For this. The hell with him.'

Matthew hung up the phone, picked up his coffee. Another bridge burned, he thought. Or maybe, just maybe, the first couple of planks set in place on a new one.

He was sailing for Hatteras in the morning.

If nothing else, he mused, it would be a good test of the *Mermaid*'s seaworthiness.

The boat was finished, painted, polished and named. He and LaRue had taken her out several times over the last few days on short runs. She sailed like a dream.

Matthew sat back now, pleasantly tired. Maybe he'd finally done something that would last.

Even the name had personal significance for him. He'd had the dream again, the one of Tate in the deep, dark sea. He didn't need Freud to explain it to him. He'd been in contact with Ray often over the last few weeks. Tate's name had come up, as had the *Isabella*, and memories of that summer.

Naturally, it had made him think, and look back, so the dream had come.

Tate might have been no more than a wistful memory, but the dream had been so immediate that he'd felt compelled to christen the boat for it. Or in a roundabout way, he supposed, for her.

He wondered if he would see her, doubted it. And letting himself slide into relaxation, told himself it didn't matter one way or the other.

The screen door whined open, slammed. LaRue came in with bags of takeout burgers and fries. 'You made your phone call?' he asked.

'Yeah. I told Ray we'd start out in the morning.' Lifting his arms over his head, Matthew linked his fingers and stretched. 'Weather looks good. Shouldn't take us more than three or four days at an easy clip. That'll give us a chance to shake her down.'

'I look forward to the meeting of him and his wife.' LaRue dug up paper plates. 'He didn't tell you more about what he found?'

'He wants me to see it in person.' Suddenly ravenous, Matthew helped himself to a burger. 'He's set on heading out for the West Indies by the middle of April. I told him that suited us.'

LaRue's gaze met Matthew's, and held. 'The sooner the better.'

'You're crazy going back there.' Face haggard, Buck stepped in from the bedroom. 'The place is cursed. The *Isabella*'s cursed. Took your father, didn't it?' His gait slow, measured, he came forward. 'Nearly took me. Should have.'

Matthew doused his fries with enough salt to make LaRue wince. 'VanDyke took my father,' he said calmly. 'A shark took your leg.'

'Angelique's Curse caused it.'

'Maybe it did.' Matthew chewed thoughtfully. 'If it did, I figure I've got a claim on it.'

'That thing's bad luck to the Lassiters.'

'It's time I changed my luck.'

Unsteady, Buck braced a hand on the tiny linoleum-topped table. 'Maybe you figure I only care what happens to you 'cause of what'll happen to me. That ain't the way it is. Your father expected I'd look after you. I did the best I could long as I could.'

'I haven't needed looking after for a long time.'

'Maybe not. And maybe I've been fucking up when it comes to you, when it comes to me the past few years. You're all I've got, Matthew. Truth is, you're all I ever gave most of a damn about.'

Buck's voice broke, causing Matthew to close his eyes and will away the worst edge of guilt. 'I'm not spending the rest of my life paying for something I couldn't stop, or watching you finish the job the shark started.'

'I'm asking you to stay. I figure we could start a business. Take tourists out, fishermen, that kind of thing.' Buck swallowed hard. 'I'd pull my weight this time around.'

'I can't do it.' Appetite gone, Matthew pushed his food aside and stood. 'I'm going after the *Isabella*. Whether I find her or not, I'm picking up my life again. There are plenty of wrecks out there, and I'm damned if I'm going to spend the rest of my life salvaging metal or chauffeuring tourists instead of hunting gold.'

'There's nothing I can do to stop you.' Buck looked down at his trembling hands. 'I didn't figure there was.' He took a deep breath, straightened his shoulders. 'I'm going with you.'

'Look, Buck–'

'I haven't had one fucking drink in ten days.' Buck fisted his hands, forced them to relax again. 'I'm dry. Maybe I'm a little rocky yet, but I'm dry.'

For the first time, Matthew looked at him. There were shadows under the eyes, but the eyes were clear. 'You've gone ten days before, Buck.'

'Yeah. But not on my own. I got a stake in this, too, Matthew. Scares the hell out of me, the thought of going back. But if you go, I go. Lassiters stick together,' he managed before his voice cracked again. 'You want me to beg you not to leave me behind?'

'No. Christ.' He rubbed a hand over his face. There were a dozen logical, viable reasons to refuse. And only one to agree. Buck was family. 'I can't baby-sit you, or worry about you sneaking a bottle. You have to work, earn your space on the boat.'

'I know what I gotta do.'

'LaRue' – Matthew turned to the man quietly eating his takeout dinner – 'you've got a stake in this. Where do you stand?'

Politely, LaRue swallowed, dabbed his mouth with a paper napkin. 'Me, I figure two more hands don't get in the way, long as they're steady.' He shrugged his shoulder. 'If they shake, you can take him for ballast.'

Humiliated, Buck set his jaw. 'I'll pull my weight. James wanted the *Isabella*. I'll help you get her for him.'

'All right.' Matthew nodded. 'Pack your gear. We leave at first light.'

Chapter Fourteen

THE LITTLE PLANE bounced on the runway and woke Tate out of a half doze. For the past thirty-eight hours she had been almost constantly on the move, juggling herself from boats to planes to cabs. She'd crossed a hefty slice of the Pacific, an entire continent, and all the varying time zones.

Her eyes told her it was day, but her body didn't have a clue.

At the moment, she felt as though she were made out of thin, fragile glass that would easily shatter at a loud noise or a careless bump.

But she was home. Or as close to home as the tiny airport in Frisco on Hatteras Island. All that was left was one quick car ride, and then, she vowed, she would avoid anything that moved for at least twenty-four hours.

Shifting carefully, she reached down for her carry-on. The tuna can with propellers she'd caught in Norfolk was empty but for her and the pilot. Once he'd taxied to a halt, he turned and gave her a thumbs-up sign which she returned with a vague gesture and an even vaguer smile.

She knew she had a great deal to think over, but her mind simply wouldn't function. Since she'd discovered the connection with VanDyke, she'd been in a tearing hurry to get home. Fate had played a hand. She'd been stuffing her gear into bags when she'd received a call from her father, asking her to come as soon as she was able to break away from the expedition.

Well, she'd broken away, she thought. In record time.

Since then, she'd done nothing but work and travel, catching snatches of sleep in between. She hoped VanDyke had already been informed she was thousands of miles from her post. She hoped he knew she'd thumbed her nose at him.

With her briefcase in one hand, the carry-on slung over her shoulder, she negotiated the narrow steps to the tarmac. Her knees wobbled, and she was grateful for the shaded glasses that cut the glare of the brilliant sun.

She saw them almost immediately, waving cheerfully while she waited for the pilot to unload her suitcase from cargo.

How little they changed, she mused. Maybe there was a touch more gray threading through her father's hair, but they were both so straight and slim and handsome. Both of them were grinning like fools, holding hands while they waved manically.

Half of Tate's travel fatigue drained just looking at them.

But what in the hell have you gotten yourselves into? she wondered. Secrets that couldn't be shared over the phone. Plots and plans and adventures. That damned amulet, that damned wreck. The damned Lassiters.

It had been Ray's enthusiasm about the possibility of hooking up with the Lassiters again that had weighed the scales in favor of Tate's trip directly to Hatteras instead of to her own apartment in Charleston. She only hoped he'd listened to her and held off contacting Matthew. It was incomprehensible to her that any of them would want a repeat of that horrendous summer.

Well, she was here now, she told herself as she gripped the strap and rolled her suitcase behind her. And she would talk some sense into her wonderful, but naive, parents.

'Oh, honey. Honey, it's so good to see you.' Marla's arms came around her, gripped tight. 'It's been so long. Nearly a year this time.'

'I know. I've missed you.' On a laugh, she let her carry-on drop so that she could pull her father into the embrace. 'I've missed both of you. Oh, and you look terrific.' Tearing up, she pulled back to take a long, close-up look. 'Really terrific. Mom, you've changed your hair. It's almost as short as mine used to be.'

'Do you like it?' Womanlike, Marla patted her sassily cropped do.

'It's great. Totally now.' And so youthfully flattering, Tate wondered how this pretty, smooth-faced woman could be her mother.

'I'm doing so much gardening now. It always seemed to be in the way. Honey, you're so thin. You've been working too hard.' Brow creased, she turned to her husband. 'Ray, I told you she's been working too hard.'

'You told me,' he agreed and rolled his eyes. 'Over and over. How was the trip, baby?'

'Endless.' She wriggled her shoulders to loosen them as they walked through the small terminal to where Ray had parked his jeep. Stifling a yawn, she shook her head. 'The bottom line is, I'm here.'

'We're glad you are.' Ray stowed the luggage in the back of the jeep. 'We wanted you in on this trip, Tate, but I feel guilty knowing you resigned from your expedition. I know it was important to you.'

'Not as important as I thought.' She climbed into the back of the jeep, let her head fall back. She didn't want to bring up VanDyke, and his connection. Not yet at least. 'I'm glad I was part of it. I really admire the people I was working with, and I'd be thrilled to work with any of them again. And the whole process was fascinating. But it was impersonal. By the time any of the artifacts got to me, they'd been through so many other hands, it was almost like taking something out of a display case to examine.' Wearily, she concluded: 'You understand?'

'Yes.' Because Marla had warned him, Ray repressed his need to rattle away about his own plans. Give her a little time, Marla had insisted. Take it slow.

'You're home now,' Marla said. 'The first thing you're going to do is have a good, hot meal and a nap.'

'No argument. Once my head clears, I want to hear all about this idea of yours to go after the *Isabella*.'

'When you've read through my research,' Ray said cheerfully as he turned toward the village of Buxton, 'you'll see why I'm so eager to get moving.' He opened his mouth to continue, noticed his wife's warning glance and subsided. 'After you've rested a bit, we'll get it all together.'

'At least tell me what you found that started the ball rolling,' she began as he turned through a break in the pines and drove up the sandy lane. 'Oh, the azaleas are blooming.'

She was caught, leaning out the window to draw in the scent of pine and bay and blooms mixed with the aroma of water. It looked, as Tate remembered, like a fairy tale.

Marla had cleverly interspersed flowering shrubs among the trees, naturalized with spring and summer bulbs so that splashes and flows of color seemed gloriously wild and unplanned.

Near the two-story cedar house with its wide-screened porch, flower beds were only slightly more formal, with low-growing rock cress, sunny primroses and flowering sage giving way to nodding columbine and larkspur. Annuals and perennials thrived, while others waited for their season.

'You've created a rock garden,' Tate observed, craning her head when the jeep turned into a widened slot facing the sound.

'My new project. We've so much shade here I have to be very choosy. And you should see my herb bed around back by the kitchen.'

'Everything looks fabulous.' Tate stepped out of the jeep and looked at the house. 'And it's so quiet,' she said softly. 'Just the water, the birds, the breeze through the pines. I don't know how you ever leave it.'

'Whenever we come back from one of our little jaunts, we love it that much more.' Ray hefted her bags. 'It'll be a great place to retire.' He winked at his wife. 'When we're ready to grow up.'

'That'll be the day.' More delighted than she'd imagined to be there, Tate started along the walking stones set into the gentle slope. 'I suppose I'll be ready for knitting or bingo long before either of–' She halted at the back door. The colorful hammock she'd bought her father during a trip to Tahiti was stretched in its usual patch of sun. But it was occupied. 'You have company?'

'No, not company. Old friends.' Marla opened the screen door. 'They arrived just before dusk last night. We're loaded with weary travelers, aren't we, Ray?'

'Got a full house.'

Tate could see little more than a mop of dark hair that flopped over mirrored glasses, a hint of a tanned, muscular body. It was enough to have her stomach clench into several painful knots.

'What old friends?' she asked in a carefully neutral tone.

'Buck and Matthew Lassiter.' Marla was already in the kitchen, checking the clam chowder she'd had heating for lunch. 'And their shipmate LaRue. An interesting character, isn't he, Ray?'

'You bet.' Ray kept a bright smile on his face. He hadn't gotten around to mentioning to Marla their daughter's objection to the renewal of the old partnership. 'You'll get a kick out of him, Tate. I'm just going to put your things in your room.' And escape.

'Where's Buck?' Tate asked her mother. Though she'd gone into the kitchen, she kept her eye on the hammock through the window.

'Oh, he's around somewhere.' She sampled the chowder, nodded. 'He looks so much better than he did the last time we saw him.'

'Drinking?'

'No. Not a drop since he's been here. Sit down, honey. Let me fix you a bowl.'

'Not just yet.' Tate set her shoulders. 'I think I'll go out and renew acquaintance.'

'That's nice. You tell Matthew his lunch is ready.'

'Right.' She intended to tell him a great deal more than that.

The sand and springy grass muffled her footsteps. Though she was certain she could have marched up with a brass band and he wouldn't have stirred. The sunlight slanted over him. Beautifully, she thought, infuriated.

He was beautiful. No amount of resentment and disdain could deny it. His hair was mussed and obviously hadn't seen a barber's care for some time. In sleep his face was relaxed, that gorgeous mouth soft. It was a bit bonier than it had been eight years ago, she supposed, deepening the hollows of his cheeks. And that only added to the instant, sexual punch. His body was trim, muscled, and looked hard as granite with its covering of ripped jeans and faded T-shirt.

She let herself take a good long look, scrupulously monitoring her own reaction as she would monitor any lab experiment. An initial jump of the pulse, maybe, she judged. But that was only natural when a woman came across a stunning animal.

She was grateful to report that after that one visceral jolt, she felt nothing but annoyance, resentment and good, old-fashioned anger at finding him napping on her turf.

'Lassiter, you bastard.'

He didn't stir; his chest continued to rise and fall rhythmically. With a grim smile, she planted her feet, took a good hold on the edge of the hammock. Putting her back into it, she heaved.

Matthew came awake halfway through the roll. He had a quick glimpse of the ground rushing up, threw his hands out instinctively to catch himself. He grunted when he hit, swore when a prickly needle of a thistle jabbed his thumb. Groggy and disoriented, he shook his head. Tossing his hair back, he shifted until he was sitting on the ground.

The first thing he saw were small, narrow feet encased in practical and well-worn walking boots. Then there were the legs. A lot of them. Long, feminine and wonderfully shaped in snug black leggings. Under different circumstances, he could have passed a great deal of time happily studying them.

Shifting his gaze a bit higher, he encountered a black shirt, mannish with its tail sweeping hips that were definitely not a man's. Lovely breasts, high, adding a nice curve to the shirt.

Then the face.

The juices the body had stirred went directly to simmer.

She'd changed, unfairly, he thought. Gorgeously. Mouth-wateringly. While she'd been fresh, lovely and sweet at twenty, the woman she'd become was heart-stopping.

Her skin was ivory, almost transparently pure with just a blush of rose. Her unpainted mouth was full, luscious, and set in a badtempered pout that had his own mouth going bone-dry. She'd let her hair grow, and it was swept back now in a no-nonsense ponytail that left that face unframed. Behind her shaded lenses, her eyes were hot with anger.

Realizing he was on the edge of gawking, Matthew unfolded himself. In defense, he tilted his head and offered a quick, careless smile.

'Hey, Red. Long time.'

'What the hell are you doing here, getting my parents tangled up in some ridiculous scheme?'

In a negligent move, he leaned on a tree. His knees were water. 'Nice to see you, too,' he said dryly. 'And you've got it backwards. Ray's got the scheme. I'm going along for the ride.'

'Taking him for a ride more likely.' Disgust fountained up. It wasn't possible to swallow all of it. 'The partnership was dissolved eight years ago, and it's going to stay that way. I want you to go back to whatever hole you climbed out of.'

'You running things around here now, Red?'

'I'll do whatever I have to, to protect my parents from you.'

'I never did anything to Ray or Marla.' He lifted a brow. 'Or to you, for that matter. Though in that area I had plenty of opportunity.'

Her cheeks heated. She hated him for it, hated those damned glasses that hid his eyes and tossed her own reflection back at her. 'I'm not a young girl with stars in her eyes now, Lassiter. I know exactly what you are. An opportunist with no sense of loyalty or responsibility. We don't need you.'

'Ray thinks differently.'

'He's soft-hearted.' She angled her chin. 'I'm not. Maybe you've conned him into putting his money into some wild plan, but I'm here to put a stop to it. You're not going to use him.'

'Is that how you see it? I'm using him?'

'You're a born user.' She said it mildly, pleased with her control. 'And when things get rough, you walk. Like you walked on Buck, leaving him in some hole-in-the-wall trailer park in Florida while you sailed off. I was there.' All but shimmering with resentment, she stepped closer. 'Almost a year ago, I went to see him. I saw that sty you dropped him in. He was all alone, sick. There was barely any food. He said he couldn't remember the last time you'd been there, that you were off diving somewhere.'

'That's true enough.' He'd have sawed off his tongue with his own pride before he would have told her differently.

'He needed you, but you were too self-involved to give a damn. You left him to drink himself half to death. If my parents knew how callous, how cold you really are, they'd pitch you out on your ass.'

'But you know.'

'Yes, I know. I knew eight years ago when you were considerate enough to show me. That's the only thing I owe you, Matthew, and I'll pay you back by letting you have the chance to bow out of this business gracefully.'

'No deal.' He folded his arms. 'I'm going after the *Isabella*, Tate, one way or the other. I've got my own debts to pay.'

'You won't use my parents to pay them.' She turned on her heel and strode off.

Alone, Matthew gave himself a minute to let the storm of emotions settle. Slowly he sat on the hammock, braced his feet to keep it from rocking.

He hadn't expected her to greet him with open arms and a sunny smile. But he hadn't expected such complete and utter loathing. Dealing with it would be difficult, but necessary.

Yet that wasn't the worst of it. Not by a long shot. He'd been so sure he was over her. She'd barely been more than a passing thought in his life for years. It was a jolt, an embarrassing, devastating jolt to realize that rather than being over her, he was desperately, foolishly in love with her.

Still.

Before Marla could repeat her offer of lunch, Tate had sailed through the kitchen, into the homey, cluttered living room, down the steps to the foyer and out the front door.

She needed to breathe.

At least she'd held on to her temper, she told herself as she stormed over the sandy soil toward the sound. She hadn't decked him the way she'd wanted to. And she'd made her position crystal clear. She would see to it that Matthew Lassiter was packed and gone by nightfall.

Tate took another gulp of air as she stepped on the narrow dock. Moored there was the *New Adventure*, the forty-two-foot cruiser her parents had christened only two years before. She was a beauty, and though Tate had only managed one brief run on her, she knew the boat to be quick and agile.

She might have gone onboard, just to spend a few minutes alone with her anger, if there hadn't been another boat on the other side of the pier.

She was frowning at it, its unusual lines and double-hull construction, when Buck came on deck.

'Ahoy there, pretty girl.'

'Ahoy yourself.' Grinning, she hurried onto the pier. 'Permission to come aboard, sir.'

'Permission granted.' He laughed, holding out a hand as she leapt gracefully down.

She could see instantly that he'd lost some of the weight the bloat of drink and bad food had ballooned on him. His color was ruddy again, his eyes clear. When she hugged him, there was no stale scent of whiskey and sweat.

'It's good to see you,' she told him. 'You look renewed.'

'I'm getting by.' He shifted uncomfortably. 'You know what they say, a day at a time.'

'I'm proud of you.' She pressed her cheek to his, but sensing his embarrassment, pulled back. 'Well, tell me about this.' She spread her arms wide to encompass the boat. 'How long have you had her?'

'Matthew finished her only a few days before we sailed up.'

Her smile faded; her arms dropped back to her sides. 'Matthew?'

'He built her,' Buck said with pride ringing in every syllable. 'Designed her, worked on her off and on for years.'

'Matthew designed and built this boat, himself?'

'Just about single-handed. I'll show you around.' As he led her around the deck from bow to stern, he ran a commentary on the design, the stability, the speed. Every few minutes, his hand would run along a rail or fitting with affection.

'I gave him grief over her,' Buck admitted. 'But the boy proved me wrong. We ran into a squall off of Georgia, and she took it like a lady.'

'Umm-hmm.'

'She carries two-hundred-gallon freshwater capacity,' he went on, bragging like a doting papa. 'And storage, the way he set her out, she's got as much as you find on a sixty-footer. Got twin motors, a hundred and forty-five shaft horsepower.'

'Sounds like he's in a hurry,' she muttered. When she stepped into the pilothouse, her eyes widened. 'God, Buck, the equipment.'

Stunned, she walked through, examining. Top-of-the-line sonar, depth finders, magnetometer. The cockpit held excellent and pricey navigational equipment, a radio-telephone, radio direction finder, a Nav Tex for offshore weather data and, to her complete amazement, an LCD-screen video plotter.

'The boy wanted the best.'

'Yes, but–' She wanted to ask how he'd paid for it, but was afraid the answer might be her parents. Instead she took a deep breath and promised to find the answer herself, later. 'It's quite a setup.'

The pilothouse boasted full visibility, access from starboard and port. There was a wide flat chart table, empty now, and glossy cabinets with brass fittings for storage. Even a settee berth with thick navy padding over wood had been built into a corner.

A far cry, she mused, from the *Sea Devil*.

'Come take a look at the cabins. Hell, guess I should call 'em staterooms. Got two of them, with heads. Sleep snug as a bug down there. And the galley's one even your ma would be proud of.'

'Sure, I'd love to see. Buck,' she began as they exited to stern. 'How long has Matthew been planning on going back to look for the *Isabella*?'

'Can't say. Probably since we left the *Marguerite*. Ask me, it's been preying on his mind all along. All he lacked was the time and the means.'

'The means,' Tate repeated. 'Did he come into some money then?'

'LaRue bought in.'

'LaRue? Who—'

'Did I hear my name?'

Tate saw a figure at the base of the companionway. As she stepped down she made out a thin, nattily dressed man somewhere between forty and fifty. Gold winked out of his grin as he offered a hand to help her down.

'Ah, mademoiselle, my head spins.' He swept her hand up to his lips.

'Don't pay this scrawny Canuk any mind, Tate. He thinks he's a ladies' man.'

'A man who reveres and appreciates women,' LaRue corrected. 'I'm enchanted to meet you at last, and to have such beauty grace our humble home.'

At a glance, the neat, shipshape deckhouse looked anything but humble. Wood gleamed on the dining bar where colorfully padded stools stood waiting. Someone had hung framed charts, yellowed with age, on the walls. She was astonished to see a vase of fresh daffodils on a table.

'Guess it's a big step up from the *Sea Devil*,' Buck commented.

'From *Sea Devil* to *Mermaid*.' LaRue grinned. 'Can I offer you tea, mademoiselle?'

'No.' She was still blinking in shock. 'Thanks. I have to get back. There are a number of things I have to talk over with my parents.'

'Ah, yes. Your father, he was thrilled that you would be going with us. Me, I'm delighted to know two such lovely ladies will be adding charm to the journey.'

'Tate's not just a lady,' Buck said. 'She's a hell of a diver, a natural born treasure hunter, and she's a scientist.'

'A woman of many talents,' LaRue murmured. 'I'm humbled.'

Baffled, she stared at him. 'You shipped with Matthew?'

'Indeed. It has been my trial to try to induce some culture into his life.'

Buck snorted. 'Shit with an accent's still shit. Begging your pardon, Tate.'

'I've got to get back,' she said again, dazed. 'Nice to have met you, Mr. LaRue.'

'LaRue only.' He kissed her hand again. 'A bientôt.'

Buck shouldered LaRue aside. 'I'll walk back with you a ways.'

'Thanks.' Tate waited until they were back on the pier and headed for shore. 'Buck, you said Matthew's been working on that boat on and off for years?'

'Yeah, whenever he had a little extra time or money. Musta done a dozen drawings and designs 'fore he settled on this one.'

'I see.' That kind of ambition, and tenacity, was more than she would have given him credit for. Unless...

'All right.' She put a friendly hand on his arm. 'I hope you won't take this the wrong way, but I'm not sure any of this is a good idea.'

'You mean us partnering up with Ray and Marla and going back?'

'Yes. Finding the *Marguerite* was practically a miracle. The odds of it happening twice are very dim. I know it took a long time for all of us to get over the disappointment before. I hate to see you, and my parents, go through all of it again.'

Buck paused to shove his glasses back into place. 'I can't say I'm happy about it myself.' Automatically, he reached down to rub the artificial leg. 'Bad memories, bad luck. Matthew's set, though. And I owe him.'

'That's not true. He owes you. He owes you his life.'

'Maybe he did.' Buck grimaced. 'Fact is, I made him pay for it. I didn't save his father. Don't know if I could have, but I

179

didn't. Never went after VanDyke. Don't know what good it woulda done, but I didn't. Then when my time came to pay, I didn't take it like a man should.'

'Don't talk like that.' She hooked a protective arm through his. 'You're doing wonderfully.'

'Now. For a couple of weeks. Don't really make up for all the years between. I let the boy shoulder it all, the work and the blame.'

'He left you alone,' Tate said furiously. 'He should have stayed by you. Supported you.'

'Done nothing but support me. Worked at a job he hated so I could have what I needed. I took it, used it and tossed it in his face every chance I got. I'm ashamed of that.'

'I don't know what you're talking about. The last time I came to see you–'

'I lied to you.' He stared down at his feet, knowing he had to risk her affection for his own self-respect. 'I made it seem like he pushed me off, didn't come around, didn't do nothing for me. Maybe he didn't come around much, but it's hard to blame him. But he sent me money, took care of things best he could. Paid to have me in detox I don't know how many times.'

'But I thought–'

'I wanted you to think. Wanted him to think it, too, 'cause it was easier for me if everybody was miserable. He did the best he could.'

Far from convinced, she shook her head. 'He should have stayed with you.'

'He did what he had to do,' Buck insisted, and Tate bowed to unshakable family loyalty.

'Regardless, this new brainstorm strikes me as being impulsive and dangerous. I'm going to do my best to talk my parents out of it. I hope you understand.'

'Can't blame you for thinking twice about hooking up with the Lassiters again. You do what you have to do, Tate, but I'll tell you, your daddy's got the wind in his sails.'

'I'll just have to change his course.'

Chapter Fifteen

BUT THERE WERE times when the wind ran strong and true and defeated even the most determined sailor.

Tate tolerated Matthew's presence at dinner. She made conversation with Buck and LaRue at the big chestnut table. She listened to their stories, laughed at their jokes.

Her heart simply wasn't hard enough to spoil the celebratory mood, or dim the light of delight in her father's eyes with cold, hard facts and logic.

Because she was sharp enough to notice her mother's occasional looks of concern in her direction, Tate managed to be marginally polite to Matthew. Though she did her best to limit contact to the obligatory 'pass the salt.'

When the meal was over, she maneuvered the situation in her favor by insisting on clearing up the dishes alone with her father.

'Bet you haven't had a meal like that in a month of Sundays,' he commented, humming under his breath as he stacked dishes.

'In a year of Sundays. I'm sorry I had to pass on the pecan pie.'

'You'll have some later. That LaRue's something, isn't he? Exchanging recipes with your mother one minute and arguing foreign policy the next with a side trip into baseball and eighteenth-century art.'

'He's a regular Renaissance man,' she murmured. But she was holding out on judgment of him. Any friend of Matthew's, she thought, required careful scrutiny. Even if he was interesting, well read and charming. Particularly if he was. 'I haven't figured out what he's doing with Matthew.'

'Oh, I think they suit each other well enough.' Ray filled the sink with soapy water for the pots as Tate loaded the dishwasher. 'Matthew's always had a lot going for him, he's just never had much chance to put it all to use.'

'I'd say he's a man who knows how to make the most of an opportunity. Which is something I want to discuss with you.'

'The *Isabella*.' Sleeves pushed up, Ray began to attack pans in the sink. 'We're going to get to that, honey. Soon as everyone's had a chance to settle in for the evening. I held off saying anything more to the rest until you got here.'

'Dad, I know how you felt when we found that virgin wreck eight years ago. I know how I felt, so I understand that you may think it's a good idea to go back. But I'm not sure you're considering all the details, the pitfalls.'

'I've thought of them a great deal over the years, and little else for the last nine months. We had our share of luck, good and bad, the last time. But we've got a hell of a lot more going for us this time around.'

'Dad.' Tate slipped another plate into the dishwasher, straightened. 'If I have the right information, Buck hasn't dived since his accident, and LaRue worked on ship as a cook. He's never had on tanks in his life.'

'That's all true. Maybe Buck won't go under, but we can always use another hand on deck. As for LaRue, he's willing to learn, and I have a feeling he's a quick study.'

'There are six of us,' Tate went on, trying futilely to chip away at the optimism. 'Only three of whom can dive. I haven't done any serious diving myself in nearly two years.'

'Like riding a bike,' Ray said easily and set a pan aside to drain. 'We need people to read and run the equipment in any case. Now we've got a professional marine archeologist on hand,

182

not one in training.' He sent her a beaming smile. 'Maybe you'll do your thesis on this expedition.'

'I'm not concerned about my thesis right now,' she said, straining for patience. 'I'm concerned about you. You and Mom have spent the last several years playing at hunting, Dad. Exploring established wrecks, pleasure diving, shell collecting. That's nothing compared to the full out physical labor needed for something like you have in mind.'

'I'm in shape,' he told her, vaguely insulted. 'I work out three times a week, dive regularly.'

Wrong tactic, she thought. 'Okay. What about the expense? It could take months of your time, plus the cost of supplies, equipment. This isn't a vacation you're talking about, or a hobby. Who's backing this venture?'

'Your mother and I are very stable financially.'

'Well.' Fighting temper, she snatched up a dishrag to swipe the counters. 'That answers my last question. You're putting your money on the line, which means you're carrying the Lassiters.'

'It's not a matter of carrying them, honey.' Genuinely puzzled, he pulled his hands out of the water and wiped them dry. 'It's a partnership, just like before. Any imbalance will be taken out of the profits once we salvage the wreck.'

'What if there isn't any wreck?' she exploded. 'I don't care if you toss your last penny away on a dream. I want you to enjoy everything you've worked for. But how can I stand by while you let that self-serving, opportunistic bastard take you for a ride?'

'Tate.' Alarmed at the way her voice carried, he patted her on the shoulder. 'I didn't know you were upset. I thought when you said you were coming back, you were committing to the idea.'

'I came back to try to stop you from making a mistake.'

'I'm not making one.' His face closed up in the way she knew it could when he was hurt. 'And there is a wreck. Matthew's father knew it, I know it. The *Isabella* is there, and Angelique's Curse is with her.'

'Not the amulet again.'

'Yes, the amulet again. That's what James Lassiter was looking for, what Silas VanDyke wants, and what we're going to have.'

'Why is it so important? This wreck, this necklace?'

'Because we lost something that summer, Tate,' he said quietly. 'More than the fortune that thief stole from us. More even than Buck's leg. We lost the joy in what we'd done, what we could do. We lost the magic of what could be. It's time we got it back.'

She let out a sigh. How could she fight dreams? Didn't she have her own, still? The museum she'd planned for, hoped for, most of her life. And someday she'd see it realized. Who was she to try to block her father's one abiding wish?

'All right. We can go back, just the three of us.'

'The Lassiters are part of it now, just as they were then. And if anyone has a right to find that wreck, and that amulet, it's Matthew.'

'Why?'

'Because it cost him a father.'

She didn't want to think of that. She didn't want to be able to visualize the young boy who had grieved helplessly over his dead father's body.

'The amulet doesn't mean any more to him than a means to an end, something to be sold to the highest bidder.'

'That's for him to decide.'

'That makes him,' she corrected, 'little better than VanDyke.'

'He hurt you that summer. Matthew.' Gently, Ray took her face in his hands. 'I knew there was something between you, but I didn't realize it had cut so deep.'

'This has nothing to do with that,' she insisted. 'It has to do with who and what he is.'

'Eight years is a long time, honey. Maybe you should step back and take another look. In the meantime, there are things I need to show you, all of you. Let's get everybody into my den.'

With reluctance, Tate joined the group in the warmly paneled room where her father did his research and wrote his articles for diving magazines. Deliberately, she moved to the opposite end of the room from Matthew and settled on the arm of her mother's chair.

With the windows open to the scents and music of the sound, it was just cool enough to indulge in a quiet fire. Ray walked behind his desk, cleared his throat like a nervous lecturer about to begin his speech.

'I know you all are curious about what prompted me to begin this venture. All of us know what happened eight years ago, what we found and what we lost. Every time I'd dive after that, I'd think about it.'

'Brood about it,' Marla corrected with a smile.

Ray smiled back at her. 'I couldn't let it go. I thought I had for a time, but then something would remind me, and set me off again. One day I had the flu, and Marla wouldn't let me out of bed. I passed the time with some television and happened across a documentary on salvaging. It was a wreck off Cape Horn, a rich one. And who was backing it, who was pulling in the glory, but Silas VanDyke.'

'Bastard,' Buck muttered. 'Probably pirated that one, too.'

'Might have, but the point is, he'd decided to film the proceedings. He wasn't on-camera much himself, but he did talk a little about some of the diving he'd done, other wrecks he'd discovered. The sonofabitch talked about the *Santa Marguerite*. He never bothered to mention it had already been found, excavated. The way he told it, he did it all, then being the generous soul he is, donated fifty percent of the proceeds to the government of St. Kitts.'

'In bribes and kickbacks,' Matthew decided.

'It got my blood up. I started researching again right then and there. I figured he'd gotten one wreck, but he wasn't going to get the other. I spent the better part of two years digging up every snatch of information I could find on the *Isabella*. No reference to that ship, that crew, that storm was too small or insignificant. That's how I found it. Or, how I found two very vital pieces to the puzzle. A map, and a reference to Angelique's Curse.'

Carefully, he lifted a book out of the top drawer. Its cover was tattered and held together by tape. Its pages were dry and yellowed.

'It's falling apart,' Ray said unnecessarily. 'I found it in a used-book store. *A Sailor's Life*. It was written in 1846, by the great-grandson of a survivor of the *Isabella*.'

'But there were no survivors,' Tate put in. 'That's one of the reasons the wreck's been so hard to find.'

'No recorded survivors.' Ray stroked the book as though it were a well-loved child. 'According to this, stories and legends the author transcribed from his grandfather's tales, José Baltazar washed ashore on the island of Nevis. He was a seaman on the *Isabella*, and he watched her go down as he clung half conscious to a plank probably from the wrecked *Santa Marguerite*. Matthew, I think your father had traced this same clue.'

'If that's true, what was he doing in Australia?'

'He was following Angelique's Curse.' Ray paused for effect. 'But he was a generation too soon. A British aristocrat, Sir Arthur Minnefield, had acquired the amulet from a French merchant.'

'Minnefield.' Buck narrowed his eyes in concentration. 'I remember seeing that name in James's notes. The night before he died he told me he'd been looking in the wrong place. He said how VanDyke had it wrong, how that damned necklace had gotten around. That's how he said it, "that damned necklace," and he was excited. When we were finished on the reef, he said how we were going to shake loose of VanDyke, turn the tables on him before he turned them on us. Said how we had to be careful of VanDyke and not move too fast. He had a lot more studying and figuring to do before we went after her.'

'My theory is he found another reference to the amulet, or to Baltazar.' Ray set the book carefully on his desk. 'You see, the amulet didn't go down on the reef, the ship did, Minnefield did, but Angelique's Curse survived. Details are sketchy for the next thirty years. Maybe it washed up on the beach or someone found it while exploring the reefs. I can't find any mention of it between 1706 and 1733. But Baltazar saw it around the neck of a young Spanish woman aboard the *Isabella*. He described it. He heard the legend, and he recounted it.'

Far from convinced, Tate folded her hands. 'If there's a reference to the amulet that places it on the *Isabella*, why hasn't VanDyke found it, and gone after the *Isabella* himself?'

'He was dead sure it was in Australia,' Buck told her. 'He was fired up about it, obsessed. He got it into his head James knew something more, dogged him about it.'

'And killed him for it,' Matthew said flatly. 'VanDyke's had teams working that wreck and that area for years.'

'But if my father found a reference that indicated the necklace was elsewhere,' Tate continued with stubborn logic, 'and your father found a reference, it's only reasonable that a man with VanDyke's resources, and his greed, would have found it as well.'

'Maybe the amulet didn't want him to find it.' LaRue spoke passively as he patiently rolled a cigarette.

'It's an inanimate object,' Tate retorted.

'So is the Hope Diamond,' LaRue said. 'The philosopher's stone, the Ark of the Covenant. Yet the legends surrounding them are vital.'

'The operative word is "legend." '

'All those degrees made you cynical,' Matthew commented. 'Too bad.'

'I think the point is,' Marla cut in, recognizing the warrior light in her daughter's eyes, 'that Ray has found something, not whether or not this amulet holds some sort of power.'

'Well put.' Ray rubbed the side of his nose. 'Where was I? Baltazar was captivated by the amulet, even after word began to pass about the curse, and the crew became uneasy. He believed the ship was wrecked because of the curse, and that he survived to tell the tale. He told it well,' Ray added. 'I've copied several pages of his reminiscences of the storm. You'll see when you read them that it was a hellish battle against the elements, a hopeless one. Of these two ships, the *Marguerite* succumbed first. As the *Isabella* broke up, passengers and crew were swept into the sea. He claims to have seen the Spanish lady, the amulet like a jeweled anchor around her neck, go down. Of course, that tidbit might have been for artistic effect.'

Ray passed out copied pages. 'In any case, he survived. The wind and the waves carried him away from land, from St. Kitts, or St. Christopher's as it was known then. He'd given up all hope, lost his sense of time when he saw the outline of Nevis. He didn't believe he could make it to shore as he was too weak to swim. But eventually he drifted in. A young native boy found him. He was delirious and near death for weeks. When he recovered, he had no desire to serve the Armada. Instead he let the world believe him dead. He remained on the island, married and passed down his stories of his adventures at sea.'

Ray took another paper from his pile. 'And, he drew maps. A map,' Ray continued, 'from an eyewitness who places the *Isabella* several degrees south-southeast from the wreck of the *Marguerite*. She's there. Waiting.'

Matthew rose to take the map. It was crude, and sparse, but he recognized the points of reference – the whale's tail of the peninsula of St. Kitts, the rising cone of Mount Nevis.

An old, almost forgotten need surged in him. The need to hunt. When he looked up, the grin he flashed was the one from his youth. Bold, reckless and irresistible.

'When do we leave?'

Tate couldn't sleep. There was too much racing inside her head, swimming in her blood. She understood, and struggled to accept, that the momentum was out of her hands. There would be no stopping her father from taking on this quest. None of the logic nor the personal doubts she used would sway him from partnering with the Lassiters.

At least the timing worked. She'd just tossed an enormous career advancement aside for principle. That gave her some satisfaction. And it also gave her the opportunity to help launch the expedition for the *Isabella*.

At least if she was there, right on hand, she could keep her eye on everyone. Matthew in particular.

So she was thinking of him when she stepped outside to face the moon and the wind that washed through the top of the pines.

She had loved him once. Over the years, she'd told herself it had been merely a crush, a young woman's infatuation with wild good looks and an adventurer's heart.

But that was a coward's lie.

She had loved him, Tate admitted, and tugged her jacket tighter against the night's moist breeze. Or had loved the man she'd thought he was, and could be. Nothing and no one had embraced her heart so completely before him. Just as nothing and no one had ever broken it so totally, and so callously.

She tugged a leaf from a fragrant bay laurel, spun it under her nose as she walked toward the water. It was a night for reflections, she supposed. The moon, nearly full, rode a sky crowded with hot stars. The air was full of perfume and promise.

Once she would have been seduced by that alone. Before her romantic side had been sliced away. She considered herself fortunate that she could now appreciate the night for what it was, and not spin dreams around it.

In a way, she knew she had Matthew to thank for opening her eyes. Rudely, painfully, but he'd opened them. She understood now that princes and pirates were for young, foolish girls to dream of. She had more solid goals than that.

If she had to put those goals aside for a time, she would. Everything she was, everything she'd accomplished, she owed to her parents' support and belief in her. There was nothing she wouldn't do to protect them. Even if it meant working shoulder-to-shoulder with Matthew Lassiter.

She stopped near the water, downcurrent from where the boats were docked. Her parents had built up the bank here with duck weed and wild grasses to fight erosion. Always the water stole from the land. Always the land adjusted.

It was a good lesson, she supposed. Things had been stolen from her. She'd adjusted.

'It's a nice spot, isn't it?'

Tate's shoulders tightened at the sound of his voice. She wondered how she hadn't sensed him. But for a man who spent his life at sea, he moved quietly on land.

'I thought you'd gone to bed.'

'We're bunked down in the boat.' He knew she didn't want him beside her, so perversely he stepped forward until their shoulders nearly brushed. 'Buck still snores like a freighter. Doesn't bother LaRue. But then, he sleeps like a corpse.'

'Try earplugs.'

'I'll just string a hammock out on deck. Like old times.'

'These are new times.' She took a bracing breath before she turned to him. As she'd expected, perhaps feared, he looked magnificent in the moonlight. Bold, exciting, even dangerous. How lucky she was that such traits no longer appealed to her. 'And we'd better lay out the ground rules.'

'You were always more into rules than me.' To suit himself he sat on a bale of duck grass, patted the space beside him in invitation. 'You go first.'

She ignored the invitation, and the half-empty bottle of beer he offered. 'This is a business arrangement. As I understand it, my parents are fronting the bulk of the expenses. I intend to keep an accurate account of your share.'

Her voice still carried those lovely liquid vowels of the south, he mused, the consonants blurring like soft shadows. 'Fine. Bookkeeping's your department.'

'You will pay them back, Lassiter. Every penny.'

He took a swallow of beer. 'I pay my debts.'

'I'll see to it you pay this one.' She paused a moment before moving from one practical matter to another. The moon mirrored prettily on the calm water, but she paid no heed to it. 'I understand you're teaching LaRue to dive.'

'I've been working with him.' Matthew moved his shoulders. 'He's catching on.'

'Will Buck dive?'

Even in the shadows, she saw his eyes glint. 'That's up to him. I'm not pushing him.'

'I wouldn't want you to.' She softened enough to move closer. 'He matters to me. I – I'm glad he's looking so well.'

'You're glad he's off the bottle.'

'Yes.'

'He's been off it before. Lasted a whole month once.'

'Matthew.' Before she'd realized it, she laid a hand on his shoulder. 'He's trying.'

'Aren't we all?' Abruptly, he grabbed her hand, tugged her down beside him. 'I'm tired of looking up at you. Besides, I can see you better down here, in the moonlight. You always had a face for moonlight.'

'Personal rule,' she said briskly. 'You keep your hands off me.'

'No problem. I don't need the frostbite. You've sure chilled down over the years, Red.'

'I've simply developed a more discerning taste.'

'College men.' His smile was a sneer. 'Always figured you'd go for the academic type.' Deliberately, he looked down at her hands, then back into her eyes. 'No rings. How come?'

'Let's keep our private lives private.'

'That's not going to be easy, seeing as we're going to be working in close quarters for some time.'

'We'll manage. And as to working arrangements, when we dive, one member of your team goes down with a member of ours. I don't trust you.'

'And you hid it so well,' he muttered. 'That's fine,' he continued. 'That suits me. I like diving with you, Tate. You're good luck.' He leaned back on his elbows, looked up at the stars. 'It's been a while since I dived in warm water. The North Atlantic's a bitch. You learn to hate her.'

'Then why did you dive there?'

He slanted her a look. 'Doesn't that come under the heading of private?'

She looked away, cursing herself. 'Yes, though it was professional curiosity that made me ask.'

So, he'd oblige her. 'There's money to be made salvaging metal wrecks. In case you haven't heard, World War II played hell with ships.'

'I thought the metal you were interested in was gold.'

'Whatever pays, sweetheart. I've got a feeling this trip's going to pay off big.' Because it pleased him almost as much as it hurt, he continued to study her profile. 'You're not convinced.'

'No, I'm not. But I am convinced this is something my father needs to do. The *Isabella* and the *Santa Marguerite* have fascinated him for years.'

'And Angelique's Curse.'

'Yes, from the moment he heard of it.'

'But you don't believe in curses anymore. Or magic. I guess you educated it out of your system.'

She couldn't have said why it stung to hear him say what was only the truth. 'I believe the amulet exists, and knowing my father, that it was aboard the *Isabella*. Finding it will be another matter altogether. And its value will come from its age and its stones and the weight of its gold, not from some superstition.'

'There's no more mermaid left in you, Tate.' He said it quietly, and stopped himself before his hand lifted to stroke her hair. 'You used to remind me of something fanciful that was as much at home in the sea as in the air. With all sorts of secrets in your eyes, and endless possibilities shimmering around you.'

Her skin shivered, not from the nippy little breeze, but from heat. In defense, her voice was flat and cool. 'I doubt very much if you had any sort of romantic flights of fancy where I was concerned. We're both aware of what you thought of me.'

'I thought you were beautiful. And even more out of reach than you are right now.'

Hating the fact that such careless lies could make her pulse jump, she rose quickly. 'It won't work, Lassiter. I'm not along on this trip to amuse you. We're business partners. Fifty-fifty since my father wants it that way.'

'Isn't that interesting?' he murmured. He set the bottle down and rose slowly until they were toe to toe. Until he could smell her hair. Until his fingers throbbed with the memory of how her skin felt under them. 'I still get to you, don't I?'

'Your ego's still in the same place.' She schooled her features to mild disdain. 'Just below the button of your jeans. Tell you what, Lassiter, if things get a little tedious and I'm desperate enough

191

to try anything to break the monotony, I'll let you know. But until that unlikely event, try not to embarrass yourself.'

'I'm not embarrassed.' He grinned at her. 'Just curious.' Hoping to loosen some of the knots in his gut, he sat again. 'Any more rules, Red?'

She needed a minute before she could trust her voice. Somehow her heart had lodged in her throat. 'If, by some miracle, we find the *Isabella*, I will, as marine archeologist, catalogue and assess and preserve all the artifacts. Everything gets logged, down to the last nail.'

'Fine. Might as well put those degrees to use.'

She bristled at his obvious lack of respect for her field. 'That's just what I intend to do. Twenty percent of whatever we find will go to the government of St. Kitts and Nevis. And though it's only fair that it be put to a vote, I'll set aside what artifacts I find appropriate to donate.'

'Twenty percent's hefty, Red.'

'Try a little fame along with your fortune, Lassiter. If things work out as we hope, I'm going to negotiate with the government to establish a museum. The Beaumont-Lassiter Museum. If the wreck's as rich as reputed, you can spare ten percent of your share and still not have to work another day in your life. It'll keep you in shrimp and beer.'

Again he flashed a grin. 'Still stewing over that sword. You surprise me.'

'As long as we keep our cards on the table, there won't be any surprises. Those are my terms.'

'I can live with them.'

She nodded. 'There's one more. If we do find Angelique's Curse, it goes to the museum.'

He picked up his beer, drained it. 'No. You've had your terms, Tate. I've only got one of my own. The amulet's mine.'

'Yours?' She would have laughed if her teeth hadn't been clenched together. 'You don't have any stronger claim on it than the rest of us. Its potential value is tremendous.'

'Then you can assess it, catalogue it and deduct it from the rest of my take. But it's mine.'

'For what?'

'To pay off a debt.' He rose, and the look in his eyes had her backing up a step before she could stop herself. 'I'm going to wrap it around VanDyke's neck, and strangle him with it.'

'That's foolish.' Her voice shook. 'Crazy.'

'That's a fact. You live with that one, Tate, because that's how it's going to be. You've got your rules.' He cupped her chin in his hand and made her tremble. Not from the touch, not this time, but from the hotblooded murder boiling in his eyes. 'I've got mine.'

'You can't expect any of us to stand by while you plan to kill someone.'

'I don't expect anything.' He'd stopped expecting long ago. 'It just wouldn't be smart to get in my way. Now you'd better get some sleep. We've got a lot of work ahead of us.'

He was lost in the shadows of the trees almost immediately. To ward off the chill, Tate wrapped her arms tight around her body.

He'd meant it. She couldn't pretend otherwise. But she could tell herself that he'd lose this thirst for revenge in the hunt.

The odds were they'd never find the *Isabella*. And if they did, the odds were even higher against finding the amulet.

For the first time, she prepared to go on an expedition hoping for failure.

Chapter Sixteen

IT WAS BLISSFULLY easy to fall back into the old routine. Tate found herself pushing the purpose of the voyage to the back of her mind and simply enjoying the ride.

They left Hatteras Island behind on a bright spring morning with the seas at a light chop. The wind was just brisk enough for a jacket and she'd pulled her hair through the hole in the back of a Durham Bulls baseball cap. At her father's insistence, she had first shift at the wheel. And took the Atlantic.

They sailed toward Ocracoke with its pirate ghosts, waving at passengers on a passing ferry as seagulls swooped and called in their wake. Then land became a shadow to the west, and there was only sea.

'How's it feel, Skipper?' Ray slipped in behind her, hugging an arm over her shoulders.

'It feels good.' Tate lifted her face to the wind that rushed through the partially open windows of the bridge. 'I guess I've been a passenger too long.'

'Sometimes your mother and I will hop aboard and sail to nowhere for a day or two. I've enjoyed that.' Eyes on the horizon, he sighed deeply. 'But it sure feels good to be sailing to somewhere. I've been wanting this for a long time.'

'I guess I thought you'd put the *Isabella*, and all of it, pretty much behind you. I didn't realize how much you still wanted her.'

'I didn't either, really.' Out of habit, he checked the course. She, the boat and his daughter, was right on the mark. 'After we lost the *Marguerite*, and you went off to college, I just drifted awhile. It seemed like the right thing to do. I felt so helpless about Buck. He and Matthew off in Chicago, and Buck just wouldn't let me connect.'

'I know that hurt you,' she murmured. 'You'd gotten so close that summer.'

'He lost a leg. I lost a friend. All of us lost a fortune. Neither Buck nor I handled it very well.'

'You did the best you could,' Tate corrected. She had lost her heart, she thought, and she, too, had done the best she could.

'I never knew what to say, or what to do. Sometimes I'd pop one of the videos your mother had taken during those months – watch and remember. It got easier to just drop a letter in the mail now and again. Matthew never let on how bad it was. We might never have found out if we hadn't taken a trip to Florida and gone by the trailer.'

He shook his head, remembering what a shock it had been to see his friend drunk, stumbling around a filthy trailer, surrounded by trash, covered in shame.

'The boy should have told us what a bind he was in.'

'Matthew?' She glanced back in surprise. 'It sounds to me as if Buck was the one in trouble. Matthew should have stayed and taken care of him.'

'If he'd stayed, he couldn't have taken care of Buck. He had to work, Tate. Hell, money doesn't just float in on the tide. It must have taken him years to pay off the medical bills. Fact is, I doubt he's managed it yet.'

'There are programs for people in Buck's situation. Subsidies, assistance.'

'Not for people like Matthew. He'd ask for a loan, but never a handout.'

Disturbed by the idea, she frowned. 'That's stupid pride.'

'Pride, anyway,' Ray agreed. 'It was after I saw Buck again that the *Isabella* started preying on my mind. I couldn't shake it.

All those what ifs. So I went back over my old research, started new.'

He looked far out, toward something she couldn't see. Or had forgotten to look for. 'I guess I started thinking if I could find some new clue, it would be a way to pay Buck back for what he'd lost as my partner.'

'Dad, that was no one's fault.'

'Not a matter of blame, honey. A matter of what's right. It's come full circle, Tate. Something tells me it was supposed to.' Shaking off the mood, he smiled down at her. 'I know, it's not logical.'

'You don't have to be logical.' She rose on her toes to kiss him. 'I'll take care of that part.'

'And your mother'll keep things shipshape.' Over the memories, the old excitement began to brew. 'We make a good team, Tate.'

'Always did.'

'*Mermaid* off the port bow,' he murmured.

So it was, Tate saw. She had to admit, it was a stunner of a boat. Those twin hulls cut through the water like diamonds through glass. Though the sun tossed light from the windows of the pilothouse, she could make out Matthew at the helm.

He pulled alongside until there was barely ten feet between them. She saw him turn his head in her direction, and sensed his challenging grin.

'Looks like he wants a race,' Ray said.

'Oh, does he?' Planting her feet a bit farther apart, she gripped the throttle. 'Well, we'll just give him one.'

'That's my girl.' With a hoot, he raced from the bridge, calling for Marla.

'Okay, Lassiter,' Tate muttered to herself. 'You're on.'

She punched the throttle, turning the wheel to give him her wake. The thrill of the competition had her laughing out loud as she felt the power hum under her hands. The *New Adventure* wasn't any Sunday cruiser, and with the Atlantic spread before her, Tate let it have its head.

At twelve knots, it was purring.

It didn't surprise her to see the *Mermaid* coming alongside. She wanted a run. When their bows were even, she shot forward again, sprinting to fifteen knots.

Again he crept steadily even with her, and again, Tate pumped her speed until his bow trailed her stern. In lieu of thumbing her nose, Tate rocked the wheel so that her boat danced. She was chuckling to herself, feeling smug until the *Mermaid* shot by like a bullet.

By the time she'd closed her mouth, he was fifty feet ahead. She bore down, took her engines to full. Her mother's wild, appreciative laughter swam up from the bow. Infectious, it had Tate giggling as she gained ground. But try as she might, she couldn't match the *Mermaid*.

'That's some boat,' she said to herself. 'Hell of a boat.'

And though she knew she should be insulted when Matthew maneuvered a wide circle and came up alongside again, she wasn't.

Damn him, he made her smile.

★

On the evening of their third day, they moored at Freeport, just ahead of a storm that swept in thundering rain and choppy seas. A group dinner was planned aboard the *Mermaid* with LaRue's shrimp jambalaya as the centerpiece.

By the time second helpings were being dispensed, LaRue and Marla were deep into cooking theories while Buck and Ray fell back into their old habit of arguing baseball. Since neither topic fell into Tate's area of expertise, she found herself uncomfortably paired with Matthew.

Because silence seemed cowardly, Tate turned to ingrained Southern manners. 'I'd forgotten you were interested in boat-building,' she began. 'Buck said you designed the *Mermaid* yourself.'

'Yeah. I toyed with a few designs over the years. This one worked for me.' He scooped up more stew. 'I guess I always figured I'd go back.'

'Did you? Why?'

His eyes shot up to hers, held. 'Because I never finished what I started. You must have thought about it now and again.'

'Not really.' Manners aside, lies were safer. 'I've been busy with other things.'

'Looks like college suited you.' She'd taken to wearing her hair in one fat braid that trailed down her back, he noted. That, too, suited her. 'I hear we'll be calling you "Doctor" Beaumont before long.'

'I have some work to do yet.'

'You earned a pretty good rep on that Smithsonian thing a couple years ago.' Her surprised look made him shrug. 'Ray and Marla passed things along.' There wasn't any point in mentioning that he'd gotten a copy of the magazine and read the five-page article twice. 'They were jazzed about the idea of you identifying artifacts from some ancient Greek ship.'

'I was hardly in charge. I was part of a team. Hayden Deel headed the archeological end. He was a professor of mine,' she added. 'He's brilliant. I was with him on the *Nomad*, my last assignment.'

'I heard about that, too.' It grated that she'd been a part of a VanDyke operation. 'A sidewheeler.'

'That's right. The depths were too great for diving. We used computers and robotics.' Comfortable with shop talk, she rested her chin on her fist. 'We have incredible film of plant and animal colonization.'

'Sounds like a barrel of fun.'

'It was a scientific expedition,' she said coolly. 'Fun wasn't a prerequisite. The equipment that was devised to search for and excavate the *Justine* was stunningly successful. We had a team of top scientists and technicians. And,' she added with a bite, 'beyond the scientific value and knowledge, we mined gold. That, I'm sure, you'd understand. A fortune in gold coins and bars.'

'So, VanDyke gets richer.'

He knew, she realized, and felt her face go cold, stiff. 'That's beside the point. The scientific and historic benefit outweighs–'

'Bullshit. Nothing VanDyke does is beside the point.' It infuriated him that she should have changed so much to believe it. 'Don't you care who writes your paycheck?'

'SeaSearch–'

'VanDyke owns Trident, which owns Poseidon, which owns SeaSearch.' Sneering, he lifted his glass of red wine, toasted. 'I'm sure VanDyke's happy with your work.'

For a moment, she could only stare. It felt as though a fist had plunged into her stomach. That he would think so little of her, of her character, and of her heart, hurt more than she had believed it could. She could see herself standing dripping and defiant, facing VanDyke on his own yacht. And she remembered the fury, the fear, and the terrible sense of loss.

Saying nothing, she pushed away from the table and walked out into the rain. On a muttered oath, Matthew shoved his bowl aside and went after her.

'Is this how you handle things now when somebody puts a mirror up to your face, Red? Walk away?'

She stood at the starboard rail, gripping it tight while the rain poured over her. To the north, lightning cracked the sky.

'I didn't know.'

'Right.'

'I didn't know,' she repeated. 'Not when I signed on. If I had, I wouldn't … I would never have been a part of anything connected with VanDyke. I wanted to work with Hayden again, to be a part of something big and important. So I never looked beyond the opportunity.' She was ashamed now, as she hadn't been when the anger and resentment had been so huge. 'I should have.'

'Why? You had a chance, you took it. That's the way things work.' He hooked his thumbs in his pockets to keep himself from touching her. 'You made your choices, and so what? Bottom line is VanDyke's not your fight anyway.'

'The hell he isn't.' Fresh fury had her whirling around. Rain streamed from her hair and face. Thunder grumbled in the distance. 'He isn't your personal demon, Matthew, whatever you think. He took from all of us.'

'So you took something back from him. You earned a little fame and fortune on the *Nomad*. Like you said, you don't care who paid for it.'

'Goddamn you, Lassiter, I said I didn't know. The minute I found out, the minute I realized he'd arranged to have me on the ship, I packed up and left.'

'You packed up and left because you were afraid I'd take advantage of your parents. Don't pull this crap, Tate. I know he called you, told you what was going down. You were on Hatteras in record time.'

'That's right, and one of the reasons I could be was because I'd already tendered my resignation and arranged for transport. The hell with you,' she said wearily. 'I don't have to prove anything to you. I don't have to justify anything to you.'

But she realized she had to justify it to herself. Impatient, she pushed dripping hair back from her face. 'I thought I'd gotten the assignment because Hayden had recommended me.'

A little kernel of jealousy glowed green just under his heart. 'You and this Hayden got a thing going?'

'He's a colleague,' she said between her teeth. 'A friend. He told me that my name was on the approved list before it got to him.'

'So?'

'Follow the logic, Lassiter. I did. Why would someone have done that? I wanted to know why, and who, and I found out. VanDyke chose me. He didn't strike me as a man who forgets. How many Tate Beaumonts with a master's in marine archeology do you figure are out there?'

Because it was starting to make sense, he began to feel like a fool. 'At a guess, I'd say one.'

'Right.' She turned back to the rail. 'He had to know who I was,' she said quietly. 'And he wanted me on the *Nomad*. Whether you believe me or not, I was leaving the expedition before my father contacted me.'

He let out a long breath, rubbed his hands over his wet face. 'I believe you. Maybe I was out of line, but I was steamed over the idea that you'd work for him just to build your rep.' The quick, cold look she shot over her shoulder had him feeling like a worm. 'I said I was out of line. I should have known better.'

'Yes, you should have known better.' Now she sighed. Why should he have trusted me? she asked herself. They didn't really know each other anymore. 'It doesn't matter. I'm glad we cleared the air about it, anyway, I've been stewing over it. I don't like knowing he'd used me. I like knowing less he's been looking over my shoulder all these years.'

It was a possibility that hadn't occurred to him. As it took root, the violent emotion that bloomed from it dimmed jealousy. He gripped her arms, lifting her to her toes. 'Did he ever contact you, try anything?'

'No.' To keep her balance, Tate splayed her hands on Matthew's chest. Rain beat down on them in fat, warm drops. 'I haven't seen him since the day he threatened to have us shot. But obviously, he's kept track of me. My first postgraduate expedition was for Poseidon, in the Red Sea. For Poseidon,' she repeated.

'And now I have to wonder how many projects I've been involved with he's had a hand in. How many doors he opened for me, and why.'

'Why's easy. He saw you had potential, and he could use it.' He recognized the look on her face and gave her a quick shake. 'He wouldn't have opened a door if he hadn't been sure you could have done it for yourself. He doesn't do favors, Red. You got where you are because you're smart and went after what you wanted.'

'Maybe. But that doesn't change the fact that he's been there, behind the scenes.'

'No, it doesn't.' His grip had gentled. He hadn't forgotten he was holding her. It crossed his mind that she was upset enough that she might not freeze if he drew her to him. Instead, he ran his hands from her shoulders to her wrists. And let her go. 'There's something else to consider.'

'What?' Distracted, she fought off a shiver. That small, careless gesture had been so familiar.

'If he knew you were aboard the *Nomad*, he knows you left. By now, he knows you've teamed up with me again, and where we're going.'

She was cold now, icily so. 'What are we going to do about it?'

'We're going to beat him.'

'How?' She turned away again, clamped her hands on the wet rail. 'He has the resources, the contacts, the means.' And he would, she realized as her insides quaked, use her to get to Matthew. 'Our best hope is to throw him off track. If I left, went back to the *Nomad*, or someplace, anyplace else, he might follow my trail. I could even leak something about your talking my parents into a wild-goose chase toward Anguilla, or Martinique.' She spun back. 'I could lead him away.'

'No. We stick together.'

'It only makes sense, Matthew. If he respects me professionally, wouldn't he believe that if I had no interest in this hunt, there wasn't anything to it? He'd be more likely to leave you alone.'

'We stick together,' he repeated. 'And we beat him together. Face it, Tate, we need each other.' He took her arm and pulled her with him.

'Where are you going?'

'We're going to the bridge. There's something I want to show you.'

'We need to tell the others about this. I should have told them before.' She clattered up the short flight of stairs. 'Everyone has a right to input, to the decision.'

'The decision's made.'

'You're not in charge here, Lassiter.'

He kicked the door shut behind him, grabbed a jacket off a hook. 'If you think anyone's going to vote that you go off on your own, you're not as smart as you look. Put this on.' He tossed the jacket at her. 'You're shivering.'

'I'm angry,' she corrected, but jammed her arms into the windbreaker. 'I'm not going to let VanDyke use me to hurt you.'

He stopped in the process of pouring the brandy he'd taken from a cupboard. 'I wouldn't think that would bother you.'

She angled her chin. 'I don't mind seeing you hurt, but I'd prefer doing it myself, not as someone's tool.'

His lips curved. He brought her a stubby glass with two fingers of brandy. 'You know, Red, you always did look terrific wet, especially when you were indignant on top of it. The way you are now.' He clinked his glass to hers. 'I know you'd like to slice me up and use me for chum. Just like I know you'll wait until the job's done.'

'I wouldn't use you for chum, Lassiter.' With a smile, she sipped the brandy. 'I have too much respect for fish.'

He laughed, and threw her off balance by giving her wet braid a quick, friendly tug. 'You know what you have, Tate, besides a good brain, a fierce sense of loyalty and a stubborn chin?'

She moved her shoulders and walked over to stand at the wheel and watch the rain.

'Integrity,' he murmured. 'It flatters you.'

Closing her eyes, she fought off a wave of emotion. He still had a way of sneaking past any defense and seducing the heart of her. 'It sounds as though you're flattering me, Matthew.' Steadying, she turned to face him again. 'Why?'

'Just calling it as I see it, Tate. And wondering if, with all those other fine virtues, you've managed to hang on to that shining sense of curiosity and empathy that made you special.'

'I was never special to you.'

'Yes, you were.' He shrugged again to cover the painful truth. 'If you hadn't been, you wouldn't have left St. Kitts a virgin.'

Color rose in her cheeks like flags of war. 'Why, you arrogant, conceited bastard.'

'Facts are facts,' he countered, pleased that he'd distracted her from her worry over VanDyke. Setting his brandy aside, he crouched to open a storage compartment under a padded bench. 'Stay put,' he said mildly when she headed for the door. 'You'll want to see this. And believe me …' Still crouched, he glanced over his shoulder at her. 'I'm not interested in seducing you. At least not right now.'

Tate's fingers tightened on the glass she'd neglected to set down. It was a pity, she thought, that there were only a few drops left in it. Not enough to make an impression if she poured them over his head.

'Lassiter, you've got as much chance of seducing me as a rabid skunk does of becoming my favored pet. And there's nothing you could have that I want to see.'

'A few pages of Angelique Maunoir's diary.'

It stopped her in her tracks, her hand on the door. 'Angelique Maunoir. Angelique's Curse.'

'VanDyke has the original diary. He tracked it down almost twenty years ago and had it translated.' Matthew took a small metal box from the compartment and straightened. 'I heard him tell my father he traced the descendants of Angelique's maid. Most of them were in Brittany. That's where the legend started. It was VanDyke's father who told him about it. Import-export, shipping, lots of tales and legends get passed around in those types of industries. And they had a personal interest as they were supposed to be some distant relations to Angelique's father-in-law. That's why VanDyke considers the amulet his.'

Though he realized she was staring at the box, Matthew sat, set it in his lap. 'VanDyke liked the idea of being descended from a count, even one, or maybe especially one, with an unsavory reputation. The way VanDyke told it, the count got the amulet back. He had to kill the maid to do it, but she was only a maid. He still had it when he died, quite miserably, I imagine, of syphilis a year later.'

Tate moistened her lips. She didn't want to be fascinated. 'If you knew all this, why didn't you tell us before?'

'Some I knew, some I didn't. My father talked to Buck, and Buck kept most of it to himself. He kept most of my father's papers to himself, too. I didn't come across them until a couple of years ago when he was in rehab and I was shoveling out the trailer. The whole business spooked him.'

Matthew watched her as he tapped a finger on the box. 'See, the problem was VanDyke told my father too much. Arrogance made him careless. I imagine he thought he was close to finding the amulet, and he wanted to gloat. He told my father how he'd traced the amulet through the count's family. Several of whom died young and violently. Those who lived suffered poverty. The amulet was sold, began its journey and developed its reputation.'

'How did your father copy pages of the diary?'

'According to his journal, he was worried about VanDyke. He suspected a double-cross, or worse, and decided to do some research on his own. He had a chance when winter set in and they had to take a break from diving. He used the time to work on his own. That's when he must have come across the *Isabella*. His notes were cryptic after that. Maybe he was worried VanDyke would find them.'

The old frustration came back, rough around his heart. 'It's mostly speculation, Tate. I was a kid, there was a lot he didn't tell me. Shit, he didn't tell me anything. Putting it together is like trying to put him together. And I'm not even sure I knew who he was.'

'Matthew.' Her voice was gentle now, Drawn, she went to sit beside him, lay a hand over his. 'You were only a boy. You can't blame yourself for not having a clear picture.'

He stared at their hands, hers narrow and white, his beneath it big, scarred and rough. That, he supposed, illustrated the difference between them as well as anything could.

'I didn't know what he was planning. I guess I knew something was going on. I know I didn't want him to go down with VanDyke that day. I'd heard them going at each other the night before. I asked him not to dive, or at least to let me go with him. He just laughed it off.'

He shook off the memory. 'But that doesn't answer your question. The best I can piece together is that my father got into VanDyke's cabin and searched it. He found the diary and copied down the relevant pages. It couldn't have been long before he did, because that's part of what they were arguing about. The diary, the amulet.'

'Why are you telling me this, Matthew? Why go back over something so painful that can't be changed?'

'Because I know you won't stay because I tell you to.'

She withdrew her hand. 'So it's a play on my sympathies.'

'It's background. Scientists need background, facts and theories, right? I know you don't believe we'll find the *Isabella*.' His gaze held hers, measuring. 'You're not convinced we'll ever find the amulet, or, if we do, that it's anything but an interesting and valuable piece of antique jewelry.'

'All right, that's true. Nothing you've told me convinces me otherwise. I understand why you need to believe, but it doesn't change the facts.'

'But we're not hunting facts, Tate.' He opened the box and handed her papers covered with cramped, hurried writing. 'I don't think you've forgotten that. If you have, maybe this will remind you.'

October 9, 1553
In the morning they will kill me. I have only one night left on earth, and spend it alone. They have taken even my dear Colette from me. Though she went weeping, it is for the best. Not even her prayers, as pure and selfless as they are, can aid me now, and she would have suffered needlessly in this cell, waiting for dawn. Companionship. I have already learned to live without it. With Etienne's death six long weeks ago, I lost not only my dearest companion, my love, my joy, but also my protector.

They say I poisoned him, plying him with one of my witch brews. What fools they are. I would have given my life for his. Indeed, I am doing so. His illness was deep within, and beyond my powers to cure. So quickly it came on him, so violently, the fever, the pain. No potion, no prayer I devised could halt his death. And I as his wife am condemned. I, who once treated the ills and suffering of the village, am reviled as a murderess. And a witch. Those whose fevers I cooled, whose pains I eased have turned against me, shouting for my death like beasts howling at the moon.

205

It is the count who leads them. Etienne's father who hates and desires me. Does he watch from his castle window as they build the pyre that will be my deathbed? I'm sure he does with his greedy eyes glinting and his thin, wicked fingers twisted in prayer. Though I will burn tomorrow, he will burn for eternity. A small but useful revenge.

If I had succumbed to him, if I had betrayed my love even after his death and gone to the bed of Etienne's father, perhaps I would live. So he promised me. I have faced the tortures of this damnable Christian court with more joy than that.

I hear my jailers laughing. They are drunk with the excitement of tomorrow. But they do not laugh when they come into my cell. Their eyes are wide and frightened as they fork their fingers in the sign against witchcraft. Such fools to believe that such a small, pitiful gesture could stop true power.

They have cut my hair. Etienne often called it his angel fire and ran his fingers through its length. It was my vanity, and even that is stripped from me. My flesh is wasting on my bones from sickness, scarred from their relentless tortures. For this one night, they will leave me in peace. That is their mistake.

However weak my body now, my heart grows stronger. I will be with Etienne soon. And that is comfort. I no longer weep at the thought of leaving a world that has become cruel, that uses God's name to torture and condemn and murder. I will face the flames, and I swear on Etienne's soul that I will not cry out for mercy from the merciless or call out to the God they use to destroy me.

Colette has smuggled the amulet to me. They will find it and steal it, of course. But for tonight I wear it around my neck, the heavy gold chain, its bright tear-shaped ruby framed in more gold and etched with Etienne's name and mine, studded with more rubies and diamonds. Blood and tears. I close my hand around it and feel Etienne close to me, see his face.

And with it, I curse the fates that killed us, that will kill the child only I and Colette know stirs within me. A child who will never know life, with its pleasures and its pains.

206

For Etienne and our child I gather what strength I have, I call on whatever forces listen, loose whatever power I hold. May those who condemn me suffer as we have suffered. May those who would take from me all that I value never know joy. I curse whoever wrests this amulet from me, this last earthly link between myself and my love. I pray to all the forces of heaven and hell that he who takes this, Etienne's last gift to me, will know strife and pain and tragedy. He who seeks to profit will only lose what is most precious, most dear. My legacy to my murderers and those who follow them is generations of grief.

Tomorrow they burn me as a witch. I pray they are right, and my powers, like my love, are enduring.

Angelique Maunoir

Tate couldn't speak for a moment. She handed Matthew back the papers and rose to go to the window. The rain had slowed, nearly stopped without her being aware.

'She was so alone,' Tate murmured. 'How cruel for her to be in that cell knowing she would die so horribly in the morning. Still grieving for the man she loved, not being able to feel joy for the child she carried. No wonder she prayed for retribution.'

'But did she get it?'

With a shake of her head, Tate turned to see he had risen as well and was standing with her. Her eyes were wet. The words written so long ago tore at her heart. But when Matthew lifted a hand and laid it on her damp cheek, she jerked back.

'Don't.' She watched his eyes go flat before she stepped away. 'I stopped believing in magic, black or white, a long time ago. The necklace was obviously vitally important to Angelique, a link to the man she'd loved. A curse is a different matter altogether.'

'Funny, I'd have thought someone who spends her time handling and researching old things would have more imagination. Haven't you ever picked up something that has been buried for centuries and felt the punch of it? The power.'

She had. Indeed she had. 'My point is,' she continued, evading, 'that I'm convinced. We stick together, beat him together. We do whatever it takes to keep the amulet out of VanDyke's hands.'

Matthew acknowledged this with a nod that was much more casual than his jerking pulse. 'That's the answer I wanted. I'd offer to shake on it, but you don't like me to touch you.'

'No, I don't.' She started to step around him, but he shifted to block her. Her eyes went cold. 'Really, Matthew, let's not be any more ridiculous than necessary.'

'When we start diving, you're going to have to tolerate me touching you when it's necessary.'

'I can work with you. Just don't crowd me.'

'That's what you used to say.' He moved back, gestured. 'There's plenty of room.'

She took advantage of it and crossed to the door. She shrugged out of the borrowed windbreaker, replaced it on its hook. 'I appreciate your showing me the papers, Matthew, and giving me more of the background.'

'We're partners.'

She glanced back. Odd how alone he looked standing there with the wheel at his back and the sea behind him. 'So it seems. Good night.'

Chapter Seventeen

SILAS VANDYKE WAS extremely disappointed. The reports he'd just read had completely ruined his morning. He tried to recapture some of the charm of the day by having lunch on his patio overlooking the sea.

It was certainly a spectacular spot, the crash of waves thundering, Chopin soaring from the speakers hidden cannily among the lush spread of his tropical gardens. He sipped champagne and picked at a succulent fruit salad, knowing his companion of the moment would be back from her shopping expedition shortly.

Naturally, she'd be willing to distract him with an afternoon of sex. But he simply wasn't in the mood.

He was calm, he assured himself. Still in charge. He was simply disappointed.

Tate Beaumont had betrayed him. He took it quite personally. After all, he'd watched her blossom as any of his well-tended blooms. Like a kindly uncle, he'd given her career little boosts along the way. Always anonymously, of course. He hadn't been looking for gratitude.

Just loyalty.

Her work on the *Nomad* would have catapulted her to the very top of her field. With her looks, her enthusiasm, her youth, she would have outstripped such quietly respected scientists as Hayden Deel. Then, when she was at her peak, he would have stepped out of the shadows and offered her the world.

She would have headed his expeditions. His labs, his funding, his finest equipment would have been at her disposal. She would have joined him in his quest for Angelique's Curse. Since that day eight years before, when she had stood on the deck of the *Triumphant*, he had known intuitively that she was his link to it. Over the years, he'd come to realize that the fates had put her in his path as a sign, a symbol. And he had kept her there, patiently waiting for the moment to come.

With her, he would have succeeded. He was sure of it.

But she had betrayed him. Left her post.

Betrayed him.

His teeth clenched and sweat popped out hot on his skin. Fury hazed his vision, overtook him so that he hurled the crystal over the sea wall, heaved the table so that china and silver and luscious fruit smashed and splattered onto the patio.

Payment, there would be payment. Desertion was a highly punishable offense. A killing offense. His nails dug red welts into his palms. She would have to pay for that, and more, for the bad taste of aligning herself once more with his enemies.

They thought they'd outwitted him, VanDyke raged as he stalked the patio, yanked a creamy hibiscus from the bush beside him. Their mistake, of course. Tate's mistake.

She owed him loyalty, and he would have it. He demanded it. A feral grin on his lips, he ripped the delicate blossom. Then he ripped off more, still more, until the bush and his beautiful suit were in tatters.

Panting, his head swimming with the volcanic fury inside him, he yanked himself back, back. As his vision cleared, he saw the shattered remains of his elegant lunch, the ruin of his possessions. His head ached abominably, and his hands were raw.

He couldn't quite remember causing the destruction, only the black cloud that had smothered him.

For how long? he wondered in jittering panic. For how long had he been lost?

He looked desperately at his watch, winking gold on his wrist, but he couldn't remember when the mood had taken him away.

It didn't matter, he soothed himself. The servants would say nothing, would think nothing but what he ordered them to think. In any case, he hadn't caused this nasty destruction of food and china.

It was they who had caused the destruction, he reminded himself. The Lassiters. The Beaumonts. He'd simply reacted, perhaps a bit rashly, to his keen disappointment. But he'd cleared his mind again. As he always did. As he always would.

Now that he was calm, he would think, and he would plan. He'd give them time, he decided. He'd give them room. Then, he'd destroy them. This time, he would destroy them utterly for causing him to lose his dignity.

He would have control, VanDyke told himself, breathing slow and deep. His father had not been able to control his mother. His mother had been unable to control herself.

But he had learned strength and will.

It was slipping now, and he feared that the way a child fears the monsters in the closet. There were monsters, he remembered, and had to force himself to stop his eyes from darting in search of them. The monsters in the dark, the monsters in the doubt. In failure.

He was losing the control over self that he had fought so hard to develop.

Angelique's Curse. He knew now, was sure now, that the amulet was the answer. With it, he would be strong, fearless, powerful. He believed the witch had put her soul into it. Oh yes, he believed that now, and wondered why he had ever doubted it, ever considered it simply a valuable, much-desired trinket.

It was his destiny, of course. He laughed a little, taking a linen handkerchief from his pocket with a trembling hand to wipe his face. His destiny, and perhaps his salvation. Without it, he would taste failure, and more. He might find himself trapped in that black, numbing world of slathering rage without a key.

The amulet was the key. Gently now, he plucked another blossom, stroked it delicately to prove he could.

Angelique had put her soul into metal and stone. She had haunted him for years, taunted him, teased him by letting him get just so close and no further.

Well, he would beat her, as his long-dead ancestor had beaten her. He would win because he was a man who knew how to win.

And as for Tate … He crushed the flower in his hand, letting his neatly manicured nails rip through the dewy petals.

She'd made her choice.

The West Indies. Tropical islands lush with flowers and palms, towering with cliffs. White sand glittering in the sun and kissed by gilded blue water. Fragrant breezes swaying majestic palms. It was everyone's image of paradise.

As Tate stepped on deck just after sunrise, she was no exception. The cone of Nevis's sleeping volcano was shrouded in mists. The gardens and cabanas of the resort that had been built since her last visit seemed to sleep as well. Nothing stirred but the gulls.

She decided she would go ashore later that morning on the supply run. But for now, she would enjoy a quiet, solitary swim.

She slipped into the water, letting it flow over her shoulders as she tipped her head back. It was just cool enough to refresh. Treading water lazily, she turned a slow circle. Her sigh of delight turned into a gasp as something grabbed her leg and pulled her under.

She sputtered furiously to the surface. Behind his mask, Matthew's eyes glinted.

'Sorry, hard to resist. I was just doing some free diving and saw these legs poke through the water. You've got great legs, Red. All the way up.'

'It's a very big sea, Matthew,' she said primly. 'Go play somewhere else.'

'Why don't you go get a mask and come down with me?'

'Not interested.'

'I've got a bag of crackers in the pocket of my trunks.' He reached over to pluck a strand of wet hair from her face. 'Don't you want to feed the fish?'

She did, but only if she'd thought of it first. 'No.' Giving him her shoulder, she swam deliberately away.

He did a neat surface dive, swam under her and came up in her face again. 'You used to be fun.'

'You used to be marginally less annoying.'

He matched his pace to hers. 'Of course, you'd be out of practice diving, spending all your time with computers and robots. That's probably why even a little snorkeling worries you.'

'I'm not worried. I dive as well as I ever did. Better.'

'We'll have to do some swim-overs while we're looking for the *Isabella*. I say you need the practice.'

'I do not need to practice snorkeling.'

'Prove it,' he challenged and kicked away from her.

She lectured herself, cursed him, but she ended up hauling herself back aboard the boat for snorkel gear. The man was an idiot, of course, she told herself, as she dropped into the water again. But he knew what buttons to push. Her only satisfaction would be to show him just how good she was.

Adjusting her mouthpiece, she skimmed onto the surface. She'd forgotten, until the moment her gaze swept through water to fish and sand, how long it had been since she'd dived – free or scuba – for pleasure only.

She paddled along dreamily, the challenge forgotten. Until Matthew streaked past beneath her, rolling until they were nearly mask-to-mask. He was grinning, then water fountained out of his pipe above the surface. He cocked his head, gestured down. Without waiting, he jackknifed and left her behind.

It was all the motivation she needed. She filled her lungs with air and kicked after him.

This was a world that always lived in her heart. Waving patches of sea grass, clear water, the plains and hillocks of sand. And when Matthew released the broken crackers from the bag he carried, teams of greedy fish.

They swarmed around her, bodies bright as they nipped and gobbled the feast. One or two were curious enough to stare into her face mask before darting off to join the competition for food. Her lungs were aching before she kicked up, blew her pipe clear and drew in more air.

Nearly an hour passed before she kicked to the surface. Tate pulled up her mask and lay contentedly on her back to float.

'Maybe you haven't lost your touch,' Matthew commented.

'I haven't spent all my time in a lab.'

Because her eyes were closed, he indulged himself and let his fingers comb through the hair that flowed red and silky on the water. 'You didn't come in when we docked at San Juan.'

'I was busy with other things.' But she'd seen him, swimming powerfully through the water, and working with LaRue on diving lessons.

'Your thesis.'

'That's right.' A faint tug on her hair had her brushing a hand back. Her fingers collided with his.

'Sorry. What's your thesis on?'

Cautious, she let herself drift a few inches away from where he trod water. 'You wouldn't be interested.'

He said nothing for a moment, surprised by the hot surge of resentment. 'You're probably right.'

Something in his tone had her opening her eyes again.

'I barely got through high-school term papers. What would I know about doctorates and theses?'

'I didn't mean it that way.' Ashamed of herself, she reached out for his arm before he could go under again. 'I didn't. I only meant I didn't think you'd care about some long-winded technical paper when you've already done everything I could write about. And the truth is, I want the damned thing over.'

'I thought you liked that stuff.'

'I do. I–' Annoyed with herself, she floated again, closed her eyes again. 'I don't know what I mean. My thesis is on the inherent versus the monetary value of artifacts. It's not terribly original, but I thought I might focus on one piece, tracing it from its beginnings through to its discovery and analysis. Or I might scrap the whole thing and go back to my first idea of how technological advancements have improved and depersonalized the science of marine archeology. Or… '

She opened one eye. 'You can see why I'm not thrilled you tried to pin me down.'

'So, you haven't made up your mind yet. What's the hurry?'

'I thought there was one.' How could she explain that she felt as though she'd been on a treadmill for years. One of her own choosing, certainly. But that she'd suddenly, and impulsively, leapt off. She didn't have her feet under her yet, and wasn't sure how to get back on when the time came.

'You always got that line, right there, when you tried to out-think yourself.' He skimmed a fingertip between her brows.

She batted his hand aside. 'Go away, Lassiter. I'm having a good time stewing over a professional crisis.'

214

'Looks to me like you have to be taught how to relax all over again.' He planted a hand firmly on her face and pushed.

She went under, but she was quick enough to snag him on the way down. She got her chin above water, and would have been more successful pulling in air if she hadn't been giggling. When he closed a hand over her ankle, she kicked out with her other foot and had the satisfaction of meeting flesh before he dragged her down again.

Rather than struggle, she went limp. The instant his grip loosened, she gave him a solid butt, then struck out for the boat. She wasn't certain if he was quicker than he'd once been, or if she was slower, but she didn't make it four strokes.

By the time she clawed her way to the surface again, she was weak and out of breath.

'You're drowning me.'

'I'm saving you,' he corrected. Indeed he was holding her up. Their legs were tangled so he used one arm to keep them buoyant while the other stayed wrapped around her.

'Maybe I am out of shape.' She fought to get her breath back and used one hand to swipe hair out of her eyes.

'Not from where I'm swimming.'

It took a moment for the laughter to fade from her face, a moment before she realized she was clinging to him, that his body was hard, nearly naked and pressed close to hers. It took a moment to read the desire in his eyes and for the raw echo of it to sound through her.

'Let me go, Matthew.'

He could feel her trembling now, and she'd gone pale. But he knew it wasn't from fear. She'd often looked and felt just like this before. When she'd wanted him.

'Your heart's pounding, Tate. I can practically hear it.'

'I said–'

He leaned forward, caught her bottom lip lightly between his teeth and watched her eyes cloud. 'Go ahead,' he challenged against her mouth. 'Say it again.'

He didn't give her the chance. His lips were devouring hers, crushing then nibbling, then seducing apart so that he could take the kiss into the deep and the dark and the dangerous.

By Christ, he'd please himself. That's what he thought, even as he suffered. She was everything he'd remembered and sought to forget. Everything and more. Even as they sank beneath the surface, kicked back into air wrapped in each other, he knew it wasn't the sea that would drown him. But his desperate, endless need for her.

The taste of her, the smell and the feel. The sound of her breath catching on confused pleasure. The memories of the past and the reality of now tangled until he could almost forget there had been time between.

She hadn't known she could still feel like this. So hungry and out of control. She didn't want to think, not when her body was so intensely alive and every nerve in it on shivering edge.

It was just physical. She could cling to that as well as him. A man's hard, demanding mouth, that wet, slippery flesh, a tough, ready body molded to hers. No, she didn't want to think. But she had to.

'No.'

She managed one breathless syllable before his mouth came back and sent her mind reeling again. She felt her will slipping and struggled against both him and herself.

'I said no.'

'I heard you.' A dozen separate wars waged inside him. He wanted her, and knew by the way her mouth had fit on his that he could have her. He needed her, and read the mirror of that in her dazed eyes. If want and need had been all, the war would have been over quickly.

But he loved her. And that left him a victim bleeding on his own battlefield.

'I didn't do that alone, Tate. But you can pretend I did if it makes you feel better.'

'I don't have to pretend anything. Let go of me.'

He already had. And that helped curve his lips into something close to a smile. 'You're holding me, sweetheart.' He brought his hands out of the water, palms facing her.

On an oath, she released the grip her arms had somehow taken around him. 'I know the cliché, Lassiter, but this time history isn't going to repeat itself. We work together, we dive together. That's all we do together.'

'It's your choice, Red. It always was.'

'Then there shouldn't be a problem.'

'No problem.' He struck out in a lazy backstroke. 'Unless you're worried you won't be able to resist me.'

216

'I can manage,' she called after him.

He'd have been pleased to see the line was between her brows again. Muttering to herself, Tate went under to cool her head, then swam in the opposite direction.

'You're not going down again until you pass the written test.' Matthew shoved papers under LaRue's nose. 'That's the way it is.'

'I'm not a schoolboy.'

'You're a trainee. I'm your instructor, and you're going to take the written test. Pass it, you dive. Fail it, you're grounded. The first part's equipment identification.' Matthew leaned forward. 'You remember what a regulator is, don't you, LaRue?'

'It gives the air from the tank to the diver.' LaRue pushed the papers aside. 'So?'

Matthew pushed them back. 'And consists of?'

'Consists of, consists of.' Scowling, LaRue snatched his tobacco pouch. 'The, ah, mouthpiece, the hose, the what is it, stages?'

'What's a stage?'

'This is pressure-reducing unit. Why do you worry me with this?'

'You don't dive until you know the equipment inside-out, until I'm sure you understand the physics and physiology.' He offered LaRue a sharpened pencil. 'Take all the time you need, but remember, you don't dive until you're done. Buck, give me a hand on deck.'

'Sure, be right there.'

LaRue glanced over his test sheets, glanced at Matthew's retreating back. 'What is Boyle's Law?' he whispered to Buck.

'When the pressure—'

'No cheating,' Matthew called back. 'Jesus, Buck.'

'Sorry, LaRue, you're on your own.' Shamefaced, Buck followed Matthew out on deck. 'I was just giving him a little hint.'

'Who's going to give him a little hint if he forgets the basics when he's forty feet under?'

'You're right – but he's doing good, isn't he? You said he had a knack for diving.'

'He's a fucking fish down there,' Matthew said with a grin. 'But he's not skipping the details.'

217

He was already wearing his wetsuit and now zipped it. He gave his tanks and gauges a last check, then let Buck help him strap them on.

'We're just going down for a little recognizance,' Matthew commented as he adjusted his weight belt.

'Yeah.'

Buck knew they were over the site of the *Marguerite*. Both he and Matthew avoided discussing the wreck, or what had happened. Buck avoided Matthew's eyes as his nephew sat to put on his flippers.

'Tate wants some pictures,' Matthew said, for lack of anything better. Everyone knew they wanted a firsthand look at what VanDyke had left behind.

'Sure. She was always big on getting pictures. Kid grew up nice, didn't she?'

'Nice enough. Don't give LaRue any more hints.'

'Not even if he begs.' Buck's smile faded when Matthew slipped on his mask. Panic reared up and grabbed him by the throat. 'Matthew...'

Matthew paused, one hand on his mask as he prepared to roll into the water. 'What?' He saw the anxiety, struggled to overlook it.

'Nothing.' Buck wiped a hand over his mouth, swallowed hard while nightmare visions of sharks and blood swam in his head. 'Good diving.'

With a brief nod, Matthew slipped into the water. He ignored the impulse to dive deep, lose himself in the silence and solitude. He crossed the distance to the *New Adventure* in an easy crawl, gave up a hailing shout.

'Ready to roll up there?'

'Just about.' Ray, full-suited, came to the rail with a grin. 'Tate's checking her camera.' He lifted a hand in a wave to Buck. 'How's he doing?'

'He'll be all right,' Matthew said. The last thing he wanted to do was dwell on his uncle's fears. Now that they were here, he was impatient to begin. 'Let's go, Red!' he shouted. 'The morning's wasting.'

'I'm coming.'

He caught a glimpse of her before she sat to pull on her flippers. Moments later, he watched her graceful entry. With a quick pike dive, Matthew was following her down even as Ray dropped into the water.

The three of them descended, nearly side by side.

Matthew hadn't expected the memories to swarm up at him like the bright, quick fish. Everything about that summer came back, unbidden and unwelcomed. He remembered the way she had looked when he'd first seen her. The wary suspicious eyes, the quick flares of anger, resentment.

Oh, and he remembered his instant attraction, one he'd smothered, or tried to. The sense of competition when they'd teamed as diving partners, an edge that had never really dulled even after they'd melded into a unit.

There was the thrill he'd experienced when they'd found the wreck. Those times with her that had opened both his heart and his hopes as nothing and no one ever had before. Or had again. All the sensations of falling in love, of working together, of discovery and promise spun through him as they neared the shadow of the wreck.

As did the jarring aches of horror and loss.

VanDyke had left little but the shredded shell of the galleon. Matthew knew at one glance it would be a foolish waste of time to bring down the airlift and dig. Nothing of any value would have been left behind. The wreck itself had been destroyed, ripped apart in search of that last doubloon.

It surprised him to feel sorrow for that. With careful excavation, the *Marguerite* might have been saved. Instead she was in pieces, left for the worms.

When he glanced at Tate, Matthew could see clearly that whatever vague regret he felt for the ship was nothing to what she was experiencing.

It shattered her. Tate stared at the scattered planks, not bothering to attempt to block the wave of grief. She let it wash over her until she felt it deep inside.

He'd killed her, she thought. VanDyke hadn't been content with his rape, but had destroyed the *Marguerite*. No one would see what she had been, what she had meant. Because of one man's greed.

She might have wept if tears hadn't been so late and so useless. Instead, she shook off the comforting hand Matthew put on her shoulder, and lifted her camera. If nothing else, she'd record the devastation.

Catching Matthew's eye, Ray shook his head, gestured so that they swam a short distance away.

There was still beauty surrounding her. The coral, the fish, the waving plants. But it didn't touch her now as she recorded the scene that had once been the stage for such great joy.

It was fitting, she supposed, that it had been ruined, destroyed, neglected. Just like the love she'd once offered Matthew.

So, she thought, that summer was finally and completely over. It was past time to bury it, and start new.

When they surfaced, the first thing she saw was Buck's pale, anxious face leaning over the rail.

'Everything okay?'

'Everything's fine,' she assured him. Because it was closer, she pulled herself aboard the *Mermaid*. She stopped, turned and waved to her mother, who was recording the event on video aboard the *New Adventure*. 'Pretty much what we expected,' she told Buck after she had dropped her weight belt.

'Bastard tore her apart, didn't he?'

'Yes.' She glanced over as Matthew climbed on deck.

'Ray wants to head south right away.' He pulled off his mask, ran a hand through his hair. 'You might as well stay put,' he told Tate before she could rise. 'It won't take long. Buck?'

With a nod, Buck headed up to the bridge to take the wheel.

'Best plan is to do some swim-overs.' After tugging down the zipper of his wetsuit, Matthew sat beside her. 'We could get lucky.'

'Are you feeling lucky, Lassiter?'

'No.' He closed his eyes as the engine purred. 'She meant something to me, too.'

'Fame and fortune?'

The words cut, but not as keenly as the edge of her voice. His gaze, hot and hurt, swept up to hers before he stood and strode toward the companionway.

'Matthew.' Shame had her springing up after him. 'I'm sorry.'

'Forget it.'

'No.' Before he could take the stairs, she grabbed his arm. 'I am sorry. That was hard on all of us – going down, seeing what was left. Remembering. Taking it out on you is easy, but it doesn't help.'

In impotent fury, Matthew's hands whitened on the rail. 'Maybe I could have stopped him. Buck thought so.'

'Buck wasn't there.' She kept her hand firm on his arm until he turned to face her again. Odd, she thought, she hadn't

220

realized he would blame himself. Or that he had room in the cold heart she'd assigned to him for guilt. 'There was nothing any of us could have done. Looking back doesn't help either, and certainly doesn't change anything.'

'The *Marguerite's* not all we're talking about, is it?'

She was tempted to back off, to shrug his words away. But evasions were foolish, and she hoped she was no longer a fool. 'No, it's not.'

'I wasn't what you wanted me to be, and I hurt you. I can't change that either.'

'I was young. Infatuations pass.' Somehow her hand had found its way to his, and linked. Realizing it, she flexed her fingers free and stepped back. 'I understood something when I was down there, looking at what was left. There is nothing left, Matthew. The ship, that summer, that girl. All that's gone. We have to start with what's now.'

'Clean slate.'

'I don't know if we can go that far. Let's just say we've turned a page.'

'Okay.' He offered a hand. When she took it, he brought hers unexpectedly to his lips. 'I'm going to work on you, Red,' he murmured.

'Excuse me?'

'You said we've got a new page. I figure I've got some say in what gets written on it. So I'm going to work on you. Last time around, you threw yourself at me.'

'I did no such thing.'

'Sure you did. But I can see I've got my work cut out for me this time. That's okay.' He skimmed his thumb over her knuckles before she jerked her hand free. 'In fact, I think I'm going to enjoy it.'

'I don't know why I waste my time trying to mend fences with you. You're as arrogant as you ever were.'

'Just the way you like me, sweetheart.'

She caught the lightning flash of his grin before she whirled away. Try as she might, she couldn't quite suppress the answering upward tug of her lips.

It was hell knowing he was right. That was exactly the way she liked him.

Chapter Eighteen

SWIM-OVERS TURNED UP nothing impressive. Tate spent most of the afternoon closeted with her father and his research while Matthew took LaRue, fresh from passing his written certification, on a practice dive.

She had already organized the heaps of notes, the snippets from the National Archives, wreck charts, the material Ray had culled from the *Archivo General de Indias* in Seville.

She'd separated his maps, charts, storm records, manifests, diaries. Now she concentrated on his calculations.

Already she'd figured and refigured a dozen times. If their information was correct, they were certainly in the right area. The problem was, of course, that even with a location, finding a wreck was like separating that one special grain of sand from a fat fistful.

The sea was so huge, so vast, and even with the leaps in technology, a man's abilities were limited. It was highly possible to be within twenty feet of a wreck, and miss it entirely.

They had been almost foolishly lucky with the *Marguerite*. Tate didn't want to calculate the odds of lightning striking twice, not with the hope and excitement she could see whenever she looked into her father's eyes.

They needed the *Isabella*, she thought. All of them did, for all manner of differing reasons.

She knew the magnetometer aboard the *Mermaid* was in use. It was a fine and efficient way of locating a wreck. So far the sensor being towed behind the *Mermaid* had picked up no readings of iron such as would be found in cannon, riggings, anchor.

They had depth finders on both bridges so that any telltale change in water depth caused by a wreck would be distinguished. They had set out buoys to mark the search pattern.

If she was down there, Tate thought, they would find her.

She stayed in the deckhouse after her father had gone out to starboard.

'You're not going to put roses in your cheeks in here, Red.'

She looked up, surprised when Matthew held out a glass of her mother's lemonade. 'You're back. How did LaRue check out?'

'He's a good diving partner. How many times are you going to go over all this?'

She tidied papers. 'Until I'm finished.'

'How about taking a break?' Reaching out, he toyed with the sleeve of her T-shirt. He'd been working on this approach all day, and still wasn't sure he had it right. 'Why don't we take a run into Nevis, have dinner?'

'Dinner?'

'That's right. You.' He tugged the sleeve. 'And me.'

'I don't think so.'

'I thought we'd turned the page.'

'That doesn't—'

'And I'm not keen on the big pinochle game that's being planned for tonight. As I remember, you weren't big on cards either. The resort has a reggae band out on the terrace. Some dinner, a little music. There won't be time for much of that once we find the *Isabella*.'

'It's been a long day.'

'You're going to make me think you're afraid to spend a couple of hours with me.' His eyes flashed on hers, blue as the sea and just as arrogant. 'Of course, if you're afraid you'll throw yourself at me again.'

'That's pathetic.'

'Well, then.' Satisfied he nailed the approach after all, he headed back for the companionway. 'Wear your hair down, Red. I like it.'

She wore it up. Not to spite him, she assured herself. But because she wanted to. She'd changed into a sundress the color of crushed blueberries borrowed from her mother's closet, at Marla's insistence. The full skirt made it easy to climb in and out of the tender.

Once she was settled in and the little tender was speeding toward the island, she admitted that she looked forward to an elegant restaurant meal, with a little music tossed in.

The air was balmy, the sun still bright as it traveled west. Behind the protection of her shaded glasses, she studied Matthew. His hair was whipping around his face. On the tiller, his hand was broad and competent. If there had been no history between them, she would have been pleased to have such an attractive companion for an evening's relaxation.

But there was history. Rather than diluting the pleasure, it added an edge to it. Competition again, she supposed. If he thought she would fall for that rough-and-ready charm a second time, she was only too happy to prove him wrong.

'The weather's supposed to hold all week,' she said conversationally.

'I know. You still don't wear lipstick.' When she instinctively flicked her tongue over her lips, he dealt with the resulting hitch in his pulse. 'It's a pity most women don't realize how tempting a naked mouth is. Especially when it pouts.'

Deliberately, she relaxed her mouth again. 'I'll enjoy knowing it's driving you crazy for the next couple of hours.'

She turned her attention to Nevis. The mountain's cone was swirled in clouds, a striking and dramatic contrast to the brilliant blue of the sky. Far below, the shore spread white against a calm sea. The sand was dotted with people, pretty umbrellas and lounging chairs. A novice sail-boarder struggled fruitlessly to stay upright. As she watched him fall into the water again, Tate laughed.

'Too bad.' She cocked a brow at Matthew. 'Have you ever tried that?'

'Nope.'

'I have. It's a hell of a lot of work, frustrating when you think you've got it then lose your balance and capsize. But if you catch the breeze and go, it's wonderful.'

'Better than diving?'

'No.' She continued to smile, watching the young man struggle onto his board again. 'Nothing's better than diving.'

'Things have changed around here.'

'Hmmm.' She waited as he maneuvered to the pier, tossed a line to a member of the resort's staff. 'I didn't even know they were planning to build when we were here last.' She took Matthew's offered hand and climbed to the dock. 'Now it looks as though it almost grew here.'

'Nevis isn't quite the secret it used to be.' He kept a hand on her arm as they walked down the pier to the beach.

Stone walkways offered a route through lush gardens and sloping green lawns where pretty two-story cabanas sat. They passed the pool-side restaurant, moving toward the marble stairs that led to the main building.

Tate glanced over her shoulder. 'We're not eating out here?'

'We can do a little better than light fare by the pool. The restaurant inside has terrace dining.' He led Tate inside toward the reservation pedestal, where a woman in the bright-patterned shirt of the staff beamed at him. 'Lassiter.'

'Yes, sir. You requested the terrace.'

'That's right. I called ahead,' he told Tate when she frowned at him. Her frown only deepened when he held out her chair. If memory served, his manners had smoothed out considerably. 'Can you handle champagne?' he murmured, leaning down so that his breath tickled her ear.

'Of course, but–'

He was ordering a bottle even as he took the seat across from her. 'Nice view.'

'Yes.' She took her gaze from his face and looked out over the gardens to the sea.

'Tell me about the last eight years, Tate.'

'Why?'

'I want to know.' Needed to know. 'Let's say it'll fill in some of the blanks.'

'I studied a lot,' she began. 'More than I bargained for. I guess I had the idea that I knew so much going in. But I

225

knew so little really. The first couple of months I …' Was lost, unhappy, missing you so terribly. 'I needed to adjust,' she said carefully.

'But you caught on pretty quick.'

'I suppose.' Relax, she ordered herself and made herself turn back and smile at him. 'I liked the routine, the structure. And I really wanted to learn.'

She looked over as the waitress brought the champagne to the table to show off its label.

'Let her taste it,' Matthew ordered.

Obliging, the waitress uncorked the bottle and poured a swallow into Tate's flute. 'It's lovely,' Tate murmured, much too aware that Matthew's eyes never left her face.

When their glasses were filled, she started to drink again, but he laid a finger on her wrist. Gently, he tapped the glasses together. 'To the next page,' he said and smiled.

'All right.' She was a grown woman, Tate reminded herself. Experienced now. She had all the defenses necessary to resist a man. Even one like Matthew.

'So you learned,' Matthew prompted.

'Yes. And whenever I had an opportunity to use what I'd learned on an expedition, I took it.'

'And the *Isabella*, isn't she an opportunity?'

'That remains to be seen.' She opened her menu, skimmed it, looked up at him with wide eyes. 'Matthew.'

'I managed to hold on to a few bucks over the years,' he assured her. 'Besides, you've always been my lucky charm.' He picked up her hand. 'This time, Red, we go home rich.'

'So, that's still the bottom line? All right.' She shrugged. 'It's your party, Lassiter. If you want to live for today, we'll do it.'

While they ate, and the wine fizzed in their glasses, the sun lowered. It sank red into the sea, giving the air that brief and painfully lovely twilight of the tropics. On cue, the music from the patio beyond began.

'You haven't told me about your eight years, Matthew.'

'Nothing very interesting.'

'You built the *Mermaid*. That's interesting.'

'She's a beauty.' He looked out to the sea where, beyond his sight, she rocked. 'Just like I imagined her.'

'Whatever happens here, you'd have a career in boat design and building.'

'I'm never working to make ends meet again,' he said quietly. 'Never doing what needs to be done and forgetting what I want.'

It struck her, that fierceness in his eyes, so that she reached out to touch his hand. 'Is that what you did?'

Surprised, he looked back. With a careless shrug, he linked his fingers with hers. 'It's not what I'm doing. That's what counts. You know something, Red?'

'What?'

'You're beautiful. No.' He smiled slowly when she tried to slip her hand free. 'I've got you now. For now,' he corrected. 'Get used to it.'

'The fact that I chose you over pinochle has obviously gone to your head.'

'Then there's that voice,' he murmured, delighted by the way confusion flickered with the candlelight in her eyes. 'Soft, slow, smooth. Like honey spiked with just the right amount of good bourbon. A man could get drunk just listening to you.'

'I think you got a headstart with the champagne. I'll pilot us back.'

'Fine. But we'll have at least one dance.' He signaled for the bill.

A dance wouldn't hurt, Tate decided. If anything, she could use the close contact to convince him that she wasn't about to be seduced into the brief affair he was obviously after.

She could enjoy him without losing herself or her heart this time around. And if he suffered a little, she wasn't above enjoying that as well.

To show how little it mattered, she let her hand stay in his as they left the screened terrace for the open patio below.

The music was slow, sexy, with the vocalist adding a teasing interpretation to the words. A couple sat huddled together at a table in the shadows, but there were no other dancers when Matthew took her into his arms.

He took her close, so their bodies molded, so that her cheek had little choice but to rest on his. Without thinking, she closed her eyes.

She should have known that he would be smooth, that he would be clever. But she hadn't expected that her steps would match his so perfectly.

'I didn't know you could dance.'

227

He skimmed a hand up her back to where material gave way to flesh, flesh that shivered at the touch. 'There's a lot we didn't know about each other. But I know the way you smelled.' He nuzzled just under her ear. 'That hasn't changed.'

'I've changed,' she said, struggling not to react as fire licked along her vulnerable flesh.

'You still feel the same.' He reached up to pull pins out of her hair.

'Stop that.'

'I liked it short.' His voice was as quiet as the breeze, just as seductive. 'But this is better.' Softly, his mouth skimmed over her temple. 'Some changes are.'

She was trembling, those quick, involuntary shivers he remembered so well.

'We're different people now,' she murmured. She wanted it to be true, needed it to be. And yet, if it was, how could it be so easy to move into his arms as if not a moment had passed since the last time?

'Lots of other things are just the way they were. Like the way you fit against me.'

She jerked her head back, then shuddered when his lips brushed over hers.

'You still taste the same.'

'I'm not the same. Nothing's the same.' She broke away and darted down the steps toward the beach.

She couldn't seem to draw in enough air. The balmy night had suddenly turned traitor, making her skin shiver. It was anger – she wanted to believe it was anger that made her stomach clench and her eyes tear. But she knew it was need, and could only hate him for rekindling a long-dead spark.

When he caught her, she was sure she would round on him, clawing and spitting. Somehow her arms were around him, her mouth seeking his.

'I hate you for this. God, I hate you for this.'

'I don't give a damn.' He dragged her head back to plunder. It was all there, that energy, that verve, that passion. He had a wild, desperate thought to drag her off into the bushes, to plunge himself into the heat that vibrated from her.

'I know you don't.' And it was that which still hurt, a scar that throbbed under a fresh wound. 'But I do.'

She broke away, throwing her hands up to ward him off when he would have taken her into his arms again. She fought to even her breathing, fought to resist that reckless, compelling light in his eyes.

'You wanted to prove you could still strike a spark between us.' She pressed an unsteady hand to her stomach. 'Well, you did. But what we do or don't do about it is my choice, Matthew. And I'm not ready to make a choice.'

'I want you, Tate. Do you need to hear me say it?' He stepped forward, but didn't touch her. 'Do you need to hear me tell you I can't sleep at night for wanting you?'

The words, the rough, impatient delivery, spun in her head, swam in her blood. 'Maybe I do, but it doesn't change the fact that I'm taking whatever time I need to decide. I'd have gone anywhere, done anything for you once, Matthew. Once. What I do now, I do for myself.'

He hooked his tensed hands in his pockets. 'That's fair enough. Because this time around what I do, I do for myself.'

'This time around.' She gave a quick laugh and pulled her fingers through her tumbled hair. 'That part looks the same from where I'm standing.'

'Then you know what you're dealing with.'

'I'm not sure I do,' she said wearily. 'You keep shifting on me, Matthew. I'm not sure what's real and what's shadow.'

'This is real.' He cupped a hand behind her neck, lifting her to her toes until their mouths met.

'Yes, that's real.' As she eased away, she let out her breath. 'I want to go back now, Matthew. We start early tomorrow.'

She really didn't mind the way the teams split so that her father and LaRue worked together, leaving her and Matthew as the second team. She and Matthew had always worked well together underwater. After their first dive, she realized they still had the same natural and instinctive communication and rhythm.

The electronic equipment was the most efficient method of locating the *Isabella*, but Tate was grateful to have the chance to dive, to search by sight and by hand as she had learned to do.

Hours of fanning sand didn't bore her. Nor did hauling chunks of conglomerate to the surface for her mother and Buck to hammer apart. As far as she was concerned she was home again, with the fish as both audience and playmates. Every lovely sculpture of coral pleased her eye. Even disappointment was part of the whole. A rusted chain, a soda can might turn a quickly beating heart into a sigh. But it was all part of the hunt.

And there was Matthew, always close at hand to share some small delight with. A garden of sea plants, a grumpy grouper disturbed from his feeding, the bright silver flash of a fish in flight. If he tended to touch her just a bit too often, she told herself to enjoy it.

If she was strong enough to resist seduction, she was certainly strong enough to resist romance.

The days slipped by into weeks, but she wasn't discouraged. The time here was soothing a need she hadn't realized she'd held inside – to revisit the sea she loved, not as a scientist, an objective observer trained to record data. But as a woman enjoying her freedom, and the companionship of a man who intrigued her.

She examined a formation of coral, fanning sand away. Glancing over her shoulder, she saw Matthew tucking conglomerate into his lobster bag. She started to smile at him, the way she reserved for herself when she knew he wasn't looking. A sharp pain stabbed the back of her hand.

Jolted, she jerked back just as the head of a moray eel retreated into its slitted home in the coral. Almost before Tate could register the insult, and curse her own carelessness, Matthew was there, grabbing the fingers of her wounded hand as blood swirled into the water. The alarm in his eyes pierced through her own shock. She started to signal that she was fine, but he already had an arm around her waist and was kicking toward the surface.

'Just relax,' he ordered the minute he spat out his mouthpiece. 'I'm going to tow you in.'

'I'm all right.' But the throbbing pain made her eyes water. 'It's just a nick, really.'

'Relax,' he said again. His face was as pale as hers by the time he reached the ladder. Hailing Ray, he began unhooking Tate's tanks.

'Matthew, for goodness sake, it's a scratch.'

'Shut up. Ray, goddamn it.'

'What? What's wrong?'

'She got bit. Moray.' Matthew passed her tanks over. 'Help her in.'

230

'Lord, you'd think I'd been chewed in half by a shark,' she muttered, then winced as she realized what she'd said. 'I'm okay,' she hurried on as her mother came rushing over.

'Let me see. Oh, honey. Ray, get the first-aid kit so I can clean this up.'

'It only nicked me,' Tate insisted when Marla pushed her down on a bench. 'It was my own fault.' She blew out a breath and watched Matthew pull himself aboard. 'There's no need to get everyone in an uproar, Lassiter.'

'Let me see the damn thing.' In a move that had Marla blinking in surprise, he shouldered her aside and took Tate's hand himself. He smeared blood away from the shallow puncture with his thumb. 'Doesn't look like it'll need stitches.'

'Of course it doesn't. It's just—' Tate broke off as he snatched the first-aid kit from Ray. The next sound she made was a screech as he doused on antiseptic. 'You're not exactly Doctor Feelgood.'

His own blood pressure was gradually leveling as he was able to get a good look at the cleaned wound. 'Probably scar.' Annoyance was an easier emotion than fear, so he scowled up at her. 'Stupid.'

'Listen, it could have happened to anyone.'

'Not if they were paying attention.'

'I was.'

'You were daydreaming again.'

Ray and Marla exchanged glances as the argument and doctoring continued.

'I suppose you've never taken a bite. Your hands are riddled with scars.'

'We're talking about you.' It infuriated him that those lovely, narrow hands might be marred.

She sniffled, flexed her fingers. The bandage was small, neat and efficient. She'd have swallowed her tongue before saying so. 'Aren't you going to kiss it and make it better?'

'Sure.' In answer, he hauled her to her feet. While her astonished parents looked on, he fixed his mouth on hers in a long, hard, demanding kiss.

When Tate could speak again, she scrupulously cleared her throat. 'You missed,' she said, holding up her bandaged hand.

'No, I didn't. Your mouth's what needs the work, sweetheart.'

231

'Really?' Her eyes narrowed to slits. 'Now you're an expert on what I need?'

'I've always known what you need, Red. Anytime you want to–' Abruptly, he remembered they were a long way from alone. Getting a grip on his temper, he stepped back. 'You might want to take a couple of aspirin to take the edge off the pain.'

Her chin was angled like a sword. 'It doesn't hurt.' She turned and hefted her tanks.

'Where do you think you're going?'

'I'm going back down.'

'The hell you are.'

'Just try to stop me.'

As her husband opened his mouth, Marla patted his arm. 'Let them fight it out, honey,' she murmured. 'Looks like it's been simmering awhile.'

'You want me to try to stop you? Okay.' Letting temper lead, Matthew grabbed the tanks out of her hands and heaved them overboard. 'That ought to do it.'

For a moment, all Tate could manage was an openmouthed gape. 'You idiot. You ignorant son of a bitch. You'd better get your butt in there and haul my tanks in.'

'Get them yourself, you're so anxious to dive.'

It was a small mistake, turning his back on her. And he paid for it. She launched herself at him. At the last instant, he realized her intent. In an effort to save himself, he shifted. But she dodged. The ensuing crash sent them both over the side.

'Shouldn't we do something, Marla?' Ray asked, as they stood at the rail.

'I think they're doing fine. Oh, look, she almost caught him with that punch. And with her bad hand, too.'

Matthew jerked back from the jab at the last moment. But he didn't quite avoid the fist to his midsection. Even slowed by the water, it earned a grunt.

'Cut it out,' he warned, snagging her injured hand by the wrist. 'You're going to hurt yourself.'

'We'll see who gets hurt. Go get my tanks.'

'You're not going down until we're sure you don't have a reaction to the bite.'

'I'll show you my reaction,' she promised and popped him on the chin.

'Okay, that does it.' He dunked her once, then hauled her up with an arm under her chin in a not-so-gentle rescue position. Every time she clawed or cursed at him, he shoved her under again. By the time they reached the ladder, she was wheezing. 'Had enough?'

'Bastard.'

'I guess one more good dunk–'

'Ahoy the *Adventure!*'

Matthew shifted his grip on her as Buck hailed from the *Mermaid*. She was coming in a good clip from her position to the southeast, where Buck and LaRue had been hunting with the sensor.

'Ahoy,' Buck shouted again from the bridge. LaRue leaned smugly on the rail at the bow. 'We got something.'

'Get aboard,' Matthew muttered to Tate and all but carried her up the ladder.

Buck piloted the *Mermaid* neatly alongside, cut her engines. 'Sensors picked up a pile of metal down there. Depth finder shows something, too. Marked it with a buoy – southeast, thirty degrees. Jesus, I think we might've found her.'

Tate took a deep breath. 'I want my tanks, Matthew.' Her eyes glittered as she turned to him. 'Don't even think about stopping me from going down now.'

Chapter Nineteen

THERE WERE SEVERAL ways to range a wreck for return to site. Standard methods included angular measurements taken from three fixed objects with a sextant, compass bearings with a nine-degree spread or simply ranging the wreck by using distant objects as gunsights. Matthew had used them all.

Though Buck had employed a simple buoy marker as a practical target, Matthew knew that had its drawbacks. A buoy could sink or drag. Or more important in this case, a buoy could be seen by other interested parties. For the sake of secrecy, he logged the compass bearings, targeted the distant Mount Nevis as a gunsight, then ordered Buck to move the buoy well away from the estimated position of the wreck.

'We'll keep the buoy on line with that group of trees on that point of the island,' he told Ray, passing over binoculars so that his partner could verify position by the point on Nevis.

They stood on the deck of the *New Adventure*, Matthew in his gear, Ray in cotton slacks and polarized glasses. Ray was already busy with his compass, marking the position for his ship's daily log.

'We're not going to moor here.' Matthew swept his gaze over the sea, noting the pretty catamaran carrying tourists on a snorkeling cruise from Nevis to St. Kitts. The cheerful sound of the ondeck band carried festively across the water. 'We'll use the buoy as a line and move inshore toward Mount Nevis.'

While Ray nodded and scribbled the marks, Matthew continued. 'Tate can make sketches of the bottom, and we can read them as we go.'

Ray slung the binoculars around his neck and studied Matthew's determined face. 'You're thinking of VanDyke.'

'Damn right. If he gets wind of us, he's not going to be able to drop right down on the wreck. He won't know the distances or the landmarks we select, or even if we're diving inshore or offshore of the buoy. That gives him plenty of possibilities to work through.'

'And buys us time,' Ray agreed. 'If this isn't the *Isabella*–'

'We'll soon find out,' Matthew interrupted. He didn't want to speculate. He wanted to know. 'One way or the other, we take precautions.' He pulled on his flippers as he spoke. 'Come on, Red, let's move.'

'I needed to reload my camera.'

'Forget the camera. We're not developing any film.'

'But–'

'Look, all it takes is one clerk passing the word along. Take all the pictures you want, but no film gets sent off until we're finished here. Got the board and graphite pencil?'

'Yes.' Assuming a nonchalantly professional pose, she patted her goody bag.

'Let's dive.'

Before she'd adjusted her mask, he was in the water. 'Impatient, isn't he?' She sent a quick smile toward her parents that revealed only a portion of the excitement humming through her. 'Keep your fingers crossed,' she told them, and splashed into the sea.

Following his trail of bubbles, she dived deep. Her inner sensor told her when she'd passed thirty feet, then forty. She began to make note of the landscape of the seafloor, knowing her assignment was to sketch it carefully. Every bed of sea grass, every twist of coral.

With her graphite pencil, she began to reproduce them, meticulously keeping to scale, marking distances in degrees, resisting the urge to add artistic flourishes. Science was exacting,

235

she reminded herself even as she watched the dance of an angelfish duet.

She saw Matthew signal, and waved back querulously at the interruption. Efficient sketches took time and care, and since he was the one who'd insisted on them rather than photographs, he could damn well wait. When the clang of his knife on his tank intruded again, she cursed him mildly then stowed her board and pencil.

Just like a man, she thought. Always come here, and make it now. Once they surfaced, she'd tell him just what she thought of the arrangement. And then …

Her thoughts trailed off, went limp as her suddenly numb fingers as she saw what he was investigating.

The cannon was the lovely pale green of corrosion and alive with colonizing animals. She snatched her camera and recorded it, with Matthew at the mouth. But that didn't make it real. Not until she had touched it with her own hand, felt the solid iron beneath her exploring fingers, did it become real.

Her breath exploded in bubbles when he grabbed her, swung her around. Tate prepared herself for an exuberant embrace, but he was only pointing her toward the rest of the find.

More cannon. This was what the magnetometer had recorded. As Matthew towed her along, she counted four, then six, then eight, spread over the sandy floor in a rough semicircle. Her heart spun into her throat. She knew that cannon often literally pointed to a wreck.

They found her nearly fifty feet south, crushed, battered, and smothered by the drifting sand.

She'd been proud once, Tate thought as she plunged her hand into the sand and felt the soft give of worm-eaten wood. Even regal like the queen she'd been named for. For so long, she'd been lost, a victim of the sea that had come to be a part of its continuity.

Broken, what was left of the *Isabella* – for Tate never doubted it was the *Isabella* – was spread over more than a hundred feet of seabed, buried, encrusted. And waiting.

Her hand was steady enough as she began to sketch again. Matthew was already fanning, so she alternated her drawing with quick snapshots while he stuffed small finds into his lobster bag.

She ran out of boards, worked her pencils down to nubs and used every frame of film. And still, her heart thrummed and jittered.

Once in a lifetime, she thought with an ache in her throat, had become twice.

When he headed back toward her, she smiled, delighted that he would think to bring her a token. He gestured for her to hold out her hand, close her eyes. She rolled them first, but obeyed, only to have them spring open again when a heavy disk was dropped into her palm.

Heavy only because she'd been expecting a coin or a button, she realized. The round, biscuit-shaped object weighed no more than two pounds at her educated guess. But her eyes went wider still at that unmistakable and stunning flash of pure and glorious gold.

He winked at her, signaled for her to put the ingot into her bag, then jerked a thumb toward the surface. She started to object. How could they leave when they had just begun?

But of course, there were others waiting. It jabbed her conscience a bit to realize she'd forgotten everything and everyone but what was here. Matthew's hand closed over hers as they kicked to the surface.

'You're supposed to throw yourself at me now,' he told her with a wicked laugh in his eyes that was more triumph than humor. 'That's what you did eight years ago.'

'I'm much more jaded now.' But she laughed and did exactly what he'd hoped by throwing her arms around him. 'It's her, Matthew. I know it.'

'Yeah, it's her.' He had felt it, known it, as if he had seen the *Isabella* whole, flags flying, as in his dream. 'She's ours now.' He had time to give Tate only a quick kiss before they were hailed. 'We'd better go give them the news. You haven't forgotten how to work an airlift, have you?'

Her lips were still tingling from his. 'I haven't forgotten anything.'

The routine was so familiar. Diving, digging, gathering. Onboard the *Mermaid*, Buck and Marla pounded away at conglomerate, separating pieces of treasure for Tate to examine and record. Each find, from a gold button set with a pink conch pearl to a gold bar a foot long, was meticulously tagged, sketched, photographed and then logged in her portable computer.

Tate put her education and experience to use preserving their finds. She knew that in the fairly shallow Caribbean, a wreck rotted, was further damaged by storm and wave action. The wood would be eaten by teredo worms.

She also knew that the history of the wreck could be read in the very damage it had sustained.

This time, she would see that every scrap brought up was protected. Her responsibility, she felt, toward the past, and the future.

Small, fragile items were stored in water-filled jars to keep them from drying out. Larger pieces would be photographed and sketched underwater, then stockpiled on the bottom. She had cushioned boxes for the fragile, such as onion-skinned bottles she hoped to find. Wooden specimens would be left in a bath to protect against warping in the small tank she'd rigged on the boat deck.

Tate delegated Marla to the position of apprentice chemist. They worked together, with daughter instructing mother. Even artifacts that resisted chemical change were soaked thoroughly in fresh water, then dried. Marla painstakingly sealed everything with a coat of wax. Only gold and silver required no special handling.

It was time-consuming work, but never, to Tate's mind, tedious. This was what she had missed and pined for aboard the *Nomad*. The intimacy, the propriety, and surprise of it all. Every spike and spar was a clue, and a gift from the past.

Ordinance marks on cannonballs corroborated their hopes that they'd found the *Isabella*. Tate added to her log all the information she had on the ship, its voyage, cargo and its fate. Painstakingly, she checked and rechecked the manifests, cross-referencing with each new discovery.

Meanwhile, the airlift was vacuuming off enough sediment to disclose the tattered hull. They dug. She drew. They hauled buckets filled with conglomerate to the surface. Matthew's sonar located the ballast stones before they found them by sight and hand. While Tate worked in the deckhouse and boat deck of the *New Adventure*, her father and LaRue were laboriously searching the ballast for artifacts.

'Honey?' Marla poked her head in. 'Don't you want to take a break? I've finished the waxing.'

'No, I'm fine.' Tate continued to add details to her sketch of a set of jet Rosary beads. 'I can't believe how fast it's going. It's been barely two weeks, and we just keep finding more. Look at this, Mom. Look at the detail on this crucifix.'

'You've cleaned it. I'd have done that.'

'I know, but I couldn't wait.'

Fascinated, Marla leaned over her daughter's shoulder to run a finger along the heavy, carved silver depiction of Christ on the cross. 'It's stunning. You can see the sinew in His arms and legs, count each wound.'

'It's too fine to have belonged to a servant. You see, each decade is perfectly matched, and the silver work is first rate. It's masculine,' she mused. 'A man's piece. One of the officers, perhaps, or maybe a rich priest on his way back to Cuba. I wonder if he held it, prayed with it as the ship went down.'

'Why aren't you happy, Tate?'

'Hmm?' She'd been dreaming again, Tate realized. Brooding. 'Oh, I was thinking of the *Santa Marguerite*. She was salvageable. I mean the wreck itself could have been preserved with enough time and effort. She was nearly intact. I'd hoped, if we did find the *Isabella*, she would be in a similar state, but she's ruined.'

'But we have so much of her.'

'I know. I'm greedy.' Tate shrugged off the gloom and set her sketch aside. 'I had this wild notion we could raise her, the way my team raised the Phoenician ship a few years ago. Now, I have to be content with the pieces the storm and time have left behind.' She toyed with her pencil and tried not to think about the amulet.

No one spoke of it now. Superstition, she supposed. Angelique's Curse was on everyone's mind, as VanDyke was. Sooner or later, she was afraid both would have to be dealt with.

'I'll let you get back to work, dear. I'm heading over to the *Mermaid* to work with Buck.' Marla smiled.

'I'll swim over later and see what you've come up with.'

Tate turned back to her keyboard to log in the Rosary. Within twenty minutes, she was lost in an examination of a gold necklace. Its bird in flight pendant had survived the centuries, the tossing waves, the abrasive sand. She estimated the relic to be worth easily fifty thousand dollars, and efficiently noted it down and began her sketch.

Matthew watched her for a moment, the competent and graceful way she moved pencil over paper. The way the sun was slanting he could make out her ghostly profile in the reflection of her monitor.

He wanted to press his lips to that spot just at the nape of her neck. He wanted to wrap his arms around her, to have her lean back into him, relaxed, easy and just a little eager for his touch.

But he'd been cautious for the last few weeks. Hoping to move her toward him without tugging. Patience was costing him dozens of restless nights. It seemed only when they were beneath the sea that they moved in concert.

Every part of him was aching for more.

'They sent up a couple of wine jugs. One's intact.'

'Oh.' Startled, she looked around. 'I didn't hear you come in. I thought you were on the *Mermaid*.'

'I was.' But all he'd been able to think about was that she was here, alone. 'Looks like you're keeping up with the haul.'

'I get antsy if I fall behind.' She brushed her braid off her shoulder, hardly aware she'd inched away when he sat beside her. But he was aware, and irritated. 'I can usually get in several hours in the evening, when everyone's turned in.'

He'd seen the light in the deckhouse every night when he'd restlessly paced his own deck. 'Is that why you never come over to the *Mermaid*?'

'It's easier for me to work in one spot.' Much easier not to risk sitting in the moonlight with him on his own turf. 'By my calculations, we're well ahead of where we were in the same amount of time in our excavation of the *Marguerite*. And we haven't hit the mother lode.'

He leaned over to pick up the gold bird, but was more interested in the way her shoulder stiffened when his brushed it. 'How much?'

Her brow creased. It was no more than expected, she supposed, that he could look at such a fabulous relic and think in dollars and cents. 'At least fifty thousand, conservatively.'

'Yeah.' With his eyes on hers, he jiggled the necklace in his hand. 'That ought to keep us afloat.'

'That's hardly the issue.' Possessively, she took the necklace back, laid it gently on the padded cloth she had covering her worktable.

'What is the issue, Red?'

'I'm not going to waste my time discussing that with you, but there is something we need to talk about.' She shifted, angling herself so that she could face him and still keep a fair distance.

'We could talk about it over dinner.' He trailed a fingertip down her shoulder. 'We haven't taken a break in more than two weeks. Why don't we take another run over to Nevis tonight?'

'Let's not cloud business with your libido, Lassiter.'

'I can manage both.' He picked up her hand, kissed her fingers, then the small scar the moray had given her. 'Can you?'

'I believe I have been.' But she drew her hand free, just to be safe. 'I've given this a lot of thought,' she began. 'We missed our chance to preserve the *Marguerite*. The *Isabella* is badly broken up, but we still have the opportunity to salvage some of her.'

'Isn't that what we're doing?'

'I don't mean just her cargo, I mean her. There are treatments to preserve ships' timbers, prevent their shrinking in open air. She can even be partially reconstructed. I need polyethylene glycol.'

'I don't happen to have any on hand.'

'Don't be cute, Matthew. Planks immersed in a bath of that solution are permeated with it. Even wood riddled with marine borers can be preserved. I want to call Hayden, ask him to get what's needed, and to come and help me salvage the ship.'

'Forget it.'

'What do you mean forget it? She's an important find, Matthew.'

'She's our find,' he tossed back. 'No way in hell I'm sharing her with some college professor.'

'He's not some college professor. Hayden Deel is a brilliant marine archeologist. One who's dedicated himself to study and preservation.'

'I don't give a damn what he's dedicated to, he's not coming in on this deal.'

'That's the bottom line, isn't it? The deal.' Disgusted, she shoved away so that she could scoot around the worktable and stand. 'I'm not asking for him to have a share of your all-important booty. He wouldn't expect it. Some of us don't measure everything in dollars.'

'Easy for you to say when you've never had to scrape one together. You always had Mom and Dad to fall back on, a nice cozy home with supper on the stove.'

Anger paled her cheeks. 'I made my way, Lassiter. On my own. If you'd ever bothered to think past the next wreck, you might have more than the loose change rattling around in your pocket. Now all you can think about is cashing in and living the good life. There's more to this expedition than auctioning artifacts.'

'Fine, when we've auctioned those artifacts, you can do whatever the hell you want, with whoever you want.' He'd damn well kill anyone who touched her. 'But until then, you don't contact anyone.'

'That's all it is to you, isn't it?' She slapped her palms on the table, leaning forward until her angry eyes were level with his. 'Just the money matters.'

'You don't know what matters to me. You never did.'

'I thought you'd changed, just a little. I thought finding the *Isabella* meant more to you than what you could take from her.' Straightening again, Tate shook her head. 'I can't believe I could be so wrong about you twice.'

'Looks like you can.' He pushed away from the table. 'You always accuse me of being self-involved, Tate, but what about you? You're so wrapped up in what you want, the way you want it, even if it blocks off what you feel.'

Driven, he grabbed her arms, dragged her against him. 'What do you feel? Damn it, what do you feel?' he repeated and closed his mouth over hers.

Too much, she thought as her heart went spinning. Too painfully much. 'That isn't the answer,' she managed.

'It's one of them. Forget the *Isabella*, the amulet, your god-damn Hayden.' His eyes were dark and fierce. 'Answer that one question. How do you feel?'

'Hurt!' she shouted over quick, useless tears. 'Confused. Needy. Yes, I have feelings, damn you, Matthew, and you stir them up every time you touch me. Is that what you want to hear?'

'It'll do. Pack a bag.'

He released her so suddenly, she stumbled. 'What?'

'Pack a bag. You're coming with me.'

'I – what? Where?'

'The hell with the bag.' She'd told him what he'd wanted to hear, and he wasn't going to let her rethink it. Not this time. He grabbed her hand again and pulled her on deck. Before she had a clue what he was planning, he'd scooped her into his arms and was lowering her over the rail into the tender.

'Have you lost your mind?'

'I should have lost it weeks ago. I'm taking her to Nevis,' he shouted to the *Mermaid*. 'We'll be back in the morning.'

'In the morning.' Shading her eyes, Marla stared at her daughter. 'Tate?'

'He's lost his mind,' Tate called out, but was forced to sit when Matthew leapt nimbly down. 'I'm not going with you,' she began, but was drowned out by the tender's engine. 'Stop the boat right now, or I'll just go overboard.'

'I'll pull you back,' he said grimly. 'You'll just get wet.'

'If you think I'm going to spend the night with you on Nevis–' She broke off when he whipped his head around. He looked too dangerous for arguments. 'Matthew,' she said more calmly. 'Get ahold of yourself. We had a disagreement, this is no way to settle it.' Her breath hitched when he cut the engine back. For one humming moment, she wondered if he would simply pitch her over the side.

'It's long past time we finish what we started eight years ago. I want you, and you've just said you want me right back. You've had plenty of time to think about it. Until we settle this, it's going to keep getting in the way.' His hand ached from his rough grip on the tiller. 'You look at me, Tate, and you tell me you didn't mean what you said, that it doesn't affect you, and everything we're doing here, and I'll turn around and go back. That'll be the end of it.'

Shaken, she dragged a hand through her tousled bangs. He'd shanghaied her, tossed her into a boat, and now he was putting the choice back in her hands. 'You expect me to sit here like this and discuss the effects of sexual attraction.'

'No, I expect you to say yes or no.'

She looked back toward the *Mermaid*, where her mother still stood at the rail. Then toward the smoky peak of Nevis. Oh, hell.

'Matthew, we don't have any clothes, luggage, we don't have a room.'

'Is that a yes?'

She opened her mouth, heard herself babble. 'This is crazy.'

'That's a yes,' he decided, and gunned the engine. He didn't speak to her again. They reached the pier, docked. As they crossed the beach at arm's length, he pointed to an empty lounge chair. 'Sit,' he told her. 'I'll be back.'

Too bemused to argue, she sat, staring at her bare feet, offering the wandering waitress who stopped by with a tray a vague shake of her head and a baffled smile at the offer of a drink.

Tate looked out to sea, but the *Mermaid* and the *New Adventure* were beyond sight. It seemed she'd cut her line.

If this was an answer, she could no longer think of the question. But when Matthew came back, held out his hand, she took it. They walked in silence through the gardens, across the slope of green lawn.

He unlocked a sliding glass door, pulled it closed behind them and flipped the latch.

The room was bright, airy, dreamy in pastels. The bed was neatly made, plumped with generous pillows. She stared at it, jerking only once when he pulled the blinds and tossed the room into shadows.

'Matthew—'

'We'll talk later.' He reached behind her to undo her braid. He wanted her hair loose, flowing through his fingers.

She closed her eyes and would have sworn the floor tilted beneath her feet. 'And if this is a mistake?'

'Haven't you ever made one?'

His grin flashed, and she found herself smiling in response. 'One or two. But—'

'Later.' He lowered his head and found her lips.

He'd been sure he needed to dive into her, the way he sometimes needed to dive into the sea, as if to save, or at least to find, his sanity. His hands had itched to tug at her clothes, to touch the skin beneath and possess what he'd once given up.

But the hot-edged hunger that had driven him to bring her here mellowed as her taste flowed through him. As sweet as yesterday, as fresh as the instant. Love, never quite conquered, swarmed through him in triumph.

'Let me see you,' he murmured. 'I've waited so long to see you.'

Lightly, gently, mindful of her trembling, he loosened her blouse, slipped it aside. She was pale ivory and soft satin beneath, a delicate feast for hands and eyes.

'All of you.' As his mouth skimmed over her bare shoulder, he tugged at her shorts, at the practical swatch of cotton under them.

His mermaid, he thought, almost dizzy with discovery. So slim and white and beautiful.

'Matthew.' She dragged his shirt over his head, desperate for flesh to find flesh. 'Touch me. I need you to touch me.'

With those words humming in his head, he lowered her to the bed and quietly, cleverly, pleasured them both.

Tenderness was so unexpected. So seductive. She had seen it once, hidden in the brash young man she had fallen in love with. But to find it now, after so long, was a treasure. His hands brushed and stroked and aroused while his mouth patiently swallowed her sighs.

Her own exploring fingers found muscle and scar, skin that heated under her curious caress. She tasted it, letting her lips and tongue skim over that flesh and savor the flavor of man and sea.

So she went dreaming, floating on a sea of shifting passions, thrilling to his murmurs of pleasure as he traveled over her. She arched to meet him, shuddering with delight when his mouth closed over her breast. So hot, so firm, so exquisitely controlled. All the while his hands moved steadily over her, sending tiny, eager pulses soaring.

When her sea began to toss, he soothed her back from the edge, teased her up again to the narrow verge until her breath came in gasps and she would have begged had she had the power. Storms brewed inside her so that the air was hot and heavy and throbbed with the threat.

He watched her, fascinated by the rapid flickers of pleasure, confusion and finally desperation on her face. His own mind was reeling when he sent her up and flying. His groan merged with hers as he felt her body tighten and shudder into wild release.

Fighting against a vicious slap of need, he closed his mouth over hers. When her breath began to settle, he nudged her gently, devastatingly over the edge again, into the tempest.

She couldn't stop the shudders. It seemed her body would break apart. So she clung to him as wave after wave of sensation battered her. She had ridden out a hurricane in the Indian Ocean, crawled through a blinding sandstorm thirty feet beneath the sea. She had felt the heat and need of a man's body meshed mindlessly with hers.

But nothing had touched her, stirred her blood or enticed her mind like this long, relentless loving. She had no secrets left to hide, no pride under which she might have buried them.

Whatever she was, whatever he wanted from her, was there for him. Weak and wrecked and willing, she offered.

He slipped inside her slowly, savoring. Now he trembled as she did, resting his brow on hers as she took him deep, held him fast.

'Tate.' Emotions erupted inside him. 'Just this,' he whispered. 'Just you.'

His hands sought hers, fingers locking. He rocked inside her, struggling to keep the pace easy, to draw out the moment. He could feel his heart thudding in his chest, the blood that pounded, the deliriously soft, wet give of her.

Her nails dug into his shoulders, her body bucked and jerked. A sob tore from her throat and ended on his name.

Finally, when he was so steeped in her he'd lost himself, he dived.

While the sun lowered in the West Indian sky, VanDyke sipped Napoleon brandy thousands of miles away. He had the latest report on the activities of the Beaumont-Lassiter expedition on his desk.

It far from satisfied him.

From all appearances, they were still exploring the remains of the *Marguerite*. None of his contacts on St. Kitts or Nevis knew anything of importance. A busman's holiday, the report indicated, but VanDyke wasn't convinced.

His instincts were humming.

Perhaps it was time he followed them, he considered. A little trip to the West Indies might be in order. It would at least provide him with the opportunity to express his displeasure to Tate Beaumont.

And, if the Lassiters weren't going to lead him to Angelique's Curse after all these years, it was time he disposed of them.

Part Three

Future

The future is purchased by the present.
—Samuel Johnson

Chapter Twenty

TATE WONDERED IF it would be awkward. In her experience, mornings after routinely were. She'd been grateful to find herself alone when she'd awakened. It gave her the opportunity to shower and think.

They'd done very little talking the night before, she remembered. Then again, it was hard to hold a reasonable conversation while your brain was being fried with hot, demanding sex.

She let out a breath as she shrugged into the thick bathrobe the hotel provided. As far as the sex went, she thought, new precedents had been set in her body. Matthew Lassiter was going to be a very tough act to follow.

As she reached for the blow-dryer, she caught a glimpse of herself in the foggy mirror. Grinning.

Well, why not? she asked herself. She'd spent an incredible night having her system rocked. And, unless she was very mistaken, doing some rocking of her own.

But the sun was up, and it was time to deal with the reality of what happened next. They had a job to do, and though the tension had been wonderfully diffused, they were still bound to clash when it came to the bottom line.

It didn't seem fair that two people who could meld so gloriously together under one set of circumstances couldn't find solid mutual ground elsewhere.

Compromise, she supposed, sighing over the word, was the only solution.

Once her hair was nearly dry, she ran her tongue over her teeth and wished the pretty room included the amenity of a toothbrush. Worrying over it, she stepped back into the bedroom just as Matthew came through the glass doors.

'Oh, hi.'

'Hi back.' He tossed her a small bag. A glance inside had her shaking her head.

'You read my mind,' she said, taking out a toothbrush.

'Good. Now you can read mine.'

It wasn't difficult as he came to her, picked her up and dropped her back on the bed.

'Matthew, really.'

'Yeah.' Grinning, he stripped off his shirt. 'Really.'

It was an hour later before she could put the toothbrush to use.

'I was wondering,' she began as they crossed the beach toward the pier.

'What were you wondering?'

'How we're going to handle this.'

'This?' He took her hand as they crossed the planks to the tender. 'Being lovers? How much do you want to complicate it?'

'I don't want to complicate it, I just want to—'

'Establish the rules,' he finished, then turned to kiss her in front of several grinning crew of the resort's tour boat. 'Never change, Red.'

Once she was in the tender, he cast off, sent a cheery wave to the crew and kicked the engine to life. He felt incredible.

'Is there something wrong with rules?' she asked.

He grinned again, turned the boat skillfully. 'I'm crazy about you.'

That tugged a little too acutely at her heart. 'That's rule number one. Let's not confuse physical attraction and compatibility.'

'With?'

'Anything.'

'I've always been crazy about you.'

'I mean it, Matthew.'

'I can see you do.' And it stung. But he wasn't going to allow anything to dim his mood, or to wither the hope he'd begun to nourish while she'd slept beside him. 'Okay, how's this? I want to make love with you at every possible opportunity. Is that better?'

Her insides went liquid at the possibility, but she kept her voice brisk. 'It may be more honest, but it's hardly practical. There are six of us on two boats.'

'So, we'll be inventive. You up to diving this morning?'

'Of course I am.'

To entertain himself, he studied her. Windblown, tousled, barefoot. 'I wonder what it would be like to get you naked underwater.' He held up a hand. 'Just kidding. For now.'

If he thought the idea shocked her, he was wrong. But before she fantasized about it too deeply, she wanted to set the record straight. 'Matthew, there are still issues we have to resolve.'

He slowed the tender. Damned if she wasn't going to pick at it until she managed to spoil the mood. 'You want to get back to the idea of calling in your associate, or whatever he was to you.'

'Hayden would be invaluable on a project like this, if he's willing to take the time.'

'My answer stands, Tate. Listen to me before you start pissing me off again. We can't risk it.'

'Risk involving one of the top scientists in the field?'

'Risk VanDyke getting wind of it.'

'You're paranoid about this,' she said impatiently. 'Hayden understands the necessity for discretion.'

'Hayden worked for Trident.'

Her chin shot up. 'So did I. I'm sure Hayden was as unaware of the politics as I was. And even if he has been associated with VanDyke, he'd say nothing to anyone if I asked him.'

'You want to take the chance of losing it all again?'

She started to speak, hesitated because she was certain he was speaking about more than the hunt. 'No,' she said quietly. 'I don't. We'll table calling Hayden for now, but it's something I feel strongly about.'

'Once we've played her out, you can call every scientist you know. I'll even help you bring her up piece by piece if that's what you want.'

She stared, speechless. 'You would?'

He cut the engine with a jerk of the hand as they came alongside the *New Adventure*. 'You don't get it, do you, Red? Even now.'

Baffled, she lifted a hand toward his. 'Matthew.'

'Work on it,' he snapped out, and jerked a thumb toward the ladder. 'And be ready to dive in twenty minutes.'

Women, he thought as he steered the tender toward the *Mermaid*. They were supposed to be the sensitive, emotional ones. What a joke. There he'd been, all but dribbling with love like a sap and all she could talk about were rules and science.

LaRue, gold tooth gleaming, caught the line Matthew heaved to secure the tender. 'So, *mon ami*, you feel refreshed this morning, eh?'

'Cram it,' Matthew suggested. He landed lightly on deck, stripping off his shirt as he went. 'Save the comments. I want coffee.'

Not bothering to hide the grin, LaRue strolled toward the galley. 'Me, when I spend the night with a woman we both smile in the morning.'

'Keep it up,' Matthew muttered, checking his gear. 'You'll lose another tooth.' After grabbing swimming trunks, he moved to the port side.

She'd gone to bed with him, he thought, bitterly. She'd let him have her until they had both been delirious. And she still thought he was one small step up from slime. He tugged off his shorts, yanked on his trunks. What the hell kind of woman was she?

When he stalked back for his wetsuit, Buck was waiting.

'Just hold on a minute, boy.' After a night of soul-searching and worry, Buck was primed. He jabbed a finger in Matthew's chest. 'You've got some explaining to do.'

'What I've got is work to do. Get the airlift ready.'

'I never interfered with that – that hormone part of your life.' To keep Matthew in place, Buck jabbed again. 'Figured you knew what was what. But when you start taking advantage of that sweet little girl.'

'Sweet,' Matthew interrupted. 'Oh yeah, she's real sweet when she's tearing strips off you or kicking your guts out.' He grabbed his wetsuit and sat to begin the process of stretching it over his legs. 'What goes on between me and Tate isn't any of your business.'

'Hell it isn't. We're all part of a team, and her daddy's the best friend I ever had.' Buck rubbed a hand over his mouth and wished actively for a drink so that he could slide painlessly through the rest of the lecture. 'I ain't saying a man don't have needs, and maybe it ain't easy for you being out here all these weeks without any way to meet them.'

Eyes narrowed against the sun, Matthew stood to work the suit to his hips. 'I got a hand if that's all I need.'

Buck scowled. He didn't like talking about such matters. But he had a duty. 'Then why the hell didn't you use it instead of using Tate? I told you this eight years ago, and I'll tell you again. She ain't no throwaway, boy, and I'm not going to stand around–'

'I didn't use her, goddamn it.' He jammed an arm through the sleeve. 'I'm in love with her.'

'Don't you–' Buck stopped, blinked and decided he'd be better off sitting down. He waited, getting his bearings, while Matthew grabbed the coffee LaRue brought out. 'You mean that?'

'Just get off my back.'

Buck looked toward LaRue, who was busying himself studying the compressor. 'Look, Matthew, I don't know much about that kind of thing, but … Well, Jesus, when did that happen?'

'About eight years ago.' Most of his anger drained, but the tension remained fierce in his shoulders. 'Don't hassle me about this, Buck. Did you get the weather report?'

'Yeah, yeah. We got no problem.' Knowing he was out of his depth, Buck rose awkwardly to help Matthew with his tanks. 'Ray and the Canadian brought up some porcelain after you went ashore. Marla was going to clean it up.'

'Fine. Signal the *Adventure*, LaRue. I want to get started.'

'Better to finish,' LaRue commented, but walked to starboard to send up the hail.

*

'Of course I'm all right.' Tate strapped on her diving knife and tried to reassure her mother. 'I'm sorry if you were worried.'

'I wasn't worried, exactly. More concerned. I know Matthew would never hurt you.'

'Wouldn't he?' Tate mumbled.

'Oh, honey.' Marla gathered her close for a quick, hard hug. 'You're a grown woman. I know that. And I know that you're sensible and careful and responsible. All the things you should be. But are you happy?'

'I don't know.' Wishing she did, Tate hitched on her tanks, tugged the strap snug. 'I haven't figured that out.' She glanced up at LaRue's hail. 'Matthew isn't an easy man to understand.' Sighing, she hooked on her weight belt. 'But I can handle it. And I can handle him.' She pulled on her flippers and frowned. 'Dad's not going to do anything crazy about this, is he?'

With a light laugh, Marla offered Tate her face mask. '*I* can handle *him*.' She lifted her gaze, looked across the water to where Matthew stood on deck. 'Matthew Lassiter is an attractive and intriguing man, Tate. There are pockets in him the right woman could plumb.'

'I'm not interested in plumbing Lassiter's pockets.' Tate adjusted her mask, then grinned. 'But I wouldn't mind getting my hands on him again.'

He didn't give her much of an opportunity. The instant they were down at the wreck, he had the airlift sweeping. He worked fast and hard. At times the sand, shells and debris machine-gunned over her back and shoulders. She had to scramble to keep up with his progress, shifting through the fallout, filling buckets, tugging on the line that would signal Buck to haul them up. He gave her little time to delight in the finds.

A chunk of conglomerate struck her shoulder hard enough to bruise. Rather than wincing over the sting, she soothed herself by cursing him as she reached for the calcified form. The blackened silver coins fused together in an insane sculpture changed her mood. Swimming through the murk, she rapped sharply on Matthew's tank.

He turned, easing back when she stuck the conglomerate in his face in triumph. He barely glanced at it. With a watery shrug, he went back to work.

What the devil was the matter with him? she wondered, and dropped the monied find in a bucket. He should have grinned, tugged her hair, touched her face. Something. Instead, he was working like a maniac without any of the pleasure that always flowed through their partnership.

She thought he was only interested in money; meanwhile, Matthew fumed and played the airlift over the sand. Did she really believe a hunk of silver would make him rear up and dance? She could keep every fucking coin as far as he was concerned. Turn every last one of them over to her precious dream museum or her precious Hayden Deel.

He'd wanted her, damn it. But he hadn't known sex without her love, and goddamn it, her respect, would be hollow. Would leave him hollow.

Well, now he knew. That left him with only one goal. Angelique's Curse. He'd search every inch of sand, every crevice, every foot of coral. And when he had it, he'd take his revenge on his father's killer.

Revenge, Matthew decided, was a more satisfying goal than the love of a woman. God knew, it couldn't hurt as much to fail.

He worked until his arms sang with fatigue, and his mind went numb with the monotony of it. Then the pipe whisked away sand, and he saw that first stunning flash of gold.

He drew the pipe back, glanced toward Tate. He could see she was scrambling through the cloudy water, her eyes sharp behind her mask, even though Matthew could sense the dragging fatigue in her movements.

He'd worked her too hard, and he knew it. Yet not once had she asked him to stop, or slow down. Has pride always been our problem? he wondered, then looked back at the shining coins, tossed like a god's careless pocket change on the seafloor.

Smiling, he turned the pipe so that it would suck the coins. They flew back, clinking against Tate's tanks, bulleting against her back. He saw the moment the first glint caught her eye, watched her hand dart. She scooped up doubloons like a child scoops up candy from a shattered piñata.

And she turned to him. It soothed his edgy heart that she would seek his face with her hands full of old gold.

He grinned as she swam toward him, tugged the neck of his suit open just enough to slip coins down his suit. Her eyes brimmed with laughter as he turned the pipe aside. Curious fish watched them wrestle, spin, then clumsily embrace.

Matthew jerked a thumb toward the surface, but she shook her head, pointed toward the airlift. With a nod, he shouldered it again while she scooped handfuls of coins from the sand to the bucket.

She had filled two to overflowing, and was happily exhausted when she spotted the pouch. It had been velvet and was tattered and worn. Even as her fingers touched it, the corners crumbled in her hand. Through the thready hole, stars fell.

Her breath literally stopped. With a trembling hand, she reached down and lifted the necklace. Diamonds and sapphires exploded through the murk. It was three strands, ridiculously heavy and ornate. The gems had held their fire through the centuries and flashed now before her dazzled eyes.

Stunned, she held it out to Matthew.

For one numbing moment, he thought they'd found it. He would have sworn he saw the amulet dripping from her hands, felt the power humming from the bloody stone. But when he touched it himself, it changed. Priceless, sumptuous, it was. But it held no magic. In a careless gesture, he tossed it over her head so that gems sparkled against her snug, dark suit.

This time when he signaled to surface, she nodded. She gave a tug on the ropes. Together they followed the buckets.

'We found the mother lode.' Exhaustion forgotten, Tate reached out for him as they broke the surface.

'I don't think there's any doubt of that.'

'Matthew.' Reverently, she slipped her fingers under the necklace. 'It's real.'

'Looks good on you.' He closed a hand over hers. 'You still bring me luck, Tate.'

'Holy God Almighty!' came the shout from the *Mermaid*. 'We got gold here, Ray,' Buck yelled. 'We got ourselves buckets of gold.'

Tate grinned and squeezed Matthew's hand. 'Let's go let them pat us on the back.'

'Good idea. I was thinking' – he kicked lazily toward the *Mermaid* – 'if I were to swim over, say about midnight, go up to the bridge. There's a lock on that door.'

She reached for the ladder ahead of him. 'Now, that's a good idea.'

Within two days, they had hauled up over a million dollars in gold. There were jewels that Tate was struggling to appraise and catalogue. The more stunning their success, the more precautions they took.

They moored the boats more than a hundred feet from the site, and Buck made a show of fishing off the bow at least twice a day when the tour boats passed within hailing distance. Tate took countless rolls of film and stored them. She sketched, and filed the drawings away.

She knew her dream of a museum was almost within her grasp. There would be articles to be written, papers to be published, interviews. She and her father debated plans and ideas. To Matthew, she said nothing of her hopes. His dreams, she knew, were different from hers. They worked together, hunted together. In the quiet of midnight, they made restless love on a padded blanket.

And if he sometimes seemed moody, if she would catch him studying her with unreadable eyes, she told herself they'd reached their compromise.

The expedition, and the quiet flow of spring into summer, couldn't have been more perfect.

LaRue strolled, whistling, out of the deckhouse. He paused a moment, watching Buck and Marla hammer conglomerate. He admired the very attractive Mrs. Beaumont. Not only for her looks and slim, lovely body, but for her seamless class. The women who had flowed in and out of LaRue's life had been interesting, intriguing, but very rarely had they been classy.

Even sweaty and grimy-handed, the pedigreed Southern belle shone through.

It was a pity the woman was married, he thought. One of the few rules LaRue never broke was to seduce a married woman.

'I must take the tender,' he announced. 'We need supplies.'

'Oh.' Marla sat back on her heels, brushed beads of perspiration from her brow. 'Are you going to St. Kitts, LaRue? I was hoping to run in myself. I could really use some fresh eggs and fruit.'

'I would be happy to pick up whatever you would like.'

'Actually …' She offered him her most charming smile. 'I'd love to go ashore for a little while. If you wouldn't mind the company.'

His smile flashed as he quickly adjusted his plans. '*Ma chère* Marla, it would be my greatest pleasure.'

'Could you wait just a few minutes while I clean up?'

'My time is your time.'

All chivalry, he assisted her into the tender, watched her efficiently zip across the distance to the *New Adventure*. Nothing, he knew, would induce the lovely Mrs. Beaumont to swim even a few feet.

'You're wasting your charm on her, Frenchie,' Buck grumbled and whacked his hammer.

'But, *mon ami*, I have so much to spare.' Amused, LaRue glanced back. 'And what would you like me to bring you back from the island?'

A bottle of Black Jack, Buck thought, nearly tasting that first shock of whiskey in his throat. 'I don't need nothing.'

'As you wish.' He patted his pocket where his tobacco was stashed, then wandered back to the rail. 'Ah, here comes my lovely shopping companion. *A bientôt.*'

Gallantly, LaRue took the tiller, executed a sweeping turn so that Marla could wave to Ray before they cruised toward St. Kitts.

'I really appreciate this, LaRue. Ray's so wrapped up with his charts and inventory I didn't have the heart to ask him to run me in.' Delighted with the prospect of poking through markets, she lifted her face to the wind. 'And everyone's so busy.'

'You work very hard yourself, Marla.'

'It hardly seems like work. Now, the diving.' She rolled her eyes. 'That's work. You enjoy it, though.'

'Matthew is an excellent teacher. After so many years on the water, it's become a pleasure for me to explore beneath. Ray is the best of diving partners.'

'He's always loved it. Now and again, he still tries to convince me to try it. I actually tried snorkeling once. The reefs off Cozumel were very exciting, but I forgot myself and paddled out a bit. Before I knew it, I was looking down at open water. It's the oddest sensation.' She shuddered. 'A kind of vertigo.' Amused at herself, she patted the life jacket she'd strapped on. 'I'll stick with boats.'

'It's a shame you can't see for yourself the *Isabella*.'

'With all the sketches Tate's done, I feel as though I have. What will you do with your share, LaRue? Will you go back to Canada?'

'Spare me. Such cold.' He studied the shoreline in the distance. White sand, swaying palms. 'Me, I prefer a warmer clime.

258

Perhaps I will build a home here, and look down on the water. Or sail the world.' He grinned at her. 'But whatever, I will enjoy being a rich man.'

It was, after all, a fine ambition.

Once he'd docked the boat, he escorted Marla into town, charmingly insisted on paying for their cab. Enjoying himself, he strolled through fruit and vegetable stands with her.

'Would you mind terribly if I took a turn through a couple shops, LaRue? I'm ashamed to admit such a female failing, but I'm feeling deprived. I'd just love to look at some trinkets. And I do need to buy some more tapes for my camcorder.'

'Then you must. I would like nothing more than to go with you, but I have an errand or two to take care of myself. Is it convenient to meet you here, in, oh, forty minutes?'

'That would be perfect.'

'Until then.' He took her hand, kissed it charmingly, then ambled off.

As soon as he was out of sight, he slipped into the lobby of a small hotel. He needed the privacy of a phone booth, and settled inside. The number he needed was inside his head. Such things were dangerous to write down for other eyes to see.

He waited patiently, humming to himself as the operator connected the call. Collect, of course. He sneered as the pompous voice announced, 'VanDyke residence.'

'I have a collect call for Silas VanDyke from a Mr. LaRue. Will you accept the charges?'

'One moment, please.'

'One moment, please,' the operator repeated in her lovely island voice for LaRue's benefit.

'I have nothing but time, mademoiselle.' To pass it, he rolled a cigarette.

'This is VanDyke, I'll accept the charges.'

'Thank you. Go ahead, Mr. LaRue.'

'*Bonjour*, Mr. VanDyke, you are, I hope, well?'

'Where are you calling from?'

'The lobby of a little hotel on St. Kitts. The weather is quite wonderful.'

'The rest of them?'

'The lovely Mrs. Beaumont is souvenir shopping. The others are at sea.'

'What are they looking for? The *Marguerite* is played out. I saw to it personally.'

'So she is. You left little even for the worms. Tate was very upset.'

'Was she?' A trace of malevolent pleasure crept into his voice. 'She should have stayed where I put her. But that's another problem to be dealt with. I want a full report, LaRue. I'm paying you very well to keep tabs on the Lassiters.'

'And I'm delighted to do so. You may be interested to know that Buck has gone on the wagon. He suffers, but he's yet to reach for a bottle.'

'He will.'

'Perhaps.' LaRue blew out smoke, watched it curl toward the top of the booth. 'He doesn't dive. When others do, he bites his nails and sweats. You might be interested that Matthew and Tate are lovers. They rendezvous nightly.'

'I'm disappointed in her taste.' The lovely, cultured voice tightened. 'Gossip is entertaining, LaRue, but I don't like to pay for it. How long do they intend to stay with the *Marguerite*?'

'We left the *Marguerite* weeks ago.'

The pause was brief. 'Weeks ago, and you didn't bother to inform me?'

'I have, as I always have, relied on my own instincts. I enjoy dramatic timing, *mon ami*. Now it seems more appropriate to tell you we have found the wreck of the *Isabella*. And, she is rich.' He drew in more fragrant smoke, blew it out. 'My diving companion, Ray Beaumont, believes quite strongly that she holds something most precious.'

'Which is?'

'Angelique's Curse.' LaRue smiled to himself. 'I think it would be wise for you to wire a bonus of one hundred thousand American dollars into my Swiss account. I will check in twenty minutes to see that the transaction has taken place.'

'A hundred thousand dollars, for a fantasy.' But there was a breathlessness in the words that came clearly over the wire.

'When I'm assured the money is in place, I will use the fax from this charming little hotel and send you copies of the documentation Ray has worked so hard and long to gather. I believe you will find it well worth the price. I will contact you again, soon, with our progress. *A bientôt.*'

Very pleased with himself, he hung up before VanDyke could finish the next sentence.

The money would come, LaRue thought. VanDyke was too much the businessman to ignore the investment.

LaRue rubbed his hands together and exited the booth, hoping the hotel ran a little coffee shop where he could pass a quiet twenty minutes.

It was so amusing, he decided, to stir the pot, and watch just how it simmered.

Chapter Twenty-one

She was late. Matthew paced the bridge, telling himself it was ridiculous to feel disappointed that she hadn't been waiting for him. He'd seen the light in the deckhouse when he'd started his swim over. Obviously, she was involved in something. Eventually, her concentration would break, she'd glance at the clock and realize it was after midnight.

Eventually.

He moved quietly to the pilot window again to stare out at the sea and stars.

Like any sailor, he could map the world with those stars. With them, he could find his way to any point of land or body of water. But he had no map, no guide to show him the route to what he coveted most. On that journey, he was blind and without direction.

All of his life it had been helplessness that had shamed him more than any emotion, any failing. He had been helpless to prevent his mother's desertion, his father's murder, Buck's mutilation. And he was helpless now to defend himself against his own heart, and the woman who didn't want it.

He wished he could blame this restlessness that chewed at him on something as simple as sex. But that basic thirst had been slaked. He still wanted her, he couldn't look at her and not want her. Yet it went so far beyond the physical.

He supposed it had always been beyond the physical.

How could he explain that he was a different man with her? Could be a different man if she felt even a shadow for him of what he felt for her. Living without her was possible. He'd done it before and knew he would do it again. But he would never be what he wanted to be, or have what he wanted to have, unless she was part of it.

There was nothing he could do but take what she gave him, and let her go when the time came.

He knew what it was like to exist for the moment. Most of his life had been like that. It was demeaning to realize that one woman could make him yearn for a future, for boundaries and responsibilities.

A woman, he knew, who didn't believe him capable of accepting any responsibility.

There was no way to prove her wrong. They both under-stood that if he found what he was looking for, he would take it. And he would use it. Once he possessed Angelique's Curse, he would lose Tate. There was no way he could hold both of them, and no way he could live with himself if he ignored his debt to his father.

Now, alone, watching the stars mirror themselves on the water, he could hope that the necklace and all it stood for remained buried under the grasping sea.

'I'm sorry.' She came in quickly, her hair flying as she turned to close and lock the door. 'I was sketching the ivory fan and lost track. It's fantastic to realize something so delicate could survive untouched and perfect for all these years.'

She stopped. He was staring at her in the way he some-times did that made her feel awkward and terrifyingly trans-parent. What was in his mind? she wondered. How did he hide those emotions that drove him? It was like looking at a volcano and knowing that far beneath the surface, lava was boiling.

'Are you angry? It's only quarter past.'

'No, I'm not angry.' Those eyes, with all the secrets glinting, held hers relentlessly. 'Do you want some wine?'

263

'You brought wine?' Suddenly nervous, she shook back her hair. 'That's nice.'

'I filched it from LaRue. He picked up some fancy French kind when he went ashore with Marla the other day. It's already opened.' Matthew picked up the bottle and poured two glasses.

'Thanks.' She took the glass and wondered what to do next. Normally, they simply dived to the floor and tore off their clothes, as greedy as children unwrapping gifts. 'There's a storm brewing west of here. It could be trouble.'

'It's still early for hurricanes. Buck's keeping his eye on it, though. Tell me about the fan LaRue brought up this afternoon.'

'It's probably worth two or three thousand. More to a serious collector.'

He reached out to touch her hair. 'Tate, tell me about the fan.'

'Oh. Well.' Off balance, she wandered to the port window. 'It's ivory, sixteen spikes, carved in a swirl pattern that forms a rose in full bloom when it's opened. I'd gauge it at mid-seventeenth century. It was already an heirloom when the *Isabella* went down.'

He twined a lock of her hair around his finger, kept his eyes on hers. 'Who owned it?'

'I don't know.' Sighing, she turned her cheek toward his hand. 'I wondered if it might have belonged to a young bride. It would have been passed down to her. She might have held it on her wedding day, as something old. She'd never use it; it would be too precious to her. But now and again, she'd take it out of the box she kept in her dressing table. She'd open it, run her finger over the rose and think of how happy she'd been when she'd carried it down the aisle.'

'Do women still do that?' Touched by the vision, he took her untasted wine, set it aside. 'Something old, something new?'

'I suppose they do.' Her head fell back as he skimmed his lips along the line of her jaw. 'If they want a traditional wedding. The once-in-a-lifetime white dress and train. The music, the flowers.'

'Is that what you want?'

'I don't–' Her heart stuttered when his mouth cruised over hers. 'I haven't thought about it. Marriage isn't a priority for me.' Pulse quickening, she stroked her hands under his shirt to run them along his back. 'God, I love your body. Make love with me, Matthew.' Greedily, and a little rough, she nuzzled his throat, nibbling the skin. 'Now. Right now.'

If that was all there could be, he'd take it. He'd take her. But she wouldn't forget, by God, she'd never forget it had been he who had stripped away every layer of that logic.

In one fierce move, he wrapped her hair around his hand, used it to yank her head back. As she opened her mouth in surprise at the sudden ruthlessness, he plundered it.

She made a sound in her throat, part protest, part arousal. Her hands came to his shoulders to pry herself free, but his darted up the baggy leg of her shorts. His fingers drove into her and shot her into a shocking and violent orgasm.

Her legs buckled. He took no time for the niceties of a blanket this time, but dragged her to the floor. Even as she gasped for breath, he was on her. His hands and mouth were everywhere, tugging, tearing at her clothes to ravish the flesh beneath.

She writhed beneath him, clawed, but not in defense. Some part of her mind realized that the volcano had finally erupted. She churned in the dark, mindless pleasure as it poured its lethal heat over her. His mouth and tongue were on her, forcing her to accept a new and terrifying level of madness. As voracious as he, she arched against him, felt the hot spurt of her own jittery climax.

'Now.' She wanted to scream it. Desperate, she fumbled for him. 'Oh God, now.'

But he streaked up her body, pinned her hands over her head. When she opened her eyes, the light dazzled them.

'No, you look at me,' he demanded when her lashes fluttered down again. 'You look right at me.' His lungs were burning and the words ground in his throat like glass. But her eyes opened, an unfocused, swimming green. 'Can you think?'

'Matthew.' Her hand strained against his. 'Take me now. I can't stand it.'

'I can.' Linking her wrists in one hand, he cupped the other over her hot center so that she bucked wildly under him. She came again, violently. He bit back his own groan when her arms went to water under his grip. 'Can you think?' he repeated.

But she was beyond words, beyond sight. Her senses were scattered, a tangle of live wires that sparked and sizzled through her system. When he released her hands, she didn't move, but lay defenseless against the next onslaught.

He devoured her, inch by inch, pale flesh, delicate curves. When he could feel himself all but being absorbed into her, when her mouth was as hungrily avid as his again, he thrust into her.

She felt battered and bruised and blissful. His weight pinned her to the unforgiving floor, and she thought vaguely of the aches she would have in the morning. Somehow she found the strength to stroke a hand over his hair.

She felt sorry for every woman who didn't have Matthew Lassiter as a lover.

'I could use that wine,' she managed in a voice that came huskily through a dry throat. 'Any chance you can reach it? Or if not, if you can roll off, I might be able to crawl a few feet.'

He pushed himself up and wondered how he could feel drained, satisfied, pleased and ashamed all at once. He brought both glasses back, sat beside her on the floor.

With effort, she lifted rockily to her elbow and took the glass. A long, cooling sip did a great deal to steady her. 'What,' she asked slowly, 'was that?'

He jerked a shoulder. 'Sex.'

After a long, appreciative breath, she smiled. 'Not that I'm complaining, but it seemed a little more like war.'

'As long as we both won.' Since he'd already drained his glass, he rose to fetch the bottle.

The last thing she'd expected after such wild intimacy was the cool tone. Concerned, she laid a hand on his knee. 'Matthew, is something wrong?'

'No. Everything's dandy.' He tossed back more wine, stared into the glass. 'Sorry if I got too rough.'

'No.' Though she couldn't have said where it had sprung from, tenderness welled inside her. Very gently, she cupped his cheek. 'Matthew …' Words fumbled inside her head, inside her heart. She struggled to choose the ones best suited to what they had together. 'Making love with you is extraordinary, every time. No one's ever …' No, it seemed wise to back off from that. 'I've never,' she corrected, 'felt more free with anyone.' She tried a smile, a lightness. 'I guess it comes from both of us knowing where we stand.'

'Right, we know where we stand.' He cupped the back of her head, held firm as his gaze drilled into hers. 'Sometimes, you can stand in one place too long.'

'I don't know what you mean.'

He pulled her up, crushed his mouth against hers until he tasted his own mistakes. 'Maybe I don't, either. I'd better go.'

'Don't.' Compelled by emotions fighting to be free, she took his hand. 'Don't go, Matthew. I ... it's a nice night for a swim. Will you come with me? I don't want to be without you yet.'

He turned her hand over, pressed his lips to the palm in a way that made her eyes film. 'I don't want to be without you, either.'

All this time, VanDyke thought. All these years, the Lassiters had played him for a fool. It was all clear now.

Unwilling to waste time with sleep, he pored over the papers LaRue had sent him, reading the words again and again until he all but knew them by rote. He had underestimated the Lassiters, he decided, and blamed himself for so careless a mistake.

Too many mistakes, he thought, carefully dabbing at the sweat that beaded above his lip. All because the amulet remained out of reach.

James Lassiter had known where to find Angelique's Curse, and had likely died laughing at his murderer. VanDyke was not a man to be laughed at.

Curling a fist around a jeweled letter opener, he viciously and mindlessly hacked through the creamy upholstery of a Queen Anne occasional chair. Brocade ripped like flesh, sounding like tiny screams as horsehair vomited out. The oval mirror on the wall reflected his face, wild and white, as he stabbed and tore.

His fingers were cramped and aching when the lovely little seat was no more than rags. His breath heaved in and out, sobbing on the air over the sounds of Mozart from the recessed speakers.

Shuddering once, he let the antique weapon drop onto the carpet, stumbled back from his latest work. It was only a chair, he thought as the sweat dried calmly on his skin. Only a thing, easily replaced. To help settle his uneasy stomach, he poured a soothing brandy.

That was better, he assured himself. It was natural for a man to let his temper out, especially a strong man. Holding it in only caused ulcers and headaches and self-doubt.

That's what his father had done, VanDyke recalled. Rather than making him strong, it had weakened him. It seemed he was thinking of his father, and his mother, more and more lately. Remembering how flawed they were, finding comfort in the fact that he had escaped all their weaknesses. No, no, had triumphed over the weaknesses of mind and body.

His mother's brain had betrayed her; his father's heart had killed him. But their son had learned to keep both strong.

Yes, it was better, much better to vent. Sipping, he took a calming turn around his office aboard the *Triumphant*.

Momentary physical release was sometimes necessary, he told himself, pursing his lips as he studied the rags of silken material that were scattered over the floor. It purged the blood.

But a cool head was imperative. And, of course, he rarely lost his.

Perhaps, just perhaps, he admitted, he had been a bit impulsive when he'd killed James Lassiter. But he'd been younger then, less mature. And he really had hated the bastard so.

Yet now to know that even in death James had tricked him … Fury clawed through him again, so ferociously that VanDyke had to close his eyes, struggle through his deep-breathing exercises to prevent himself from hurling the snifter and shattering the lovely Baccarat.

No, the Lassiters would cost him nothing more, he promised himself. Not even the price of a glass of brandy. Settled again, he walked out on deck to let the balm of the night air caress him.

The yacht moved swiftly through the Pacific, Costa Rica to the east.

He'd nearly taken his jet to the West Indies before he'd controlled the impatience. The time it would take to get there by sea would be put to very good use. His plans were already formulating, and with his own man part of Lassiter's team, it was almost like being there himself.

Of course, LaRue was a bit of a nuisance with his periodic demands for bonuses. VanDyke smiled to himself and swirled brandy. Then again, he, too, would be dealt with, after his usefulness had passed.

The ultimate termination of an employee, he thought with a low, long chuckle. And that would be a small but sweet pleasure.

The man had no ties, no family, just as VanDyke preferred his tools. No one would miss a middle-aged French Canadian ship's cook.

Ah, but that little diversion was for later. The real joy would come from disposing of the Lassiters, and their partners. He would use them first, let them dig and dive and work. The effort would give them a sense of satisfaction, the belief that they were deceiving him would delight them.

Oh, he could imagine their laughter, their excited meetings discussing their cleverness. They would be so smug and self-congratulatory that they had had the patience to wait so long when they had known just where to strike.

Matthew had worked eight years, VanDyke mused, in bone-chilling water, doing the kind of salvage work true treasure hunters scoffed at, certain his nemesis would lose interest. To be fair, VanDyke had to admire him for his efforts and long-range view of the prize.

But the prize would never belong to anyone but Silas VanDyke. It was his legacy, his property, his triumph. The owning of it would shove every possession he'd ever had into the shadows.

Once they had the amulet, held the prize in their trembling hands, were filled with the elation of success, it would be so much more satisfying to destroy them.

Chuckling to himself, VanDyke polished off his brandy. In one sharp strike, he shattered the delicate crystal on the rail and let the shards tumble glittering into the water. Not because he was angry, not because he was violent, he mused.

Simply because he could.

The storm came in hard, with sheeting rain and howling wind. Ten-foot seas buffeted both boats and made diving impossible. After a debate and vote, the Lassiter-Beaumont team opted to ride it out. Once she'd accustomed herself to the movement of the boat, Tate settled down with her computer and a jug of hot tea.

There would be no midnight rendezvous tonight, she mused. It surprised her how much the lack disappointed her. Perhaps

269

the storm was a lucky break, she decided. Without realizing it, she'd let herself get entirely too used to having Matthew beside her.

It wasn't wise to become used to anything that included Matthew.

After a great deal of internal debate, she'd convinced herself it was all right, at least safe, to care about him. Affection and attraction didn't have to be a dangerous combination. However much they clashed, however much he tended to irritate her, she liked him. They had too much in common to remain truly at odds.

At least her heart was her own this time around. For that, she was grateful. To care and to want were a far cry from being in love. Logically, practically, sex was more satisfying when a woman felt affection, even friendship for her lover. Just as logically, practically, only a fool loved when the end had already been written.

Matthew would take his share of the *Isabella* and go. Just as she would take hers. It was a pity that what they wanted from that long doomed ship was so diverse. Still, it didn't matter as long as neither interfered with the other's goals.

Frowning, she switched documents so that the article she was drafting out on Angelique's Curse popped on screen.

Legends such as the one surrounding the Maunoir amulet, also known as Angelique's Curse, often have their roots in fact. Though it is illogical to ascribe mystical powers to an object, the legend itself has life. Angelique Maunoir lived in Brittany and was known as the village wise woman, or healer. She did indeed own a jeweled necklace such as described above, a gift from her husband, Etienne, the youngest son of the Count DuTashe. Documentation indicates that she was arrested, charged with witchcraft and executed in October of 1553.

Excerpts from her personal journal relate her story and her intimate thoughts on the eve of her execution. On October the tenth of that year, she was burned at the stake as a witch. Limited available data indicates she was sixteen. It is not indicated that, as was often done to show mercy, she was strangled first rather than burned alive.

On reading her words written the night before her execution, one can speculate on how the legend of Angelique's Curse grew and spread.

NOTE: transcribe last portion of diary.

A deathbed curse, from a woman distraught and desperate? An innocent woman grieving over the loss of her beloved husband, betrayed by her father-in-law and facing a horrible death. Not only her own, but her unborn child's. Such truths lead to myth.

Dissatisfied with her own take on the matter, Tate leaned back and reread. When she reached for her Thermos of tea, she saw Buck in the doorway.

'Well, hi. I thought you were battened down with Matthew and LaRue on the *Mermaid*.'

'Damn Canuk makes me nuts,' Buck grumbled. His yellow slicker ran with water, his thick lenses were fogged with it. 'Thought I'd come over and hang out with Ray.'

'He and Mom are up in the bridge, I think, listening to the weather reports.' Tate poured the tea, held up the half filled lid of the Thermos. She could see that it wasn't just LaRue that had Buck nervous. 'The last I heard, the storm was blowing herself out. We should be clear by midday tomorrow.'

'Maybe.' Buck took the tea, then set it down without tasting it.

Reading him well, Tate pushed back from the monitor. 'Take that wet thing off, Buck, and sit down, will you? I could really use the break and the company.'

'Don't want to mess up your work.'

'Please.' With a laugh, she rose to get another cup from the galley. 'Please mess up my work, just for a few minutes.'

Reassured, he stripped off his dripping slicker. 'I was thinking maybe Ray'd be up for some cards or something. Don't seem to have a lot to do with my time.' He slipped onto the settee, drummed his fingers on the table.

'Feeling restless?' she murmured.

'I know I'm letting the boy down,' he burst out, then flushed and picked up the tea he didn't want.

'That's just not true.' She hoped her basic psych course in college, and her understanding of the man beside her, would guide her instincts. No one spoke of the fact that he didn't

271

dive. Perhaps it was time someone did. 'None of us could get along without you, Buck. Not diving doesn't mean you're not productive or an essential part of the team.'

'Checking equipment, filling tanks, hammering rocks.' He winced. 'Taking videos.'

'Yes.' She leaned forward to lay a hand over his restless one. 'That's as important as going down.'

'I can't go down, Tate. Just can't.' He stared miserably at the table. 'And when I watch the boy go, it dries up the spit in my mouth. I start thinking about taking a drink. Just one.'

'But you don't, do you?'

'Guess I figured out just one'd be the end of me. But it doesn't stop the wanting.' He glanced up. 'I was gonna talk to Ray about this. Didn't mean to hit you with it.'

'I'm glad you did. It gives me the chance to tell you how proud I am of the way you've pulled yourself together. And that I know you're doing it more for Matthew than for anyone else, even yourself.'

'At one time, all we had was each other. Some wouldn't think so, but there were good times. Then I cut him off, or tried to. But he stuck by me. He's like his dad was. He's got loyalty. He's stubborn, and he keeps too much inside. That's the pride working there. James always figured he could handle whatever came, that he could do it on his own. And it killed him.'

He lifted his eyes again. 'I'm afraid the boy's heading the same way.'

'What do you mean?'

'He's got his teeth in this, nothing's going to shake him loose. What he brings up day after day, oh, it's exciting for him. But he's waiting and wanting just one thing.'

'The amulet.'

'It's got hold of him, Tate, just like it got hold of James. It scares me. The closer we get, the more it scares me.'

'Because if he finds it, he'll use it against VanDyke.'

'Fuck VanDyke. Sorry.' He cleared his throat, sipped at the tea. 'I ain't worried about that son of a bitch. That the boy can handle just fine. It's the curse.'

'Oh, Buck.'

'I'm telling you,' he said stubbornly. 'I feel it. It's close.' He looked out the window at the lashing rain. 'We're close. Could be this storm's a warning.'

Struggling not to laugh, Tate folded her hands. 'Now listen to me. I understand the seafaring superstitions, but the reality here is that we're excavating a wreck. This amulet is very likely an artifact of that wreck. With luck and hard work, we'll find it. I'll sketch it and tag it and catalogue it just the way I do every other piece we bring up. It's metal and stone, Buck, with a fascinating and tragic story attached. But that's all it is.'

'Nobody who ever owned it lived to see a happy old age.'

'People often died young, violently and tragically during the sixteenth, seventeenth and eighteenth centuries.' She gave his hand a squeeze and tried another tack. 'Let's say, just for argument's sake, that the amulet does hold some sort of power. Why would it have to be evil? Buck, have you read Angelique's diary? The part your brother copied down?'

'Yeah. She was a witch, and she put a curse on the necklace.'

'She was a sad, grieving and angry woman. She was facing a terrible death, convicted of witchcraft and of murdering her husband, a man she loved. An innocent woman, Buck, helpless to change her fate.' Seeing he was far from convinced, she blew out a breath. 'Damn it, if she'd been a witch, why didn't she just disappear in a puff of smoke or turn her jailers into toads?'

'Don't work that way,' he said stubbornly.

'Fine, it doesn't work that way. So she put a spell or whatever on the necklace. If I read correctly, she cursed those who condemned her, those who would take her last link with her husband through greed. Well, Matthew didn't condemn her, Buck, and he didn't take her necklace. What he may do is find it again, that's all.'

'And when he does, what'll it do to him?' Desperate concern made his eyes glossy and dark. 'That's what eats at me, Tate. What'll it do to him?'

A shiver raced through her. 'I can't answer that.' Surprised at how uneasy she'd become, she picked up her cup and tried to warm her suddenly chilly hands. 'But whatever happens, it will be Matthew's doing, his choosing, not an ancient curse on a piece of jewelry.'

273

Chapter Twenty-two

Long after Buck had gone off to find her father, his words and his worries haunted Tate. She couldn't dismiss them as absurd or mildly hysterical. She understood that the belief itself, the reality of it was what created legends.

And she'd believed once. When she'd been young and soft-hearted and ready to dream, she'd believed in the possibility of magic and myth and mystery. She'd believed in a great many things.

Annoyed with herself, she poured more tea, tepid now as she'd forgotten to close the Thermos. It was foolish to regret a loss of naïveté. Like childhood games, it was something that was set aside with time and knowledge and experience.

She'd learned the reasons behind such legends as Angelique's Curse. Indeed that was part of her fascination for her work. The whys and hows and whos were as important to her as the weight and date and fashion of any artifact she had ever held in her hands.

Innocence and wide eyes were lost perhaps, but her education hadn't diminished her curiosity or her imagination. It had only enhanced it, and given it a channel.

Over the years she, too, had gathered information on Angelique's Curse. Bits and pieces of research she had eventually filed away on disk. More, or so she had thought, out of a sense of organization than curiosity.

It didn't have the renown of the Hope Diamond, or the cachet of the philosopher's stone, yet its story and travels were interesting. Following the trail of any artifact gave a scientist facts, dates and a glimpse of the humanity of history.

From Angelique Maunoir to the count who had condemned her, from the count after his death to his eldest daughter, who had fallen from her horse and broken her neck on the way to a tryst with a lover.

Nearly a century had passed before it had turned up again in verified documentation. In Italy, Tate mused, where it survived a fire that had destroyed its owner's villa and left him a widower. Eventually it had been sold, and traveled to Britain. The merchant who purchased it committed suicide. It came into the hands of a young duchess who apparently wore it happily for thirty years. But when her son inherited the necklace, along with her estate, he drank and gambled away his fortune and died penniless and insane.

And so the necklace had been purchased by Minnefield, who had lost his life on the great Australia reef. The necklace had also been assumed to be lost there, buried in sand and coral.

Until Ray Beaumont had found an old, tattered book and had read of a sailor and an unknown Spanish lady who faced a hurricane aboard the galleon *Isabella*.

Those were the facts, Tate thought now. Death was always cruel, but rarely mysterious. Accidents, fires, illnesses, even poor luck were simply part of the cycle of living. Stones and metal could neither cause nor change it.

But despite all the facts, the scientific data, Buck's fears had translated to her, and had that well-groomed imagination working in overdrive.

Now the storm seemed eerie with its keening wind and lashing waves. Every distant flash of lightning was a warning that nature continued to thrive on possibilities.

The night seemed to warn that certain of those possibilities were best left untapped.

More than ever she wanted to contact Hayden, to call on a fellow scientist to help her put the *Isabella* and its treasures, all of its treasures, back into perspective. She wanted someone to remind her just what it was they had. An archeological find of significant importance. Not a witch's curse that seduced.

But the night was wild and full of voices.

'Tate.'

She had the unpleasant experience of discovering just what it felt like to jump out of her skin. After she'd knocked over her cup, spilled lukewarm tea into her lap, she had the presence of mind to swear as Matthew laughed at her.

'Little jumpy?'

'It's hardly a night for visitors, and you're number two.' She rose to grab a towel from a storage cabinet to mop up the spill. 'Buck's probably upstairs, trying to wrangle a card game. What are you–'

She looked at him for the first time, saw that he was soaking wet. His shirt and worn jeans clung to him and dripped water heedlessly on the floor.

'You swam over? Are you insane?' She was already grabbing more towels as she berated him. 'For Christ's sake, Lassiter, you might have drowned.'

'Didn't.' He stood cooperatively as she rubbed the towel over his hair and muttered at him. 'I had an uncontrollable urge to see you.'

'You're old enough to control your urges. Go to Dad's cabin and get some dry clothes before you catch a chill to go with your insanity.'

'I'm fine.' He took the towel, looped it around her neck and used it to pull her to him. 'You didn't really think a little squall would stop me from keeping our date?'

'I had the mistaken belief that common sense would outweigh lust.'

'Wrong.' His lips curved as they met hers. 'But I wouldn't turn down a drink. Got any whiskey?'

She sighed. 'There's brandy.'

'Good enough.'

'Put a towel on the bench before you sit,' she ordered as she turned into the adjoining galley to locate the bottle and a glass. 'You just left LaRue alone on the *Mermaid*?'

'He's a big boy. The wind's dropping some anyway.' Pumped up by the swim and the storm, he took the brandy, and her hand. 'Want to sit on my lap and neck?'

'No, thanks very much. You're wet.'

Grinning, he tugged her down and nuzzled. 'Now we're both wet.'

She laughed, and found it amazingly easy to give in. 'I guess I should consider the fact that you risked life and limb. Here.' She angled his face with her hand so that her lips could fit nicely over his. On a little murmur of approval, she sank into the kiss. 'Warming up?'

'You could say that. Mmm, come back,' he muttered when she lifted her head.

When he was satisfied, he cuddled her head on his shoulder, smiling as she toyed with the silver disk on the chain around his neck.

'I could see the light in here from the *Mermaid*. I kept thinking, she's in there, working away, and I'm never going to get any sleep.'

Finding it lovely to be snuggled in his lap, she sighed. 'I don't think anyone's going to get very much sleep tonight. I'm glad you're here.'

'Yeah?' His hand slipped nimbly up to cup her breast.

'No, not because of that. I wanted to … mmm.' Her mind slipped quietly out of gear as his thumb teased her nipple through her dampened shirt. 'How is it you always know just where to touch me?'

'I've done a study on it. Why don't you turn off that machine of yours, Red? We'll go lock ourselves in your cabin. I can show you a terrific way to ride out a storm at sea.'

'I'm sure you could.' And it was ridiculously easy for her to envision them tucked into her bunk, riding the waves, and each other. 'I need to talk to you, Matthew.' Greedily she angled her head to give his busy mouth freer access to her throat. 'I never realized I had such a hair trigger sex drive.'

'Looks like you needed my finger on your trigger, sweetheart.'

'Apparently.' Because that idea was more than a little unnerving, she shifted and rose. 'We do have to talk.' Determined to remember her priorities, she took a steadying breath and tugged her shirt back into place. 'I was going to try to find a way to get you alone tomorrow.'

'That sounds promising.'

'I think I'll have a brandy, too.' It would give her a minute to compose herself, she decided. At a safe distance, she poured a second glass, easily adjusting to the sway of the boat. 'Matthew, I'm worried about Buck.'

'He's getting his balance.'

'You mean he's not drinking. Okay that's good, that's important, even if he is facing his problem for you instead of for himself.'

'What are you talking about?'

'Take the blinders off.' She scooted onto the bench from the opposite side. 'He's here and he's dry because of you. He feels he owes you.'

'He doesn't owe me jack,' Matthew said flatly. 'But if it helps keep him from drinking himself to death, that's fine.'

'I agree, to a point. Eventually, he'll have to keep himself sober for himself. That's not going to happen as long as he's so worried about you.'

'About me?' With a half laugh, Matthew sampled the brandy. 'What's he got to be worried about?'

'About you finding Angelique's Curse, and paying for it.'

Annoyed to have the recklessly cheerful mood that had driven him into a stormy sea shattered, he dragged a hand through his wet hair. 'Look, as long as I've partnered with him, he's wanted that damn necklace. He worried about it, sure, but he wanted it. Because my father wanted it.'

'And now you do.'

'That's right.' He knocked back more brandy. 'Now I do.'

'And for what purpose, Matthew? Underlying it all, the nonsense about spells and witches, I really think that's what's eating at Buck.'

'So, now it's nonsense.' He smiled a little. 'You didn't always think so.'

'I used to believe in the Tooth Fairy, too. Listen to me.' With some urgency, she closed her hand over his. 'Buck's not going to feel easy in his mind or his heart as long as the amulet is an issue.'

'Don't ask me to forget it, Tate. Don't ask me to make a choice like that.'

'I'm not.' She sat back, sighed again. 'Even if I could convince you, I have to work on my father, probably LaRue. Even myself.' With a restless movement of her shoulders, she glanced over to the monitor. 'I'm not immune to the fascination, Matthew.'

278

'You've been writing about it.' Intrigued, he nudged at her to get a better look. 'Let me read it.'

'It's not finished. It's rough. I was just–'

'Let me read it,' he repeated, 'I'm not going to grade you on it.'

Huffing a bit because she felt exactly like a schoolgirl facing a quiz, she sat back out of his way.

'How does this thing work?' he asked after a moment. 'I never had much use for computers. How do you turn the page?' Absently, he glanced down as her fingers quickly tapped. 'Got it.'

Thoughtful, he read from beginning to end. 'Pretty cut and dried,' he murmured, and put her back up.

'It's a paper,' she said testily, 'not a romance novel.'

'Until you read between the lines,' he finished, and looked back at her. 'You've been giving it a lot of thought.'

'Of course I have. Everyone has, though nobody talks about it.' With a few expert taps, she saved her file and shut down. 'The fact is I want very much to find the amulet, see it myself, examine it. It would be the find of any professional lifetime. Truthfully, it's been playing on my mind so much that I've revised my entire thesis around it.'

She turned back with a weak smile. 'Myth versus science.'

'What are you asking me, Tate?'

'To reassure Buck, and I guess to reassure me, that finding it will be enough for you. Matthew, you have nothing to prove. If your father loved you even a fraction of the amount that Buck does, he wouldn't want you to ruin your life on some useless vendetta.'

Torn between comforting and convincing, she framed his face in her hands. 'It won't bring him back, give you the years you lost with him. VanDyke's out of your life. You can beat him if that's still important to you just by finding the necklace. Let that be enough.'

He didn't speak for a moment. The war inside was so familiar he barely registered the rip of battle. In the end it was he who broke contact.

'It isn't enough, Tate.'

'Do you really think you could kill him? Even if you managed to get close enough, do you really believe you're capable of taking a life?'

279

His eyes glinted as they sliced to hers. 'You know I am.'

She shivered as her blood chilled. There was no doubt in her mind that the man looking at her now was capable of anything. Even murder.

'You'd ruin your life? And for what?'

He shrugged. 'For what's right. I've ruined it before.'

'That's so incredibly ignorant.' Unable to sit, she shoved out and paced the room. 'If there's a curse on that damned thing, this is it. It blinds people to their better selves. I'm calling Hayden.'

'What the fuck does he have to do with it?'

'I want another scientist here, or at least I want to be able to consult with one. If you won't find a way to re-assure Buck, I will. I can find a way to prove to him that the amulet is just an amulet, and that if and when it's found, it will be treated as a relic. With the scientific community backing me, that necklace will be put in a museum where it belongs.'

'You can toss it back into the sea when I'm done with it,' Matthew told her, and his voice was cold and final. 'You can call a dozen scientists. They're not going to stop me from dealing with VanDyke my way.'

'It always has to be your way, doesn't it?' If it would have done any good, she would have thrown something.

'This time it does. I've been waiting half my life for this.'

'So you'll waste the rest of your life. Not just waste,' she said furiously. 'But throw it away.'

'It's still my life, isn't it?'

'No one's life is theirs alone.' How could he be so blind? she wondered bitterly. How could he turn the beauty of these past weeks into something as ugly as vengeance. 'Can't you stop and think, for just a moment, what it would do to other people if you manage to succeed in this insane idea? What would happen to Buck if you get yourself killed or spend the rest of your miserable life in prison for murder? How do you think I would feel?'

'I don't know, Tate. How would you feel?' He pushed away from the table. 'Why don't you tell me? I'm interested. You're always so goddamn careful not to tell me anything you feel.'

'Don't turn this around on me, make it my responsibility. We're talking about you.'

'Sounds like we're talking about us. You put up the rules from the get-go,' he reminded her. 'No emotions or pretty words cluttering up nice, companionable sex. You didn't want me interfering with your life or your ambitions. Why should I let you interfere with mine?'

'Damn it, you know it's not as cold as that.'

'No?' He lifted a brow. 'It looks like that from where I'm standing. I don't remember you saying any different.'

She was very pale now, her eyes too dark against the white skin. He had to know how he was making everything they had together sound. Everything she'd given to him.

'You know I have feelings for you. I wouldn't sleep with you if I didn't.'

'News to me. Best I can figure, you're just scratching an itch.'

'Bastard.' Stunned by the sting, she'd swung out and slapped him hard before she could stop herself.

His eyes flashed, narrowed, but his voice was icily calm. 'Did that help? Or was that your answer to the question?'

'Don't attribute your own motivations and lack of sensitivity to me,' she shot back, both furious and ashamed. 'Do you think I'd pour out my heart and soul to you the way I did once? Not a chance. Nobody hurts me, especially you.'

'You think you're the only one who got hurt?'

'I know I was.' She jerked at her arm when his fingers wrapped around it. 'You'll never get a second chance to shrug me off again. I loved you, Matthew, with the kind of innocent, unrestricted love that only comes around once. You tossed it back in my face like it was nothing. Now your pride's ruffled because I won't put myself in the position where you can do it again when you're ready to move on. Well, the hell with you.'

'I'm not asking you for a second chance. I know better than that. But you've got no right to ask me to settle for sex then expect me to give up the one thing that's kept me going. I gave you up, now I'm taking what's left.'

'You didn't give me up,' she tossed back. 'You never wanted me.'

'I never wanted anything the way I wanted you. I loved you.' He dragged her painfully to her toes. 'I've always loved you. I cut my own heart out when I sent you away.'

She couldn't breathe, was afraid if she did everything inside her would shatter like glass. 'What do you mean, you sent me away?'

281

'I–' He caught himself. Shaken, appalled, he loosened his grip and stepped back. He needed a minute, he told himself, to get his balance. 'Nothing. It doesn't matter. Digging up old ground doesn't change where we stand now. I won't give you what you want. That's the bottom line.'

She stared at him, one part of her brain fascinated by the way he was able to close off. All those vivid emotions were dimming behind carefully shuttered eyes one by one. No, she thought. Oh no, not this time.

'You started digging this ground, Lassiter. Now we'll finish the excavation.' She balled her unsteady hands into fists. 'Eight years ago you laughed in my face, Matthew. You stood there on that beach and told me that it had all been for fun. Just a way to pass a summer. Was that a lie?'

His gaze never faltered, never changed, never sparked. 'I said it doesn't matter. The past is past.'

'If you really believed that, you wouldn't be so hell-bent on evening the score with VanDyke. Answer me,' she demanded. 'Was it a lie?'

'What the hell was I supposed to do?' he exploded. Outside the windows, the sky erupted in frenzied light. 'Let you throw everything away on some idiotic dream? I didn't have anything to give you. I ruined everything I touched. Christ, we both knew I wasn't good enough, but you were too stupid to admit it.'

Thunder grumbled, a nasty old woman's chuckling.

'But you would have,' he continued. 'And then you'd have hated me. I'd have hated myself.'

Unsteady, she braced a hand on the table. The storm outside was nothing compared to the one pitching inside her. Everything she'd believed, everything that had kept her from looking back in misery was shattered at her feet.

'You broke my heart.'

'I saved your life,' he snapped back. 'Get a picture, Red. I was twenty-four years old, I had no future. I had nothing but an uncle who was going to need every penny I could scrape together, maybe for the rest of my life. You had potential. You had brains, ambitions. All of a sudden, you're talking about ditching college and hooking up with me, like we'd just sail off into the sunset.'

'I never thought that. I wanted to help you. I wanted to be with you.'

'And you'd have ended up saving nickels and wondering what the hell you'd done to your life instead of making something out of it.'

'And you made that choice for me.' Oh, she could breathe now. She could breathe just fine. In fact, the air that filled her lungs was hot and pure. 'You arrogant son of a bitch. I cried myself empty over you.'

'You got over it.'

'Damn right I did.' She could lash back with that and be thankful. 'I got way over it. And if you think I'm going to weep gratefully on your shoulder because you see yourself as some self-sacrificing hero, you're mistaken, Lassiter.'

'I don't see myself as anything but what I am,' he said, wearily now. 'You were the one who saw something that wasn't there.'

'You had no right to make that choice for me. No right to expect me to be grateful for what you did.'

'I don't expect anything.'

'You expect me to believe you're in love with me.'

What the hell, he thought, he'd already ruined it. 'I am in love with you. Pathetic, isn't it? I never got over you. Seeing you again, eight years later, carved a hole in me I've been trying to fill ever since with whatever you'd toss my way. No chance.'

'We had one once.'

'Hell, Tate.' He reached out to rub his thumb over a tear on her cheek. 'We never had a chance. The first time it was too soon. This time it's too late.'

'If you'd been honest with me—'

'You loved me,' he murmured. 'I knew you loved me. You'd never have left me.'

'No.' Her vision blurred with more tears, but she could see so clearly what had been lost. 'I'd never have left you. Now we'll never know what we might have had.' She turned away. 'So, what now?'

'That's up to you.'

'Ah, this time it's up to me.' She wished she could find even one small laugh inside her. 'That's only fair, I suppose. Only this time I don't have all that simple, innocent faith.'

And this time, she realized, she didn't know what to do, except protect herself from being so horribly hurt again.

'I guess the only answer here is to be practical. We can't go back, so we go forward.' She drew a deep breath. 'It would be unfair to the others, and shortsighted, to scuttle the expedition because of something that happened eight years ago. I'm willing to continue.'

He'd never expected otherwise. 'And?'

'And.' She blew out the breath. 'We can't afford to let personal problems undermine the excavation. Under the circumstances, I don't think it's in your best interest or in mine to continue the intimate aspect of our relationship.'

Again, it was no less, and no more than expected. 'All right.'

'This hurts,' she whispered.

He shut his eyes, knowing he couldn't hold her. 'Would you feel better if we switched teams? I can dive with Ray or LaRue.'

'No.' She pressed her lips together before turning back. 'I think the less upheaval, the better. We both have some sorting out to do, but I don't think we have to let it affect the others.' Impatiently, she brushed the heels of her hands over her face to dry it. 'But we can make some excuse to switch if you're uncomfortable ...'

He did laugh. It was such an absurd word for what he was feeling. 'You were always a piece of work, Red. We'll keep things status quo.'

'I'm only trying to make all of this as simple as I can.'

'Fuck.' Nearly undone, he scrubbed his hands over his face. 'Yeah, you go ahead and simplify. We keep the schedule as is, we cut out the sex. How's that for simple?'

'You won't make me fall apart,' she said, terrified she would do just that. 'I'm going to see this through. It'll be interesting to find out if you can do the same.'

'I'm game if you are, sweetheart. I guess that covers it.'

'Not quite. I want to contact Hayden.'

'No.' He lifted a hand before she could spit at him. 'Let's try this. We haven't found the amulet, and can't say that we will. If and when we do, we'll bring up the idea of calling in your backup scientist.'

It was a compromise that made sense, which was why she was instantly suspicious. 'I have your word? When we find it, I can contact another archeologist?'

'Red, when we find it, you can take out an ad in *Science Digest*. Until then, the lid's on.'

'All right. Will you promise to reconsider your plot for revenge?'

'That sounds pretty dramatic for something so straightforward. I'll give you a straightforward answer. No. I lost everything that mattered to me in my life, and VanDyke had a part in all of it. Leave it alone, Tate,' he said before she could speak again. 'The ball started rolling sixteen years ago. You're not going to stop it. Look, I'm tired. I'm going to bed.'

'Matthew.' She waited until he'd stopped at the companion-way and turned back. 'You might consider the idea that rather than your ruining my life, I might have made a difference in yours.'

'You did,' he murmured, and walked out into the dying storm.

Chapter Twenty-three

THE ROUGH CHOP postponed the morning's dive. Tate was grateful to have some time alone, so she closed herself in her cabin with her work.

But work wasn't on her mind.

She indulged herself, lying on her bunk, watching the ceiling. A woman had a right to sulk when she discovered that eight years of her life had been determined by someone else's decision.

She'd already gone over all the standard lines in her head. He'd had no right. He'd broken her heart for what he'd deemed her own good. Every relationship in her life had been shadowed by what had happened on that beach in her twentieth year.

It did no good to go over it all again and again. But the arrogance of it, the unfairness of it stewed inside her.

Now he claimed he'd loved her. Loved her still.

What a crock, she thought and flopped over on her stomach. Obviously he'd seen her as a dim-witted child who hadn't been capable of making her own choices. She'd been young, yes, but she hadn't been stupid.

What games had fate been playing to have brought them full circle?

The hiatus had made her stronger, she acknowledged. She had used her opportunities and her brains to make her mark. There were degrees tucked away in the window seat in her room in Hatteras, an apartment in Charleston that was tastefully decorated and rarely used. She had a reputation, colleagues whose companionship she enjoyed, offers to teach, to lecture, to join expeditions.

Professionally, she had everything she'd ever wanted.

But she had no real home, no man to hold through the night. No children to love.

And she might have, she would have, if Matthew had only trusted her.

That was behind her now, she thought, and rolled over again. Who knew better than an archeologist that the past could be examined, analyzed and recorded, but it couldn't be changed. What had been, and might have been, was as calcified as old silver in seawater. It was the moment that had to be faced.

She hoped it was true, that he did love her. Now he could suffer, as she had, when a heart was offered and turned aside. He'd had his chance with her. This would be a case in point where history did not repeat itself.

But she wouldn't be cruel, she decided, rising to glance at herself in the oval mirror over her dresser. It wasn't necessary to pay him back in kind. After all, her own emotions weren't involved this time around. She could afford to be generously, certainly politely, forgiving.

Not loving him would help her be carefully detached. They would continue to dive together, work to salvage the *Isabella* as partners, colleagues. She was certainly able to turn aside her personal past in order to explore history.

Satisfied that she'd reached the only logical solution, she left her cabin. She found her father on the port deck, busily checking gauges.

'Wild night, huh, honey?'

In more ways than one, she thought. 'You'd hardly know it now.'

Above, the sky was blue and clear with no more than a few tattered powder-puff clouds. She glanced over atop the bridge to study the wind gauge. 'Wind's coming from the south now.'

287

'Bringing in drier air. The sea's calming, too.' He set a regulator aside. 'I've got a good feeling about today, Tate. Woke up full of energy, a kind of anticipation.' He rose, took a deep gulp of air. 'Your mother said it was leftover electricity from the storm.'

'You're thinking about the amulet,' she murmured and wanted to sigh. 'What is it about that one piece that pulls everyone so?'

'Possibilities.' Ray looked out to sea.

'Last night Buck was panicked at the thought of finding it. All Matthew can think about is using it to settle the score with VanDyke. VanDyke himself, a rich, powerful, successful man, is so obsessed by it he'll do anything to have it. And you.' She pushed impatiently at her hair. 'And you. You've realized a dream of a lifetime with the *Isabella*. There's a fortune down there, for you, for the museum we've always wanted. But it's the amulet that brought you back here.'

'And that makes no sense to you.' He slipped an arm around her shoulders. 'When I was a boy, I was fortunate to have a beautiful home, a yard with rich green grass and big shady trees to climb. I had a jungle gym, sliding board, pals. Everything a kid could want. But beyond the fence and just over the hill there was a swampy area. Dark, junglelike kudzu and ugly trees, a slow, almost stagnant river. There were snakes. I was forbidden to go there.'

'So, of course, that's where you most wanted to go.'

He laughed and kissed Tate on top of the head. 'Of course. Legend had it that it was haunted, which only added to the allure. Little boys went in, so I was told, and never came out again. I would stand at the back fence, smelling the honeysuckle that climbed there and think, what if.'

'Did you ever go in?'

'I got as far as the edge once, where you could smell the river and see the vines clogging the trees. But I lost my nerve.'

'Just as well. You'd likely have been snake bit.'

'But what if,' he murmured. 'I've never lost that curiosity.'

'You know it wasn't haunted. Your mother told you those stories so that you'd stay out of it. Otherwise you could have fallen in the river or lost your way. It wasn't ghosts she was worried about.'

'I'm not at all sure it wasn't.' He watched a gull soar overhead, then turn restlessly toward the horizon. 'I think it would be very sad if we lost our wonder, if we knew there was no possibility of magic-good or evil. I suppose you could say Angelique's Curse has become my haunted swamp. This time I want to go in and see for myself.'

'And if you find it?'

'I'll stop regretting I didn't take that next step through the kudzu.' Laughing at himself, Ray gave her a quick squeeze. 'Maybe Buck will stop believing he's not the man he was. Matthew might stop blaming himself for his father's death. And you …' He turned her to face him. 'You might let a little magic into your life again.'

'That's an awful lot to ask of one necklace.'

'But what if.' He drew her close for a hug. 'I want you happy, Tate.'

'I am happy.'

'All the way happy. I know you closed something off inside eight years ago. I've always worried that I handled things badly because I wanted the best for you.'

'You've never handled anything badly.' She drew her head back to study his face. 'Not where I was concerned.'

'I knew how Matthew felt about you. How you felt about him. It worried me.'

'You had nothing to worry about.'

'You were so young.' He sighed and touched her hair. 'I see the way he feels about you now.'

'Now I'm not so young,' she pointed out. 'You still have nothing to worry about.'

'I see the way he feels about you,' Ray repeated, his eyes sober and seeking. 'What worries me, what surprises me, is that I can't see the way you feel about him.'

'Maybe I haven't decided. Maybe I don't want to decide.' She shook herself, drummed up a smile for him. 'And maybe you shouldn't worry about something I have completely under control.'

'Maybe that's what worries me.'

'I can't win with you.' Rising on her toes, she gave Ray a quick kiss. 'So, I'm going to see if Matthew's up for diving.' She turned to walk away, but something stopped her, made her look back.

Ray was standing, one hand on the rail, a far-off look in his eyes as he gazed toward open sea.

'Dad. I'm glad you didn't walk through the kudzu. If you had then, you might not need to take the step now.'

289

'Life's all timing, Tate.'

'Maybe it is.' Mulling that over, she headed around to starboard. Timing, she supposed, could stop or start a war, save or end a marriage, take or give a life.

There was Matthew on the *Mermaid*, an elbow on the rail, a coffee mug in his hand. She didn't want that jolt of emotion, the stir and simmer. But they came nonetheless. Her heart went butter soft in her breast and melted out a sigh.

Did he have to look so lonely?

It wasn't her problem, she assured herself. She wouldn't let it be her worry.

But he turned his head. Across the choppy waves, his eyes met hers. There was nothing in them to read. Like the storm, whatever raged inside him had calmed, or was controlled. She saw nothing but that deep, enigmatic blue.

'We're down to a light chop,' she called out. 'I'd like to dive.'

'Could smooth out more if we wait an hour or two.'

Something was swelling in her throat. 'I'd like to go down now. If it's too rough once we do, we can scrub the dive.'

'All right. Get your gear.'

Turning, she walked blindly away. Damn him, damn the *Isabella*, damn Angelique and her cursed necklace. Her life had been manageable without them. She was afraid it would never be manageable again.

There was nothing to decide, nothing to control. She was still in love with him after all.

The storm had stirred and shifted the sand. Several of the excavation trenches needed to be cleared again. Matthew was grateful for the extra work. The skill and delicacy required to work the airlift left no room for deep personal thoughts.

He'd had enough of them during the night.

It gave him some small pleasure to suck away sand and see the hilt of a sword.

Déjà vu, he thought, almost amused. He turned the airlift aside. A glance around showed him that Tate was efficiently picking through the debris.

Matthew clanged on his tank, waited for her to look around. He signaled her over. Once she'd joined him, he gestured toward the hilt.

Take it, he indicated. This one's yours.

He watched her hesitate, knew she was remembering. Then her fingers closed around it, tugged it free.

Halfway down, the blade came to a jagged halt.

That, he supposed, studying the shattered sword, told the whole story. Struggling against keen disappointment, he lifted a shoulder. With the pipe, he widened the trench.

They saw the plate at the same moment. Even as she grabbed his arm to signal him to stop, Matthew was turning the pipe away. Hand fanning, Tate uncovered three quarters of the plate.

It was nearly transparent china, delicately painted with violets dancing around the rim. The rim itself was gold. With great care, she closed her fingers over the edge and tried to ease the plate free.

It was stuck fast. Frustrated, she looked at Matthew, shook her head. They both knew that dislodging it with the airlift was as chancy as cutting a diamond with an ax. If the plate was whole, which would be a miracle itself, the flow from the pipe could snap it.

They debated their options with hand signals until it was decided that they had to try. Ignoring the murk and discomfort, Tate kept her fingers lightly on the edge of the plate while Matthew removed the sand and debris, almost a grain at a time.

It was probably missing a fist-sized chunk, he thought, but ignored the strain in his back and shoulders. Degree by degree, he cleared the translucent china, exposing another sprig of violets, and the first swirl of a monogram.

Feeling a give, she stopped him. Working to keep her breathing steady, she eased the plate out another fraction before it jammed again. She could read the first ornate letter, painted in gold. *T*. Taking it as a sign, she nodded for Matthew to resume.

It would have a bite out of it, he was certain. The steel sword less than a foot away had been shattered. How could something as fragile as a china plate survive intact? Frowning in concentration he watched the next letter emerge. *L*.

If the *L* stood for Lassiter's luck, they were wasting their time. He wanted to stop, roll out the ache from his shoulders, but a glimpse at Tate's excited face had him keeping the flow steady.

The final letter came clear so that the monogram read *TLB*. She'd barely had time to consider the oddity of that when the plate, whole and miraculously undamaged, slipped effortlessly free.

Stunned, she nearly dropped it. With it held between her and Matthew, she could see the play of her own fingers under the base. The plate, so fine, so elegant, had once graced a gleaming table, she imagined. It had been part of a cherished set, carefully packed for the voyage to a new life.

And hers were the first hands to hold it in more than two hundred years.

In wonder, she looked up at Matthew. For an instant they shared the silent and intimate thrill of discovery. Then his face changed, became remote. They were only professionals again.

Sorry for it, Tate swam clear to set the plate beside the broken sword out of the range of fallout. She studied the two pieces lying side by side on the sand.

They had been on the same ship, through the same storm, had been tossed, then buried by the same sea. Two different kinds of pride, she mused. Force and beauty. Only one had survived.

What whim had chosen between them? she wondered. Snapping steel and leaving the fragile undamaged? Mulling through it, she went back to the chore of sifting debris.

Later, she would ask herself just what had made her look up and around at just that moment. There'd been no movement to catch her eye. Perhaps there had been a tickle at the back of her neck, or that visceral sensation of being watched.

But she looked up through the murk. The steely eyes and toothy grin of the barracuda gave her a jolt. Amused at herself for the reaction, she reached into the fallout again. And again found herself looking where the fish continued to hover – patient and watching. And familiar.

Surely it couldn't be the same fish that had joined them daily on their excavation of the *Marguerite*?

She knew it was foolish to think so, but the idea of it made her smile. Wanting to get Matthew's attention, she reached for her knife to rap on her tanks. Suddenly something flew out of the fallout and landed less than an inch from her hand.

It glittered and pulsed and gleamed. Fire and ice and the regal shine of gold. The water seemed to heat around her, move around her and grow clear as glass.

The ruby was a spreading of blood, surrounded by the iced tears of diamonds. The gold was as polished and bright as the day it had been fashioned into those heavy links and ornate setting.

There was such clarity to it that she could read the French inscribed around the stone perfectly.

Angelique. Etienne.

The roar in her head was her own blood singing. For there was no sound at all in the sea. No hum from the pipe, no clatter from the stone and shells that rained over her tanks. The silence was so perfect, she could hear her own words echo in her head as if she'd spoken aloud.

Angelique's Curse. We've found it, and freed it, at last.

With numbed fingers, she reached down for it. It was her imagination, of course, that made her think she could feel heat radiating toward her. An invitation, or a warning. When she held it in her hands, it was only fantasy that made it seem as though the necklace vibrated like something alive taking a long greedy breath.

She felt a terrible grief, and anger and fear. Almost, the wild flood of sensation made her drop it again. But there was love welling through all the rest, a fierce and desperate love that tore at her heart.

Tate closed a hand around the chain, another around the stone and absorbed the war of emotion.

She could see the cell, the thin light through the single barred window set high in the thick stone. She could smell the filth and the fear, and hear the screams and pleas of the damned.

And the woman in a dingy tattered dress, her red hair dull and chopped off rudely at her neck, sat at a tiny table. She wept, and she wrote while around her thin throat, the amulet hung like a bleeding heart.

For love. The words drifted through Tate's mind. Only and always for love.

Fire swept up greedily and consumed her.

Matthew. It was her first coherent thought. Tate had no idea how long she had clutched the necklace while debris fell like rain around her.

He was working steadily, his face angled away. Here it is, she thought. What you're searching for is right here. How did you miss it? Why, she thought with a shiver, didn't you see it?

She knew she should signal to him, show him what she held. The object that had drawn them together, twice, was right there in her hands.

And what would it do to him? she wondered. What would it cost him? Before she could question her own motives, she jammed the necklace in her goody bag, drew the drawstring tight.

Struggling for calm, she looked toward the barracuda. But the fish was gone, as if it had never been. There was only murk.

Five hundred miles away, VanDyke rolled off his surprised lover and got out of bed. Ignoring her complaints, he swung into a silk robe and hurried from the master suite. His mouth was dry, his heart throbbing like a wound. Stalking past a white-suited steward, he rushed up the companionway to the bridge.

'I want more speed.'

'Sir.' The captain looked up from his charts. 'There's weather due east. I was about to alter our course to swing below it.'

'Hold your course, goddamn you.' In one of his rare leaps of public temper, VanDyke swept a hand over the table and sent charts scattering. 'Hold your course and give me more speed. You'll have this ship to Nevis by morning or I'll see you captain nothing larger than a two-man paddle boat.'

He didn't wait for an answer, didn't need to. VanDyke's commands were always followed, his wishes always granted. But the flush of humiliation that had come across the captain's face didn't calm or appease VanDyke as it should have.

His hands were trembling, the bitter cloud of rage threatening to close over him. The signs of weakness infuriated him, frightened him. To prove his strength, he marched into the lounge, cursed at the bartender always on duty and grabbed a bottle of Chevis himself.

The amulet. He would have sworn he'd seen it flashing, felt its weight around his own neck as he'd ranged himself over the woman in his bed. And the woman in his bed had not been the increasingly tedious companion of the last two months, but Angelique herself.

Snarling at the bartender to leave, VanDyke poured the liquor, drank it down, poured again. His hands continued to tremble, to curl themselves of their own accord into fists looking for something to pummel.

It had been too real to have been a simple fantasy. It was, he was sure, a premonition.

Angelique was taunting him again, snickering at him from centuries past. But he would not be tricked, or outwitted, this time. His course was set. He accepted now that it had been set from the moment he'd been born. Destiny beckoned so that he could nearly taste it along with the liquor. And it was sweet and strong. He would soon possess the amulet, its power. With it he would have his legacy, and his revenge.

'Tate seems preoccupied,' LaRue commented, tugging up the zipper of his wetsuit.

'We put in a long shift.' Matthew hauled tanks over to the tender. Buck would be taking them to the island to be refilled. 'I guess she's tired.'

'And you, *mon ami?*'

'I'm fine. You and Ray want to work on that southeast trench.'

'As you say.' Taking his time, LaRue hooked on his tanks. 'I noticed she did not linger on deck after you surfaced, as is her habit. She went inside quickly.'

'So what? You writing a book?'

'I am a student of human nature, young Matthew. It is my opinion that the lovely mademoiselle has something to hide, something that worries her mind.'

'Worry about your own mind,' Matthew suggested.

'Ah, but the study of others is so much more interesting.' He smiled at Matthew as he sat to put on his flippers. 'What one does, or doesn't do. What that one thinks or plans. You understand?'

'I understand you're wasting your air.' He nodded toward the *New Adventure*. 'Ray's waiting on you.'

'My diving partner. This is a relationship that must have full trust, eh? And you know, young Matthew …' LaRue pulled on his mask. 'You can rely on me.'

'Right.'

LaRue saluted, then went into the water. Something told him he would need to make another phone call very soon.

She didn't know what to do. Tate sat on the edge of her bunk staring at the amulet in her hands. It was wrong for her to keep the discovery to herself. She knew it, and yet …

If Matthew knew she had it, nothing would stop him from taking it. He'd alert VanDyke that he had it in his possession. He'd demand a showdown.

She knew without doubt that only one of them would walk away from it.

All this time. Slowly, she ran her fingers over the carved names. She hadn't really believed they would find it. What she hadn't realized was that, against all logic, all scientific curiosity, she had hoped they wouldn't find it.

Now it was real, in her hands. She had a foolish urge to open her window and heave it back into the sea.

She didn't have to be an expert on gems to know that the center ruby alone was priceless. It was certainly easy enough to judge the gram weight of the gold and figure that worth in current market value. Add the diamonds, the antiquity, the legend, and what did she have? Four million dollars in her hands? Five?

Enough, certainly, to satisfy any greed, any lust, any vengeance.

Such a stunning piece of work, she mused. Surprisingly simple despite the flash and fire. A woman would wear it and draw eyes and admiration. Displayed, it would be the centerpiece of any museum. Around it she could build the most impressive, the most spectacular collection of marine salvage in the world.

Her professional dreams would be realized beyond any of her wildest imaginings. Her reputation would soar. Any and all funding she desired for an expedition would flow to her like river to sea.

All of this and more would come. She had only to hide the amulet, to go to Nevis and make a single phone call. Within hours she and her prize could be on their way to New York or Washington to stun the world of ocean exploration.

She jerked back, letting the necklace spill onto the bed. Shocked, she stared at it.

What had she been thinking? How could she have even considered such actions? When had fame and fortune become more important to her than loyalty, than honesty? Than even love.

With a shiver, she pressed her hands to her face. Maybe the damn thing was cursed if having it for so short a time skewed her integrity.

She turned her back on it, walked to the window and, opening it, took deep gulps of sea air.

The truth was, she would give up the amulet, the museum, everything, if it would turn Matthew away from this course of self-destruction. She would hand it over to VanDyke personally if the betrayal would save the man she loved.

Perhaps it would. Turning, she studied the amulet again, spread like stars over the serviceable cover of her bunk. Driven by instinct, she scooped it up, pushed it under the neatly folded clothes in her middle drawer.

She needed to act quickly. Through the doorway leading to the bridge, she spied out at the *Mermaid*. She could see her mother hammering conglomerate to the rhythm of some top-forty station on the portable radio. Buck was on his way to St. Kitts, she knew, and her father and LaRue were at the wreck.

That left only Matthew, and of him she saw no sign. There was no better time, she decided, and no better way.

Heart pounding, she slipped up the stairs to the bridge. She hoped the operator on Nevis could help her contact Trident Industries. Failing that, she would work to track down Hayden. Surely between them, they could find a way to get through to VanDyke.

She made the ship-to-shore call, wishing she'd thought quickly enough to hitch a ride with Buck to the island. It would certainly have simplified the contact.

After twenty frustrating minutes, and countless transfers, she was able to reach Trident, Miami. For all the good it did, Tate thought when she disconnected. No one there would even acknowledge that Silas VanDyke was associated with them. All she could do was insist the silky voiced receptionist take her message and see that it was passed to the proper source.

Remembering the man she had faced years before, she had no doubt it would be. But there was little time.

That left Hayden, she decided, and hoped that he was off the *Nomad* and back in North Carolina. Again, she made the ship-to-shore, waited while the call was transferred north and over the Atlantic.

For all her trouble, her call was taken by Hayden's answering service.

'I need to get a message to Dr. Deel. It's urgent.'

'Dr. Deel is in the Pacific.'

'I'm aware of that. This is Tate Beaumont, his associate. It's imperative that I reach him as soon as possible.'

'Dr. Deel checks in for his messages periodically. I'll be glad to relay your message to him when he contacts me.'

'Tell him Tate Beaumont needs to speak with him urgently. Urgently,' she repeated. 'I'm at sea in the West Indies aboard the *New Adventure*. HTR-56390. He can contact the operator on Nevis for the transfer. Have you got that?'

Precisely, the service repeated the location and the call numbers.

'Yes. Tell Dr. Deel that I must speak to him, that I urgently need his help. Tell him I've found something of vital importance, and I need to contact Silas VanDyke. If I haven't heard from Dr. Deel in a week, no, three days,' she decided, 'I'll make arrangements to join the *Nomad*. Tell him I need his help badly.'

'I'll see that he gets your message the moment he calls in, Ms. Beaumont. I'm sorry I can't tell you how long that might be.'

'Thank you.' She could back up the message with a letter, Tate thought. God knew how long it would take to reach the *Nomad*, but it was worth a try.

She spun around, then stopped dead when she saw Matthew blocking the doorway.

'I thought we had a deal, Red.'

Chapter Twenty-four

DOZENS OF EVASIONS and excuses ran through her head. Plausible evasions, reasonable excuses.

She was sure the man who faced her now would swat them aside like pitiful gnats. Still, by the way he leaned negligently against the jamb, she thought there was a small chance.

'I want to check some data with Hayden.'

'Is that so? How many times have you felt the need to check some data with Hayden since we found the *Isabella?*'

'This is the first–' She yelped and instinctively stumbled back when he straightened. It wasn't the move, which had been slow and controlled. It had been the vicious temper that had leapt into his eyes. In all the time she'd known him, she'd never seen it fully unleashed.

'Goddamn you, Tate, don't lie to me.'

'I'm not.' She pressed back against the wall, for the first time in her life fully physically terrified. He could hurt her, she realized. Something in his eyes warned her that he'd like to. 'Matthew, don't.'

'Don't what? Don't tell you you're a lying, double-crossing bitch?' Because he did want to hurt her, was afraid he would if he let that last link of control snap, he slapped his hands on the wall at either side of her head to cage her in. 'When did he get to you?'

'I don't know what you mean.' She swallowed on a dry throat. 'I just needed to ask Hayden …' Her excuse ended on a whimper when he closed a hand over her jaw and squeezed.

'Don't lie to me,' he said, spacing each word deliberately. 'I heard you. If I hadn't heard you myself, no one could have convinced me you'd turn this way. What for, Tate? The money, the prestige, a promotion? A fucking museum with your name on it?'

'No, Matthew, please.' She closed her eyes and waited for the blow when his grip vised on her flesh.

'What were you so anxious to pass on to VanDyke? Where is he, Tate? Keeping a safe distance until we play out the *Isabella?* Then with your help he'll come along and take everything we've worked for.'

Her eyes swam with useless frightened tears. 'I don't know where he is. I swear it. I'm not helping him, Matthew. I'm not giving him the *Isabella.*'

'Then what? What the hell else would you have to give him?'

Staggered, she cringed back from the ripe violence in his face. 'Please, don't hurt me.' Cowardice had tears of shame spilling down her cheeks. Humiliated, she fought to keep her breath from sobbing.

'You can face down a shark, but you can't face yourself.' He let his hand drop, stepped back. 'You know, maybe you figure you've got a lot to pay me back for. I wouldn't argue with that. But I'd never have thought you'd betray the whole expedition just to get to me.'

'I didn't. I haven't.'

'What were you going to tell him?' She opened her mouth, shook her head. 'Fine. You tell him this for me, sweetheart. If he comes within a hundred feet of my boat, of my wreck, he's a dead man. You got that?'

'Matthew, please listen.'

'No, you listen. I've got a lot of respect for Ray and Marla. I know as far as they're concerned the sun rises and sets in you. For their sake, we'll keep this between the two of us. I'm not going to be responsible for them finding out what you really are. So you're going to come up with a real good reason why you've got to ditch this expedition. You make them believe you had to go back to the university, or back to the *Nomad*, or wherever, but you're out of here within twenty-four hours.'

'I'll go.' She dashed at tears. 'If you'll just listen to me first, I'll go as soon as Buck gets back with the tender.'

'You don't have anything to say I want to hear. You can consider it a job well done, Tate.' The heat had died from both his eyes and his voice. They were viciously cold again. 'You paid me all the way back.'

'I know what it's like to hate you. I can't bear knowing you'd hate me now.' She would have thrown herself at him when he turned for the door. It wasn't pride that stopped her, but fear that even begging wouldn't sway him. 'I love you, Matthew.'

It stopped him, sliced at him. 'That's a trick that would have worked even a couple of hours ago. Check your timing, Red.'

'I don't expect you to believe me. I just needed to say it. I don't know what's right.' She squeezed her eyes shut so that she didn't have to see his hard, unyielding face. 'I thought this was. I was scared.' Fighting for courage, she opened her eyes again. 'I was wrong. Before you walk away, before you send me away a second time, there's something I need to give you.'

'You don't have anything I want anymore.'

'Yes, I do.' She took a quick, shuddering breath. 'I have the amulet. If you come with me to my cabin, I'll give it to you.'

He turned slowly, completely around 'What kind of bullshit is this?'

'I have Angelique's Curse in my cabin.' She let out a thin, watery laugh. 'It seems to be working.'

He lunged forward, grabbed her arm. 'Show me.'

She didn't whimper this time, or complain though his fingers dug painfully into her flesh. Beyond tears now, she led the way into her cabin. Once inside, she opened the drawer and took out the amulet.

'I found it this afternoon, shortly after we dug out the monogrammed plate. It was just there, all of a sudden, lying on the sand. I didn't clean it,' she murmured, rubbing a thumb over the center stone. 'There was no calcification, no encrustation. It might have been lying on velvet in a display case. That's funny, isn't it? When I picked it up I thought I could feel … well, I don't suppose you're very interested just now in the tricks a mind can play.'

She lifted her head, held out her hands with the necklace dripping from them. 'You've got what you wanted.'

He took it. Glittering, gleaming, it was as stunning as he'd ever imagined. It was warm, almost hot, he thought. But perhaps his hands were chilled. Of course that didn't explain the sudden clenching in his gut, or the odd image of leaping flames that jumped into his head.

Nerves, he told himself. A man was entitled to be nervous when he'd found the treasure of his lifetime.

'My father died for this.' He didn't hear himself say it, wasn't even conscious that he'd thought it.

'I know. I'm afraid you will, too.'

Distracted, he glanced up. Had she said something? It had sounded more like weeping than words. 'You weren't going to tell me you'd found it.'

'No, I wasn't.' She would face his fury now, his hate, even his disgust. But in doing so, she would make him listen. 'I don't really know what made me keep it from you when we were down, I just felt compelled to.'

On unsteady legs, she crossed to her dresser, picked up a bottle of water to slake her burning throat. 'I started to signal you, then I didn't. Couldn't. I hid it in my pouch, and brought it in here. I needed to think.'

'To figure out how much VanDyke would pay you for it?'

The fresh barb dug deep. Tate set the bottle down again, turned back. Her eyes were eloquent with sorrow. 'However much I've disappointed you, Matthew, you have to know better than that.'

'I know you have ambitions. Ambitions VanDyke could turn into fact.'

'Yes, I'm sure that's true. And I admit, for a few minutes sitting in here alone with that, I indulged in speculating just what having that amulet could do for me.' She wheeled away to stand at the small window. 'Do I have to be flawless to be acceptable to you, Matthew? I'm not allowed to have any selfish needs.'

'You're sure as hell not allowed to double-cross your family, and your partners.'

'You really are a fool if you think I could. But you're right about one thing, I was trying desperately to contact VanDyke,

302

to tell him I'd found it. I'd hoped I could arrange to meet him somewhere and give it to him.'

'Do you sleep with him?'

The question was so absurd, so unexpected, she nearly laughed. 'I haven't laid eyes on Silas VanDyke in eight years. I haven't spoken with him much less slept with him.'

Where was the sense in this? he wondered. Where was the logic that was so intricate a part of her makeup? 'But the first thing you did when you found this was to try to contact him?'

'No, the first thing I did was worry over what you would do to him if you had it.' She closed her eyes and let the light breeze that danced through the window play over her face. 'Or worse, what he might do to you. And I panicked. I even thought about throwing it back into the water, pretending I'd never found it, but that wouldn't really solve the problem. Giving it to VanDyke, I thought, asking him only to give his word that he'd leave you alone in exchange for it, would solve everything.

'I didn't know I still loved you,' she said, staring hard at the shifting water. 'I didn't know, and when I did, I guess I panicked there, too. I don't want to feel this way about you, and I know I'll never feel this way about anyone else.'

Grateful her eyes were dry again, she made herself turn. 'I guess you could say I thought I was saving your life, doing what was best for you. That should sound familiar. And it was as stupid for me to take the choice out of your hands as it was for you to take it out of mine.'

She lifted her hands, let them fall. 'Now you have it, and you can do what you need to do. But I don't have to watch.' Sliding open the door on the closet, she took out her suitcase.

'What are you doing?'

'I'm going to pack.'

He picked up the case, tossed it across the room. 'Do you think you can hit me with all of this then just walk away?'

'Yes, I do.' How odd it was, she realized, to be so utterly calm again. As if she'd punched her way through a hurricane to the thick, quiet air of the eye. 'Just as I think we both need to take time to sort through the mess we've made out of things.' She started to walk past him to retrieve her case, then lifted her chin when he blocked her path. 'You're not going to push me around again.'

'If I have to.' To settle the matter he turned and flicked the lock on her cabin door. 'The first thing we have to settle is this.' He held up the amulet so that it caught the light and exploded with color. 'We've all got a stake in it, but mine's the oldest. When I've done what I need to do, you can have it.'

'If you're still alive.'

'That's my problem.' He slipped the necklace into his pocket. 'You've got an apology coming for the things I said to you on the bridge.'

'I don't want your apology.'

'You've got it anyway. I should have trusted you. Trusting people isn't one of my strong suits, but it should have been where you're concerned. I frightened you.'

'Yes, you did. I suppose I deserved it. Let's just say we're even.'

'We're not finished,' he murmured and laid a hand, gently this time, on her arm.

'No, I guess we're not.'

'Sit down.' When she looked up, her eyes were guarded. 'I'm not going to hurt you. I'm sorry I did. Sit down,' he repeated. 'Please.'

'I don't know what else there is to say, Matthew.' But she sat, folded her tensed hands in her lap. 'I understand your reaction to what you heard and what you saw perfectly.'

'I heard you tell me you loved me.'

'Poor timing. Again. I don't want to,' she said with undertones of tired anger. 'I can't seem to help it.'

He sat beside her, but didn't touch her. 'Eight years ago, I did what I had to do. I did the right thing. I've screwed up enough to know when I manage to do the right thing. I wasn't going to drag you down with me. When I look at you now, what you are, what you've done with your life, I know it was right.'

'There's no point—'

'Let me finish. There're some things I didn't tell you last night. Maybe I didn't want to admit them to you. When I first started salvaging for Fricke, I thought about you all the time. I didn't do much but work, pay bills and think about you. I'd wake up in the middle of the night and miss you so much it hurt. After a while, things were so fucking bad, I didn't have the energy to hurt anymore.'

Remembering, he stared down at his hands. 'I told myself it wasn't such a big deal, a couple of months out of my life with a pretty girl. I didn't much think about you anymore. Now and again it would grab me by the throat, tear right down into the gut. But I'd shake it off. I had to. Things with Buck were as bad as they could get, and I hated every minute of what I was doing to make a lousy dollar.'

'Matthew.'

He shook his head to hold her off. 'Let me get it out. It's not easy stripping down this way. When I saw you again, it ripped my heart open. I wanted all those years back, and knew I couldn't have them. Even when I got you into bed there was this hole. Because all I really wanted was for you to love me back.

'I want a chance with you again. I want you to give it to me.' Now, at last, he looked at her, laid a hand on her cheek. 'I might even be able to convince you that you like being in love with me.'

She managed a shaky smile. 'You probably could. I'm already beginning to lean in that direction.'

'I'd start out by telling you that what I felt for you eight years ago was the biggest thing in my life. And it's not even close to what I feel for you now.'

She was near tears again, and more desperately in love than she'd thought possible. 'What took you so long to tell me all of this?'

'I was pretty sure you'd laugh in my face. Christ, Tate, I wasn't good enough for you then. I'm no better for you now.'

'Not good enough,' she said quietly. 'In what possible way?'

'In every possible way. You've got brains, an education, family.' Frustrated at trying to explain intangibles, he dragged his hand through his hair. 'You've got – it's … class.'

She remained silent a moment while it all simmered. 'You know, Matthew, I'm just too worn out to be angry with you, even for something that ignorant. I really had no idea you, of all people, had a problem with self-esteem.'

'It's not self-esteem.' The idea made him feel ridiculous. 'It's just fact. I'm a treasure hunter, broke most of the time. I've got nothing but a boat, and even that's part LaRue's. I'll make a fortune on this hunt and probably blow it in a year.'

She might have sighed if she hadn't begun to understand. 'And I'm a scientist with a carefully balanced portfolio. I don't have a boat, but I have an apartment that I rarely use. This hunt's going to make me famous, and I intend to use both that and my share of the fortune to make my mark a little deeper. Given those run-downs it appears we have very little in common and no logical reason to cultivate a long-term relationship. Want to give it a shot anyway?'

'I figure this,' he said after a moment. 'You're old enough and smart enough to live with your mistakes. So yeah, I want to give it a shot.'

'Me, too. I loved you once blindly. I see you much clearer now, and I love you more.' She framed his face with her hands. 'We must be crazy, Lassiter. But it feels good.'

He turned his head, pressing his lips to the center of her palm. 'It feels right.' Joy, he couldn't remember when he'd last felt the simple lift of it. Gathering her close, he nuzzled his face in her hair. 'I'd gotten over you, Red. Mostly.'

'Mostly?'

'I could never quite forget the way you smell.'

With a chuckle, she leaned back so that she could see his face. 'The way I smell?'

'Fresh. Cool. Like a mermaid.' He touched his lips to hers, lingered. 'I named her for you.'

His boat, she realized. The boat he'd built with his own hands. 'Matthew, you make my head spin.' Content, she laid her head on his shoulder. This time, she thought, they would sail off into the sunset. 'We'd better go out on deck before someone comes looking for us. We've got something to tell the rest of the team.'

'There's that practical streak.' He brushed a hand over her hair. 'And I was just thinking about getting you in bed.'

'I know.' A quick, satisfying shiver coursed through her at the pleasure of being desired. 'And that's definitely something I'm looking forward to. But for now … ' She took his hand and pulled him to the door. 'I like the way you locked this,' she said, flipping the latch. 'Very macho.'

'You like macho, huh?'

'In small, tasteful doses.' Outside, she hooked her arm through his and walked to the rail. She could hear the radio jingling from the deck of the *Mermaid*, and her mother's brisk, tireless hammering. The compressor kicked on, grinding. The air was filled with the sulfuric perfume of undersea excavation.

'They're all going to be shocked and excited when you show them the amulet.'

306

'We show them,' Matthew corrected.

'No, it's yours. I can't explain rationally how I feel about this, Matthew,' she continued over his protest. 'It seems I'm starting to accept that this whole business isn't meant to be rational. I felt the pull of that necklace, a kind of lust of ownership. When I was holding it earlier, I could actually see, vividly see,' she added, turning to look at him, 'just what it could bring me. The money, the outrageous fortune, the fame and respect. The power. It shakes me to realize that under all the fine lofty motives of education and knowledge, I want those things.'

'So, you're human.'

'No, it was very strong, that desire to keep it, to use it to gain my own ends.'

'What stopped you? What made you decide to turn it over to VanDyke?'

'I love you,' she said simply. 'I'd have done anything to protect you.' She smiled a little. 'Sound familiar?'

'Sounds to me like it's time we started trusting each other. The fact remains you found the amulet.'

'Maybe I was meant to, so that I could give it to you.'

'Meant to?' He took her chin in his hand. 'This from a scientist.'

'A scientist who knows her Shakespeare. "There are more things in heaven and earth." ' Keeping her eyes on his, she suppressed a shudder. 'It's in your hands now, Matthew. And for you to decide.'

'None of this — if you loved me you'd …?'

'I know you love me. A woman can go her whole life and never hear the kind of things you've just said to me. That's why you're going to marry me.'

His hand dropped away from her face. A knee-jerk reaction that made her lips curve wryly. 'I am?'

'Damn right you are. It shouldn't be too difficult to arrange the necessary paperwork on Nevis. I'm sure we'd both prefer to keep it simple. We can have a small ceremony right here on the boat.'

His stomach jittered, then settled smooth. 'You've got it all worked out.'

'Working things out is my life, Lassiter.' Smug, she linked her arms around his neck. 'I've got you, from where I'm standing, exactly where I want you. You're not getting away again.'

307

'I'd probably be wasting my time arguing.'

'Totally,' she agreed, almost purring when he slipped his arms around her. 'Might as well give up now.'

'Sweetheart, I hoisted the white flag the minute you knocked me out of that hammock onto my butt.' The smile faded from his eyes. 'You're my luck, Tate,' he murmured. 'There's nothing I can't do if you're with me.'

She settled into his arms, closed her eyes. And tried not to think about the weight of the curse in his pocket.

The teams gathered on the deck of the *Mermaid* in the thinning light of dusk. The weeks of treasure-hunting had been prosperous. On the generous foredeck, bits and pieces of the latest haul were separated from debris. There were sextants, octants, tableware, a simple gold locket containing a lock of hair.

Tate did her best to keep her mind off the amulet Matthew still held and answered questions on the two porcelain statues her father was examining.

'They're Ching dynasty,' she said. 'They're called Immortals, depicting saintly human figures from Chinese theology. In all there are eight, and these two are wonderfully undamaged. We may find the other six, if indeed there was a complete set. They're not listed in the manifest.'

'Valuable?' LaRue tossed out.

'Very. In my opinion, it's time we started thinking about transferring the more valuable and the more fragile items to a safer place.' Deliberately, she kept her eyes averted from Matthew's. 'And that we call in at least one other archeologist. I need corroboration, and more extensive facilities in order to complete a proper study. And we have to begin work on preserving the *Isabella* herself.'

'The minute we make any move like that, VanDyke would be on us,' Buck objected.

'Not if we take the precaution of notifying the proper institutions. The Committee for Nautical Archeology in England, its counterpart in the States. If anything, keeping this to ourselves is more dangerous than going public. Once we're on record, it would be impossible for VanDyke or anyone like him to sabotage our operation.'

'You don't know pirates,' Buck said grimly. 'And government's the biggest pirate of all.'

'I'm leaning with Buck on this.' Frowning, Ray studied the Chinese figures. 'I won't dispute that we have an obligation to share what we've found, but we haven't finished yet. We have weeks more excavating, maybe months, before we've played her out. And we've yet to find the main thing we came for.'

'Angelique's Curse,' Buck said under his breath. 'Maybe she doesn't want to be found.'

'If she's there,' LaRue corrected, 'we'll find her.'

'I think you're all missing the point.' Marla spoke quietly. It was so rare she offered an opinion on excavation policy, everyone stopped and turned to her. 'I know I don't dive, don't work the airlift, but I understand the heart of all of this. Look what we've done, what we've found already. A small operation with only two diving teams, working frantically to keep it all so quiet and secret. Yet we've uncovered a kind of miracle. And we've made Tate responsible for caring for that miracle. Now that she's asking for help, we're all worried someone might come along and steal our thunder. Well, they can't,' she added. 'Because we've done it. And if we focus so narrowly on one piece, aren't we losing sight of the whole? Angelique's Curse might have drawn us here, but we don't have to find it to know we've done something incredible.'

With a sigh, Ray draped an arm over her shoulders. 'You're right. Of course you're right. It's foolish to think we haven't succeeded because we haven't found the amulet. Still, every time I go down and come up again without it, I feel as though I've failed. Even with all this.'

Tate's hot gaze skimmed over Matthew before settling on her father. 'You haven't failed. None of us have.'

Saying nothing, Matthew rose. He took the gold chain from his pocket, let it dangle. For an instant, Tate thought she saw light flash from the stone.

Ray got shakily to his feet. His vision seemed to blur and fracture as he reached out to touch the center ruby. 'You found it.'

'Tate found it. This morning.'

'It's a devil's tool,' Buck whispered, backing away. 'It'll bring you nothing but grief.'

'It may be a tool,' Matthew agreed, and his glance flicked over LaRue. 'And I'll use it. My vote goes with Tate. We make arrangements to transfer what we have. She can contact her committees.'

'So that you can lure VanDyke,' she murmured.

'VanDyke's my problem. This is what he wants.' Matthew slipped the necklace from Ray's hands. 'He won't find it easy going through me to get it. It might be best to suspend operations for a while. You and Marla and Tate could go on the island.'

'And leave you here to face him down alone?' Tate tossed back her head. 'Not a chance, Lassiter. Just because I'm stupid enough to want to marry you doesn't mean I'll let you bundle me off.'

'You're getting married?' Marla pressed a hand to her lips. 'Oh, honey.'

'I had intended to make the announcement a little more smoothly.' Annoyance glittered in Tate's eyes. 'You jerk.'

'I love you, too.' Matthew hooked an arm around her waist while the amulet dripped from his free hand. 'She asked me this afternoon,' he explained to Marla. 'I decided to give her a break and go along with it, since it means I get you in the bargain.'

'Thank goodness the two of you have come to your senses.' With a sob, Marla threw her arms around both of them. 'Ray, our baby's getting married.'

He patted his wife awkwardly on the shoulder. 'I guess this is my cue to say something profound.' Emotions warred through him, regret mixed with joy. His little girl, he thought, was another man's woman. 'I can't think of a damn thing.'

'If you will pardon me,' LaRue said. 'I suggest a celebration.'

'Of course.' Marla wiped at her eyes and stepped back. 'I should have thought of it.'

'Allow me.' LaRue strolled off into the galley to unearth the bottle of Fume Blanc he'd hidden away.

After the glasses were poured, the toasts drunk and the tears dried, Tate walked to the starboard rail to join Buck.

'It's a pretty big night,' she murmured.

'Yeah.' He lifted his glass of ginger ale.

'I thought – I'd hoped that you'd be happy for us, Buck. I do love him so much.'

He shifted uncomfortably. 'Guess I know you do. I got used to thinking about him like my own the past fifteen years. I ain't been much of a substitute father–'

'You've been wonderful,' she interrupted hotly.

'Screwed up more than once, but mostly I done my best. I always knew Matthew had something special in him. More'n me, more'n James. I never knew how to make it come out. You do,' he added, turning to her at last.

'He's a better man with you than he would be without. He'll try harder with you there, and turn off that bad Lassiter luck. You gotta make him get rid of that damned necklace, Tate, before it curses your lives. Before VanDyke kills him for it.'

'I can't do that, Buck. If I tried, and he changed himself because I'd asked, what would I leave him?'

'I should never have told him about it. I made him think we could make James's death worth something if we found it. That was stupid. Dead's dead.'

'Matthew's his own man, Buck. What he does can't be because of me, or you, or anyone. If we love him, we have to accept that.'

Chapter Twenty-five

TATE STRUGGLED TO take her own advice to heart. As Matthew slept beside her in his cabin on the *Mermaid*, she tried to put her fears to rest.

He'd said it was time they trusted each other. She knew trust could be as strong a shield as love. She would make hers strong enough, she promised herself, to defend them both against any-one or anything.

Whatever happened, whatever he did, they would face it together.

'Stop worrying,' he murmured and nudged her closer.

The heat of his body, the hard length of it against hers, soothed. 'Who said I was?'

'I can feel it.' To distract them both, he ran his hand over her hip. 'You keep sending out all these nasty little worry darts. They're keeping me awake.' His hand inched back up, over her rib cage. 'And since I'm awake anyway ...' He rolled on top of her to send kisses and shivers down her throat.

'Next time I build a boat, I'm going to make the master cabin bigger.'

She sighed as his lips nibbled their way to her ear. 'Next time?'

'Mmm-hmm. And I'm soundproofing it.'

She let out a chuckle. Buck's snoring from the next cabin battered the walls like thunder. 'I'll help you. How does LaRue stand it?'

'He says it's like the boat rocking in the current. It's just there.' Circling a finger around her breast, Matthew studied her face in the moonlight that drifted through the open window. 'When I designed the living quarters, I didn't have a wife in mind.'

'You'd better keep one in mind now,' she warned him. 'This one. And I think the living quarters are just fine.' Teasingly, she flicked her tongue over his jaw. 'Especially the captain's cabin.'

'You know, if I'd figured out that this engagement business would clear the way for this, I'd have tried it sooner.' To please himself, he spread her hair over the pillow. 'It beats the floor of the bridge.'

'All to hell.' She curved her lips under his. 'But I kind of liked those nights. Don't think this engagement business is going to last long,' she added. 'We're going to Nevis tomorrow to start the formalities.'

'Christ, you're bossy.'

'Yeah, and I've got you, Lassiter.' She vised her arms around him. 'I've really got you.'

Nothing, absolutely nothing, she vowed, was going to take him away from her.

'The minute you're finished, I want you to meet me in the boutique.' Under the bright morning sun, Marla shook the sand out of her sandals as she stepped from the beach onto the stone walkway of the resort. Small, informal wedding or not, she intended to take her duties as mother of the bride, and surrogate mother of the groom, seriously.

Tate sighed and flipped her braid over her shoulder. 'I don't suppose it's any use telling you again that I don't need a new dress.'

'No use at all.' Happily, Marla beamed. 'We're getting you a wedding dress, Tate Beaumont. If the boutique here at the resort doesn't have anything suitable, we're going to St. Kitts. And Matthew' – she patted him gently on the cheek – 'you could use a haircut – and a decent suit.'

'Yes, ma'am.'

'Suck up,' Tate muttered.

Ignoring that, Marla continued to smile. 'Now y'all go see the concierge. I'm sure he can help you find the way to push through the paperwork. Matthew, you and I will look into that suit later this afternoon. Oh, and Tate, ask him about shoes.'

'Shoes?'

'We'll want to get some to match your dress.' With a cheery wave, she headed up the steps toward the boutique.

'She's off and running,' Tate said under her breath. 'Thank God we're doing this here and now. Can you imagine what she'd be planning if we were getting married back on Hatteras? Showers and bridal shows. Flowers, caterers, cakes.' She shuddered delicately. 'Wedding consultants.'

'Sounds kind of nice.'

'Lassiter.' Bemused, Tate stared up at him. 'You're not telling me you'd like all that fuss and bother. If she had the chance, she'd stuff you into a tux, maybe tails.' She gave his butt a friendly pat. 'Not that you wouldn't look wonderfully dashing.'

'I thought women were supposed to want a big, splashy wedding.'

'Not sane women.' Amused, she paused halfway up the steps. 'Matthew, is that what you want, all the pomp and circumstance?'

'Look, Red, I'll take you any way I can get you. I just don't see what's so wrong with the fancywork. A new dress, a haircut.'

Tate narrowed her eyes wickedly. 'She's going to make you wear a tie, pal.'

He couldn't quite control the wince. 'Not such a big deal.'

'You're right.' With a little laugh, she pressed a hand to her stomach. 'I guess I'd better just come clean and admit it. I'm scared.'

'Good.' He clasped his hand over hers. 'That makes two of us.'

Together they went into the lobby to track down the concierge.

Fifteen minutes later, they walked out again, dazzled.

'It's going to be awfully easy,' Tate managed. 'Proof of citizenship, sign a few papers.' She blew the hair out of her eyes. 'We could pull this off in two or three days.'

'Cold feet?'

'They're blocks of ice, but I can handle it. You?'

'I never welch on a deal.' To prove it, he scooped her off her feet. 'Are you going to be Doctor Lassiter or Doctor Beaumont?'

314

'I'm going to be Doctor Beaumont and Mrs. Lassiter. Suit you?'

'Suits me. Ah, I guess we'd better head to the boutique.'

'I can save you from that.' Understanding, she gave him a hard, smacking kiss. 'If we manage to find a dress in there, you aren't allowed to see it. Mom will have a fit if we don't follow at least one tradition.'

Hope bloomed. 'I don't have to go shopping?'

'You don't have to go shopping until she snags you. Why don't you swing by in about a half hour? Wait, I forgot I was dealing with Marla the mad shopper Beaumont. Give us an hour. And since I'm feeling so generous where you're concerned, if Mom decides to drag me off to St. Kitts, we'll detour back to the boat and drop you off.'

'I owe you big, Red.'

'I'll collect. Put me down.'

He gave her one last kiss, then set her on her feet. 'I bet they carry lingerie up there.'

'I bet they do.' She laughed and gave him a shove. 'I'll surprise you. Get lost, Lassiter.'

Smiling, she watched him disappear back into the lobby. Suddenly the idea of a new dress, something flowing and romantic, didn't seem so frivolous. Something that would be flattered by a little gold heart with a single pearl dripping from its point.

Lassiter, she decided, I'm going to knock your socks off.

Flushed with pleasure, she started across the patio. The hand that clamped on her arm made her laugh. 'Matthew, really–'

The words, and her breath, clogged in her throat as she stared into the smoothly handsome face of Silas VanDyke.

Reality tilted on its edge for a moment. He looked exactly the same, she thought dumbly. The years had laid lightly on him. The thick, glossy pewter hair, the smooth, elegant face and pale eyes.

His hand was soft as a child's on her arm, and she could smell the subtle, expensive cologne he'd dabbed on his skin.

'Ms. Beaumont, what a pleasure to run into you like this. I must say, the years have been overwhelmingly generous with you.'

It was the sound of his voice, faintly European and coldly pleased, that snapped her back. 'Let go of me.'

'Surely you have a moment or two for an old friend?' Still smiling benignly, he steered her sharply around the garden of brilliant annuals as he spoke.

There were dozens of people around, she reminded herself as she fought back fear. Guests, staff, the early diners who lounged in the poolside restaurant. She only had to shout.

The realization that she was afraid, here, in the bright sunlight, had her digging in her heels. 'Oh, I've got a moment or two for you, VanDyke. In fact, I'd enjoy dealing with you very much.' Alone, she thought, without Matthew shouldering her aside. 'But if you don't let me go, right now, I'll start screaming.'

'Now that would be an unfortunate mistake,' he said mildly. 'And you're a sensible woman, I know.'

'Keep pawing at me and I'll show you just how sensible.' Furious, she jerked her arm free. 'I'm sensible enough to know there's nothing you can do to me in a public place.'

'Do to you?' He looked shocked, and vaguely offended. But his head was aching, pounding at the idea that she would defy him. 'Tate, my dear, what a foolish thing to say. I wouldn't dream of doing anything to you at all. I'm simply inviting you to come out and spend an hour or two on my yacht.'

'You must be insane.'

His fingers closed so quickly, so painfully over her arm, she was too surprised to shout. 'Be careful. I don't care for poor manners.' His face smoothed out again with a smile. 'We'll try again, shall we? I'd like you to accompany me for a short, friendly visit. If you refuse, or if you insist on making a scene here in, as you say, a public place, your fiancé will pay the price.'

'My fiancé will scrape your face over the pavement, VanDyke, unless I do it first.'

'What a pity that your mother's gentle breeding seems to have skipped a generation.' He sighed, leaned closer, keeping his teeth clenched to control his voice. 'I have two men watching your Matthew as we speak. They'll do nothing unless you force me to signal them otherwise. They're quite skilled and quite discreet.'

The blood drained from her face, leaving it cold and stiff. 'You can hardly have him killed in the lobby of the resort.' But he'd planted the seed of terror, and it was blossoming.

'You can always take that chance. Oh, and wasn't that your mother up in the boutique? She's chosen several lovely things for you.'

Numb with fear, Tate glanced up. She could see the glass doors and windows of the shop tossing back sun. And the man, broad shouldered, neatly dressed, loitering outside. He inclined his head slowly.

'Don't hurt her. You have no reason to hurt her.'

'If you do what I tell you, I'll have no reason to hurt anyone. Shall we go? I've instructed my chef to prepare a very special lunch, and now I have someone to share it with.' With a horrible gallantry, he tucked a hand under her elbow and led her toward the pier. 'The trip will only take a short time,' he assured her. 'I'm moored just west of you.'

'How did you know?'

'Oh, my dear.' Jaunty in his white suit and panama, pleased with his victory, he clucked her under the chin. 'How naive of you to think I wouldn't.'

Tate jerked her arm from his grip, gave one last look back at the resort before stepping down into the waiting tender. 'If you hurt them, if you so much as touch either of them, I'll kill you myself.'

She planned the ways she would do it as the tender cut through the water.

In the boutique, Marla sighed. After instructing the clerk to put aside her selections, she set out to track down her daughter. She searched the restaurants and lounges, scanned the beach and the pool. Mildly irked, she went through the gift shop, then back to the boutique.

When there was no sign of Tate, she marched back to the lobby intending to have the concierge do a page.

She spotted Matthew jumping out of a cab.

'Matthew, for goodness sake, where have you been?'

'Something I had to take care of.' He patted his pocket where the contract he'd just signed was neatly folded. 'Hey, I'm only a little late.'

'Late for what?'

'We said an hour.' Unconcerned, he glanced at his watch. 'It's just over that. So, did you talk her into a dress or is she still fighting it?'

'I haven't seen her,' Marla said grumpily. She was hot, frustrated. 'I thought she was with you.'

'No, we separated. She was going to meet you.' He shrugged. 'We were talking about different kinds of weddings, flowers and stuff. She probably got involved in something.'

'I know – the beauty salon,' Marla said, inspired. 'She probably wanted to check about getting her hair and nails done, getting a facial.'

'Tate?'

'It's her wedding.' Baffled by the casualness of youth, she shook her head. 'Every woman wants to look her best as a bride. She's down there right now going through pictures of hairstyles.'

'If you say so.' The idea of Tate getting herself polished and painted for him had him grinning. This he had to see. 'Let's go smoke her out.'

'I'm going to give her a piece of my mind, too,' Marla muttered. 'I was starting to worry.'

'Champagne?' VanDyke lifted a flute from the tray his steward had set beside a pair of peacock blue lounge chairs.

'No.'

'I think you'll agree that it sets the palate for the lobster dish we're having for lunch.'

'I'm not interested in champagne or lobster or your transparent politeness.'

Ignoring the little tremors of fear, Tate kept her shoulders braced. If she'd gauged it correctly they were about a mile west of the *Mermaid*. She could swim it if necessary.

'What I am interested in is why you kidnapped me.'

'Such a hard word.' VanDyke sampled the champagne, found it perfectly chilled. 'Please sit.' His eyes frosted when she stayed braced against the rail. 'Sit, now,' he repeated. 'We have business to discuss.'

Bravery was one thing. But when his eyes looked as flat and mindless as a shark's, she thought it wise to obey. She sat stiffly and forced herself to accept the second flute he held out.

She'd been wrong, she realized. He had changed. The man she had faced eight years ago had seemed sane. This one …

'To … destiny, perhaps?'

She'd have preferred to dash the contents of the glass into his face. Whatever small satisfaction that might bring her, she knew that it would cost dearly. 'Destiny?' It bolstered her to find her voice could be calm and even. 'Yes, I could drink to that.'

Relaxed, he sat back, holding the stem of the flute between his fingers. 'It's so charming to visit with you again. You know, Tate, you made quite a favorable impression on me during our last encounter. I've enjoyed watching your professional progress over the years.'

'If I had known you were associated with the *Nomad*'s last expedition in any way, I would never have been a part of it.'

'So foolish.' He crossed his ankles to better enjoy the wine and the company. 'Surely you know that I've financed a number of scientists, labs, expeditions. Without my backing, numerous projects would never have reached fruition. And the charities I support, worthwhile causes.' He paused to sip again. 'Would you deny those causes, Tate, charitable and scientific, because you disapprove of the source?'

She tipped her glass and sipped as delicately as he. 'When the source is a murderer, a thief, a man without conscience or morals, yes.'

'Fortunately few share your opinion of me, or your rather naive ethics. You disappointed me,' he said in a tone that had her pulse going thick. 'You betrayed me. And you've cost me.' Absently, he glanced up as a steward appeared. 'Lunch is served,' VanDyke told her, smoothly genial again. 'I thought you'd enjoy dining al fresco.'

He rose, offering a hand, which she ignored. 'Don't try my patience, Tate. Small rebellions only irritate me.' He demonstrated by clamping his hand over her wrist. 'You've already disappointed me deeply,' he continued as she struggled against his hold. 'But I'm hoping you'll take this last chance I'm giving you to redeem yourself.'

'Take your hands off me.' Temper spiked, propelling her around. Her fist was poised, ready to strike when he grabbed her braid and yanked sharply enough to have stars exploding in front of her eyes. When her body was dragged against him, she discovered the elegant clothes masked a tough, hard body.

'If you think I have any qualms about striking a woman, think again.' His eyes glittered as he shoved her roughly into a chair. He leaned over her, his breath hitching, his eyes blind. 'If I wasn't a reasonable, civilized man, if I let myself forget that, I'd break you, a bone at a time.'

Like a light switched, his eyes changed. The vicious temper turned into a smile that was edgy and thin. 'There are those who believe that corporal punishment is unwise, even uncivilized.' Daintily he fussed with his lapels, then sat. Brushing a hand back, he signaled for the stone-faced steward to retrieve the wine and glasses. 'However, I disagree. I'm a firm believer that pain and punishment are very effective for instilling a sense of discipline. And certainly respect. I demand respect. I've earned it. Do try one of these olives, dear.' The avuncular host once more, he offered her a crystal dish. 'They're from one of my groves in Greece.'

Because her hands were shaking badly she kept them locked under the table. What kind of man threatened to inflict pain one moment, and offered exotic tidbits the next? A mad one.

'What do you want?'

'First, to share a congenial meal in a lovely spot with an attractive woman.' His brow lifted when her cheeks went white. 'Don't fret, dear Tate. My feelings for you are much too paternal for me to entertain any sexual notions. Your honor, as you might think of it, is more than safe.'

'I'm supposed to be relieved that rape isn't on your itinerary?'

'Another ugly word.' Mildly annoyed with her choice of it, he helped himself to the dish of olives and the antipasto. 'A man who stoops to forcing himself on a woman sexually isn't a man at all in my opinion. One of my executives in New York browbeat and intimidated his assistant into having sex with him. She had to be hospitalized when he'd finished.'

VanDyke sliced through a piece of prosciutto. 'I arranged to have him fired – after I'd had him castrated.' He dabbed at his mouth with a pale blue linen napkin. 'I like to think he would have thanked me. Please, try the lobster. I guarantee it's superb.'

'I don't seem to have much of an appetite.' Tate shoved her plate aside in a gesture she knew was foolishly defiant. 'You got me here, VanDyke, and obviously you can keep me here. At least until Matthew and my family start looking for me.' Lifting her chin, she stared directly into his eyes. 'Why don't you tell me what you want?'

'We will have to discuss Matthew,' he mused, 'but that can wait. I want what I've always wanted. I want what belongs to me. Angelique's Curse.'

Worry gnawed at her stomach as Marla paced the hotel lobby. No matter how many times she told herself that Tate couldn't

320

have simply disappeared, she was terrified. She watched people come and go, staff bustling along to perform duties, guests strolling from pool to lounge to garden.

She heard laughter, the splash of children swimming, the whirl of the blender that mixed frosty island drinks for those waiting at the bar.

She and Matthew had separated – she, to ask at the front desk, to question the doormen, the cab drivers, anyone who might have seen Tate leave the resort, he to check the beach and the dock.

When she spotted Matthew coming toward her, Marla's heart leapt. Only when she saw that he was alone, when she saw the grim look in his eyes, did it sink again.

'Tate.'

'Several people saw her. She met someone, left with him by tender.'

'Left? Who did she meet? Are you sure it was her?'

'It was her.' The panic that raced through him could be controlled. But not so easy was it to control the need to kill. 'The description I got fits VanDyke.'

'No.' Weak with fear, she reached out to take his arm. 'She wouldn't have gone with him.'

'She wouldn't unless he hadn't given her a choice.'

'The police,' she said faintly. 'We'll call the police.'

'And tell them that she left the island, without putting up any struggle, with the man who endowed her last project?' Eyes hard and hot, he shook his head. 'We don't know how many cops he owns either. We do this my way.'

'Matthew, if he hurts her …'

'He won't.' But they both knew he said it only to soothe. 'He has no reason to. Let's get back. My guess is that he won't be far from where we're moored.'

He doesn't know. Tate's mind whirled with possibilities. He'd known where to find them. Had somehow known what they were doing. But he didn't know what they'd found. Stalling, she reached for her glass again.

'Do you think, if I had it, I'd give it to you?'

'Oh, I think when you have it you'll give it to me to save Matthew and the others. It's time we worked together, Tate, as I've planned for some time.'

321

'You've planned?'

'Yes. Though not in quite the way I had hoped.' He brooded over that for a moment, then brushed it aside. 'I'm willing to overlook your mistakes, I'm even willing to let you and your team reap the rewards of the *Isabella*. All I want is the amulet.'

'You'd take it and walk away? What assurance do I have of that?'

'My word, of course.'

'Your word means less than nothing to me.' She gasped involuntarily when he crushed her fingers in his hand.

'I don't tolerate insults.' When he released her, her hand throbbed like a bad tooth. 'A man's word is sacred, Tate,' he said with eerie calm. 'My proposition stands. The amulet is all I want from you. In exchange for it, you'll have the fame and the fortune that goes with the *Isabella*. Your name will be made. I'm even willing to assist on that point wherever I have influence.'

'I don't want your influence.'

'You benefited from it many times in the past eight years. But I did that for my own pleasure. Still it wounds to have generosity met with ingratitude.' His face darkened. 'Lassiter's doing. I understand that. You realize that by aligning yourself with him you're lowering your expectations, your standards, your social and professional opportunities. A man like him will never be an asset to you on any level.'

'A man like Matthew Lassiter makes you look like a child. A spoiled, evil child.' Her head snapped back and her eyes watered when the back of his hand slashed across her cheek.

'I warned you.' Furious, he shoved his plate aside. The force of it sent it bulleting off the table to smash on the deck. 'I won't tolerate disrespect. I've made allowances as I admire your courage and intelligence, but you will mind your tongue.'

'I despise you.' She braced for another blow. 'If I found the amulet, I'd destroy it before turning it over to you.'

She watched him snap. The way his hands trembled as he surged to his feet. There was murder in his eyes. More than that, she understood. There was a kind of terrible delight. He would hurt her, she knew, and he would enjoy it.

The survival instinct kicked in over the numb fear. She sprang to her feet, leaping back when he grabbed for her. Without pausing, she sprinted for the rail. Water was safety. The sea would save her. But even as she poised to dive, she was dragged back.

She kicked, screamed, fought to find flesh that her teeth could sink into. The steward simply pinned her arms, yanking them viciously up behind her back until her vision grayed.

'Leave her to me.'

Dimly, she heard VanDyke's voice as she fell bonelessly to the deck.

'You're not as sensible as I'd hoped.' With the rage still in him, VanDyke snagged her abused arm and yanked her to her feet. Fresh agony had a sob catching in her throat. 'Your loyalty is displaced, Tate. I'll have to teach you—'

He broke off as the sound of a motor caught his attention. Hearing it, Tate swayed, turned her face toward the noise.

Matthew.

Terror and pain stripped aside all pride. She wept weakly when VanDyke let her drop to the deck a second time.

He'd come. She curled into a ball, nursing bruises. He'd take her away, and it wouldn't hurt anymore. She wouldn't be afraid anymore.

'Again,' VanDyke said, 'you're late.'

'It wasn't a simple matter to leave.' LaRue landed lightly on deck. He glanced briefly at Tate before reaching for his tobacco. 'You have a passenger, I see.'

'Fortune smiled on me.' Nearly steady again, VanDyke sat back down. He picked up a napkin to dab at his sweaty face. 'I was handling a few details on the island when who should cross my path but the delightful Ms. Beaumont.'

LaRue clucked his tongue and helped himself to Tate's champagne. 'There's a mark on her face. I disapprove of the rough treatment of women.'

VanDyke's teeth bared. 'I don't pay you for your approval.'

'Perhaps not.' LaRue decided to postpone his cigarette and enjoy the antipasto. 'When Matthew discovers you have her, he'll come looking.'

'Of course.' That would make up for everything. Nearly everything. 'Have you come only to tell me what I already know?'

'LaRue.' Trembling, Tate struggled to her knees. 'Matthew, where's Matthew?'

'I would guess he is speeding back from Nevis to search for you.'

323

'But–' She shook her head to clear it. 'What are you doing here?' Slowly it began to register that he was alone, that he was sitting comfortably at the table, nibbling.

He smiled when he saw the knowledge seep into her eyes, and with it disgust. 'So, the light dawns.'

'You work for him. Matthew trusted you. We all trusted you.'

'I would hardly have earned my keep if you hadn't.'

She wiped the weak tears from her cheek. 'For money? You've betrayed Matthew for money?'

'I have a great fondness for money.' Dismissing her, he turned back, popped an olive into his mouth. 'And speaking of my great fondness, I will require another bonus.'

'LaRue, I'm growing tired of your added demands.' VanDyke held up a finger. In answer, the steward stepped forward, flipped open his sharply creased white jacket and took out a highly polished .32. 'I might redeem myself in Tate's eyes by having you shot in several painful places and thrown overboard. I believe you'd draw sharks nicely.'

Lips pursed, LaRue contemplated his choice of peppers. 'If you kill me, your hopes for Angelique's Curse die with me.'

VanDyke clenched his fist until he calmed again. Another quick signal had the .32 disappearing under the tailored coat. 'I also grow tired of you dangling the amulet.'

'Two hundred and fifty thousand American dollars,' LaRue began, and shut his eyes briefly to savor the hot, sweet flavor of the pepper. 'And the amulet is yours.'

'Bastard,' Tate whispered. 'I hope he does kill you.'

'Business is business,' LaRue said with a shrug. 'I see that she has yet to tell you of our luck, *mon ami*. We have Angelique's Curse. For a quarter of a million, I'll see that it is safely in your hands by tomorrow, nightfall.'

Chapter Twenty-six

ANGELIQUE'S CURSE GLITTERED in Matthew's hands. He stood on the bridge of the *Mermaid*, his fingers wrapped tight around the chain. The hot white sun poured over the ruby, flashed the diamonds, sparkled the gold. Here was the treasure of a lifetime, fortune and fame in metal and stone.

Here was misery.

Everyone he'd loved had been hurt by it. Holding it, he could see the lifeless body of his father, crumpled on the deck of a boat. The face, so like his own, bleached white in death.

He could see Buck in the jaws of a shark, blood swirling in the water.

He could see Tate, tears in her eyes, offering him the amulet, offering him the choice of salvation or destruction.

But he couldn't see her now. He couldn't know where she'd been taken or what had been done to her. All he knew was that he would do anything, give anything to get her back.

The cursed necklace weighed like lead in his hands and mocked him with beauty.

Eyes blazing, he turned as Buck came onto the bridge.

'Still no sign of LaRue.' Spotting the amulet, Buck took a jerky step back.

Matthew swore and laid the necklace on the chart table. 'Then we move without him. We can't wait.'

'Move where? What the hell are we going to do? I'm with Ray and Marla on this, Matthew. We gotta call in the cops.'

'Did the cops do us any good last time?'

'This ain't piracy, boy, it's kidnapping.'

'It was murder once, too,' Matthew said coldly. 'He's got her, Buck.' He leaned against the chart table, warring against the old helplessness. 'In front of dozens of people he walked right off with her.'

'He'd trade her for that.' Wetting his lips, Buck forced himself to look at the necklace. 'Like a ransom.'

Hadn't he been waiting, praying by the radio, for VanDyke to make contact? Matthew thought. 'I can't afford to count on that. Can't afford to wait any longer.'

He grabbed binoculars, shoved them at Buck. 'Due west.'

Stepping up, Buck lifted the binoculars, skimmed the sea. He focused in on the yacht, hardly more than a glimmer of sleek white. 'A mile off,' he murmured. 'Could be him.'

'It's him.'

'He'd be waiting for you. Expecting you to come after her.'

'I wouldn't want to disappoint him, would I?'

'He'll kill you.' Resigned now, Buck set the glasses aside. 'You could give him that fucking thing wrapped in a bow and he'd still kill you. Just like he did James.'

'I'm not giving it to him,' Matthew returned. 'And he's not killing anyone.' Impatient, he seized the binoculars, searched the sea for a sign of LaRue. Time was up.

'I need you, Buck.' He set the glasses down again. 'I need you to dive.'

Terror and pain were no longer important. Tate watched LaRue eat heartily as he betrayed his partners. She no longer thought of escape as she lunged to her feet and flew at him.

The attack was so unexpected, her prey so complacent, that she was able to knock him out of his chair. Her nails scraped viciously down his cheek, drawing blood before he managed to flip and hold her down.

326

'You're even worse than he is,' she spat out, wriggling like an eel under him. 'He's just crazy. You're revolting. If VanDyke doesn't kill you, Matthew will. I hope I get to watch.'

Amused, excited by the display, VanDyke sipped champagne. He let the wrestling match play on, enjoying LaRue's grunts as he fought to restrain Tate. Then with a sigh, he signaled the steward. He couldn't afford to have LaRue overly damaged. Quite yet.

'Show Ms. Beaumont her stateroom,' he ordered. 'And see that she's not disturbed.' He smiled as his man hauled Tate to her feet. She kicked, cursed and struggled, but she was outweighed by a hundred pounds of solid muscle. 'I think you should have some rest, my dear, while LaRue and I complete our business. I'm sure you'll find your accommodations more than suitable.'

'Burn in hell,' she shouted, choking on tears of frustration as she was carried off. 'Both of you.'

VanDyke squirted a bit of lemon on his lobster. 'An admirable woman all in all. Not easily cowed. A pity her loyalties are so misplaced. I could have done great things with her. For her, as well. Now she's bait.' He nibbled delicately. 'Nothing more.'

LaRue wiped at the blood on his cheek with the back of his hand. The furrows she'd dug burned like fire. Though VanDyke frowned in annoyance, he used the linen napkin to staunch it.

'Next to money, love is the most powerful motivator.' More shaken than he cared to admit, LaRue poured the flute full and drank it down.

'You were telling me about Angelique's Curse before we were interrupted.'

'Yes.' Surreptitiously LaRue rubbed at his ribs where Tate's elbow had jabbed. Damned if he wasn't going to bruise. 'And about two hundred and fify thousand dollars. American.'

The money was nothing. He'd spent a hundred times that in his search already. But it bubbled in his blood to pay it. 'What proof is there that you have the amulet?'

Lips curled, LaRue lifted a hand to his shredded cheek. 'Come now, *mon ami*. Tate found it herself only yesterday, and with love guiding her, handed it selflessly to Matthew.' To soothe his frayed nerves, LaRue began to roll a cigarette. 'It is magnificent, more so than you had led me to believe. The center stone ...' LaRue made a circle with his thumb and forefinger to indicate size. 'Red as blood, the diamonds around it iced tears. The

327

chain is heavy but delicately wrought, as is the sentiment etched around the jewel.'

He struck a match, cupping it against the soft breeze, to light his cigarette. 'You can feel the power humming in it. Against your fingers it seems to throb.'

VanDyke's eyes glazed, his mouth went slack. 'You touched it?'

'*Bien sûr.* I am trusted, eh?' He blew out a lazy stream of smoke. 'Matthew guards it close, you see, but he doesn't guard against me. We are shipmates, partners, friends. I can get it for you, once I am assured the money is in place.'

'You'll have your money.' Need had VanDyke's hands trembling. His face was white and still as he leaned forward. 'And this promise, LaRue. If you cross me, if you try to bleed more money from me or if you fail, there is no place you can hide that I won't find you. When I do, you'll pray for death.'

LaRue dragged in more smoke and smiled. 'It's difficult to frighten a rich man. And rich is what I'll be. You'll have your curse, *mon ami*, and I my money.' Before he could rise, VanDyke held up a hand.

'We aren't finished. A quarter of a million is a great deal.'

'A fraction of the worth,' LaRue pointed out. 'Would you try to negotiate now when it is all but in your hands?'

'I'll double it.' Pleased to see LaRue's eyes widen, VanDyke leaned back. 'For the amulet, and for Matthew Lassiter.'

'You want me to bring him to you?' With a laugh, LaRue shook his head. 'Not even your precious amulet could protect you from him. He means to kill you.' He gestured in the direction where Tate had been taken. 'And you have the tool to bring him down already in your possession.'

'I don't want you to bring him to me.' That was a pleasure he would have to deny himself, VanDyke realized. The fact that he could make such a practical choice over an emotional one proved he was still in control of his fate. Business, he thought, was business. 'I want you to dispose of him. Tonight.'

'Murder,' LaRue mused. 'This is interesting.'

'An accident at sea would be appropriate.'

'You think he dives when Tate is missing? You underestimate his feelings for her.'

'Not at all. But feelings make a man careless. It would be a pity if something happened to his boat, when he and his

328

drunken uncle were aboard. A fire perhaps. An explosion – tragic and lethal. For an extra quarter million, I'm sure you can be inventive.'

'I am known for a certain quickness of mind. I want the first two hundred and fifty deposited this afternoon. I will not move further until I am assured of it.'

'Very well. When I see the *Mermaid* destroyed, I'll make a second payment into your account. Make it tonight, LaRue, midnight. Then bring me the amulet.'

'Transfer the money.'

Hours passed. Tate resisted the fruitless urge to batter her fists on the door and shout for release. There was a beautiful wide window offering a spectacular view of the sea and sun sinking toward it. The chair she'd thrown had bounced off the glass without making a scratch.

She'd tugged and yanked until her already aching arms had wept with fatigue. But the window stayed firmly in place, and so did she.

She paced, she cursed, she planned revenge and she listened desperately to every creak and footfall.

But Matthew didn't come.

Fairy-tale heroes rescued damsels in distress, she reminded herself. And damned if she wanted to be some whiny damsel. She'd get herself out, somehow.

She spent nearly an hour searching every inch of the cabin. It was large and lovely, decorated in cool pastels under a ceiling of pale-gold wood. Her feet sank into ivory carpet, her fingers skimmed over smoothly lacquered mauve walls, around trim painted seafoam green.

In the closet she found a long silk robe in a brilliant pattern of cabbage roses, a matching nightdress. A linen jacket, a spangled wrap and a black evening coat had been provided for those cool night breezes. A simple black cocktail dress, an assortment of casual cruise wear completed the inventory.

Tate pushed clothes aside and examined every inch of the closet wall.

It was as solid as the rest of the cabin.

He hadn't skimped on the amenities, she observed grimly. The bed was king-sized, plumped with satin pillows. Glossy magazines fanned on the glass-topped coffee table in the sitting area. In the entertainment center under the TV and VCR were an assortment of the latest available movies on video. A small refrigerator held soft drinks, splits of wine and champagne, fancy chocolate and snacks.

The bathroom boasted an oversized whirlpool tub in mauve, a sink shaped like a scallop, brass lights around a generous mirror. On the pale green counters were a variety of expensive creams, lotions, bath oils.

Her search for a jerry-built weapon turned up nothing but a leather travel kit with all the necessities.

There were bath sheets, loofahs, a hotel-style terry-cloth robe and dainty soaps shaped like starfish, conch shells and seahorses.

But the brass towel rack she envisioned wielding as a club was bolted firmly in place.

Desperate, she raced back into the main cabin. Her search through the elegant little writing desk unearthed thick creamy stationery, envelopes, even stamps. The perfect fucking host, she fumed, then closed her fingers over a slim gold pen.

How much damage, she wondered, could a designer ballpoint inflict? A good shot to the eye – the thought made her shudder, but she slipped the pen into the pocket of her slacks.

She slumped into a chair. The water was so close, so close, she wanted to weep.

And where was Matthew?

She had to find a way to warn him. LaRue, the bastard LaRue. Every precaution they'd taken over the last months had been for nothing. LaRue had passed every movement, every plan, every triumph, along to VanDyke.

He'd eaten with them, worked with them, laughed with them. He'd told stories of his days at sea with Matthew with the affection of a friend in his voice.

All the while he'd been a traitor.

Now he would steal the amulet. Matthew would be frantic, her parents wild with worry. He would pretend concern, even anger. He would be privy to their thoughts, their plans. Then he would take the amulet and bring it to VanDyke.

She wasn't a fool. It had already fixed in her mind that once VanDyke had what he wanted, her usefulness was over. He would have no reason to keep her, and couldn't afford to set her free.

He would certainly kill her.

Somewhere in the open sea, she imagined, coolly logical. A blow to the head most likely, then he would dump her, dead or unconscious, into the water. The fish would do the rest.

In all those miles, in all that space, no one would ever find a trace of her.

He assumed it would be simple, she thought, and closed her eyes. What could one unarmed woman do to defend herself? Well, he would be surprised what this woman could do. He might kill her, but it wouldn't be simple.

Her head jerked up as the lock on her door clicked. The steward opened it, his shoulders filling the doorway.

'He wants you.'

It was the first time he'd spoken in her hearing. Tate detected the Slavic song in the brusque tone.

'Are you Russian?' she asked. She rose but didn't come toward him.

'You will come now.'

'I worked with a biologist a few years ago. She was from Leningrad. Natalia Minonova. She always spoke fondly of Russia.'

Nothing flickered on his wide, stony face. 'He wants you,' the steward repeated.

She shrugged, slipping her hand in her pocket, closing her fingers over the pen. 'I've never understood people who take orders blindly. Not much of a self-starter, are you, Igor?'

Saying nothing, he crossed to her. When his beefy hand closed over her arm, she let herself go limp. 'Doesn't it matter to you that he's going to kill me?' It was easy to put the fear back into her voice as he dragged her across the room. 'Will you do it for him? Snap my neck or crush my skull? Please.' She stumbled, turned into him. 'Please, help me.'

As he shifted his grip, she pulled the pen out of her pocket. It was a blur of movement, the slim gold dart plunging, his hand shooting up.

She felt the sickening give as her weapon sank into flesh, and the warm wetness on her hand before she was hurled against the wall.

Her stomach roiled as she watched him stoically yank the pen from his cheek. The puncture was small but deep, and blood ran. Her only regret was that she'd missed the eye.

Without a word he clamped her arm and dragged her out on deck.

VanDyke was waiting. It was brandy this time. Glass-shielded candles glowed prettily on a table beside a bowl of dewy fruit and a fluted plate offering delicate pastries.

He had changed into formal evening attire to suit the celebration he planned. Beethoven's *Pathétique* flowed subtly from the outdoor speakers.

'I had hoped you might avail yourself of the wardrobe in your stateroom. My last guest left rather hurriedly this morning and neglected to pack all of her belongings.' His brow lifted when he saw his steward's bloody cheek.

'Go to the infirmary and have that dealt with,' he said impatiently. 'Then come back. You never cease to surprise me, Tate. What did you use?'

'A Mont Blanc. I wish it had been you.'

He chuckled. 'Let me give you a logical choice, my dear. You can be restrained or drugged, both of which are distasteful. Or you can cooperate.' He saw her glance involuntarily toward the rail and shook his head. 'Jumping overboard would hardly be productive. You have no gear. One of my men would be in the water in moments to bring you back. You wouldn't make it fifty yards. Why don't you sit?'

Until she could formulate a better plan, she saw no point in defying him. If he drugged her, she'd be lost.

'Where did you find LaRue?'

'Oh, it's amazingly easy to find tools when you can pay for them.' He paused a moment to choose the perfect glossy grape.

'A study of Matthew's shipmates showed LaRue to be a likely candidate. He's a man who enjoys money and the transient pleasures it buys. To date, he's been a good if occasionally expensive investment.'

He paused, eyes half closed in pleasant relaxation, and swirled his brandy.

'He kept close tabs on Matthew aboard ship, was able to develop a friendship with him. Through LaRue's reports I was able to determine that Matthew continued to keep contact with your parents, and that he never quite gave up the idea of finding Angelique's Curse. He knew where it was, of course, always, but he'd never tell LaRue where. Even friendship has its limits. He'd boast of it, but never drop his guard enough to tell the tale.'

VanDyke chose a second dark purple grape from the bowl. 'I do admire that. His tenacity and his caution. I wouldn't have thought it of him, holding onto the secret all these years, working like a dog when he could have lived like a prince. Still, he slipped when he resumed his partnership with your parents, and you. Women often cause a man to make foolish mistakes.'

'Firsthand experience, VanDyke?'

'Not at all. I adore women, much in the same way I adore a good wine or a well-played symphony. When the bottle is done, or the music over, one can always arrange for another.' He smiled as Tate tensed. The boat had begun to move.

'Where are we going?'

'Not far. A few degrees east. I'm expecting a show, and I want a closer seat, so to speak. Have a snifter of brandy, Tate. You may feel the need for it.'

'I don't need brandy.'

'Well, it's here if you change your mind.' He rose and crossed to a bench. 'I have an extra pair of binoculars. Perhaps you'd like them.'

She snatched them, rushed to the rail to scan east. Her heart leapt when she found the dim outline of the boats. There were lights glowing on the *New Adventure*, another holding steady on the bridge of the *Mermaid*.

'You must realize if we can see them, they'll be able to see us.'

'If they know where to look.' VanDyke stepped beside her. 'I imagine they'll scan this way eventually. But they're going to be very busy shortly.'

'You think you're clever.' Despite her best efforts, her voice broke. 'Using me to lure them here.'

'Yes. It was a stroke of luck well used. But now plans have changed.'

'Changed?' She couldn't stop staring at the lights. She thought she saw movement. A tender? she wondered. Cutting away toward shore. LaRue, she thought with a sinking heart, taking the amulet to some hiding place.

'Yes, and I believe the change is imminent.'

The excitement in his voice shivered over her skin. 'What are you—'

333

Even at nearly a mile's distance, she heard the blast. The lenses of the binoculars exploded with light, dazzling her shocked eyes. But she didn't look away. Couldn't look away.

The *Mermaid* was engulfed in flames.

'No. No, God. Matthew.' She'd nearly leapt over the rail before VanDyke yanked her back.

'LaRue is efficient as well as greedy.' VanDyke wrapped a wiry arm around her throat until her frantic struggles drained into wild weeping. 'The authorities will do their best to piece it together, what there is left to piece. Any evidence they find will indicate that Buck Lassiter, in a drunken haze, slopped gas too near the engine, then carelessly lit a match. As there's nothing left of him, or his nephew, there will be no one to dispute it.'

'You were going to get the amulet.' She stared at the fire licking at the dark sea. 'You were going to get it. Why did you have to kill him?'

'He would never have stopped,' VanDyke said simply. The flames dancing toward the sky mesmerized him. 'He stared at me over his father's body, with knowledge and hate in his eyes. I knew then that one day this would come.'

The pleasure of it shivered through him like wine, iced and delicious. Oh, he hoped there had been pain and understanding, even only an instant of it. How he wished he could be sure.

Tate sank to her knees when he released her. 'My parents.'

'Oh, safe enough, I imagine. Unless they were on board. I have no reason at all to wish them ill. You're terribly pale, Tate. Let me get you that brandy.'

She braced a hand on the rail, leveled herself up on her trembling legs. 'Angelique cursed her jailers,' she managed. 'She cursed those who had stolen from her, who persecuted her and cut off the life of her unborn child.'

Fighting to speak over her shuddering breaths, she watched his eyes in the glow of candlelight. 'She'd have cursed you, VanDyke. If there's any justice for her, and power left, the amulet will destroy you.'

There was a chill around his heart that was fear and deadly fascination. With the flickers of the distant fire behind her, grief and pain dark in her eyes, she looked powerful and potent.

Angelique would have looked so, he thought, and lifted the brandy to his suddenly icy lips. His eyes were almost dreamy on Tate's. 'I could kill you now.'

Tate gave a sobbing laugh. 'Do you think it matters to me now? You've killed the man I love, destroyed the life we would have had together, the children we would have made. There's nothing else you can do to me that matters.'

With the grief trapped inside her, Tate stepped forward. 'You see, I know how she felt now, sitting in that cell waiting for morning, waiting to die. It was anticlimactic really, because her life had ended with Etienne's. I don't care if you kill me. I'll die cursing you.'

'It's time you went back to your cabin.' VanDyke lifted tensed fingers. The steward, his cheek neatly bandaged, stepped out of the shadows. 'Take her back. Lock her in.'

'You'll die slowly,' Tate called as she was led away. 'Slowly enough to understand hell.'

She stumbled into her cabin and collapsed weeping onto the bed. When the tears were dry and her heart empty of them, she moved to a chair to watch the sea and waited to die.

Chapter Twenty-seven

SHE SLEPT FITFULLY and dreamed.

The cell stank of sickness and fear. Dawn sneaked stealthily through the barred window, signaling death. The amulet was cold under her stiff fingers.

When they came for her, she rose regally. She would not disgrace her husband's memory with cowardly tears and pleas for mercy that would never be granted.

He was there, of course. The count, the man who had condemned her for loving his own son. Hot greed, lust, an appetite for death gleamed in his eyes. He reached out, dragged the amulet over her head, slipped it over his own.

And she smiled, knowing she had killed him.

They bound her to the stake. Below, the crowds gathered to watch the witch burn. Eager eyes, vicious voices. Children were held up to afford them a better view of the event.

She was offered a chance to renounce, to pray for God's mercy. But she remained silent. Even as the flames crackled beneath, bringing heat and dazing smoke, she spoke no word. And thought only one.

Etienne.

From fire to water, so cool and blue and soothing. She was free again, swimming deep with golden fish. There was such joy her eyes teared in sleep and she had drops slipping down her cheeks. Safe and free, with her lover waiting.

She watched him swim effortlessly through the water toward her, and her heart almost burst with happiness. She laughed, reached out for him, but couldn't close the distance.

They broke the surface, feet apart, into air perfume sweet. The moon wheeled overhead, silver as an ingot. Stars were sparkling jewels displayed on velvet.

He climbed up the ladder of the *Mermaid*, turned and held out a hand for her.

The amulet was a spot of dark blood on his chest, as a wound drained from the heart.

Her fingers reached for his an instant before the world exploded.

Fire and water, blood and tears. Flames rained out of the sky and plunged into the sea until it boiled with heat.

Matthew.

His name circled her mind as she stirred in sleep. Lost in dreams and grief, she didn't see the figure creeping silently toward her, or the glint of the knife in his hand as the moonlight struck the blade. She didn't hear the whisper of his breath as he came close, leaning over the chair where she slept.

The hand clamped over her mouth shocked her awake. Tate struggled instinctively, her eyes going wide as she saw the silver gleam of the knife.

Even knowing it was futile, she fought, vising her fingers over the wrist before the blade could slash down.

'Be quiet.' The harsh whisper hissed next to her ear. 'Goddamn it, Red, can't you even let me rescue you without an argument?'

Her body jerked and froze. Matthew. It was a hope too painful to contemplate. But she could just make out the silhouette, smell the sea that clung to the wetsuit and dripped from the dark hair.

'Quiet,' he repeated when her breath sobbed against his muffling palm. 'No questions, no talking. Trust me.'

She had no words. If this were another dream, she would live in it. She clung to him as he led her out of the cabin, up

337

the companionway. Shudders racked her like earth tremors, but when he signaled her to climb over the side, she did so without question.

Clinging to the base of the ladder was Buck. Under that ingot moon, his face was white as bone. In silence, he hitched tanks over her shoulders. His hands trembled as hers did as he helped her with her mask. Beside them Matthew hooked on his own gear.

And they dived.

They stayed close to the surface to use the moonlight as a guide. A flashlight would mark a trail Matthew knew they couldn't risk. He'd been afraid she'd be too frightened to handle the dive and the demanding swim, but she matched the pace he set stroke for stroke.

It was nearly four miles to where they had moved the *New Adventure*. There were squid and other night feeders, spots of color, blurs of movement in the shadowy sea. She never flagged.

He could have fallen in love with her for that alone, for the dogged way she swam, her hair and clothes floating around her, her eyes dark and determined behind her mask.

From time to time he checked his compass, corrected their course. It took more than thirty minutes of steady strokes to reach the boat.

Tate surfaced, fountaining water.

'Matthew, I thought you were dead. I saw the *Mermaid* explode and I knew you were on it.'

'Doesn't look like it,' he said lightly, but supported them both gratefully as she held onto him. 'Let's get you on deck, Red, you're shaking pretty bad, and your mom and dad are crazy with worry.'

'I thought you were dead,' she said again and sobbed as she crushed her mouth to his.

'I know, baby. I'm sorry. Buck, give me a hand with her.'

But Ray was already reaching over the side. His eyes, wet with relief, roamed over his daughter as he hauled up the tanks. 'Tate, are you hurt. Are you all right?'

'I'm fine. I'm fine,' she said again as Marla reached down to take her hand. 'Don't cry.'

But she was crying herself when her mother embraced her. 'We were so worried. That horrible man. That bastard. Oh, let

338

me look at you.' Marla framed Tate's face, nearly smiled before she saw the bruising. 'He hurt you. I'm going to get you some ice, some hot tea. You sit down, honey, and let us take care of you.'

'I'm all right now.' But it felt wonderfully good to sink onto the bench. 'The *Mermaid*–'

'It's gone,' Ray said gently. 'Don't worry about that now. I want to take a good look at you, see if there's any shock.'

'I'm not in shock.' She sent Buck a grateful smile when he wrapped a blanket over her shoulders. 'I need to tell you. LaRue–'

'At your service, mademoiselle.' With a jaunty smile, he came out of the galley with a bottle of brandy.

'Son of a bitch.' Fatigue, fear and the fogginess of shock snapped clear. With a snarl she was on her feet and leaping. Matthew barely caught her before she could sink nails and teeth into LaRue's face.

'Did I tell you?' LaRue shivered and drank the brandy himself, straight from the bottle. 'She'd have clawed my eyes out if she'd had the chance.' He tapped his free hand on the medicated scratches scoring his cheek. 'Another inch north and I would be wearing a patch, eh?'

'He's working for VanDyke,' Tate spat out. 'He's been VanDyke's worm all along.'

'Now she insults me. You give her the brandy,' he said, shoving it into Ray's hand. 'LaRue, she'd hit over the head with it.'

'I'd tie you to the stern and use you for chum.'

'We'll talk about that later,' Matthew suggested. 'Sit down, take a drink. LaRue isn't working for VanDyke.'

'He only pays me,' LaRue said cheerfully.

'He's a traitor, a spy. He blew up your boat, Matthew.'

'I blew up my boat,' Matthew corrected. 'Drink.' He all but poured a shot of brandy down her throat.

She sputtered, and the heat hit her stomach like a fist. 'What are you talking about?'

'If you'd sit and calm down, I'll tell you.'

'You should have told her, and all of us, months ago,' Marla said testily as she bustled out with a steaming mug. 'Here's some soup, honey. Did you eat?'

'Did I–' In spite of everything, Tate began to laugh. It was only when she couldn't seem to stop that she realized it was borderline hysteria. 'I didn't care much for the menu.'

'Why the hell'd you waltz off with him?' Matthew exploded. 'A half a dozen people saw you get into his tender without a murmur.'

'Because he said he'd have one of his men kill you if I didn't,' she shot back. 'He had another right outside the boutique where Mom was.'

'Oh, Tate.' Shaken all over again, Marla sank to her knees beside her daughter.

'I didn't have any choice,' she said, and between sips of hot chicken soup, did her best to fill them all in on the events that had taken place since VanDyke had found her.

'He wanted me outside,' she finished. 'He even provided binoculars so I could watch the boat blow up. I thought you were dead,' she murmured, looking up at Matthew. 'And there was nothing I could do.'

'There was no way to tell you what was going on here.' Matthew sat beside her, took her hand. 'I'm sorry you were worried.'

'Worried. Yes, I suppose I was a bit concerned when I thought pieces of you were floating on the Caribbean. And why did you blow up your boat?'

'So VanDyke would think pieces of me were floating on the Caribbean. He's paying LaRue an extra quarter mill for it.'

'I will enjoy collecting.' LaRue's cocky smile faded. 'I apologize for not killing him for you when I found you on his boat. It was an unexpected turn of events. I didn't yet know you were missing. When I returned to tell Matthew, he was already making plans to get you back.'

'You'll excuse me if I'm confused,' Tate said coolly. 'Have you or have you not been passing information about Matthew to VanDyke during this expedition?'

'Filtering information is more accurate. He knew only what Matthew and I chose for him to know.' Squatting on the deck, LaRue took the brandy bottle again. 'I'll tell you the beginning. VanDyke offered me money to keep watch on Matthew, to become his companion and to pass along any salient information. I am fond of money. I am fond of Matthew. It seemed to me there was a way to take the first and assist the second.'

'LaRue told me months ago about the deal.' Matthew picked up the story, and the bottle. 'Of course LaRue had already been

340

collecting for what, about a year, before he decided to let me in on the arrangement.'

With a flash of gold, LaRue grinned. 'Who is counting, *mon ami?* When the time was necessary, I shared with you.'

'Yeah.' To settle the stomach that had just begun to jitter in reaction, Matthew drank from the bottle. 'We figured we'd play along, split the profit.'

'Seventy-five, twenty-five, of course.'

'Yeah.' Matthew shot him a sour look. 'Anyway, the extra cash came in handy, and it did me a lot of good knowing we were bleeding it out of VanDyke. When we decided to come back after the *Isabella*, we knew we'd have to up the ante. And if we played it right, we'd harpoon VanDyke at the same time.'

'You knew he was watching us?' Tate said dully.

'LaRue was doing the watching,' Matthew corrected. 'All VanDyke knew was what we wanted him to know. When you found the amulet, LaRue and I agreed that it was time to reel him in with it. Only it got a little complicated when he reeled you in first.'

'You kept this from me, from all of us?'

'I didn't know how you'd react, or even if you'd be interested in my personal agenda. Then things moved pretty fast. It seemed logical,' he decided with a lift of brow, 'that the fewer people who were in on it, the better.'

'You know what, Lassiter?' She rose stiffly to her feet. 'That hurts. I need dry clothes,' she murmured and stalked off to her cabin.

She'd no more than slammed the door when he was shoving it open again. One look at her face decided him. He flipped the lock.

'You put me through hell.' She slapped open her closet, yanked out a robe. 'All because you didn't trust me.'

'I was playing it by ear, Red. I couldn't even trust myself. Look, it's not the first mistake I've made where you're concerned.'

'Hardly.' She fumbled to unbutton her wet shirt.

'And it won't be the last. So why don't we …' His words trailed off as she dragged off the shirt. There were purpling bruises on her arms and shoulders. When he spoke again, his voice was icily detached. 'Did he put those marks on you?'

'Him and his ham-fisted henchman from hell.' Still simmering, she peeled off her slacks, shrugged into the robe. 'I stabbed that Slavic robot with a hundred-dollar pen.'

341

He was staring at her face now, at the bruise along her cheekbone. 'What?'

'I aimed for his eyes, but I guess I froze up. Put a damn good hole in his cheek. Scraped a few layers off LaRue, too. I suppose I should be sorry for that now. But I'm not. If you had told me—' She squeaked in painful surprise when Matthew lurched forward and wrapped her tight in his arms.

'Yell at me later. He put his hands on you.' Eyes fierce, he framed her face. 'I swear to God he'll never touch you again.' He laid his lips gently on her cheekbone. 'Never again.'

Strapping on control, he stepped back again. 'Okay, you can yell now.'

'You know damn well you've ruined that for me. Matthew.' She reached out, let herself be folded in his arms. 'I was so scared. I kept telling myself I'd get away, then I thought you were dead. It just didn't matter anymore.'

'It's okay. It's over now.' Lifting her, he carried her to the bed to cradle her. 'When LaRue got back he told me how rough it was going on you. I never knew what it meant to be sick from fear until then.'

To comfort them both, he brushed kisses over her hair. 'We were already working on springing you when LaRue came onboard. Buck and I would swim over, he'd handle the tanks and gear while I looked for you. I figure it might have worked, but LaRue made it easier.'

'How?'

'For one, he found out which cabin you were in before he left, and snagged one of the duplicate keys. In his defense,' Matthew added, 'he was crazy at the thought that he had to leave you alone with that bastard.'

'I'll try to keep that in mind.' She heaved a long sigh. 'You had a key. And here I was imagining you swinging onboard like a privateer. Kicking in doors with a knife between your teeth.'

'Maybe next time.'

'Nope, I've had enough excitement for the next fifty or sixty years.'

'That's fine with me.' He took a breath. 'So, I laid everything out to Buck, then to Ray and Marla. The best I could think of was to use VanDyke's plan to burn the boat to our advantage. If we hadn't given him a show, he might have taken off, or done something to you.' Eyes closed, he pressed his lips to her hair. 'I couldn't risk it.'

'Your beautiful boat.'

'Hell of a distraction, and a foolproof way of making him believe everything was going his way. He'd see it go up, figure everything was going according to plan. I had to hope he'd relax enough thinking I was dead so that I could get on the yacht and get you off without risking a fight.'

He'd have loved a fight, he thought. He'd craved one. But not with her in the middle.

'Now we—' She stopped, jerked her head up. 'Buck. It just hit me. He went in.'

'It was tough on him. I wasn't sure he was going to make it. When LaRue got back, I thought about him going with me, but I wasn't sure I could keep you quiet if you spotted him. And Ray, well, he and Marla needed to stick together. That left Buck. He did it for you.'

'Looks like I've got a whole basket of heroes.' She touched her lips to his. 'Thanks for scaling the castle wall, Lassiter.' With a sigh, she settled her head on his shoulder again. 'He's not sane, Matthew. It's not just obsession or greed. He slips in and out of sanity like a shadow. He's only partially the man I met eight years ago, and it's terrifying to watch.'

'You won't have to watch again.'

'He won't stop. When he finds out you weren't blown up with the boat, he'll keep coming after you.'

'I'm counting on it. It'll be over this time tomorrow.'

'You still mean to kill him.' Chilled, she shifted away, moved out of his arms. 'I understand something of what you feel now. I would have killed him myself if I'd had the means when I thought you were dead. When I knew he was responsible for taking you from me. I could have done it then, in the heat of all that grief.'

Taking a steadying breath, she turned back to him. 'I don't think I could do it now, when the blood's cooled. But I know why you feel you have to.'

He looked at her for a long time. Her eyes were swollen from weeping, even in her sleep. Her skin was still pale so that the mark on her cheek stood out like a brand. She had, he knew, forgiven him any mistake he'd made.

'I'm not going to kill him, Tate. I could,' he continued almost thoughtfully as she stared at him. 'For my father, for the helpless

343

kid who stood there doing nothing. For taking you, for touching you, for every bruise, every second you were afraid, I could cut out his heart without a flinch. Do you understand that?'

'I–'

'No.' His smile was thin as he rose to face her. 'You don't understand that I could kill him coldly, the way I've planned it for years. All those years I stared at the ceiling over my bunk on that fucking boat, with nothing to hold me together but the idea that one day I'd have his blood on my hands. I even used his money, setting what I could aside so I'd have enough to finish the boat, to buy equipment, to tide me over. Because I was going to find that amulet if it took a lifetime.'

'Then my father speeded things up.'

'Yeah. I could practically see "X" marking the spot. I knew I'd have it, and him. Then you …' He reached out to touch her face. 'Then you tipped the scales. You can't imagine how shocked I was to realize I was still in love with you. To know that the only thing inside me that had changed where you were concerned was that there was more.'

'Yes, I can,' she said quietly. 'I can imagine that perfectly.'

'Maybe you can.' He took her hand, brought it to his lips. 'I wasn't going to let that stop me though. I couldn't let it stop what had started sixteen years ago. Even when you put the amulet in my hand, I wasn't going to let it stop me. I told myself you loved me, you'd understand and come to accept what I had to do. You'd try to understand, but you'd have to live with it.'

Watching her face, he linked his fingers with hers. 'If I killed him, he'd always be between us. I realized that more than anything else, I want a life with you. The rest just doesn't come close.'

'I love you so much.'

'I know. I want to keep it that way. You can call the Smithsonian, or one of your committees.'

'You're sure?' she began.

'I'm sure it's what's best for us. What's right for us. The amulet's going into a vault for safekeeping until we get that museum off the ground. Make sure whoever you call hits the media hard. I want it to be worldwide news.'

'A publicity safety net.'

'It'll be tough for him to get around it. Meanwhile, I'm going to arrange to meet him.'

Panic grabbed her by the throat. 'You can't. God, Matthew, he's already tried to have you killed.'

'It has to be done. This time it'll be VanDyke who'll have to back down and sail away. A dozen news agencies will be sending reporters out here. The scientific world will be buzzing with the discovery. He'll know the amulet is out of his reach. There'll be nothing he can do.'

'It sounds reasonable, Matthew. But he's not a reasonable man. I wasn't exaggerating before. He's not completely sane.'

'He's sane enough not to risk his reputation, his position.'

She wished she could be so sure of that. 'He kidnapped me. We can have him arrested.'

'How are you going to prove it? Too many people saw you go with him, without a struggle. The only way to end it is to face him, to make him see he's lost.'

'And if he doesn't see, doesn't accept?'

'I'll make him.' He smiled again. 'When are you going to trust me, Red?'

'I do. Promise me you won't meet him alone.'

'Do I look stupid? I said I wanted a life with you. He's going to be meeting me, along with a couple of my pals, in the hotel lobby. We'll have drinks, a nice quiet chat.'

She gave a quick shudder. 'That sounds too much like him.'

'Whatever it takes.' He kissed her brow. 'After tomorrow, we're finished with him.'

'And then?'

'And then I guess we're going to be pretty busy for a while, putting this museum together. There's a piece of land at Cades Bay that ought to do.'

'Land? How do you know?'

'I checked it out the other day.' His eyes heated again as he stroked her bruised cheek. 'If I hadn't gone off to hunt up a realtor, VanDyke would never have gotten near you.'

'Hold on. You found a realtor and went out to look at land without telling me?'

Sensing trouble, he shifted back. 'It's not like you're committed to it. I just put a deposit on it to hold it for thirty days. I thought it would be like a wedding present.'

'You thought you would buy the land for the museum as a wedding present?'

345

Irritated, he jammed his hands in his pockets. 'You don't have to take it. It was just an impulse so— ' She moved so fast he didn't have time to yank his hands free and brace himself before she tumbled him onto the bed. 'Hey.'

'I love you.' Straddling him, she rained kisses over his face. 'No, I adore you.'

'That's good.' Pleased, if baffled, he pried his hands loose and cupped them comfortably over her hips. 'I thought you were mad.'

'I'm mad about you, Lassiter.' Bracing his hands on either side of his head she lowered to cover his mouth with hers in a deep, dreamy kiss that turned his brain to mush. 'You did this for me,' she murmured. 'You don't even care about a museum.'

'I don't have anything against it.' His hands slipped under her robe to flesh as her mouth jolted his system. 'In fact, I'm starting to like the idea. More and more.'

She skimmed her lips over his jaw and down his throat. 'I'm going to make you so happy.'

He let out a shaky breath as she peeled his T-shirt over his head. 'You're doing a good job so far.'

'I can do better.' She leaned back, her eyes on his, and slowly unbelted the robe. 'Just watch me.'

She was his oldest and most vivid fantasy, rising over him, slim and agile. Flame-colored hair, milky skin, eyes that echoed the sea. She was his to touch wherever he desired. His to hold when his heart thundered. His to watch as passion shimmered over her.

It was so quiet, so peaceful, so easy to join body and heart with hers. They might have been in that long-ago underwater dream, weightless, anchored only to each other. Every sense, every cell, every thought was tied to her, and only her.

He belonged, finally and completely.

Chapter Twenty-eight

TATE ROSE EARLY, and leaving Matthew sleeping, slipped from the cabin. She needed to think. The idea of a solitary cup of coffee in the galley seemed the best way to start.

Trusting Matthew was one thing, but letting him handle VanDyke on his own was another.

When she walked into the galley she found her mother already at the stove with the radio playing Bob Marley at low volume.

'I didn't think anyone was up.' Following the scent, Tate walked to the coffeepot and poured.

'I had an urge to bake bread. Kneading helps me think.' Marla vigorously massaged the dough on her floured board. 'And I thought I'd cook everyone a full breakfast. Eggs, bacon, sausage, biscuits. Cholesterol be damned.'

'You cook like that during emotional upheavals.' Concerned, Tate studied her mother over the rim of her mug. However carefully Marla had made up her face, Tate spotted the signs of a disturbed night. 'I'm okay, Mom.'

'I know.' Marla bit her lip, surprised tears were threatening again. Like most mothers facing a crisis, she hadn't broken down until Tate had been safe. Then she'd crumbled. 'I know everything's all right. But when I think of those hours that vile, unprincipled–' Rather than give in to tears, she punctuated each word with a sharp punch to the dough. 'Evil, conniving, murdering jackal had you I want to peel his skin away from his bones with a paring knife.'

'Whoa.' Impressed, Tate rubbed her mother's shoulder. 'Great image. You're a scary woman, Marla Beaumont. That's why I love you.'

'Nobody messes with my baby.' She let out a long breath, grateful there was no betraying hitch in it. The kneading and the venting had worked wonders. 'Your father talked about drawing and quartering and keelhauling.'

'Dad?' Tate set her mug down and chuckled. 'Good old mild-mannered Ray?'

'I wasn't sure Matthew was going to be able to convince him to stay aboard when they went after you. They fought about it.'

That brought her up short. 'Fought? Dad and Matthew?' Tate decided she needed more coffee after all.

'Well, they didn't come to blows, though it was close there for a minute or two.'

It took a conscious effort to close her mouth at the image of her father and her lover squaring off on the foredeck. 'You're joking.'

'Buck got between them until they'd both cooled off,' Marla remembered. 'I was afraid Ray would pop him instead.'

'Come on, Dad's never hit anyone in his life.' She lowered her mug again. 'Has he?'

'Not in the last few decades. Tempers were a bit heightened.' Marla's eyes softened as she brushed at her daughter's tumbled hair. 'You've got two men who love you sick with worry. And Matthew busy blaming himself.'

'He always does that,' Tate muttered.

'It's his nature to believe he has to protect his woman. Don't knock it,' Marla added with a chuckle at Tate's derisive snort. 'No matter how strong and self-reliant, a woman who has a man who loves her enough that he would literally give his life for hers is very lucky.'

'Yes.' Equality and common sense aside, she couldn't help but smile over it. Damned if she didn't have a white knight after all.

'If I could choose someone for you to spend your life with, it would be Matthew. Even eight years ago when you were both so young, too young, I knew you'd be safe with him.'

Intrigued now, Tate leaned a hip on the counter. 'I'd have thought the reckless, go-to-hell, adventurous type would have been every mother's nightmare.'

'Not when there's solid ground beneath.' Marla put the dough in a bowl to rise, covered it with a cloth. Finding her hands empty again, she looked around the already spotless galley. 'I guess I'll start breakfast.'

'I'll give you a hand.' Tate pulled a pack of sausage from the fridge. 'That way the guys'll have to clean up.'

'Good thinking.'

'Well, I wouldn't have time anyway. After we eat, I've got a lot of calls to make. The university, the Cousteau Society, *National Geographic* – maybe a dozen others.' Glad for the busywork, Tate chose a skillet. 'Matthew told you of his plan to make the discovery public before he confronts VanDyke?'

'Yes, we talked about it after you'd fallen asleep last night.'

'I wish I thought it was enough,' Tate murmured. 'I wish I thought it would ensure that VanDyke would just go away and stay away.'

'The man should be in prison.'

'I agree, completely. But knowing the things he's done and proving them are different matters.' As dissatisfied as her mother, Tate set the skillet on a burner to heat. 'We have to accept that and move on. He'll never pay for what he did to Matthew, to all of us. But we'll have the pleasure of seeing to it that he'll never have the necklace either.'

'Still, what might he do to pay you back for that?'

Tate lifted a shoulder as she set sausage to grilling. 'The necklace will be out of his reach, and I'll have to make sure I am, too. Along with my white knight.'

Absently, Marla reached into a bin and selected potatoes for home fries. 'Tate, I've been thinking. I had an idea – I know it's probably full of flaws, but …'

'An idea about what?'

'About VanDyke,' Marla said, gritting her teeth over the name as she scrubbed potatoes.

'Does it involve a paring knife?'

'No.' There was a giggle at that, followed by a self-deprecating shrug. 'Oh, it's probably stupid.'

'Why don't you tell me about it?' Tate flipped the browning meat with a spatula. 'You never know.'

'Well, I was just thinking …'

Ten minutes later, with sausage sizzling in the pan, Tate shook her head.

'It's so simple.'

Marla sighed and poked at her frying potatoes. 'It's a silly idea. I don't know what made me think of it, or that it could work.'

'Mom.' Tate took her mother's shoulders, turned her around. 'It's brilliant.'

Taken off guard, Marla blinked. 'It is?'

'Absolutely. Simple and brilliant. Keep cooking,' she said, adding a cheerful kiss. 'I'm going to wake everybody up so they can see I come by my genius naturally.'

With a sound of pleased surprise, Marla went back to her home fries. 'Brilliant,' she said to herself and gave her back a congratulatory pat.

'This may work.' LaRue took another scan of the spacious hotel lobby. 'But you're sure, Matthew, you wouldn't like to go back to your early idea of cutting VanDyke into small pieces and feeding him to the fish?'

'It's not about what I'd like.' Matthew stood out of view in the cozy library off the main lobby. 'Besides, it'd probably kill the fish.'

'True.' LaRue sighed deeply. 'It is the first sacrifice of the married man, *mon jeune ami*. The giving up of what he likes. A variety of women, the occasional drunken brawl, eating at the sink in underwear. Those days are over for you, young Matthew.'

'I'll live with it.'

Gingerly, LaRue touched his wounded cheek, and was able to smile. 'She is, I believe, worth even such wrenching sacrifices.'

'Maybe not eating in my underwear, but we'll work out a compromise. Everything set from your viewpoint?'

'All's well.' LaRue scanned the capacious lobby with its generous sitting areas, lush foliage and wide windows. 'The weather is so fine there is little traffic inside. And the timing, of course,' he added. 'We're late for lunch, early for the cocktail hour. Our man is prompt as a rule. He'll be here in ten minutes.'

'Sit down and order a drink. We don't want him choosing the table.'

LaRue straightened his shoulders, brushed at his hair. 'How do I look, eh?'

'Gorgeous.'

'*Bien sûr.*' Satisfied, LaRue moved off. He took a table by the patio window, across from a deeply cushioned sofa. He glanced toward a breakfront that held a variety of board games to amuse guests on rainy days, then took out his tobacco pouch.

He was enjoying the last of his cigarette with a frothy mai tai and a chapter of Hemingway when VanDyke walked in, tailed by his stoic steward.

'Ah, prompt, as expected.' He toasted VanDyke, sneered at the steward. 'I see you feel the need for protection, even from a loyal associate.'

'For precaution.' With a wave of the hand, VanDyke gestured his man toward the sofa. 'You feel the need for the protection of a public place for our business meeting?'

'For precaution,' LaRue countered, meticulously marking his page in his book before setting it aside. 'How fares your guest?' he asked casually. 'Her parents are terrified for her safety.'

VanDyke folded his hands, felt them relax. He had been fighting off a rage all morning after Tate's disappearance had been discovered. Obviously, he thought, she never made it back to the bosom of her family. Drowned, he supposed and glanced up at the waitress. A pity.

'A champagne cocktail. My guest is no concern of yours,' he added to LaRue. 'I'd prefer to get straight to our business.'

'I'm in no hurry.' Demonstrating, LaRue tilted back in his chair. 'Were you able to see the fireworks I displayed for you last night?'

'Yes.' Fussily, VanDyke flicked a speck of lint from his starched cuffs. 'I assume there were no survivors.'

LaRue's smile was thin and cool. 'You didn't pay me for survivors, eh?'

'No.' VanDyke let out a long, almost reverent breath. 'Matthew Lassiter is dead. You've earned your money, LaRue.' He broke off and gifted the waitress with his most charming smile as she served his drink.

'Your orders were to destroy his boat, along with him and his uncle, and your price, I believe, was two hundred and fifty thousand.'

'A bargain, to be sure,' LaRue murmured.

'Your payment will be transferred to your account before the close of the business day. Do you think he died instantly?' VanDyke said dreamily. 'Or do you think he felt the blast?'

LaRue contemplated his drink. 'If you had wanted him to suffer, you should have made it clear in the contract. For a slightly larger fee, it could have been arranged.'

'It hardly matters. I can assume he suffered. And the Beaumonts?'

'Eaten with grief, of course. Matthew was like a son to them, and Buck a dear friend. *Ils sont désolés.* For myself I pretend guilt and misery. If I had not chosen to take the launch to St. Kitts for a bit of nightlife …' He touched his heart, shook his head. 'They reassure me, tell me there was nothing I could have done.'

'Such generous spirits.' VanDyke pitied them for their open hearts. 'An attractive couple,' he mused. 'The woman in particular is quite lovely.'

'Ah.' LaRue kissed his fingers. 'A true blossom of the south.'

'Still …' Contemplating, VanDyke sipped his drink. 'I wonder if an accident on their voyage home might not be best.'

Surprised, LaRue sloshed his mai tai. 'You want the Beaumonts eliminated?'

'Clean slate,' VanDyke murmured. They had touched the necklace, he thought. His necklace. It was reason enough for them to die. 'Smaller prey, however. I'll pay you fifty thousand apiece to take care of them.'

'A hundred thousand for a double murder. Oh, *mon ami*, you are stingy.'

'I can handle it myself for nothing,' VanDyke pointed out. 'A hundred thousand to spare me the trouble of making other arrangements. I'd prefer that you wait a week, perhaps two.' To give me time, he mused, to plan your disposal as well. 'Now, with that settled, where is the amulet?'

'Oh, it's safe.'

The easy smile faded, hardened to stone. 'You were to bring it.'

'*Mais non*, money first.'

'I've transferred your asking price for the amulet, as agreed.'

'All of the money.'

VanDyke bit back on fury. It was the last time, he promised himself, that the little Canadian bastard would bleed him. In his mind murder flashed, the kind of murder that wasn't neat, wasn't practical. And wasn't handled by someone else.

'I told you you'd have the money by the end of the business day.'

'Then you'll have your treasure when the payment clears.'

'Damn you, LaRue.' With temper flushed on his cheeks, he pushed back from the table, nearly sent his chair toppling before he caught himself. Business, he repeated in his head like a chant. It's only business. 'I'll arrange it immediately.'

LaRue took the unexpected bonus philosophically. 'As you wish. Through that alcove you will find a phone.' Chuckling to himself, he watched VanDyke stride off. 'Another quarter million,' he murmured into his drink, while his gaze roamed idly around the lobby, paused very briefly on the opening to the library. 'That's very sweet.'

Feeling generous, he decided to up Matthew's share to fifty percent, as a wedding present. It seemed, after all, only just.

'It's done,' VanDyke snapped when he returned a few minutes later. 'The money is being transferred immediately.'

'As always, it's a pleasure to do business with you. When I've finished my drink, I'll make my own call, see that the transfer is complete.'

VanDyke's knuckles were white against the table. 'I want the amulet. I want my property.'

'Only a few minutes longer,' LaRue assured him. 'I have something to amuse you until then.' From the pocket of his shirt, LaRue took a sheet of drawing paper. He unfolded it and laid it on the table.

The sketch was meticulously detailed, each link of the chain, each stone, even the tiny letters of the engraving.

The flush died from VanDyke's face until it was as white as his knuckles. 'It's magnificent.'

'Tate is quite skilled. She captured the elegance of it, eh?'

'The power,' VanDyke whispered as he skimmed his fingers over the sketch. He could all but feel the texture of the stones. 'Even in a drawing you can see it. Feel it. For almost twenty years I've searched for this.'

'And killed for it.'

'Lives are nothing compared to this.' Saliva pooled in his mouth and the champagne was forgotten. 'No one who's coveted it understood what it means. What it can do. It took me years to realize it myself.'

LaRue's eyes glinted at the opening. 'Not even James Lassiter knew?'

'He was a fool. He thought only of its monetary value, and of the glory he would reap if he could find it. He thought he could outwit me.'

'Instead, you killed him.'

'It was so simple. He trusted his son to check the gear. Oh, and the boy was careful, efficient, even suspicious of me. But just a boy for all that. It was ridiculously easy to sabotage the tanks, a matter of negating a contract.'

Resisting the urge to glance toward the library, LaRue kept his eyes on VanDyke's face. 'He must have known. Lassiter was an experienced diver, eh? When he began to feel the effects of the excess nitrogen, he would have surfaced.'

'I had only to restrain him for a short time. There was no violence in it, none at all. I'm not a violent man. He was confused, even happy. Once the raptures had overtaken him, it was only a matter of enjoyment. He smiled when I took the mouthpiece away. He drowned in ecstasy – my gift to him.'

VanDyke's breath quickened as he stared at the sketch of the necklace, as he steeped himself in it. 'But I didn't know then, couldn't be sure then, he died with knowledge.'

As he came out of his own spell, VanDyke reached for his drink. The memory had tripped his heartbeat pleasantly. And the realization that what he had done all those years before hadn't been a mistake after all. Only one of many steps to this point.

'All these years the Lassiters have kept what is mine from me. Now all of them are dead, and the amulet will come home to me.'

'I think you're mistaken,' LaRue murmured. 'Matthew, will you join us for a drink?'

As VanDyke gaped in shock, Matthew dropped into a chair. 'I could use a beer. Hell of a piece, isn't it?' he commented and lifted the sketch just as VanDyke lurched to his feet.

'I saw your boat go up in flames.'

'Planted the charge myself.' He glanced toward the steward, who had lunged to attention. 'You might want to call off your dog, VanDyke. A classy place like this frowns on brawls.'

'I'll kill you myself for this.' To keep from scrambling across the table, VanDyke gripped it until the bones in his fingers ached. 'You're a dead man, LaRue.'

'No, I'm a rich man, thanks to you. Mademoiselle.' LaRue smiled at the waitress, who'd hurried up and stared with anxious eyes. 'My companion is a bit overwrought. If you would be so kind as to bring us another round, and a Corona, with lime, for my friend.'

'Do you think you can walk away from this?' Shaking with fury, VanDyke snarled at his bodyguard until the man sat silently on the sofa again. 'Do you think you can cheat me, amuse yourselves at my expense, take what belongs to me by blood right? I can crush you.'

He couldn't quite get his breath, could see nothing but Matthew's cold and calm eyes. James Lassiter's eyes.

The dead came back.

'Everything you have can be mine within a week. I've only to whisper the right words in the right ears. And after I have, after you've lost everything you own, I'll have you hunted down, slaughtered like animals.'

'This is as close as you'll ever get to Angelique's Curse.' Matthew folded the sketch, slipped it into his pocket. 'And you'll never touch me or mine.'

'I should have killed you when I killed your father.'

'Your mistake.' Matthew could see the boy he had been, sick and trembling with grief, with rage, with helplessness. Now, it seemed the boy was dead as well. 'I'm going to make you a proposition, VanDyke.'

'A proposition?' He all but spat it as his head threatened to explode. 'You think I would do business with you?'

'I think you will. Come on out, Buck.'

Red-faced from crouching in a jungle of decorative palms beside the breakfront, Buck puffed his way into the clear. 'I tell you, Matthew, them Japanese are geniuses.' He grinned at the palm-sized video recorder he held, then flipped out the tiny tape. 'I mean to tell you, the clarity's crystal, and the sound? I could almost hear the ice melting in that sissy drink of LaRue's.'

355

'I really prefer my brand.' Stripping a huge, floppy brimmed hat from her head, Marla strolled to the table. 'The zoom is superior. All the way across the lobby, and I could count the pores in his skin.' She too ejected the tape. 'I don't think we missed anything, Matthew.'

'Technology.' Matthew bounced the minicassette in his hand. 'It's amazing. On these little tapes we have video and sound recording, from two angles, of you confessing to racketeering. You know what racketeering is, don't you, VanDyke? That's when you pay somebody to do the crime.'

He smiled thinly as he palmed the tapes. 'I guess they'd get you for conspiracy to murder along with it.' He considered. 'That would be two counts. Then there's murder, that would be the first-degree murder of James Lassiter. Last I heard there was no statute of limitations on murder. Nobody forgets,' he added quietly.

He handed the cassettes to LaRue. 'Thanks, partner.'

'My pleasure, I assure you.' Gold flashed in his grin. 'My very *rich* pleasure.'

Matthew looked at his uncle. 'Buck, you and LaRue go take care of these.'

'On our way.' Buck paused, looked back at VanDyke. 'I thought the necklace was evil. I figured it had done in James, and that it hounded me and the boy here all our lives. But it was just you. Now we've done in you, VanDyke, and I gotta figure James is having a good laugh over it.'

'No one will take you or your tapes seriously.' VanDyke blotted his mouth with a handkerchief and sent a subtle signal to his steward.

'I think they will. Hold on a minute.' Wanting the entertainment, Matthew swiveled in his chair. He was in time to see LaRue bend down as if to tie his shoe. He came up like a bullet, directly between the legs of the bodyguard.

Two hundred and sixty-eight pounds of muscle bounced off the glossy floor, with barely a whimper, then curled up like a boiled shrimp.

'That was for Tate,' LaRue told him, then fluttered his hands helplessly as several staff members rushed over. 'He just fell over,' LaRue began. 'A heart attack perhaps. Someone should call a doctor.'

'You always underestimated the Canuk.' Matthew swiveled back. 'Thanks,' Matthew added as the now visibly nervous waitress brought the drinks. 'Marla, looks like you've got a mai tai.'

'Why, I'd love one, honey.' She settled at the table, smoothed the full skirt of her sundress, then aimed her frosty Southern gaze on VanDyke. 'I really want you to know this was my idea. The rough idea,' she temporized. 'It had to be refined a bit. You're very pale, Mr. VanDyke. You may want some cheese, a quick protein lift.'

'Isn't she terrific?' Madly in love, Matthew snatched Marla's hand and kissed it lavishly. 'Now, business. There are going to be copies of those tapes in various safe deposit boxes, vaults, law firms around the world. With the classic instructions – you know the drill – if anything should happen to me, et cetera. Me includes myself, my gorgeous future mother-in-law.'

'Oh, Matthew.'

'Ray,' Matthew continued after winking at her. 'Buck, LaRue, and of course, Tate. Oh, and speaking of Tate.'

Matthew's hand flashed out like a snake, snagged the meticulous Windsor knot of VanDyke's silk tie. With his eyes bullet hot, he twisted it like a noose.

'If you ever go near her again, if you ever have one of your walking dead put a finger on her, I will kill you – after I've broken every bone in your body, and peeled your skin with one of Marla's paring knives.'

'Tate wasn't supposed to tell you about that.' Flushing, Marla sucked mai tai through her straw.

'I think we understand each other.' Finished, if far from satisfied, Matthew loosened his grip.

'How nice. You're still here.' Tate strolled into the lobby. Despite the bruise, her face was glowing. 'Hello, lover.' Almost singing it, she bent to kiss Matthew's cheek. 'We're a bit late,' she went on. 'The plane was delayed. I'd like you to meet my friends and colleagues, Dr. Hayden Deel and Dr. Lorraine Ross.' She beamed at both of them. 'Also known as the new Mr. and Mrs. Deel. Dad.' Tate put a restraining hand on her father's arm when she saw him bare his teeth at VanDyke. 'Behave.'

'Nice to meet you.' Matthew rose and effectively blocked VanDyke in. 'Did you have a good trip?'

'Enjoyed every minute of it,' Lorraine told him. 'Jet lag included.'

Tate slipped off her sunglasses. 'It's very exciting. The captain of the *Nomad* married them just a few days ago.'

'We're going to combine a honeymoon here with business.' Hayden kept an arm around Lorraine's shoulder as if she might disappear without the contact. 'When we got Tate's message we were concerned enough to make the trip immediately.'

'It was great to be able to surprise them at the airport. When I called the university this morning to start the ball rolling on announcing the discovery of the wreck, they told me Hayden and Lorraine were already on their way.'

'Gives us a chance to beat out the others.' Lorraine leaned against Hayden's arm and struggled not to yawn. 'Nevis will be lousy with scientists and reporters in a couple of days. We're anxious to examine the relics from the *Isabella* before it gets crowded.'

'That's the plan.' Tate smiled sourly at VanDyke. 'I don't believe you've met my associates face-to-face, VanDyke, but you certainly know them by reputation. Oh, and wasn't that your servant I saw being loaded into an ambulance outside? He looked terribly pale.'

White with a choking, smothering fury, VanDyke rose. 'This doesn't end here.'

'I agree.' In restraint and unity, Tate laid a hand on Matthew's shoulder. 'It's just a beginning. Several very important institutes are sending representatives to observe the rest of our operation, and to examine the artifacts. Of particular interest is a certain amulet known as Angelique's Curse. The *Smithsonian Magazine* is going to do an extensive article on its history, its discovery and its lore. The *National Geographic* is considering a documentary.'

As all the pieces fell neatly into place, she smiled. 'It's very much on record now where the amulet was found, by whom, and to whom it belongs. Checkmate, VanDyke.'

'Want a beer, Red?'

'Yeah.' She squeezed Matthew's shoulder. 'Love one.'

'Take the rest of mine. I don't think the waitress will be coming back. I think that pretty much concludes our business, VanDyke. Anything else comes to mind, get in touch. Through our lawyer. What was that name again, Red?'

'Winston, Terrance and Blythe, Washington, D.C. You might have heard of them. I believe they're one of the top firms on the East Coast. Oh, and darling, the American consul was very enthusiastic when I spoke with him a couple of hours ago. He'd like to visit the site himself.'

God, Matthew thought, she was something. 'We'll have to accommodate him. Now if you'll excuse us, VanDyke, we have a lot of plans to make.'

VanDyke scanned the faces surrounding him. He saw triumph, confusion, challenge. He could meet none of them here, alone. With the sour taste of failure burning his throat, he turned stiffly and left.

He still had control.

'Kiss me,' Tate demanded and dragged Matthew hard against her. 'And make it good.'

'Ah …' Hayden fiddled with his glasses. 'Would someone tell me what's going on?'

'It feels like we walked in on the last act,' Lorraine agreed. 'Was that Silas VanDyke, entrepreneur, benefactor and friend to marine scientists?'

'That was Silas VanDyke.' Tate gave Matthew a violent squeeze. 'Loser. I'm crazy about you, Lassiter. Let's find that waitress and bring the newlyweds up to date.'

Chapter Twenty-nine

'It's a story with everything,' Lorraine mused.

On the deck of the gently rocking boat she studied the stars and the lovely silver moon. It was past midnight, the explanations, exclamations, victory dinner and celebratory toasts were over.

She'd left her new husband poring over treasures with the others and had slipped away for a quiet moment with her former shipmate.

'The ending's the best part.' Content to play truant, Tate lingered over the last glass of the last bottle of champagne.

'I don't know. You've got murder, greed, lust, sacrifice, passion, sex—'

'Okay, maybe the sex is the best part.'

With a chuckle, Lorraine tried to squeeze a few more drops from the bottle standing between their chairs. 'I left out witchcraft. Do you think Angelique Maunoir was really a witch?'

'This from a scientist.' But Tate sighed. 'I think she was strong and powerful, and that love can work magic of all sorts.'

'Maybe you should worry about owning that amulet, gorgeous as it is.'

'I like to think she would have approved of who found it, and what we intend to do with it. We'll be able to tell her story. And speaking of stories …' Generously, Tate poured half her glass of wine into Lorraine's. 'What about yours and Hayden's?'

'It's not as legendary, but I like it.' Pursing her lips, Lorraine held up her hand to study her wedding ring. There was just enough starlight to make it glint. 'I hooked him on the rebound.'

'Don't be ridiculous.'

'Well, maybe it's not quite like that. You know, when you and I were working together, I never really understood you. There was Hayden, watching your every move with those wonderful cow eyes, and you never blinked. Of course now, meeting Matthew, it all comes clear.' She gave a dreamy little sigh.

'I hope you won't take this the wrong way, but I was thrilled when you were called away from the *Nomad*. Lorraine, I told myself, the coast just cleared.' Gesturing with her glass, she nearly sloshed out champagne. 'Get to work.'

'You worked fast.'

'I just love him. I swear, Tate, he made me feel like a clumsy puppy begging for scraps the whole time we were working together. I'd always been in control with men, you know? With Hayden, all bets were off. I finally had to swallow any semblance of pride. I cornered him in the lab one night when he was working late, and seduced him.'

'In the lab?'

'You bet. Actually, I'd made a few moves before, just to get his attention. I told him I loved him, that I was going to dog his heels wherever he went.

'He studied me very seriously before he said that it seemed best if we got married.'

'He said that?'

'Exactly that.' Lorraine sighed over the romance of it. 'And then he smiled. And then I cried like a baby.' Lorraine sniffled and tossed back the rest of her champagne. 'If I'm not careful, I'll cry again.'

'Don't, you'll set me off. I guess we both got lucky.'

'It's taken me practically my whole life to get lucky. Shit.' With a shrug she slurped more champagne. 'I'm just drunk enough to admit it. Forty-three years. I'm a goddamn middle-aged marine chemist who's really in love for the first time. Damn it, I am going to cry.'

'Okay.' Tate sniffled. 'Are you up to playing matron of honor in a couple of days?'

'Yeah.' Lorraine blubbered sentimentally into her empty glass. She looked up with a watery smile and misty eyes as Hayden and Matthew came on deck.

'What's going on out here?' Hayden asked.

'We're drunk and happy,' Lorraine told him. 'And in love.'

'That's nice.' Hayden patted her on the head. 'You be sure to mix yourself up something to fix the hangover you're going to have in the morning. We've got a busy day ahead.'

'He's so …' Lorraine rose, rocked and draped herself over him. 'Organized. Turns me to mush.'

'Lorraine, there are important people flying in from all over the world in the next day or two. We have to prepare.' When she only continued to beam at him, Hayden glanced at Matthew. 'Can I impose on you for a lift back to Nevis? I think Lorraine needs to lie down.'

'Buck and LaRue'll help you pour her into the tender, run you back.' He held out a hand. 'It's good to have you on our team.'

When the tender skimmed back toward the island, Tate leaned against Matthew. 'They look wonderful together.'

'I guess I can see why you kept tossing his name in my face. He catches on fast and he focuses in on what's most important.'

Resting her head on Matthew's shoulder, she watched the tender's light grow smaller. 'He's the best in the field, and his name carries a lot of weight. Lorraine's not small potatoes either. Having the two of them onboard cloaks the whole operation with efficiency and respect, and scientific purpose.' She let out a satisfied breath. 'And the more influential people who know about the *Isabella* and the amulet, the more impossible it is for VanDyke to interfere in any way.'

'Let's not lower our guard just yet. We're a lot better moored here, off island, miles from the site.'

'VanDyke's skulking off with his tail between his legs. He can call out every politician, every institute and official in his pocket. It won't change things now.' Turning, she wrapped her arms around him. 'I know you'd rather have handled things differently, but this is the best way for us.'

'Doing it this way was more satisfying than I thought. We win, he loses. All the way around.' He reached in his pocket, took out the amulet. 'It's really yours now.'

'Ours.'

'Rules of salvage,' he murmured and slipped it around her neck. 'I think when he had it made for her, he chose a ruby as the heart, for passion. The diamonds around it for endurance. The gold for strength.' Gently, he kissed her brows, her cheek, her lips. 'Love needs all those things.'

'Matthew.' She closed her hand around the stone. 'That's lovely.'

'I thought you might want to wear it for the wedding.'

'I would, yes, if I didn't have something else I treasure even more. It's a little gold locket with a pearl.'

Absurdly touched, he ran a finger down her cheek. He had to clear his throat before he could trust his voice. 'You kept that?'

'I tried to throw it away a dozen times, and never could. Nothing I've ever brought up from the sea was more precious to me. Not even this.'

'We're going to make it work.' He kissed her lightly. 'You're my luck, Red. Why don't we go in? Hayden's right about that long day coming up.'

'I'll be right along. I want to go over my records, make sure everything's perfect. Shouldn't take more than a half hour.'

'You're going to be practical when I was planning on driving you crazy?'

'Make that twenty minutes.' She laughed and gave him a nudge. 'I really need to be sure all my documents are in order. No way I'm going to look half-baked when the rep from the Cousteau Society shows up.'

'Ambitious and sexy.' He nipped her bottom lip. 'I'll wait for you.'

'Fifteen minutes,' she called after him, then hugged herself.

Everything she'd ever wanted was only a step away. The man she loved and a life with him, a career suddenly on fast forward, the museum that would showcase their work.

She closed her hand around the amulet, shut her eyes. And after four hundred years, perhaps Angelique would finally be at rest.

Nothing, she realized, was impossible.

She walked over to pick up the bottles and glasses she and Lorraine had left behind. The quiet footsteps behind her had her chuckling.

'Fifteen minutes, Lassiter. Maybe ten if you don't distract me.'

The hand that clamped around her mouth was damp and smooth. Her own had jerked up to claw at it even before true alarm registered.

'There's a gun at your back, Tate.' The sharp jab just above her kidneys had her going still. 'Silenced. No one will hear if I shoot you right here. If you scream or call out I'll kill you, and anyone who runs to your aid. Do you understand?'

The voice, the threat were sickeningly familiar. She could only nod.

'Be very careful.' VanDyke shifted his rough grip from her mouth to her throat. 'You can be dead in an instant.' Perhaps he could just snap her neck. He considered it, toyed with it, discarded it. Murder could wait. 'An instant later I'm in the water and away.'

'What do you hope to prove by this?' The words were weak and gasping as he squeezed her throat. 'The *Isabella* and everything she held is out of your reach. You can kill me, kill all of us, it won't change that. You'll be hunted down, thrown in prison for the rest of your life.'

'Don't you know that no one will be able to touch me once I have the amulet? You know the power it holds, you've felt it.'

'You're insane–' Her scream was involuntary and carried no more than a foot when his fingers crushed brutally over her windpipe.

'It's mine. Has always been mine.'

'You'll never get away. They'll know it was you. All your money and all your influence won't be able to protect you this time.' She wheezed out a breath as he loosened his grip.

'The amulet will be enough.'

'You'll have to go into hiding for the rest of your life.'

As she spoke, she shifted her eyes wildly in search of a weapon. The champagne bottle with its thick heavy glass was out of reach.

'We have the tapes, we've announced the find.' She hurried on. 'Hayden and Lorraine know, as do dozens of others. You can't kill them all.'

'I can do anything. I can do anything, and there's nothing and no one to touch me. Give me the amulet, Tate, and I'll spare your parents.'

Her head whirled as she remembered. She closed her hand protectively around the stone. It seemed to pulse quietly against her palm.

'I don't believe you. You'll kill me, you'll kill all of us, and for what, some wild notion that a necklace will bring you power and impunity?'

'And perhaps immortality.' Yes, he'd begun to believe that, begun to see the truth of that. 'Others have believed it, but they were weak, unable to control what they held in their hands. I'm different, you see. I'm used to command, to harnessing power. That's why it belongs to me. What would it be like to live with every wish, every thought possible? To win everything. To live forever if you wanted it.'

His breath quickened, coming hard against her ear. 'Yes, I'll kill you for that. I'll kill all of you for that. Do you want me to make you suffer first?'

'No.' She closed her eyes, straining her ears for the sound of the returning tender. If she could somehow signal them, or Matthew, there might be a way to stop VanDyke from killing all of them. 'I'll give it to you, and pray to God it gives you the life you deserve.'

'Where is the amulet?'

'Here.' She lifted the stone she still held in her hand. 'Right here.'

Stunned, he loosened his hold enough for her to jerk away. But she didn't run. There was nowhere to run. Instead she faced him, eyes cold and defiant, her fingers still circling the brilliant center gem. She could see his face go lax, soften like glass heated. But the gun never wavered.

'It's beautiful, isn't it?' she said quietly. She couldn't appeal to his reason. So she would appeal to his madness. Perhaps, just perhaps, she had a weapon after all.

'For centuries it's waited to be held again, worn again, admired again. Do you know there wasn't a mark on it when I took it from the sand?'

She turned the stone so that it caught the white beam of the moon. Light and shadows danced. It was quiet, suddenly so quiet, she could hear each separate whisper of the waves kissing the hull.

'Time, water hadn't touched it. It would have looked just like this, bright and gleaming, the last time she wore it around her neck.'

When he continued to stare, his eyes locked, hypnotized, on the amulet, she inched back, still holding the stone out. 'I think she wore it that morning. The morning they came to execute her. And he, the man responsible for condemning her, waited outside the cell, and took it.'

Her voice was quiet, almost soothing. 'He couldn't have her, but he could have that last physical link she had to the man she loved. Or so he thought. But he just couldn't break that very intimate connection between them. Neither could death. She spoke his name in her mind as the smoke filled her lungs and the flames licked at her feet. Etienne's name. I can hear her, VanDyke, can't you?'

Caught like a rat by the gaze of a snake, he stared. His tongue darted out to lick his lips. 'It's mine.'

'Oh no, it's still hers. It always will be. That's the secret, VanDyke, that's the magic and the power. The ones who didn't understand that, and coveted it for their own ends are the ones who brought the curse on their own heads. If you take it,' she said softly and with sudden certainty, 'you're damned.'

'It's mine,' he repeated. 'I'm the only one it was meant for. I've spent a fortune to find it.'

'But I found it. You're only stealing it.' She was nearly at the rail now. Was that a motor? she wondered. Or just her wishing? If she shouted now, would she save the people she loved, or kill them?

VanDyke's eyes snapped back to hers, and her heart sank like a stone in the sea. Those eyes were clear again, calm again, without that thin glaze of madness.

'You think I don't know what you're doing? Stalling for time until your broad-shouldered hero charges to your aid. A pity he hasn't so you could die together, romantically. Now I've indulged you long enough, Tate. Take off the amulet and give it to me or I'll put the first bullet in your gut instead of your heart.'

'All right.' Her fingers were oddly light and steady as she drew the chain from around her neck. It was almost as if they weren't her own, as if she were floating somewhere beyond her own flesh. 'If you want it so desperately. Get it, and pay the price.'

Braced for the bullet, she tossed it high and far over the sea.

He howled. The sound was inhuman, like a beast tasting blood. And like a beast he shambled to the rail and plunged into the dark water. Before he'd disappeared beneath, she was after him.

As she cut through the water, part of her brain registered the dangerous folly of the act. Yet she was compelled, driven to fill her lungs with air and dive blind.

Reason told her he would never find the amulet in the night sea without mask or tanks or time. Nor would she find him or the treasure she'd flung away.

Even as logic began to balance impulse, she saw the shadow of movement. Rage she hadn't even known had rooted inside her burst free. She was on him like a shark.

Here, in the airless world, his superior strength was countered by her youth and skill. His blind greed by her fury. There was no gun now, only hands and teeth. She used hers viciously.

He clawed at her, desperate to reach the surface and breathe again. With her own lungs aching, she dragged him back, until a kick sent her spinning away.

Up again through the dark water she rose, nearly despairing that she would reach the surface.

He waited for her there, lashing out wildly, and she fought to fill her empty lungs. His face was distorted by the water and salt in her eyes, obscenely feral as he struck out. They fought in a terrible silence broken only by gasping breaths and swirling water.

His eyes rolled white as he pulled her under. The sea embraced them greedily.

She swallowed water, choked. The salt stung her eyes as he held her down and gulped air for himself. Fumbling, her hands lost purchase on his slick wetsuit. The buzzing in her ears became a roar. There were lights glowing, bursting in her head, in front of her eyes.

No, she thought, fighting free. A light. A single light shining against the sand. He was racing toward it, diving, diving through the glassy black water to white sand where the amulet lay like a bloody star.

She watched him lift it, saw his hand close around it greedily. The soft red glow shone luminescently through his fingers, and deepened, darkened. Bled.

He turned his head, looked at her in triumph. Their eyes met, held.

Then surely he screamed.

'She's coming around. That's it, Red, cough it up.'

367

Through the harsh sounds of her own racking heaves, she heard Matthew's voice, the tremor in it. She could feel the solid wood of the deck beneath her, his big hands cradling her head, the damp rain of water leaking onto her skin.

'Matthew.'

'Don't try to talk. Christ, where's the damn blanket?'

'Here, right here.' With calm efficiency, Marla covered her daughter. 'You're all right, honey, just lie still now.'

'VanDyke—'

'It's all right.' Matthew glanced around to where the man sat hudled under LaRue's ready bangstick. He was half drowned and quietly chuckling to himself.

'The amulet.'

'Jesus, it's still around her neck.' Matthew slipped it off with an unsteady hand. 'I didn't even notice.'

'You were a little busy saving her life.' Ray squeezed his eyes tight and absorbed the relief. When Matthew had dragged Tate from the water, he'd been sure his only child was dead.

'What happened?' Tate finally found the strength to open her eyes. Overhead was a circle of pale, concerned faces. 'God, I hurt all over.'

'Just be quiet for a minute. Her pupils look normal. She's not shaking.'

'There could be delayed shock. I think we should get her out of those wet clothes and into bed.' Marla bit her lip, and though she knew it was foolish, checked Tate's brow for fever. 'I'll make you some nice chamomile tea.'

'Okay.' A little woozy, Tate smiled. 'Can I get up now?'

Muttering an oath, Matthew picked her up, blanket and all. 'I'll put her in bed.' He paused briefly for a last glance at VanDyke. 'LaRue, you and Buck better get what's left of him over to Nevis, give him to the cops.'

Vaguely curious, Tate stared. 'Why is he laughing?'

'That's all he's done since Ray hauled him in. He laughs and mutters about witches burning in water. Let's get you in a hot bath.'

'Oh, let's.'

He was patient. Matthew drew her bath, massaged her shoulders. He even washed her hair himself. Then he dried her, tucked her into a night-shirt and robe and put her to bed.

'I could get used to this,' she murmured, letting her still light head rest against plumped pillows while she sipped the tea her mother had brought in.

'You stay put,' Marla ordered, fussing with the blanket. She glanced up at Matthew. 'Ray went along to Nevis. He didn't want to let VanDyke out of his sight until he was in a cell. Do you want me to let you know when they get back?'

'I'll come up shortly.'

Marla only lifted a brow. She had a feeling Tate had one more crisis to deal with. 'I think I'll go brew a big pot of coffee. You rest, honey.' She kissed Tate's forehead and closed the door quietly behind her.

'Isn't she the best?' Tate began. 'Nothing ever shakes that wonderful Southern panache.'

'You're about to find out what shakes a Yankee temperament. What the hell did you think you were doing?'

She winced at the volume. 'I don't know, exactly. It all happened so fast.'

'You weren't breathing.' He caught her chin in fingers tensed and trembling like plucked wires. 'You weren't breathing when I pulled you out.'

'I don't remember. Everything after I dived in after him is jumbled and kind of surreal.'

'You dived in after him,' Matthew repeated, spacing each word.

'I didn't mean to,' she said quickly. 'I threw the amulet into the water. I had to take the chance that he'd go after it instead of shooting me.'

His heart, which had already suffered violently, stopped again. 'He had a gun?'

'Yes.' She could feel her mind begin to float again and struggled to concentrate. 'He must have lost it in the water. I was coming inside.' Gently she took his hand in hers. 'He was just there. Just there behind me, Matthew, with the gun jammed into my back. He must have come over from starboard. His gear's probably still there on the ladder. I couldn't call for you, Matthew. He'd have killed all of us.'

As calmly as she could, she told him what had happened on deck.

'I took the necklace off,' she murmured and closed her eyes to try to see it all again.

The play of light, the shifting shadows. The way the stone seemed to throb like a heart in her hand.

'I didn't even have to think about it. I just threw it. He ran past me; he never even looked at me. Just went in.'

'Why the hell did you go after him? I was right here, Red.'

'I know. I can't explain it. One minute I was thinking I'll get Matthew, and the next I was in the water. Even as I was diving I was thinking it didn't make sense. But I couldn't stop myself. I caught him, and we struggled.'

To bring the picture clearer, she closed her eyes again. 'I remember thrashing around with him on the surface, under it. I remember losing air, knowing he would drown me. Then there was this light.'

'Christ.' He dragged a hand through his hair. 'You're telling me you had a near-death experience? The white light, the tunnel, the works?'

As puzzled as he, she opened her eyes again. 'No, but it was just as odd. I must have been hallucinating. I saw this glow, and the glow was the necklace. The sand was perfectly white, and I could see it as clearly as I see you. I know it's not possible, but I did. So did he.'

'I believe you,' Matthew said quietly. 'Go on.'

'I watched him dive for it. I was just hovering there in the water.' Her brows drew together, forming a faint line between them. 'It was as if I had to be there, had to watch. I'm not explaining this very well.'

'You're doing fine.'

'I watched, waited,' she continued. 'He picked it up and held it, and I could see it bleed through his fingers, as if the stone had gone to liquid. He looked up. He looked right at me. I saw his eyes. Then ...'

Because she trembled, he stroked her hair. He wanted to gather her close, tell her to forget all of it. But he knew she had to finish. 'Then what?'

'He screamed. I heard it. It wasn't muffled by the water. It was piercing, terrified. He kept looking at me and screaming. There was fire, everywhere. The light and color from it, but no heat. I wasn't afraid, not at all. So I took the amulet from him and let him go.'

She stopped on a nervous laugh. 'I don't know – I guess I blacked out. I must have. I must have been unconscious all along because it couldn't have happened that way.'

'You were wearing the amulet, Tate. When I pulled you out, you were wearing it.'

'I must have ... found it.'

He brushed her hair back from her face. 'And that makes sense to you?'

'Yes, of course. No,' she admitted and reached for Matthew's hand. 'It doesn't.'

'Let me tell you what I saw. When I heard you calling for me, I ran out on deck. VanDyke was in the water. He was flailing around, and yeah, he was screaming. I knew you must be in the water, so I went in.'

There was no point in telling her that he dived until his lungs had all but burst, had never given a thought to surfacing unless she was with him.

'When I found you you were on the bottom, lying on your back the way you do when you sleep. And you were smiling. I almost expected you to open your eyes and look at me. I realized when I was pulling you up that you weren't breathing. It couldn't have been more than three, four minutes tops from the time you yelled for me to come, but you weren't breathing.'

'So you brought me back to life.' She leaned forward, set the cup aside so that her hands were free to frame his face. 'My personal white knight.'

'It wasn't like Prince Charming. Nothing romantic about mouth-to-mouth and CPR.'

'Under the circumstances, it beats a bouquet of lilies.' She kissed him gently. 'Matthew, one thing. I never called out.' She shook her head before he could protest. 'I didn't call out. But I did say your name in my head when I thought I was drowning.' She laid her cheek on his and sighed. 'I guess you heard me.'

Chapter Thirty

THROUGH THE BARS of the small cell, Matthew studied Silas VanDyke. Here, he thought, was the man who had plagued his life, taken his father, plotted to murder him and who had nearly killed the woman he loved.

He'd been a man of power, of far-reaching financial, social and political strength.

Now he was caged like an animal.

They'd given him a cotton shirt and pants, both faded and baggy. He wore no belt, no shoelaces, certainly no mono-grammed silk tie.

Still he sat on the narrow bunk as if he sat in a custom-made chair, as if the dingy cell were his lushly decorated office. As if he were still in charge.

But it seemed to Matthew that he had shrunken somehow, that his body looked frail in the oversized prison clothes. The bones of his face had sharpened and pressed skeletally against the skin as if flesh had melted away overnight.

He was unshaven, his hair matted from seawater and sweat. Livid scratches scarred his face and hands, reminding Matthew of Tate's desperate fight for her life.

For that alone he wanted to break through the bars himself, to hear VanDyke's bones snap in his hands.

But he made himself stand, and study.

And he saw that the dignity and appearance of power VanDyke struggled to maintain were stretched over him like thin, fragile glass. The hate was still there, Matthew realized, ripe, alive and burning in his eyes. He wondered if it was enough to keep the man alive, if he could feed on it through all the years he'd be locked away.

He hoped it would be.

'How does it feel,' Matthew wondered aloud, 'to lose everything?'

'Do you think this will stop me?' VanDyke's voice was barely a whisper that slithered through the bars like a snake. 'Do you think I'll let you keep it?'

'I came here to tell you that you don't matter anymore.'

'Don't I?' His eyes flickered. 'I should have killed her. I should have put a hole in her gut and let you watch her die.'

Matthew leapt toward the bars, nearly ripped at them, until the gleam of satisfaction in VanDyke's eyes stopped him. No, not this way, Matthew told himself. Not *his* way. 'She beat you. She's the one who finally brought you down. You saw it, didn't you? The fire in the water. You saw her watching you,' he continued, drawing on the scene Tate had described to him. 'She was so beautiful, so terrifying caught in that wild light. And you screamed like a child in a nightmare.'

Color that rage had washed into his cheeks had now drained, leaving them white as paper. 'I saw nothing. Nothing!' His voice rose as he jerked off the cot. In his mind a blur of terrifying images swam, took shape and threatened to tear at his sanity like eager claws.

The screams wanted to pump, wild and hot, out of his throat.

'You saw it.' Calm settled over Matthew once more. 'And you'll see it over and over again. Every time you close your eyes. How long can you live with the fear of that?'

'I'm afraid of nothing.' Terror was an icy ball in his belly. 'They won't keep me in prison. I have position. I have money.'

'You have nothing,' Matthew murmured, 'but years to think about what you did, and what in the end you couldn't do.'

'I'll get out, and I'll find you.'

'No.' This time, Matthew smiled, sharp and fast. 'You won't.'

'I've already won.' He came close, wrapped his fingers around the bars until they were white as his face. His breath came fast, and the eyes that burned into Matthew's held the bright edge of madness. 'Your father's dead, your uncle's a cripple. And you're nothing but a second-rate scavenger.'

'You're the one in the cage, VanDyke. And I'm the one with the amulet.'

'I'll deal with you. I'll finish the Lassiters and take what's mine.'

'She beat you,' Matthew repeated. 'A woman started it, and a woman ended it. You had it in your hands, didn't you? But you couldn't keep it.'

'I'll get it back, James.' His lips peeled back. 'And I'll deal with you. You think you can outwit me?'

'I'll protect what's mine.'

'Always so sure of yourself. But I've already won, James. The amulet's mine. It was always mine.'

Matthew backed away from the bars. 'Stay healthy, VanDyke. I want you to live a long, long time.'

'I won.' The shrill, furious voice followed Matthew as he walked away. 'I won.'

Because he needed the sun, Matthew walked outside the station-house. He scrubbed his hands over his face and hoped Tate wouldn't be much longer giving her statement.

The air was hot and still, and he had a deep craving for the sea – for something fresh and scented. For Tate.

It was nearly twenty minutes later before she came out. He thought she looked exhausted, all pale skin and haunted eyes. Saying nothing, he held out a bouquet of vivid pink and blue flowers.

'What's this?'

'They're called flowers. They sell them at the florist down the street.'

That made her smile, and when she buried her face in them, her spirits lifted. 'Thanks.'

'I thought we could both use them.' He ran a hand down her braid. 'Rough morning?'

'Well, I've had better. Still, the police were very sympathetic and patient. With my statement, yours, LaRue's, the tapes, they have so many charges I'm not sure what they'll do first.' She lifted a shoulder. It hardly mattered now. 'I suppose he'll be extradited eventually.'

With his hand linked with hers, Matthew walked her to the rental car. 'I think he's going to spend what's left of his life in a padded cell. I just saw him.'

'Oh.' She waited until he'd climbed into the driver's seat. 'I wondered if you would.'

'I wanted to see him in a cage.' Thoughtfully, Matthew put the car in gear and pulled away from the curb. 'I guess since I couldn't pound his face in, I wanted to have the chance to gloat at least.'

'And?'

'He's right on the edge, and I might have given him a little shove to take him closer to it.' He glanced toward her. 'He tried to convince me – or maybe himself, that he'd won.'

Tate lifted the flowers to rub the fragrant blooms over her cheek. 'He hasn't. We know that, and it's what matters.'

'Right before I left, he called me by my father's name.'

'Matthew.' Concerned, she laid a hand over his on the gear shift. 'I'm sorry.'

'No. It's all right. It seemed just somehow. Like a closure. Almost half my life, I've wanted to turn the clock back to that day, do something to change what happened. I couldn't save my father, and I couldn't be him. But today, for a few minutes, it was like standing in for him.'

'Justice instead of revenge,' she murmured. 'It's easier to live with.'

As he turned the car toward the sea, she let her head fall back against the cushion. 'Matthew, I remembered something when I was talking to the police. Last night, when I was on deck with VanDyke, I had my hand on the amulet and I told him I hoped it gave him the life he'd earned.'

'Twenty or thirty years locked away from everything he wants most. Good call, Red.'

'But who called it?' She let out a long breath. 'He doesn't have the amulet, Matthew, but he certainly has Angelique's Curse.'

It felt good to be back at sea again, back at work. Warding off all suggestions that she take the remainder of the day to rest, Tate closeted herself with Hayden and her cataloguing.

'You've done a top-notch job here, Tate.'

'I had a good teacher. There's still so much to do. I have miles of film to be developed. We already have the videos, of course, and my sketches.'

Briskly, she ran a finger down one of her lists. 'We desperately need storage space,' she continued. 'More holding tanks and preserving solutions. And now that we've made the announcement, we can start bringing up the cannon. We couldn't risk using inflatables and cranes before.'

She blew out a breath and sat back. 'We need the equipment for handling the rest, and of course, for preserving and reconstructing what we can of the *Isabella*.'

'You've got your work cut out for you.'

'I've got a great team.' She reached for coffee, smiled at the vase of cheery flowers beside her monitor. 'Even better now that you and Lorraine are signing up.'

'Neither one of us would miss it.'

'I think we're going to need a bigger boat, certainly until Matthew can build one.'

But it wasn't that which preyed on her mind while Hayden muttered over her notes. Tate braced her shoulders and screwed up her courage.

'Tell me honestly, Hayden, when the reps and other scientists get here, am I prepared for them? Are my notes and papers organized and detailed enough? Without being able to use outside resources, I've had to guess on so many of the artifacts that I—'

'Are you looking for a grade?' he interrupted.

The amusement in his eyes had her squirming. 'No. Well, maybe. I'm nervous.'

He took off his glasses, rubbed the bridge of his nose, then replaced them. 'You spent last night fighting a madman, all morning talking to police, and giving a presentation to colleagues makes you nervous?'

'I've had more time to think about the colleagues,' she said dryly. 'I'm greedy, Hayden. I want to make a huge splash with this. It will be the foundation for the Beaumont-Lassiter Museum of Marine Archeology.'

She picked up the necklace that lay on the table. She'd needed, for reasons she no longer felt required analysis, to keep it close.

It was cool in her hands now. Beautiful, priceless and, she thought, quiet at last.

'And I … well, I want Angelique's Curse to have the home it deserves after four hundred years of waiting.'

'Then I can honestly tell you in my professional opinion, you have a very strong foundation.'

Very gently, she laid the necklace back in its padded box. 'But do you think that –' She broke off, glancing toward the window at the sound of clanging and motorized hiccoughing. 'What the hell is that?'

'Whatever it is, it sounds bad.'

They went on deck together where Matthew and Lorraine were already at the rail. Ray and Marla bolted out of the galley.

'What an awful noise,' Marla began, then her eyes widened. 'Oh my God, what is that thing?'

'I think it's supposed to be a boat,' Tate murmured. 'But don't take my word for it.'

It was painted a virulent pink which clashed interestingly with the heavy rust. The flying bridge shuddered each time the engine belched. As it drew alongside, Tate estimated that it was forty feet of warped wood, cracked glass and corroding metal.

Buck stood at the wheel, waving wildly. 'Ain't she something?' he shouted. He cut the engines, which showed their appreciation by vomiting a spew of smoke. 'Weigh anchor.'

There was a horrible grinding sound, a shudder and screech. Buck shoved up his shaded glasses and grinned.

'Going to christen her *Diana*. LaRue says she was a hell of a hunter.'

'Buck.' Matthew coughed and waved at the smoke carried cheerfully by the breeze. 'Are you telling me you bought that thing?'

'*We* bought this thing,' LaRue announced and strolled out on the slanted deck. 'We are partners, me and Buck.'

'You're going to die,' Matthew decided.

'Just needs some paint, little sanding, some mechanical work.' Buck started down the steps to the deck. Fortunately, it was the second riser from the bottom that snapped under his weight. 'Some carpentry,' he added, still grinning.

'You gave someone money for that?' Tate wondered.

'She was a bargain.' LaRue tapped the rail cautiously. 'When she's shipshape and our work is done here, we are off to Bimini.'

'Bimini?' Matthew repeated.

'There's always another wreck, boy.' He beamed at Matthew. 'Been too many years since I had a boat of my own under me.'

'How's it going to stay under him?' Tate murmured beneath her breath. 'Buck, wouldn't it be better to—'

But Matthew put a hand over hers and squeezed. 'You'll make her shine, Buck.'

'Coming aboard for inspection,' Ray called out. He stripped off his shoes and shirt and plunged into the water.

'They do love their toys,' Marla decided. 'I'm making lemon tarts if anyone wants a snack.'

'Right behind you.' Lorraine grabbed Hayden's hand.

'Matthew, that boat is a mess. They'll have to replace every board and spur.'

'So?'

Tate blew her bangs out of her eyes. 'Wouldn't it be more practical to put their money into something in better condition? Into something in any kind of condition?'

'Sure. But it wouldn't be as much fun.' He kissed her, and when she started to speak, kissed her again, thoroughly. 'I love you.'

'I love you, too, but Buck—'

'Knows just what he's doing.' Matthew grinned over the rail where the three men were busy laughing and examining the broken step. 'Charting a new course.'

Bemused, she shook her head. 'I think you'd like to go with them, bailing all the way to Bimini.'

'Nope.' He scooped her into his arms, spun a circle. 'I've got my own course. Straight ahead full. Want to get married?'

'Yeah. How about tomorrow?'

'Deal.' The reckless light came into his eyes. 'Let's dive.'

'All right, I—' She squealed when he carried her to the rail. 'Don't you dare throw me in. I'm still dressed. Matthew, I mean it. Don't—'

She gave a scream of helpless laughter as he leapt out into the water.

Read the opening chapter of
Nora Roberts' new bestseller

Tribute

978-0-7499-3922-9
Now available from Piatkus

One

According to legend, Steve McQueen once swam buck-naked among the cattails and lily pads in the pond at the little farm. If true, and Cilla liked to think it was, the King Of Cool had stripped off and dove in post The Magnificent Seven and prior to The Great Escape.

In some versions of the legend, Steve had done more than cool off on that muggy summer night in Virginia—and he'd done the more with Cilla's grandmother. Though they'd both been married to other people at the time, the legend carried more cheer than disdain. And since both parties were long dead, neither could confirm or deny.

Then again, Cilla thought as she studied the murky water of the lily-choked pond, neither had bothered—as far as she could ascertain—to confirm or deny while they'd had the chance.

True or false, she imagined Janet Hardy, the glamorous, the tragic, the brilliant, the troubled, had enjoyed the buzz. Even icons had to get their kicks somewhere.

Standing in the yellow glare of sun with the dulling bite of March chilling her face, Cilla could see it perfectly. The steamy summer night, the blue wash from the spotlight moon. The gardens would've been at their magnificent peak and stunning the air with fragrance. The water would've been so cool and silky on the skin, and the color of chamomile tea with pink and white blossoms strung over it like glossy pearls.

Janet would have been at her stunning peak as well, Cilla mused. The spun-gold of her hair tumbling free, spilling over white shoulders … No, those would have been spun-gold, too, from her summer tan. Gilded shoulders in the tea-colored water, and her Arctic blue eyes bright with laughter—and most likely a heroic consumption of liquor.

Music darting and sparkling through the dark, like the fire-flies that flashed over the fertile fields, the velvet lawns, Cilla imagined. The voices from the weekend guests who wandered over the lawns, the porches and patios as bright as the music. Stars as luminous as the ones that gleamed overhead like little jewels scattered away from that spotlight moon.

Dark pockets of shadows, streaming colored lights from lanterns.

Yes, it would've been like that. Janet's world had been one of brilliant light and utter dark. Always.

Cilla hoped she dove into that pond unapologetically naked, drunk and foolish and happy. And utterly unaware her crowded, desperate, glorious life would end barely a decade later.

Before turning away from the pond, Cilla listed it in her thick notebook. It would need to be cleaned, tested and eco-logically balanced. She made another note to read up on pond management and maintenance before she attempted to do so, or hired an expert.

Then the gardens. Or what was left of them, she thought as she crossed through the high, lumpy grass. Weeds, literal blankets of vines, overgrown shrubs with branches poking through the blankets like brown bones, marred what had once been simply stupendous. Another metaphor, she supposed, for the bright and beautiful choked off and buried in the grasping.

She'd need help with this part, she decided. Considerable help. However much she wanted to put her back into this project, get her hands into it, she couldn't possibly clear and hack, slash and burn, and redesign on her own.

The budget would have to include a landscaping crew. She noted down the need to study old photographs of the gardens, to buy some books on landscaping to educate herself, and to contact local landscapers for bids.

Standing, she scanned the ruined lawns, the sagging fences, the sad old barn that stood soot-gray and scarred from weather. There had been chickens once—or so she'd been told—a couple of pretty horses, tidy fields of crops, a small, thriving grove of fruit trees. She wanted to believe—maybe needed to believe—she could bring all that back. That by the next spring, and all the springs after, she could stand here and look at all the budding, the blooming, the business of what had been her grandmother's.

Of what was now hers.

She saw how it was, and how it once had been through her own Arctic blue eyes shaded by the bill of a Rock the House ball cap. Her hair, more honey than gold dust, threaded through the back of the cap in a long, messy tail. She wore a thick hooded sweatshirt over strong shoulders and a long torso, faded jeans over long legs, and boots she'd bought years before for a hiking trip through the Blue Ridge Mountains. The same mountains that rolled up against the sky now.

Years ago, she thought. The last time she'd come east, come here. And when, she supposed, the seeds for what she would do now had been planted.

Didn't that make the last four—or was it five—years of neglect at least partially her doing? She could've pushed sooner, could have demanded. She could have done something.

"Doing it now," she reminded herself. She wouldn't regret the delay any more than she would regret the manipulation and bitter arguments she'd used to force her mother to sign over the property.

"Yours now, Cilla," she told herself. "Don't screw it up."

She turned, braced herself, then made her way through the high grass and brambles to the old farmhouse where Janet Hardy had hosted sparkling parties, or had escaped to between roles. And where, in 1973, on another steamy summer night, she took her own life.

So claimed the legend.

There were ghosts. Sensing them was nearly as exhausting as evaluating the ramshackle three stories, facing the grime, the dust, the disheartening disrepair. Ghosts, Cilla supposed, had kept the vandalism and squatting to a minimum. Legends, she thought, had their uses.

She'd had the electricity turned back on, and had brought plenty of light bulbs along with what she hoped would be enough cleaning supplies to get her started. She'd applied for her permits and researched local contractors.

Now, it was time to start something.

Lining up her priorities, she tackled the first of the four bathrooms that hadn't seen a scrub brush in the last six years.

And she suspected the last tenants hadn't bothered overmuch with such niceties during their stint.

"Could be more disgusting," she muttered as she scraped and scrubbed. "Could be snakes and rats. And God, shut up. You're asking for them."

After two sweaty hours and emptying countless buckets of filthy water, she thought she could risk using the facilities without being inoculated first. Chugging bottled water, she headed down the back stairs to have a whack at the big farmhouse kitchen next. And eyeing the baby blue on white laminate on the stubby counters, she wondered whose idea that update had been, and why they'd assumed it would suit the marvelous old O'Keefe & Merritt range and Coldspot refrigerator.

Aesthetically, the room was over the line of hideous, but sanitary had to take precedence.

She braced the back door open for ventilation, tugged rubber gloves back on and very gingerly opened the oven door.

"Oh, crap."

While the best part of a can of oven cleaner went to work, she tackled the oven racks, the burners, the stove top and hood. A photograph flitted through her memory. Janet, a frilly apron over a wasp-waisted dress, sunlight hair pulled back in a sassy tail, stirring something in a big pot on the stove. Smiling at the camera while her two children looked on adoringly.

Publicity shoot, Cilla remembered. For one of the women's magazines. Redbook or McCall's. The old farmhouse stove, with its center grill, had sparkled like new hope. It would again, she vowed. One day, she'd stir a pot on that same stove with probably as much faked competence as her grandmother.

She started to squat down to check the oven cleaner, then yipped in surprise when she heard her name.

He stood in the open doorway, with sunlight haloing his silvered blond hair. His smile deepened the creases in his face, still so handsome, and warmed those quiet hazel eyes.

Her heart took a bound from surprise to pleasure, and another into embarrassment.

"Dad."

When he stepped forward, arms opening for a hug, she tossed up her hands, wheeled back. "No, don't. I'm absolutely disgusting. Covered with … I don't even want to know." She swiped the back of her wrist over her forehead, then fumbled off the protective gloves. "Dad," she repeated.

"I see a clean spot." He lifted her chin with his hand, kissed her cheek. "Look at you."

"I wish you wouldn't." But she laughed as most of the initial awkwardness passed. "What are you doing here?"

"Somebody recognized you in town when you stopped for supplies and said something to Patty. And Patty," he continued, referring to his wife, "called me. Why didn't you tell me you were coming?"

"I was going to. I mean I was going to call you." At some point. Eventually. When I figured out what to say. "I just wanted to get here first, then I …" She glanced back at the oven. "I got caught up."

"So I see. When did you get in?"

Guilt pricked her conscience. "Listen, let's go out on the front porch. It's not too bad out front, and I have a cooler sitting out there holding a coldcut sub with our names on it. Just let me wash up, then we'll catch up."

It wasn't as bad in front, Cilla thought when she settled on the sagging steps with her father, but it was bad enough. The overgrown, weedy lawn and gardens, the trio of misshaped Bradford pears, a wild tangle of what she thought might be wisteria could all be dealt with. Would be. But the wonderful old magnolia rose, dense with its deep, glossy leaves, and stubborn daffodils shoved up through the thorny armor of climbing roses along the stone walls.

"I'm sorry I didn't call," Cilla began as she handed her father a bottle of iced tea to go with half the sub. "I'm sorry I haven't called."

He patted her knee, opened her bottle, then his own.

It was so like him, she thought. Gavin McGowan took things as they came—the good, the bad, the mediocre. How he'd ever fallen for the emotional morass that was her mother eluded her. But that was long ago, Cilla mused, and far away.

She bit into her portion of the sub. "I'm a bad daughter."

"The worst," he said, and made her laugh.

"Lizzy Bordon."

"Second worst. How's your mother?"

Cilla bit into her sub, rolled her eyes. "Lizzy's definitely running behind me on Mom's scale at the moment. Otherwise, she's okay. Number Five's putting together a cabaret act for her." At her father's quiet look, Cilla shrugged. "I think when your marriages average a three-year lifespan, assigning numbers to husbands is practical and efficient. He's okay. Better than Numbers Four and Two, and considerably smarter than Number Three. And he's the reason I'm sitting here sharing a sub with the never-to-be-matched Number One."

"How's that?"

"Putting the song and dance together requires money. I had some money."

"Cilla."

"Wait, wait. I had some money, and she had something I wanted. I wanted this place, Dad. I've wanted it for a while now."

"You—"

"Yeah, I bought the farm." Cilla tossed back her head and laughed. "And she's so pissed at me. She didn't want it, God knows. I mean, look at it. She hasn't been out here in years, in decades, and she fired every manager, every overseer, every custodian. She wouldn't give it to me, and it was my mistake to ask her for it a couple years ago. She wouldn't sell it to me then, either."

She took another bite of the sub, enjoying it now. "I got the tragedy face, the spiel about Janet. But now she needed seed money and wanted me to invest. Big no on that followed by big fight, much drama. I told her, and Number Five, I'd buy this place, named an amount and made it clear that was firm."

"She sold it to you. She sold you the little farm."

"After much gnashing of teeth, much weeping, various sorrowful opinions on my daughterly behavior since the day I was born. And so on. It doesn't matter." Or hardly mattered, Cilla thought. "She didn't want it; I did. She'd have sold it long before this if it hadn't been tied up in trusts. It could only be sold and transferred to family until, what, 2012? Anyway, Number Five calmed her down, and everyone got what they wanted."

"What are you going to do with it, Cilla?"

Live, she thought. Breathe. "Do you remember it, Dad? I've only seen the pictures and old home movies, but you were here when it was in its prime. When the grounds were gorgeous and the porches gleaming. When it had character and grace. That's what I'm going to do with it. I'm going to bring it back."

"Why?"

She heard the unspoken how? and told herself it didn't matter that he didn't know what she could do. Or hardly mattered.

"Because it deserves better than this. Because I think Janet Hardy deserves better than this. And, because I can. I've been flipping houses for almost five years now. Two years pretty much on my own. I know none of them was on the scale of this, but I have a knack for it. I've made a solid profit on my projects."

"Are you doing this for profit?"

"I may change my mind in the next four years, but for now? No. I never knew Janet, but she's influenced almost every area of my life. Something about this place pulled her here, even at the end. Something about it pulls me."

"It'a a long way from what you've known," Gavin said. "Not just the miles, but the atmosphere. The culture. The Shenandoah Valley, this part of it, is still fairly rural. Skyline Village boasts a few thousand people, and even the larger cities like Front Royal and Culpepper, it's far and away from LA."

"I guess I want to explore that, and I want to spend more time with my East Coast roots." She wished he'd be pleased instead of concerned that she'd fail or give up. Again.

"I'm tired of California, I'm tired of all of it, Dad. I never wanted what Mom wanted, for me or for herself."

"I know, sweetie."

"So I'll live here for a while."

"Here?" Shock covered his face. "Live here? At the Little Farm?"

"I know, crazy. But I've done plenty of camping, which is what this'll be for a few days anyway. Then I can rough it inside for a while longer. It'll take about nine, ten months, maybe a year to do the rehab, to do it right. At the end of that, I'll know if I want to stay or move on. If it's moving on, I'll figure out what to do about it then. But right now, Dad, I'm tired of moving on."

Gavin said nothing for a moment, then draped his arm around Cilla's shoulder. Did he have any idea, she wondered, what that casual show of support meant to her? How could he?

"It was beautiful here, beautiful and hopeful and happy," he told her. "Horses grazing, her dog napping in the sun. The flowers were lovely. Janet did some of the gardening herself when she was here, I think. She came here to relax, she said. And she would, for short stretches. But then she needed people—that's my take on it. She needed the noise and the laughter, the light. But now and again, she came out alone. No friends, no family, no press. I always wondered what she did during those solo visits."

"You met Mom here."

"I did. We were just children, and Janet had a party for Dilly and Johnnie. She invited a lot of local children. Janet took to me, so I was invited back whenever they were here. Johnnie and I played together, and stayed friends when we hit our teens, though he began to run with a different sort of crowd. Then Johnnie died. He died, and everything went dark. Janet came here alone more often after that. I'd climb the wall to see if she was here, if Dilly was with her, when I was home from college. I'd see her walking alone, or see the lights on. I spoke to her a few times, three or four times, after Johnnie died. Then she was gone. Nothing here's been the same since.

"It does deserve better," he said with a sigh. "And so does she. You're the one who should try to give it to them. You may be the only one who can."

"Thanks."

"Patty and I will help. You should come stay with us until this place is habitable."

"I'll take you up on the help, but I want to stay here. Get a feel for the place. I've done some research on it, but I could use some recommendations for local labor—skilled and not. Plumbers, electricians, carpenters, landscapers. And just people with strong backs who can follow directions."

"Get your notebook."

She pushed to her feet, started inside, then turned back. "Dad, if things had worked out between you and Mom, would you have stayed in the business? Stayed in LA?"

"Maybe. But I was never happy there. Or I wasn't happy there for long. And I wasn't a comfortable actor."

"You were good."

"Good enough," he said with a smile. "But I didn't want what Dilly wanted, for herself or for me. So I understand what you meant when you said the same. It's not her fault, Cilla, that we wanted something else."

"You found what you wanted here."

"Yes, but—"

"That doesn't mean I will, too," she said. "I know. But I just might."

First, Cilla supposed, she had to figure out what it was she did want. For more than half her life she'd done what she was told, and accepted what she had as what she should want. And most of the remainder, she admitted, she'd spent escaping from or ignoring all of that, or sectioning it off as if it had happened to someone else.

She'd been an actor before she could talk because it was what her mother wanted. She'd spent her childhood playing another child—one who was so much cuter, smarter, sweeter than she was herself. When that went away, she'd struggled through what the agents and producers considered the awkward years, where the work was lean. She cut a disastrous mother-daughter album with Dilly, and did a handful of teen slasher films in which she considered herself lucky to have been gruesomely murdered.

She'd been washed up before her eighteenth birthday, Cilla thought as she flopped down on the bed in her motel room. A has-been, a whatever-happened-to who copped a scattering of guest roles on TV and voice-overs for commercials.

But the long-running TV series and a few forgettable B-movies provided a nest egg. She'd been clever about feathering that nest, and using those eggs to allow her to poke her fingers into various pies to see if she liked the flavor.

Her mother called it wasting her God-given, and her therapist termed it avoidance.

Cilla called it a learning curve.

Whatever you called it, it brought her here to a fairly crappy hotel in Virginia, with the prospect of hard, sweaty and expensive work over the next several months. She couldn't wait to get started.

She flipped on the TV, intending to use it as background noise while she sat on the lumpy bed to make another pass through her notes. She heard a couple of cans thud out of the vending machine a few feet outside her door. Behind her head, the ghost sounds of the TV in the next room wafted through the wall.

389

While the local news droned on her set, she made her priority list for the next day. Working bathroom, number one. Camping out wasn't a problem for her, but moving out of the motel meant she required the basic facilities. Sweaty work necessitated working shower. Plumbing, first priority.

Halfway through her list her eyes began to droop. Reminding herself she wanted to be checked out and on site by eight, she switched off the TV, then the light.

As she dropped into sleep, the ghosts from the next room drifted through the wall. She heard Janet Hardy's glorious voice lift into a song designed to break hearts.

"Perfect," Cilla murmured as the song followed her into sleep.

She sat on the lovely patio with the view full of the pretty pond and the green hills that rolled back to the blue mountains. Roses and lilies stunned the air with perfume that had the bees buzzing drunkenly and a hummingbird, bold as an emerald, darting for nectar. The sun poured strong and bright out of cloudless skies to wash everything in the golden light of fairy tales. Birds sang their hearts out in Disneyesque harmony.

"I expect to see Bambi frolicking with Thumper any minute," Cilla commented.

"It's how I saw it. In the good times." Young, beautiful in a delicate white sundress, Janet sipped sparkling lemonade. "Perfect as a stage set, and ready for me to make my entrance."

"And in the bad times?"

"An escape, a prison, a mistake, a lie." Janet shrugged her lovely shoulders. "But always a world away."

"You brought that world with you. Why?"

"I needed it. I couldn't be alone. There's too much space when you're alone. How do you fill it? Friends, men, sex, drugs, parties, music. Still, I could be calm here for a while. I could pretend here, pretend I was Gertrude Hamilton again. Though she died when I was six and Janet Hardy was born."

"Did you want to be Gertrude again?"

"Of course not." A laugh, bright and bold as the day, danced through the air. "But I liked to pretend I did. Gertrude would have been a better mother, a better wife, probably a better woman. But Gertrude wouldn't have been nearly as interesting as Janet. Who'd remember her? And Janet? No one will ever forget her." With her head tilted, Janet gave her signature

390

smile—humor and knowledge with sex shimmering at the edges. "Aren't you proof of that?"

"Maybe I am. But I see what happened to you, and what's happened to this place, as a terrible waste. I can't bring you back, or even know you. But I can do this."

"Are you doing this for you or for me?"

"Both, I think." She saw the grove, all pink and white blossoms, all fragrance and potential. And the horses grazing in green fields, gold and white etched against hills. "I don't see it as a perfect set. I don't need perfect. I see it as your legacy to me and, if I can bring it back, as my tribute to you. I come from you, and through my father, from this place. I want to know that, and feel it."

"Dilly hated it here."

"I don't know if she did, always. But she does now."

"She wanted Hollywood—in big, shiny letters. She was born wanting it, and lacking the talent or the grit to get it and hold it. You're not like her, or me. Maybe …" Janet smiled as she sipped again. "Maybe you're more like Gertrude. More like Trudy."

"Who did you kill that night? Janet or Gertrude?"

"That's a question." With a smile, Janet tipped back her head and closed her eyes.

But what was the answer? Cilla wondered about that as she drove back to the farm in the morning. And why did it matter? Why ask questions of a dream anyway?

Dead was dead, after all. The project wasn't about death, but about life. About making something for herself out of what had been left to ruin.

As she stopped to unlock the old iron gates that blocked the drive she debated having them removed. Would that be a symbol to throwing open again what had been closed off, or would it be a monumentally stupid move that left her, and the property, vulnerable? They protested when she walked them open, and left rust on her hands.

Screw symbols and stupidity, she decided. They should come down because they were a pain in the ass. After the project, she could put them back up.

Once she'd parked in front of the house, she strode up to unlock the front door, and left it wide to the morning air. She drew on her work gloves. She'd finish tackling the kitchen, she thought. And hope the plumber her father had recommended showed up.

Either way, she'd be staying. Even if she had to pitch a damn tent in the front yard.

She'd worked up her first sweat of the day when the plumber, a grizzle-cheeked man named Buddy, showed up. He made the rounds with her, listened to her plans, scratched his chin a lot. When he gave her what she thought of as a pull-it-out-of-his-ass estimate for the projected work, she countered with a bland stare.

He grinned at that, scratched some more. "I could work up something a little more formal for you. It'd be considerable less if you're buying the fixtures and such."

"I will be."

"Okay then. I'll work up an estimate for you, and we'll see what's what."

"That's fine. Meanwhile, how much to snake out the tub in the first bath upstairs? It's not draining right."

"Why don't I take a look-see? Estimate's free and I'm here for that anyway."

She hovered, not so much because she didn't trust him but because you could never be sure what you might learn. She learned he didn't dawdle, and that his fee for the small task—and a quick check of the sink and john—meant he wanted the job enough that his estimate would probably come into line.

By the time Buddy climbed back into his truck, she hoped the carpenter and electrician she'd lined up for estimates worked out as well.

She dug out her notebook to tick her meeting with Buddy off her day's to-do list. Then she hefted her sledgehammer. She was in the mood for some demo, and the rotted boards on the front porch were just the place to start.

midnight
bayou

For Leslie Gelbman,
a woman who understands
the value of time

God stands winding His lonely horn,
And time and the world are ever in flight;
And love is less kind than the gray twilight,
And hope is less dear than the dew of the morn.

William Butler Yeats

Prologue

Death, with all its cruel beauty, lived in the bayou. Its shadows ran deep. Cloaked by them, a whisper in the marsh grass or rushes, in the tangled trap of the kudzu, meant life, or fresh death. Its breath was thick and green, and its eyes gleamed yellow in the dark.

Silent as a snake, its river swam a sinuous line – black water under a fat white moon where the cypress knees broke the surface like bones piercing skin.

Through the dark, moon-dappled water, the long, knobby length of an alligator carved with barely a ripple. Like a secret, its threat was silent. When it struck, its tail whipping a triumphant slice through the water, when it clamped the unwary muskrat in its killing jaws, the bayou echoed with a single short scream.

And the gator sank deep to the muddy bottom with its prey.

Others had known the cruel, silent depths of that river. Knew, even in the vicious summer heat, it was cold, cold.

Vast with secrets, the bayou was never quite still. In the night, under a high hunter's moon, death was busy. Mosquitoes, voracious vampires of the swamp, whined in a jubilant cloud of greed. Players of the marsh music, they blended with the buzzes, hums and drips that were punctuated by the shocked squeals of the hunted.

In the high limbs of a live oak, shadowed by moss and leaves, an owl hooted its two mournful notes. Alerted, a marsh rabbit ran for his life.

A breeze stirred the air, then was gone, like the single sigh of a ghost.

The owl swooped from its perch with a swift spread of wings.

Near the river, while the owl dived and the rabbit died, an old gray house with a swaying dock slept in shadows. Beyond, rising over a long, lush spread of grass, a great white manor stood watchful in the moonlight.

Between them, teeming with life, vigorous with death, the bayou laid its line.

Chapter One

Manet Hall, Louisiana
December 30, 1899

The baby was crying. Abigail heard it in dreams, the soft, unsettled whimper, the stirring of tiny limbs under soft blankets. She felt the first pangs of hunger, a yearning in the belly, almost as if the child were still inside her. Her milk came down before she was fully awake.

She rose quickly and without fuss. It gave her such pleasure – that overfull sensation in her breasts, the tenderness of them. The purpose of them. Her baby needed and she would provide.

She crossed to the *recamier*, lifted the white robe draped over its back. She drew in the scent of the hothouse lilies – her favorite – spearing out of a crystal vase that had been a wedding present.

Before Lucian, she'd been content to tuck wildflowers into bottles.

If Lucian had been home, he would have woken as

well. Though she would have smiled, have stroked a hand over his silky blond hair as she told him to stay, to sleep, he would have wandered up to the nursery before she'd finished Marie Rose's midnight feeding.

She missed him – another ache in the belly. But as she slipped into her night wrapper, she remembered he would be back the next day. She would start watching for him in the morning, waiting to see him come galloping down the *allée* of oaks.

No matter what anyone thought or said, she would run out to meet him. Her heart would leap, oh, it always leaped, when he sprang down from his horse and lifted her off her feet into his arms.

And at the New Year's ball, they would dance.

She hummed to herself as she lit a candle, shielding it with her hand as she moved to the bedroom door, out into the corridor of the great house where she had once been servant and was now, well, if not daughter of the house at least the wife of its son.

The nursery was on the third floor of the family wing. That was a battle she'd fought with Lucian's mother, and lost. Josephine Manet had definite rules about behavior, domestic arrangements, traditions. Madame Josephine, Abigail thought as she moved quickly and quietly past the other bedroom doors, had definite ideas on everything. Certainly that a three-month-old baby belonged in the nursery, under the care of a nursemaid, and not in a cradle tucked into the corner of her parents' bedroom.

Candlelight flickered and flew against the walls as Abigail climbed the narrowing stairs. At least she'd managed to keep Marie Rose with her for six weeks. And had used the cradle that was part of her own family's traditions. It had been carved by her *grand-père*. Her own mother had slept in it, then had tucked Abigail in it seventeen years later.

Marie Rose had spent her first nights in that old cradle, a tiny angel with her doting and nervous parents close at hand.

Her daughter would respect her father's family and their ways. But Abigail was determined that her child would also respect her mother's family, and learn their ways.

Josephine had complained about the baby, about the homemade cradle, so constantly that she and Lucian had given in. It was, Lucian said, the way water wears at rock. It never ceases, so the rock gives way or wears down.

The baby spent her nights in the nursery now, in the crib made in France, where Manet babies had slept for a century.

It was a proper if not cozy arrangement, Abby comforted herself. Her *petite* Rose was a Manet. She would be a lady.

And as Madame Josephine had pointed out, again and again, other members of the household were not to have their sleep disturbed by fretful cries. However such matters were done in the bayou, here in Manet Hall, children were tended in the nursery.

How her lips curled when she said it. Bayou – as if it were a word to be spoken only in brothels and bars.

It didn't matter that Madame Josephine hated her, that Monsieur Henri ignored her. It didn't matter that Julian looked at her the way no man should look at his brother's wife.

Lucian loved her.

Nor did it matter that Marie Rose slept in the nursery. Whether they were separated by a floor or a continent, she felt Marie Rose's needs as she felt her own. The bond was so strong, so true, it could never be broken.

Madame Josephine may win battles, but Abigail knew she herself had won the war. She had Lucian and Marie Rose.

There were candles glowing in the nursery. Claudine, the nursemaid, didn't trust the gaslight. She already held Marie Rose and was trying to quiet her with a sugar tit, but the baby's fists were shaking, little balls of rage.

'Such a temper she has.' Abigail set the candle down and was laughing as she crossed the room, her arms already outstretched.

'Knows what she wants, and when she wants it.' Claudine, a pretty Cajun with sleepy dark eyes, gave the baby a quick cuddle, then passed her off. 'She hardly made a fuss yet. Don't know how you hear her way off downstairs.'

'I hear her in my heart. There now, *bébé*. *Maman's* here.'

'Diaper's wet.'

'I'll change her.' Abigail rubbed her cheek on the baby's and smiled. Claudine was a friend – a battle won. Having her established in the nursery, in the household, gave Abigail comfort and the companionship none of Lucian's family would offer her.

'Go on back to bed. Once she's nursed, she'll sleep till morning.'

'Good as gold, she is.' Claudine brushed fingertips over Marie Rose's curly hair. 'If you don't need me, maybe I'll take a walk down to the river. Jasper, he's gonna be there.' Her dark eyes lit. 'I told him maybe, if I can get away, I come down around midnight.'

'You oughta make that boy marry you, *chère*.'

'Oh, I'm gonna. Maybe I run down for an hour or two, if you don't mind, Abby.'

'I don't mind, but you be careful you don't catch nothing more than some crawfish. Anything more,' she corrected as she prepared to change Marie Rose's soiled linen.

6

'Don't you worry. I'll be back before two.' She started out through the connecting door and glanced back. 'Abby? You ever think, when we were kids, that you'd be mistress of this house one day?'

'I'm not mistress here.' She tickled the baby's toes and had Marie Rose gurgling. 'And the one who is'll probably live to a hundred and ten off of spite just to make sure I never am.'

'If anybody could, it'd be that one. But you will be, one day. You fell into the luck, Abby, and it looks real fine on you.'

Alone with the baby, Abby tickled and cooed. She powdered and smoothed, then tidily fastened the fresh diaper. When Marie Rose was tucked into a fresh gown and swaddled, Abby settled in the rocker, bared her breast for that tiny, hungry mouth. Those first greedy tugs, the answering pull in her womb, made her sigh. Yes, she'd fallen into the luck. Because Lucian Manet, the heir of Manet Hall, the shining knight of every fairy tale, had looked at her. And loved.

She bent her head to watch the baby nurse. Marie Rose's eyes were wide open, fixed on her mother's face. A tiny crease of concentration formed between her eyebrows.

Oh, she had such hope those eyes would stay blue, like Lucian's. The baby's hair was dark like her own. Dark and curling, but her skin was milk white – again like her papa's rather than the deeper tone, the dusky gold of her Cajun mama's.

She would have the best of both of them, Abby thought. She would have the best of everything.

It wasn't only the money, the grand house, the social position, though she wanted that for her children now that she had tasted it herself. It was the acceptance, the learning, the *knowing* you belonged in such a place. Her

7

daughter, and all the children who came after, would read and write, would speak proper English, proper French, in fine voices.

No one would ever look down on them.

'You'll be a lady,' Abigail murmured, stroking the baby's cheek as Marie Rose's hand kneaded her breast as if to hurry the milk along. 'An *educated* lady with your papa's sweet heart and your mama's good sense. Papa'll be home tomorrow. It's the very last day of a whole century, and you have your whole life to live in it.'

Her voice was quiet, a singsong rhythm to lull both of them.

'It's so exciting, Rosie, my Rosie. We're going to have a grand ball tomorrow night. I have a new gown. It's blue, like your eyes. Like your papa's eyes. Did I tell you I fell in love with his eyes first? So beautiful. So kind. When he came back to Manet Hall from the university, he looked like a prince coming home to his castle. Oh, my heart just pounded so.'

She leaned back, rocking in the fluttering light of the candles.

She thought of the New Year's celebration the next evening, and how she would dance with Lucian, how her gown would sweep and swirl as they waltzed.

How she would make him proud.

And she remembered the first time they had waltzed.

In the spring, with the air heavy with perfume from the flowers, and the house alight like a palace. She'd sneaked into the garden, away from her duties, because she'd wanted to see it so much. The way the gleaming white hall with its balusters like black lace stood against the starry sky, the way the windows flamed. Music had spilled out of those windows, out of the gallery doors where guests had stepped out for air.

8

She'd imagined herself inside the ballroom, whirling, whirling, to the music. And so had whirled in the shadows of the garden. And, whirling, had seen Lucian watching her on the path.

Her own fairy tale, Abby thought. The prince taking Cinderella's hand and drawing her into a dance moments before midnight struck. She'd had no glass slipper, no pumpkin coach, but the night had turned into magic.

She could still hear the way the music had floated out through the balcony doors, over the air, into the garden.

'*After the ball is over, after the break of morn …*'

She sang the refrain quietly, shifting the baby to her other breast.

'*After the dancers leaving, after the stars are gone …*'

They had danced, to that lovely, sad song in the moon-lit garden with the house a regal white and gold shadow behind them. Her in her simple cotton dress, and Lucian in his handsome evening clothes. And as such things were possible in fairy tales, they fell in love during that lovely sad song.

Oh, she knew it had started before that night. For her it had begun with her first glimpse of him, astride the chestnut mare he'd ridden from New Orleans to the plantation. The way the sun had beamed through the leaves and the moss on the live oaks along the *allée*, surrounding him like angel wings. His twin had ridden beside him – Julian – but she'd seen only Lucian.

She'd been in the house only a few weeks then, taken on as an undermaid and doing her best to please Monsieur and Madame Manet so she might keep her position and the wages earned.

He'd spoken to her – kindly, correctly – if they passed each other in the house. But she'd sensed him watching her. Not the way Julian watched, not with hot eyes and a

9

smirk twisting his lips. But, she liked to think now, with a kind of longing.

In the weeks that went by she would come upon him often. He'd sought her out. She knew that now, prized that now, as he'd confessed it to her on their wedding night.

But it had really begun the evening of the ball. After the song had ended, he'd held her, just a moment longer. Then he bowed, as a gentleman bows to a lady. He kissed her hand.

Then, just as she thought it was over, that the music would dim, he tucked the hand he'd kissed into the crook of his arm. Began to walk with her, to talk with her. The weather, the flowers, the gossip of the household.

As if they were friends, Abby thought now with a smile. As if it were the most natural thing in the world for Lucian Manet to take a turn in the garden with Abigail Rouse.

They'd walked in the garden many nights after that. Inside the house, where others could see, they remained master and servant. But all through that heady spring they walked the garden paths as young lovers, telling each other of hopes, of dreams, of sorrows and joys.

On her seventeenth birthday he brought her a gift, wrapped in silver paper with a bright blue bow. The enameled watch was a pretty circle dangling from the golden wings of a brooch. Time flew, he told her as he pinned the watch to the faded cotton of her dress, when they were together. And he would rather have his life wing by than spend it apart from her.

He'd gotten down on one knee and asked her to be his wife.

It could never be. Oh, she'd tried to tell him through the tears. He was beyond her reach, and he could have anyone.

10

She remembered now how he'd laughed, how the joy had burst over his beautiful face. How could he be beyond her reach when she had his hand in hers even now? And if he could have anyone, then he would have her.

'So now we have each other, and you,' Abby whispered and shifted the drowsing baby to her shoulder. 'And if his family hates me for it, what does it matter? I make him happy.'

She turned her face into the soft curve of the baby's neck. 'I'm learning to speak as they speak, to dress as they dress. I will never think as they think, but for Lucian, I behave as they behave, at least when it shows.'

Content, she rubbed the baby's back and continued to rock. But when she heard the heavy footsteps on the stairs, the stumbling climb, she rose quickly. Her arms tightened in a circle of protection around the baby as she turned toward the crib.

She heard Julian come through the door and knew without seeing he would be drunk. He was nearly always drunk or on his way to becoming so.

Abby didn't speak. She lay the baby in the crib, and when Marie Rose whimpered restlessly, stroked her quiet again.

'Where's the nursemaid?' he demanded.

Still, Abby didn't turn. 'I don't want you in here when you've been drinking.'

'Giving orders now?' His voice was slurred, his balance impaired. But he was thinking clearly enough. Liquor, he'd always believed, helped clarify the mind.

And his was clarified when it came to his brother's wife. If Lucian had a thing – and what was a woman but a thing? – Julian wanted it.

She was small, almost delicate of build. But she had good strong legs. He could see the shape of them where

11

the firelight in the nursery grate shimmered through her thin nightclothes. Those legs would wrap around him as easily as they did his brother.

Her breasts were high and full, fuller now since she'd had the whelp. He'd gotten his hands on them once, and she'd slapped him for it. As if she had a say in who touched her.

He closed the door at his back. The whore he'd bought that night had only whetted his appetite. It was time to sate it.

'Where's the other bayou slut?'

Abby's hand fisted at her side. She turned now, guarding the crib with her body. He looked so like Lucian, but there was a hardness in him Lucian lacked. A darkness.

She wondered if it was true, what her *grand-mère* said. That with twins, sometimes traits get divvied up in the womb. One gets the good, the other the bad.

She didn't know if Julian had come into the world already spoiled. But she knew he was dangerous when drunk. It was time he learned she was dangerous as well.

'Claudine is my friend, and you have no right to speak of her that way. Get out. You have no right to come in here and insult me. This time Lucian will hear of it.'

She saw his gaze slide down from her face, watched lust come into his eyes. Quickly, she tugged her wrapper over the breast still partially exposed from nursing. 'You're disgusting. *Cochon*! To come in a child's room with your wicked thoughts for your brother's wife.'

'Brother's whore.' He thought he could smell her anger and her fear now. A heady perfume. 'You'd have spread your legs for me if I'd been born fifteen minutes sooner. But you wouldn't have stolen my name the way you stole his.'

Her chin came up. 'I don't even see you. No one does.

12

You're nothing beside him. A shadow, and one that stinks of whiskey and the brothel.'

She wanted to run. He frightened her, had always frightened her on a deep, primal level. But she wouldn't risk leaving him with the baby. 'When I tell Lucian of this, he'll send you away.'

'He has no power here, and we all know it.' He came closer, easing his way like a hunter through the woods. 'My mother holds the power in this house. I'm her favorite. Timing at birth doesn't change that.'

'He *will* send you away.' Tears stung the back of her throat because she knew Julian was right. It was Josephine who reigned in Manet Hall.

'Lucian did me a favor marrying you.' His voice was a lazy drawl now, almost conversational. He knew she had nowhere to run. 'She's already cut him out of her will. Oh, he'll get the house, she can't change that, but I'll get her money. And it's her money that runs this place.'

'Take the money, take the house.' She flung out her hands, dismissing them, and him. 'Take it all. And go to hell with it.'

'He's weak. My sainted brother. Saints always are, under all the piety.'

'He's a man, so much more a man than you.'

She'd hoped to make him angry, angry enough to strike her and storm out. Instead he laughed, low and quiet, and edged closer.

When she saw the intent in his eyes, she opened her mouth to scream. His hand whipped out, gripped a hank of the dark hair that curled to her waist. And yanking had her scream gurgling into a gasp. His free hand circled her throat, squeezed.

'I always take what's Lucian's. Even his whores.'

She beat at him, slapped, bit. And when she could draw

13

in air, screamed. He tore at her wrapper, pawed at her breasts. In the crib, the baby began to wail.

Fueled by the sound of her child's distress, Abby clawed her way free. She spun, stumbled over the torn hem of her nightgown. Her hand closed over the fireplace poker. She swung wildly, ramming it hard against Julian's shoulder.

Howling in pain, he fell back against the hearth, and she flew toward the crib.

She had to get the baby. To get the baby and run.

He caught her sleeve, and she screamed again as the material ripped. Even as she reached down to snatch her daughter from the crib, he dragged her back. He struck her, slicing the back of his hand over her cheek and knocking her back into a table. A candle fell to the floor and guttered out in its own wax.

'Bitch! Whore!'

He was mad. She could see it now in the feral gleam in his eyes, the drunken flush on his cheeks. In that instant fear turned to terror.

'He'll kill you for this. My Lucian will kill you.' She tried to gain her feet, but he hit her again, using his fist this time so the pain radiated from her face, through her body. Dazed, she began to crawl toward the crib. There was blood in her mouth, sweet and warm.

My baby. Sweet God, don't let him hurt my baby.

His weight was on her – and the stench of him. She bucked, called for help. The sound of the baby's furious screams merged with hers.

'Don't! Don't! You damn yourself.'

But as he yanked up the skirt of her nightgown, she knew no amount of pleading, no amount of struggle, would stop him. He would debase her, soil her, because of who she was. Because she was Lucian's.

'This is what you want.' He drove himself into her, and

14

the thrill of power spurted through him like black wine. Her face was white with fear and shock, and raw from the blows of his hands. Helpless, he thought, as he pounded out his raging envy. 'This is what all of you want. Cajun whores.'

Thrust after violent thrust, he raped her. The thrill of forcing himself into her spumed through him until his breathing turned to short bursts grunted between clenched teeth.

She was weeping now, huge choking sobs. But screaming, too. Somehow screaming as he hammered his fury, his jealousy, his disgust into her.

As the great clock began to chime midnight, he closed his hands around her throat. 'Shut up. Damn you.' He rammed her head against the floor, squeezed harder. And still the screaming pierced his brain.

Abby heard it, too. Dimly. The baby's frantic cries pealed through her head along with the slow, formal bongs of the midnight hour. She slapped, weak protests against the hands that cut off her air, tried to shut her body off from the unspeakable invasion.

Help me. Mother of Jesus. Help me. Help my baby.

Her vision dimmed. Her heels drummed wildly on the floor as she convulsed.

The last thing she heard was her crying daughter. The last thing she thought was, *Lucian.*

The door of the nursery burst open. Josephine Manet stood just inside the nursery. She summed up the scene quickly. Coldly.

'Julian.'

His hands still vised around Abby's throat, he looked up. If his mother saw madness in his eyes, she chose to ignore it. With her gilt hair neatly braided for the night, her robe sternly buttoned to the neck, she stepped over, stared down.

15

Abby's eyes were wide and staring. There was a trickle of blood at the corner of her mouth, and bruises blooming along her cheeks.

Dispassionately, she leaned down, laid her fingers against Abby's throat.

'She's dead,' Josephine announced and moved quickly to the connecting door. She opened it, glanced into the maid's room. Then closed it, locked it.

She stood for a moment, her back against it, her hand at her own throat as she thought of what could come. Disgrace, ruin, scandal.

'It was ... an accident.' His hands began to shake as they slid away from Abby's throat. The whiskey was whirling in his head now, clouding it. It churned in his belly, sickening it.

He could see the marks on her skin, dark and deep and damning. 'She ... tried to seduce me, then, she attacked ...'

She crossed the room again, her slippers clicking on wood. Crouching down, Josephine slapped him, one hard crack of flesh on flesh. 'Quiet. Be quiet and do exactly as I say. I won't lose another son to this creature. Take her down to her bedroom. Go out through the gallery and stay there until I come.'

'It was her fault.'

'Yes. Now she's paid for it. Take her down, Julian. And be quick.'

'They'll ...' A single tear gathered in the corner of his eye and spilled over. 'They'll hang me. I have to get away.'

'No. No, they won't hang you.' She brought his head to her shoulder, stroking his hair over the body of her daughter-in-law. 'No, my sweet, they won't hang you. Do what Mama says now. Carry her to the bedroom and wait for me. Everything's going to be all right. Everything's going to be as it should be. I promise.'

'I don't want to touch her.'

'Julian!' The crooning tone snapped into icy command. 'Do as I say. Immediately.'

She rose, walked over to the crib, where the baby's wails had turned to miserable whimpers. In the heat of the moment, she considered simply laying her hand over the child's mouth and nose. Hardly different than drowning a bag of kittens.

And yet …

The child had her son's blood in her, and therefore her own. She could despise it, but she couldn't destroy it. 'Go to sleep,' she said. 'We'll decide what to do about you later.'

As her son carried the girl he'd raped and murdered from the room, Josephine began to set the nursery to rights again. She picked up the candle, scrubbed at the cooling wax until she could see no trace.

She replaced the fireplace poker and, using the ruin of Abby's robe, wiped up the splatters of blood. She did it all efficiently, turning her mind away from what had caused the damage to the room, keeping it firmly fixed on what needed to be done to save her son.

When she was certain all was as it should be, she unlocked the door again, left her now-sleeping grandchild alone.

In the morning, she would fire the nursemaid for dereliction of duty. She would have her out of Manet Hall before Lucian returned to find his wife missing.

The girl had brought it on herself, Josephine thought. No good ever came from trying to rise above your station in life. There was an order of things, and a reason for that order. If the girl hadn't bewitched Lucian – for surely there was some local witchery involved – she would still be alive.

17

The family had suffered enough scandal. The elopement. Oh, the embarrassment of it! Of having to hold your head high when your firstborn son ran off with a penniless, barefoot female who'd grown up in a shack in the swamp.

Then the sour taste of the pretense that followed. It was essential to save face, even after such a blow. And hadn't she done all that could be done to see that creature was dressed as befitted the family Manet?

Silk purses, sow's ears, she thought. What good were Paris fashions when the girl had only to open her mouth and sound of the swamp? For pity's sake, she'd been a servant.

Josephine stepped into the bedroom, shut the door at her back, and stared at the bed where her son's dead wife lay staring up at the blue silk canopy.

Now, she thought, Abigail Rouse was simply a problem to be solved.

Julian huddled in a chair, his head in his hands. 'Stop screaming,' he muttered. 'Stop the screaming.'

Josephine marched to him, clamped her hands on his shoulders. 'Do you want them to come for you?' she demanded. 'Do you want to drag the family through disgrace? To be hanged like a common thief?'

'It wasn't my fault. She enticed me. Then she attacked me. Look. Look.' He turned his head. 'See how she clawed my face?'

'Yes.' For a moment, just for a moment, Josephine wavered. The heart inside the symbol she'd become reared up in protest against the horror of the act all women fear.

Whatever she was, she'd loved Lucian. Whatever she was, she'd been raped and murdered within feet of her own child's crib.

18

Julian forced her, struck her, defiled her. Killed her.

Drunk and mad, he'd killed his brother's wife. God's pity.

Then she shoved it viciously aside.

The girl was dead. Her son was not.

'You bought a prostitute tonight. Don't turn away from me,' she snapped. 'I'm not ignorant of the things men do. Did you buy a woman?'

'Yes, Mama.'

She nodded briskly. 'Then it was the whore who scratched you, should anyone have the temerity to ask. You were never in the nursery tonight.' She cupped his face in her hands to keep his eyes level with hers. And her fingers dug into his cheeks as she spoke in low, clear tones. 'What reason would you have to go there? You went out, for drink and women, and having your fill of both, came home and went to bed. Is that clear?'

'But, how will we explain – '

'We'll have nothing to explain. I've told you what you did tonight. Repeat it.'

'I – I went into town.' He licked his lips. Swallowed. 'I drank, then I went to a brothel. I came home and went to bed.'

'That's right. That's right.' She stroked his scored cheek. 'Now we're going to pack some of her things – some clothes, some jewelry. We'll do it quickly, as she did it quickly when she decided to run off with a man she'd been seeing in secret. A man who might very well be the father of that child upstairs.'

'What man?'

Josephine let out a long sigh. He was the child of her heart, but she often despaired of his brain. 'Never mind, Julian. You know nothing of it. Here.' She went to the chifforobe, chose a long black velvet cloak. 'Wrap her in this. Hurry. Do it!' she said in a tone that had him getting to his feet.

His stomach pitched, and his hands trembled, but he wrapped the body in velvet as best he could while his mother stuffed things in a hatbox and a train case.

In her rush she dropped a brooch of gold wings with a small enameled watch dangling from it. The toe of her slipper struck it so that it skittered into a corner.

'We'll take her into the swamp. We'll have to go on foot, and quickly. There are some old paving bricks in the garden shed. We can weigh her down with them.'

And the gators, she thought, the gators and fish would do the rest.

'Even if she's found, it's away from here. The man she ran away with killed her.' She dabbed her face with the handkerchief in the pocket of her robe, smoothed a hand over her long, gilded braid. 'That's what people will believe if she's found. We need to get her away from here, away from Manet Hall. Quickly.'

She was beginning to feel a little mad herself.

There was moonlight. She told herself there was moonlight because fate understood what she was doing, and why. She could hear her son's rapid breathing, and the sounds of the night. The frogs, the insects, the night birds all merging together into one thick note.

It was the end of a century, the beginning of the new. She would rid herself of this aberration to her world and start this new century, this new era, clean and strong.

There was a chill in the air, made raw with wet. But she felt hot, almost burning hot as she trudged away from the house, laden with the bags she'd packed and weighed down. The muscles of her arms, of her legs, protested, but she marched like a soldier.

Once, just once, she thought she felt a brush against

her cheek, like the breath of a ghost. The spirit of a dead girl who trailed beside her, accusing, damning, cursing her for eternity.

Fear only made her stronger.

'Here.' She stopped and peered out over the water. 'Lay her down.'

Julian obeyed, then rose quickly, turned his back, covered his face with his hands. 'I can't do this. Mama, I can't. I'm sick. Sick.'

He tumbled towards the water, retching, weeping.

Useless boy, she thought, mildly annoyed. Men could never handle a crisis. It took a woman, the cold blood and clear mind of a female.

Josephine opened the cloak, laid bricks over the body. Sweat began to pour down her face, but she approached the grisly task as she would any other. With ruthless efficiency. She took the rope out of the hatbox, carefully tied hanks around the cloaked body, top, bottom, middle. Using another, she looped the line through the handles of the luggage, knotted it tight.

She glanced over now to see Julian watching her, his face white as bone. 'You'll have to help. I can't get her into the water alone. She's too heavy now.'

'I was drunk.'

'That's correct, Julian. You were drunk. Now, you're sober enough to deal with the consequences. Help me get her into the water.'

He felt his legs buckle and give with each step, like a puppet's. The body slid into the water almost soundlessly. There was a quiet plop, a kind of gurgle, then it was gone. Ripples spread on the surface, shimmered in the moonlight, then smoothed away again.

'She's out of our lives,' Josephine stated calmly. 'Soon she'll be like those ripples. Like she never was. See that you clean your boots thoroughly, Julian. Don't give them to a servant.'

She slid her arm through his, smiled, though her smile was just a little wild. 'We need to get back, get some rest. Tomorrow's a very busy day.'

Chapter Two

Manet Hall, Louisiana
January 2002

His mother was right – as always. Declan Fitzgerald stared through the mud-splattered windshield into the driving winter rain and was glad she wasn't there to gloat.

Not that Colleen Sullivan Fitzgerald ever stooped to a gloat. She merely raised one perfect eyebrow into one perfect arch and let her silence do the gloating for her.

She'd told him, very succinctly, when he'd stopped by before driving out of Boston, that he'd lost his mind. And would rue the day. Yes, he was pretty sure she'd said 'rue the day.'

He hadn't sunk as low as ruing – yet – but studying the jungle of weeds, the sagging galleries, the peeling paint and broken gutters of the old plantation house, he was no longer confident of his mental health.

What had made him think he could restore this rambling old derelict into its former splendor? Or, more to the point, that he should? For God's sake, he was a lawyer, a Fitzgerald of the Boston Fitzgeralds, and more tuned to swinging a nine-iron than a hammer.

Rehabbing a town house in his spare time over a two-year period was a far cry from relocating to New Orleans and pretending he was a contractor.

Had the place looked this bad the last time he'd been down here? Could it have? Of course that was five, no, six years before. Certainly it couldn't have looked this bad the first time he'd seen it. He'd been twenty and spending a crazed Mardi Gras interlude with his college roommate. Eleven years, he thought, dragging his fingers through his dark blond hair.

The old Manet Hall had been a niggling germ in his brain for eleven years. As obsessions went, it was longer than most relationships. Certainly longer than any of his own.

Now the house was his, for better or for worse. He already had a feeling there was going to be plenty of worse.

His eyes, as gray, and at the moment as bleak, as the rain, scanned the structure. The graceful twin arches of the double stairs leading to the second-floor gallery had charmed him on that long-ago February. And all those tall arched windows, the whimsy of the belvedere on the roof, the elegance of the white columns and strangely ornate iron balusters. The fanciful mix of Italianate and Greek Revival had all seemed so incredibly lush and Old World and *southern*.

Even then he'd felt displaced, in a way he'd never been able to explain, in New England.

The house had pulled him, in some deep chamber. Like a hook through memory, he thought now. He'd been able to visualize the interior even before he and Remy had broken in to ramble through it.

24

Or the gallon or two of beer they'd sucked down had caused him to think he could.

A drunk boy barely out of his teens couldn't be trusted. And neither, Declan admitted ruefully, could a stone-sober thirty-one-year-old man.

The minute Remy had mentioned that Manet Hall was on the block again, he'd put in a bid. Sight unseen, or unseen for more than half a decade. He'd *had* to have it. As if he'd been waiting all his life to call it his own.

He could deem the price reasonable if he didn't consider what he'd have to pour into it to make it habitable. So he wouldn't consider it – just now.

It was his, whether he was crazy or whether he was right. No matter what, he'd turned in his briefcase for a tool belt. That alone lightened his mood.

He pulled out his cell phone – you could take the lawyer out of Boston, but . . . Still studying the house, he put in a call to Remy Payne.

He went through a secretary, and imagined Remy sitting at a desk cluttered with files and briefs. It made him smile, a quick, crooked grin that shifted the planes and angles of his face, hollowed the cheeks, softened the sometimes-grim line of his mouth.

Yes, he thought, life could be worse. He could be the one at the desk.

'Well, hey, Dec.' Remy's lazy drawl streamed into the packed Mercedes SUV like a mist over a slow-moving river. 'Where are you, boy?'

'I'm sitting in my car looking at this white elephant I was crazy enough to buy. Why the hell didn't you talk me out of it or have me committed?'

'You're here? Son of a bitch! I didn't think you'd make it until tomorrow.'

'Got antsy.' He rubbed his chin; heard the scratch of stubble. 'Drove through most of last night and got an early start again this morning. Remy? What was I thinking?'

'Damned if I know. Listen, you give me a couple of hours to clear some business, and I'll drive out. Bring us some libation. We'll toast that rattrap and catch up.'

'Good. That'd be good.'

'You been inside yet?'

'No. I'm working up to it.'

'Jesus, Dec, go on in out of the rain.'

'Yeah, all right.' Declan passed a hand over his face. 'See you in a couple hours.'

'I'll bring food. For Christ's sake, don't try to cook anything. No point burning the place down before you've spent a night in it.'

'Fuck you.' He heard Remy laugh before he hung up.

He started the engine again, drove all the way to the base of what was left of those double stairs that framed the entranceway. He popped the glove compartment, took out the keys that had been mailed to him after settlement.

He climbed out and was immediately drenched. Deciding he'd leave the boxes for later, he jogged to the shelter of the entrance gallery, felt a few of the bricks that formed the floor give ominously under his weight, and shook himself like a dog.

There should be vines climbing up the corner columns, he thought. Something with cool blue blossoms. He could see it if he concentrated hard enough. Something open, almost like a cup, with leaves shaped like hearts.

Must've seen that somewhere, he mused, and turned to the door. It was a double, with carvings and long arched panels of glass on either side and a half-moon glass topper. And tracing his fingers over the doors, he felt some of the thrill sneak into him.

'Welcome home, Dec,' he said aloud and unlocked the door.

The foyer was as he remembered it. The wide loblolly pine floor, the soaring ceiling. The plaster medallion overhead was a double ring of some sort of flowers. It had probably boasted a fabulous crystal chandelier in its heyday. The best it could offer now was a single bare bulb dangling from a long wire. But when he hit the wall switch, it blinked on. That was something.

In any event, the staircase was the focal point. It rose up, wide and straight to the second level, where it curved right and left to lead to each wing.

What a single man with no current prospects or intentions of being otherwise needed with two wings was a question he didn't want to ask himself at the moment.

The banister was coated with gray dust, but when he rubbed a finger over it, he felt the smooth wood beneath. *How many hands had gripped there? How many fingers had trailed along it?* he wondered. These were the sort of questions that fascinated him, that drew him in.

The kind of questions that had him climbing the stairs with the door open to the rain behind him, and his possessions still waiting in the car.

The stairs might have been carpeted once. There probably had been runners in the long center hallway. Some rich pattern on deep red. Floors, woodwork, tabletops would have been polished religiously with beeswax until they gleamed like the crystal in the chandeliers.

At parties, women in spectacular dresses would glide up and down the stairs – confident, stylish. Some of the men would gather in the billiard room, using the game as an excuse to puff on cigars and pontificate about politics and finance.

And servants would scurry along, efficiently invisible, stoking fires, clearing glasses, answering demands.

27

On the landing, he opened a panel. The hidden door was skillfully worked into the wall, the faded wallpaper, the dulled wainscoting. He wasn't certain how he'd known it was there. Someone must have mentioned it.

He peered into the dim, dank corridor. Part of the rabbit warren of servants' quarters and accesses, he believed. Family and guests didn't care to have underfoot those who served. A good servant left no trace of his work, but saw to his duties discreetly, silently and well.

Frowning, Declan strained his eyes to see. Where had that come from? His mother? As tight-assed as she could be from time to time, she'd never say something that pompous.

With a shrug, he closed the door again. He'd explore that area another time, when he had a flashlight and a bag of bread crumbs.

He walked along the corridor, glancing in doorways. Empty rooms, full of dust and the smell of damp, gray light from the rain. Some walls were papered, some were down to the skeletal studs.

Sitting room, study, bath and surely the billiard room he'd imagined, as its old mahogany bar was still in place.

He walked in to circle around it, to touch the wood, to crouch down and examine the workmanship.

He'd started a love affair with wood in high school. To date, it was his most lasting relationship. He'd taken a summer job as a laborer even though his family had objected. *He'd* objected to the idea of spending those long summer days cooped up in a law office as a clerk, and had wanted to work outdoors. To polish his tan and his build.

It had been one of the rare times his father had over-ruled his mother and sided with him.

He'd gotten sunburn, splinters, blisters, calluses, an aching back. And had fallen in love with building.

Not building so much, Declan thought now. Rebuilding. The taking of something already formed and enhancing, repairing, restoring.

Nothing had given him as big a kick, or half as much satisfaction.

He'd had a knack for it. A natural, the Irish pug of a foreman had told him. Good hands, good eyes, good brain. Declan had never forgotten that summer high. And had never matched it since.

Maybe now, he thought. Maybe he would now. There had to be more for him than just getting from one day to the next doing what was expected and acceptable.

With pleasure and anticipation growing, he went back to exploring his house.

At the door to the ballroom he stopped, and grinned. 'Wow. Cool!'

His voice echoed and all but bounced back to slap him in the face. Delighted, he walked in. The floors were scarred and stained and spotted. There were sections damaged where it appeared someone had put up partitions to bisect the room, then someone else had knocked them out again.

But he could fix that. Some moron had thrown up drywall and yellow paint over the original plaster walls. He'd fix that, too.

At least they'd left the ceiling alone. The plasterwork was gorgeous, complicated wreaths of flowers and fruit. It would need repairing, and a master to do it. He'd find one.

He threw open the gallery doors to the rain. The neglected, tumbled jungle of gardens spread out, snaked through with overgrown and broken bricked paths. There was likely a treasure of plantings out there. He'd need a landscaper, but he hoped to do some of it himself.

Most of the outbuildings were only ruins now. He could see a portion of a chimney stack, part of a vine-smothered wall of a derelict worker's cabin, the pocked bricks and rusted roof of an old *pigeonnier* – Creole planters had often raised pigeons.

He'd only gotten three acres with the house, so it was likely other structures that had belonged to the plantation were now tumbling down on someone else's land.

But he had trees, he thought. Amazing trees. The ancient live oaks that formed the *allée* dripped with water and moss, and the thick limbs of a sycamore spread and twisted like some prehistoric beast.

A wash of color caught his attention, had him stepping out into the rain. Something was blooming, a tall, fat bush with dark red flowers. What the hell bloomed in January? he wondered, and made a mental note to ask Remy.

Closing his eyes a moment, he listened. He could hear nothing but rain, the whoosh and splash of it on roof, on ground, on tree.

He'd done the right thing, he told himself. He wasn't crazy after all. He'd found his place. It *felt* like his, and if it wasn't, what did it matter? He'd find another. At least, finally, he'd stirred up the energy to look.

He stepped back in and, humming, walked back across the ballroom toward the family wing, to check out each of the five bedrooms.

He caught himself singing under his breath as he wandered through the first of them.

'*After the ball is over, after the break of morn; After the dancers leaving, after the stars are gone …*'

He stopped examining baseboard and looked over his shoulder as if expecting to see someone standing behind him. Where had that come from? he wondered. The tune, the lyrics. With a shake of his head, he straightened.

'From the ballroom, idiot,' he mumbled. 'Ballroom on the mind, so you start singing about a ball. Weird, but not crazy. Talking to yourself isn't crazy, either. Lots of people do it.'

The door to the room across the hall was closed. Though he expected the creak of hinges, the sound still danced a chill up his spine.

That sensation was immediately followed by bafflement. He could have sworn he smelled perfume. Flowers. Lilies. Weddings and funerals. And for an instant he imagined them, pure and white and somehow feral in a tall crystal vase.

His next feeling was irritation. He'd only sent a few pieces ahead, including his bedroom furniture. The movers had dumped it in the wrong room, and he'd been very specific. His room would be the master at the corner, overlooking the garden and pond at the rear, and the avenue of oaks from the side.

Now he'd have to settle for this room, or haul the damn stuff himself.

The scent of lilies was overpowering when he shoved the door all the way open. Almost dizzying. Confused, he realized it wasn't even *his* furniture. The bed was a full tester draped in deep blue silk. There was a carved chifforobe, a tall chest of drawers, all gleaming. He caught the scent of beeswax under the floral. Saw the lilies in that tall, crystal vase on a woman's vanity table, its legs curved like the necks of swans. The chair was delicate, its seat an intricate needlepoint pattern of blue and rose.

Silver-backed brushes, a brooch of gold wings with an enameled watch. Long blue draperies, ornate gaslight sconces set on a low, shimmering light. A woman's white robe tossed over the back of a blue chaise.

Candlesticks on the mantel, and a picture in a silver frame.

31

He saw it all, snapshot clear. Before his brain could process the how of it, he was staring into an empty room where rain streamed outside uncurtained windows.

'Jesus Christ.' He gripped the doorjamb for balance. 'What the hell?'

He drew in a breath. There was nothing in the air but must and dust.

Projecting, he told himself. Just projecting what the room might have looked like. He hadn't seen anything, or smelled anything. He'd just gotten caught up in the charm of the place, in the spirit of it.

But he couldn't make himself step over the threshold.

He closed the door again, walked directly down to the corner room. His furniture was there, as ordered, and the sight of it both relieved and steadied him.

The good, solid Chippendale bed with its headboard and footboard unadorned. The one point of agreement he'd had, always, with his mother was a love of antiques, the respect for the workmanship, the history.

He'd bought the bed after he and Jessica had called off the wedding. Okay, after he'd called it off, he admitted with the usual tug of guilt. He'd wanted to start fresh, and had searched out and purchased the pieces for his bedroom.

He'd chosen the bachelor's chest not only because it appeared he was going to remain one, but also because he'd liked the style of it, the double herringbone inlay, the secret compartments, the short, turned legs. He'd selected the armoire to conceal his television and stereo, and the sleek Deco lamps because he'd liked the mix of styles.

Seeing his things here in the spacious room with its handsome granite fireplace in dark green, the arched gallery doors, the gently faded wallpaper, the pitifully scarred floors, clicked him back into place again.

The adjoining dressing area made him smile. All he needed was a valet, and white tie and tails. The connecting bath, modernized from the look of it sometime in the woeful seventies, had him wincing at the avocado-green decor and yearning for a hot shower.

He'd take a quick walk through the third floor, he decided, do the same on the main level, then take the ugly green tub for a spin.

He headed up. The tune was playing in his head again. Around and around, like a waltz. He let it come. It was company of sorts until Remy showed up.

Many the hopes that have vanished, after the ball.

The staircase was narrower here. This level was for children and staff, neither of whom required fancy touches.

He'd save the servants' wing for later, he decided, and circled around toward what he assumed were nursery, storage, attics.

He reached for a doorknob, the brass dull with time and neglect. A draft, cold enough to pierce bone, swept down the corridor. He saw his breath puff out in surprise, watched it condense into a thin cloud.

As his hand closed over the knob, nausea rose up so fast, so sharp, it stole his breath again. Cold sweat pearled on his brow. His head spun.

In an instant he knew a fear so huge, so great, he wanted to run screaming. Instead he stumbled back, braced himself against the wall while terror and dread choked him like murderous hands.

Don't go in there. Don't go in.

Wherever the voice in his head came from, he was inclined to listen to it. He knew the house was rumored to be haunted. He didn't mind such things.

Or thought he didn't mind them.

But the idea of opening that door to whatever was

33

behind it, to whatever waited on the other side, was more than he cared to face alone. On an empty stomach. After a ten-hour drive.

'Just wasting time anyway,' he said for the comfort of his own voice. 'I should be unloading the car. So, I'm going to unload the car.'

'Who you talking to, *cher?*'

Declan jumped like a basketball center at the tip-off, and barely managed to turn a scream into a more acceptable masculine yelp. 'God *damn* it, Remy. You scared the shit out of me.'

'You're the one up here talking to a door. I gave a few shouts on my way up. Guess you didn't hear.'

'Guess I didn't.'

Declan leaned back against the wall, sucked in air, and studied his friend.

Remy Payne had the cocky good looks of a con artist. He was tailor-made for the law, Declan thought. Slick, sharp, with cheerful blue eyes and a wide mouth that could, as it was now, stretch like rubber into a disarming smile that made you want to believe everything he said, even as you caught the distinctive whiff of bullshit.

He was on the skinny side, never had been able to bulk up despite owning the appetite of an elephant. In college he'd worn his deep-brown hair in a sleek mane over his collar. He'd shortened it now so it was almost Caesarean in style.

'I thought you said a couple hours.'

'Been that. Damn near two and a half. You okay there, Dec? Look a little peaky.'

'Long drive, I guess. God, it's good to see you.'

''Bout time you mentioned that.' With a laugh, he caught Declan in a bear hug. 'Whoo, boy. You been working out. Turn around, lemme see your ass.'

'You idiot.' They slapped backs. 'Tell me one thing,' Declan remarked as he took a step back. 'Am I out of my fucking mind?'

''Course you are. Always have been. Let's go on down and have ourselves a drink.'

They settled in what had once been the gentlemen's parlor, on the floor with a pepperoni pizza and a bottle of Jim Beam.

The first shot of bourbon went down like liquid silk and untied all the knots in Declan's belly. The pizza was good and greasy, and made him decide the strangeness he'd experienced had been a result of fatigue and hunger.

'You planning on living like this for long, or buying yourself a chair or two?'

'Don't need a chair or two.' Declan took the bottle back from Remy, swigged down bourbon. 'Not for new anyway. I wanted to cut things down to the bone for a while. I got the bedroom stuff. Might toss a table up in the kitchen. I start buying furniture, it'll just be in the way while I'm working on this place.'

Remy looked around the room. 'Shape this place is in, you'll need a fucking wheelchair before you're finished.'

'It's mostly cosmetic. People who bought it last got a good start on the big work, from what I hear. Seems they had an idea about turning it into a fancy hotel or some such thing. Gave it nearly six months before they turned tail. Probably they ran out of money.'

Lifting his eyebrows, Remy ran a finger over the floor, studied the layer of dust he picked up. 'Too bad you can't sell this dirt. You'd be filthy rich. Ha. Oh yeah, I forgot. You already are filthy rich. How's your family?'

'About the same as always.'

'And they think, Our boy Dec, *il est fou.*' Remy circled a finger by his ear. 'He's gone round the bend.'

'Oh yeah. Maybe they're right, but at least it's finally *my* damn bend. If I'd gone to one more deposition, faced one more meeting, handled one more pretrial negotiation, I'd have drowned myself in the Charles.'

'Corporate law's what stifled you, *cher*,' Remy licked sauce from his fingers. 'You should've tried criminal, like me. Keeps the blood moving. You say the word, we'll hang out a shingle together tomorrow.'

'Thanks for the thought. You still love it.'

'I do. I love the slippery, sneaking angles of it, the pomp and ceremony, the sweaty wrestling, the fancy words. Every damn thing.' Remy shook his head, tipped back the bottle. 'You never did.'

'No, I never did.'

'All those years busting ass through Harvard, tossed aside. That what they're saying to you?'

'Among other things.'

'They're wrong. You know that, Dec. You're not tossing anything aside. You're just picking up something different. Relax and enjoy it. You're in New Orleans now, or close enough. We take things easy here. We'll wear some of that Yankee off you soon enough. Have you doing the Cajun two-step and stirring up some red beans and rice on wash day.'

'Yeah, that'll happen.'

'You come on into town once you're settled in, Effie and I'll take you out to dinner. I want you to meet her.'

Remy had pulled off his tie, shucked his suit jacket, rolled up the sleeves of his lawyerly blue shirt. Except for the hair, Declan thought, he didn't look that different than he did when they'd been at Harvard sucking down pizza and bourbon.

'You're really doing it? Getting married.'

Remy let out a sigh. 'Twelfth of May, come hell or

36

high water. I'm settling my bad ass down, Dec. She's just what I want.'

'A librarian.' It was a wonder to Declan. 'You and a librarian.'

'Research specialist,' Remy corrected and hooted out a laugh. 'Damn prettiest bookworm I ever did see. She's a smart one, too. I'm crazy in love with her, Dec. Out of my mind crazy for her.'

'I'm happy for you.'

'You still got the guilts over … what was her name? Jennifer?'

'Jessica.' Wincing, Declan took another swig to cut the taste her name brought to his tongue. 'Calling off a wedding three weeks before you're due to walk down the aisle ought to give you the guilts.'

Remy acknowledged this with a quick shrug. 'Maybe so. Feel worse if you'd gone through with it.'

'Tell me.' Still, his gray eyes remained broody as he stared at the bottle. 'But I think she'd have handled it better if we'd done the thing, then gone for a divorce the next day.' It still gave him a twinge. 'Couldn't have handled it any worse, anyway. She's seeing my cousin James now.'

'James … James … That the one who squeals like a girl or the one with the Dracula hair?'

'Neither.' Declan's lips twitched. Jesus, he'd missed this. 'James is the perfect one. Plastic surgeon, polo player, collects stamps.'

'Short guy, receding chin, broad Yankee accent.'

'That's him, but the chin doesn't recede anymore. Implant. According to my sister, it's starting to look serious between them, which just serves me right, I'm told.'

'Well, hell, let your sister marry Jennifer.'

'Jessica, and that's what I told her,' he said, gesturing with the bottle for emphasis. 'She didn't speak to me for two weeks. Which was a relief. I'm not very popular with the Fitzgeralds right now.'

'Well, you know, Dec, I'd have to say, given the circumstances and such … screw 'em.'

With a laugh, Declan handed Remy the bottle. 'Let's drink to it.'

He took another slice of pizza from the box. 'Let me ask you something else, about this place. I've researched the history, did a chunk of it way back after we came here the first time.'

'Stumbling around like drunken fools.'

'Yeah, which we may do again if we keep hitting this bourbon. Anyway, I know it was built in 1879 – after the original structure burned down in an unexplained fire, which was very likely set due to politics, Reconstruction and other post-Civil War messiness.'

'That's the War of Northern Aggression, son.' Remy pointed a warning finger. 'Remember which side of the Mason-Dixon Line you're plopping your Yankee ass down on now.'

'Right. Sorry. Anyway. The Manets scooped up the land, cheap, according to the old records, and built the current structure. They farmed sugar and cotton primarily and divvied off plots to sharecroppers. Lived well for about twenty years. There were two sons, both died young. Then the old man died and the wife held on until she apparently stroked out in her sleep. No heirs. There was a granddaughter on record, but she was cut out of the will. Place went to auction and has passed from hand to hand ever since. Sitting empty more than not.'

'And?'

Declan leaned forward. 'Do you believe it's haunted?'

Remy pursed his lips, copped the last piece of pizza. 'That whole history lesson was your way of working around to asking that one question? Boy, you got the makings for a fine southern lawyer. Sure it's haunted.' His eyes danced as he bit into the pizza. 'House been here this long and isn't, it'd have no self-respect whatsoever. The granddaughter you mentioned. She was a Rouse on her mama's side. I know that, as I'm fourth or fifth cousins with the Simones, and the Simones come down from that line. Girl was raised, I believe, by her maternal grandparents after her mama took off with some man – so it's said. Don't know if I recollect what happened to her daddy, but others will if you want to know. I do know that Henri Manet, his wife, Josephine, and the one son – damned if I know what his name was – all died in this house. One of them doesn't have the gumption to haunt it, that's a crying shame.'

'Natural causes? The people who died here?'

Curious, Remy frowned. 'Far as I know. Why?'

'I don't know.' Declan had to fight off a shudder. 'Vibes.'

'You want someone to come through here? Little gris-gris, little voodoo, chase off your ghost, or maybe summon the spirit for a little conversation? You can find yourself a witch or psychic every second corner in town.'

'No, thanks.'

'You let me know if you decide different.' Remy winked. 'I'll put you onto somebody who'll give you a fine show.'

He didn't want a show, Declan decided later. But he did want that shower, and bed. With Jim Beam buzzing pleasantly in his blood, he hauled in boxes, pawed through them to find sheets and towels. He carted what he figured he'd need for the night upstairs.

It was good old Catholic guilt rather than any need for order that had him making the bed. He treated himself to a ten-minute shower, then climbed into the fresh sheets to the sound of the incessant rain.

He was asleep in thirty seconds.

There was a baby crying. It didn't strike him as odd at all. Babies tended to cry in the middle of the night, or whenever they damn well pleased. It sounded fretful and annoyed more than alarmed.

Someone ought to go pick it up … do whatever people did with crying babies. Feed it. Change it. Rock it.

When he'd waked from nightmares as a child, his mother or his nanny, sometimes his father, had come in to stroke his head and sit with him until the fear faded away again.

The baby wasn't frightened. The baby was hungry.

It didn't strike him as odd that he thought that. That he knew that.

But it did strike him as odd, very odd, to wake, bathed in sweat, and find himself standing outside the door with the dull brass knob on the third floor.

Chapter Three

Sleepwalking. That was something he hadn't done since childhood. But in the watery light of day it was simple enough to see how it had happened. Jim Beam, pepperoni pizza and talk of ghosts.

A little harder to accept was the gut-clenching terror he'd felt when he'd surfaced and found himself outside that third-level door. He'd snapped out of the fugue and into a nightmare of panic – one where he'd been certain he'd heard the fading echoes of a baby's restless crying.

He'd run. He couldn't have opened that door if he'd had a gun to his head. So he'd run, with his own bright fear chasing him, to lock himself back in the bedroom. Like a mental patient, he thought now over a lukewarm cup of instant coffee.

At least there'd been no one around to see it.

But if you thought about it, it was a rather auspicious first night. Cold spots, baby ghosts, fugues. It sure beat sitting in his empty town house in Boston, sucking on a beer and watching ESPN.

Maybe he would spend some time digging deeper into the history of the house. His house, he corrected, and with his coffee, he leaned on the damp iron rail of the gallery outside his bedroom.

His view. And it was a beaut once you skimmed over the wreck of the gardens.

Leaves dripped from the rain in steady, musical plops, and the air shimmered with the weight the storm had left behind. Mists crawled over the ground, smoky fingers that trailed and curled around the trees to turn them into romantic and mysterious silhouettes.

If the sun broke through, the glittery light would be spectacular, but it was nothing to sneeze at now.

There was a pond, a small one, choked with lily pads, and fields – some fallow, some already planted for a spring that came so much sooner here. He could see the thin curve of the river that ribboned its way through the deep shadows of the bayou.

A rickety little bridge crossed the water in a hump, then a dirt road pushed into the trees toward a house mostly hidden by them. He could just make out a puff of smoke that rose up to mix with the hazy air.

He'd already been up on the belvedere that morning, and had been relieved to find it, the roof, the chimneys, all in good repair. The last owners had seen to that and this second-floor gallery before they'd thrown in the towel.

It looked as if they'd started on the rear gallery as well, had started preliminary work on closing it into a screened porch.

Which might not be a bad idea. He'd think about it.

Declan wasn't certain if they'd run out of money or energy, or both, but he considered it his good fortune.

He had plenty of money, and just now, watching the steam rising over the weeds and water, plenty of energy.

He lifted the cup to his lips, then lowered it again as he saw a woman – a girl? – slip through the trees toward the curve of the river. A huge black dog lumbered along beside her.

She was too far away from him to make out features. He saw she wore a red checked shirt and jeans, and her hair was long and dark and madly curling. Was she old? he wondered. Young? Pretty or plain?

He decided on young and pretty. It was, after all, his option.

She tossed a ball in the air, fielded it smartly when the dog gave a leap. She tossed it twice more while the dog jumped and ran in circles. Then she reared back like a pitcher in the stretch and bulleted it through the air. The dog gave chase and didn't hesitate, but leaped toward the pond, shagging the ball with a snap of teeth an instant before he hit the water.

Hell of a trick, Declan thought and, grinning, watched the girl applaud.

He wished he could hear her. He was sure she was laughing, a low, throaty laugh. When the dog swam to the edge, scrambled out, he spit the ball at her feet, then shook himself.

It had to have drenched her, but she didn't dance away or brush fussily at her jeans.

They repeated the routine, with Declan a captive audience.

He imagined her walking with the dog closer to the Hall. Close enough that he could wave from the gallery, invite her in for a cup of bad coffee. His first shot at southern hospitality.

Or better yet, he could wander down. And she'd be wrestling with the dog. She'd slip on the wet grass, tumble into the pond. He'd be right at hand to pull her out. No, to dive in after her and save her because she couldn't swim.

Then one thing would lead to another, and they'd have sex on that damp grass, in the watery sunlight. Her body, wet and sleek, would rise over his. He'd fill his hands with her breasts, and …

'Jeez.' He blinked, saw her disappearing into the trees again.

He wasn't sure if he was embarrassed or relieved to find himself hard. He'd had sex only once in the six months since he'd broken things off with Jessica. And that had been more a reflex than real desire.

So if he could find himself fully aroused over some ridiculous fantasy of a woman whose face he hadn't seen, that area was coming back to normal.

He could check worry over his manhood off his list of concerns.

He tossed the last swallows of cold coffee away. He didn't mind starting the day with a stray erotic fantasy, but he did mind starting it with bad coffee. It was time to get down to practicalities.

He went back in, grabbed his wallet and keys, and headed into town for supplies.

It took him most of the day. Not just to get the supplies, but to reacquaint himself with the city he was going to call his own.

If Boston was a respectable wife, with a few seamy secrets, New Orleans was a sensual mistress who celebrated her darker side.

He treated himself to an enormous breakfast, so loaded with cholesterol he imagined his heart simply keeling over from the shock.

He bought coffee beans and a grinder. Bagels and

beignets. He loaded up on the single-male cuisine of packaged dinners, frozen pizza, dry cereal. Hit the liquor store for beer, bourbon and some good wine.

He loaded it into his car, then struck out again, as much for the joy of wandering the streets as the recollection he needed something to eat on and with. He settled for paper plates and plastic ware, and stopped to watch a street musician set out his trumpet case, prime it with a few coins, then fill the air with a stream of magic.

Declan gave him his first dollar of the day.

He avoided the temptation of the antique shops and the lure of the Quarter. Lunchtime music was already pumping out of clubs and exotic scents wafted from restaurants. He bought himself a muffuletta – that marvel of meat and cheese and oil on Italian bread – to take back home for later.

As he walked to his car again, he noted the tourists with their bags from Café du Monde or the Riverwalk shops, the card readers sitting at folding tables around the perimeter of Jackson Square who would tell your fortune for ten dollars a pop. He caught the faint drift of marijuana under the ripening stench of garbage as he walked by an alleyway.

And saw an enormous black woman, smoking in indolent puffs, on the plant-jammed gallery above a shop that advertised erotic candles.

He bought one for Remy of a naked woman with breasts like torpedoes, and grinned over it all the way back to his car.

He drove home energized. He hauled in supplies, stuffed them wherever seemed logical at the time, then began a serious room-by-room inspection of the main level. He made notes on problems, on potentials, on plans and on priorities.

The kitchen was a definite first. He had experience there from his own house in Boston, and from two remodels where he'd assisted friends.

He couldn't claim to cook more than the occasional omelette or toasted sandwich, but he thought of the kitchen as the heart of any home. The latest transition of the Manet Hall kitchen was early eighties – stark white and chrome with a slablike island work counter and blinding white flooring.

The good points were the generous windows, the old and serviceable brick hearth and the pretty coffered ceiling. He liked the enormous pantry, but thought it would serve better as a mudroom. He'd hack down to the original wood flooring, strip off the overly sweet teapot-themed wallpaper, yank out the island in favor of an antique baker's table or some such thing.

Decorating wasn't his strong point. He'd left that to Jessica, who'd favored pale colors and classic lines.

And now that he thought about it, he preferred stronger colors and the charm of the fanciful. He *liked* details and fuss. It was his house, damn it, and he'd do it his way. Top to bottom.

He'd put in some old glass-fronted cabinets where he could display antique kitchen appliances. Cracked, mismatched dishes, bottles and Mason jars. Cluttered.

Good solid surface countertops. Copper faucets. He didn't care if they tarnished. They'd just look more real.

Big-ass refrigerator. State of the art dishwasher and range. All fronted with distressed wood.

Now, we're cooking.

He took reams of notes, measured, remeasured. He dragged out his research books and pored over them on the floor of the empty library while he ate half his sandwich and drank enough coffee to make his ears ring.

He could see it, so perfectly. The floor-to-ceiling shelves jammed with books, the deep green walls and the soft cream of the plaster ceiling with trim. Thick silver candlesticks on the mantel. He'd have to have all the chimneys checked professionally so he could start building fires, knock the chill out of the air.

The trim would be restored where it needed it, sanded smooth as satin. The pocket doors here, and the massive ones separating the gentlemen's and ladies' parlors were in excellent shape.

Someone along the way had refinished the library flooring.

He crawled around, running his hands over the wood. Sand it down lightly, slap on a couple coats of clear varnish, and they'd be set. The area rugs had protected it well – the good, thick Aubussons Josephine had ordered from Paris.

He smelled brandy, leather, beeswax and roses, but thought nothing of it. His eyes were cloudy and distant when he stopped at the tiled hearth, flicked his thumb over the chip at the corner. That section would have to be replaced, or if it couldn't be matched, rounded off. They'd been hand painted and glazed in Italy, at considerable expense.

Julian had knocked the candlestick off the mantel, and it had chipped the tile. Drunk again. Raging again.

The cell phone in his pocket rang and had Declan sitting back on his heels. Blinking, displaced, he gazed around the empty room. What had he been doing? Thinking? He glanced down at his thumb and saw he'd rubbed it raw on the jagged tile. Disoriented, he dragged out his phone.

'Yeah. Hello?'

'There he is. I was about to give you up.' Remy's cheerful voice jangled in his head as Declan stared at the tile. He'd been thinking about the tile. Something …

47

'I'm, ah, doing a room by room. Measuring. Stuff.'

'How about you get yourself out of there for a while? I got me a late meeting, thought you could meet me for a drink after. Effie, too, if I can drag her out.'

'What time is it?' Declan turned his wrist to check his watch. 'Midnight? It's midnight?'

'Not yet it's not. You been drinking already?'

'Just coffee.' He frowned at his watch, tapped the face. 'Battery must've gone.'

'It's just after six. I should be able to wiggle loose by nine. Why don't you come on in? I'll meet you at Et Trois, in the Quarter, on Dauphine about a block off Bourbon.'

'Yeah.' Absently, he shoved at his hair, found his forehead was lightly beaded with sweat. 'Yeah, that sounds fine.'

'You need directions, Yankee boy?'

'I'll find it.' He rubbed his throbbing thumb. 'Remy?'

'That's my name.'

Declan shook his head, laughed at himself. 'Nothing. See you later.'

He drove in early. He wasn't particularly interested in drinking, but wanted to see the metamorphosis of New Orleans from day to night. The streets gleamed under the carnival of lights, teemed with the crowds who streamed along, looking for entertainment.

It was neither the tourists nor the merchants who ran the show, in Declan's opinion. It was the city itself. And its wheels turned on music.

It pumped from doorways, cool jazz, hot rock, melting blues. Overhead, restaurant galleries were thick with diners who warded off the January chill with spicy sauce and alcohol. The strip club hawkers promised all manner of visual delights, and in the shops cash registers rang as tourists gorged on T-shirts and Mardi Gras masks. The bars served hurricanes to the Yankees, and beer and liquor to those who knew better.

But it was the music that kept the parade marching.

He soaked it in as he strolled down Bourbon, past doorways, bright lights, and sudden, unexpected court-yards. He skirted around a group of women who clutched together on the sidewalk chattering like magpies.

He caught the scent of them – flowers and candy – and felt the typical male reaction of pleasure and panic when they burst into giggles.

'Nice ass,' one of them commented, and Declan kept on walking.

Women in packs were dangerous and mysterious entities.

It occurred to him that if he were going to meet Effie, he should take her a token. Some sort of engagement gift. He didn't know what she liked, or what she *was* like, come to that. But if there was one thing he was good at, it was buying gifts.

Wishing he'd thought of it earlier, he poked through a couple of shops without much hope. Nearly everything in this section was geared for the tourist trade, and he didn't think a wind-up, plastic penis was quite the thing for a first introduction. A gift could wait, he reflected, or he could just fall back on the basket of girl lotions and potions.

Then he saw it. The silver frog squatted on all fours as if it was about to take a good, springy hop. It had a cheer-fully wicked face and a big, smart-ass grin. And reminded Declan instantly of Remy.

If this Effie had fallen for his old college pal, she had to appreciate whimsy. He had it wrapped in fancy paper with a big red bow.

It was still shy of nine when he turned onto Dauphine.

He was ready to sit in a bar, away from the center ring of the circus. Maybe listen to some music and work on a beer. For the next several weeks, he was going to have to tow the line. Spend his days tearing into the kitchen, his evenings planning his next point of attack. He had to track down specific craftsmen. Get bids. Get started.

For tonight, he'd spend some time with friends, then go home and get a solid eight hours' sleep.

He spotted the sign for Et Trois. It was hard to miss as it danced cheerfully in cool blue over the scarred wooden door of a building barely two good strides from the street.

The second floor boasted the typical gallery and lacy iron baluster. Someone had decked it out with fat clay pots of hot pink geraniums and strung little white fairy lights along the eaves. It made a pretty, feminine picture. The kind of spot where you might sit, drink a glass of wine, and contemplate the people strolling by below.

He opened the door to a blast of jumpy zydeco, the scent of garlic and whiskey.

On the small stage was a five-piece band – washboard, fiddle, drums, guitar, accordion. The little dance floor was already packed with people executing the quick, fancy two-step the music cried for.

Through the dim light he could see that none of the round wooden tables scooted to the side were free. He turned toward the bar. The wood was nearly black with age, but it gleamed. A dozen backless stools were jammed together. Declan copped the single one left before some-one beat him to it.

Bottles lined the mirror behind the bar, and inter-spersed with them were salt and pepper shakers in a vari-ety of themes. An elegant couple in evening dress, dogs, Rocky and Bullwinkle, Porky and Petunia, the round, naked breasts of a reclining woman, carnival masks and winged fairies.

He contemplated them, considered the sort of person who would collect and display fairies and body parts, and decided it was someone who understood New Orleans.

Onstage, the fiddle player began to sing in Cajun. She had a voice like a rusty saw that was inexplicably appealing. Tapping his foot, Declan glanced down to the end of the bar. The man tending had dreadlocks down to his waist, a face that might have been carved by a very skilled hand out of a polished coffee bean, and hands that moved with balletic grace as he worked taps and poured shots.

He started to lift his hand to get the bartender's attention. And then she walked out of the door behind the bar.

Later, when he could think clearly, he would decide it had been like having a sledgehammer plowed into his chest. Not stopping his heart, but jump-starting it. His heart, his blood, his loins, his brain. Everything went from holding pattern to quick march in an instant.

There you are! something in his mind shouted. *Finally*.

He could hear the race of his body like a hard hum that drowned out the music, the voices. His vision focused in on her so completely it was as if she were spotlighted on a black stage.

She wasn't beautiful, not in any classic sense. What she was, was spectacular.

Her hair was midnight black, a gypsy mane that spilled wild curls over her shoulders. Her face was fox-sharp – the narrow, somewhat aristocratic nose, the high, planed cheeks, the tapered chin. Her eyes were long and heavy-lidded, her mouth wide, full and painted blood-lust red.

It didn't quite go together, he thought as his brain jumbled. The elements in the face shouldn't work as a whole. But they were perfect. Striking, sexy, superb.

51

She was small, almost delicately built, and wore a tight scooped-neck shirt the color of poppies that showed off the lean muscles of her arms, the firm curve of her breasts. Tucked into the valley of those breasts was a silver chain with a tiny silver key.

Her skin was dusky, her eyes, when they flicked to his, the deep, rich brown of bitter chocolate.

Those red lips curved – a slow, knowing smile as she strolled over, leaned on the bar so their faces were close enough for him to see the tiny beauty mark just above the right curve of her top lip. Close enough for him to catch the scent of night-blooming jasmine, and start to drown in it.

'Can I do something for you, *cher*?'

Oh yeah, he thought. *Please*.

But all that came out was: 'Um ...' She gave her head a little toss, then angled it as she sized him up. She spoke again, in that easy Cajun rhythm. 'You thirsty? Or just ... hungry tonight?'

'Ah ...' He wanted to lap his tongue over those red lips, that tiny mole, and slurp her right up. 'Corona.'

He watched her as she got the bottle, snagged a lime. She had a walk like a dancer, somewhere between ballet and exotic. He could literally feel his tongue tangling into knots.

'You want to run a tab, handsome?'

'Ah.' *God, Fitzgerald, pull yourself together*. 'Yeah, thanks. What's it unlock?' When she lifted her eyebrows, he picked up the bottle. 'Your key?'

'This?' She reached down, trailed a finger over the little key and sent his blood pressure through the roof. 'Why, my heart, *cher*. What'd you think?'

He reached out a hand for hers. If he didn't touch her, he was afraid he might break down and sob. 'I'm Declan.'

'Is that right?' She left her hand in his. 'Nice name. Not usual.'

'It's … Irish.'

'Uh-huh.' She turned his hand over, leaned down as if reading the palm. 'What do I see here? You haven't been in New Orleans long, but you hope to be. Got yourself out of the cold, cold North, did you, Declan?'

'Yeah. Guess that's not hard to figure.'

She looked up again, and this time his heart did stop. 'I can figure more. Rich Yankee lawyer down from Boston. You bought Manet Hall.'

'Do I know you?' He felt something – like a link forged onto a chain – when his hand gripped hers. 'Have we met before?'

'Not in this life, darling.' She gave his hand a little pat, then moved down the bar filling more orders.

But she kept an eye on him. He wasn't what she'd expected from Remy's description. Though she was damned if she knew what she'd expected. Still, she was a woman who liked surprises. The man sitting at her bar, watching her out of storm-gray eyes, looked to be full of them.

She liked his eyes. She was used to men looking at her with desire, but there'd been more in his. A kind of breathless shock that was both flattering and sweet.

And it was appealing to have a man who looked like he could handle anything you tossed at him fumble when you smiled at him.

Though he'd barely touched his beer, she worked her way back to him, tapped a finger to the bottle. 'Ready for another?'

'No, thanks. Can you take a break? Can I buy you a drink, coffee, a car, a dog?'

'What's in there?'

53

He glanced at the little gift bag he'd set on the bar. 'It's just a present for someone I'm meeting.'

'You buy gifts for lots of women, Declan?'

'She's not a woman. I mean, not my woman. I don't actually have one – it's just … I used to be better at this.'

'Better at what?'

'At hitting on women.'

She laughed – the low, throaty sound of his fantasies.

'Can you take a break? We'll kick somebody away from a table and you can give me another chance.'

'You're not doing so bad with the first one. I own the place, so I don't get breaks.'

'This is your place?'

'That's right.' She turned as one of the waitresses came to the bar with a tray.

'Wait. Wait.' He reached for her hand again. 'I don't know your name. What's your name?'

'Angelina.' She said softly. 'But they call me Lena, 'cause I ain't no angel. *Cher.*' She trailed a finger down his cheek, then stepped away to fill orders.

Declan took a deep, long swallow of beer to wash back the saliva that had pooled in his mouth.

He was trying to work out another approach when Remy slapped him on the back. 'We're going to need us a table, son.'

'View's better from here.'

Remy followed the direction of Declan's gaze. 'One of the best the city offers. You meet my cousin Lena?'

'Cousin?'

'Fourth cousins, I'm thinking. Might be fifth. Angelina Simone, one of New Orleans's jewels. And here's another. Effie Renault. Effie darling, this is my good friend Declan Fitzgerald.'

'Hello, Declan.' She wiggled between him and Remy and kissed Declan's cheek. 'I'm so happy to meet you.'

She had a cloud of blond hair around a pretty, heart-shaped face, and eyes of clear summer blue. Her lips had a deep, Kewpie doll curve and were a rosy pink.

She looked like she should be leading cheers at the local high school.

'You're too pretty to waste yourself on this guy,' Declan told her. 'Why don't you run away with me instead?'

'When do we leave?'

With a chuckle, Declan slid off the stool and returned her kiss. 'Nice job, Remy.'

'Best work I ever did.' Remy pressed his lips to Effie's hair. 'Sit on down there, darling. Place is packed. Bar might be the best we do. You want wine?'

'The house white'll be fine.'

'Get you a refill there, Declan?'

'I'll get it. I'm buying.'

'If that's the case, get my girl here the good chardonnay. I'll have what you're having.'

'Look what the cat dragged.' Lena sent Remy a grin. 'Hey, Effie. What's everybody drinking tonight?'

'A glass of chardonnay for the lady. And two more Coronas,' Declan told her. 'Then maybe you can call nine-one-one. My heart stops every time I look at you.'

'Your friend's got himself a smooth way once he gets rolling, Remy.' Lena took a bottle of wine from the cooler.

'Those Harvard girls were putty in his hands.'

'We southern girls are too used to the heat to melt easy.' She poured wine, topped the beers with lime wedges.

'I do know you.' It bounced back in his memory. 'I saw you, this morning, playing with your dog. Big black dog, near the pond.'

'Rufus.' It gave her a little jolt to realize he'd watched her. 'He's my grandmama's dog. That's her house back the bayou. I go out sometimes and stay with her if she's feeling poorly. Or just lonely.'

'Come by the Hall next time you're out. I'll give you the tour.'

'Just might. I've never been inside.' She set a fresh bowl of pretzels on the bar. 'Y'all want something from the kitchen?'

'We'll think about that,' Remy said.

'Just let us know.' She swung around and through the back door.

'You gonna want to mop that drool off your chin, Dec.' Remy squeezed Declan's shoulder. 'It's embarrassing.'

'Don't tease him, Remy. A man doesn't get a little worked up around Lena, he's got some essential parts missing.'

'You definitely should run away with me,' Declan decided. 'But meanwhile. Best wishes.' He nudged the gift bag in front of her.

'You bought me a present? Aren't you the sweetest thing!' She tore into it with an enthusiasm that made Declan grin. And when she held up the frog, she stopped, stared. Then threw back her head and let out a hooting laugh. 'It looks like Remy. Look here, honey, he's got your smile.'

'I don't see it.'

'I do. Dec did.' She swiveled on the stool and beamed up into Declan's face. 'I like you. I'm so glad I like you. I love this moron here so much I can hardly stand it, so I'd've pretended I liked you even if I didn't. But I don't have to pretend.'

'Oh now, don't start watering up, Effie.' Remy dug out a handkerchief as she sniffed. 'She does that when she's happy. Night I asked her to marry me, she cried so much it took her ten minutes to say yes.'

He pulled her off the stool. 'Come on, *chère*, you dance with me till you dry up again.'

Declan got back on the stool, picked up his beer, and watched them circle the floor.

'They look good together,' Lena commented from behind him.

'Yeah. Yeah, they do. Interested in seeing how we look together?'

'You are persistent.' She let out a breath. 'What kind of car you going to buy me?'

'Car?'

'You offered to buy me a drink, coffee, a car or a dog. I can buy my own drinks, and I like my own coffee. I got a dog, more or less. A car, too. But I don't see why I shouldn't have two cars. What car are you buying me?'

'Your choice.'

'I'll let you know,' she replied, then moved down the bar once more.

Chapter Four

He worked solidly for three days. There was little, in Declan's opinion, more satisfying than tearing something apart. Even putting it back together again didn't reach into the gut with the same primal zing.

He gutted the kitchen, ripping out the center island, the counters and cabinets. He steamed off wallpaper and yanked up linoleum.

He was left with a shell of plaster and wood, and endless possibilities.

In the evenings he nursed his blisters and strained muscles, and pored through design books.

Every morning, before he started the day, he took his first cup of coffee out on the gallery and hoped for a glimpse of Lena and the big black dog she'd called Rufus.

He contacted workmen and craftsmen, ordered materials, and in a frenzy of enthusiasm, bought a full-sized pickup truck straight off the lot.

The first night he was able to build a fire in the down-river parlor, he toasted the occasion, and himself, with a solitary glass of Merlot.

There'd been no more sleepwalking, but there had been dreams. He could remember only snatches of them upon waking. Music – often the tune had seemed to be lodged in his brain like a tumor. Or raised voices.

Once he'd dreamed of sex, of soft sighs in the dark, of the lazy glide of flesh over flesh, and the need rising up like a warm wave.

He'd woken with his muscles quivering and the scent of lilies just fading from his senses.

Since dreaming about sex seemed to be the best he could manage, he put his energies into the work.

When he did take a break, it was to pay a call, and he went armed with a bouquet of white daisies and a rawhide bone.

The bayou house was a single-story cypress, shotgun style. Tobacco-colored water snaked around it on three sides. A small white boat swayed gently at a sagging dock.

Trees hemmed it in where the water didn't. The cypress and live oak and pecan. From the limbs hung clear bottles half-filled with water. And nestled into the gnarled roots of a live oak stood a painted statue of the Blessed Virgin.

There were purple pansies at her feet.

A little porch faced the dirt drive, and there were more potted flowers on it along with a rocking chair. The shutters were painted a mossy green. The screen door was patched in two places, and through the checkerboard net came the strong, bluesy voice of Ethel Waters.

He heard the deep, warning barks of the dog. Still, Declan wasn't prepared for the size and speed as Rufus burst out the door and charged.

'Oh, Jesus,' was all he managed. He had an instant to wonder if he should dive through the window of the pickup or freeze when the black mess the size of a pony skidded to a halt at his feet.

Rufus punctuated those ear-splitting barks with rumbling growls, liquid snarls and a very impressive show of teeth. Since he doubted he could beat the dog off with a bunch of daisies, Declan opted for the friendly approach.

'Hey, really, really big Rufus. How's it going?'

Rufus sniffed at his boots, up his leg and dead into the crotch.

'Oh man, let's not get that personal right off.' Thinking of those teeth, Declan decided he'd rather risk his hand than his dick, and reached out slowly to give the massive head a little shove and pat.

Rufus looked up with a pair of sparkling brown eyes, and in one fast, fluid move, reared up on his hind legs and planted his enormous paws on Declan's shoulders.

He swiped a tongue about the size of the Mississippi over Declan's face. Braced against the side of the truck, Declan hoped the long, sloppy licks were a greeting and not some sort of tenderizing.

'Nice to meet you, too.'

'Get on down now, Rufus.'

At the mild order from the front doorway, the dog dropped down, sat, thumped his tail.

The woman standing on the porch was younger than Declan had expected. She couldn't have been far into her sixties. She had the same small build as her granddaughter, the same sharp planes to her face. Her hair was black, liberally streaked with white, and worn in a mass of curls.

She wore a cotton dress that hit her mid-calf with a baggy red sweater over it. Stout brown boots covered her feet with thick red socks drooping over them. He heard the jangle of her bracelets as she fisted her hands on her narrow hips.

'He liked the smell of you, and the sound of you, so he gave you a welcome kiss.'

'If he didn't like me?'

She smiled, a quick flash that deepened the lines time had etched on her face. 'What you think?'

'I think I'm glad I smell friendly. I'm Declan Fitzgerald, Mrs. Simone. I bought Manet Hall.'

'I know who you are. Come on inside and sit for a spell.' She stepped back, opened the rickety screen door.

With the dog plodding along beside him, Declan walked to the porch. 'It's nice to meet you, Mrs. Simone.'

She studied him, a frank and cagey stare out of dark eyes. 'You sure are a pretty one, aren't you?'

'Thanks.' He held out the flowers. 'You, too.'

She took the flowers, pursed her lips. 'You come courting me, Declan Fitzgerald?'

'Can you cook?'

She laughed, a thick foggy sound, and he fell a little in love. 'I got some fresh corn bread, as you can see for yourself.'

She led the way in, down the wire-straight center hall. He caught glimpses of the parlor, of bedrooms – one with an iron crucifix over a simple iron bed – a sewing room, that all managed to be cozily cluttered and pin-neat.

He smelled furniture polish and lavender, then a few steps from the kitchen, caught the country scent of baking.

'Ma'am? I'm thirty-one, financially solvent, and I got a clean bill of health my last physical. I don't smoke, I usually drink in moderation, and I'm reasonably neat. If you marry me, I'll treat you like a queen.'

She chuckled and shook her head, then waved to the kitchen table. 'Sit yourself down there and stretch those long legs under the table so they don't trip me up. And since you're sparking me, you can call me Miss Odette.'

She uncovered a dish on the counter, got plates out of a cupboard. While she cut squares of corn bread, Declan looked out her kitchen door.

The bayou spread, a dream of dark water and cypress knees with the shadowy reflection of trees shimmering on the surface. He saw a bird with bright red wings spear through the air and vanish.

'Wow. How do you get anything done when you could just sit here and look all day?'

'It's a good spot.' She took a pitcher of dark tea from an old refrigerator that was barely taller than she was. 'My family's been here more'n a hundred-fifty years. My grandpapa, he had him a good still out back that stand of oaks. Revenuers never did find it.'

She set the glass, the plate in front of him. '*Manger*. Eat. What your grandpapa do?'

'He was a lawyer. Actually, both of them were.'

'Dead now, are they?'

'Retired.'

'You, too, huh?' She got out a fat, pale blue bottle as he took the first bite of corn bread.

'Sort of, from the law anyway. This is wonderful, Miss Odette.'

'I got a hand with baking. I like daisies,' she added as she put them in the bottle she'd filled with water. 'They got a cheerful face. You gonna give Rufus that bone you brought along, or make him beg for it?'

As Rufus was currently sitting at his feet with one weighty paw on his thigh, Declan decided he'd begged enough. He pulled the bone out of its bag. The dog took it with a surprisingly delicate bite, wagged his tail from side to side twice, like a whip, then plopped down and began to gnaw.

Odette put the flowers in the center of the table, then sat in the chair next to Declan's. 'What're you going to do with that big old place, Declan Fitzgerald?'

'All kinds of things. Put it back the way it used to be, as much as I can.'

'Then what?'

'I don't know. Live there.'

She broke off a corner of her corn bread. She'd already decided she liked the look of him – the untidy hair, the stone-gray eyes in a lean face. And the sound of him – Yankee, but not prim. And his manners were polished but natural and friendly.

Now she wanted to see what he was made of.

'Why?'

'I don't know that, either, except I've wanted to since the first time I saw it.'

'And how's the Hall feel about you?'

'I don't think it's made up its mind. Have you ever been inside?'

'Hmm.' She nodded. 'Been some time ago. Lotta house for one young man. You got you a girl back up there in Boston?'

'No, ma'am.'

'Handsome boy like you, past thirty. Not gay, are you?'

'No, ma'am.' He grinned as he lifted the glass of tea. 'I like girls. Just haven't found the right fit yet.'

'Let me see your hands.' She took one in hers, turned it over. 'Still got city on them, but you're taking care of that right quick.' Her thumb passed over healing blisters, scrapes, the ridge of forming callus. 'I got some balm I'll give you before you go, keep these blisters from troubling you. You got a strong hand, Declan. Strong enough that you changed your fate. Took yourself a new road. You didn't love her.'

'I'm sorry?'

'This woman.' Odette smoothed her fingernail over the side of his palm. 'The one you stepped back from. She wasn't for you.'

Frowning, he leaned closer, stared down at his own hand. 'You see Jessica on there?' Fascinating. 'Does she end up with James?'

'What do you care? She didn't love you, either.'

'Well, ouch,' he said and laughed a little.

'You've got love coming, the kind that'll knock you flat on your behind. It'll be good for you.'

Though she continued to stroke her thumb over his palm, her gaze lifted to his face. Her eyes seemed to deepen. It seemed he could see worlds in them.

'You've got strong ties to Manet Hall. Strong, old ties. Life and death. Blood and tears. Joy, if you're strong enough, smart enough. You're a clever man, Declan. Be clever enough to look front and back to find yourself. You're not alone in that house.'

His throat went dry, but he didn't reach for his tea. He didn't move a muscle. 'It's haunted.'

'What's there's kept others from settling in. They'd say it was the money, the time or some such, but what's in that house frightened them away. It's been waiting for you.'

The chill shot up his spine in a single, icy arrow. 'Why?'

'That's for you to find out.' She gave his hand a squeeze, then released it, picked up her tea.

He curled his fingers into his tingling palm. 'So you're, like, a psychic?'

Amused, she rose to bring the pitcher of tea to the table. 'I see what I see from time to time. A little kitchen magic,' she said as she refilled the glasses. 'It doesn't make me a witch, just a woman.' She noted his glance at the silver cross she wore, tangled with colored beads around her neck. 'You think that's a contradiction? Where do you think power comes from, *cher*?'

'I guess I never thought about it.'

'We don't use what the good Lord gave us, whatever talent that might be, we're wasting his gift.' She angled her head, and he saw she wore earrings as well. Fat blue stones dangling from tiny lobes. 'I hear you called Jack Tripadoe about maybe doing some plumbing work in that place of yours.'

'Ah …' He struggled to shift his brain from the fantastic to the practical, while his palm continued to vibrate from the skim of her fingers. 'Yes. My friend Remy Payne recommended him.'

'That Remy.' Her face lit, and any mystery that had been in it vanished. 'He's a caution. Jack, he's a cousin of my sister's husband's brother's wife. He'll do good work for you, and if he doesn't give you a fair price, you tell him Miss Odette's gonna want to know why.'

'I appreciate that. You wouldn't happen to know a plasterer? Somebody who can handle fancy work?'

'I'll get you a name. It'll cost you a pretty bag of pennies to put that place back to what it was and keep it that way.'

'I've got a lot of pennies. I hope you'll come by sometime so I can show you around. I can't make corn bread, but I can manage the tea.'

'You got a nice manner, *cher*. Your mama, she raised you right.'

'Would you mind writing that down, signing it? I can mail it to her.'

'I'm going to like having you around,' she declared. 'You come back to visit anytime.'

'Thank you, Miss Odette.' Reading his cue, he got to his feet. 'I'm going to like having you around, too.'

The sun beamed across her face as she looked up at him. The angle of it, the amusement in her dark eyes, the teasing curve of lips, shot him back to the dim bar in the Quarter. 'She looks so much like you.'

'She does. You got your eye on my Lena already?'

He was a little flustered to realize he'd spoken out loud, so he tried a grin. 'Well, we established I like girls, right?'

She gave the table a little slap to punctuate the laugh as she rose. 'I like you just fine, Declan.'

He liked her, too. Enough that he decided to buy a couple of chairs after all, so she'd have somewhere to sit when she came by. He'd find something on Saturday, he thought as he went back to prepping the kitchen walls. He could hunt some down in the afternoon, before he was due to have dinner with Remy and Effie.

Then, he'd cap off the evening with a drink at Et Trois.

And if Lena wasn't working that night, he'd just walk back out and throw himself in front of a speeding car.

He worked until well after dark, then treated himself to a beer along with his Hungry-Man chicken dinner. He ate sitting on a sawhorse and admiring the progress of the kitchen.

The walls were stripped, repaired and prepped for paint. His pencil marks on them indicated the measurements of the cabinets he would start to build the next day. He'd even tried his hand at pointing up the bricks in the hearth, and didn't think he'd done a half-bad job of it. The old pine flooring was exposed and protected now with drop cloths. He'd finally settled on the traffic pattern, and had earmarked the spots for the range and the refrigerator.

If he couldn't find the right china cabinet for the long wall, he'd damn well build that, too. He was on a roll.

He carried a bottle of water upstairs, took his now-traditional nine-minute shower, then stretched out on the bed with his notes, drawings and books. Halfway through adjusting his plans for the front parlor, he conked out.

And woke, shivering with cold, in full dark. The baby had wakened him. The thin cries were still in his ears as he sat straight up with his heart banging like a hammer against his ribs.

He didn't know where he was, only that he was on the floor instead of in bed. And it was cold enough that he could see the white mist of his own breath pluming into the inky dark.

He rolled over, gained his feet. Reaching out like a blind man, he felt at the air as he took a cautious step forward.

Lilies. His body shuddered as he registered the scent. He knew where he was now – in the room down the hall from his own. The room, like the one on the third floor, he'd so carefully avoided over the last several days.

He was in it now, he thought as he took another shuffling step. And though it was insane, he knew he wasn't alone.

'You can scare me. But you won't scare me away.'

His fingers brushed something solid. He yelped, snatched them back an instant before he realized it was a wall. Taking several steadying breaths, he felt his way along it, bumped over trim, tapped over glass. Fumbling, he found the knob for the gallery doors and flung them open.

The January air felt warm and heavy against his chilled skin. He stumbled forward, gripped the rail. The night was like the inside of a cave. The old adage was true, he decided. There was no dark like country dark.

When his eyes adjusted to it, he turned back, pulled the door to the room firmly closed.

'This is my house now.' He said it quietly, then walked down the gallery, opened the door of his bedroom, and went back inside.

'Sleepwalking?' Remy scooped up another forkful of rice.

'Yeah. I went through it for about six months when I was around eleven.' Declan shrugged, but couldn't quite dismiss the weight of it.

He hadn't meant to bring it up, at least no more than in passing. The dinner Effie had fixed in Remy's Garden District apartment was welcome, as was the company. But somehow he'd gone from telling them about the progress of the rehab to his nighttime adventures.

'It must be terrifying,' Effie said, 'to wake up and find yourself somewhere else.'

'Spooky anyway. It's funny I'd end up at the two rooms that make me the most uneasy. Or, I guess it's logical. Some subconscious deal.'

'As long as you stay inside the house,' Remy put in. 'I don't want to hear you've sleepwalked your way into the swamp.'

'That's a nice thought. Thanks.'

'Remy.' Effie slapped his hand. 'I think you should see a doctor,' she told Declan. 'You could take something to help you sleep better.'

'Maybe. Been there a week, and it's only happened twice. Anyway, taking a couple of tranqs isn't going to do anything about the ghost.'

'It's just drafts and old wood settling.'

Remy grinned. 'Effie doesn't believe in ghosts.'

68

'Or in tarot cards or reading tea leaves or any such nonsense.' Her voice was prim, and just a little defensive.

'My girl, she's very grounded in the here and the now.'

'Your girl just has good sense,' she shot back. 'Dec, it just stands to reason you'd have some strange feelings, staying away out there in that big old house all alone. And I bet you're not eating right, either. You ought to live here with Remy for a while, until you get used to things.'

'She won't.' Remy jerked his head in Effie's direction. 'I'll live with you when we're married, and not before.'

'Oh, but, *chère*. May's so far away. I miss you when you're not here.' He took her hand, kissing it lavishly as he spoke.

'Tell you what, Effie, you come out and stay with me for a few nights. Strictly platonic,' he said with a grin as Remy narrowed his eyes. 'I bet you shift your stand on ghosts after one or two nights.'

'Sorry. I'm a city girl. What do you do out there all by yourself, Declan, when you're not working?'

'Read. And speaking of that, I need to come by the library, see if you can help me dig up more about Manet Hall. I've been taking a few whacks at the garden, too. Take walks. Drove over to visit Miss Odette.'

'You met Miss Odette?' Remy asked as he polished off his dinner. 'Something, isn't she?'

'I really liked her. Truth is, the house is keeping me so busy I usually drop off by ten at night. I finally got a TV hooked up, and I never think to turn it on. But I did buy a table and chairs this afternoon, and some other things.'

It was always a mistake, he chided himself, to let him through the door of an antique shop.

'We're not going to have you locking yourself out there and working yourself to the bone,' Effie decided. 'I expect you to come into town and see us at least once a week from now on. And Remy, you should start going out there on Saturdays and giving Dec a hand. Spending too much time alone,' she declared as she pushed back from the table. 'That's what's wrong with you. Now, y'all ready for pie?'

Maybe she was right, Declan thought as he hunted up a place to park. If she wasn't right, Effie was certainly definite. He'd try mixing it up a little more. He could drive into town once or twice a week for a real meal. Maybe have Remy and Effie out for one – a very informal one.

He could spend an evening reading something other than research.

More, he thought. He was going to gear himself up soon and push himself through the mental block he'd erected about the third-floor room.

He had to park a block and a half from Et Trois, but when he stepped in, saw Lena at the bar, he thought the walk had been worth it.

He couldn't even snag a stool tonight, but he did manage to squeeze between customers and claim a corner of the bar. The music was loud and lively, and so was the crowd.

There was a blond behind the bar tonight in addition to its owner and Dreadlock Guy. Each of them was hopping.

Lena flicked him a glance as she served two drafts and a gin fizz.

'Corona?'

'Better make it a Coke.'

She looked just as good as he remembered. Just exactly as good. She wore blue tonight – a shirt that was unbuttoned low and rolled to the elbows. Her lips were still red, but she'd scooped her hair back on the sides with silver combs. He could see the glint of hoops at her ears.

She set a tall glass in front of him. 'Where y'at?'

'Ah, I think I'm right here.'

'No.' She gave him that quick smoky laugh. 'Don't you speak New Orleans, *cher*? When I say "where y'at," I'm asking how you're doing.'

'Oh. Fine, thanks. Where you at?'

'There you go. Me, I'm fine, too. Busy. Let me know if you want anything else.'

He had to content himself with watching her. She worked her third of the bar, filling orders, having a quick word, slipping into the kitchen and out again without ever seeming to rush.

He never considered going home. When a stool freed up, he climbed on, settled in.

It was like being studied by a big, handsome cat, Lena thought. Steady and patient and just a little dangerous. He nursed his Coke, took a refill, and was still sitting when the place began to thin out.

She swung by again. 'You waiting for something, handsome?'

'Yeah.' He kept his eyes on hers. 'I'm waiting.'

She wiped up a spill with her bar rag. 'I heard you went by to see my grandmama.'

'A couple of days ago. You look like her.'

'They say.' Lena tucked the end of the rag in her back pocket. 'You go over there so you could lay on your Yankee charm and she'd put in a good word for you with me?'

'I was hoping that'd be a side benefit, but no. I went over because she's a neighbor. I expected she was an *old* neighbor – elderly woman, living alone – and thought she'd like to know someone was around who could give

71

her a hand with things. Then I met her and realized she doesn't need me to give her a hand with anything.'

'That's nice.' Lena let out a breath. 'That was nice. Fact is, she could do with a strong back now and again. Dupris, honey?' she called out with her gaze locked on Declan's. 'You close up for me, okay? I'm going on home.'

She pulled a small purse from behind the bar, slung its long strap over her shoulder.

'Can I walk you home, Lena?'

'Yeah, you can do that.'

She came out from behind the bar, smiled when he opened the door for her.

'So, I hear you're working hard on that house of yours.'

'Night and day,' he agreed. 'I started on the kitchen. I've made serious progress. Haven't seen you near the pond in the mornings.'

'Not lately.' The truth was she'd stayed away deliberately. She'd been curious to see if he'd come back. She strolled down the sidewalk.

'I met Rufus. He likes me.'

'So does my grandmama.'

'What about you?'

'Oh, they like me fine.'

She turned toward the opening of a tall iron gate when he laughed. They moved into a tiny, paved courtyard with a single iron table and two chairs.

'Lena.' He took her hand.

'This is where I live.' She gestured back toward the steps leading to the second-floor gallery he'd admired the first night.

'Oh. Well, so much for seducing you with my wit and charm on the long walk home. Why don't we—'

'No.' She tapped a finger on his chest. 'You're not

coming up, not tonight. But I think we'll get this out of the way and see what's what.'

She rose on her toes, swayed in. Her hand slipped around to the back of his neck as she brought his mouth down to hers.

He felt himself sink. As if he'd been walking on solid ground that had suddenly turned to water. It was a long, steep drop that had a thousand impressions rushing by his senses.

The silky slide of her lips and tongue, the warm brush of her skin, the drugging scent of her perfume.

By the time he'd begun to separate them, she eased back.

'You're good at that,' she murmured, and laid a fingertip on his lips. 'I had a feeling. 'Night, *cher.*'

'Wait a minute.' He wasn't so shell-shocked he couldn't function. He grabbed her hand. 'That was practice,' he told her, and spun her stylishly into his arms.

He felt the amused curve of her lips against his and, running his hands up her back, into her hair, let himself drown.

Whoops! That single thought bounced into her head as she felt herself slip. His mouth was patient, but she felt the quick flashes of hunger. His hands were gentle, but held her firmly against him.

The taste of him, like something half remembered, began to seep into her blood.

Someone opened the door of the bar. Music jumped out, then shut off again. A car gunned by on the street behind her, another blast of music through the open windows.

Heat shimmered over her skin, under it, so that the hands she rested on his shoulders trailed around, linked behind his neck.

73

'Very good at it,' she repeated, and turned her head so her cheek rubbed his. Once, then twice. 'But you're not coming up tonight. I have to think about you.'

'Okay. I'll keep coming back.'

'They always come back for Lena.' *For a while*, she thought as she eased away. 'Go on home now, Declan.'

'I'll just wait until you get inside.'

Her brows lifted. 'Aren't you the one.' Because it was sweet, she kissed his cheek before she walked to the steps and headed up.

When she unlocked the door and glanced back, he was still there. 'You have sweet dreams now, *cher*.'

'That'd be a nice change,' he muttered when she closed the door behind her.

Chapter Five

Manet Hall
January 2, 1900

It was lies. It had to be lies, of the cruelest, coldest nature. He would not believe, *never* believe that his sweet Abby had run away from him. Had left him, left their child.

Lucian sat on the corner of the bed, trapped in the daze that had gripped him since he'd returned home two days before. Returned home to find the Hall in an uproar, and his wife missing.

Another man. That's what they were saying. An old love she'd met in secret whenever Lucian had gone into New Orleans on business.

Lies.

He had been the only man. He had taken an angel to wife, a virgin to their wedding bed.

Something had happened to her. He opened and closed his hand over the watch pin he'd given her when he'd asked her to marry him. Something terrible.

But what? What could have pushed her to leave the house in the night?

A sick relation, he thought as he rose to pace and pace and pace.

But he knew that wasn't the case. Hadn't he ridden like a wild man into the marsh, to ask, to demand, to beg her family, her friends, if they knew what had become of her?

Even now people were searching for her, on the road, in the swamp, in the fields.

But the rumors, the gossip, were already rushing along the river.

Lucian Manet's young wife had run off with another man.

And he could hear the whispers behind the whispers. *What did he expect? Cajun trash. Likely that girl-child got started in the bayou and she passed it off as his.*

Horrible, vicious lies.

The door opened. Josephine hadn't bothered with even a cursory knock. Manet Hall was hers, now and always. She entered any room at her whim.

'Lucian.'

He spun around. 'They've found her?' He'd yet to change the clothes soiled from his last search, and hope shone through the dirt on his face.

'They have not.' She closed the door at her back with a testy snap. 'Nor will they. She is gone, and is probably at this moment laughing at you with her lover.'

She could almost believe it. Soon, she thought, it would be the truth.

'She did not run away.'

'You're a fool. You were a fool to marry her, and you remain a fool.' She strode to the armoire, threw it open. 'Can't you see some of her clothes are missing? Hasn't her maid reported as much?'

All he could see was the blue ball gown with the flounces and rosettes she'd been so proud of.

'The maid is mistaken.' But his voice shook.

'You're mistaken. What of her jewelry?' Josephine pulled the leather box from the shelf, tossed the lid up. 'Where are the pearls you gave her for Christmas? The diamond bracelet you bought her when she had the child?'

'Someone stole them.'

On a sound of disgust, Josephine upended the jewelry on the bed. 'She took whatever sparkled the most. A girl of her type knows nothing but glitter. She bewitched you, caused you to embarrass your family, your name, now she has disgraced us all.'

'No.' He squeezed his eyes shut as his heart ripped to pieces. 'She wouldn't leave me. She would never leave Marie Rose.'

'However much affection she might have had for the child, I doubt either she or her lover wanted to be saddled with a baby. How do you know, Lucian, that the child is yours?'

The red rage of fury stained his cheeks. 'How can you ask such a question? How could you have lived in the same house with her for a year, and say such a thing about her?'

The doubt, Josephine thought coldly, had been planted. She would help it bloom. 'Because I did live in the same house with her, but I wasn't blinded by lust or bewitched by whatever spell she put on you. This is your fault as much as hers. If you had satisfied your appetites as other men, paid her, given her a few trinkets, we would not have this new scandal on our hands.'

'Paid her. Like a whore. Like Julian pays his women.' Lucian stepped forward, so angry his hands trembled. 'My wife is not a whore.'

'She used you,' Josephine said in a vicious whisper. 'She took your dignity, and smeared ours. She came into this house a servant, and left it with the spoils of her deception. Like a thief in the night, with her child crying behind her.'

She gripped his arms and shook. 'You tried to change what cannot be changed. You expected too much of her. She could never have been mistress of Manet Hall.' *I am.* 'At least she had the sense to know it. Now, she's gone. We will hold our heads up until the gossip dies down. We are Manets, and we will survive this.'

She turned away, walked to the door. 'I expect you to make yourself presentable and join the family for dinner. Our lives have been disrupted long enough.'

Alone, Lucian sat on the bed and, with the watch pin in his hand, fell to weeping.

'I gotta hand it to you, boy.' With his hands on his hips, Remy turned a circle in the kitchen. 'You made a hell of a mess here.'

'Come back in a couple weeks,' Declan called out from the adjacent dining room, where he'd set up what he thought of as his carpentry shop.

Effie lifted a corner of the drop cloth. 'The floor's going to be beautiful. It's a blank canvas,' she said as she looked around the gutted kitchen. 'He had to wipe it clean so he could paint the right picture.'

'Effie, ditch that moron and come live here with me.'

'You stop trying to make time with my girl.' Remy walked to the doorway. Declan stood at a power saw, a tool belt slung at his hips and a carpenter's pencil behind his ear. It looked to Remy as if his friend hadn't used a razor in a good three days.

And damned if the scruffy, handyman look didn't suit him.

'You got something you want me to do around here, or should we just stand around admiring how manly you look?'

'I could sure use one or two laborers.' He ran the saw through wood with a satisfying buzz and a shower of sawdust, switched it off before he glanced over. 'You really up for it?'

'Sure.' Remy slung an arm around Effie's shoulder. 'We'll work for beer.'

Four hours later, they sat on the gallery outside the freshly painted kitchen. Effie, dwarfed in the old denim shirt Declan had given her for a smock, had freckles of paint on her nose. The beer was cold and crisp, and on Declan's countertop stereo, Foghat was taking a slow ride.

As he worked his latest splinter out of his thumb, Declan decided it didn't get much better.

'What's that bush blooming out there?' He gestured toward the wreck of gardens.

'Camellia,' Effie told him. 'These gardens are a sin, Dec.'

'I know. I've got to get to them.'

'You can't get to everything. You ought to get someone out here to clean it up.'

'Big Frank and Little Frankie.' Remy took a long swallow of beer. 'They'd do the job for you. Do good work.'

'Family business?' He always trusted family businesses. 'Father and son?'

'Brother and sister.'

'A brother and sister, both named Frank?'

'Yeah. Frank X. – that's for Xavier – he's got him some ego. Named both his kids after him. I'll give you the number. You tell them Remy told you to call.'

'I'm going to go clean up.' Effie looked down at her paint-speckled hands. 'Is it all right if I wander around the house some?'

79

'Sweetheart.' Declan took her hand, kissed it. 'You can do anything you want.'

'Good thing I saw her first,' Remy commented as Effie went inside.

'Damn right.'

'Seems to me you got your mind on another woman, the way you keep looking toward the bayou.'

'I can't have Effie unless I kill you, so I'm courting Miss Odette as a testament to our friendship.'

'Yeah, you are.' With a laugh, Remy leaned back on his elbows. 'That Lena, she tends to stir a man up, get him thinking all kinds of interesting things.'

'You got a girl.'

'Don't mean my brain stopped working. Don't you worry, though, Effie's all I want.' He let out a long sigh of a contented man. 'Besides, Lena and me, we did our round some time back.'

'What do you mean?' Declan set his beer back down and stared at his friend. 'You and Lena. You … and Lena?'

Remy winked. 'One hot, sweaty summer. Must've been close to fifteen years ago. Ouch.' He leaned up to rub his heart. 'That hurts. I was about … yeah, I was seventeen, just graduated high school. That'd make her fifteen, seems to me. We spent some memorable evenings in the back-seat of my old Chevy Camaro.'

He noted Declan's brooding look. 'Hey, I saw her first, too. I was in a hot trance over that girl, a good six months. Thought I'd die if I didn't have her. You know how it is at seventeen.'

'Yeah. I know how it is at thirty-one, too.'

Remy chuckled. 'Well, I mooned over her, danced around her, sniffed at her heels. Took her to the movies, for long drives. To my senior prom. God, what a picture she was. Then one moonstruck June night, I finally got her clothes off in the back of that Camaro. It was her first time.' He shot Declan a look. 'You know, they say a woman never forgets her first. You got your work cut out for you, *cher*.'

'I think I can do better than a randy teenager.' Despite, he admitted, the fact that she made him feel like one. 'What happened between you?'

'Drifted is all. I went up North to school, she stayed here. Fever burned itself out, and we slid into being friends. We are friends, Dec. She's one of my favorite people.'

'I know a warning when I hear one. You want all the girls, Remy?'

'Just thinking to myself that I'd hate to see two of my friends hurt each other. The two of you, boy, you come with a lot of baggage.'

'I know how to store mine.'

'Maybe. God knows she's worked hard to keep hers locked in the attic. Her mother –' He broke off when Effie screamed.

Beer spewed over the floor when Remy kicked the bottle over as he leaped up. He was through the kitchen door one stride ahead of Declan and shouting Effie's name.

'Upstairs.' Declan veered left and charged up the kitchen stairway. 'She's upstairs.'

'Remy! Remy, come quick!'

She sat on the floor, hugging her arms, and threw herself into Remy's the instant he crouched beside her. 'Baby, what happened? Are you hurt?'

'No. No. I saw …' She turned her face into his shoulder. 'In there. On the bed in there.'

Declan looked at the open door. The only bed in there was the one he'd imagined. Slowly, he pushed the door open the rest of the way. He could see the layer of dust on the floor, where it had been disturbed when Effie had started to go in. The sun beamed through the windows onto nothing but wood and faded wallpaper.

'What did you see, Effie?' Declan asked.

'On the bed. A woman – her face. She was dead.'

'Baby.' Staring into the room, Remy stroked her hair. 'There's nothing in there. Look now. There's nothing there.'

'But I saw …'

'Tell me what you saw.' Declan knelt down beside her. 'What did you see in there?'

'I saw …' She shuddered, then pressed her lips into a firm line. 'Help me up, Remy.'

Though her face was stark white, she got to her feet and stepped to the doorway.

'Effie darling, you're shaking. Let's get you downstairs.'

'No. No, wait.' Her eyes were wide, and her heart continued to beat wildly as she scanned the room. 'I couldn't have seen anything. It's an empty room. Just an empty room. I must've imagined …'

'A tester bed? Blue drapes? A chest of drawers and mirrored bureau. A woman's vanity and a blue chaise. Gaslight sconces, candles on the mantel and a framed picture.'

'How do you know what I saw?'

'Because I saw it, too. The first day I was here. I smelled lilies.'

'White lilies in a tall vase,' Effie continued, and a tear trickled down her cheek. 'I thought it was odd, and sort of sweet, that you'd have flowers in there. Then I thought, for just a minute, well, how did he fix this room up so beautifully, why didn't he mention it? And I stepped in and saw her on the bed. I'm sorry. I really need some air.'

Without a word, Remy scooped her off her feet.

'My hero,' she murmured as he carried her toward the stairs.

'You gave me a hell of a fright, *chère*. Declan, you get my girl some water.'

For a long moment, Declan stared into the room. Then he followed them down.

He fetched a glass of water, took it out to the gallery where Remy sat with Effie cradled in his lap.

'How do you feel about ghosts now?'

She took the water, sipped while she studied Declan over the rim. 'I imagined it.'

'A white robe over the chaise. A silver brush set, some sort of gold and enamel pin.'

'Watch pin,' she said quietly. She let out a shuddering breath. 'I can't explain it.'

'Can you tell me about the woman?'

'Her face was all bruised and bloody. Oh, Remy.'

'Ssh now.' He stroked her hair, gathered her closer. 'You don't have to think about it. Let her be, Declan.'

'No, it's all right.' Taking slow breaths, Effie laid her head on Remy's shoulder. Her eyes met Declan's and held. 'It's just so strange, so awful and strange. I think she was young, but it was hard to tell. Dark hair, a lot of dark, curling hair. Her clothes – nightgown – it was torn. There were terrible bruises on her neck – like … God, like she'd been strangled. I knew she was dead. I screamed and stumbled back. My legs just gave out from under me.'

'I need to find out who she was,' Declan declared. 'There's got to be a way to find out who she was. Family member, servant, guest. If a young woman died violently in there, there's a record somewhere.'

'I can do some research.' Effie lowered the water and managed a smile. 'That's my job, after all.'

'If there was a murder, it seems we'd have heard stories over the years.' Remy shook his head. 'I never have. Honey, I'm going to take you home.'

'I'm going to let you.' Effie reached out, touched Declan's arm. 'Come on with us. I don't know if you should be staying here.'

'I've got to stay. I want to stay.'

Needed to stay, he thought when he was alone and the whooshing sound of his nail gun echoed through the dining room. He wasn't just restoring the house, he was making it his own. If a murdered girl was part of it, then she was his, too.

He wanted to know her name, to know her story. Where had she come from? Why had she died? Maybe he'd been meant to come here, to find those things out.

If those images, those feelings, had driven others away, they were only locking him in.

He could live with ghosts, Declan thought as he ran his hand over the side of his first completed cabinet. But he wouldn't rest until he knew them.

But when he finally called it a day and went to bed, he left the lights on.

For the next few days, he was too busy to think about ghosts or sleepwalking, or even those nights out he'd promised himself. The electrician and plumber he'd hired were hard at work with their crews. The house was too full of noise and people for ghosts.

Frank and Frankie, who were as alike as their names, with beefy shoulders and mud-colored hair, trudged around his gardens, made mouth noises that may have been approval or disgust. Little Frankie seemed to be the brains of the operation, and after an hour's survey gave Declan a bid for clearing out underbrush and weeds. Though he wondered if they intended to retire on the profit from the job, Declan trusted Remy and hired them.

They came armed with shovels, pickaxes and mile-long clippers. From the dining room where he worked on cabinets, Declan could hear the lazy rise and fall of their voices, the occasional thump and tumble.

When he glanced out, he noticed that the tangle was disappearing.

The plasterer Miss Odette sent him was a rail-thin black man whose name was Tibald, and his great-grandpappy, so Declan was told, once worked as a field hand for the Manets.

They toured the house with Tibald scribbling in a tiny, dog-eared notepad. When they reached the ballroom, Tibald looked up at the ceiling with a dreamy expression.

'I always think I've put a picture in my head that isn't there,' he said. 'Don't think I'd ever get used to seeing this kind of work.'

'You've been in here before.'

'Have. The Rudickers took a bid for me on plaster-work. They'd be the people you bought the Hall from. They had big, fine ideas, the Rudickers. But they never did much about them. Anyhow, they were going to hire someone from Savannah. So I heard.'

'Why?'

Tibald just kept smiling at the ceiling. 'They had those big, fine ideas, and didn't see how locals could put a polish on them. Seems to me they figured the more money they spent, the higher the gloss. If you know what I mean.'

'Yeah, I get it. The way I look at it, you hire local, you're liable to get people who're more invested in the job. Can you repair and duplicate this kind of work?'

'I did the plasterwork in the Harvest House down on the River Road. I got pictures out in my truck, like a reference. You maybe want to take a look at them, maybe go on down to Harvest House and take a study. They give public tours and hold fancy events there now. Do some work in New Orleans, in Baton Rouge and Metairie. Can give you names.'

'Let's take a look at the pictures.'

One look at the before and after shots of various cornices, walls, medallions, showed Declan his man was an artist. For form, he asked for a bid, and after promising to have one written up by the end of the week, Tibald offered his hand.

'I admit, I'd love to get my hands on that ballroom.' Tibald glanced back over at the house. 'You doing any work on the third floor?'

'Eventually.'

'Maybe you want to talk to my sister, Lucy. She cleans houses.'

'I'm a long way from needing a housekeeper.'

Tibald laughed, took out a pack of Big Red chewing gum. 'No, sir, I don't mean that kind of clean.' He offered Declan a stick before taking one himself, folding it in half, and sliding it into his mouth. 'Spirit clean. You got some strong spirits in that place.' He chewed contemplatively. ''Specially on the third floor.'

'How do you know?'

'Feel it breathing on my neck. Can't you? When the Rudickers were working on the place, they lost two laborers. Those men just hightailed it out and kept on going. Never went back. Could be one of the reasons they looked farther afield for workers here.'

Tibald shrugged, chewed his Big Red. 'Could be the reason they never finished up those big, fine ideas.'

'Do you know what happened on the third floor?'

'Nope. Don't know of anyone who does. Just know a

few who wouldn't go up there, no matter what you paid them. Any plasterwork needs doing on the third floor, you give my sister Lucy a call first.'

They both turned at the sound of a car coming down the drive. 'That's Miss Lena's car, and Miss Odette with her.' Tibald's grin spread as the ancient MG stopped beside his truck.

'Afternoon, ladies.' Tibald walked to the passenger's side to open the door for Odette. 'Where y'at?'

'Oh, fine and well, Tibald. How's that family of yours?'

'Nothing to complain about.'

Lena climbed out as Declan opened the door. Her jeans were intriguingly snug, worn with a shirt the color of polished turquoise. 'My grandmama thought it was time to pay a call.' She scanned the drive, noted the number of pickups. 'What did you do, *cher*? Hire yourself an army?'

'Just a battalion.' She smelled of jasmine, he thought. She smelled of night. He had to concentrate on basic manners or swallow his gum. 'Can I give you a tour?'

'Mmm. We'll get to it. Tibald, you say hey to Mazie for me, won't you?'

'I will. Gotta be on my way. I'll get that bid to you, Mr. Fitzgerald.'

'Declan. I'll be looking for it. Miss Odette.' Declan took her hand as Tibald climbed into his truck. She wore a cotton dress the color of ripe squash, and a dark green sweater against the mid-winter chill. Today's socks matched it.

She smelled of lavender and jingled with her chains and bracelets. Everything about her relaxed him. 'Welcome to Manet Hall. Such as it is.'

Odette winked at Lena when Declan kissed her hand. 'We'll take a look at it when we've finished out here. Heard you hired Big Frank and Little Frankie,' she said, nodding toward their pickup. 'How're they working out for you?'

'They seem to be doing the job. I don't know how.' He studied the patchy front gardens with his thumbs hooked through his belt loops. 'I can't catch them actually doing anything, but I blink and a couple truckloads of underbrush is gone. Would you like to walk around the grounds?'

'I would. Lena honey, get those spirit bottles out of the trunk. We'll hang them on these live oaks to start.'

'Spirit bottles?'

'To keep the evil spirits away.' Lena began lifting bottles half filled with water from her trunk.

'Should I be worried about evil spirits?' Declan asked.

'An ounce of prevention.' And taking two, Odette moved off toward the trees.

'Spirit bottles,' Declan reported, lifting one. He'd seen them hanging outside the shotgun house. 'Just how do they work?'

'It's an old voodoo trick,' Lena told him. 'The clanking sound they make scares the evil spirits away.'

Testing, he bumped two together. It sounded pleasant enough, he thought, and not particularly scary. 'You believe in voodoo?'

'I believe in that ounce of prevention.' She strolled off, small and curvy, to join her grandmother.

Voodoo or old glass bottles, he liked the way they looked hanging from his trees. And when he tapped two together again, he liked the sound they made.

It took nearly an hour to wind their way around the house and into it as there had to be conversations with the landscapers, inquiries about their family, speculation on the weather, discussion of the garden.

When he finally got them into the kitchen, Odette fisted her hands on her hips and nodded. 'That's a good color, like a nicely baked pastry crust. Most men, they don't know anything but white. Brings out these good pine floors.'

'I should have the cabinets ready to install next week.' He gestured toward the dining room. 'I'm using pine there, too. With glass fronts.'

Lips pursed, Odette walked in, ran her hand over a cabinet. 'This is nice work, Declan. You got a talent.'

'Thanks.'

'And it makes you happy.'

'It sure does. Would you like to go into the parlor? I've got a table in there. We'll have some tea.' He glanced up as something heavy hit the floor above. 'Sorry about the noise.'

'Work's rarely a quiet activity. Lena and I will just wander along, if you don't mind. We'll find the parlor.'

'You can't miss it. It's the only room with a table.'

'He's a very nice young man,' Odette commented as she and Lena walked out of the dining room.

'He is.'

'Good-looking, too.'

'Very.'

'Got a hot eye for you, *chère*.'

Now Lena laughed. 'He does.'

'What're you going to do about it?'

'I'm still thinking. Lord, what a place.' Lena trailed her hands over a wall. 'Doorways wide enough to drive a car through. It makes you cry to see how it's been let go.'

'Let go? I don't know. Seems to me it's just been waiting. Isn't this just like a man,' she said when they stepped into the parlor. 'Living with one table and two chairs. Bet he hasn't fixed a decent meal for himself since he got here.'

Lena cocked an eyebrow. 'Grandmama, you're not going to make me feel sorry enough for him to cook his dinner.' Amused, Lena wandered to the window. 'It's beautiful, what you see from here. Imagine what it would've been like to stand here when the house was in its glory. Horses coming through the *allée*, those funny old cars rumbling up the drive.'

'It'll be beautiful again. But it needs a woman – just like that boy needs one.'

Lena toyed with the little key that hung around her neck. 'I said I'm still thinking. Chilly in here yet,' she added. 'Needs a fire going.'

'I'll build one,' Declan told her as he came in with a pitcher of over-steeped tea and plastic cups.

Chapter Six

It was a good hour, Declan thought. And not counting Remy and Effie, his first real company.

He liked having them there, the female presence in his parlor with the fire he'd built crackling cheerfully and the late afternoon sun fighting through the dust on the windows.

'I'm going to come back,' Odette told him, 'to see your kitchen when it's finished.'

'I hope you'll come back often. I'd be glad to show you the rest of the house.'

'You go on and show Lena. Me, I'm going to walk on home.'

'I'll take you home, Grandmama.'

'No, you stay awhile.' However casual her tone, there was a sly look in her eye. 'I want to walk, then it'll be time for my nap.' As she started to rise, Declan got up, offered his hand. And made her smile. 'You got a pretty manner about you. You come back and see me when you're not busy. I'll make you some *sauce patate* – potato stew – before you get so skinny your clothes fall off your bones.'

'I got the phones hooked up.' He dug in his pocket for a scrap of paper, found a pencil in his shirt pocket and wrote down the number. 'If you need anything, just call.'

'Yes, indeed, a very pretty way.' She turned her cheek up, inviting his kiss. When he walked her to the door, she gestured for him to lean down again. 'I approve of you sparking my Lena. You'll have a care with her, and most don't.'

'Is that your way of telling me I don't have a chance with you, Miss Odette?'

She laughed and patted his cheek. 'Oh. If I was thirty years younger, she'd have a run for her money. Go on now, and show her your house.'

He watched her walk by the trees with the spirit bottles dangling.

'You like my grandmama,' Lena said from the parlor doorway.

'I'm love-struck. She's wonderful. Listen, it's a long walk to her place. You ought to—'

'If she wants to walk, she walks. There's no stopping her from doing anything.' She wandered to the front door to stand beside him. 'Look there, it's Rufus come to walk her home. I swear, that dog has radar when it comes to her.'

'I kept hoping he'd come around.' He turned to Lena. 'Bring you with him. I started out two nights this week to go to your place, and talked myself out of it.'

'Why's that?'

'There's persistence, and there's stalking.' He reached up to twirl her hair around his finger. 'I figured if I could hold out until you came by here, you wouldn't consider getting a restraining order.'

'If I want a man to go away, I tell him to go away.'

'Do men always do what you tell them?'

Her lips curved into that cat smile that made him want to lick at the little black mole. 'Mostly. You going to show me this big house of yours, *cher*?'

'Yeah.' He caught her chin in his hand, kissed her. 'Sure. By the way.' Now he took her hand as he led her toward the staircase. 'I have Miss Odette's permission to spark you.'

'Seems you need my permission, not hers.'

'I intend to charm you so completely, we'll slip right by that step. Fabulous staircase, isn't it?'

'It is.' She trailed a red-tipped finger along the banister. 'Very grand, this place of yours, Declan. And from what I've seen of it, I realize you're not a rich lawyer after all.'

'Ex-lawyer. And I don't follow you.'

'You got enough to put this place back, to keep it – you do mean to keep it?'

'Yeah, I do.'

'Then you're not rich. Step up from rich. You're wealthy. Is that the case?'

'Well, money's not a problem. It doesn't buy happiness, either.'

She stopped on the landing and laughed. 'Oh, *cher*, you think that, you just don't know where to shop.'

'Anytime you want to help me spend some of it.'

'Maybe.' She looked down over the banister toward the grand foyer. 'You'll be needing furniture eventually. There's some places I know.'

'You have a cousin?'

'One or two.' She lifted her eyebrows at the noise and cursing from the end of the long hall.

'Plumber,' Declan explained. 'I had him start on the master bath. It was … well, it was an embarrassment of avocado. If you know anyone who wants some really ugly bathroom fixtures, let me know.'

He started to steer her away from the door of what he now thought of as his ghost room. But she turned the knob, opened it. Declan found himself holding his breath as she stepped inside.

'Cold in here.' She hugged her arms, but couldn't stop the shiver. 'You ought to try to save the wallpaper. It's a pretty pattern. Violets and rosebuds.'

She was halfway to the gallery doors when she stopped, and the shiver became a shudder. The feeling that poured into her was grief. 'It's a sad room, isn't it? It needs light. And life.'

'There's a ghost. A woman. I think she was killed here.'

'Do you?' She turned back to him. Her face was a little pale, her eyes a little wide. 'It doesn't feel … violent. Just sad. Empty and sad.'

Her voice had thickened. Without thinking, he went in, went to her. 'Are you all right?'

'Just cold.'

He reached down to rub her arms, and at the contact, felt a quick shock.

With a half-laugh, she stepped back. 'I don't think that's what Grandmama meant by you sparking me, *cher*.'

'It's this room. There's something strange in this room.'

'Ghosts don't worry me. Shouldn't worry you. They can't hurt you.' But she walked to the door, had to fight a need to rush her steps.

She wandered through the other bedrooms, but experienced none of that grief, the dread, the dragging loneliness that had driven her out of the first.

At the door to Declan's room, she smiled. 'Well, not so rough in here. You got taste, *cher*.' She poked her head in the bathroom, where workmen clanged and cursed.

'Which is more than I can say for whoever did this bathroom. That you there, Tripadoe? Your mama know you eat with that mouth?'

She leaned on the doorjamb, spent a few minutes chatting with his plumbers. And Declan could stand back and just look at her.

It was pathetic, he told himself. This puppy-dog crush he'd developed.

And when she glanced at him over her shoulder, he felt the jolt right down to the soles of his feet.

'Why don't I show you the ballroom. It's going to be the showcase.'

'Sure, I'd like to see that.' But when they started out, she gestured toward the stairs. 'What's up there?'

'More empty rooms. Storage, some of the servants' quarters.'

'Let's have a look.'

'It's nothing special.' He made a grab for her hand, but she was already going up.

'Can you get to the belvedere from here?' she asked. 'I used to look over at that and imagine standing up there.'

'It's easier from the – don't!'

His sharp order had her hand freezing on the dull brass knob of the nursery. 'What's wrong? You got a woman chained in here? All your secrets locked inside here, *cher*?'

'No, it's just ...' He could feel the panic rising, burning the base of his throat. 'There's something wrong with that room.'

'Something wrong with most of them,' she tossed back, and opened the door.

He was right. It hit her immediately, that same throbbing sense of grief and loss and loneliness. She saw walls and floor and windows, dust and neglect. And felt as if her heart were breaking.

Even as she started to speak, the cold swept in. She felt it blow over her skin like breath, pass through her hair like fingers.

'It's the center,' she declared, though she was far from sure what she meant, or how she knew. 'Can you feel it? Can you?'

He swayed in the doorway. Bearing down, he dug his fingers into the jamb. His fear was unreasonable, spearing like knives into bones. It was his house, he reminded himself grimly. His goddamn house. He took a step inside, then a second.

The room spun. He heard a scream, saw Lena's face, the alarm that leaped over it. He thought he saw her mouth move, form his name. Then his vision grayed, white spots dancing through the mist.

'Declan. Here now, *cher*. Here, darling.'

Someone was stroking his hair, his face. He felt lips brush over his. He opened his eyes to a blur, so simply closed them again.

'No you don't.' She tapped his cheeks now with fingers that trembled lightly. He'd gone down like a tree under the ax, right after his face had drained of color and his eyes had rolled back white. 'Open your eyes.'

'What the hell happened?'

'You fainted.'

His eyes opened now, focused on her face. Mortification warred with a vague nausea. 'Excuse me, men don't faint. We do, on occasion, pass out or lose consciousness. But we do not faint.'

The breath she let out was a shudder of relief. He may have cracked his head, she thought, but he'd come to with his wits about him. 'I beg your pardon. You passed out. Cold. Hit the floor hard enough to bounce your head off it.' She leaned down again, brushed her lips over the raw scrape on his forehead. 'You're going to have a bruise, *bébé*. I couldn't catch you. I guess if I had, you'd've taken us both down.'

She had managed to roll him over, and now stroked her fingers over his pale cheeks. 'You do a lot of passing out?'

'Usually I have to drink myself into oblivion first, which I haven't done since college. Look, at the risk of embarrassing myself twice in a matter of minutes, I really have to get the hell out of this room.'

'Okay. All right. Can you stand? I don't think I can haul you up, *cher*. You're a pretty big guy.'

'Yeah.' He got to his knees, tried to catch his breath, but it was clogging again. It felt like a semi had parked on his chest, and his heart was tripping to try to find a beat. He staggered up, stumbled.

Lena wrapped an arm around his waist, took as much of his weight as she could manage. 'One step, two steps. We'll just get you downstairs so you can lie down.'

'It's okay. I'll be okay.' His ears were ringing. The minute he got out of the room, he headed for the steps, then just sank down and put his head between his knees. 'Jesus.'

'There now, sweetheart.' She stroked his hair.

'Close that door, would you? Just close it.'

She hurried back, slammed it shut. 'You get your breath back, then we'll get you down and into bed.'

'I've been wanting to hear you say that since the first time I laid eyes on you.'

The clutching in her belly eased a bit. 'You're coming back, aren't you?'

'Better.' He could breathe again, and the nausea was fading. 'I'll just have to go beat someone up, or shoot some small mammal so I can regain my manhood.'

'Let me see your face.' She tipped his head back, studied him. 'Still a little pale, but you got some color again. I bet Grandmama's right. You don't eat. What'd you eat today, *cher*?'

'Wheaties. Breakfast of champions.' He managed a wan smile. 'Doesn't seem to have worked.'

'I'm going to fix you a sandwich.'

'Really?' The simple pleasure of the idea trickled through him. 'You're going to cook for me?'

'A sandwich isn't cooking.'

'In my world it is. Lena, that room …'

'We'll talk about that – after you get something in your stomach.'

The pickings were sparse. One look in the secondhand refrigerator currently gracing the dining room had Lena sending Declan one long, pitying look. 'How old are you? Twelve?'

'I'm a guy.' He replied with a shrug. 'Guys' grocery habits never age. I've got peanut butter to go with that jelly.' He glanced around the room. 'Somewhere.'

He also had one lonely slice of deli ham, two eggs, some anemic-looking cheese and a half bag of pre-cut salad. 'Looks like I'm going to cook for you after all. Where's the stove?'

'Right here.' He tapped the top of a microwave.

'Well, we'll make do. Bowl? Knife? Fork?'

'Ah …' He rooted through the box of his current kitchen supplies and came up with the plastic ware.

'Honey, this is just sad. Sit yourself down, and Lena'll take care of you. This one time,' she added.

He hitched onto a sawhorse and watched her beat some eggs, shred in the ham, the cheese, sprinkle in some of the contents of the salad bag.

'You got any herbs, *cher*? Any spices?'

'I got salt and pepper. That counts,' he muttered when she sighed. 'Explorers discovered whole continents for salt.'

98

'Grew up with a cook, didn't you?'

'Yeah. So?'

'What did you do when you moved out on your own?'

'Takeout, delivery and the microwave. With those three things, no man need starve.'

She set the bowl in the microwave, programmed it, then turned back to him. 'Living out here, you'd best hire yourself another cook.'

'Name your price.'

'You're a funny man, Declan.' His color was good now, his eyes clear. The knot that had been in her belly since he'd pitched over loosened. 'How come you don't have a woman?'

'I had one, but it turned out I didn't really want her.'

'That so?' She opened the oven when it beeped, whisked the egg mixture around, then programmed it again. 'What happened?'

'Remy didn't tell you?'

'He doesn't tell me everything.'

'I was engaged. I called it off three weeks before the wedding, which makes me, you know, a cad. A lot of people in Boston are still cursing my name.'

He was trying to make it a joke, she thought, but wasn't quite pulling it off. 'Is that why you left?'

'No, it's why I realized I could leave.'

'You didn't love her.'

'No, I didn't love her.'

'It makes you sad to say that.' She drew out the bowl, got a fresh plastic fork, then handed it to him. His eyes were stormy again, she noted. With regret. 'She love you?'

'No. We looked good together. We were used to each other. She thought we wanted the same things.'

'But you didn't.'

99

'We never did. And the closer it got to D-Day, the more I saw my life just … narrowing down until I was squeezed into this tiny slot. No room, no air. No light. I realized I felt the same way about marrying Jessica as I did about practicing corporate law, and if that was going to be the rest of my life, I could jump off a bridge or get out of the slot while I had the chance.'

She brushed the hair from his forehead. 'It was braver to get out than to jump.'

'Maybe. This is good,' he said as he scooped up more egg. 'Why don't you have a man?'

She cocked her head. 'Who says I don't?'

He grabbed her hand before she could turn away. 'I need to know if you do.'

She looked down at his hand, back to his face. 'Why is that?'

'Because I can't stop thinking about you. I can't get you out of my head, from under my skin. Because every time I see you, my heart kicks in my chest.'

'You're good at that, too. At saying things that stir a woman up.' If it had just been that, just a matter of being stirred by him, she might have eased in between those long legs and satisfied them both. But this wasn't a simple man, she thought.

Being with him wouldn't be simple.

'Eat your eggs,' she told him, and slid her hand free of his. 'Why are you starting with the kitchen if you eat peanut butter and don't have a single dish to your name?'

'I've got dishes, just not the kind you wash. The kitchen's the heart of a house. The house where I grew up - this big, old wonderful house with big, wonderful rooms. We had that cook, but it was the kitchen where we ended up if there was a crisis or a celebration, or just something to talk over. I guess I want that here.'

'That's nice.' She leaned back on a cabinet to study him. 'You want to have sex with me, *cher*?'

His pulse lurched, but he managed to hop nimbly off the sawhorse. 'Sure. Just let me kick the plumber out.' He loved the way she laughed. 'Oh, you didn't mean right this minute. That was, what, like a true or false type of question. Let me check.' He laid his fingers on his wrist. 'Yeah, I'm still alive, so the answer is true.'

She shook her head, took the empty bowl from him and dumped it in the box he was using for trash. 'You're an interesting man, Declan. And I like you.'

'Uh-oh. Hold on a minute.' He glanced around, picked up the screwdriver lying on a plank. 'Here you go,' he said as he handed it to her.

'What's this for?'

'So you can plunge it into my heart when you tell me you just want to be friends.'

'I bet Jessica's still kicking herself for letting you slip away. I do want to be friends.' She turned the screwdriver in her hand, then set it down again. 'I don't know yet if I just want to be friends. I have to think about it.'

'Okay.' He took her arms, ran his hands up to her shoulders. 'Think about it.'

She didn't try to pull away, but lifted her face so his lips could meet hers. She liked the easy glide from warmth to heat, the fluid ride offered by a man who took his time.

She understood desire. A man's. Her own. And she knew some of those desires could be sated only in quick, hot couplings in the dark.

From time to time, she'd sated hers in just that fashion.

There was more here, and it came like a yearning. Yearnings, even met, could cause a pain desire never could.

Still, she couldn't resist laying her hands on his face, letting the kiss spin out.

Inside her, deep inside her, something sighed.

'Angelina.'

He said her name, a whisper of sound, as he changed the angle of the kiss. As he deepened it. A thousand warnings jangled in her brain and were ignored. She gave herself over for one reckless moment, to the heat, to the need. To the yearning.

Then she drew back from all of it. 'That's something to think about, all right.'

She pressed a hand to his chest when he would have pulled her into him again. 'Settle down, *cher*.' She gave him a slow, sleepy smile. 'You've got me worked up enough for one day.'

'I was just getting started.'

'I believe it.' She let out a breath, pushed her hair back. 'I've got to go. I'm working the bar tonight.'

'I'll come in. Walk you home.'

However calm his voice, his eyes had storms in them. The sort, she imagined, that would provide a hell of a thrill before they crashed over your head. 'I don't think so.'

'Lena. I want to be with you. I want to spend time with you.'

'Want to spend time with me? You take me on a date.'

'A date?'

'The kind where you pick me up at my door and take me out to a fancy dinner.' She tapped a finger on his chest. 'Take me dancing after, then walk me back to my door and kiss me good-night. Can you handle that?'

'What time do you want me to pick you up?'

She smiled, shook her head. 'I'm working tonight. I got Monday night off. Place isn't so busy Monday nights. You pick me up at eight.'

'Monday. Eight o'clock.'

He grabbed her arms again, jerked her against him. There was no glide into heat this time, but a headlong dive into it.

Oh yeah, she thought, it would be quite a thrill before the crash.

'Just a reminder,' he told her.

A warning, more like, she thought. He wasn't nearly as tame as he pretended to be. 'I won't forget. See you later, *cher*.'

'Lena. We didn't talk about what happened upstairs.'

'We will,' she called back, and kept going.

She didn't breathe easy until she was out of the house. He wasn't going to be as simple to handle as she'd assumed. The good manners weren't a veneer, they went straight through him. But so did the heat, and the determination.

It was a package she admired, and respected.

Not that she couldn't handle him, she told herself as she got into her car. Handling men was one of her best skills.

But this man was a great deal more complicated than he seemed on the surface. And a great deal more intriguing than any she'd met before.

She knew what men saw when they looked at her. And she didn't mind it because there was more to her than what they saw. Or wanted to see.

She had a good brain, a strong back and a willingness to use both to get what she wanted. She ran her life the same way she ran her bar. With an appreciation for color and a foundation of order beneath the chaos.

She glanced in her rearview mirror at Manet Hall as she drove away. It worried her that Declan Fitzgerald could shake that foundation the way no one had before.

It worried her that she might not find it so easy to shore up the cracks when he walked away.

They always walked away. Unless you walked first.

★

He fell asleep thinking of Lena, and drifted into dreams of her. Strong, full-bodied dreams where she lay beneath him, moved under him with hard, quick jerks of her hips. Damp skin, like liquid gold. Dark chocolate eyes, and red, wet lips.

He could hear the sound of her breath, the catch and release, little gulps of pleasure. He smelled her, that siren's dance of jasmine that made him think of harems and forbidden shadows.

He dropped deeper into sleep, aching for her.

And saw her hurrying along a corridor, her arms full of linens. Her hair, all that gorgeous hair, was ruthlessly pinned back, and that tempting body covered from neck to ankle in a baggy dress covered with tiny, faded flowers.

Her lips were unpainted and pressed tightly together. And in the dream, he could hear her thoughts as if they were his own.

She had to hurry, to get the linens put away. Madame Manet was already up and about, and she didn't care to see any of the undermaids scurrying in the hallways. If she wasn't quick, she could be noticed.

She didn't want Madame to notice her. Servants stayed employed longer when they were invisible. That's what Mademoiselle LaRue, the housekeeper, said, and she was never wrong.

She needed the work. Her family needed the money she could bring in, and oh, but she loved working in the Hall. It was the most beautiful house she'd ever seen. She was so happy and proud to have some part of tending to it.

How many times had she stared at it from the shadows of the bayou? Admiring it, longing for a chance to peek in the windows at all the beauty inside.

And now she *was* inside, responsible in some small way for the tending of that beauty.

She loved to polish the wood, to sweep the floors. To see the way the glass sparkled after she'd scrubbed it.

In his dream, she came out of the corridor through one of the hidden doors on the second level. Her eyes tracked everywhere as she hurried along – the wallpaper, the rugs, the wood and glass. She slipped into a dressing room, put the linens away in a cupboard.

But as she turned back toward the door, something caught her attention, and she tiptoed to the window.

He saw, as she saw, the riders approaching through the grand oaks of the *allée*. He felt, as she felt, a stumble of heart as her gaze locked on the man who rode a glossy chestnut. His hair was gold, and streamed as he galloped. Straight as a soldier in the saddle, with a gray coat over his broad shoulders and his black boots shining.

Her hand went to her throat, and she thought, quite clearly, *Here is the prince come home to his castle.*

She sighed, as girls sigh when they fall foolishly in love. He smiled, as if smiling at her, but she knew it was the house that caused that joy to fill his handsome face.

With her heart pounding, she hurried out of the room, back to the servants' door and into the maze.

The young master was home, she thought. And wondered what would happen next.

Declan woke with a jolt, in the dark, in the cold. He smelled damp and dust and felt the hard wood of the floor under him.

'What the hell?' Groggy, disgusted, he stretched out a hand and hit wall. Using it for reference, he got to his feet. He felt along, waiting to come to a corner, to a door. It took a moment to register that the wall wasn't papered.

He wasn't in his ghost room this time. He was in one of the servants' passageways, as the girl in his dream had been.

Somehow, he thought, he'd walked as she had walked.

The idea of stumbling around in the dark until he found a way out had little appeal, but slightly more than the idea of spending the next few hours in there, waiting for dawn.

He inched along. By the time he felt the seam of a door, he was drenched in sweat.

He shoved his way out, offered up a prayer of thanksgiving when he gulped in fresher air, saw in the faint light the shape of the second-level corridor.

There were cobwebs in his hair, his hands and feet were filthy.

If this kept up, he told himself, he was going to see a doctor and get some sleeping pills. Hoping the night's adventures were over, he went to wash, to chug down water for his burning throat. And to lock himself in the bedroom.

Chapter Seven

Declan took the load of books out of Effie's arms, then kissed her cheek. 'You didn't have to come all this way to bring me these. I'd've come to you.'

'I didn't mind. I had a meeting cancel, and some time to spare. And the fact is …' Breathing slowly, she turned a circle. 'I had to prove to myself I wouldn't just turn tail and run when I started to come in this place.'

'Doing okay?'

'Yeah.' She let out one of those slow breaths, then nodded briskly. 'Doing just fine.' Then she frowned at the shadows dogging his eyes. 'Now, you on the other hand look worn out.'

'Not sleeping so well.' But he didn't want to talk about the dreams, the sleepwalking. The sounds that so often wakened him in the dead of night. 'Come on back to the kitchen so I can show off. I've got some lemonade – not from actual lemons, but it's wet and it's cold.'

'All right.' She touched his arm in a kind of silent acknowledgment and, because she understood, lightened her tone. 'I've only got about half an hour, but I've got some information for you. Information and speculation. What's going on in here?'

She glanced into the front parlor. There were papers stacked on the floor, books spread open, a pile of paint and fabric samples.

'My next project. I thought I'd start on a room where people could actually sit down when it was finished. What kind of information?'

'On the Manets. Facts were easy enough,' she said as they continued through the house. 'Henri Manet married Josephine Delacroix. They both came from wealthy and prominent Creole families. Henri was active politically. It's rumored his father profited handsomely by running supplies during the War between the States. The family became staunch Republicans during Reconstruction, and again it's rumored they used their power and influence to buy votes and politicians. Oh my goodness, Dec, just look at this!'

She stepped into the kitchen and beamed at the base cabinets he'd installed. 'Why, they're beautiful.'

He hooked his thumbs in his back pockets, and his grin was crooked. 'You sound surprised.'

'Well, I am, but in a very complimentary sort of way. Remy can barely hammer a nail in the wall to hang a picture.' She ran her hand over the wood, opened and closed a door. 'These are really fine. You must be so proud.'

'I'm feeling pretty pleased with myself. Counter guys just left. I'm going with solid surface. It'll look like slate. Ordered this giant Sub-Zero refrigerator – for reasons I've yet to explain to myself – and a range, a dishwasher. I'm going to make panels so all you'll see is wood.'

He set the books down on a sheet of plywood he had over the top of the base cabinets. 'Want that lemonade?'

'That'd be nice.' She wandered into the dining room behind him. He had two of the top cupboards finished, and a third started. 'My, aren't they going to be pretty. You must be working night and day.'

Losing weight, she thought. *Getting a gaunt look in your face.*

'Better than sleepwalking.' He was jittery, and found himself dipping hands into his pockets again to keep them still. 'Tell me more, Effie.'

'All right.' She suppressed the urge to fuss over him and went back to the facts. 'The original owners had lost most of their money during the war. They hung on, selling off parcels of land, or renting it out to sharecroppers. Their politics and the Manets' were in opposition. There was a fire, burned the house down to the ground. Wiped them out. The Manets bought the land, and had this place built. They had two sons, twins. Lucian and Julian. Both went to Tulane, where Lucian did very well and Julian majored, you could say, in drinking and gambling. Lucian was the heir, and was meant to run the family businesses. Most of the Manet money had dwindled, but Josephine had a considerable inheritance. Both sons died before their twenty-third birthday.'

Declan handed her a glass. 'How?'

'Here we have rumors and speculation.' She sipped. 'The strongest speculation is they killed each other. No one seems to know why, family argument gone violent. It's said Lucian went into New Orleans, on his mother's orders, to fetch his brother back out of one of the brothels he frequented. Julian didn't want to be fetched, they argued, and one of them – odds are on Julian here – pulled a knife. They fought, struggled for the knife, were both wounded. Julian died on the spot. Lucian lingered about another week, then somehow got out of bed, wandered outside, and fell into the pond, where he drowned.'

The pond, he thought, choked with lily pads, steaming with mists at dawn. 'That had to be rough on the parents.'

'The father's heart gave out a few years later. Josephine lived several years more, but had a reversal of financial fortune. She had the house, some land, but had all but run out of money. Again, speculation is Julian had gambled a large part of it away, and it was never fully recouped.'

'Remy said there was a granddaughter. Lucian's or Julian's?'

'There's speculation there, too. Though the records show that Lucian married an Abigail Rouse in 1898, and that a daughter was born the next year, there's no record of Abigail's death. After Lucian was killed, the Manets declaimed the child, legally. Had her written out of the will. She was, apparently, raised by the Rouses. I can't find anything on Abigail Rouse beyond the legal records of her birth and her marriage.'

'Maybe they kicked her out when Lucian died.'

'Maybe. I talked to Remy about it.' She wandered toward the windows, stared out at the messy gardens. 'He's a little vague, but seems to recall hearing stories about how she ran off with another man.'

She turned back. 'Stories from the Rouse side differ sharply. They lean toward foul play. You'd get a fuller picture of her, and what might've happened, if you talk to someone from the Rouse or Simone families.'

'A clear picture about a girl who ran off or died a hundred years ago.'

'Honey, this is the South. A hundred years ago was yesterday. She was seventeen when she married Lucian. She was from the bayou. His family could not have approved of such a match. I doubt her life in this house was rosy. Running off might've been just what she did. On the other hand … I saw something, someone, in that room upstairs. I don't believe in that sort of thing. Didn't.' Effie fought back a shiver. 'I don't know what I think about it now, but I sure would like to find out.'

'I'll ask Miss Odette. And Lena. I've got a date with her Monday.'

'Is that so?' The idea brightened her mood. 'Looks like we'll have more rumor and speculation.' She handed him back the glass. 'I have to get on. I'm sending Remy out here tomorrow to give you a hand and keep him out of my hair. I've got a fitting for my wedding gown and other bridal things to take care of.'

'I'll keep him busy.'

'Why don't you come back into town with him?' she said as she headed out. She wanted to lock her arm around his and tug him through the door and away. 'We'll have some dinner, go out to the movies.'

'Stop worrying about me.'

'I can't help it. I think about you way out here, alone in this house, with that room up there.' She glanced uneasily up the staircase. 'It gives me the shivers.'

'Ghosts never hurt anybody.' He kissed her forehead. 'They're dead.'

But in the night, with the sound of the wind and rain, and the bang of spirit bottles, they didn't seem dead.

He gave himself Sunday. He slept late, woke to a sky fighting to clear, and spent another hour in bed with the books Effie had brought him.

She'd marked pages she felt would have the most interest for him. He scanned and studied old photographs of the great plantation houses. And felt a thrill race through him as he looked at the old black-and-white picture of Manet Hall in its turn-of-the-century splendor.

Formal photographs of Henri and Josephine Manet didn't bring the same thrill. With those there was curiosity. The woman had been undeniably beautiful, very much in the style of her day with the deep square bodice of her ball gown edged with roses, and the high, feathered comb adorning her upswept hair.

The gown, tucked into an impossibly small waist, gave her a delicacy accented by the sweep of the brocade skirts, the generously poofed sleeves that met the long white gloves.

But there was a coldness to her face, one Declan didn't think was a result of the rigidity of the pose or the quality of the print. It overwhelmed that delicacy of build and made her formidable.

But it was the photograph of Lucian Manet that stopped him in his tracks.

He'd seen that face, in his dream. The handsome young man with streaming gold hair, riding a chestnut horse at a gallop through the moss-laced Oaks.

The power of suggestion? Had he simply expected the face in the dream to be real, and was he projecting it now onto the doomed Lucian?

Either way, it gave him the creeps.

He decided he'd drive into New Orleans and treat himself to a few hours' haunting the antique shops.

Instead, less than an hour later, he found himself walking into Et Trois.

It did a strong Sunday-afternoon business, he noted. A mix of tourists and locals. He was pleased he was learning to distinguish one from the other. The jukebox carried the music now, a jumpy number by BeauSoleil that do-si-doed around the chatter from tables and bar.

The scent of food, deeply fried, reminded his stomach he'd skipped breakfast. Recognizing the blond tending bar from his second visit, Declan walked up, tried a smile on her. 'Hi. Lena around?'

'Back in the office. Door to the right of the stage.'

'Thanks.'

'Anytime, cutie.'

He gave the door marked PRIVATE a quick knock, then poked his head in. She was sitting at a desk, working at a computer. Her hair was clipped back and made him want to nibble his way up the nape of her neck.

'Hi. Where y'at?'

She sat back, gave a lazy stretch of her shoulders. 'You're learning. What're you doing at my door, *cher*?'

'I was in the neighborhood and thought I'd see if you'd let me buy you lunch. Like a prelude to tomorrow night.'

She'd been thinking about him, more than was comfortable. Now here he was, all tall and rangy and male. 'I'm doing my books.'

'And I've interrupted you. Don't you hate that?' He came in anyway, sat on the edge of the desk. 'Bought you a present.'

It was then that she noticed the little gift bag he carried. 'I don't see how you could've fit a new car in there.'

'We're working up to the car.'

She kept her eyes on his a moment longer as she took the bag from him. Then she dipped in for the box. It was wrapped in gold paper, with a formal white bow. She took her time with it, she'd always believed the anticipation was as important as the gift.

The bow and ribbon she tucked neatly back into the bag, and after she'd picked at the top, slid the box out, folded the paper precisely.

'How long does it take you to open your presents Christmas morning?' he asked.

'I like taking my time.' She opened the box, felt her lips twitch, but kept her expression sober as she took out the grinning crawfish salt and pepper shakers. 'Well now, aren't they a handsome pair?'

'I thought so. They had alligators, too, but these guys seemed friendlier.'

'Are these part of your charm campaign, *cher*?'

'You bet. How'd they work?'

'Not bad.' She traced a finger over one of the ugly grins. 'Not bad at all.'

'Good. Since I've interrupted you, and charmed you, why don't you let me feed you? Pay you back for the eggs.'

She eased back in her chair, swiveled it as she considered. 'Why do I get the feeling, every time I see you, I should start walking fast in the opposite direction?'

'Search me. Anyway, my legs are longer, so I'd just catch up with you.' He leaned over the desk, lifted his brows. She was wearing a skirt, a short one. His legs might've been longer, but they wouldn't look half as good in sheer stockings. 'But you could eat up some ground with those. How come you're dressed up?'

'I'm not dressed up. Church clothes. I've been to Mass.' Now she smiled. 'Name like yours, I figure you for a Catholic boy.'

'Guilty.'

'You been to Mass today, Declan?'

He could never explain why a question like that made him want to squirm. 'I'm about half-lapsed.'

'Oh.' She pursed her lips. 'My grandmama's going to be disappointed in you.'

'I was an altar boy for three years. That ought to count.'

'What's your confirmation name?'

'I'll tell you if you come to lunch.' He reached over for the crawfish, made them dance over her desk. 'Come

114

on, Lena, come out and play with me. It's turned into a nice day.'

'All right.' Mistake, her practical mind said, but she got to her feet, picked up her purse. 'You can buy me lunch. But a quick one.' She leaned over, saved her file, and closed down her computer.

'It's Michael,' he said, holding out a hand. 'Declan Sullivan Michael Fitzgerald. If I was any more Irish, I'd bleed green.'

'It's Louisa. Angelina Marie Louisa Simone.'

'Very French.'

'*Bien sûr*. And I want Italian.' She put her hand in his. 'Buy me some pasta.'

From his previous visits Declan knew you had to work very hard to find a bad meal in New Orleans. When Lena led the way to a small, unpretentious restaurant, he didn't worry. All he had to do was take one sniff of the air to know they were going to eat very well.

She waved a hand at someone, pointed to an empty table, and apparently got the go-ahead.

'This isn't a date,' she said to him when he held her chair.

He did his best to look absolutely innocent, and nearly succeeded. 'It's not?'

'No.' She eased back, crossed her legs. 'A date is when we have a time arranged and you pick me up at my house. This is a drop-on-by. So tomorrow, that's our first date. Just in case you're thinking of that three-date rule.'

'We guys don't like to think you women know about that.'

Her lips curved. 'There's a lot y'all don't like to think we know about.' She kept her eyes on his, but lifted up a hand to the dark-haired man who stopped at the table. 'Hey there, Marco.'

'Lena.' He kissed her fingers, then handed her a menu. 'Good to see you.'

'This is Remy's college friend from Boston. Declan. I brought him by so he can see how we do Italian food here in the Vieux Carre.'

'You won't do better.' He shook Declan's hand, gave him a menu. 'My mama's in the kitchen today.'

'Then we're in for a treat,' Lena said. 'How's your family, Marco?'

Declan saw how it happened then. When she shifted in her chair, lifted her face, looked at Marco, it was as if the two of them were alone on a little island of intimacy. It was sexual, there was no question about it, but it was also … attentive, he decided.

'Good as gold. My Sophie won a spelling bee on Friday.'

'That's some bright child you got.'

They chatted for a few moments, but Declan entertained himself by watching her face. The way her eyebrows lifted, fell, drew together according to the sentiment. How her lips moved, punctuated by that tiny mole.

When she turned her head, he shook his. 'Sorry, did you say something to me? I was looking at you. I get lost.'

'They got some smooth talkers up North,' Marco said.

'Pretty, too, isn't he?' Lena asked.

'Very nice. Our Lena here's having the seafood linguini. You know what you want, or you need some time to decide?'

'You don't get the same.' Lena tapped a finger on the menu Declan had yet to read. 'Else it's no fun for me picking off your plate. You try the stuffed shells, maybe. Mama makes them good.'

'Stuffed shells, then.' He had a feeling he'd have tried crushed cardboard if she'd requested it. 'Do you want wine?'

'No, because you're driving and I'm working.'

'Strict. San Pelligrino?' He glanced at Marco.

'I'll bring you out a bottle.'

'So …' She tucked her hair behind her ear as Marco left them. 'What're you up to today, *cher*?'

'I thought I'd hit some of the antique stores. I'm looking for a display cabinet for the kitchen, and stuff to stick in it. I thought I might go by and see Miss Odette on the way back. What does she like? I want to take her something.'

'You don't have to take her anything.'

'I'd like to.'

Lena hooked an arm over the back of her chair, drummed her fingers on the table as she studied him. 'You get her a bottle of wine, then. A good red. Tell me something, *cher*, you wouldn't be using my grandmama to get to me, would you?'

She saw the temper flash into his eyes – darker, hotter than she'd expected from him. Should've known, she thought, that all that easy manner covered something sharp, something jagged. It was impressive, but more impressive was the lightning snap from mild to fury, and back to mild again.

A man who could rein himself in like that, she decided, had a will of iron. That was something else to consider.

'You've got it backwards,' he told her. 'I'm using you to get to Miss Odette. She's the girl of my dreams.'

'I'm sorry.'

'Good, you should be.'

Lena waited until their water and bread were served. His tone had raised her hackles. Mostly, she could admit, because she'd deserved the quick slap. Folding her arms on the table, she leaned toward him.

'I am sorry, because that was nasty. I'm going to tell you something, Declan, nasty words have a habit of popping

117

right out of my mouth. I don't always regret saying them. I'm not a sweet-mannered, even-tempered sort of woman. I don't have a trusting nature. I've got good points, but I've got just as many bad. I like it that way.'

He mimicked her posture. 'I'm single-minded, competitive and moody. I've got a mean temper. It takes a lot to get it going, which is a fortunate thing for the general population. I don't have to have my way in the little things, but when I decide I want something, really want it, I find a way to get it. I want you. So I'll have you.'

She'd been wrong. He hadn't snapped back to mild. Anger was still simmering behind his eyes. As the one person she tried to be honest with at all times was herself, she didn't bother to pretend it didn't excite her.

'You're saying that to make me mad.'

'No, that's just a side benefit.' He eased back, picked up the basket of bread, and offered it. 'You want to fight?'

Feeling sulky, she picked out a piece. 'Maybe later. Getting riled up spoils my appetite. Anyway.' She shrugged, bit into the bread. 'You don't want to go by Grandmama's today. She's over visiting her sister this afternoon.'

'I'll stop in later this week. I got the kitchen counters installed. Remy gave me a hand, so to speak, with the wall units yesterday. It should be finished in a couple of weeks.'

'Good for you.' She wanted to brood, and could see by his amused expression that he knew it. 'You been back up on the third floor?'

'Yeah.' He'd had to prime himself with a good shot of Jim Beam first, but he'd gone back. 'Didn't fall on my face this time, but I had a major panic attack. I'm not prone to panic attacks. I found out more about the Manet family history, but there are pieces missing. Maybe you've got them.'

'You want to know about Abigail Rouse.'

'That's right. How much do –' He broke off because she'd turned her attention away from him and back to Marco, who brought out their pasta. He reminded himself as they fell into a lazy discussion about the food, that the wheel turned more slowly in the South.

'How much do you know about her?' he asked when they were alone again.

Lena rolled up a forkful of pasta, slid it between her lips. She sighed deep, swallowed. 'Mama Realdo. She's a goddess in the kitchen. Try yours,' she ordered, and leaned over to sample from his plate.

'It's great. Best meal I've had since a microwave omelette.'

She smiled at him, one long, slow smile that lodged in his belly. Then went back to eating. 'I know the stories that came down in my family. Nobody can say for sure. Abigail, she was a maid in the big house. Some of the rich families, they hired Cajun girls to clean for them, to fetch and carry. Story is that Lucian Manet came home from Tulane and fell in love with her. They ran off and got married. Had to run off, because nobody's going to approve of this. His family, hers.'

She broke off a chunk of bread, nibbled on it as she studied him. 'Mixing classes is an uneasy business. He moved her into the Hall after, and that was an uneasy business, too. People say Josephine Manet was a hard woman, proud and cold. People started counting on their fingers, but the baby, she don't come for ten months.'

'That room upstairs. It must've been the nursery. They'd have kept the baby there.'

'Most like. There was a nursemaid. She married one of Abigail's brothers later. Most of the stories about the Hall come from her. It seems a couple days before the

119

end of the year, Lucian was off in New Orleans on business. When he came back, Abigail was gone. They said she'd run off with some bayou boy she'd been seeing on the side. But that doesn't ring true. The nursemaid, her name was … Claudine, she said Abigail never would've left Lucian and the baby. She said something bad had to have happened, something terrible, and she blamed herself because she was off meeting her young man down by the river the night Abigail disappeared.'

A dead girl on the tester bed in a cold room, Declan thought, and the pasta lodged in his throat like glue. He picked up the fizzy water, drank deep. 'Did they look for her?'

'Her family looked everywhere. It's said Lucian haunted the bayou until the day he died. When he wasn't looking there, he was in town trying to find a trace of her. He never did, and didn't live long himself. With him gone, and the twin his mother favored by all accounts, dead as well, Miss Josephine had the baby taken to Abigail's parents. You've gone pale, Declan.'

'I feel pale. Go on.'

This time, when she broke off a hunk of bread, she buttered it, handed it to him. Her grandmama was right, Lena thought, the man needed to eat.

'The baby was my grandmama's grandmama. The Manets cast her out, claiming she was a bastard and no blood of theirs. They brought her to the Rouses with the dress she had on, a small bag of crib toys. Only thing she had from the Hall was the watch pin Claudine gave to her that had been Abigail's.'

Declan's hand shot out to cover hers. 'Is the pin still around?'

'We hand such things down, daughter to daughter. My grandmama gave it to me on my sixteenth birthday. Why?'

120

'Enameled watch, hanging from small, gold wings.'

Color stained her cheeks. 'How do you know?'

'I saw it.' The chill danced up his spine. 'Sitting on the dresser in the bedroom that must have been hers. An empty room,' he continued, 'with phantom furniture. The room where Effie saw a dead girl laid out on the bed. They killed her, didn't they?'

Something in the way he said it, so flat, so cold, had her stomach dropping. 'That's what people think. People in my family.'

'In the nursery.'

'I don't know. You're spooking me some, Declan.'

'You?' He passed a hand over his face. 'Well, I guess I know who my ghost is. Poor Abigail, wandering the Hall and waiting for Lucian to come home.'

'But if she did die in the Hall, who killed her?'

'Maybe that's what I'm supposed to find out, so she can … you know. Rest.'

He wasn't pale now, Lena thought. His face had toughened, hardened. That core of determination again. 'Why should it be you?'

'Why not? It had to be one of the Manets. The mother, the father, the brother. Then they buried her somewhere and claimed she ran away. I need to find out more about her.'

'I imagine you will. You've got a mulish look about you, *cher*. Don't know why that should be so appealing to me. Talk to my grandmama. She might know more, or she'll know who does.'

She nudged her empty plate back. 'Now you buy us some cappuccino.'

'Want dessert?'

'No room for that.' She opened her purse, pulled out a pack of cigarettes.

'I didn't know you smoked.'

'I get one pack a month.' She tapped one out, ran her fingers up and down its length.

'One a month? What's the point?'

She put the cigarette between her lips, flicked the flame on a slim silver lighter. As she had with the first bite of pasta, she sighed over that first deep drag. 'Pleasure, *cher*. There are twenty cigarettes in a pack, thirty or thirty-one days to a month. 'Cept for February. I dearly love the month of February. Now, I can smoke up the whole pack in a day, and just about lose my mind for the rest of the month. Or I can dole them out, slow and careful, and make them last. Because there's no buying another pack before the first of the month.'

'How many do you bum from other people during the month?'

Her eyes glittered through the haze of smoke. 'That would be cheating. I don't cheat. Pleasure's nothing, sugar, unless you got the willpower to hold off until you really appreciate it.'

She trailed a fingertip over the back of his hand, and for the hell of it, rubbed the side of her foot against his leg under the table. 'How are you on willpower?' she asked.

'We're going to find out.'

It was dusk when he got back to the house. The back of his four-wheel was loaded with treasures he'd hunted up in antique shops. But the best was the kitchen cabinet he'd found, and had begged and bribed to have delivered the next day.

He carried what he could on the first trip and, when he stepped inside, set everything down in the foyer. He closed the door behind him, then stood very still.

'Abigail.' He said the name, listened to it echo through the house. And waited.

But he felt no rush of cold air, no sudden shift in the silence.

And standing at the base of the grand staircase, he couldn't explain how he knew he wasn't alone.

Chapter Eight

He woke to a crashing thunderstorm, but at least he woke in his own bed. Lightning slashed outside the windows and burst a nova of light through the room.

A glance at the bedside clock showed him a minute to midnight But that had to be wrong, Declan thought. He hadn't gone to bed until after one. Wondering if the storm had knocked out his power, he turned the switch on the bedside lamp.

Light speared out, half blinding him.

'Damn it.' He rubbed his shocked eyes, then grabbed the bottle of water he'd set on the table next to the bed. And rising, went out on the gallery to watch the show.

It was worth the price of a ticket, he decided. Lashing rain, pitchfork lightning, and a wind that was whipping through the trees in moans and howls. He could hear the excited clanging of the spirit bottles and the fierce jungle war of thunder.

And the baby crying.

The water bottle slid out of his fingers, bounced at his feet and soaked them.

He wasn't dreaming, he told himself, and reached out to grip the wet baluster. He wasn't sleepwalking. He was awake, fully aware of his surroundings. And he heard the baby crying.

He had to order himself to move, but he walked back into the bedroom, dragged on sweats, checked his flashlight. Barefoot, shirtless, he left the security of his room and started toward the third floor.

He waited for the panic to come – that clutching in the belly, the sudden shortness of breath, the pounding of his heart.

But it didn't come this time. The steps were just steps now, the door just a door with a brass knob that needed polishing.

And the baby wasn't crying any longer.

'Come this far,' he grumbled.

His palms were sweaty, but it was nerves instead of fear. He reached out, turned the knob. The door opened with a whine of hinges.

There was a low fire in the hearth. Its light, and the light of candles, danced in pretty patterns over walls of pale, pale peach. At the windows were deep blue drapes with lacy under curtains. The floor was polished like a mirror with two area rugs in a pattern of peaches and blues.

There was a crib with turned rails, a small iron cot made up with white linen.

She sat in a rocking chair, a baby at her breast. He could see the baby's hand on it, white against gold. Her hair was down, spilling over her shoulders, over the arms of the rocker.

Her lips moved, in song or story he didn't know. He couldn't hear. But she stared down at the child as she nursed, and her face was lit with love.

'You never left her,' Declan said quietly. 'You couldn't have.'

She looked up, toward the doorway where he stood so that for one heart-stopping second, he thought she'd heard him. Would speak to him. When she smiled, when she held out a hand, he took a step toward her.

Then his knees went loose as he saw the man cross the room – pass through him like air – and walk to her.

His hair was golden blond. He was tall and slim of build. He wore some sort of robe in a deep burgundy. When he knelt by the rocker, he stroked a fingertip over the baby's cheek, then over the tiny fingers that kneaded at the woman's breast.

The woman, Abigail, lifted her hand, pressed it over his. And there, surrounded by that soft light, the three of them linked while the baby's milky mouth suckled and the woman gently rocked.

'No. You never left them. I'll find out what they did to you. To all of you.'

As he spoke, the door slammed shut behind him. He jolted, spun and found himself plunged back into the dark, with only the lightning blasts and the beam of his flashlight. The weight fell into his chest like a rock, cutting off his air. The room was empty, freezing, and the panic leaped at his throat

He dragged at the doorknob, his sweat-slicked hands sliding off the icy brass. He could feel his choked gasps wanting to rise into shouts and screams, pleas and prayers. Dizziness drove him down to his knees, where he fumbled frantically with the knob, wrenched and tugged at the door.

When he managed to pull it open, he crawled out on his hands and knees, then lay facedown on the floor with his heart thundering in his chest as the storm thundered over the house.

126

'Okay, I'm okay. I'm okay, goddamn it, and I'm getting up off the floor and going back to bed.'

He might be losing sleep, Declan thought as he got shakily to his feet, but he'd learned a couple of things.

If what he'd seen inside the nursery was truth and not some self-generated fantasy, Abigail Rouse Manet hadn't left Manet Hall of her own free will.

And he had more than one ghost on his hands.

She was probably making a mistake, Lena thought as she slicked a little black dress down her body. She'd already made several small mistakes where Declan Fitzgerald was concerned. It irritated her, as she rarely made mistakes when it came to men.

If there was one thing she'd learned from her mother, it was how to handle the male species. It was a reverse tutelage. She made a habit of doing exactly the opposite of what Lilibeth did and had done when it came to relationships.

The process had kept Lena heart-whole for nearly thirty years. She had no desire, and no intention, of putting herself into a man's hands. Metaphorically speaking, she thought with a smirk as she painted her lips.

She liked being in the right man's hands well enough, when she was in the mood to be handled.

A woman who didn't enjoy sex, in her opinion, just didn't know how to pick her partners cannily enough. A smart woman culled out men who were willing and able to be shown how that woman wanted to be pleasured. And a woman pleasured tended to give a man a good, strong ride.

Everybody ended up winning.

The problem was, Declan had the talent for putting her in the mood for sex all the damn time. She was *not* in the habit of being guided by her hormones.

The wisest, safest thing for a woman to do about sex was to be in control of it. To decide the when, the where, the who and how. Men, well, they were just randy by nature. She couldn't blame them for it.

And women who claimed not to try to stir men up were either cold-blooded or liars.

If she'd believed she and Declan were headed toward a simple affair that began and ended with a mutual buzz, she wouldn't have been concerned. But there was more to him than that. Too many layers to him, she thought, and she couldn't seem to get through them all and figure him out.

More, and much more worrying, there was another layer to her reaction to him than simple lust. That, too, was complicated and mysterious.

She liked the look of him, and the Yankee bedrock sound of his voice. And then he'd gone and hit her soft spot with his obvious affection for her grandmama.

Got her blood heated up, too, she admitted. The man had a very skilled pair of lips.

And when he wasn't paying attention, a wounded look in his eyes. She was a sucker for hurting hearts.

Best to take it slow. She arched her neck and ran the crystal wand of her perfume bottle over her skin. Slow and easy. No point in getting to the end of the road unless you'd enjoyed the journey.

She trailed the wand over the tops of her breasts and imagined his fingers there. His mouth.

It had been a long time since she'd wanted a man quite this ... clearly, she realized. And since it was too late for a quick, anonymous roll in the sheets, it would be wise to get to know him a little better before she let him think he'd talked her into bed.

'Right on time, aren't you, *cher*?' she commented aloud

at the knock on her door. She gave her reflection a last check, blew herself a kiss, and walked to the front door.

He looked good in a suit. Very classy and *GQ*, she decided. She reached out, ran the stone-gray lapel between her thumb and fingers. 'Mmm. Don't you clean up nice, *cher*.'

'Sorry, all the blood just drained out of my head so the best I can come up with is, wow.'

She sent him that sassy, under-the-lashes look and turned a slow circle on stiletto heels. 'This work okay for you, then?'

The dress clung, dipped and shimmied. His glands were doing a joyful jig. 'Oh yeah. It's working just fine.'

She crooked her finger. 'Come here a minute.'

She stepped back, then slid a hand through his arm and turned toward an old silver-framed mirror. 'Don't we look fine?' she said, and her reflection laughed at his. 'Where you taking me, *cher*?'

'Let's find out.' He picked up a wide, red silk scarf, draped it over her shoulders. 'Are you going to be warm enough?'

'If I'm not, then this dress isn't working after all.' With this she strode out on her little gallery. She started to hold out a hand for his, then just stared down at the white stretch limo at the curb.

She was rarely speechless, but it took her a good ten seconds to find her voice, and her wits. 'You buy yourself a new car, darling?'

'It's a rental. This way, I figure we can both have all the champagne we want.'

As first dates went, she thought as he led her down, this one had potential. It only got better when the uniformed driver opened the door and bowed her inside.

There were two silver buckets. One held a bottle of champagne and the other a forest of purple tulips.

'Roses are obvious,' he said and pulled a single flower out to offer her. 'And you're not.'

She twirled the tulip under her nose. 'Is this how you charm the girls in Boston?'

He poured a flute of champagne, held it out to her. 'There are no other girls.'

Off balance, she took a sip. 'You're dazzling me, Declan.'

'That's the plan.' He tapped his glass to hers. 'I'm really good at seeing a plan through.'

She leaned back, crossed her legs in a slow, deliberate motion she knew would draw his gaze down to them. 'You're a dangerous man. You know what makes you really dangerous? It doesn't show unless you take a good look under all the polish.'

'I won't hurt you, Lena.'

'Oh, hell you won't.' But she let out a low, delightful laugh. 'That's just part of the trip, sugar. Just part of the trip. And so far, I'm enjoying it.'

He went for elegant, Old-World French where the waiters wore black tie, the lighting was muted, and the corner table was designed for intimacy.

Another bottle of champagne arrived seconds after they were seated, telling her he'd prearranged it. And possibly a great deal more.

'I'm told the food is memorable here. The house is early twentieth century,' he continued. 'Georgian Colonial Revival, and belonged to an artist. A private home until about thirty years ago.'

'Do you always research your restaurant's history?'

'Ambience matters. Especially in New Orleans. So does cuisine. They tell me the *caneton à l'orange* is a house specialty.'

'Then one of us should have it.' Intrigued, she set her menu aside. He wasn't just fun, she thought. He wasn't just sexy and smart. He was *interesting*. 'You choose. This time.'

He ordered straight through from appetizers to chocolate soufflé with the ease of a man accustomed to fine dining in exclusive restaurants.

'You have good French, at least for ordering food. Do you speak it otherwise?'

'Yes, but Cajun French can still throw me.'

'Have you been to Paris?'

'Yes.'

She leaned forward in that way she had, her arms folded on the edge of the table, her gaze fastened to his. 'Is it wonderful?'

'It is.'

'One day I'd like to go. To Paris and Florence, to Barcelona and Athens.' They were hot, colorful dreams of hers, and the anticipation of them as exciting as the wish. 'You've been to those places.'

'Not Athens. Yet. My mother liked to travel, so we went to Europe every year when I was growing up. Every other to Ireland. We still have family there.'

'And what's your favorite?' She rested her elbows on the table and her chin in her laced fingers. 'Of all the places you've been.'

'Hard to say. The west coast of Ireland, the hills in Tuscany, a sidewalk café in Paris. But at the moment, right here is my favorite place.'

'There's that silky tongue again. All right then, tell me about Boston.'

'It's a New England harbor city of great historical importance.' When she laughed, he sat back and soaked it in. 'Oh, that's not what you meant.'

'Tell me about your family. You have brothers, sisters?'

'Two brothers, one sister.'

'Big family.'

'Are you kidding? My parents were pikers in the

go-forth-and-multiply area. Mom has six brothers and sisters, my father comes from a family of eight. None of their siblings had less than five kids. We are legion.'

'You miss them.'

'I do? Okay, I do,' he admitted reluctantly. 'From this nice, safe distance, I've realized I actually like my family.'

'They'll come visit you?'

'Eventually. Everyone will wait for my mother to start actually speaking to me again. In our house if it's not one thing, it's your mother.'

She sampled the appetizer he'd ordered for her. She wore no rings, and he wondered why. She had lovely hands, slim, elegant, delicate. The silver key rested against that smooth, dusky skin, and there was a glint of silver at her ears. But her fingers, her wrists were bare. Beautifully bare, he realized, and wondered if the lack of ornamentation was some sort of female ploy to make a man notice every line, every curve, every sweep of her.

It was sure as hell working that way on him.

'You think she's mad at you? Your mama?'

He had to blink himself back to the threads of conversation. 'Not mad. Irritated, annoyed, baffled. If she was really angry, she'd be down here in my face, chipping away until I crumbled to her terrifying will.'

'Does she want you to be happy?'

'Yes. We love each other like idiots. She'd just be more satisfied if my happiness aligned with her point of view.'

Her head angled, and again he caught that wink of silver through the thick, dark curls of her hair. 'Why don't you let her know she hurts your feelings?'

'What?'

'If you don't let her know she hurts them, how is she going to stop?'

'I let them down.'

'Oh, you did not,' she replied, with a kind of impatient sympathy. 'You think your family wants you to be miserable and unfulfilled? Married to a woman you don't love, working at a career that you don't want?'

'Yes. No,' he answered. 'I don't honestly know.'

'Then it seems to me you ought to ask them.'

'Do you have any siblings?'

'No. And tonight we're going to talk about you. We'll save me for another time. Did you find what you wanted at your antique shops?'

'And then some.' More comfortable talking about acquisitions than family, he gave her a blow-by-blow that took them into the main course.

'How do you know what you want before you have the room done?'

'I just do.' He moved his shoulders. 'I can't explain it. I've got this great davenport on hold for the upriver parlor. That's where I'm starting next, and it's not nearly as big a job as the kitchen. Walls and floors mostly. I want to get a good start on the interiors so I can concentrate on the galleries, the double stairs, have the place painted starting in April, if I'm lucky. That way, we should be able to shift back inside before the summer heat.'

'Why are you pushing so hard? The house isn't going anywhere.'

'Remember the single-minded, competitive nature I told you about?'

'Doesn't mean you can't relax a bit. How many hours are you putting in in a week?'

'I don't know. Ten, twelve a day generally.' Then he grinned and reached for her hand. 'You worried about me? I'll take more time off if you'll spend it with me.'

'I'm not that worried about you.' But she left her hand in his, let it be held against that hard, calloused palm. 'Still,

133

Mardi Gras's coming. If you don't take some time to enjoy that, you might as well be in Boston.' She looked at the double soufflé their waiter set in the middle of the table. 'Oh my. My, my.' She leaned forward, closed her eyes, and sniffed. And was laughing when she opened them again. 'Where's yours?'

He took her dancing. He'd found a club that played the slow fox-trots and jazzy swings of the thirties, and surprised her by whirling her around the floor until her legs were weak.

'You're full of surprises.'

'Bet your ass.' He swung her into his arms, had her blood pressure spiking when he ran his hands down her body and gripped her hips. Her body rolled against his, a wave sliding under a wave while a tenor sax wailed.

He dipped her, had her laughing even as her pulse went thick. She let her head fall back, her hair stream down as he lowered his face toward hers. His lips skimmed over her chin, just a hint of teeth, then he swept her up again, circled her, seduced her.

The lights were a warm, smoky blue, and his movements fluid so it was like moving underwater. The yearning she wasn't ready for crawled into her belly. With her eyes half closed, she skimmed a hand into his hair, brought his face closer, that last inch closer so his mouth met hers.

'You fit, Lena. We fit.'

She shook her head, turned it so her cheek rested against his. 'You make love half as well as you dance, you must have a trail of female smiles in your wake.'

'Let me show you.' He nipped at her earlobe, and felt her quick shiver. 'I want to touch you. I know how your skin will feel under my hands. I dreamed about it.'

She kept her eyes closed, tried to lock away the yearning. 'Just dance with me. It's getting late, and I want one more dance.'

She rested her head on his shoulder in the limo. The music, the wine, the soft lights were all still playing in her head. She felt drenched in romance, and knowing that had been his intention didn't diminish the effect. It only enhanced it.

He was a man who would trouble himself with the details. The large and the small. With the house he'd chosen, with the woman he wanted.

She admired that. Admired him.

'You show a girl a good time, *cher*.'

'Let me show you one tomorrow night.'

'I work tomorrow night.'

'Your next night off, then.'

'I'm going to think about that. I'm not being coy, Declan.' She sat up so she could look at him. 'I don't like coy. I'm being cautious. I can't say I care much for that, either, but where you're concerned I think it's the smart thing to be. And I do like being smart.'

As the limo glided to the curb in front of her home, she trailed a finger down his cheek. 'Now you walk me to my door, and kiss me good-night.'

He carried the silver bucket with the purple tulips. He set them down in front of her door, then framed her face in his hands.

The kiss was sweeter than she'd expected. She'd been prepared for heat, the persuasive, pervasive heat that might melt her resistance. Instead he gave her the sweet, and the gentle, ending the evening as he'd begun it. With romance.

'How about before you go to work?' He lifted her hand to his lips now. 'I'll take you on a picnic.'

Undone, she stared at him. 'A picnic?'

'It should be warm enough. We can spread a blanket by the pond. You can bring Rufus along as chaperone. I like watching him jump in.'

'Damn it.' She caught his face in her hands now. 'Damn it. I want you to go on down to that big white limo.'

'Okay.' He touched her hair. 'I'll just wait until you're inside.'

'Go down to the limo,' she repeated. 'And pay that driver, and tell him to go on home. Then you come back up.'

He closed his hands over her wrists, felt the trip of her pulse. 'Five minutes. Don't change your mind. Two minutes,' he amended. 'Time me.'

As he bolted down the stairs, she picked up her flowers, let herself inside. If it was a mistake, she thought, it wouldn't be her first. Or her last.

She lit the candles, put on some Billie Holiday. Sex should be easy, she reminded herself. When it was between two unattached adults with, well, at least some affection along with the lust, it should be a celebration.

Whether or not she'd been persuaded, the decision was hers. There was no point in regretting it before it had even begun.

He knocked. The idea that he would, rather than just walking in, made her smile. Good manners and hot blood. It was an interesting combination. Irresistible.

She opened the door, and Billie Holiday's heartbreak streamed out. Declan slid his hands into his pockets and smiled at her.

'Hi.'

'Hi back, handsome.' Lena reached out and grabbed his tie. 'Come on in here.' She tugged, and pulled him in the door. And, walking backward, would have pulled him straight into the bedroom.

But he laid his hands on her hips, drew her to him. 'I like your music.' He eased her into a dance. 'When I can see something besides you, I'll tell you if I like your place.'

'Did you take lessons on what to say to have women falling for you?'

'Natural gift.' He brushed his lips at each corner of her mouth. Over that sexy little mole. 'The streets of Boston are littered with my conquests. It was playing hell with traffic, so the city council asked me to leave.' He skimmed his cheek over hers. 'I smell you in my sleep. And wake up wanting you.'

Her heart began to shiver, like something feeling warmth after a long freeze. 'I knew you were trouble, the minute you stepped up to my bar.' She stretched under the hand that ran down her back. 'I just didn't know how much trouble.'

'Plenty.' He scooped her off her feet, crushed his mouth to hers until they both moaned. 'Which way?'

'Mmm. I've got a number of ways in mind.'

What blood was left in his head shot straight down to his loins. 'Ha. I meant which way is your bedroom.'

With a low laugh, she chewed on his bottom lip. 'Door on the left.'

He had a number of impressions as he carried her across the room, through the doorway. Vibrant colors, old wood. But most of his senses were wrapped around the woman in his arms. The weight of her, the shape and scent. The surprise that flickered over her face when he set her on her feet beside the bed instead of on it.

'I'd like to take my time with this, if it's all the same to you.' He trailed a fingertip down her collarbone, over the lovely curve of breast the dress displayed. 'You know, like unwrapping a present.'

'I can't say I mind that.'

She'd expected a rush – fast hands, hungry mouth – to match the reckless lust she'd seen in his gaze. When his hands took hers, linked fingers, and his lips lay silky on her lips, she remembered how ruthlessly he'd controlled his temper the day before.

It seemed his control reached to other passions as well.

She wasn't prepared for romance. He'd realized it when she'd seen the tulips. More than surprise, there'd been suspicion in her eyes. Just as there was now as he slowed the pace, lingered over the quiet pleasure of a kiss.

Seducing her into bed was no longer enough. He wanted to seduce that suspicion into helpless pleasure.

Her lips were warm and willing. It was no hardship to mate his with them, to float on that lazy slide of tongues while their bodies swayed together as if they were still dancing.

He knew when her fingers went limp in his that she floated with him.

He lowered the zipper of her dress in one slow glide and traced his fingers over the newly exposed flesh. She arched her back, and all but purred.

'You've got good hands, *cher*, and very sexy lips.' Watching him now, as he watched her, she loosened the knot of his tie. 'Let's see about the rest of you.'

There was something about undressing a man in a suit, she thought. The time it took to remove all the layers to get to skin, built anticipation, honed curiosity. He touched her as she unbuttoned his shirt, easing the dress off her shoulders so that it clung, erotically, to the curve of her breasts. He nibbled at her mouth, never hurrying, never groping.

And when she opened his shirt, ran her hands over his

chest with a little hum of approval, she felt the heavy beat of his heart under her palms.

'Some build you've got for a lawyer.'

'Ex-lawyer.' It was like dying, he thought, dying by inches to have those long, slender fingers with those hot red nails running over him. She pinched lightly at his biceps, licked her lips.

'Yes indeed, you're just full of surprises. I like a strong man.'

She tapped her nails on his belt buckle, and her smile was female. Feline. 'Let's see what other surprises you've got for me.'

They were dancing again, the oldest dance, and somehow she'd taken the lead. His stomach muscles quivered when she whipped the belt off, tossed it over her shoulder.

In his mind he saw himself throwing her down on the bed, pounding himself and this outrageous need into her. She'd accept it.

She'd expect it.

Instead, he took both her hands before she could unhook his trousers and lifted them to his lips. Watching her over them, he saw the surprise – and again the suspicion.

'I seem to be falling behind,' he said playfully. 'And since I've been wondering what you've got on under that dress, I'd like to find out how close my speculations were to reality.'

He laid his lips on her bare shoulder, used them to nudge the material down her arm. And blessed the laws of gravity when it slid down and puddled at her feet.

She wore black lace.

She was every man's fantasy. Dusky skin, tumbled hair, full, high breasts barely restrained in that fancy of lace. The slim torso, the gently rounded hips with more midnight lace riding low. Shapely legs in sheer black stockings and man-killer heels.

'Close.' The breath was already burning in his lungs. 'Very close. What's this?' He traced a fingertip over the tattoo on her inner thigh, just above the lacy edge of her stocking.

'That's my dragon. He guards the gates.' She was trembling, and wasn't ready to tremble. 'A lot of men think they can get past him. 'A lot of men get burned.'

He stroked his finger up, along that sensitive valley between lace and thigh. 'Let's play with fire.'

He yanked her against him, devoured her mouth. And when that wasn't enough, whirled her around to scrape his teeth along her shoulder, the side of her neck. With his face buried in her hair he ran his hands up her body, filled them with her lace-covered breasts.

She arched back to him, hooked her arms around his neck and offered. The spin from patient to urgent left her dizzy, brutally aroused and ready to be taken. She felt the greed from him now, and felt her own rise to match it.

His hand slid down, cupped between her legs, pressed, and brought her to the jagged edge of release. Before she could fall, he trailed his fingers down her thigh and with one fast flick, unhooked a garter.

Her breath caught. Her body strained. '*Mon Dieu.*'

'When I'm inside you, you won't be able to think about anything else.' He unhooked a second garter. 'But first, I need to touch you, the way I've been dreaming of touching you.' He rubbed his lips over her shoulder, nudged the strap of her bra aside. 'Angelina.'

He turned her to face him, let his fingers dive into her hair, draw her head back. 'You're mine tonight.'

Denial, defiance, fought their way through seduction. 'I belong to myself.'

He scooped her up, laid her back on the bed. 'Tonight, we're going to belong to each other.'

He closed his mouth over hers, stopping her words, drugging her brain. She turned her head to take a breath, to try to steady herself again. But his lips trailed down to her breast, over flesh, over lace, under it. The long, liquid tugs in her belly loosened her muscles, melted her will.

She yielded, telling herself she was surrendering to her own needs, and not to him.

He felt her give, the softening of her. Heard it in the low, throaty moan that was pleasure and acceptance.

So he took what he'd been aching for since the first moment he'd seen her in the morning mist.

Her body was a treasure, scented skin, female curves. He fed himself on the taste of it in slow sips and long gulps. Then freed her breasts to his hands, his mouth. His blood raged like a firestorm, but he let himself burn and tortured them both.

When he rolled the lace down her hips, she arched. Opened. He traced his fingers over her, watching her face in the candlelight as her eyes closed, her lips trembled on a groan. And when he slid them into her, into the hot wet velvet of her, she bowed up, cried out. Drove him mad.

Pressing his face to her belly, he sent her flying.

Her body was a mass of aches, of joys, with the sharp edge of sensation slicing through like a bolt of light. It burst in her, sent her helplessly hurtling.

She reached for him, closed her hand around him. He was hard as stone. She wanted him inside her as much as she wanted her next breath.

'Now. I want you.' She felt him quiver, even as she quivered. Saw herself in his eyes as he rose over her. 'I want you to fill me. Fill me up.'

He clung to that slippery line of control, and as her legs wrapped around him, slid slowly, very slowly into her. Slid deep when she rose to meet him. Held there with

141

his breath caught in his throat and everything he was lost in her.

Sighs now, and a quick, rushing gasp. They kept their eyes on each other and moved, an almost lazy pace that spread pleasure like a warm pool. Their lips met, and he felt hers curve against his before he lifted his head to see her smile.

Flesh glided over flesh, silky friction. Music, the tragic sob of it from her living room, a sudden celebratory burst of it from the street below, merged together in his head with her quickening breaths.

She tensed beneath him, her head going back to bare the line of her throat for his lips. She tightened around him, shuddered, shuddered. Once again he buried his face in her hair, and this time, let himself fly with her.

Later, he lay watching the light play on the ceiling, stroking his hand along her back. Drenched in her. 'Are you going to let me stay?' he asked. 'Or do I catch a cab?'

She stared into the shadows. 'Stay.'

Chapter Nine

He woke just after daybreak. She'd curved into him in sleep, but he saw that she had her arm between them and a fist curled over her heart. As if she were guarding it, he thought. The little silver key lay against the side of her hand.

He wanted to lift that hand, gently uncurl the fingers. Bare her heart to him, he realized. He'd already lost his to her. Had lost it, he decided, the moment he'd seen her.

It was a jolt, and a shock for a man who'd come to believe he simply wasn't capable of love. Unless it was family or friendship. His personal crisis over Jessica, who everyone – including Jessica – had claimed was perfect for him, had convinced him he'd blown his one chance at a lasting, content relationship with a woman.

It had been tough to swallow for a man who, at the core, believed strongly in family, in home, in marriage. And swallowing it, he realized, had been largely responsible for the restless unhappiness that had trailed after him like a faithful dog for months.

Now he was looking at the woman who was the answer. And he didn't think she was going to be willing to listen to the question.

So, he'd have to persuade her. One way or the other, and sooner or later. Because he'd meant what he'd said the night before. They were going to belong to each other.

He considered waking her up and reminding her how good they were together in bed. He couldn't think of a better way to start the day, especially since she was warm and soft and draped around him.

But it didn't seem quite fair to wake her when they'd barely slept. Her workday started a great deal later than his.

He slid away from her, with no little regret, and eased out of bed. She stirred, sighing in sleep, and rolled into the warmth he'd left behind.

He grabbed his trousers and headed into the shower.

In his opinion, you could tell a lot about a person by their bathroom. Hers was both rigorously clean and indulgent. Thick towels of forest green offset the white fixtures and picked up the small diamond chip pattern scattered through the floor tile.

Lush green plants lined the windowsill, and a trio of daffodils speared out of a slim bottle of pale green.

There were other bottles, jewel colors, and covered boxes that held fragrant oils and lotions, bath salts. She liked fancy soaps, he noted, and kept them in a pretty bowl.

He also discovered her hot water lasted longer than his. He smiled through the bliss of a fifteen-minute shower that steamed up the room like a Turkish bath.

She was still sleeping when he stepped out. Sprawled now over the sheets with the morning sun slanted over the lean length of her naked back. He turned his mind firmly from sliding back into bed with her and focused it on finding coffee.

Her living area had lofty ceilings and dark wood floors. She'd sponged the walls with a bluish paint that made them look like faded denim. Against one stood a fireplace framed in that same dark wood with a sunburst mantelpiece he immediately coveted. Its woodwork was distressed, its cream-colored paint peeling.

He understood why she'd left it that way. Its history and character came through.

To complement the faded walls, she'd hung colorful framed posters. Advertising posters, he noted. Elegant women selling champagne, sleek-looking men toting cigars.

A high-backed sofa in royal blue sat in the center of the room covered, as women mysteriously cover sofas and beds, with pillows.

He admired the style she'd formed here. Old, subtly battered tables and slashing colors. And he liked seeing his tulips on her coffee table.

He wandered through to the kitchen and found himself grinning. It wasn't often you found black-and-white photos of nudes – male and female – on kitchen walls.

But he was happier yet to find coffee.

He closed the pocket door so the sound of grinding beans wouldn't carry to the bedroom. And while the coffee brewed, he stood at her kitchen window, looking out at her section of New Orleans.

He heard the slide of the kitchen door.

She wore a short red robe, and her eyes were heavy with sleep, her smile lazy with it.

'Sorry, I thought I'd muffled the coffee grinder.'

'I didn't hear it.' She drew a deep breath. 'But I smelled the results. You making breakfast, *cher*?'

145

'Want toast? It's my best thing.'

'Oh, I think I had a taste of your best thing last night.' Still smiling, she sauntered toward him, slid her hands around his neck. 'Gimme another,' she said and lifted her mouth to his.

She'd woken lonely, sure he'd gone. She never let men stay the night in her bed. It was too easy for them to slip out the door. Better to send them along, to sleep alone than to wake lonely.

Then she'd seen his shirt, his jacket, his shoes, and had been delighted. Too delighted. When a man had that much power, it was time to take some back. The surefire way was to cloud his mind with sex.

'Why didn't you just roll over and wake me up, sugar?'

'Thought about it.' Was still thinking about it. 'I figured since you're working tonight, you need more than ten minutes' sleep. But since you're awake ...' She laughed and slipped away. 'Since I'm awake I want coffee.' She opened a cupboard door, sent him that knowing glance over her shoulder. 'Maybe if you ask nice, I'll fix you some breakfast.'

'Do you want me to beg standing up, on my knees or completely supine?'

'You tickle me, Declan. I'll make you some toast. *Le pain perdu*,' she added when his face fell. 'French toast. I got me most of a nice baguette.' She handed him a thick white mug filled with black coffee.

'Thanks. Since you're good in the kitchen, we won't have to hire a cook when we get married and raise our six kids.'

'Six?'

'I feel obligated to uphold the Sullivan-Fitzgerald tradition. I really like your kitchen art. Not the usual spot for nudes.'

'Why?' She got out a black iron skillet. 'Cooking's an art, and it's sexy if you do it right.'

She got out a blue bowl. He watched her crack an egg on its side, slide white and yolk in, one-handed.

'I see what you mean. Do it again.'

She chuckled and cracked a second egg. 'Why don't you go on out and put some music on? This won't take long.'

They ate at a little gateleg table she had tucked under one of the living room windows.

'Where'd you learn to cook?' he asked her.

'My grandmama. She tried to teach me to sew, too, but that didn't stick so well.'

'I'm surprised you didn't open a restaurant instead of a bar.'

'I like to cook when I like to cook. Do it for a living, do it all the time.'

'There's that How did you end up running a bar?'

'I wanted my own business. You work for somebody else, they say do this, don't do that, come here, go there. That doesn't set with me. So I went to business school, and I think, what business do I want to have? I don't want to sell souvenirs, don't want a gift shop, don't want to sell dresses. I think, all those things sell in New Orleans, but what sells even more? Pleasure sells. A little harmless sin and a good time, that's what people come to the Big Easy for. So … Et Trois.'

'How long have you had it?'

'Let's see now.' She'd already eaten her single slice, so speared a forkful of one of the four she'd piled on his plate. 'Going on six years now.'

'You opened a bar when you were twenty-three?'

'Hey, how do you know how old I am?'

'Remy.'

She looked up at the ceiling. '*Et là*! Gonna have to take a strip off his ass for that. Man oughta know better than flapping about a woman's age. What else he flap about?'

Declan gave his breakfast his undivided attention. 'This is really great. What do you put in this stuff?'

She said nothing for a full ten seconds. 'I see. Men just can't stop themselves from crowing about their sexual exploits.'

Uneasy, for himself and his friend, Declan replied, 'It wasn't like that. It was nostalgic. And it was sweet. You meant something to him. You still do.'

'It's a good thing for him I know that. And that I feel the same. Do you remember the first girl you got into the backseat, Declan? Do you remember her fondly?'

'Sherry Bingham. A pretty little blond. I loved her desperately through most of my junior year in high school.'

She liked him for coming out with a name, instantly. Even if he'd made it up. 'What happened?'

'She dumped me for a football player. Left tackle. Jesus, a football player with no neck and the IQ of a pencil. I'm still pissed off at her. But to get back to you – and by the way, you're really good at deflecting personal questions, but I was a lawyer. Anyway, how did you manage to pull it off? Twenty-three's pretty young to establish a business, one that's proven itself out when most go under within three years.'

She leaned back. 'What difference does it make? Counselor.'

'Okay.' He shrugged and kept eating. 'I'll just assume you robbed a bank, paid off the Mob, seduced then murdered the previous owner – after he left you the building in his will. And continue to run illegal gambling and prostitutes out of the back room.'

'Why I've been so busy. But I like your version better. Mine's very dull in comparison. I worked after school and summers, saved my pennies. I'm very good at saving pennies

148

if I need to. Then I worked, tending bar, serving drinks, and went to business school part-time. Just before I turned twenty-two, my grandpapa died. Fell off a ladder, broke his damn fool neck.'

Her eyes filled as she said it. 'Guess I'm still pissed off at him.'

'I'm sorry.' He covered her hand with his. 'You were close.'

'I loved him more than any man in the world. Pete Simone, with his big laugh and his big hands. He played the fiddle and always carried a red bandanna. Always. Well ...' She blinked away the tears. 'He had an insurance policy, bigger than it ought to have been considering. Half for me, half for Grandmama. In the end she made me take all of it. Nothing you can do to change her mind when she digs her heels in. So I invested the money, and a year later I opened my place.'

'There's nothing dull about that. You run a good bar, Lena.'

'Yes, I do.' She rose, picked up the plates. 'You'd best get yourself dressed, *cher*, if you want a ride home.'

He couldn't talk her into coming inside. He had to settle for a mind-numbing kiss before she pushed him out of her car and drove away.

Arriving home at nine in the morning in a wrinkled suit gained him a grin and a wink from Big Frank as the man carted dead tree limbs to a burn pile.

'You fell into some luck last night, Mister Dec.'

Into something, Declan thought and, rubbing his heart, went into the house to get to work.

She wouldn't see him that night, or the next. He had to content himself with phone calls that made him feel like a teenager as he wandered the house with his portable phone and rattled his brains for any conversational ploy that would keep her on the line.

Mardi Gras celebrations, and business, were under way, she told him. While they were, she didn't have time to come out and play.

He knew when he was being tested and stalled and tangled. And decided he'd let her string out his line. Until he reeled her in.

Remy dropped by one afternoon wearing Hugo Boss and gold beads. He took the beads off, tossed them over Declan's head. 'When you coming into town?'

'I thought I might join the insanity over the weekend.'

'*Cher*, it's Mardi Gras. Every night's the weekend.'

'Not out here. Come take a look.' He led the way into the parlor, where Tibald was high on a ladder patiently detailing the ceiling plasterwork.

'Hey, Tibald.' Remy hooked his thumbs into his pockets and craned his neck back. 'That's some job.'

'It surely is. How's Effie doing these days?'

'Driving me to drink with wedding plans. Picked out the cake yesterday, and you'd think it was a matter of life and death whether it has yellow rosebuds or full-blown roses around the edges.'

'Best thing a man can do in these situations is nod at whatever she likes best, and just show up on the day.'

'You might've said something of that nature before I told her I liked the big, fat roses when it turned out she had her mind set on the buds.' He pulled a small bottle of Tylenol out of his pocket. 'You got something I can down this with, Dec? That woman's given me the mother of all headaches.'

Declan picked up a half-empty bottle of water. 'Did you come out here to hide?'

'Till she cools off.' Gulping down the pills and water,

Remy wandered over the drop cloth. 'You do these walls in here, Dec, or you hire them out?'

'I did them.' Pleased, Declan ran his fingers over the smooth surface of the Paris green walls. 'Spent the last three days on this room.' And nights, he thought. 'I think this color will make the room seem cooler than a patterned paper and I like the way it looks with the trim.'

'You're a regular Bob Vila and Martha Stewart combined. What do you tackle next?'

'The library. Still some details to deal with in here, and the kitchen, but the library's on the slate for next week. After that, I'm hoping to move outside for a while. Give me a couple of those aspirin.'

'Sure.' Remy handed over the pills and the water. 'You got work problems or female problems?'

'A little of both. Come out on the back gallery, take a look at what the Franks have done with the rear gardens.'

'Heard you escorted our Lena around in a big, white limo a few nights ago,' Remy said as they walked toward the back of the house. 'Classy stuff.'

'I'm a classy guy.' He handed the water back to Remy and opened the French doors of the dining room.

'You got romancing her in mind, that's a good start.'

'I've got more than that in mind,' Declan said as Remy tipped back the bottle. 'I'm going to marry her.'

Water spewed out as Remy choked.

'Pretty good spit take,' Declan commented. 'Keep the bottle.'

'Jesus, Dec. Jesus Christ, you and Lena are getting married?'

'I'd like to have the wedding here, in the fall. September maybe.' He scanned his gallery, his gardens. He wondered what kind of bird it was that was currently singing its lungs out. 'The place won't be finished, but that'd be part of the charm. Of course, if it takes me longer to pin her down, we could do it next spring.'

'That's some fast work.'

'Not really. It's just a matter of keeping at it.' He smiled now as he studied Remy's baffled face. 'Oh, you don't mean the house. Lena. I haven't asked her yet. She'd just say no. Look out there, bulbs coming up. Daffodils, tulips, calla lilies, the Franks tell me. Buried under all those weeds and vines, maybe blooming under it for years. That's something.'

'Dec, I think you need something stronger than Tylenol.'

'I'm not crazy. I'm in love with her. I'm starting to think I was in love with her before I even met her. That's why there was never anyone else who really mattered. Not like this. Because she was here, and I just hadn't found her yet.'

'Maybe I need something stronger.'

'Bourbon's in the kitchen. Ice is in the cooler. New frig is due to come in tomorrow.'

'I'm fixing us both a drink.'

'Make mine short and weak,' Dec told him absently. 'I've got work to do yet today.'

Remy brought back two glasses and took a long sip of his as he studied Declan's face. 'Declan, I love you like a brother.'

'I know you do.'

'So, I'm going to talk to you like I would a brother – if I had one instead of being plagued with sisters.'

'You think I've lost my mind.'

'No. In some situations, hell, in most situations, a man thinks with his dick. By the time that thought process works all the way to his head, he usually sees that situation more clearly.'

'I appreciate you explaining that to me, Dad.'

Remy only shook his head and paced up and down the gallery. 'Lena's a very sexy woman.'

'No argument there.'

'She just sort of exudes those pheromones or whatever the hell they are the way other women do the perfume they splash on to get a man stirred up. She stirs you up just by breathing.'

'You're trying to tell me I'm infatuated, or in the heavy wave of first lust.'

'Exactly.' Remy laid a supportive hand on Declan's shoulder. 'Not a man alive would blame you for it. Add to that, son, you've had a rough few months on the relationship train, and knowing the way you cart guilt around like it was your personal treasure chest, I don't imagine you've been clearing your pipes regular since you broke it off with Jennifer.'

'Jessica, you asshole.' Amused, touched, Declan leaned back on the baluster. 'It's not infatuation. I thought it was, with a good dose of that lust tossed in. But that's not it. It's not a matter of clogged pipes, and I'm not thinking with my dick. It's my heart.'

'Oh, brother.' Remy took another good gulp of whiskey. 'Dec, you haven't been down here a full month yet.'

'People are always saying something like that, as if time is a factor.' And because the critical part of his brain had said the same thing, he was irritated to hear the sentiment from his closest friend. 'What, is there a law somewhere that states you can't fall in love until a reasonable, rational period of time has passed during which the parties will socialize, communicate and, if possible, engage in sexual intercourse in order to assure compatibility? If there is, and it worked, explain the divorce rate.'

'A couple of lawyers stand here debating the subject, we'll be here till next Tuesday.'

'Then let me say this. I've never felt like this before, never in my life. I didn't think I could. I figured something inside me just didn't work the way it was supposed to.'

'Well, for Christ's sake, Dec.'

'I couldn't love Jessica.' The guilt slid back into his voice. 'I just couldn't, and I tried to. I damn near settled for affection, respect and mutual backgrounds because I thought it was all I'd get, or be able to give. But it's not. I've never felt like this, Remy,' he said again. 'And I like it.'

'If you want Lena, then I want her for you. The thing is, Dec, no matter how you feel, it doesn't guarantee she's going to feel the same.'

'Maybe she'll break my heart, but feeling too much is a hell of a lot better than feeling nothing.' He'd been telling himself that, repeatedly, since he'd realized he was in love with her. 'One way or the other, I've got to try.'

He swirled the whiskey he'd yet to drink. 'She doesn't know what to make of me,' Declan murmured. 'It's going to be fun letting her find out.'

That night, he heard weeping. A man's raw and broken sobs. Declan tossed in sleep, weighed down with the grief, unable to stop it, unable to give or seek comfort.

Even when silence came, the sorrow stayed.

Chapter Ten

Bayou Rouse
March 1900

He didn't know why he came here, to stare at the water while thick green shadows spread around him, as night gathered to eat away at the day.

But he came, time and again, to wander through the marsh as if he would somehow come upon her, strolling along the curve of the river where the swamp flowers blossomed.

She would smile at him, hold out her hand.

And everything would be right again.

Nothing would ever be right again.

He was afraid he was going mad, that grief was darkening his mind as night darkened the day. How else could he explain how he could hear her whispering to him in the night? What could he do but shut off the sound of her, the pain of her?

He watched a blue heron rise from the reeds like a ghost, beautiful, pure, perfect, to skim over the tea-colored water and glide into the trees. Away from him. Always away from him.

She was gone. His Abby had winged away from him, like the ghost bird. Everyone said it. His family, his friends. He'd heard the servants whispering about it. How Abigail Rouse had run off with some no-account and left her husband and bastard baby daughter behind.

Though he continued to look in New Orleans, in Baton Rouge, in Lafayette, though he continued to haunt the bayou like a ghost himself, in the loneliest hours of the night, he believed it.

She'd left him and the child.

Now he was leaving, in all but body. He walked through each day like a man in a trance. And God help him, he could not be a father to the child, that image of Abigail he secretly, shamefully doubted carried his blood. Just looking at her brought him unspeakable sorrow.

He no longer went up to the nursery. He hated himself for it, but even the act of climbing the stairs to the third floor was like drowning in a sea of despair.

They said the child wasn't his.

No. In the dimming light of dusk, with the night coming alive around him, Lucian covered his face with his hands. No, he could not, would not believe that of her. They had made the child together, in love, in trust, in desire.

If even that was a lie …

He lowered his hands, stepped toward the water. It would be warm, as her smile had been warm. Soft, as her skin had been soft. Even now the color was deepening and was almost the color of her eyes.

'Lucian!'

He froze, on the slippery edge.

Abby. She was rushing toward him, pushing through the fronds of a willow, with her hair spilling over her shoulders in midnight curls. His heart, deadened with grief, woke in one wild leap.

Then the last shimmer of sunlight fell over her face, and he died again.

Claudine gripped his hands. Fear made her fingers cold. She'd seen what had been in his eyes, and it had been his death.

'She would never want this. She would never want you to damn your soul by taking your life.'

'She left me.'

'No. No, that isn't true. They lie to you. They lie, Lucian. She loved you. She loved you and Marie Rose above all things.'

'Then where is she?' The rage that lived under the numbness of his grief leaped out. He gripped Claudine's arms, hauled her to her toes. Part of him, some dark, secret part, wanted to pound his fists into her face. Erase it for its connection to Abigail, and his own drowning despair. 'Where is she?'

'Dead!' She shouted it, and her voice rang in the warm, sticky air. 'They killed her. Death is the only way she would leave you and Rosie.'

He shoved her aside, staggered away to lean against the trunk of a live oak. 'That's just another madness.'

'I tell you I know it. I *feel* it. I've had dreams.'

'So did I.' Tears stung his eyes, turned the light watery. 'So did I have dreams.'

'Lucian, you must listen. I was there that night. She came to the nursery to tend the baby. I've known Abby since we were babies ourselves. There was nothing in her but love for you and Marie Rose. I should never have left the Hall that night.' Claudine crossed her hands over her breast, as if to hold together the two halves of her broken heart. 'The rest of my life I'll beg her forgiveness for not being there.'

157

'She took clothes, jewelry. My mother is right.' He firmed his lips on what he believed was an act of strength, but was only his weakened faith. 'I have to accept.'

'Your mama hated Abby. She kicked me out the next day. She's afraid to keep me in the house, afraid I might find out—'

He whirled around, his face so contorted with fury, Claudine stepped away. 'You want me to believe my mother somehow killed my wife, then disguised the crime, the sin, the horror, by making it appear Abby ran away?'

'I don't know what happened. But I know Abby didn't leave. Mama Rouse, she went to Evangeline.'

Lucian waved a hand, turned away again. 'Voodoo nonsense.'

'Evangeline's got power. She said there was blood, and pain, and fear. And a dark, dark sin. Death, she said, and a watery grave. She said you got two halves, and one is black as a cave in Hell.'

'I killed her then? I came home in the night and murdered my wife?'

'Two halves, Lucian, that shared one womb. Look to your brother.'

The chill stabbed through him, bringing a raw sickness to the belly, a vile roaring in his head. 'I won't listen to any more of this. Go home, Claudine. Keep away from the Hall.'

He dug into his pocket, took out the watch pin, pressed it into Claudine's hand. 'Take this, keep it for the child.' He could no longer call her by name. 'She should have something that was her mother's.'

He stared down, grieving, at the symbol in her hand. Time had stopped for Abigail. 'You kill her again by not believing in her.'

'Stay away from me.' He staggered away, toward Manet Hall, toward his chosen hell. 'Stay away.'

'You know!' Claudine shouted after him. 'You know she was true.'

Clutching the watch to her breast, Claudine vowed to pass it, and the truth, along to Abigail's daughter.

Manet Hall
February 2002

From his gallery, Declan watched the day come to life. Dawn was a rosy blush on the eastern sky, with hints of mauve, like sleepy bruises, just beneath. The air was warming. He could feel the rise of it almost every day. It wasn't yet March, but winter was bowing out.

The gardens that a month before had been a sorrowful wreck, showed hints of their former grandeur. Strangling vines, invasive weeds, deadwood and broken bricks had been hauled away, revealing foot by foot the wandering paths, the shrubs, even the bulbs and plants that had been too stubborn to die away.

An old iron arbor was wild with what the Franks told him was wisteria, and there was an island of massive azaleas that showed the beginning of hopeful buds.

He had magnolia, crape myrtle, camellia, jasmine. He'd written down everything he could remember the Franks reeled off in their lazy voices. When he'd described the vine he imagined on the corner columns, they'd told him what he wanted was morning glory.

He liked the sound of it. Mornings here were full of glory.

He thought his body was adjusting to the five or six hours of disturbed sleep a night he was able to snatch. Or maybe it was just nervous energy that was fueling him.

Something was pushing him, driving him step by step through the transformation of the house that was his. Yet somehow, not only his.

If it was Abigail hovering, she was a damn fickle female. There were times he felt utterly comfortable, totally at peace. And others when cold fear prickled the back of his neck. Times when he felt in his gut he was being watched.

Stalked.

Well, that was a woman for you, he thought as he sipped his morning coffee. All smiles one minute, and slaps the next.

Even as he thought it, he saw Lena and the big black dog step out of the trees.

He didn't think twice, but set his coffee aside and started for the gallery steps.

She'd seen him long before he'd seen her. From the shelter of the trees and morning mists, she'd stood, idly rubbing Rufus's head, and had studied the house. Studied him.

What was it about the place and the man that pulled at her so? she wondered. There were any number of great old houses here, along the River Road, on toward Baton Rouge.

God knew there were any number of good-looking men, if a woman was in the market for one.

But it was this house that had always snagged her interest and imagination. Now it seemed it was this man, jogging down the thick stone stairs in a ratty shirt, rattier jeans, his face rough, with the night's beard, who had managed to do the same.

She didn't like to want. It got in the way of things. And when that want involved a man, well, it was just bound to mess up your life.

She'd built her life brick by goddamn brick. And she liked it, just as it was. A man, no matter how amiable he was, would, at best, alter the design. At worst, he'd send those bricks tumbling down to ruin.

She'd kept away from him since the night she'd taken him into her bed. Just to prove she could.

But she had a smile ready for him now, a slow, cat-at-the-mouse-hole smile, and stood her ground as the dog raced over, tearing through the ground fog, to meet him.

Rufus leaped, slopped his tongue over Declan's face, then collapsed, belly up, for a rub.

It was, Lena knew, Rufus's way of showing unconditional love.

Charms dogs, too, she thought as Declan crouched down to rub and wrestle. The man had entirely too much appeal for anybody's good. Especially hers.

'Rufus!' she called out, bringing the dog to his feet in a flurry of muscle and limbs that nearly put Declan on his ass. And laughing, she tossed the ball she carried high in the air, nipped it handily on its fall. Rufus charged her, a blur of black fur and enthusiasm. She hurled the ball over the pond. Rufus sailed up, over the water, and nabbed the ball with his teeth seconds before his massive splash.

'The Bo Sox could use you two.' As the dog paddled his way to shore, Declan strode up, cupped his hands under Lena's elbows, and lifted her off her feet. He had an instant to see her blink in surprise before he covered her mouth with his, and took her under.

She gripped his shirt, not for balance, though her feet were dangling several inches off the ground. But because he was under it, all that muscle and heat and man.

She heard the dog bark, three deep throaty rumbles, then the water he shook off himself drenched her. She wouldn't have been surprised if it had steamed off her skin.

'Morning,' Declan said and dropped her back on her feet. 'Where y'at?'

'Woo.' She had to give him credit for both greetings, and pushed a hand through her hair. 'Where y'at?' she responded, then reached up and rubbed a hand over his rough cheek. 'Need a shave, *cher*.'

'If I'd known you'd come walking my way this morning, I'd have taken care of that.'

'I wasn't walking your way.' She picked up the ball Rufus had dropped at her feet and sent it, and the dog, flying again. 'Just playing with my grandmama's dog.'

'Is she all right? You said you stayed over with her when she wasn't feeling well.'

'She gets the blues sometimes, is all.' And damn it, *damn* it, his instant and genuine concern touched her. 'Missing her Pete. She was seventeen when they got married, and fifty-eight when he died. More'n forty years is a long time to mesh lives.'

'Would she like it if I went by later?'

'She likes your company.' Because Rufus was thumping his tail impatiently, she winged the ball again.

'You said she has a sister. Any other family?'

'Two sisters, a brother, all still living.'

'Children?'

Her face shut down. 'I'm all she's got there. You been into town for any of the partying?'

Off limits, he decided. He let it go, for the moment. 'Not yet. I figured I'd go in tonight. Are you working?'

'Nothing but work till Ash Wednesday. People do like to drink before Lent comes.'

'Late hours for you. You look a little tired.'

'I don't much care for being up this early, but Grandmama, she's an early bird. She's up, everybody's up.'

She lifted her arms high, stretched. 'You're an early bird yourself, aren't you, *cher*?'

'These days. Why don't you come back to the house with me, have some coffee, see what I've been doing with my time since I haven't been able to spend any with you.'

'I've been busy.'

'So you said.'

Her brows knit, forming a long, shallow line of annoyance between them. 'I say what I mean.'

'I didn't say different. But I'm making you edgy. I don't mind that, Lena.' He reached out to tug on her hair, amused and delighted to see temper darken her face. 'But I would mind if you think I'd settle for one night with you.'

'I sleep with you if I want, when I want.'

'And I'd mind,' he continued mildly, though the hand that gripped her arm before she could spin away was very firm. 'I'd mind a great deal if you think all I want is to get you in the sheets.'

'Men don't touch me unless I tell them they can touch me.' She shoved at his hand.

'You've never dealt with me before, have you?' There was steel in his fingers, in his tone. 'Just simmer down. Picking a fight isn't going to shake me loose, either. You wanted to keep your distance this week, okay. I'm a patient man, Lena, but I'm not a doormat. Don't think you're going to walk over me on your way out the door.'

Anger, she realized, wasn't the way to handle him. She had no doubt she could scrape away at that control and stir him up into a good shouting match of a fight. It would be interesting, even entertaining. But she had a fifty-fifty chance of losing it.

She didn't care for the odds.

Instead, she stroked a hand over his cheek. 'Aw now, *cher.*' Her voice was liquid silk. 'What you getting so het up about? You got me irritable, that's all. I'm not at my best so early in the day, and here you being all tough and surly. I don't mean to hurt your feelings.'

She rose on her toes and kissed his cheek.

'What *do* you mean to do, Angelina?'

There was something about the way he used her whole name that put her back up. A kind of warning. 'Now, Declan honey, I like you. I truly do. And the other night, why, you just about swept me off my feet. We had ourselves a real good time, too, didn't we? But you don't want to be making more out of it than it was.'

'What was it?'

She lifted her shoulders. 'A very satisfying interlude, for both of us. Why don't we leave it at that and be friends again?'

'We could. Or, we could try it this way.'

He yanked her to him, dragged her up to her toes. And plundered her mouth. No patience this time, no reason, no dreamy mating of lips. It was a branding, and they both knew it.

Rufus gave a warning growl as she struggled. Even when the growl turned to a snarl, Declan ignored it. He fisted a hand in her hair, pulled her head back, and took them both deeper. Temper, hurt and hunger all stormed inside him and flavored the kiss.

She couldn't resist it. Not when the punch of emotions slammed into her system, liberating needs she'd hoped to lock down. On a muffled oath, she wrapped her arms around his neck and met the ferocity of the kiss.

With a whine, Rufus settled down to chew at the ball.

'We're not done with each other.' Declan ran proprietary hands down her arms.

'Maybe not.'

'I'll come in tonight, take you home after you close. Wednesday, after things quiet down, I'd like you to come out here. We'll have dinner.'

She managed to smile. 'You cooking?'

He grinned, touched his lips to her brow. 'I'll surprise you.'

'You usually do,' she retorted when he walked away.

She was irritated with herself. Not just for losing a battle, but for cowardice. It was cowardice that had pushed her to start the fight in the first place.

She trudged through the marsh while Rufus raced into the trees, through the thick green undergrowth in hopes of scaring up a rabbit or a squirrel.

She stopped at the curve of what had been known as far back as memory stretched as Bayou Rouse. This mysterious place with its slow-moving, shadowy water, its cypress bones and thick scents, was as much her world as the crooked streets and lively pace of the Quarter.

She'd run in this world as a child, learned the difference between a wren and a sparrow, how to avoid a copperhead nest by its cucumber whiff, how to drop a line and pull up a catfish for supper.

It was the home of her blood, as the Quarter had become the home of her ambition. She didn't come back to it only when her grandmother was feeling blue, but when she herself was.

She caught a glimpse of the knobby snout of an alligator sliding by. It was, she thought, what was under the surface that could take you down, one quick, ugly snap, if you weren't alert and didn't keep your wits about you.

There was a great deal under the surface of Declan Fitzgerald. She'd have preferred if he'd been some spoiled,

165

rich trust-fund baby out on a lark. She could've enjoyed him, and dismissed him when they were both bored.

It was a great deal more difficult to dismiss what you respected. She admired his strength, his purpose, his humor. As a friend, he would give her a great deal of pleasure.

As a lover, he worried the hell out of her.

He wanted too much. She could already feel him sucking her in. And it scared her, scared her that she didn't seem able to stop the process.

Toying with the key around her neck, she started back toward the bayou house. It would run its course, she told herself. Things always did.

She pasted on a smile as she neared the house and saw her grandmother, shaded by an old straw hat, fussing in her kitchen garden.

'I smell bread baking,' Lena called out.

'Brown bread. Got a loaf in there you can take home with you.'

Odette straightened, pressed a hand lightly to the small of her back. 'Got an extra you could take on by the Hall for that boy. He doesn't eat right.'

'He's healthy enough.'

'Healthy enough to want a bite outta you.' She bent back to her work, her sturdy work boots planted firm. 'He try to take one this morning? You've got that look about you.'

Lena walked over, dropped down on the step beside the garden patch. 'What look is that?'

'The look a woman gets when a man's had his hands on her and didn't finish the job.'

'I know how to finish the job myself, if that's the only problem.'

With a snorting laugh, Odette broke off a sprig of rosemary. She pinched at its needle leaves, waved it under her

166

nose for the simple pleasure of its scent. 'Why scratch an itch if someone'll scratch it for you? I may be close to looking seventy in the eye, but I know when I see a man who's willing and able.'

'Sex doesn't run my life, Grandmama.'

'No, but it sure would make it more enjoyable.' She straightened again. 'You're not Lilibeth, *'t poulette.*'

The use of the childhood endearment – little chicken – made Lena smile. 'I know it.'

'Not being her doesn't mean you have to be alone if you find somebody who lights the right spark in you.'

She took the rosemary Odette offered, brushed it against her cheek. 'I don't think he's looking for a spark. I think he's looking for a whole damn bonfire.' She leaned back on her elbows, shook back her hair. 'I've lived this long without getting burned, and I'm going to keep right on.'

'It always was right or left for you. Couldn't drive you to middle ground with a whip. You're my baby, even if you are a grown woman, so I'll say this: Nothing wrong with a woman walking alone, as long as it's for the right reasons. Being afraid she might trip, that's a wrong one.'

'What happens if I let myself fall for him?' Lena demanded. 'Then he has enough of swamp water and trots on back to Boston? Or he just has his fill of dancing with me and finds himself another partner?'

Odette pushed her hat back on the crown of her head, and her face was alive with exasperation. 'What happens if it rains a flood and washes us into the Mississippi? Pity sakes, Lena, you can't think that way. It'll dry you up.'

'I was doing fine before he came along, and I'll do fine after he goes.' Feeling sulky, she reached down to pet Rufus when he butted his head against her knee. 'That house over there, Grandmama, that house he's so set on bringing back, it's a symbol of what happens when two people don't belong in the same place. I'm her blood, and I know.'

'You don't know.' Odette tipped back Lena's chin. 'If they hadn't loved, if Abby Rouse and Lucian Manet hadn't loved and made a child together, you and I wouldn't be here.'

'If they'd been meant, she wouldn't have died the way she did. She wouldn't be a ghost in that house.'

'Oh *chère*.' Both the exasperation and all the affection colored Odette's voice. 'It isn't Abby Rouse who haunts that place.'

'Who, then?'

'I expect that's what that boy's there to find out. Might be you're here to help him.'

She gave a sniff of the air. 'Bread's done,' she said an instant before the oven buzzer sounded. 'You want to take a loaf over to the Hall?'

Lena set her jaw. 'No.'

'All right, then.' Odette walked up the steps, opened the back door. 'Maybe I'll take him one myself.' Her eyes were dancing when she glanced over her shoulder. 'And could be I'll steal him right out from under your nose.'

Declan had every door and window on the first level open. Ry Cooder blasted out of his stereo with his lunging rhythm and blues. Working to the beat, Declan spread the first thin coat of varnish on the newly sanded floor of the parlor.

Everything ached. Every muscle and bone in his body sang with the same ferocity as Ry Cooder. He'd thought the sheer physical strain of the sanding would have worked off his temper. Now he was hoping the necessary focus and strain of the varnishing would do the job.

The rosy dawn hadn't lived up to its promise.

The woman pushed his buttons, he thought. And she knew it. One night she'd wrapped herself all over him in bed, and the next she won't give him more than some conversation on the phone.

Snaps out in temper one minute, melts down to sexy teasing the next. Trying to turn the night they'd spent together into the classic one-night stand.

Fuck that.

'Aw, *cher*, what you wanna get all het up about?' he muttered. 'You haven't seen het up, baby. But you're going to before this is done.'

'You look to be in the middle of a mad.'

He spun around, slopping varnish. Then nearly went down to his knees when he saw Odette smiling at him from the doorway.

'I didn't hear you come in.'

'Not surprising.' With the privilege of age, she leaned down and turned down the volume on his portable stereo as Cooder switched pace, lamenting falling teardrops. 'Like Cooder myself, but not that loud. Brought you by a loaf of the brown bread I baked this morning. You go on and finish what you're doing. I'll put it back in the kitchen for you.'

'Just give me a minute.'

'You don't have to stop on my account, *cher*.'

'No. Please. Five minutes. There's … something, I forget what, to drink in the fridge. Why don't you go on back, help yourself?'

'I believe I will. It's a bit close out already, and not even March. You take your time.'

When he'd finished up enough to join her, Odette was standing in front of his kitchen display cabinet, studying the contents.

'My mama had an old waffle iron just like this. And I still got a cherry seeder like the one you got in here. What do they call these dishes here? I can't remember.'

'Fiestaware.'

'That's it. Always sounds like a party. You pay money for these old Mason jars, *cher*?'

'I'm afraid so.'

She clucked her tongue at the wonder of it. 'There's no accounting for things. Damn if they don't look pretty, though. You come look through my shed sometime, see if there's anything in there you want.' She turned now, nodded at the room. 'This is fine, Declan. You did fine.'

'It'll come together when the counters are in and I finish the panels for the appliances.'

'It's fine,' she said again. 'And the parlor where you're working, it's as lovely as it can be.'

'I've already bought some of the furniture for it. A little ahead of myself. Would you like to sit down, Miss Odette?'

'For a minute or two. I've got something from the house you might like to have, maybe put on the mantel in the parlor or one of the other rooms.'

She took a seat at the table he'd moved in, and pulled an old brown leather frame from a bag. 'It's a photograph, a portrait, of Abigail Rouse.'

Declan took it and gazed down on the woman who haunted his dreams. It might have been Lena, he thought, but there was too much softness, too much yet unformed in this face. Her cheeks were rounder, her long-lidded eyes too gullible, and far too shy.

So young, he mused. And innocent despite the grown-up walking dress with its high, fur-trimmed collar, despite the jaunty angle of the velvet toque with its saucy feathers.

170

This was a girl, he reflected, where Lena was a woman.

'She was lovely,' Declan said. 'Lovely and young. It breaks your heart.'

'My grandmama thought she was 'round about eighteen when this was taken. Couldn't've been more, as she never saw her nineteenth birthday.'

As she spoke, a door slammed upstairs, as if in temper. Odette merely glanced toward the ceiling. 'Sounds like your ghost's got mad on, too.'

'That just started happening today. Plumber's kid shot out of here like a bullet a couple hours ago.'

'You don't look like you're going anywhere.'

'No.' He sat across from her as another door slammed, and looked back down at Abigail Rouse Manet's shy, hopeful smile. 'I'm not going anywhere.'

Chapter Eleven

There was a madness about Mardi Gras. The music, the masks, the mayhem all crashing together into a desperate sort of celebration managed to create a tone that was both gleefully innocent and rawly sexual. He doubted the majority of the tourists who flocked here for the event understood or cared about the purpose of it. That rush to gorge on pleasures before the forty days of fasting.

Wanting a taste of it himself, Declan opted to wander through the crowds, even snagged some beads when they were tossed in a glitter of cheap gold from one of the galleries. His ears rang with the blare of brass, the wild laughter.

He decided the sight of naked breasts, which a couple of coeds flashed as they followed tradition and jerked up their shirts, would be less alarming after a couple of drinks.

As would being grabbed by a total stranger and being treated to a tonsil-diving kiss. The tongue currently invading his mouth transferred the silly sweetness of many hurricanes and happily drunken lust onto his.

'Thanks,' he managed when he freed himself.

'Come on back here,' the masked female shouted. '*Laizzez les bon temps rouler!*'

He didn't want to let the good times roll when it involved strange tongues plunged into his mouth, and escaped into the teeming crowds.

Maybe he was getting old, he thought – or maybe it was just the Boston bedrock – but he wanted to get someplace where he could sit back and observe the party rather than being mobbed by it.

The doors to Et Trois were flung open, so the noise from within poured out and tangled with the noise of the streets. He had to weave his way through the revelers on the side-walk, those packed inside, and squeeze his way to a standing spot at the bar.

The place was full of smoke, music and the slap of feet on wood as dancers shoehorned together on the dance floor. Onstage, a fiddler streamed out such hot licks, Declan wouldn't have been surprised to see the bow burst into flame.

Lena was pulling a draft with one hand, pouring a shot of bourbon with the other. The two other bartenders were equally busy, and from what he could see, she had four waitresses working the tables.

He spotted his crawfish grinning from their spot on the shelf behind the bar and was ridiculously pleased.

'Beer and a bump,' she said and slid the glasses into waiting hands. When she spotted Declan, she held up a finger, then served three more customers as she worked her way down to him.

'What's your pleasure, handsome?'

'You are. You're packed,' he added. 'In here and out on the sidewalk.'

'Banquette,' she corrected. 'We call them banquettes 'round here.' She'd pulled her hair back, wound purple and gold beads through it. The little silver key dangled against skin dewed with perspiration. 'I can give you a drink, *cher*, but I don't have time to talk right now.'

'Can I give you a hand?'

She pushed at her hair. 'With what?'

'Whatever.'

Someone elbowed in, shouted out a request for a tequila sunrise and a Dixie draft.

Lena reached back for the bottle, shifted to pull the draft. 'You know how to bus tables, college boy?'

'I can figure it out.'

'Redheaded waitress? She's Marcella.' She nodded in the general direction of mayhem. 'Tell her you're hired. She'll show you what to do.'

By midnight, he figured he'd carted about a half a ton of empties into the kitchen, and dumped the equivalent of Mount Rainier in cigarette butts.

He'd had his ass pinched, rubbed, ogled. What *was* it with women and the male behind? Someone ought to do a study on it.

He'd lost track of the propositions, and didn't care to think about the enormous woman who'd hauled him into her lap.

It had been like being smothered by a three-hundred-pound pillow soaked in whiskey.

By two, he was beyond amazement at the human body's capacity for vice, and had revised any previous perception of the skill and endurance required in food-service occupations.

He made sixty-three dollars and eighty-five cents in tips, and vowed to burn his clothes at the first opportunity.

The place was still rolling at three, and he decided Lena hadn't been avoiding him. Or if she had, she'd had a reasonable excuse for it.

'What time do you close?' he asked when he carted another load toward the kitchen.

'When people go away.' She poured bottled beer into the plastic to-go cups, handed them off.

'Do they ever?'

She smiled, but it was quick and distracted as she scanned the crowd. 'Not so much during Mardi Gras. Why don't you go on home, *cher*? We're going to be another hour or more in here.'

'I stick.'

He carried the empties into the kitchen and came back in time to see a trio of very drunk men – boys really, he noted – hitting on Lena and hitting hard.

She was handling them, but they weren't taking the hint.

'If y'all want to last till Fat Tuesday, you gotta pace yourself a bit.' She set to-go cups under the taps. 'Y'all aren't driving now, are you?'

'Hell no.' One, wearing a University of Michigan T-shirt under an avalanche of beads, leaned in. Way in. 'We've got a place right over on Royal. Why don't you come back there with me, baby? Get naked, take a spin in the Jacuzzi.'

'Now, that's real tempting, *cher*, but I've got my hands full.'

'I'll give you a handful,' he said and, grabbing his own crotch, had his two companions howling and hooting.

Declan stepped forward, ran a proprietary hand over Lena's shoulder. 'You're hitting on my woman.' He felt her stiffen under his hand, saw the surly challenge in the Michigan boy's eyes.

Under other circumstances, Declan thought as he sized the kid up – six-one, a toned one-ninety – he might be the type to make his bed every morning, he might visit old ladies in nursing homes. He might rescue small puppies. But right now, the boy was drunk, horny and stupid.

To prove it, Michigan bared his teeth. 'Why don't you just fuck off? Or maybe you want to take it outside, where I can kick your ass.'

Declan's voice dripped with bonhomie. 'Now, why would I want to go outside and fight about it, when all you're doing here is admiring my taste? Spectacular, isn't she? You didn't try to hit on her, I'd have to figure you're too drunk to see.'

'I see just fine, fuckface.'

'Exactly. Why don't I buy you and your pals a drink? Honey, put those drafts on my tab.'

Declan leaned conversationally on the bar, nodded toward the T-shirt. 'Spring break? What's your major?'

Baffled and boozy, Michigan blinked at him. 'Whatzit to ya?'

'Just curious.' Declan slid a bowl of pretzels closer, took one. 'I've got a cousin teaching there, English department. Eileen Brennan. Maybe you know her.'

'Professor Brennan's your cousin?' The surly tone had turned to surprised fellowship. 'She damn near flunked me last semester.'

'She's tough, always scares the hell out of me. If you run into her, tell her Dec said hi. Here's your beer.'

It was past four when Lena let them into her apartment over the bar. 'Pretty smooth with those college jerks, *cher*. Smooth enough I won't give you grief for the "my woman" comment.'

'You are my woman, you just haven't figured it out yet. Besides, they were easy. My cousin Eileen has a rep at the U of M. Odds were pretty good he'd heard of her.'

176

'Some men would've flexed their muscles.' She set her keys aside. 'Gone on outside and rolled around in the street to prove who had the biggest dick.' Weary, she reached up to tug the beads loose as she studied him. 'I guess it's the lawyer in you, so you just talk yourself out of a confrontation.'

'Kid was maybe twenty-two.'

'Twenty-one last January. I carded them.'

'I don't fight with kids. Plus, I really hate having bare knuckles rammed into my face. It seriously hurts.' He tipped her chin up. She looked exhausted. 'Had a long one, didn't you?'

'Going to be a long time till Wednesday. I appreciate the help, sugar. You pulled your weight.'

More than, she thought. The man had slid right into the rhythm of her place and *worked*. Charmed her customers, tolerated the grab-hands, and avoided a potentially ugly situation by using his wit instead of his ego.

The longer she knew him, she reflected, the more there was to know.

She tugged an envelope out of her back pocket.

'What's this?'

'Your pay.'

'Jesus, Lena, I don't want your money.'

'You work, I pay. I don't take free rides.' She pushed the envelope into his hands. 'Off the books, though. I don't want to do the paperwork.'

'Okay, fine.' He stuffed it into his own pocket. He'd just buy her something with it.

'Now, I guess I'd better give you a really good tip.' She wound her arms around his neck, slithered her body up his. Eyes open, she nibbled on his lip, inching her way into a kiss.

His hands ran down her sides, hooked under her hips, then hitched them up until her legs wrapped around his waist. 'You need to get off your feet.'

177

'Mmm. God, yes.'

He nuzzled her neck, her ear, worked his way back to her mouth as he carried her into the bedroom. 'Know what I'm going to do?'

Lust was a low simmer under the bright glory of being off her aching feet. 'I think I have a pretty good notion.'

He laid her on the bed, could almost feel her sigh of relief at being horizontal. He pried off one of her shoes. 'I'm going to give you something women long for.' He tossed the shoe aside, then climbing onto the bed, removed the other.

Weary or not, her face went wicked. 'A sale at Saks?'

'Better.' He skimmed a finger over her arch. 'A foot rub.'

'A what?'

Smiling, he flexed her foot, rubbed her toes, and saw her eyes go blurrier yet with pleasure.

'Mmmm. Declan, you do have a good pair of hands.'

'Relax and enjoy. The Fitzgerald Reflexology Treatment is world famous. We also offer the full-body massage.'

'I bet you do.'

The worst of the aches began to evaporate. When he worked his way up to her calves, overworked muscles quivered with the combination of pain and pleasure.

'Do you take any time off after Mardi Gras?'

She'd been drifting, and struggled to focus at the sound of his voice. 'I take Ash Wednesday off.'

'Boy, what a slacker.' He tapped a careless kiss to her knee. 'Here, let's get your clothes off.'

He unbuttoned her jeans. She lifted her hips, gave a lazy stretch. He doubted she realized her voice was husky, her words slurring. 'What else you got in mind to rub, *cher*?'

He indulged himself by cupping her breasts, enjoyed her easy response, the way she combed her fingers through

178

his hair, met his lips. He tugged her shirt up and away, snapped open the front catch of her bra. Kissed his way down to her breasts while she arched back to offer.

Then he flipped her onto her stomach. She jerked, groaned, then all but melted when he kneaded her neck. 'Just as I thought,' he announced. 'Carry most of your tension here. Me, too.'

'Oh. God.' If she'd had a single wish at that moment, it would've been that he keep doing what he was doing for a full week. 'You could make a good living out of this.'

'It's always been my fall-back career. You've got yourself some serious knots here. Doctor Dec's going to fix you up.'

'I just love playing doctor.'

She waited for him to change the tone, for his hands to become demanding. He was a sweetheart, she thought sleepily. But he was a man.

She'd just take herself a little catnap, and let him wake her up.

The next thing she knew, the sun was beating through her windows. A groggy glance at her bedside clock showed her it was twenty after ten. Morning? she thought blearily. How did it get to be morning?

And she was tucked into bed as tidily as if her grandmother had done the job. Tucked in alone.

She rolled over on her back, stretched, yawned. And realized with a kind of mild shock that nothing ached. Not her neck, not her feet, not her back.

Doctor Dec, she mused, had done a very thorough job. And was probably at home sulking because she hadn't paid his fee. Hard to blame him, when he'd been such a sweetie pie, and she'd done nothing but lie there like a corpse.

Have to make it up to him, she told herself, and crawled out of bed to put coffee on before she hit the shower.

She walked into the kitchen, stared at the full coffeepot on her counter, and the note propped in front of it. Frowning, she picked up the note, switched the pot back to warm as she read.

> *Had to go. Counter guys coming this morning. Didn't know when you'd surface, so I was afraid to leave the pot on. But it's fresh as of seven-ten a.m., that is, if you end up sleeping 'round the clock. By the way, you look pretty when you sleep.*
>
> *I'll give you a call later.*
>
> *Declan.*

'Aren't you the strangest thing,' she muttered as she tapped the note against her palm. 'Aren't you just a puzzlement.'

She needed to stop into the bar to check on her lunch shift, to check on supplies. Then, needing her curiosity satisfied, she drove out to Manet Hall.

The door was open. She imagined he was one of the few who'd lived here who would leave that impressive front door open to whoever might wander in. Country living or no, someone should put a bug in his ear about a security system.

She could hear the racket of workmen from the back of the house, but took her time getting there.

The parlor grabbed her attention. She crouched down, touched her fingers to the glossy floors, and found them hard and dry, and, stepping in, just looked.

He took care, was all she could think. He took care of what was his. Paid attention to details and made them matter.

Color, and wood, the elegant fireplace, the gleam of the windows, which she imagined he'd washed personally.

Just as she imagined he would furnish this room personally – and with care and attention to detail.

She'd never known a man to take so much … bother, she supposed, with anything. Or anyone. And maybe, she was forced to admit, she'd spent too much time with the wrong kind of man.

'What do you think?'

She turned and, framed by the windows, by the light, looked at him as he stood in the doorway. 'I think this house is lucky to have you. I think you see it as it should be, and you'll work to make it come to life again.'

'That's nice.' He crossed to her. 'That's very nice. You look rested.'

'A man's not supposed to tell a woman she looks rested. He's supposed to tell her she looks gorgeous.'

'I've never seen you look otherwise. Today you look rested on top of it.'

'You are the smoothie.' She wandered away, toward the fireplace. She trailed a palm over the mantel, stopped when she came to the brown leather frame holding the photograph of a young woman. 'Abigail,' she whispered, and the ache went into her. Went deep.

'Miss Odette gave it to me. You look like her, a little.'

'No, I never looked as innocent as this.' Compelled, Lena traced a fingertip over the young, hopeful face.

She'd seen the photograph before, had even studied it, point by point, during a period in her life when she'd found the story, the mystery of it, romantic. During a period when she herself had been young enough to see romance in tragedy.

'It's odd,' Lena said, 'seeing her here. Seeing part of me here.'

'She belongs here. So do you.'

She shook that off, and the sorrow those dark, clear eyes coated over her heart. Turning, she gave Declan a long, considering look. Work clothes, she thought, tool belt, a night's stubble. It was getting harder and harder to picture him wearing a pin-striped suit and carrying a fancy leather briefcase.

It was getting harder and harder to picture her life without him in it.

'Why did you leave my place this morning?'

'Didn't you see the note? Counter guys.' He jerked a thumb back toward the kitchen. 'I had to beg and pay extra to get them to schedule me for a Saturday morning. I had to be here.'

'That's not what I meant. You didn't come into the city, work – what was it, about six hours busing tables? – and give me a foot rub because you didn't have anything better to do on a Friday night. You came in for sex, *cher*, and you left without it. Why is that?'

He could feel his temper prick holes in his easy mood. 'You're a piece of work, Lena. You've got a real talent for turning something simple into the complicated.'

'That's because things are rarely as simple as they look.'

'Okay, let's clear it up. I came into the city because I wanted to see you. I bused tables because I wanted to help you. I rubbed your feet because I figured you'd been on them about twelve hours straight. Then I let you sleep because you needed to sleep. Hasn't anyone ever done you a favor?'

'Men don't, as a rule, unless they're looking for one in return. What're you looking for, Declan?'

He gave himself a moment, waiting for the first lash of anger to pass. 'You know, that's insulting. If you're worried about your pay-for-work ethic, I can spare about twenty minutes now. We can go up, have sex, even the score. Otherwise, I've got a lot to do.'

'I didn't mean to insult you.' But she saw, quite clearly, she had. 'I just don't understand you. The men I've known, on an intimate level, would have been irritated by what didn't happen between us this morning. I expected you to be, and I wouldn't have blamed you. I would've understood that.'

'It's harder for you to understand that I could care about you enough to put sex on the back burner so you could get a few hours' sleep?'

'Yes.'

'Maybe that's not insulting. Maybe that's just sad.' He saw the color deepen in her cheeks as the words bit her. Embarrassed color, he realized. 'Everything doesn't boil down to sex for me. It helps things percolate, but it's not all that's in the pot.'

'I like knowing where I stand. If you don't know where you stand, you can't decide if that's where you want to be, or which direction you'd like to go from there.'

'And I'm fucking up your compass.'

'You could say that.'

'Good. I'm a pretty agreeable guy, Lena, but I'm not going to be lumped in with others you've dealt with. In fact, you won't deal with me at all. We'll deal with each other.'

'Because that's the way you want it.'

'Because that's the way it is.' His tone was flat, final. 'Nothing between us is like, or going to be like, anything either of us has had before. You may need some time to get used to that.'

'Is this how you get your way?' she demanded. 'By listing off the rules in that annoyingly reasonable tone.'

'Facts, not rules,' he corrected in what he imagined she would consider that annoyingly reasonable tone. 'And it's

183

only annoying because you'd be more confident having a fight. We've already eaten into the twenty minutes we could've earmarked for sex. Good sex, or a good fight, take time. I'm going to have to take a rain check on both.'

She stared at him, tried to formulate any number of withering remarks. Then just gave up and laughed. 'Well, when you cash in your rain checks, let's do the fight first. Then we can have make-up sex. That's like a bonus.'

'Works for me. Do you have to get right back, or have you got a few minutes? I could use a hand hauling in and unrolling the rug I've got for in here. I was going to snag one of the counter guys, but with what I'm paying them, I'd as soon they stick with the counters.'

'Pinching pennies now? And you with all those big tubs of money.'

'You don't keep big tubs of money if you let yourself get hosed. Besides, this way I'd get to keep you here and look at you a little while longer.'

'That's clever.' And the fact was, she wanted to stay, wanted to be with him. 'All right, I'll help you with your rug before I go. Where is it?'

'Next parlor.' He gestured to the connecting doors. 'I've got most of what I've bought so far stuffed in here. I'm working in the library next, so I can clean out what goes in the front parlor and in there before I start on this one.'

Lena moved to the pocket doors he opened, then just goggled. Aladdin's cave, she thought, outfitted by a very rich madman with very eclectic taste. Tables, sofas, carpets, lamps, and what her grandmother would call doodads were spread everywhere.

'God Almighty, Declan, when did you get all this?'

'A little here, a little there. I tell myself no, but I don't listen. Anyway' – he began to pick his way through the narrow aisles his purchases formed – 'it's a big house. It needs lots of … stuff. I thought about sticking with the era when the house was originally built. Then I decided I'd get bored. I like to mix things up.'

She spotted a brass hippo on what she tagged as a Hepplewhite side table. 'Mission accomplished.'

'Look at this lamp.' He ran his fingers over the shade of a Tiffany that exploded with gem colors. 'I've got a weakness for lamps.'

'*Cher*, looking 'round here, I'd say you've got a weakness for every damn thing.'

'I sure have one for you. Here's the rug.' He patted the long, rolled carpet leaning against the wall. 'I think we can drag it, snake it through. I should've put it closer to the door, but I wasn't sure where I was going to use it when I bought it. Now I am.'

Between them, they managed to slide it to the floor, then with Declan walking bent over and backward, they wove it around the islands of furniture. He had to stop once to move a sofa, again to shove a table aside.

'You know,' Lena said as they both went down on their knees, panting a little, in the parlor, 'in a couple months you're going to be rolling this up again. Nobody leaves rugs down through the summer around here. Too damn hot.'

'I'll worry about that in June.'

She sat back on her heels, patted his cheek. '*Cher*, you're going to start thinking summer before April's over. Okay.' She pushed up her sleeves, put her palms on the roll. 'Ready?'

On their hands and knees, they bumped along, pushing the carpet, revealing the pattern. She could catch only glimpses of the colors and texture, but it was enough to see why he wanted it here.

The greens of leaves were soft, like the walls, and blended with faded pink cabbage roses against a deeper green background. Once it was unrolled, she got to her feet to study the effect while he fussed with squaring it up.

'You bought yourself a rose garden, Declan. I can almost smell them.'

'Great, huh? Really works in here. I'm going to use the two American Empire sofas, and I think the Biedermeier table. Start with those, then see.' He looked up at the ceiling medallion. 'I saw this great chandelier – blown glass, very Dale Chuhuly. I should've bought it.'

'Why don't we see how your sofas do first?'

'Hmm? Oh, they're heavy, I'll get Remy to give me a hand with them later. He's supposed to come by.'

'I'm here now.'

'I don't want you to hurt yourself.'

She merely shot him a look and started back into his makeshift storeroom.

They'd just set the second one in place, she'd only stepped back to ponder the arrangement, when she heard the baby crying.

She glanced over at Declan, but he seemed lost in thought.

'Did one of your counter men bring a baby with him?' she asked, and Declan closed his eyes, sank down on the sofa.

'You hear it? Nobody else hears it. The doors slamming, yeah. And water running when there's nobody in the room to turn on the taps. But nobody hears the baby.'

A chill whipped up her back, had her glancing uneasily toward the hallway. 'Where is it?'

'The nursery, mostly. Sometimes in the bedroom on the second floor. Abigail's room. But usually the nursery.

It stops when I get to the door. Remy's been here twice when it started. He didn't hear it. But you do.'

'I have to see. I can't stand hearing a baby crying that way.' She walked into the foyer, started up the stairs. And it stopped.

For an instant, it seemed the whole house hushed. Then she heard the clamor from the kitchen, the stream of music from a radio, the hum of men's voices as they worked.

'That's so strange.' She stood on the staircase, one hand on the banister. And her heart thumping. 'I was thinking, I wanted to pick up the baby. People say you need to let babies cry, but I don't know why they should. I was thinking that, and she stopped crying.'

'It's weird, isn't it, that you were thinking about picking-ing up your great-great-grandmother? It's Marie Rose,' he said when Lena turned on the stairs to look down at him. 'I'm sure of it. Maybe you can hear her because you're blood. I guess I can because I own the house. I have a call in to the previous owners. I wanted to ask them, but they haven't gotten back to me.'

'They may not tell you.'

'Well, they can't tell me if I don't ask. Does it scare you?'

She looked up the stairs again and asked herself the same question. 'I guess it should, but no, it doesn't. It's fascinat-ing. I think—' She broke off as a door slammed upstairs. 'Well, no baby did that.' So saying, she ran upstairs.

'Lena.' But she was already rounding the curve to the landing and gave him no choice but to bolt after her.

Marching down the hall, she flung doors open. As she reached Abigail's room, the cold swept in. The shock of it had her breath huffing out. Mesmerized by the vapor it caused, she wrapped her arms tightly over her chest.

'This isn't like the baby,' she whispered.

'No. It's angry.' When he laid his hands on her shoulders to warm her, to draw her away, the door slammed in their faces.

She jumped — she couldn't help it. And heard the nerves in her own strangled laugh. 'Not very hospitable, this ghost of yours.'

'That's the first time I've seen it.' There was a hard lump at the base of his throat. His heart, Declan thought as he took two steadying breaths. 'Whoever it is — was — is seriously pissed off.'

'It's Abigail's room. We Cajuns can have fierce tempers if we're riled.'

'It just doesn't feel like a girl's anger. Not that pretty young thing in the photograph downstairs.'

'A lot you know about girls then, *cher*.'

'Excuse me, I have a sister, and she can be mean as a scalded cat. I meant it feels more ... full-blown. More vicious.'

'Somebody killed me and buried my body in some unmarked grave, I'd be feeling pretty vicious.' Lena made herself reach out, grip the icy knob. 'It won't turn.'

Declan laid his hand over hers. The cold swept out again; the knob turned easily. And when they opened the door, there was only an empty room, full of sunlight and shadows.

'It's a little scary, isn't it?' But she stepped over the threshold.

'Yeah, a little bit.'

'You know what I think, *cher*?'

'What?'

'I think that anybody who stays in the house alone, night after night, who goes out and buys rugs and tables and lamps for it ...' She turned around and slid her arms

188

around his waist. 'I think a man who does that has big steel balls.'

'Yeah?' Reading invitation, he lowered his head and kissed her. 'I could probably carve out another twenty minutes for that sex now.'

She laughed and gave him a hard hug. 'Sorry, sugar. I've got to get on back. Saturday night's coming on. But if you happened to be in the neighborhood, say, at three, four in the morning, I think I could stay awake long enough to …' She cupped her hand between his legs and stroked over denim. 'Stay awake long enough to give those big, steel balls a workout.'

He managed not to whimper, but it was a close call. 'Wednesday,' he told her. 'When you're clear.'

She still had her hand between his legs, could feel the hard line of him. 'Wednesday?'

'When you're clear.' But he did crush his mouth to hers to give her some taste of what he was feeling. 'Come out here. We'll have dinner. And stay.' He backed her against the wall. Used his teeth on her. 'Stay the night. I want you in my bed. Wednesday. Tell me you'll come out and be with me.'

'All right.' She wiggled free. Another few minutes of that, she thought, they wouldn't wait till Wednesday and she'd have him right here on the floor. 'I have to get back. I shouldn't have stayed so long.'

She looked up and down the hall as she stepped out of the room. 'I don't believe I've ever spent the night in a haunted house. What time should I come by?'

'Early.'

'I might do that, too. You don't need to see me to the door, *cher*.' She sent him a wicked grin. 'Walking's got to be a little bit of a problem for you, shape you're in just now. You come on into the bar if you change your mind.'

189

She laid a fingertip on her lips, kissed it, then pointed it at him like a gun before she walked away.

It was an apt gesture, Declan thought. There were times a look from her was as lethal as a bullet.

All he had to do was hold out until Wednesday, then he could get shot again.

Chapter Twelve

Rain moved in Saturday night and camped out like a squatter through the rest of the weekend. It kept Declan inside, and kept him alone. With Blind Lemon Jackson playing on his stereo, he started preliminary work on the library.

He built a fire as much for cheer as warmth, then found himself sitting on the hearth, running a finger over the chipped tile. Maybe he'd leave it as it was. Not everything should be perfect. Accidents should be accepted, and the character of them absorbed.

He wanted to bring the house to life again, but did he want to put it back exactly the way it had been? He'd already changed things, and the changes made it his.

If he had the tile replaced, was he honoring the history of the Hall, or re-creating it?

It hadn't been a happy home.

The thought ran through him like a chill, though his back was to the snapping fire.

A cold, cold house, full of secrets and anger and envy. Death.

She wanted a book. Reading was a delight to her — a slow and brilliant delight. The sight of the library, with row after row after row of books, made her think of the room as reverently as she did church.

Now, with Lucian closeted with his father in the study going over the business of land and crops, and the rain drumming against the windows, she could indulge herself in a quiet afternoon of reading.

She wasn't quite accustomed to the time to do as she pleased and so slipped into the room as if it were a guilty pleasure. She no longer had linens to fold, tables to dust, dishes to carry.

She was no longer a servant in this place, but a wife.

Wife. She hugged the word to her. It was still so new, so shiny. As the life growing inside her was new. So new, she had yet to tell Lucian.

Her curse was late, and it was never late. She'd awakened ill three days running. But she would wait, another week. To speak of it too soon might make it untrue.

And oh, she wanted a child. How she wanted to give Lucian a child. She laid a hand on her belly as she wandered along the shelves and imagined the beautiful son or daughter she would bring into the world.

And perhaps, just perhaps, a child would soften Lucian's mother. Perhaps a child would bring joy into the house as the hope for one brought joy to her heart.

She selected Austen's Pride and Prejudice. The title, she thought, spoke to her. Manet Hall had so much of both. She bit her lip as she flipped through the pages. She was a slow, painstaking reader, but Lucian said that only meant she savored the words.

Stumbled over them, she thought, but she was getting better. Pleased with herself, she turned and saw Julian slouched in one of the wine-colored chairs, a snifter in his hand, a bottle by his elbow.

Watching her.

He frightened her. Repulsed her. But she reminded herself she was no longer a servant. She was his brother's wife, and should try to be friends.

'Hello, Julian. I didn't see you.'

He lifted the bottle, poured more brandy into his glass. 'That book,' he said, then drank deep, 'has words of more than one syllable.'

'I can read.' *Her spine went arrow-straight.* 'I like to read.'

'What else do you like, chère?'

Her fingers tightened on the book when he rose, then relaxed again when he strolled to the fireplace, rested a boot on the hearth, an elbow on the mantel.

'I'm learning to ride. Lucian's teaching me. I'm not very good yet, but I like it.' *Oh, she wanted to be friends with him. The house deserved warmth and laughter, and love.*

He laughed, and she heard the brandy in it. 'I bet you ride. I bet you ride a man into a sweat. You may work those innocent eyes on my brother — he's always been a fool. But I know what you are, and what you're after.'

'I'm your brother's wife.' *There had to be a way to take the first step beyond this hate. For Lucian, for the child growing inside her, she took it, and walked toward Julian.* 'I only want him to be happy. I make him happy. You're his blood, Julian. His twin. It isn't right that we should be at odds this way. I want to try to be your sister. Your friend.'

He knocked back the rest of the brandy. 'Want to be my friend, do you?'

'Yes, for Lucian's sake, we should—'

'How friendly are you?' *He lunged toward her, grabbed her breasts painfully.*

The shock of it froze her. The insult flashed through the shock with a burning heat. Her hand cracked across his cheek with enough force to send him staggering back.

'Bastard! Animal! Put your hands on me again, I'll kill you. I'm Lucian's. I'm your brother's wife.'

'My brother's whore!' he shouted as she ran for the door. 'Cajun slut, I'll see you dead before you take what's mine by rights.'

Raging, he shoved away from the mantel. The heavy silver candlestick tumbled off, smashed against the edge of the tile, snapped off the corner.

Declan hadn't moved. When he came back to himself he was still sitting on the hearth, his back to the snapping fire. The rain was still beating on the ground, streaming down the windows.

As it had been, he thought, during the … vision? Fugue? Hallucination?

He pressed the heel of his hand between his eyes, where the headache speared like a spike into his skull.

Maybe he didn't have ghosts, he thought. Maybe he had a goddamn fucking brain tumor. It would make more sense. Anything would make more sense.

Slamming doors, cold spots, even sleepwalking were byproducts of the house he could live with. But he'd seen those people, inside his head. Heard them there – the words, the tone. More, much more disturbing, he'd felt them.

His legs were weak, nearly gave way under him as he got to his feet. He had to grip the mantel, his fingers vising on so that he wondered the marble didn't snap.

If something was wrong with him, physically, mentally, he had to deal with it. Fitzgeralds didn't bury their heads in the sand when things got tough.

Figuring he was as steady as he was going to get, he went into the kitchen to hunt up aspirin. Which, he decided as he shook out four, was going to be like trying to piss out a forest fire. But he gulped them down, then ran the cold glass over his forehead.

He'd fly up to Boston and see his uncle. His mother's baby brother was a cardiologist, but he'd know the right neurosurgeon. A couple of days, some tests, and he'd know if he was crazy, haunted or dying.

He started to reach for his phone, then stopped and shook his head. Crazy, he thought, just got one more point. If he went to Uncle Mick, word of his potential medical problems would run through the family like an airborne virus.

Besides, what was he running back to Boston for? New Orleans had doctors. He'd get the name of Remy's. He could tell his friend he just wanted to get a doctor, a dentist and so on in the area. That was logical.

He'd get himself a physical, then ask the doctor to recommend a specialist. Simple, straightforward and efficient.

If ghosts couldn't drive him out of Manet Hall, damn if a brain tumor would.

As he set the glass down, a door slammed on the second floor. He simply glanced up at the ceiling and smiled grimly.

'Yeah, well, I'm in a pretty crappy mood myself.'

By Wednesday, he had a handle on things again. Maybe it was the anticipation of seeing Lena that lifted his spirits – in combination with the work he'd managed to get done on those last days before Lent. He had an appointment with Remy's doctor the following week and, having taken that step, was able to put most of the concern about the state of his brain aside.

There had been no more fugues. At least, he thought, none he was aware of.

The rain had finally moved on to plague Florida, and had left him with the first tender trumpets of daffodils scattered along one of his garden paths.

The morning weather report had detailed a ten-inch snowfall in Boston.

He immediately called his mother to rub it in.

Sunshine and the tease of spring had him switching gears earlier than he'd intended. He postponed work on the library and set up outdoors to reinforce the second-floor gallery, to replace damaged boards.

He listened to Ray Charles, and felt healthy as a horse. He was going to have the Franks do most of the early planting, he decided. He just didn't have time. But next year, he'd do his own. Or as much as he could manage.

Next spring, he'd sit out here on the gallery on Sunday mornings, eating beignets, drinking café au lait – with Lena. Long, lazy Sundays, looking out over the lawns, the gardens. And a few years down the road, looking out at the kids in the yards, in the gardens.

He wanted a family of his own, and it was good to know it. He'd never had that need inside him before, the need to hold onto the now and look to tomorrow at the same time.

So he knew it was right, what he felt for her. What he planned for them. He'd help her in the bar if she needed it, but he'd have his own work.

He turned his hands over, studied the palms, the calluses he'd built. The little nicks and scars he looked on as personal medals of valor.

He'd use them, his back and his imagination, to transform other houses. People in the parish would think of Declan Fitzgerald when they needed a contractor.

You should've seen that old house before he got ahold of it, they'd say. You need the job done, you just call Dec. He'll fix you up.

The idea made him grin as he ripped out the next rotten board.

By four, he'd finished the long front sweep of the gallery floor and stretched out on it, belly down, to take a break. He fell asleep with B. B. King pleading with Lucille.

And was sleeping still when he rose and walked down the shaky, sagging curve of stairs to the front lawn.

The grass was thick under his feet, and the heat of the sun poured over his face, beat down on his head despite the hat he wore as protection.

The others were inside, but he'd wanted to look at the pond, at the lilies. He'd wanted to sit in the shade of the willow that danced over the water, and read.

He liked the music of the birds, and didn't mind the heat so much. The heat was honest. The air inside the Hall was cold and false.

It was heartbreaking to watch the house he loved rotting away from bitterness.

He stopped at the edge of the pond, looking down at the green plates of the pads, the creamy white lilies that graced them. He watched a dragonfly whiz by, the sun glinting off the wings so it was an iridescent blur. He heard the plop of a frog and the call of a cardinal.

When he heard his name, he turned. And smiled as his beloved crossed the velvet lawn toward him. As long as they were together, he thought, as long as they loved, the Hall would stand.

'Declan. Declan.'

Alarmed, Lena gripped his arms and shook. She'd seen him coming down those treacherous stairs as she'd driven down his lane, and how he'd walked toward the pond in an awkward, hesitant gait so unlike his usual easy stride.

His eyes were open but glazed in a way that made her think he was looking through her and seeing something – someone – else.

'Declan.' She kept her voice firm, and her hands, as she took his face in them. 'Look at me now. Hear me? It's Lena.'

'Let's sit under the willow where no one can see us.'

There was no willow, only the rotted stump of one. Fear tickled the back of her throat, but she swallowed it. Going with instinct, she rose up on her toes and laid her lips warmly on his.

His response was slow, dreamy, a kind of sliding to her. Against her. Into her. So she knew the instant he snapped back by the way his body stiffened. He started to sway, but she held on.

'Steady now, *cher*. You just hang onto me till you get your legs under you.'

'Sorry. Need to sit.' He dropped straight down on the grass, laid his brow on his knees. 'Whoa.'

'You're okay now. You're fine now.' She knelt beside him, brushing at his hair and murmuring in Cajun – her language of comfort. 'Just get your breath back.'

'What the hell's wrong with me? I was on the gallery. I was working on the gallery.'

'Is that the last thing you remember?'

He looked up now, over the pond. 'I don't know how I got out here.'

'You walked down the stairs, the ones on the right of the house. I thought you were going to go straight through them.' Her heart still hitched when she thought of how unsteady they were. 'They don't look safe, Declan. You ought to block them off.'

'Yeah.' He scrubbed his hands over his face. 'Lock myself in a padded room while I'm at it.'

'You're not crazy.'

'I'm sleepwalking – in the daylight now. I'm hallucinating. I'm hearing voices. That doesn't sound sane to me.'

'That's just the Yankee talking. Down here that doesn't even come up to eccentric. Why, my great-aunt Sissy has whole conversations with her husband, Joe, and he's been dead for twelve years come September. Nobody thinks she's crazy.'

'What do they talk about?'

'Oh, family business, current events, the weather. Politics. Great-Uncle Joe dearly loved complaining about the government. Feeling better now, *cher*?'

'I don't know. What did I do? What did you see me do?'

'You just came down the stairs and walked across the grass toward the pond. You weren't walking like you, so I knew something was wrong.'

'What do you mean?'

'You've got a smooth, lanky kind of gait, and you weren't moving like that. Then you stopped at the pond.'

She didn't tell him she'd had one shocked moment when she'd been sure he meant to walk straight into the water.

'I kept calling you. And finally you turned around and smiled at me.' Her stomach muscles tightened as she remembered. 'But not *at* me. I don't think you were seeing me. And you said you wanted to sit under the willow, where no one could see us.'

'There's no willow here.'

'Well.' She pointed toward the stump. 'There was, once. Seems like you're having dreams where maybe you can see things that happened before. That's a kind of gift, Declan.'

'Where do I return it?' He shook his head. 'I don't know, because I can't remember once I wake up. But I'm starting to think I should tie myself to the bedpost at night.'

'I can take care of that for you tonight.'

'You trying to cheer me up with bondage fantasies?'

'How'd I do?'

'Pretty good.' He let out a breath, then frowned at the smudge on her forehead. 'You've got some soot or something,' he began, and she tipped her head back before he could rub at it.

'Those are my holy ashes.'

'Oh, right.' His brain had definitely gone on holiday. 'Ash Wednesday. I not only don't know where I am, but when I am.'

She couldn't bear to watch him sink into the dark again, and kept her voice brisk, just a little lofty. 'I take it you didn't get to church today, on this holy day of obligation.'

He winced. 'You sound like my mother. I forgot. Sort of.'

She arched an eyebrow. 'Seems to me you could use all the blessings you can get.' So saying, she rubbed her thumb on the print of ash on her forehead, then rubbed it on his. It made him smile.

'That's probably sacrilegious, but thanks. What time is it?' He looked at his watch and swore. 'I have to get this sucker into the shop. It keeps stopping on me. I know it's past noon, and it sure isn't midnight.'

'It's about five. You did say to come early.'

'Yeah, I did. Why don't we go sit out back and have some wine?'

She watched him closely for the first few minutes, but he appeared to be steady again as he selected a wine. Got some lovely old stemware out of his new cupboards.

He'd frightened her, Lena could admit, and badly. She'd been certain he'd intended to walk into the water, to drown himself among the lily pads just as Lucian Manet had done.

And with the realization, a whole new realm of possibilities opened in her mind. 'Declan ...'

'I got steaks and I got a grill,' he said as he poured the wine. He needed to focus on ordinary things – to steep himself in the here and now. 'All real men can grill steaks. If you tell me you don't eat red meat, we're going to have to go for the frozen pizza.'

'If I eat meat, why should I care what color it is? Let's go out and sit. I've got an idea I want to run by you.'

They walked to the two wooden crates he was using for chairs and sat.

'What if it's not ghosts. Or not only ghosts?' she asked him.

'Oh, that's a cheering thought. What else have I got? Vampires? Werewolves? Maybe some flesh-eating zombies. I'm going to sleep much better now, thanks.'

'What do you think about reincarnation?'

'Past lives? Recycling souls?' He shrugged his shoulders. 'I don't know.'

'It always seemed efficient to me – and fair, too. Everybody deserves more than one chance, don't you think? Maybe you're remembering things that happened here because you lived here before. Maybe you're Lucian, come back after all these years for his Abigail.'

'That's a romantic notion. I'll be Lucian if you'll be Abby.'

'You don't get to choose. And if you're going to make fun of the idea, I won't say another word about it.'

'Okay, don't get testy.' He sipped his wine, brooded into space. 'So your theory is I'm here, and these things are happening because I lived a past life, as Lucian Manet.'

'It's no more far-fetched than the place being haunted, which you swallowed easy enough. It would explain why you bought this place, needed it. Why you're working so hard to restore its beauty. How you saw the furniture in his bedroom upstairs.'

'Reincarnation,' he repeated. 'Sounds better than a brain tumor.'

'What?'

He shook his head, drank again. 'Nothing.'

'You're thinking you got a tumor in your brain? That's nonsense, Declan.' Her voice was sharper than she'd intended, so she continued more gently. 'That's just non-sense, *cher*. There's not a thing wrong with your head or any other part of you.'

'Of course not. I was just thinking out loud.'

But she saw it on his face and, rising, slid onto his lap, straddling him. 'You're really worried you've got something inside your head making you see things, do things?'

'I'm not worried. I'm just … Look, I'm going to have some tests, eliminate the possibility.'

'You're not sick, *cher*.' She touched her lips to his cheek, then the other. There'd never been another man who'd so consistently, so effortlessly, nudged out her tender side. 'I guarantee it. But if having some fancy doctor tell you the same thing settles your mind, that's fine.'

'Don't mention this to Remy.' He took her hand until she eased back to meet his eyes. 'He's got the wedding coming up. That's enough for him to think about right now.'

'So, you're planning on going to have brain tests all by yourself? That's not the way we do things around here, *cher*. You don't want Remy to know, all right. But you tell me when this is set up for, and I'll go with you.'

'Lena, I'm a big boy.'

'You're not going by yourself. So I go with you, or I tell Remy and we gang up on you.'

'Okay. I'll let you know when it's scheduled and you can hold my hand. In the meantime, I'm going to put my money on your reincarnation theory. It's weird, but it's a lot less messy than brain surgery.'

'They say Lucian Manet was a handsome man, like a young golden god.' She trailed her fingers through Declan's disordered hair. It was a dark blond, she mused, thick, lush, and she bet it would streak up sexily with the summer sun. 'I think you've improved on him this time around.'

'Oh yeah?' He hooked his arms around her waist. 'Tell me more.'

'I never much cared for the golden-god type. Usually too pretty for my taste.' She cocked her head, eased forward to kiss him. 'You suit my taste, *cher*.'

He brought her closer and, sitting on the wooden crate, rested his chin on her shoulder as he looked out over the gallery railings. 'I love you, Lena.'

'If you're trying to sweet-talk me into bed before you feed me—'

He drew her back, and the grin faded from her face as she saw his. 'I love you,' he repeated. 'I never understood what that meant before, and I didn't think I could.'

He held her in place when she tried to scramble up and away. 'You need to settle down now,' she told him.

'Yeah, I do – but I don't think you mean it the same way. I need to settle down, right here, with you. I don't care if it's the first time or the fiftieth time we've gone around. You're what I've been waiting for.'

'Declan, you're making more out of this than you should.' Her voice wanted to shake. God knew, her stomach already was. 'We went out to dinner. We went to bed. We've seen each other a handful of times.'

'It only took one look at you.'

His eyes were so deep, she thought, so clear. Like the surface of a lake at twilight. 'You don't even know me.'

He pulled her back a second time, reminding her that there was steel in him, and an edge to it. 'You're wrong. I know you're smart, and you're strong. Enough to carve out your own place from almost nothing. I know you pay your debts. I know you're loyal and you're loving. I know somebody hurt you, and it wouldn't take much to knock the scab off. And I know I'm scaring you right now because you don't think you're ready to hear what I'm saying to you.'

The beat of her heart was painful, like the strike of a fist on a raw wound. 'I'm not looking for love, Declan. I'm sorry.'

'Neither was I, but there you go. We don't have to rush it. I wasn't going to say anything to you yet but … I needed to.'

'*Cher*, people, they fall in and out of love all the time. It's just a dazzle of chemicals.'

'He really hurt you.'

Frustrated, she pushed away, and this time he let her go. 'You're wrong. There's no man, no ghost of some lover who broke my heart. I look like a cliché to you?'

'You look like everything to me.'

'*Mon Dieu*.' The man made her throat fill up, then snap shut. Deliberately she fought back the sensation and spoke clearly. 'I like you, Declan, and I enjoy your company. I want you in bed. If that's not enough for you, I walk now and save us both a lot of trouble and disappointment.'

'Do you always get so pissed off when somebody tells you he loves you?'

No one ever had, she nearly said. No one ever had who meant it. 'I don't like being pushed, and when I am, I make a point of not going in that direction.'

'I have to admire that.' His grin was easy as he got to his feet. 'I like you, too, Lena. And I enjoy your company, want you in bed. That's enough for now. Are you hungry? I think I'll heat up the grill.'

If it was a trick, Lena thought, or some sort of strategy to keep her off balance, it was well done.

She just couldn't quite puzzle the man out, and his seamless shift of moods was a surefire way to push her to keep trying.

He cooked like a man who didn't trust himself in an actual kitchen. Jacketed potatoes on the grill, the steaks. And he sweet-talked her into making the salad.

He didn't say another word about love.

He asked her about work, how her business had done during the two days of rain. He put on music, kept it low, and talked through the kitchen door as the grill smoked and she chopped vegetables.

They might have been casual friends, or the most comfortable of lovers.

They ate in his pretty kitchen, by candlelight. Even the house behaved. Despite it – or perhaps because of it – she stayed on edge throughout the meal.

He took a bakery cake out of the fridge. Lena took one look, sighed. 'I can't.'

'We can save it for later.'

'I can't for forty days. I gave up chocolate for Lent. I've got a powerful taste for chocolate.'

'Oh.' He stuck it back in. 'I've probably got something else.'

'What'd you give up?'

'Wearing women's underwear. It's tough, but I think I can hold out till Easter.'

'You talk like that, I'm going to take my ashes back.' He

205

was making her itchy, she thought. The best way to solve that was to make him itch more. She stepped behind him as he searched his refrigerator, then wrapped her arms around his waist, pressed her body to his. 'You need to give something up, *cher*, something you've got a powerful taste for.'

'It sure as hell isn't going to be you.'

He let her spin him around, shove him back against the refrigerator.

Oh, he knew her, he thought as she used her lips to set off explosions in his bloodstream. He knew she was using sex to keep one step ahead of him. One step back from him.

If she didn't realize he could love her as much as he wanted her, it was up to him to show her.

'In your bed, you said.' Her mouth was reckless, restless as it raced over his face. 'In your bed.'

She pulled him toward the doorway. He nearly pulled her back, toward the kitchen stairs, but decided it might be interesting to take the long way around.

He pushed her against the wall in the hallway, assaulted her throat with his teeth. 'We'll get there.'

He reached down, yanked her shirt up, over her head, threw it aside. Wrapped together, they did a quick vertical roll along the wall, and finally stopped with their positions reversed. With impatient hands she pulled his shirt open so that buttons danced along the floor.

They fought with clothes on their way to the steps. Shoes landed with thumps. Her bra fluttered over the banister, his jeans plopped on the third step.

They were breathless before they reached the landing.

His hands were rough, a workingman's hands now that thrilled as they streaked over her. Her skin came alive.

'Hurry.' She sank her teeth into his shoulder as need raged through her, a firestorm of violent heat that burned away all caution. 'God, hurry.'

He nearly took her where they stood, but he wanted her under him. Bucking, arching.

With his mouth savaging hers, he wrapped his arms around her waist, lifted her two inches off the floor. Something raw and primitive stabbed through him at the knowledge that there was no choice now. No choice for either of them but to mate.

Shadows cloaked them as they moved toward the bedroom.

Cold from doorways seeped out, made her shiver.

'Declan.'

'This is us. This is ours.' As he spoke, his voice a snarl, as he held her, his grip like iron, the cold curled back.

They fell on his bed, a tangle of limbs and urgency. When he plunged into her, her nails dug into his back. Pleasure, dark and desperate, drenched her, the feral glory of it drove her up so that she twined herself around him and matched the furious pace.

No control, nor the desire for it. Only the wild thirst to take and take and take. And with it, the gnawing hunger to give.

She clung to him, riding through the storm of sensation, sprinting up and up toward that jagged brink again.

Dimly, she heard a clock begin to strike in deep, heavy bongs. On the twelfth, she shattered with him.

When he started to shift away, she tightened her grip. 'Mmm. Don't move yet.'

'I'm too heavy for you.' He rubbed his lips at the curve of her throat.

'I like it. I like this.' Lazily, she angled her head so he could work his way up to her jaw. Her body felt used and bruised and wonderfully loose. 'Even better than chocolate cake.'

He laughed and rolled over, taking her with him so she sprawled over his chest. 'There, now I don't have to worry about crushing you.'

'A gentleman to the last.' Content, she settled in. 'I've always liked a clock that chimes the hours,' she said. 'But you need to set it. It's not midnight yet.'

'I know.'

'Sounded like a big, old grandfather clock. Where'd you put it? In the parlor.'

'No.' He stroked a hand over her hair, down her back. 'I don't have a clock that chimes.'

'*Cher*, you absolutely ring my bells, but I heard a clock chime twelve.'

'Yeah, so did I. But I don't have a clock.'

She lifted her head, let out a slow breath. 'Oh. Well then. Does it scare you?'

'No.'

'Then it doesn't scare me, either,' she said, and laid her head back over his heart.

Chapter Thirteen

The best way, in Declan's opinion, to break through the obstacles and opposition to any goal, was not to ram headfirst against them and risk a skull fracture, but to chip away at them. Gradually, reasonably. Relentlessly. Whether it was a lawsuit, a sporting event or a love affair, it was imperative to keep the end in sight in order to select the correct means.

He found out which Mass Lena and her grandmother attended, and at which church. Research was essential in any strategy.

When he slipped into the pew beside them on Sunday morning, he got a long speculative look from Lena, and a conspirator's wink from Odette.

He figured God would understand and appreciate the ploy, and not hold it against him for using Sunday Mass as a means to his end.

But he wouldn't mention the brainstorm to his mother. She was, in Declan's experience, a lot less flexible than the Almighty.

Aiming the leading edge of his charm toward Odette, he talked them into brunch afterward, and got another cool stare from Lena when he gave his name to the hostess. He'd already made reservations for three.

'Sure of yourself, aren't you, *cher*?'

His eyes were the innocent gray of a former altar boy. 'Just prepared.'

'You ain't no Boy Scout, sugar,' she told him.

'Your granddaughter's very cynical,' Declan responded as he offered his arm to Odette.

'What she is, is smart.' Odette patted a hand on his and had her bracelets jangling. 'A woman's got to be about smooth-talking, handsome men. Man who comes into church so he can spend a Sunday morning with a woman, he's pretty smart, too.'

'I thought I'd come in and pray for a while.'

'What'd you pray for?'

'That you'd run away with me to Borneo.'

With a laugh, Odette slipped into the chair Declan held out for her. 'Aren't you the one.'

'Yeah.' He looked directly at Lena. 'I'm going to be the one.'

They settled in with mimosas and the first round from the expansive buffet. While a jazz quartet played Dixieland, Declan told them about the progress on the house.

'I'm going to stick with the outside work as long as the weather holds. Tibald's still dealing with the plastering, and I'm trying to line up a painter for the exterior. I don't want to do that myself. The guy I had paint the parlor came in to take a look at the library, but he left sort of abruptly.'

Declan's expression was rueful as he sipped his mimosa. 'I don't think he's coming back. Tile man, either. He got one bath half done when he packed it in.'

'I can do some asking around for you,' Odette offered.

'I'd appreciate it. But I think I'm going to have to start looking outside the parish or try my hand at some of this stuff myself. Things are getting a little lively at the Hall.'

'Grown men running off because a couple of doors slam.' Lena curled her lips into a sneer. 'Ought to have more spine.'

'It's a little more than that now. Clocks bonging where there aren't any clocks to bong, music playing in empty rooms. When the painter was there, the pocket doors in the library kept opening and closing. Then there was the screaming.'

'What screaming?'

'Tile guy.' Declan smiled wanly. 'Said he heard somebody come in the bedroom door, thought it was me. He's talking away, setting the tiles, listening to what he assumed was me moving around in there. Since I wasn't answering whatever questions he had, he got up, walked in. Nobody there. From what I could get out of him when he was semi-coherent, the bathroom door slammed behind him, the logs caught fire in the fireplace. Then he claims he felt somebody put a hand on his shoulder. I had to peel him off the ceiling when I got up there.'

'What do you think about it?' Odette asked.

'A couple of things. Seems to me the more the work progresses on the house, the more overt and volatile the ... paranormal activity, we'll call it. Especially, well, when I veer off from the original scheme.'

Lena scooped up a forkful of grits – a particular southern culinary custom Declan had yet to get his tastebuds around. 'What do you mean?'

'For example, the plasterwork. The areas where that is going on, things are pretty settled. I'm restoring them, replicating. But in places where I've made changes – bathroom setup, tiles – things get really interesting. It's like whatever's in the house gets royally ticked that we're not sticking with the original plan.'

'Something to think about,' Odette commented.

'I have been. I figure Josephine Manet.' Even here, with Dixieland bright in the air and champagne fizzing, the name coated his belly with dread. 'Mistress of the Hall. You only have to look at her photographs to see that was a woman who didn't like to be crossed. Now, I come along and put my fingerprints all over what's hers.'

'You resolved to living with her?' Odette asked, and watched his jaw firm.

'I'm resolved to living in the Hall, and doing it my way. She wants to kick up a fuss about it, that's her problem.'

Lena sat back. 'What do you figure, Grandmama? Brave or stubborn?'

'Oh, he's some of both. It's a good mix.'

'Thanks, but I don't know how brave it is. It's my house now, and that's that. Still, I think you can't blame a man who doesn't have any more than his time and labor invested for taking a hike. Anyway, Miss Odette, what do you think? Am I tangling with Josephine?'

'I think you've got two opposing forces in that house. The one that brought you there, the one that wants you to go away. It's going to come down to who's strongest.'

She opened her Sunday purse, took out a small muslin bag. 'I made this up for you.'

'What is it?'

'Oh, a little kitchen magic. You just keep that in your pocket. May not help, but it can't hurt.' She picked up her glass again, smiled at it. 'Imagine, drinking champagne for breakfast.'

'Come with me to Borneo, you can bathe in it.'

'*Cher*, I drink enough of this, I may take you up on it.'

'I'll get us another round.'

★

212

He was so sweet with her, Lena thought. Flirting with her grandmother until there was a flush of pleasure on Odette's cheeks throughout the long, lazy meal. He troubled himself for people, she mused. Took the time, made the effort to find out what they might enjoy, then saw to it.

He was attentive, clever, sexy, rich, tough-minded and kind.

And he said he was in love with her.

She believed she understood him well enough to be sure he wouldn't have said it unless he meant it. That's what unnerved her.

For added to those other qualities was a wide streak of honesty. And sheer stubborn grit.

He could make her fall in love with him. She was already halfway there and sliding fast. Every time she tried to dig her heels in, she lost her balance again. The tumble was as worrisome as it was thrilling.

But what would happen when she hit? Once she dropped all the way, there'd be no climbing back out. That was something she understood about herself. Relationships were easy when they didn't matter, or mattered only for the moment.

When they mattered forever, they changed everything.

Things had changed already, she admitted. It had started with that yearning for him inside her. And now with the comfort and challenge she felt when she was with him. With being able to imagine feeling it day after day, year after year.

He'd want promises she was afraid to give.

Not afraid, she corrected, irritated with herself. Reluctant to give. Unwilling to give.

Then she watched him lean over and kiss her grandmother's cheek and was afraid – there was no point in pretending otherwise – that she'd end up giving him anything he asked for.

He courted her. It seemed a particularly appealing southern word to Declan, bringing images of moonlight and porch swings, tart lemonade and country dances.

Throughout March, two things occupied his mind, his time and his plans. Lena and the house.

He celebrated the clear results of his neurological tests by taking the day off to antique. Spring had jump-started the flowers and had pedestrians strolling in shirtsleeves. The carriage horses the tourists loved prancing with bright clip-clops of hooves on pavement.

Summer would drop her heavy hand soon enough, and turn the air to molasses. The thought of it reminded him he had to have the air-conditioning upgraded, and maybe reconsider installing paddle fans in some of the rooms.

He bought with his usual surrender to impulse, brightening the day of several shopkeepers before he stopped in a place called, simply, Yesterday.

It was a hodgepodge of statuary, lamps, vintage accessories and jewelry, with three curtained booths on the side where patrons could buy a tarot card reading.

It was the ring that caught his eye first. The blood-red ruby and ice-white diamond formed two halves of an interlocking heart on a platinum band.

The minute he held it in his hand, he knew he wanted it for Lena. Maybe it was foolish to buy an engagement ring at this point in their relationship. And it was reckless to snatch at something before he'd looked at other options.

But this was the one he wanted to put on her finger. And he decided if a man could buy a house on a whim, he could sure as hell buy a ring.

'I'll take it.'

'It's beautiful,' said the shopkeeper. 'She's a lucky woman.'

'I'm working on convincing her of that.'

'I have some lovely earrings that would complement this. Is ruby her birthstone?' the clerk asked as she showed him a pair of earrings with a dangle of ruby hearts and diamonds.

'I don't know.' But he'd gotten her birthday from Odette to make sure he didn't miss it. 'July?'

'Then it is. Lucky guess.'

'No kidding.' It gave him a little tingle as he looked back at the ring. Some things were meant, he told himself. He lifted one of the earrings. He could already see them on her – just as he imagined the clerk could see *Impulse Buyer* stamped on his forehead.

He leaned on the counter and began to pit Yankee bargaining skills against southern horse-trading.

He figured they'd come to fair terms when her smile was still in place but much less brilliant.

'Will that be all for you today?'

'Yeah, I've got to get going. I'm already—' He broke off when he glanced at his watch and saw it had stopped at twelve again. 'You know, I could use a watch – a pocket watch. Mine's been acting up, and I'm doing a lot of carpentry right now. Probably smashed this one a few times on the job.'

'I've got some wonderful old pocket watches and chains. They're so much more imaginative than the new ones.'

She led him over to another display cabinet, pulled out a drawer and set it on the counter.

'Watches like this tell more than time,' she began. 'They tell a story. This one—'

'No.' The edges of his vision dimmed like smoke. The chatter of voices from other customers faded into a hum. Part of him remained aware enough to know he was sliding away from himself. Even as he tried to stop it, to pull back, he watched his own hand reach out, pick up a gold watch and its loop of chain.

The voice of the shopkeeper hovered around the rim of his consciousness. It was another voice that stabbed through, clear as a bell. Female, young, excited.

For my husband, for his birthday. He broke his. I want to give him something special. This one is so handsome. Can you engrave it?

And he already knew what he would find, exactly what he would find, before he turned the watch over to read the back.

> *To Lucian from his Abby.*
> *To mark our time together.*
> *April 4, 1899*

'Mr. Fitzgerald? Mr. Fitzgerald, are you all right? Would you like some water? You're awfully pale.'

'What?'

'Can I get you some water? Would you like to sit down?'

'No.' He closed his hand tightly over the watch, but the sensation was already fading. 'No, thanks. I'm okay. I'll take this, too.'

More than a little shaken, he headed to Remy's office. He thought some time in the sensible business district, in the rational atmosphere of law, might help settle him down.

More, he wanted a few minutes with a friend who might think he was crazy, but would love him anyway.

'If you'd told me you were coming by,' Remy began as he closed his office door, 'I'd've scooted some stuff around so we could maybe have lunch.'

'I didn't expect to head over this way today.'

'Been shopping again.' Remy nodded at the bag Declan carried. 'Boy, aren't you having anything sent down from Boston?'

'As a matter of fact, I've got some stuff coming down next week. Books mostly,' Declan said as he wandered the office. His gaze skimmed over the law books, the fat files, the memos. All of it, the debris of the lawyer, seemed very distant to him now.

'A few pieces I had in my study up there that should work in the library.'

He picked up a brass paperweight, set it down. Slipped a hand into his pocket, jiggled change.

'You going to tell me what's on your mind, or just pace until you dig a trench in my carpet?' With his suit jacket draped over the back of his chair, his tie loosened, his sleeves rolled up, Remy kicked back in his chair and began to swish a bright green Slinky from palm to palm. 'You're wearing me out.'

'I've told you some of the things that've been happening.'

'Got a firsthand account of them myself when I dropped in on Saturday. I'd still feel better if you told me that piano music we heard was from some radio you forgot to turn off.'

'I guess I'll have to get a piano for the ladies' parlor, since that seems to be the spot. I like to play anyway, when I remember to sit down at one.'

Remy shifted the Slinky to vertical, let the colorful spiral drip into itself. 'So, you came by to tell me you're in the market for a piano?'

'I bought a watch today.'

'And you want to show it off? Want me to call in my assistant, some of the law clerks?'

'It was Lucian Manet's watch.'

'No shit?' The Slinky, sloshed into a whole, was tossed aside. 'How do you know? Where'd you get ahold of it?'

'Little shop in the Quarter.' He drew out the box, set it on Remy's desk. 'Take a look at it.'

Obliging, Remy took off the lid. 'Elegant, if you want something you're going to have to dig out whenever you want to know what time it is. Heavy,' he added when he picked it up.

'You don't … feel anything from it?'

'Feel anything?'

'Look on the back, Remy.'

'Names and dates are right,' Remy concluded. 'Hell of a stroke of luck, you stumbling on this.'

'Luck? I don't think so. I go into a shop, buy Lena a ring, then –'

'Whoa, whoa, whoa, just back up there a minute. A ring?'

'I told you I was going to marry her.' Declan shrugged. 'I found the ring. It doesn't hurt to have it ahead of schedule. But that's not the point.'

'Pretty damn big point, if you ask me. She know you're up to this?'

'I told her how I felt, what I wanted. I'm letting her stew on it awhile. Can we get back to the watch?'

'*Et là*! You always were mule-headed. Go ahead.'

'I walk into that shop, decide I need a watch because mine's acting up. I decide I need a pocket watch even though I've never used one, never thought about using one. Then, I see that one, and I know. I know it was his, I know she bought it for him for his birthday. I know what it says on the back before I read it. Exactly what it says. Because I heard it in my head.'

'I don't know what to think about that.' Remy raked his fingers through his hair. 'Isn't there something about how some people touch an object and get images from it? Its history or whatever?'

'It's called psychometry. I've been doing a lot of reading up on paranormal science in my spare time,' Declan explained when Remy frowned at him. 'But I've never had anything like that happen before. Lena's got a theory. That this is a reincarnation deal.'

Remy pursed his lips, set the watch back in its box. 'I guess I'd be more inclined to put some stock in that rather than the psycho whatever.'

'If it is, then the house, now this watch, are triggering past-life memories. Pretty weird.'

'The whole thing's been weird since the get-go, *cher*.'

'Here's the kicker. If I accept that I was Lucian, then I know Lena was Abigail. What I don't know is if I'm supposed to bring her into the house, to make things right from before. Or if I'm supposed to keep her away from it, and resolve the cycle that way.'

In the Vieux Carre, where Lena prepared to leave her apartment for the bar and the afternoon shift, she opened the door and stepped into another cycle. An old one.

'Baby!' Lilibeth Simone threw open her arms.

Sluggish with shock, Lena was unable to move back before they wrapped around her like chains. Trapped, she was assaulted with impressions. Too much perfume that didn't quite cover the smell of stale smoke, the bony form honed down by years of hard living. Sticky layers of hairspray over curls dyed black as pitch.

And through it all seeped her own dark dread.

'I went downstairs first, and that handsome young man behind the bar said you were still up here. Why, I'm so glad to catch you!' The voice was a bright bubble that bounced and jerked in the air. 'Let me just *look* at you! I swear, I

219

swear you just get prettier every time I see you. Sweetie pie, I just have to sit down a minute and catch my breath. I'm just so excited to see you, I can hardly *stand* it.'

She talked too fast, Lena noted, walked too fast on the spiked backless heels she'd paired with hot-pink and skin-tight capris. Those were warnings that she'd taken a hit of her current drug of choice very recently.

'Look what you've done with this place!' Lilibeth dropped into a chair and dumped a floral suitcase beside her. She clapped her hands like a child so the plastic bracelets on her bony wrists banged together. 'Why, I just love it. Suits you, baby. It sure does suit you.'

She'd been pretty once, Lena thought as she studied her mother. She'd seen pictures. But all that prettiness had been carved down, diamond-hard, to canny.

At forty-four, Lilibeth's face showed all the wear from too much liquor, too many pills and far too many men.

Deliberately, Lena left the door open and remained standing just inside it. The sound of traffic, the scent of the bakery across the street, kept her grounded. 'What do you want?'

'Why, to see you, of course.' Lilibeth let out a trill of laughter that scraped over Lena's brain like nails on a blackboard. 'What a thing to ask. I got such a yen to see you, baby. I said to myself, My Lena's busy, but we've just got to have a little time together. So I got myself on a bus, and here I am. You just have to sit on down here, honey, and tell me everything you've been up to.'

Disgust rolled through her, and Lena clung to it. Better disgust than the despair that crept along just under it. 'I have work.'

'Oh now, you can take a little while for your own mama. After all, you own the place. I'm just so proud of my baby, all grown up and running your own business.

'Doing so well for yourself, too,' she continued as she looked around the room.

Lena caught the look, and the cunning in it. It tightened her chest, and stiffened her spine. 'I told you the last time it was the last time. You won't get any money from me again.'

'Why do you want to hurt my feelings like that?' Lilibeth widened her eyes as they filled with tears. 'I just want to spend a few days with my little girl.'

'I'm not a little girl,' Lena said dully. 'Yours in particular.'

'Don't be mean, honey, after I've come all this way just to see you again. I know I haven't been a good mama to you, darling, but I'm going to make it up.'

She jumped up, pressing a hand to her heart. The nail on the pinkie of her right hand was very long, slightly curved.

Coke nail, Lena realized without shock or regret. Now she knew Lilibeth's current drug of choice.

'I made some mistakes, I know I did, honey.' Lilibeth's voice rang with apology, with regret. 'You gotta understand, I was just so young when you came along.'

'You've used that one up.'

Lilibeth dug into her shiny red purse, pulled out a tattered tissue. 'Why you wanna be so hard on your mama, baby girl? Why you wanna hurt my heart?'

'You don't have a heart. And you're not my mama.'

'Carried you inside me for nine months, didn't I?' Sorrow became temper as if a switch had been flicked. Lilibeth's voice rose, shrilled. 'Nine months of being sick and fat and stuck back that damn bayou. Lay there in pain for hours giving birth to you.'

'And left me within a week. An alley cat spends more time with its litter than you did with me.'

'I was sixteen.'

It was that, the sad fact of it, that had caused Lena to make room, time and time again, in her heart. Until her heart had simply calcified from the blows. 'You haven't been sixteen in quite a while. Neither have I. I'm not going to waste time arguing about it. I have to work, and you have to go.'

'But, baby.' Panicked, Lilibeth shifted, back to the teary, choked voice. 'You've got to give me a chance to make things right. I'm going to get me a job. I can work for you awhile, won't that be fun? I'll just stay here with you for a couple weeks till I find a place of my own. We'll have such a fine time. Just like girlfriends.'

'No, you won't work for me, and no, you can't stay here. I made that mistake four years ago, and when I caught you turning tricks up here, you stole from me and took off again. I don't repeat myself.'

'I was sick back then. I'm clean now, honey, I swear I am. You can't just turn me out.' She held out her hands, palms up, in a gesture of pleading. 'I'm flat broke. Billy, he took almost everything I had and ran off.'

Lena could only assume Billy was the latest in the string of users, losers and abusers Lilibeth gravitated to. 'You're high right now. Do you think I'm blind or just stupid?'

'I'm not! I just took a little something because I was so nervous about seeing you. I knew you'd be mad at me.' Tears spilled out, tracking bits of mascara down her cheeks. 'You just have to give me a chance to make it up to you, Lena honey. I've changed.'

'You've used that one up, too.' Resigned, Lena walked to her purse, counted out fifty dollars. 'Here.' She stuffed it into Lilibeth's hand. 'Take this, get on a bus and ride it as far away as this takes you. Don't come back here again. There's no place for you here.'

'You can't be so mean to me, baby. You can't be so cold.'

'Yes, I can.' She picked up the suitcase, carried it over to the door and set it outside. 'It's in the blood. Take the fifty. It's all you're going to get. And get out, or I swear to God, I'll throw you out.'

Lilibeth marched to the door. The money had already disappeared into her purse. She stopped, gave Lena one last glittering look. 'I never wanted you.'

'Then we're even. I never wanted you, either.' She shut the door in her mother's face. Then flipped the locks, sat down on the floor. And cried in absolute silence.

She was certain she'd smoothed away the edges by the time she drove out to Manet Hall that evening. She'd nearly canceled the dinner plans she had with Declan, but that would have given her mother too much importance.

That would have acknowledged the grief that had slashed its way into her heart despite the locks.

She needed to put her mind to other things, and would never manage it if she stayed at home, brooding. She'd get through the night, hour by hour, and in the morning Lilibeth would be gone. From her life, and from her mind.

The house looked different, she thought. Little changes that somehow made it seem more real. It was good to look at it, to focus on it, and to contemplate that some things could change for the better. With the right vision.

Over the years, she'd come to think of Manet Hall as a kind of dream place, burrowed in the past. More than that, she decided. Of the past.

Now, with new unpainted boards checkerboarded with the old, peeling white, with some windows gleaming and others coated with dust, it was a work in progress.

Declan was bringing it back to life.

Though the front gardens were a bit straggled, a bit

lost, there were flowers blooming. And he'd plopped a huge clay pot full of begonias on the gallery.

He'd have planted them himself, she thought as she walked toward the door. He was a man who liked his hands in things. Especially when he considered them his.

She wondered if he thought of her as one of his works in progress. Probably. She couldn't quite decide if the idea amused or irritated her.

She strolled in. She figured that when two people had slept with each other a time or two, formalities were superfluous.

She smelled the lilies first, the good, strong scent bringing the garden indoors. He'd bought a lovely old table, a couple of straight-back chairs and, she saw with a grin, an enormous ceramic cow for the foyer.

Some would call it foolish, others charming, she supposed, but no one would call the entrance to the old hall sterile any longer.

'Declan?' She wandered in and out of the parlor, noting the few new additions. She circled into the library and found herself crossing to the mantel and the heavy candlesticks standing on it.

Why did her fingers tremble? she wondered as she reached out to touch. Why did those old tarnished candlesticks look so strangely familiar?

There was nothing special about them, really. Expensive perhaps, but too ornate for her taste. And yet … her fingers brushed down each of them, lightly. And yet they looked right here, so right she could imagine the slim white tapers they were waiting to hold once more; she could smell the melting wax.

Shivering, she stepped back and walked out of the room.

She kept calling his name as she started up the stairs. When she reached the first landing, the hidden door in the wall opened. She and Declan choked back simultaneous screams.

With a gasping laugh, she clutched at her heart and stared at him. He had cobwebs in his hair, dirt smeared on his cheek and hands. The flashlight he carried bobbled.

'Lord, *cher*, next time just shoot me and get it over with.'

'Same goes.' He blew out a breath, dragged at his hair and the cobwebs lacing it. 'You scared five years off me.'

'Well, I called out a couple times, then decided I'd just hunt you up.' She peered over his shoulder. 'What've you got here, secret passages?'

'No, servants' access. There are doors on every level, so I thought I'd take a look. It's kind of cool, but a real mess.' He looked down at his filthy hands. 'Why don't you go fix yourself a drink or something? I'll clean up.'

'I might be persuaded to fix us both a drink. What're you in the mood for?'

'Could use a beer.' But he was studying her face now that he'd recovered from the jolt. 'What's wrong, Lena?'

'Nothing, other than you frightening the wits out of me.'

'You're upset. I can see it.'

She tried a suggestive smile. 'Maybe I'm sulking 'cause you don't bother to kiss me hello.'

'Maybe you don't trust me enough yet, and figure all I'm looking for with you is a good time.' He used one knuckle to lift her chin, stared into her eyes until hers began to sting. 'You're wrong. I love you.' He waited a beat, then nodded when she didn't respond. 'I'll be down in a minute.'

She started down the steps, then stopped, speaking without looking back. 'Declan, I don't think you're looking for a good time, but I don't know as I have what it is you are looking for.'

'Angelina. You're what I've looked for all my life.'

★

He didn't press. If she needed to pretend she wasn't upset and skittish, he'd give her room. They took a walk through the rear gardens as dusk crept in.

'This place. All these years, people come, people go. Mostly they go. And here you are, doing more in a few months than anyone's done since before I can remember.'

She turned to study the house. Oh, it still needed work. Wood and paint. New shutters here and there. But it no longer seemed … dead, she realized. It hadn't just been abandoned, it had been dead until he'd come.

'You're bringing it back to life. It's more than the money and the work.'

'Could you live here?'

Her eyes, startled, even panicked, whipped back to his. But his gaze stayed calm and level. 'I have my own place.'

'That's not what I asked. I asked if you could. If you could be comfortable here, or if the idea of sharing the place with … ghosts or memories, whatever you'd call it, would bother you.'

'If it bothered me I wouldn't have come over tonight so you could feed me. Which reminds me, what are you feeding me, *cher*?'

'I'm going to try my hand at grilling tuna.' He pulled his pocket watch out. 'In a bit,' he said after checking the time.

She was mesmerized by the watch in his hand. Her stomach jittered as it had done when she'd seen the candlesticks. 'Where did you get that?'

'I found it at a shop today.' Alerted by her tone, fascinated by it, he held the watch out. 'Look familiar?'

'You just don't see many men using that type of watch anymore.'

'I knew it was mine as soon as I saw it. I think you bought it for me,' he said, and her head jerked up. 'A long time ago.' He turned the watch over so she could read the inscription on the back.

'Lucian's.' Because her instinct was to curl her fingers into her palms, she made herself reach out and touch the engraving. 'Very strange. Strange indeed, Declan. You think I was Abigail?'

'Yeah, I do.'

She shook her head. 'Don't you think that's a little too neat and tidy – and self-serving?'

'Murder, despair, suicide, a century of wandering souls?' He shrugged and slipped the watch back in his pocket. 'Not very tidy, if you ask me. But I think, Lena, that maybe love is patient enough to wait until its time comes around again.'

'God, you are so … appealing. And it's irritating that I have to be the sensible one around here. I like being with you, Declan.'

She toyed with the key on her neck chain as she spoke. A habit, he thought, she was probably unaware of.

'I like your company, I like your looks. And I like making love with you. That's all I have right now.'

He took her into his arms. 'I'll take it.'

Chapter Fourteen

Lena rolled over, slid along one pillow to the other. She heard singing – a deep, male voice in a dreamy refrain. And sighing, she ran her hand over the sheets.

He wasn't beside her in bed, but his warmth was.

Opening her eyes, she blinked against the misty sunlight. She hadn't meant to stay the night. But with Declan, her intentions often twisted around to meet his wishes. More, somehow his wishes circled until they ended up being hers as well.

Clever man, she mused, yawning as she burrowed into the pillow. He rarely seemed to push, never appeared to be unreasonable. And always got his way.

Damned if she didn't admire him for it.

Even now, though she'd have preferred waking in her own bed, she was glad she'd stayed. Her mood had been heavy, and a bit prickly, when she'd arrived. Seeing her mother usually had that effect on her. For a few hours, she'd forgotten about it, and had just enjoyed being with him.

That was enough – and would have to be enough for both of them for as long as it lasted. Seeing Lilibeth was a stark reminder of the promises Lena had made to herself.

To succeed, on her own terms. To live, precisely how she chose to live. And never, never to place her hopes, her needs, her wants in the hands of another.

Declan would move along sooner or later. Everyone did. But she cared more this time, and would make a genuine effort to be and to remain friends.

So, she would be very, very careful not to fall in love with him. Very careful not to hurt him while he believed he loved her.

Her brow creased. She *did* hear singing. In the shower, she realized, Declan's voice over the drum of water.

'*Long years have passed, child – I've never wed, true to my lost love, though she is dead.*'

An odd tune for a man to belt out in the shower, she thought, and found herself singing the refrain with him in her mind. *After the ball is over, after the break of morn.*

Puzzled – where had those lyrics come from? – she rose and went to the bathroom door. She knew the tune, but more, she knew the words. The sad story of lack of faith, of death, melded to the romantic melody.

And her heart was pounding. She felt the pulse of it jump in her throat.

Dancing in the moonlight with the house a white beacon against the night. A girl in faded muslin, and the young man in elegant black tie. The smell of lilacs. Heavy and sweet.

The air's thick with flowers. So thick it's hard to breathe. So thick it makes you dizzy as you spin around and around through the garden, along the bricks with the music playing.

Dizzy, dizzy from the dance. Dizzy, dizzy from the fall into love.

She swayed, reaching out to brace a hand against the door. But it opened, and steam poured out as she fell forward.

'Whoa!' Declan caught her, scooped her off her feet. Still wet from the shower, his hair dripping onto her face, he carried her back to bed.

'I'm okay. I just … lost my balance.'

'Baby, you're white as a sheet.' He brushed her hair back, rubbed her chilled hand between both of his. 'What happened?'

'Nothing.' Torn between confusion and embarrassment, she nudged him back to sit up. 'I got up too fast, is all. Then I lost my balance when I reached for the door and you opened it. I'm fine, *cher. Ça va.* It's just a little early for me to be up and around.'

'I'll get you some water.'

'Sweetheart, don't fuss. Simones aren't swooning sorts.' She ran a finger over his chin. It was all fading away now, the song, the scent of lilacs, the giddy sense of reeling. 'Though that handsome face of yours does take my breath away. You leave any hot water for me?'

'Probably not.' He eased down to sit beside her. 'I've got to replace that water heater. If you give it a half hour, it should come through for another shower.'

'Mmm. Now what could I do with a half hour?' Laughing, she pulled him into bed.

Now that, Lena decided, was a much better way to start the day. She lingered over her first cup of coffee at the little table Declan had set up on the gallery outside his bedroom. As his breakfast pickings were slim at best, she'd settled on a bowl of Frosted Flakes and had watched him load his down with sugar.

'*Cher*, why don't you just have yourself a big old candy bar for breakfast.'

'Don't have one.'

He grinned over at her, and damn it, he *did* take her breath away.

'You've got yourself a nice spot here,' she told him. 'Good morning-contemplation sort of spot.'

'It'll be better when I get some of the boards replaced and it's painted. Needs more stuff, too.' He glanced around. 'Pots, you know, flowers and things. A glider or a swing.'

She spooned up some cereal. 'You're just a homebody, aren't you, *cher*?'

'Looks like.' And it delighted him. 'Who'd've thought?'

'And what does the homebody have planned for today?'

'I want to finish the first section of the exterior stairs. If the weather holds through the weekend, I'll have a good start on the front of the house. I've got guys coming in to start on the other bathrooms. Got some more shopping to do. Want to come with me?'

'I've never seen a man so crazy to shop.' It was tempting to give in to the charming image of hunting with him for treasures. And to have some part in selecting pieces for the house.

And wouldn't that go toward forging another link in making them a couple instead of two people just enjoying the moment?

So she shook her head and denied herself the pleasure. 'Unless this shopping involves looking at shoes or earrings, you're on your own, sugar.'

'I could probably fit that in, between hunting up drawer pulls and hardware. In fact … hang on a minute.'

He rose and went inside while Lena stretched back and, cupping her mug in both hands, looked out over the gardens to the pond.

She'd distracted him, she thought. Or at least he was pretending to be distracted from what had happened that morning. She'd damn near fainted, and that would've been a first.

Something in the house, she mused, was affecting her, just as it did Declan. One side pulling her in, another pushing her out, but she was determined to stand firm.

Was it possible he was right after all? Could it be so perfectly neat? He had been Lucian in a past life, and she his doomed Abigail?

Had they danced in the moonlight to that old, sad song?

If it were true, what did it mean to them now, in this life?

Her face was clear of worry when he stepped out again. And put a small box on the table beside her bowl.

'*Cher*, you keep picking up presents like this, what're you going to do when my birthday rolls around?'

'I'll think of something.'

'Well, I don't think you're going to top my salt and pepper shakers, but ...' She opened the box, expecting to see some cute and foolish pin or silly earrings. Then just stared down at the pair of ruby and diamond hearts.

'They caught my eye.'

'You – you can't give me something like this.' For the first time since he'd known her, she stuttered. 'You can't just – just give me earrings like these. These are real stones. Do you think I'm too stupid to recognize real diamonds?'

'No.' Interesting, he thought, that she'd jump from fluster into temper at the gift of diamonds. 'I thought they'd look good on you.'

'I don't care how rich you are.' She snapped the lid back down on the sparkle of blood and ice. 'I don't care how much money you've got stuffed away in your port-folios and your bank accounts. I don't want you buying me expensive jewelry. If I want diamonds and rubies, then *alors*, I'll buy them for myself. I'm not sleeping with you for baubles and profit.'

'Well, these were a big hit.' He tipped back in his chair to meet her furious eyes, as she'd leaped to her feet as she'd shouted at him. 'So, they'd be okay with you if they were glass? Let me get the ground rules clear. If I see something I'd like to get for you, it has to be, what, under a hundred? One-fifty? Give me a ballpark.'

'I don't need you to buy me things.'

'Lena, if you needed me to buy you things, I'd buy you groceries, for Christ's sake. These were pretty, they made me think of you. And look at this.' He picked up the box, ran his free hand around it. 'No strings attached.'

'Something costs as much as a decent secondhand car's got strings, *cher*.'

'Wrong. Money's relative. I have a lot of it, so deal. You don't want them, fine.' He shrugged, picked up his coffee. 'I'll give them to someone else.'

Her eyes went to slits. 'Oh, will you?'

'They appear to upset your moral balance, but there's no point in them going to waste.'

'You're trying to make me sound like an idiot.'

'No, you're acting like an idiot. I'm just playing my part in your little drama. I'd like you to have them, but not if you're going to think they're payment for services rendered. That's just as insulting to me as it is to you, Lena,' he said when her mouth dropped open. 'Your telling me you don't want payment for sex is telling me I'm willing to buy it from you. They're just goddamn rocks.'

'They're beautiful rocks.' Damn, damn, damn! Why did the man constantly throw her off balance?

And wasn't it just like him, just exactly like him, to sit there, calmly watching her flash and burn?

She took a deep, steadying breath while he looked at her with both patience and amusement. 'I was rude, and I over-reacted. I'm not used to men handing me diamonds and rubies over bowls of cereal.'

'Okay. Want me to wait and give them to you over a nice steak dinner?'

She gave a weak laugh, dragged her hair back. 'You're entirely too good for me.'

'What the hell does that mean?' he demanded.

But she shook her head, then picked up the box. She studied the earrings against their bed of velvet for a long moment before taking them out, putting them on.

'How do they look?'

'Perfect.'

She leaned down, kissed him. 'Thank you. They just scared me a little, but I'm getting over it pretty quick now.'

'Good.'

'I'm going to have to wear my hair back with them. Show them off. Damn it,' she said as she ran for the door. 'I have to see.' She stopped at the mirror, held her hair back with one hand. 'Oh God! They're fabulous. I've never had anything so lovely in my life. You're a sweet man, Declan. A hardheaded, crazy, sweet man.'

'When you marry me,' he said from the doorway, 'I'll give you diamonds for breakfast once a week.'

'Stop that.'

'Okay, but keep it in mind.'

'I've got to get on. I want to stop by and see my grand-mama before I head back.'

'Give me a ride over? I've got something for her.'

Her eyes, when they tracked to his in the glass, were indulgent and just a little frustrated. 'You bought her another present.'

'Don't start on me,' he warned, and stepped back out to gather up the bowls.

'Why do you have to buy things all the time, *cher*?'

She knew him now, and the little ripple movement of his shoulders told her he was annoyed and uncomfortable. So she softened the question by giving him a quick kiss on the cheek.

'I've got money,' he said. 'And I like stuff. You trade money for stuff, which is more fun and interesting than having a bunch of green paper in your wallet.'

'I don't know. Me, I like that green paper just fine. But …' She fingered the diamonds at her ears. 'I could grow mighty fond of these pretty rocks. Go on, get whatever you've gone and bought for Grandmama. Bound to brighten her day, whatever it is, 'cause it's from you.'

'You think?'

'She's sweet on you.'

'I like that.' He turned, wrapped his arms around Lena's waist. 'How about you? You sweet on me?'

A long line of warmth flowed down her spine, nearly made her sigh. 'You make it hard not to be.'

'Good.' He touched his lips to hers, then eased away. 'I like that even better.'

He carried a little gift bag out to her car. It struck her as odd and charming that he would think of things like that. Not just a present, a token he could so easily afford, but the presentation of it. Pretty bags or bows, ribbons or wrappings most men – or men she'd known – would never bother with.

Any woman she knew would call Declan Fitzgerald one hell of a catch. And he wanted her.

'I'm going to ask you a question,' she began as she started the car.

'True or false? Multiple choice?'

'I guess it's more the essay type.'

He settled back, stretched out his legs as best he could as she started down the drive. He'd always aced his tests. 'Shoot.'

'How come with all those fine ladies up in Boston, and all the good-looking women here 'round New Orleans, you zeroed in on me?'

'Not one of them ever made my heart stop, or sprint like a racehorse at the starting gun. But you do. Not one of them ever made me see myself ten years, twenty years down the road, reaching out to take her hand. But you do, Lena. And what I want most in the world is to hold onto you.'

She didn't look at him, didn't dare, as everything inside her seemed to fill up so she knew one glance at his face would have it all spilling out. Warm and sweet and conquered.

'That's a good answer,' she managed.

'It's a true one.' He took one of her tensed hands off the wheel, kissed it. 'God's truth.'

'I think it is. I don't know what to do about it, Declan. You're the first man who's ever made me worry about what to do. I've got powerful feelings for you. I'd rather I didn't.'

'Here's what I think. We should elope to Vegas, then you won't have anything to worry about.'

'Oh, I'm sure the Boston Fitzgeralds would just be thrilled hearing you've eloped to Vegas with a Cajun bar owner from the bayou. That'd set them up right and tight.'

'It'd give them something to talk about for the next decade or two. My mother would like you,' he said, almost to himself. 'And she's no easy mark. She'd like that you're your own woman and don't take any crap off anyone.

236

Run your own business, look after your grandmother. She'd respect that, and she'd like that. Then she'd love you because I do. My father would take one look at you and be your slave.'

She laughed at that and it loosened some of the tightness in her chest. 'Are all the Fitzgerald men so easy?'

'We're not easy. We just have exceptional taste.'

She pulled up in front of Odette's house, and finally turned to look at him. 'Any of them coming down for Remy and Effie's wedding?'

'My parents are.'

'We'll see what we see, won't we?'

She hopped out, headed to the door ahead of him. 'Grandmama!' She bumped the door open and strolled in. 'I brought you a handsome gentleman caller.'

Odette came out of the kitchen, wiping her hands on a red checked cloth. The smells of fresh coffee and baking followed her. She was, as always, decked out in layers of jewelry and sturdy boots. But there was a strain around her eyes and mouth even Declan spotted instantly.

'A gentleman caller's always welcome. *Bébé*,' she replied and kissed Lena's cheek.

'What's wrong?'

'Baked me some brown bread this morning,' Odette said, evading Lena's question. 'Y'all come back to the kitchen.' She wrapped an arm around Lena's waist to nudge her along. 'What you got in the pretty bag, *cher*?'

'Just a little something I thought you'd like.' In the kitchen, Declan set it on the table. 'Smells fabulous in here. Maybe I ought to learn how to bake bread.'

Odette smiled as he'd hoped she would, but the tension in the air didn't lessen. 'Could be I'll teach you a thing or two. Kneading dough's good therapy. Takes your mind off your troubles, gives you thinking time.'

She took the small wrapped box out of the gift bag, turned it in her hand, then tugged the ribbon free. 'Lena, you don't nail this boy down, I may just snatch him for myself.' When she opened the box, her face softened.

The trinket box fit into the palm of her hand. It was heart-shaped and hand-painted with a couple in old-fashioned formal dress sitting on a garden bench. When she lifted the lid, it played a tune.

'I've been hearing that song in my head for weeks,' Declan told her. 'So when I saw this, I figured I'd better buy it.'

'"After the Ball,"' Odette told him. 'It's an old waltz. Sad and sweet.' She looked up at him. 'Maybe you got a nice widowed uncle you could send my way.'

'Well, there's Uncle Dennis, but he's homely as a billy goat.'

'He's got half your heart, I'll take him.'

'Isn't this a pretty picture?'

At the voice, Lena went stiff as if someone had pressed a gun to her head and cocked the hammer. Declan saw the look pass between her and her grandmother. Apologetic on Odette's part, shocked on Lena's.

Then they turned.

Lilibeth slumped against the doorjamb. She wore a short red robe, loosely belted. Her hair was a tumble around her shoulders, and her face already made up for the day with her eyes darkly lined, her lips slick and red as her robe.

'And who might this be?' She lifted one hand, languidly pushed back her hair as she sent Declan a slow, feline smile.

'What's she doing here?' Lena demanded. 'What the hell is she doing in this house?'

'It's my house as much as yours,' Lilibeth shot back. 'Some of us have more respect for blood kin than others.'

'I told you to get on a bus and go.'

238

'I don't take orders from my own daughter.' Lilibeth pushed off the jamb, sauntered to the stove. 'This here coffee fresh, Mama?'

'How could you?' Lena demanded of Odette. 'How could you take her in again?'

'Lena.' All Odette could do was take her hand. 'She's my child.'

'*I'm* your child.' The bitter fury poured out and left its horrid taste on her tongue. 'You're just going to let her come back, stay until she's sucked you dry again, until she and whatever junkie she hooks up with this time steal you blind? It's cocaine now. Can't you see it on her? And that doesn't come free.'

'I told you I'm clean.' Lilibeth slapped a mug on the counter.

'You're a liar. You've always been a liar.'

Lilibeth surged forward. Even as Lena threw out her chin to take the blow, Declan stepped between them. 'Think again.' He said it quietly, but the heat in his voice pumped into the kitchen.

'You lay a hand on her, Lilibeth, one hand on her, and I'll put you out.' Odette stepped to the stove, poured the coffee herself with hands not quite steady. 'I mean that.'

'She's got no call to speak to me that way.' Lilibeth let her lips quiver. 'And in front of a stranger.'

'Declan Fitzgerald. I'm a friend of Lena's, and Miss Odette's. I'll get that coffee, Miss Odette. You sit down now.'

'This is family business, Declan.' Lena kept her furious eyes on her mother's face. She would think of the embarrassment later. Right now it was only a dull pinch through the cushion of anger. 'You should go.'

'In a minute.' He poured coffee, brought a cup to Odette. Crouched so their faces were level. 'I'm Irish,' he

239

told her. 'Both sides. Nobody puts on a family fight like the Irish. You only have to call me if you need me.'

He squeezed her hand, then straightened. 'Same goes,' he said to Lena.

'I'm not staying. I'll drive you back.' She had to breathe deeply, to brace for the pain her own words would cause. 'Grandmama, I love you with all my heart. But as long as she's in the house, I won't be. I'm sorry this hurts you, but I can't do this again. Let me know when she's gone. And you.' She turned to Lilibeth. 'You hurt her again, you take one dollar from her or bring any of the scum you like to run with in this house, I'll hunt you down. I swear to God I will, wherever you go. And I'll take it out of your skin this time.'

'Lena baby!' Lilibeth rushed down the narrow hall as Lena strode to the door. 'I've changed, honey. I want to make it all up to you. Give me a chance to—'

Outside, Lena whirled. 'You've had your last chance with me. Don't you come near me. Don't you come near my place. You're dead to me, you hear?'

She slammed the car door, ground the engine to life, then sped off, spewing up a thin cloud of smoke that obscured her mother and the house where she'd grown up.

'Well, that was fun, wasn't it?' Lena punched the gas. 'I bet your family would just love a load of Lilibeth Simone. Whore, junkie, thief and liar.'

'You can't blame your grandmother for this, Lena.'

'I don't blame her. I don't.' The tears were rushing up from her throat. She felt the burn. 'But I won't be a part of it. I won't.' She slammed the brakes in front of the Hall. 'I need to go now.' But she lowered her brow to the wheel. 'Go on, get out. *Va t'en.*'

'No. I'm not going away.' Others had, he realized now.

And that's where the hurt came from. 'Do you want to talk about this out here, or inside?'

'I'm not going to talk about it anywhere.'

'Yes, you are. Pick your spot.'

'I told you all you need to know. My mother's a whore and a junkie. If she can't earn enough to feed her various habits on her back, she steals. She'd as soon lie as look at you.'

'She doesn't live around here.'

'I don't know where she lives. No place for long. She came to my place yesterday. Stoned, and full of lies and her usual talk about new starts and being friends. Thought I'd let her move in with me again. Never again,' she said and leaned her head back on the car seat. 'I gave her fifty dollars for bus fare. Should've known better. Likely it's already gone up her nose.'

'Let's take a walk.'

'This isn't something you walk off or kiss better, Declan. I need to get back.'

'You're not driving into town when you're still churned up. Let's walk.'

To ensure she didn't just drive away when he got out, he took the keys out of the ignition, pocketed them. Then he climbed out, walked around the car. Opening her door, he held out a hand.

She couldn't drum up the energy to argue. But instead of taking his hand, she slid out of the car and dipped hers in her pockets.

They'd walk, she figured. They'd talk. And then, it would be over.

She imagined he thought his gardens – that new blossoming, the tender fragrances – would soothe her. He would want to comfort. He was built that way. More, he'd want to know so he could find solutions.

241

When it came to Lilibeth, there were no solutions.

'Family can suck, can't it?'

Her gaze whipped to his – dark and fierce, and sheened with damp. 'She's *not* my family.'

'I get that. But it's a family situation. We're always having situations in my family. Probably because there are so many of us.'

'Not having enough canapés at a cocktail party, or having two aunts show up in the same fancy dress isn't a situation.'

He debated whether to let the insult pass. She was, after all, raw and prickly. But he couldn't quite swallow it. 'You figure having money negates personal problems? Takes the sting out of hurts, buries tragedies? That's pretty shallow, Lena.'

'I'm a shallow gal. Comes through the blood.'

'That's bullshit, but you're entitled to feel sorry for yourself after almost taking a slap in the face. Money didn't make my cousin Angie feel much better when her husband got her and his mistress pregnant the same month. It didn't help my aunt when her daughter died in a car wreck on her eighteenth birthday. Life can fuck you over, whatever your income bracket.'

She stopped, ordered herself to calm down. 'I apologize. She tends to put me in a mood that's not fit for company.'

'I'm not company.' Before she could evade, he cupped her face in his hands. 'I love you.'

'Stop it, Declan.'

'I can't.'

'I'm no good for you. No good for anybody, and I don't want to be.'

'That's the key, isn't it?'

'Yeah.' He reached down, lifted the key she wore around her neck. 'It wasn't a man, but a woman who broke your heart. Now you want to lock it up, close it off so you won't accept love when it's offered. Won't let yourself give it back. Safer that way. If you don't love, it doesn't matter if someone walks away. That makes you a coward.'

'So what if it does?' She shoved his hand aside. 'It's my life. I live it the way I want, and I get along fine. You're a romantic, *cher*. Under all that Yankee sense, that expensive education, you're a dreamer. I don't put stock in dreams. What is, that's what counts. One of these days you're going to wake up and find yourself in this big, old house in the middle of nowhere, wondering what the hell you were thinking. And you'll hightail it back to Boston, go back to lawyering, marry some classy woman named Alexandra, and have a couple pretty children.'

'You forgot the pair of golden retrievers,' he said mildly.

'Oh.' She threw up her hands. '*Merde!*'

'Couldn't agree more. First, the only woman I know named Alexandra has teeth like a horse. She sorts of scares me. Second, and more important, what I'm going to do, Angelina, is live out my life in this big, old house, with you. I'm going to raise a family with you, right here. Golden retrievers are optional.'

'You saying it, over and over, isn't going to make it so.'

Now he grinned, white and wide. 'Bet?'

There was something about him when he was like this, she realized. Something potent and just a little frightening when he wore that sheen of affability over a core of concrete stubbornness.

'I'm going to work. You just stay away from me for a while, you hear? I'm too irritated to deal with you.'

He let her walk away. It was enough, for now, that her anger with him had dried up those tears that had glimmered in her eyes.

Chapter Fifteen

New Orleans
1900

Julian was drunk, as he preferred to be. He had a half-naked whore in his lap, and her heavy breast cupped in his hand. The old black man played a jumpy tune on the piano, and the sound mixed nicely in his head with wild female laughter.

Cigar smoke stung the air, giving him a low-level urge for tobacco. But he couldn't quite drum up the gumption for a cigar, or to haul the whore upstairs.

The fact that he was broke – again – didn't worry him overmuch. He patronized this brothel habitually, and always, eventually, scraped together the funds to pay his bill. His credit was good here, for the moment.

He'd selected the prostitute because she was blond and lush of build, vacant of brain. He could tell himself that later, when he rode her, he wouldn't see Abigail's face staring back up at him.

Not this time.

He took another swig of bourbon, then pinched the blond's nipple. She squealed and slapped playfully at his hand. He was grinning when Lucian walked in.

'My sainted brother.' Though his words slurred, they were bitter on his tongue. Julian gulped more whiskey as he watched Lucian shake his head at a redhead who sidled up to him.

He looked, Julian thought, pale and gold and perfect through the hazy smoke, against the garish colors, through the raucous noise.

And he wondered if Cain had looked at Abel and felt the same violent disgust as he himself felt now.

He waited, jiggling the blond on his knee, squeezing her breast as Lucian scanned the parlor. When their eyes met – identical eyes – there was a clash. Julian would have sworn he heard it in his head. The sound two swords make when struck in battle.

'What's this?' he said as Lucian approached. 'Finally lowering yourself to the rest of us humans? My brother needs a drink, a drink and a woman for *mon frère*!' he called out. 'Though I doubt he knows what to do with either.'

'You embarrass yourself and your family, Julian. I'm sent to bring you home.'

'I'm not embarrassed to pay for a whore.' Julian set down his glass and ran his hand up the blond's thigh. 'Now if I married one, it would be a different matter. But you beat me to that, brother, as you have so many other things.'

Lucian's face whitened. 'You will not speak of her in this place.'

'My brother married a slut from the swamps,' he said conversationally, jerking the blond back when she tried to crawl off his lap. He could feel her heart pounding,

245

pounding under his hand now as the heat between him and Lucian stirred fear.

And her fear excited him as none of the promises she'd whispered in his ear had done.

'Lucian, pride of the Manets, brought his tramp into our home, and now he pines and weeps because she left him for another, and saddled him with her bastard whelp.'

He had to believe it. Over the winter he'd drowned in an ocean of bourbon the look of her staring eyes, the sound of her body sliding wetly into the bayou.

He *had* to believe it, or go mad.

'*Allez,*' Lucian ordered the blond. 'Go.'

'I like her where she is.' Julian clamped his hands on her arms as she struggled.

Neither of them noticed as the room fell silent, as the notes of the piano died away and the laughter trailed off. Lucian reached down, dragged the blond off Julian's lap. She bolted away like a rabbit even as Lucian yanked Julian from the chair.

'Gentlemen.' The madam of the house swept forward. Behind her was an enormous man in spotless evening dress. 'We want no trouble here. Monsieur Julian.' Her voice cooed, her hand glided intimately over his cheek. And her eyes were frigid. 'Go with your brother now, *mon cher ami.* This isn't the place for family squabbles.'

'Of course. My apologies.' He took her hand, kissed it. Then turned and leaped on Lucian.

The table and lamp they fell on shattered. While people rushed away, women screamed, they rolled, jabbing with fists, snapping like dogs as the violence of a lifetime sprang out of both of them.

The bouncer waded in, dragged Julian up by the scruff. He quick-marched him to the door, heaved him through. Lucian had barely gained his hands and knees when he was lifted.

Curses and screams followed him out the door. And anger was smothered by mortification. Lucian shook his head clear, gained his feet.

He looked down at his brother, that reflection of self, and felt a different kind of shame. 'Have we come to this?' he said wearily. 'Brawling in brothels, sprawling in gutters. I want peace between us, Julian. God knows I have peace nowhere else.'

He held out a hand, an offering, to help Julian to his feet.

But Julian's shame had a different color. And it was black.

He wouldn't remember drawing the knife out of his boot. Liquor and temper and guilt blinded him. Nor would he remember surging to his feet, striking out.

He felt the blade slice through his brother's flesh with a kind of wild glee. And his lips were peeled back, his eyes mad as he scented first blood.

They struggled, Lucian through the pain and shock, Julian through the black haze, with the hilt of the knife slippery in their hands.

And the bright, bright horror paralyzed him as Julian's eyes widened when the killing point turned on him, into him.

'Mère de Dieu,' Julian murmured, and stared down at the blood on his breast. 'You've killed me.'

Manet Hall
2002

The heat had pumped in from the south. It seemed to Declan that even the air sweat. Mornings and evenings, when it was bearable, he worked outside. Afternoons, he sought the cooler regions of the house.

It wasn't as efficient, dragging his tools in and out, but he was making progress. That was the name of the game.

He didn't call Lena – he figured she needed to simmer and settle. But he thought of her, constantly.

He thought of her as he nailed boards, when he studied paint samples, when he installed paddle fans.

And he thought of her when he woke, in the middle of the night, to find himself curled on the grass by the edge of the pond, Lucian's watch clutched in his fist and his face damp with tears.

He tried to put the sleepwalking out of his mind in the daylight. But he couldn't put her out.

One more day, he ordered himself as he wiped sweat off his face. Then he was going into town, banging on her door. If he had to push her into a corner to force her to talk to him, that's what he'd do.

Remy's wedding was coming up fast. Which meant not only was he going to watch his best friend get married, but … his parents were coming to town.

He was ridiculously grateful they'd declined his offer for them to stay with him. Everyone would be a hell of a lot happier with them tucked into a nice hotel suite.

Regardless, he was determined to finish the galleries, and one of the spare bedrooms. In that way, the house would look impressive when they came down the drive, and he could prove he'd *had* the room he'd offered them.

His mother would look to be sure. That was a given.

He backed down the ladder, grabbed the cooler, and gulped cold water. Then poured the rest over his head. Refreshed, he walked across the lawn, then turned back to look.

Dripping, already starting to steam, he felt the smile spread across his face.

'Not bad,' he said aloud. 'Not half bad for a Yankee amateur.'

He'd finished the dual staircases. The sweep of them curved up opposite sides of the second-floor gallery. The elegance of them negated all the nicks, cuts, scrapes, and the hours of labor.

They would be, he realized, his pride and joy.

Now all he needed was to bribe the painters to work in this heat wave. Or pray for a break in the weather.

Either way, he wasn't going to wait until he'd finished the rear of the house. He wanted the front painted, wanted to stand as he was standing now, and see it gleam in bridal white.

To please himself, he strode back, walked slowly up the right-hand stairs, crossed the gallery, and walked slowly down the left. It gave him such a kick he did it again.

Then he dug through his toolbox for his cell phone and called Lena.

He had to share his excitement with her. What did it matter if he was a day ahead of schedule?

The phone was ringing in her apartment when he glanced over and saw Lilibeth crossing his lawn. He pressed END, got to his feet, and put the phone back in his toolbox.

'I swear, this heat's just wilting.'

She beamed at him, fluttering her lashes as she waved a hand in front of her face. He noted the bracelets she wore were Odette's.

'And it's barely noon. Look at you,' she said in a slow purr.

She sauntered straight to him, trailed a fingertip down his bare chest. 'You're all wet.'

'Impromptu shower.' Instinctively, he took a step back so her finger no longer touched his skin. 'What can I do for you, Miss Simone?'

'You can start by calling me Lilibeth. After all, you're a good friend of my mama's – and my little girl's, aren't you?'

She wandered away a bit, let her eyes widen as she scanned the house. 'I just can't hardly believe what you've done with this big, old place. You must be awfully clever, Declan.' She said flirtatiously, 'I can call you Declan, can't I?'

'Sure. You don't have to be so clever,' he said. 'You just have to have plenty of time.'

And money, she thought. *Plenty of money*. 'Oh now, don't you be modest. It's just a miracle what you're doing here. I hope it wouldn't be putting you out too much to show me some of the inside. And I surely could use something cold. Just walking over here from home's left me parched.'

He didn't want her in his house. More than distaste, there was a kind of primitive dread. But whatever else she was, she was Lena's mother, and his own had drummed manners into his bones.

'Of course. I've got some tea.'

'Can't think of anything that would be more welcome.'

She followed him to the door, was pleased when he opened it for her and stepped back for her to enter ahead of him. She let her body brush his, just the faintest suggestion, then walked into the foyer and let out a gasp.

She didn't have to feign the shock, or her wonder as she gazed around the grand entrance. She'd been inside before. Remy and Declan weren't the first to get liquored up and break into Manet Hall.

She'd never liked it much. The place had given her the creeps with its shadows and dust, its cobwebs and faded glamour.

But now it was full of light and polish. Glossy floors, glossy walls. She didn't think much of the old furniture, not for looks anyway. But she had no doubt the price tags had been heavy.

Old money bought or kept old things. It was a concept that baffled her when there was so much new and glittery in the world.

'My lord, sugar, this is a showplace. Just a showplace,' she repeated and wandered into the parlor.

She might've preferred the city, where the action was, but she could see that a woman could live like a queen in such a place. And bring the action in, at her whim.

'Goodness, did I say you were clever? Why, you're just a genius. Everything's so beautiful and fresh.' She turned back to him. 'You must be awful proud.'

'It's coming along. Kitchen's back this way. We can get you that cold drink.'

'That would be lovely, but don't you hurry me along now.' She slid a proprietary hand onto his arm, clung there as she walked down the hall. 'I'm just fascinated by what you've done with this place. Mama said you'd only started on it a few months ago.'

'You can get a lot done if you stick to the plan.'

And since he seemed to be stuck with her, for the time being, he banked down on the desire to get her out again. Instead, as she turned into the library, made purring noises, he took the opportunity to study her.

He couldn't see Lena in her. There were, he supposed, some physical similarities. But where Lena had that compact, bombshell body, Lilibeth's had been whittled down with time and abuse to nearly gaunt.

Showing it off in tiny red shorts and a tight tank top only made her appear cheap and pathetic – a worn-out Kewpie doll painted up for one last night at the carnival. He felt a stir of sympathy for a woman who sought approval and attention by trying to showcase a sexuality she'd already lost.

She'd used a heavy hand with makeup, and the heat hadn't been kind. Her face seemed sallow and false under

251

all the borrowed color. Her hair had frizzed, and graying roots were streaking through it.

By the time he got her into the kitchen, he found her too pitiful to resent.

'Have a seat,' he told her. 'I'll get you that drink.'

And she mistook the kindness in his voice for attraction.

'A kitchen like this ...' She slid into a chair. It was cool here, and she tipped back her head to let the air reach her throat – and to watch him. 'Don't you go and tell me you cook, too. Why, if that's so, sugar, I'm just going to have to cut Lena out and marry you my own self.'

'Sorry.' The mention of Lena tightened him up again. But his back was to her, and she didn't see his face. 'I don't cook.'

'Well, a girl can make allowances.' She lapped her tongue over her lips. He had a good, strong build to go along with those deep pockets. And she was starting to itch for a man.

'You wouldn't have anything a little stronger than that tea, would you, honey?'

'Would you rather a beer?'

She'd rather a good glass of whiskey, but she nodded. 'That'd be just fine. You gonna join me?'

'I'll stick with tea. I've got work to do yet today.'

'Too hot to work.' She stretched back, looking at him under her lashes. 'Days like this, you just wanna soak in a cool tub, then lie on down in a dim room with a fan blowing over your skin.'

She accepted the glass of beer he'd poured her, and sipped. 'What do you do to beat the heat, honey?'

'Pour cold water over my head. How's Miss Odette?'

Lilibeth's lips pursed. 'Oh, she's fine. House is hot as hell in the morning with her baking. Gotta save her pennies. I've been helping out, best I can, but things are tight. Declan …'

She ran her finger down the condensation on the glass, drank some more. 'I wanted to apologize for that scene over at the house the other day. Lena and I, well, we just rub each other wrong half the time. I guess I can't deny I didn't do right by her when she was a little thing. But I'm trying to make it up to her.'

She widened her eyes until they stung and watered cooperatively. 'I've changed. I've come to a point in my life when I realize what's important. And that's family. You know what I mean. You've got family.'

'Yes, I've got family.'

'And now you're down here, you must miss them, and they miss you. Whatever troubles you might have between you, you'd put them aside and support each other. No matter what, ain't that right?'

'Yes.'

She dabbed delicately at her tears. 'I need Lena to see that's all I want. She doesn't trust me yet, and I can't blame her. I was hoping maybe you could help convince her to give me a chance.'

She slid her hand across the table, skimmed it over the back of his. 'I'd sure appreciate it if you did. I feel so alone. Woman in my situation, she needs a friend. A strong man in her corner. If I knew I had you on my side, it would help so much.'

'If there have to be sides, I'm on Lena's. Either way, I can't step between family – and if I was stupid enough to try it, she wouldn't listen to me anyway.'

'Maybe the two of you aren't as close as I assumed.'

'It's always risky to make assumptions,' he returned equably.

She took another swallow of beer. 'You're sleeping with her, aren't you?'

253

'I'm not going to discuss that with you.'

'Why not?' Lilibeth ran the chilly glass between her breasts, then, laughing, rose. 'You shy, honey? Don't you be shy with Lilibeth. We could be friends, you and me.' She skirted the table, leaned in behind him. 'Very good friends,' she added as her arms twined down and her teeth nipped at his ear.

'Miss Simone, you're putting me in the awkward position of asking you to get your hands off me.'

'You *are* shy.' With a chuckle that blew warm breath and beer over his cheek, she trailed her hands down toward his lap.

He clamped a hand over her wrists, jerked them up again. 'You're embarrassing yourself.' He twisted so he could lever out of the chair and onto his feet to face her. 'That's your business. But you're using me to take a shot at Lena, and that's mine.'

Angry color spotted her cheeks. 'Maybe you think you're too good for me.'

'There's no maybe about it. Get out and we'll forget this happened.'

She wanted to scream at him, to strike out. But she still had her wits about her. She hadn't had enough beer to dull them, and the hit of coke she'd had before walking over had been miserly. Playing it out, she sank into a chair, dropped her head on her folded arms and sobbed.

'I don't know what to do. I'm just so alone. I'm just so scared. I need help. I thought – I thought if I let you have me, you'd help me. I just don't know what to *do*!'

She lifted her head, and the two tears she'd managed to squeeze out tracked through her makeup. 'I'm in such awful trouble.'

He went to the sink, ran the water cold, then got a glass. 'What kind of trouble?'

'I owe some money. That's why I left Houston, and I'm afraid they'll find me. Hurt me. Maybe Lena, too. I don't want them to hurt my baby.'

He set the water in front of her. 'How much money?'

He saw it, the quick glint of satisfaction in her eyes before she lowered them. 'Five thousand dollars. It wasn't my fault. Really, it wasn't my fault. I trusted the wrong people. A man,' she said wearily. 'And he ran off with the money and left me owing. If I don't find a way to pay it back, they're going to track me down and do something to me. Something to Mama and Lena.'

He sat back down, looked at her intently. 'You're a liar. You want to try to soak me for a quick five K so you can score some drugs and get out of town. You figure me for an easy mark, but you figure wrong. If it wasn't for Lena, I'd give you a couple hundred to send you along. But you see, Lilibeth, there is Lena. She wouldn't like it.'

She hurled the water in his face. He barely blinked. 'Fuck you.'

'I thought we already established that wasn't an option.'

'Think you're so smart, don't you? So important because you come from money.' She pushed to her feet. 'Big, fancy, highfalutin family. I found out all about you, Declan Fitzgerald. Let me ask you just what that big, fancy, highfalutin family's going to think when they hear you're heating the sheets with a Cajun swamp whore?'

The phrase had something clutching in his gut, in the back of his throat, in his head. Her face changed in front of his eyes, became fuller, older. Colder.

Josephine.

'Get out.' He wasn't sure, not entirely, if he spoke to the flesh-and-blood woman or to the ghost. His hands shook as he gripped the edge of the table.

'All those fine doctors and lawyers and Indian chiefs up there in Boston, how are they gonna like the idea of their golden boy hooking up with some bastard child from the bayou? No money, no pedigree. Runs a second-rate bar and has a grandmama who sews for other people to earn extra pennies. Gonna cut you right out of the will, sugar. Leave you high and dry with this big white elephant of a house on your hands. Especially when I tell them you slept with her mama, too.'

His legs were weak as water, but he stood on them. 'Get out of my house before I hurt you.'

'Your type doesn't lay hands on a woman. Don't think I don't know the difference.' Riding on coke and confidence, she tossed back her hair. 'You wanna keep plugging your wick into my girl, and you wanna keep your family out of it, you'll write me a check, *cher*. You'll write it quick, fast and in a hurry. And we're going to make it ten thousand now, because you hurt my feelings.'

'Your feelings aren't worth a buck and a half to me, Lilibeth.'

'They will be, after I have a little chat with your mama.'

'My mother will chew you up and spit you out.' He walked to the counter, yanked open a drawer and took out a pad. Scrawled a number on it. 'Here, that's her number. Call her. You can use my phone, as long as I can listen in. It'll be a real pleasure to hear her slice you to bloodless pieces.'

'I need money!'

'You won't get it here.' Out of patience, he grabbed her arm and pulled her to the door. 'I can make a lot more trouble for you than you can for me. Believe it,' he said, and shut the door in her face.

He had to sit down until he had his legs under him again. He felt ill, physically ill. Something had happened when she'd raged at him over Lena. The face that had become her face was one he'd seen in his dreams.

The face belonged to the house, or to the part of it that slammed doors, that wished him away.

That wished him harm.

No doubt now, he told himself, that Lena's mother now wished him harm as well.

He rose, went to the phone. One positive result of the ugly incident was it had made him appreciate his own mother.

He dialed, and felt cleaner at the familiar sound of her voice.

'Hi, Ma.'

'Declan? What are you doing calling in the middle of the day? What's wrong? You had an accident.'

'No, I –'

'All those horrible tools. You've cut off a hand.'

'I still have two, and all other assigned parts. I just called to tell you I love you.'

There was a long, pregnant pause. 'You've just learned you have a terminal disease and have six months to live.'

Now he laughed. 'Got me. I'm a dead man and want to make contact with my family so I get a really cool wake.'

'Do you want Uncle Jimmy to sing "Danny Boy"?'

'I really don't. I'd as soon rest in peace.'

'So noted. What is it, really, Declan?'

'I want to tell you about the woman I'm in love with and want to marry.'

This pause was even longer. 'Is this a joke?'

'No. Got a couple minutes?'

'I think I can rearrange my schedule for this.'

'Okay.' He walked over, picked up his iced tea. The ice had melted, but he glugged it down anyway. 'Her name's Angelina Simone, and she's beautiful, fascinating, frustrating, hardheaded and perfect. She's just perfect, Ma.'

'When do I meet her?'

'Remy's wedding. There's this one minor glitch – other than the one where she isn't ready to say yes.'

'I'm sure you can overcome that minor detail. What's the glitch?'

He sat down again and told her about Lilibeth.

By the time he got off the phone, he felt lighter. Going with impulse, he went upstairs to clean up and change. He was going to confront Lena a bit ahead of schedule.

Chapter Sixteen

Declan detoured by Remy's office on the way to Et Trois. The wedding was approaching quickly, and his duties as best man included coordinating the bachelor party. Though he figured the big picture was clear enough – enough booze to float a battleship, and a strip club – there were some finer details to work out.

When reception buzzed through to Remy's office, he heard his friend's almost frantic 'Send him right in.'

The minute he opened the office door, he saw why.

Effie, tears streaking down her cheeks, sat in one of the visitor chairs with Remy crouched at her feet. Though Remy kept mopping at the tears, kept trying to comfort, he shot Declan a look of sheer male panic.

In a testament to friendship, Declan resisted the urge to back out and run. Instead he closed the door, crossed over and rubbed Effie's shoulder.

'Sweetheart, I told you I'd tell him you were dumping him for me.'

Effie merely looked up, then covered her face with her hands and sobbed.

'Okay, bad joke.' Declan scrubbed now-sweaty palms over his jeans. 'What's wrong?'

'Problem with the wedding venue,' Remy began, and Effie let out a wail.

'There *is* no wedding venue.' She snatched Remy's handkerchief, buried her face in it. 'They had … they had a kitchen fire, and the fire department came, and they … they … Oh what're we going to do!'

'Smoke and water damage,' Remy explained to Declan. 'Over and above the fire damage. They're not going to be able to put it back together in time.'

'It's my fault.'

Mirroring Remy, Declan crouched. 'Okay, honey, why'd you start the fire?'

It made her laugh – for a split second. 'I wanted to use that old plantation house. It's romantic and so lovely. Remy said it'll all be easier booking a hotel ballroom, but no, I just had to have my way. And now look. We've got less than three weeks, and we're … We're just sunk, that's all.'

'No, we're not, honey. We'll find another place. *Pleure pas, chère.*' Remy kissed the tip of her nose. 'Worse comes to worst, we'll have the wedding, then we'll have our party later. We'll have us a real *fais do-do*, after the honeymoon.'

'Where are we going to get married? City Hall?'

'I don't care where we get married.' Now he kissed her fingers. 'Long as we do.'

She sniffled, sighed, leaned into him. 'I'm sorry. I'm being silly and selfish. You're right. It doesn't matter where or how.'

'Sure it does.' Declan's statement had them both staring at him, Effie with tears still swirling, Remy with baffled frustration. 'You can't let a little fire screw up your plans. Use my place.'

'What do you mean, your place?' Remy demanded.

'The Hall. Sure as hell big enough. Ballroom needs some work, but there's time. I have to strong-arm some painters, but I finished the entrance this morning. Gardens are in really good shape, kitchen's done, parlors, library. Lots of rough spots yet, but people won't care about that. They'll get the house, the grounds, the ghosts. They'll talk about it for years.'

'Do you mean it?' Effie snagged Declan's hands before Remy could speak.

'Sure I do. We can pull it off.'

'Dec,' Remy began, but Effie rolled right over him.

'Oh God. Oh, I *love* you.' She threw her arms around Declan's neck. 'You're the most wonderful man in the world. An angel,' she said and kissed him. 'A saint.'

'Do you mind?' Declan said to Remy. 'We'd like to be alone.'

Laughing, Effie spun to her feet. 'Oh, I shouldn't let you do this. You'll have all those strangers roaming around your house, trooping all over your lawn. But I'm going to let you because I'm desperate, and it's so perfect. I swear, I swear you won't have to do any of the work. I'll take care of everything. I'm going to owe you till my dying day.'

'Giving me your firstborn son will be payment enough.'

Remy sat on the edge of the desk and shook his head. 'I say I'll marry you anywhere, anytime, all he does is give you a broken-down house and he's the one gets kissed.'

'I already got you.' But she turned, wrapped her arms around Remy and, with a sigh, rested her head on his shoulder. 'I want it to be beautiful, Remy. I want it to be special. It means a lot to me.'

'I know it does. So it means a lot to me, too. We'll have us some party, won't we?'

'We will.' She gave him one last squeeze, then whirled away. The sad, sobbing woman was replaced by a dervish. 'Can I go out now?' she asked Declan. 'I need to get my mother and my sister, and we'll go out right now and start figuring it all out.'

'Go ahead.'

'Thank you.' She kissed his cheek. 'Thank you.' Then the other. 'Thank you.' Then his mouth with a long, drawn-out smack. 'Remy, you come on out soon as you can. Oh, Dec?' She was pulling out her cell phone as she headed for the door. 'My bride colors are rose and blue. You don't mind if we have the house painted those colors, do you?'

His mouth dropped open as she shut the door behind her. 'She was kidding, right?'

'Probably.' Knowing his girl, and the pack she ran with, Remy blew out a breath. '*Cher*, you don't know what you just got yourself into. You made my girl happy, and I'm grateful, but I gotta tell you, you're in for a couple weeks of pure insanity.'

'I couldn't stand seeing her crying like that. Besides, it makes sense.' Rose and blue, he thought. How much trouble could they get into with nice, harmless colors like rose and blue? 'Anyway,' he added, rubbing a hand over his sinking heart. 'I've been through wedding plans before.'

'You haven't met her mother before.'

Declan shifted his feet. 'Is she scary?'

'Pretty scary.'

'Hold me.'

Good deeds put him in a good mood. When he walked into Et Trois, he was ready for a cold one, a self-congratulatory pat on the back. And Lena.

She was behind the bar, pulling a draft and chatting up one of her regulars. He watched her gaze wash over, then land on him. Stay on him as he walked up, flipped up the pass-through.

She had time to slide the foaming mug across the bar to waiting hands, start to turn before he lifted her off her feet and planted his lips on hers.

The scattering of applause and hoots had him grinning as he held her an inch off the floor. 'Missed you.'

She rubbed her tingling lips together. 'Your aim seemed good to me.' She patted his cheek, gave him that quick, wicked gleam. 'Now down, boy. I'm working here.'

'You're going to need someone to cover for you.'

'I'm busy, *cher*. Go on and sit down, I'll get you a beer.'

He just hitched her up, giving her legs a little swing so he could get his arm under them. He elbowed the door to the bar kitchen. 'Lena needs you to cover for her,' he called back, then nodded toward the pass-through. 'Mind?' he asked the man sipping the draft.

'Sure thing.'

'Declan.' She didn't struggle, bad for the image. 'I'm running a business here.'

'And you do a damn good job of it. Thanks,' he added when the man flipped up the pass-through. 'It ought to run fine without you for a half hour.' He nodded as his new friend hustled over and opened the door for him.

He carried her outside. They got a few glances as he walked down the sidewalk and turned into her courtyard.

'I don't like being pushed around, *cher*.'

'I'm not pushing you, I'm carrying you. Where's your spare key?' he asked as he climbed the stairs. When she said nothing, he shrugged. 'Fine. We're going to get arrested for doing what I plan on doing out here on your gallery, but I'm game.'

'Under the pot, second from the left.'

'Good.'

To her shock, he shifted her, slinging her over his shoulder as he crouched down to retrieve the key. She continually underestimated his strength and, she admitted, her reaction to it.

'You've dropped a couple of pounds,' he commented and unlocked her door. 'Good.'

'I beg your pardon?' she said in her best frigid, southern-belle tone.

'I figure it's because you've been pining for me.'

'You're going to want to get a grip, *cher*.'

'Got one,' he said and reached up to squeeze her butt as he kicked the door closed.

'I can't tell you how flattered I am that you'd take time out of your busy day to come into town for a quickie, but I—'

'Excellent idea. It wasn't my first order of business, but why wait?' He hitched her more securely on his shoulder and headed for the bedroom.

'Declan, you're starting to seriously irritate me now. You'd better just put me down and—'

She lost the rest — and the air in her lungs — when he flipped her onto the bed. He could see her eyes glittering dangerously behind her hair before she shoved it out of her face. And that, he thought, was perfect. He was in the mood for the fast and the physical, the sweaty and the sexy.

'What the *hell's* gotten into you? You come marching into my place like you own it, cart me off like I'm spoils of war. If you think I'm here to scratch your itch whenever it suits you, you're about to find out different.'

He merely grinned, yanked off a shoe and tossed it aside.

'Put that back on, or hobble out. Either way, I want you gone.'

He pulled off the other shoe, then his shirt. Her response to that was to scramble to her knees and spit out in Cajun so rapid and thick he caught only about every sixth word.

'Sorry,' he said in mild tones as he unbuttoned his jeans. 'That was a little quick for me. Did you say I was a pig who should fry in hell, or that I should go to hell and eat fried pig?'

He was ready when she leaped, and laughing as she swiped at him. It was time for a fast tumble, fast and violent, and her clawing nails and bared teeth added the perfect punch.

She slapped, cursed, kicked. Then bucked like a wild mare when he crushed her under him on the bed and covered her snarling mouth with his in a hot, hungry kiss.

'Not what you expect from me, is it?' Breathless and randy, he tore at her shirt. 'Given you too much of what you expect so far.'

'Stop it. Stop it now.' Her heart sprinted under his rough hand. No, it wasn't what she expected from him, any more than her electrified response to his dominance was what she expected from herself.

'Look at me.' He clamped her hands on either side of her head. 'Tell me you don't want me, that you don't want this. Say it and mean it, and I'm gone.'

'Let go of my hands.' Though her gaze remained steady, her voice shook. 'You let go of my hands.'

He released one. 'Say it.' His muscles quivered. 'You want, or you don't.'

She fisted a hand in his hair and dragged his mouth back to hers. '*J'ai besoin.*'

265

I need.

She used her teeth, gnawing restlessly at his lips. Used her legs, wrapping them around to chain him to her.

'Take me,' she demanded. 'Fast. Fast and rough.'

His hand shot beneath the short, snug skirt, tore away the thin panties beneath. Sweat already slicked his skin and hers as she arched to him.

'Hold on,' he warned, and plunged into her.

She cried out as the explosive sensation ripped through her, cried out again as he drove deeper, harder. Filled, invaded, took until needs, frantic, outrageous needs swarmed through her. Her nails scored down his back, pinched into his hips.

De plus en plus. More and more, her mind screamed. 'More,' she managed. 'I want more.'

So did he. He shoved her knees back, opened her and hammered himself inside her.

It burned. His lungs, his heart, his loins. The ferocious heat, the unspeakable pleasure of going wild with her hazed his vision until the world was drenched with it.

White sun beating through the windows, the brassy blast of a trumpet from the street, the mad squeak of springs as slick skin slapped rhythmically against slick skin.

And her eyes, dark and glossy as onyx, locked on his.

I love you. Endlessly.

He didn't know if he spoke, or if the words simply ran a desperate loop in his brain. But he saw her eyes change, watched emotion swirl into them, blind them.

He heard her sob for breath, felt her vise around him as she came. Helpless, half mad, he shattered. And poured into her.

Out of breath, out of his mind, he collapsed onto her. Beneath him she continued to quake, to quiver. And shudder, those aftershocks of eruption. Then she was still.

'Can't move yet,' he mumbled. He felt hollowed out, light as a husk that could be happily blown apart by the slightest breeze.

'Don't need to.'

Her lips were against the side of his throat, and their movement there brought him an exquisite tenderness. A rainbow after the storm.

'Would you believe I came in to talk to you?'

'No.'

'Did. Figured we'd get to this after. Change of plans. I owe you a shirt and some underwear.'

'I've got more.'

He'd recovered just enough to prop on his elbows and look down at her. Her cheeks were flushed and glowing. Curls of damp hair clung to her temples, spilled over the rumpled spread.

He wanted to lap her up like a cat with cream.

'Pissing you off got me hot,' he told her.

'Me too. Seems like. I wasn't going to do this with you again.'

'Weren't you?'

'No.' She laid a hand on his cheek, amazed by the wave of tenderness. 'I'd made up my mind about it. Then you come into my place, all sexy and good-looking, scoop me up that way. You mess with my mind, *cher*. You just go and unmake it for me, time and again.'

'You're everything I want.'

'And nothing that's good for you. Go on.' She gave his shoulder a little push. 'Get off me. Two of us are a sweaty mess.'

'We'll take a shower, then we'll talk. Talk,' he repeated when she raised a brow. 'Scout's honor.' He held up two fingers.

'I've got to get back to work.'

'Angelina.'

'All right.' She waved him away. It was, she knew, no use arguing with him. God *knew* why she found that mule-headed streak of his so appealing. 'Go get yourself cleaned up. I'll call down and make sure everything's covered for the next little while.'

She stepped into the shower just as he got out. He imagined she'd timed it that way, to avoid the intimacy. Giving her room, he went to the kitchen, found the expected pitcher of tea, and poured two glasses.

When she came in, wearing that same sexy skirt and a fresh shirt, he offered her a glass.

She took it into the living room.

In the last few days, she'd resigned herself to what needed to be. Throughout, part of her had indeed pined for him. And every time she'd caught herself glancing toward the bar door, looking for him, or waking up in the night reaching for him, she'd cursed herself for being a weak fool.

Then she'd glanced at the door, and there he was. Her own soaring pleasure, depthless relief, had annoyed her even before he'd nipped at her pride by plucking her out of her own bar.

'Declan,' she began. 'I wasn't fair to you the other day. I wasn't in the mood to be fair.'

'If you're going to apologize for it, save it. I wanted to make you mad, I'd rather see you angry than sad. She makes you both.'

'I suppose she does. Mostly I hate knowing she's out there with Grandmama, knowing she'll hurt her again. I can't stop it, I can't fix it. That troubles me. But you shouldn't have been brought into it.'

'You didn't bring me into it. It happened.' He angled his head. 'Correct me if I'm wrong. You've got the impression that since I come from where and who I come from, I'm not equipped to handle the darker, the more difficult, the stickier aspects of life. Your life, in particular.'

'*Cher*, I'm not saying you're not tough. But this particular aspect of life, my life, is out of your scope. You wouldn't understand someone like her.'

'Since I've been so sheltered.' He nodded. 'She came to see me today.'

The healthy flush sex and heat had put in Lena's cheeks drained. 'What do you mean?'

'Lilibeth paid me a call around noon. I debated whether to tell you about it or not, and decided that I'm not going to keep secrets from you, or tell lies. Not even to spare your feelings. She came by, invited herself in for a cold one. Then she tried to seduce me.'

'I'm sorry.' Her lips felt stiff and ice cold as she formed the words. Her throat burned like fire. 'It won't happen again; I'll see to it.'

'Shut up. Do I look like I need your protection? And save your outrage until I'm done,' he told her. 'When she reached for my zipper, I told her not to embarrass herself. Her next tack was to fling herself down on the kitchen table and cry.'

He eased down on the arm of Lena's sofa. The tone of conversation, he thought in some corner of his brain, didn't lend itself to lounging among all those soft, colorful pillows. 'She didn't manage to work up many tears along with the noise, but I give her marks for effort. The story was how bad, mean people were after her. They'd hurt her, you, Miss Odette if she didn't give them five thousand dollars. Where could she turn, what could she do?'

Color rushed back into Lena's face, rode high on her cheekbones. 'You gave her money? How could you believe—'

'First a sheltered wimp, now a moron.' He gave an exaggerated sigh and sipped his tea. 'You're really pumping up the ego here, baby. I didn't give her a dime, and let her know, clearly, I wasn't going to be hosed. That irritated her into threatening to go to my family. Seems she's asked around about me and got the picture. She figured they'd be shocked and shamed by the idea of their fair-haired boy falling under your spell. For good measure, she'd tell them I'd fucked her, too.'

'She could do it.' It was more than the cold now. The sickness roiled in her belly. 'Declan, she's perfectly capable of—'

'Didn't I tell you to wait until I was finished?' His voice didn't whip, didn't sting. It was simply implacable. 'The cost doubled to ten thousand for this spot of blackmail. I don't think she was pleased with my response. I kicked her out. That's about it, so you can be outraged now if you want. Don't cry.' He spoke roughly when her eyes filled. 'She's not worth one tear from you.'

'I'm mortified. Can't you understand?'

'Yes. Though we're both smart enough to know this had nothing to do with you, I understand. And I'm sorry for it, sorry to add to it.'

'It's not you. It's never been you.' She wiped a tear from her lashes before it could fall. 'That's what I've been trying to get through your head from the start.'

'It's not you, either, Lena. It's never been you. I looked at her. I looked close and hard, and there's nothing there that's part of you. Family's the luck of the draw, Lena. What you make of yourself, because of or despite it, that's where the spine and heart come in.'

'I'll never be rid of her, not all the way. No matter what I do.'

'No, you won't.'

270

'I'm sorry. No, damn it, I will say it,' she snapped when his face tightened. 'I'm sorry she came into your home. I'm sorry she touched on your family. I need to ask you not to say anything about this to my grandmama.'

'Why would I?'

She nodded, then rising, wandered the room. She loved this place because she'd made it herself. She respected her life for the same reasons. Now, because she cared for, because she respected the man who was so determined to be part of her life, she'd explain.

'She left me before I was two weeks old,' she began. 'Just went out one morning, got in her mama's car, and drove off. Dumped the car in Baton Rouge. I was three before she came back around.'

'Your father?'

She shrugged. 'Depends on her mood. Once she told me it was a boy she loved and who loved her, but his parents tore them apart and sent him far away. Another time, she told me she was raped on the way home from school. Still another it was a rich, older man who was going to come back for both of us one day and set us up in a fine house.'

She turned back so she could face him. 'I was about eighteen when I figured she told me the truth. She was high enough, careless enough, mean enough for it to be the truth. How the hell should she know, she said. There were plenty of them. What the hell did she care who planted me in her? One was the same as the other.

'She was whoring when she got pregnant with me. I heard talk when I was old enough to understand what the talk meant. When she got in trouble, she ran back to my grandparents. She was afraid of an abortion – afraid she'd die of it, then go to hell or some such thing. So she had me, and she left me. Those are the only two things in this world I owe her.'

She drew a breath, made herself sit again. 'Anyway, she came back when I was three, made what would become her usual promises that she'd learned her lesson, she was sorry, she'd changed. She stayed around a few days, then took off again. That's a pattern that's repeated since. Sometimes she'd come back beat up from whatever bastard she'd taken up with most recently. Sometimes she'd come back sick, or just high. But Lilibeth, she always comes back.'

She fell silent, brooding over that single, unavoidable fact.

'It hurts when she does,' Declan said quietly. 'Hurts you, hurts Miss Odette.'

'She hurts everyone. It's her only talent. She was high when she showed up on my thirteenth birthday. We were having a *fais do-do* at the house, all the friends and family, and she stoned, with some lowlife. It got ugly pretty quick, and three of my uncles turned them off. I need a smoke,' she said, and left the room.

She came back a moment later with a cigarette. 'I had a boy I was seeing, crazy about that boy. I was sixteen, and she came back. She got him liquor and drugs and had sex with him. He was hardly older than I was, so it's hard to blame him for being an idiot. She thought it was funny when I stumbled over them out in the bayou. She laughed and laughed. Still, when I got this apartment, and she came back, I took her in. Better me than Grandmama, I thought. And maybe this time … Just maybe.

'But she turned tricks in my bed and brought her drugs into my home. She stole from me, and she left me again. From then I've been done with her. I'm done with her. And I'll never be done with her, Declan. Nothing I can do changes her being my mother.'

'And nothing she does can change who you are. You're a testament to your own grit, Lena, and a credit to the people who raised you. She hates you for what you are.'

She stared at him. 'She hates me,' she whispered. 'I've never been able to say that to anyone before. Why should saying such a thing, such an awful thing, help so much?'

'I won't say she can't hurt you any more, because she can. But maybe now she won't be able to hurt you as much, or for as long.'

Thoughtfully, she tapped out her cigarette. 'I keep underestimating you.'

'That's okay. That way I can keep surprising you. How's this one? She's connected to Manet Hall.'

'What do you mean?'

'I don't know, exactly, and can't explain it. I just know she is. And I think maybe she was meant to come back now, to say what she said to me. One more link in the chain. And I think she's pretty well done around here, this time out. Call your grandmother, Lena. Don't let this woman put a wedge between you.'

'I've been thinking of it. I guess I will. Declan.' She picked up her glass, set it down again. The useless gesture made him raise his eyebrows. 'I was going to end things between us.'

'You could've tried.'

'I mean it. We'd both be better off if we stepped back a ways, tried to be friends of some sort.'

'We can be friends. I want our children to have parents who like each other.'

She threw up her hands. 'I have to get back to work.'

'Okay. But listen, speaking of weddings, slight change of plans in Remy and Effie's. We're having the whole deal at my place.'

She rubbed her temple, tried to switch gears and moods as smoothly as he did. 'In … with half finished rooms and tools and lumber, and—'

'That's a very negative attitude, and not at all helpful, especially since I was going to ask you for a hand. How are you with a paintbrush?'

She let out a sigh. 'Do you save everyone?'

'Just the ones who matter.'

Somewhere between Declan's leaving the Hall, and Effie's arrival, Lilibeth paid another call. She was riding on coke and insult. The lousy son of a bitch couldn't spare a few bucks for the mother of the woman he was screwing, she'd just help herself.

She'd cased the first floor when he'd led her back to the kitchen, and going in through the back, she arrowed straight to the library and the big rolltop desk she'd spotted.

People with money kept cash handy, in her experience. Moving quickly, she yanked open drawers, riffled through, then let out a shout when she found a neat pile of fifties. Those she stuffed into her pocket.

She figured the books he'd shelved and the ones yet in boxes were probably worth something. But they'd be heavy, and hard to sell. He'd likely have more cash, a few pieces of jewelry up in his bedroom.

She raced up the main stairs. The fact that he could come back at any time only added to the thrill of stealing.

A door slammed, had her falling straight to her knees. Just a draft, she told herself as she caught her breath, as the pulse in her throat began to pop. Big, drafty old house. In fact, she felt cold air whisk over her as she jumped to her feet again.

She touched a doorknob, yanked her hand away again. The knob was so cold it all but burned.

Didn't matter. What the fuck? His room was down the hall. She wasn't as stupid as people thought she was. Hadn't she watched the house over the last few days? Hadn't she seen him come out on the gallery from the room at the far corner?

Laughing out loud, the sound rolling back over her, she dashed down, streaked through the open door. She yanked open the top drawer of a dresser and hit pay dirt with the old carved box inside.

Gold cuff links – at least she assumed they were real gold. Silver ones, too, with some sort of fancy blue stone. Diamond studs, a gold watch. And in a box inside the box, a woman's ring of … ruby maybe, diamond and ruby, fashioned in interlocking hearts.

She set the box on the dresser, hunted through a couple more drawers until she found another wad of cash.

Paid anyway, didn't you, you bastard. Paid just fine.

She tossed the bills into the jewelry box, tucked the box under her arm.

Standing there, her breath whistling out in excitement, cocaine dancing in her blood, she debated the satisfaction of trashing the place. It would be satisfying – more payment. But it wasn't smart. And she was smart.

She needed time to turn the jewelry into cash, time to turn some of the cash into drugs. Time to get the hell out of Dodge. Best to leave things as they were.

She'd go out the other side, just in case her long-nosed mama was looking this way.

But when she stepped back into the hall, she found herself staring at the third-floor stairs.

What was up there? she wondered. Maybe something good. Maybe something she could come back for later. Something that would make her rich.

Her breath wasn't just whistling now, but wheezing. Her skin was ice cold. But she couldn't resist the urge to climb those stairs. She was alone in the house, wasn't she? All alone, and that made it *her* house.

It was her house.

Swallowing continually to wet her dry throat, she started up. Shivering.

Voices? How could she hear voices when there was no one there? But they stopped her, urged her to turn back. *Something wrong here, something bad here. Time to go.*

But it seemed hands pressed to her back, pushed her on until, with trembling fingers, she reached for the door.

She meant to ease it open, slowly – just take a peek. But at the touch of her hand, it swung violently open.

She saw the man and woman on the floor, heard the baby screaming in the crib. Saw the woman's eyes – staring and blind. And dead.

And the man, his hair gold in the dim light, turned to look at her.

Lilibeth tried to scream, but couldn't grab the air. As she opened her mouth, something *pushed* into her. For one horrifying moment it became her. Then it swept through her. Cold, vicious, furious.

Another figure formed in the room. Female, sturdy, in a long night robe.

Julian.

And in speechless terror, Lilibeth turned and ran.

Chapter Seventeen

Within twenty-four hours, Declan discovered he had more help on the house than he knew what to do with. Apparently everyone in Louisiana was invited to the wedding, and they were all willing to lend a hand.

He had painters, plumbers, carpenters and gofers. And though it occurred to him in the middle of the melee that if half that amount had pitched in to repair the original venue, the job would have been done in about twenty minutes, he decided to keep the thought to himself.

It seemed rude to voice it.

And he appreciated the labor, sincerely. Reminded himself of it whenever he felt certain pieces of the house slipping away from him into someone else's charge.

He'd been looking forward to screening in the lower rear gallery himself, but comforted himself that one good hurricane would demand rescreening.

He'd intended to sand and varnish the ballroom floors, but bucked up when he thought of all the other floors waiting for him throughout the house.

And he sure as hell didn't mind turning over the exterior painting to others. It was a hot, exacting and laborious job, and crossing it off his list left him free to tackle the downstairs powder room, and to hang the blown-glass chandelier he'd bought for the foyer, and to finish plans for the mud room. And …

Well, there was plenty to go around, he reflected.

Then there was the pure pleasure of watching Effie zip in and out on her lunch hour or after work. Even when she brought her mother in tow. Mrs. Renault was a spit-and-polished older version of her daughter with an eye like an eagle and a voice like a drill sergeant.

Remy was right, she was pretty scary. Declan hid from her, whenever possible and without shame.

On the second day of the full-out campaign, Declan strode toward the rear gallery to check progress. He was feeling pretty peppy from the tile he'd just set, was covered with ceramic dust from cutting it.

The noise level was amazing. Voices, radios, power tools. As much as he enjoyed people, he'd have given a thousand dollars for five minutes alone in his house.

'Jim Ready? I want those windows sparkling, you hear? How's it going to look in the wedding pictures if those windows are dull? Put your back into it, boy!'

The sound of Mrs. Renault's voice had Declan turning sharply on his heel and changing direction. He all but bowled over Odette.

'Hey, sorry. You all right? I didn't see you. I was running away.'

'You got a houseful.'

'You're right about that. If this place isn't fixed up enough to suit General Renault by D-Day, we're all going to be shot.' He took her arm as he spoke and, thinking only of self-preservation, hustled her into the library. Shut the doors.

'Can I come live at your house?'

She smiled – a curve of lips that didn't reach her eyes. 'You're such a good boy, Declan, doing all this for your friend.'

'I'm not doing much more right now than staying the hell out of the way.'

'And you'd rather all these people go back where they came from, and leave you be so you can play with your house.'

'Yeah, well.' He shrugged, pushed his dusty hand through his dusty hair. 'There'll still be plenty to do once they go. We're not touching the third floor or the servants' area, and only doing one other room on the second. Tell me what's wrong, Miss Odette?'

'I gotta work up to it.' She set down the shopping bag she carried, then walked over to look at some of his books. There were still boxes of them to be shelved, but she saw what it would be. Towers of words, some old and worn, some fresh and new. Small treasures, deep colors.

'You got vision,' she said at length. 'You picture what you want, then you make it happen. That's a fine skill, *cher.*'

'Some people call it single-minded.'

'You're anything but. You've got a lot of channels in that head of yours. Working on one at a time till it's done shows character to me. I'm awful fond of you, Declan.'

'I'm awful fond of you, too. I wish you'd sit down, Miss Odette. You look tired.' And troubled. 'Why don't I get us a cold drink?'

'No, don't you trouble and risk getting shanghaied by Sarah Jane Renault. Now that's a single-minded individual, and I don't fault her for it.'

'She told me to get a haircut by the end of the week so I don't look shaggy or freshly shorn for the wedding.'

Sulking over it a little, Declan ran a testing hand through his hair. 'And that she'll be putting fancy soaps, towels and so on in all the bathrooms the day before the wedding. I'm not to use them under penalty of death. And I'm to get more green plants inside the house. A house can't breathe without green plants.'

'She's just nervous, honey. Effie's her baby. Her youngest daughter.' Odette pressed her lips together. 'Declan, I'm shamed to say what I have to say to you, and I won't blame you if, after I'm done, you ask me not to come back in your home again.'

The words alarmed him, nearly as much as the pain in her eyes. 'There's nothing you can say that would make you unwelcome in my home, Miss Odette. Who hurt you?'

'Oh, *mon Dieu*, if this spoils what I see between you and my Lena, I'll never forgive myself. My daughter stole from you,' she blurted out. 'She came in your house and took what was yours.'

With a heavy heart she reached into her bag, took out his carved box. 'This was in her room. I knew it was yours even before I looked in and saw a set of cuff links with your initials. I don't know if it's all here, but that's all there was. If anything's missing—'

'Let's just see. I want you to sit down now. I mean it.'

She nodded, sank into a chair.

He chained down his rage as he set the box on a table, opened it. He saw the ring box first, opened it, and felt the worst of the anger fade when the stones glittered up at him.

'Okay.' He breathed out. 'The most important thing's still here.' As was, as far as he could see, everything else but the couple thousand in twenties he kept secured with the money clip that had been his great-grandfather's.

'It's all here.'

'You're not telling me the truth,' Odette said dully.

'A little cash, that's all.'

'I need to know how much so I can pay it back.'

'Do you think I'd take money from you?' Some of the anger lashed out, made her wince. 'Look at my face. Do you think I'd take money from you for this, for anything?'

Her lips wanted to quiver, so she pressed them into a firm line. 'She's my responsibility.'

'The hell she is. Don't insult me again by talking about restitution.'

Despite her promise not to shed one in front of him, a tear spilled over. 'I know what she is. And I know she'll never be what I hoped for, worked for, wished for from the moment I knew she was inside me. But she gave me Lena.'

She dug out a tissue, patted her cheeks. There would be no more tears. 'I expected she'd steal from me before she took off again, but I didn't think she'd take from you. I never thought of it, and I'm sorry for that.'

'You want to look at my face again and see if I blame you?'

'No, you don't blame me. Oh, I want you for my Lena. I'm sitting here knowing my child stole from you, and all I can think is I want you for my baby.'

'Good thing, because I want me for her, too.' He picked up the ring box, crossed over to her chair. 'I bought this for her. Maybe you could put in a good word for me so when I give it to her, she takes it.'

Odette looked at the ring and sighed. 'Suits her. Sure does suit her. She's got a good heart, Declan, but it's got scars on it. She's so strong. Sometimes I worry she's too strong, and she'll forget how to give. I'll have to tell her about this.'

'Yes.'

'And you'll have to figure out how to keep her from pulling away from you when she knows. That's what she'll want to do.'

'Don't worry. Where's Lilibeth?'

'Gone. I found this in her room this morning. She's barely come out of there since the day before. When I went in and found it, I put it away where she wouldn't find it. Then we had words about it. She packed up and left. She'll come back,' she said in the same hollow tone he'd heard from Lena. 'In a year or two. And we'll go through it once more.'

'We'll deal with it when it happens.' He leaned down, kissed her cheek. 'I love you.' When her eyes filled again, he took her hand. 'Whether Lena's ready for it or not, we're family now. Family sticks.'

'When I meet your mama,' Odette managed, 'I'm gonna give her one big, rib-cracking hug.'

'That'll set her up. Why don't we take a look at what's happening around here, and you can protect me from General Renault.'

He didn't expect it to take long, and wasn't disappointed. About the time most of his free labor was packing up for the day, and Effie and her mother had him out in the back garden, Lena strode around the side of the house.

Since he was in the middle of the series of: uh-huhs, you-bets and no-problems that had become his litany of responses to the Renault women's wedding agenda, he decided the confrontation in Lena's eyes would be a relief.

'The railings and baluster will be wrapped in tulle and lace.'

'Uh-huh.'

'And we'll have baskets – white baskets – of flowers set out on the gallery there.'

'You bet.'

'The florist will need to start early on the day of the wedding, so you just scoot out of the way and make sure they have access to all the areas of the house I've got marked off on my chart here.'

'No problem. Lena.' He reached out and clutched her hand. A drowning man grabbing a rope. 'We're just talking about flower arrangements.'

'Flowers are the landscape of a wedding,' Mrs. Renault declared, and made more notations on the clipboard she carried everywhere. 'How are you, Lena?'

'I'm just fine, Miss Sarah Jane. Isn't this exciting? Counting right down to the big day. Effie, you must be half mad with the details.'

'I've passed half, working toward pure insanity.'

'It'll all be beautiful.' She kept her smile bright, her voice light even as the dark heat coursed through her. 'Those rhododendrons are going to be spectacular on your day.'

'The gardens are going to be a sight,' Mrs. Renault agreed, and ran down her checklist again. 'Pity, though, there wasn't time to put up an arbor, train some sweet peas up.' She looked over the tops of her reading glasses at Declan with a faintly accusatory gleam.

'Maybe the Franks can rig something. Ah, can you excuse me a minute? There's something I need to show Lena.'

He escaped, pulling her toward the steps to the second-floor gallery. There was still some of General Renault's militia on the lower level. 'They're like ants,' he babbled. 'Crawling out of the woodwork when you're not looking.'

'What're you talking about?'

'People. Everywhere. Watch that bucket. I think the ballroom's safe.'

'Feeling a little pressed, are you, *cher*?'

'I'm thinking of a nice vacation in Maui until this is over. I've got to say, I admire women.'

'Really.' She glanced down at the ladders, the tarps, the debris of construction – and the two women picking their way through it with visions of tulle and lace in their heads. 'Why is that?'

'You can be spitting mad, and still carry on a polite conversation about rhododendrons.' He peeked through the ballroom doors, sighed. 'All clear. Anyway, when most guys work up a head of steam, it spews. Well …' He stepped inside. 'What do you think?'

The walls were a pale rose, the floor gold and gleaming.

'It's big.'

'It'll need to be for this little do. The General says we've got two-fifty coming. Otherwise, you can use the pocket doors to turn it into a couple of parlors.'

He crossed the floor, drew one of the big doors out of its slot. 'Isn't this amazing?' He trailed his fingers over the carved wood reverently. 'The craftsmanship in these. More than a hundred years ago. I hate hiding them. See how the pattern matches the ceiling medallions? Tibald did a hell of a job restoring those.'

She had worked up a head of steam since her conversation with her grandmother, but found it dispersing now as she watched his undiluted pleasure and pride.

'It's true love, isn't it? You and this house. Most men don't look at a woman the way you look at those doors.'

'I look at you that way.'

She had to turn away. 'You make it damn hard to hold onto a mad. Tell me why you're not mad, Declan. Why aren't you mad she stole from you?'

'I am. And if I have occasion to see her again, she'll know it.'

'You should go to the police.'

'I thought about it. I might get some of the money back, but it would embarrass Miss Odette.'

'She's already embarrassed.'

'I know. Why add to it? I got back the things that mattered.'

The bitterness gushed through her anew. 'She came in your house, she went through your things. She *took* from you.'

He lifted a brow at the tone of her voice. 'Working up that steam again?'

'Goddamn it. Goddamn it, Declan, she violated your home. It's not like taking from me or Grandmama. How much did she take?'

'Couple thousand.'

The muscles in Lena's jaw tightened. 'I'll have you a check tomorrow.'

'You know I'll tear it up. Put it away, Lena. I figure it was a cheap lesson. If you're going to live in the country, have a houseful of valuables and spare cash, you don't walk off and leave it unlocked and unattended.'

'She'd have broken a window.'

'Yeah. That's why I'm getting a couple of dogs. Always wanted a pack of dogs. I thought I'd go to the shelter after the wedding. Want to come with me?'

She just shook her head. 'You lose two thousand dollars – and I bet it was more – to a thieving junkie, and your response is to buy some dogs.'

'Figured I'd get some fun out of it. How about it? They'll be your dogs, too.'

'Stop it, Declan.'

'Uh-uh.' With a satisfied smirk on his face, he walked

toward her. 'Let's get us a couple mongrel puppies, Lena. They'll be good practice before the kids come along.'

'You get your own puppies.' But he'd teased a smile out of her. 'And run around after them when they pee on your rugs and chew on your shoes.'

'Maybe Rufus will teach them their manners. You're wearing my earrings,' he said as he slipped his arms around her and glided into a dance.

'They're my earrings now.'

'You think of me when you put them on.'

'Maybe. Then I think how nice they look on me, and I forget all about you.'

'Well, then I'll have to find other ways to remind you.'

'A necklace.' She skimmed her fingers up the nape of his neck, into his hair. 'Couple of nice glittery bracelets.'

'I was thinking of a toe ring.'

She laughed, eased in closer so that she could rest her cheek on his. They were waltzing, and a tune was playing in her head. One she'd heard him hum or whistle countless times. She could smell his workday on him – the sweat, the dust – and under it the faint, faint drift of soap from his morning shower. His cheek was a little rough against hers as he'd neglected to shave.

If life were a fairy tale, she thought, they could stay just like this. Waltzing around and around on the satiny floor, while the sun slid down, the flowers rioted, and the lights from hundreds of tiny crystal prisms showered over them.

'I've got such feelings for you. More than I ever had for anyone, or wanted to. I don't know what to do with them.'

'Give them to me,' he pleaded, turning his lips into her hair. 'I'll take good care of them.'

She hadn't realized she'd spoken aloud. Hadn't meant to. Now, when she would have drawn back, he pulled her closer. So close, so tight, she couldn't get her breath.

Her head spun, and the music inside it soared. The strong scent of lilies rose up and almost smothered her.

'Do you hear it?' His hands trembled as he gripped her arms. 'Violins.'

'I can't …' His voice sounded far off, and as she fought to focus on his face, another seemed to float over it. 'I'm dizzy.'

'Let's sit down.' He kept his hands on her arms, lowered them both to the floor. 'You heard it, too. The music. You felt it, too.'

'Just hold on a minute.' She had to regain her bearings. The room was empty but for the two of them. There was no music, no crystal light, no pots heaped with fragrant white lilies. Yet she had heard, seen, smelled. 'I didn't know hallucinations were catching.'

'It's not hallucination. It's memory. Somehow, it's memory. They'd have danced here, Lucian and Abigail, like we were. Loved each other, like we do.' When she shook her head, he swore. 'All right, damn it, he loved her, the way I love you. And there's something still alive between them. Maybe something that needs to be finished, or just acknowledged. We're here, Lena.'

'Yes, we're here. And I'm not living someone else's life.'

'It's not like that.'

'It *felt* like that. And living someone else's life might just mean dying someone else's death. He drowned himself in that pond outside there, and she—'

'She died in this house.'

Lena took a calming breath. 'Depending on whose story you believe.'

'I know she did. Upstairs, in the nursery. Something happened to her up there. And he never knew. He grieved himself to death not knowing. I need to find out for him. And for myself. I need you to help me.'

'What can I do?'

'Come to the nursery with me. We're closer now. Maybe you'll remember this time.'

'Declan.' She took his face in her hands. 'There's nothing for me to remember.'

'You hang witch bottles out in my tree, but sit here denying any possibility of reincarnation, which you brought into the mix in the first place.'

'That's not what I'm doing. There's nothing for me to remember because I'm not Abigail. You are.'

She might as well have slipped on a pair of brass knuckles and plowed her fist into his stomach. The shock of her words had him reeling.

'Get out. That's not possible.'

'Why not?'

'Because …' Flustered, oddly embarrassed, he pushed to his feet. 'You're trying to say I was a girl?'

'I don't know why that's such a shock to your system. A lot of us get along just fine female.'

'I don't. I'm not. I wasn't.'

'It makes the most sense, if any of this makes sense.'

'No sense. None. No way.'

'You're the one who keeps hearing the baby cry.' She'd never seen him quite so flustered. 'Mothers do, before anyone else. And you're drawn to that room upstairs, the way a mother would be to her baby. Even though the room scares you, you're pulled back. You said how you wandered through the servants' wing, how easy it was to find your way. She'd have known it, but why would Lucian?'

'It was his house.' But he remembered how he'd imagined looking out the window, imagined seeing the two men riding toward the house. Why would he imagine seeing Lucian riding home if he'd *been* Lucian?

'A couple other things,' Lena continued. 'One telling one. That day when I came along and saw you walking toward the pond. Trancelike. You walked oddly. I couldn't figure out what it was about the way you walked that struck me. But now I know. You were walking the way a very pregnant woman walks. Waddling a bit,' she said as he turned and gaped at her with something like horror. 'A hand pressed to the small of your back. Small, careful steps.'

'Now you're saying I wasn't just a girl, but a pregnant girl?'

'Oh for heaven's sake, *cher*, some people believe you can come back as a poodle. What's so bad about a pregnant woman?'

'Because pregnant women go into labor at a certain point, then have to push several pounds of baby out of a very limited space.'

The horror on his face was comical, and enough to have her relaxing into the theory. 'I don't think you'll have to repeat that performance in this life. Have you considered that if you look at this puzzle from this new angle, you might find the answers you want?'

He found himself wanting to rub at his crotch just to make sure everything was where it should be. Maybe work up a good, manly belch. 'I like it better the other way.'

'Keep an open mind, *cher*. I've got to get to work.'

'Wait a minute, wait a minute.' He dashed after her. 'You're just going to drop this bombshell on me, then leave?'

'I've got to work for a living.'

'Come back after closing. Stay.'

'I need to stay at Grandmama's for a night or two, till she's feeling steadier.'

'Okay. Okay.' He let out a breath when they reached the main floor. 'Let me try this.' He spun her around,

289

crushed his mouth to hers. Then took the kiss deep and dreamy.

'You didn't get any lesbian-type vibe from that, did you?' he asked when he drew back.

'Hmm.' She touched her tongue to her top lip, pretended to consider. 'No. I can attest that you're all man this time around. Now, shoo. You've got plenty to do the next few days to keep your mind occupied. This whole thing's waited a hundred years, it can wait till after Remy's wedding.'

'Come back and stay when Miss Odette's feeling better.'

'All right.'

'I love you, Lena.'

'I'm afraid you do,' she whispered, and walked away.

Lena left the bar as early as she could manage, but it was still after one in the morning when she pulled up to the bayou house. The porch light was burning, and the moths seduced to death by it. She sat for a moment, listening to the music of the frogs and night birds, and the teasing whisper of a faint breeze.

This was the place of her girlhood. Perhaps the place of her heart. Though she'd made her life in the city, it was here she came when she was most happy, or most troubled. Here she came to think her deepest thoughts or dream her most secret dreams.

She'd let herself dream once – those innate female dreams of romance and a handsome man to love her, of home and children and Sunday mornings.

When had she stopped?

That sticky summer afternoon, she admitted. That hot, hazy day when she'd seen the boy she'd loved with all her wild heart and foolish youth coupling like an animal with her mother on a ragged blanket in the marsh.

The marsh that was hers, the boy that was hers. The mother that was hers.

It had sliced her life in two, she thought now. The time before, when there was still hope and innocent dreams and faith. And the time after, where there was only ambition, determination and a steely vow never, never to believe again.

The boy didn't matter now, she knew. She could barely see his face in her mind. Her mother didn't matter, not at the core of it. But the *moment* mattered.

Without it, who knew what direction her life would have taken? Oh, she and the boy would have parted ways soon enough. But it might've been with some sweetness, it might have left her with some soft memory of first loves.

But that stark vision of sex and betrayal had forged her. She'd understood then what it might have taken her years to learn otherwise. That a woman was smarter, safer, to drive the train herself. Men came, men went, and enjoying them was fine.

Loving them was suicide.

Suicide? she shook her head as she climbed out of the car. That was overly dramatic, wasn't it? Heartbreak wasn't death.

He'd died from it.

She all but heard the voice in her head. It hadn't been the knife wound, it hadn't been the pond that had killed Lucian Manet.

It had been a broken heart.

She let herself into the house and immediately saw the spill of light from Odette's room. Even as she approached, Lena heard the quick thump-thump of Rufus's tail on the floor.

She stepped to the doorway, cocked her head. Odette was sitting up in bed, a book open on her lap, the faithful dog curled on the floor.

'What are you doing up so late?'

'Waiting for my baby. I didn't think you'd be back for another hour or more.'

'Business was light enough to spare me.'

Odette patted the side of the bed in invitation. 'You took off early because you were worried about me. You shouldn't.'

'You used to tell me worrying was your job.' Lena lay down on top of the sheets, her head in the curve of her grandmother's arm. 'Now it's mine, too. I'm sorry she hurt you.'

'Oh, baby, I think that must be her job. God knows she's good at it.' Odette stroked Lena's hair. 'I got you, though. I got my Lena.'

'I was thinking what it was like for you and Grandpapa to raise a baby after you'd already raised your own.'

'You were nothing but pure pleasure to both of us.'

'It made me think about how the Manets brought your grandmama back here when she was a baby. You remember her pretty well, don't you?'

'I remember her very well. You've the look of her. You've seen the old pictures, so you know that.'

'Did she ever say how the Hall should've been hers?'

'Never heard her say anything like. She was a happy woman, Lena. Maybe happier here than she would've been in the Hall, had things been different. She had a fine hand with baking, and that she passed to me. She told good stories, too. Sometimes when I'd come spend time with her, she'd make them up just like they were real. I think she could've been a writer if she'd wanted that for herself.'

'She must've thought of her parents, and the Manets. No matter how happy she was here, she must've thought of them.'

292

'I expect so. She used to take flowers to her papa's grave. Took them every year on her birthday.'

'Did she? You never told me that.'

'Said she owed him life – hers, her children, her grand-children. She even laid flowers on the graves of Josephine and Henri Manet. Though she never stopped there to say a prayer. And she did one more thing on her birthday, every year until she died. She took flowers and tossed them into the river. And there she said a prayer.'

'For her mother, you think?'

'She never said, but that's what I think.'

'And do you think that's where Abigail is? In the river?'

'Some say.'

Lena raised her head. 'I'm not asking some. I'm asking you.'

'I know sometimes I walk along the bank, and I feel an awful sadness. And I think, sometimes, old souls search for new life. And keep searching until it comes out right. What're you searching for?'

Lena laid her head down again, closed her eyes. 'I thought I'd found it. Now I'm not so sure. He loves me, Grandmama.'

'I know he does.'

'If I love him back, everything changes.'

Odette smiled, leaned over to shut off the light. 'It surely does,' she murmured and continued to stroke Lena's hair. 'It surely does.'

Chapter Eighteen

As host of Remy's bachelor party, Declan felt socially obligated to stay till the bitter end. The bitter end was some dingy, backstreet dive in the Quarter where the liquor burned holes in what was left of a man's stomach lining and the strippers were woefully past their prime.

Nobody seemed to care.

In the spirit of good-fellowship, Declan tucked a final dollar in the frayed garter on a flabby white thigh, then hauled a glassy-eyed Remy to his feet.

'Let's go, pal of mine.'

'Huh? What? Is it morning?'

'Close enough.'

As they stumbled out, arm in arm as much for necessity as friendship, Remy looked around. His head bopped like a puppet's on a jerked string. 'Wherez everybody?'

'Passed out, in jail, dead in an alley.'

'Oh. Wimps.' Remy grinned his rubber grin. 'You 'n me, Dec, we still got it.'

'I'm starting a course of antibiotics in the morning to get rid of it.' He tripped and had to wrap both arms around Remy to keep from falling on his face. 'Too much gravity. There's entirely too much gravity out here.'

'Let's go find us another naked woman.'

'I think we found all of them already. Time to go home, old buddy, old pal.'

'I'm getting married in three days.' Remy held up four fingers to demonstrate. 'No more carousing for Remy.' He looked around. The streets were nearly deserted and oily with the light drizzle. 'Do we have to bail anybody out?'

'Screw 'em.'

'Damn right. Where's my girl? Effie!' He shouted it, and the name echoed back, making Declan snort drunkenly.

'Stella!' Cracked up by his own wit, he sat down hard in a puddle. 'Fuck it, Remy. Let's just sleep here.'

'Gotta go find my girl, gonna make sweet, sweet love to my Effie.'

'You couldn't get it up right now with a hydraulic pump.'

'Bet?' Remy fumbled for his zipper, and Declan had just enough brain cells left to stagger up and stop him.

'Put that thing away before you hurt yourself. Get us arrested for decent exposure.'

''S okay. We're lawyers.'

'Speak for yourself. Find cabs. We must find cabs.'

'Cab to Effie. Where's my blushin' bride?'

'Home in bed, like every other good woman is at …' He lifted Remy's wrist, tried to focus on the watch. 'Whatever o'clock in the morning. Lena, she's in bed. She thinks I'm a woman.'

'You must not be fucking her right then.'

'No, you ass. And remind me to punch you for that later. She thinks I'm Abigail.'

'You haven't been trying on her underwear or anything weird like that, have you, son?'

'I like the little black lace panties with the roses best. They slim down my hips.'

'Pretty sure you're joking. Wait.' He stopped, leaned over the curb, hands braced on his knees. Then slowly straightened again. 'False alarm. Not gonna puke.'

'There's good news. Cab!' Declan waved desperately when he saw one cruising. 'In the name of God. You first,' he said and all but shoved Remy inside before diving in after.

'Where do I live?' Remy demanded. 'I used to know, but I forgot. Can I call Effie and ask her?'

Fortunately Declan remembered, and as Remy snoozed on his shoulder, he concentrated on remaining conscious until he fulfilled the last of his duties and got his friend home alive.

At the curb, he elbowed Remy and brought him up like an arrow from a bow. 'What? Where? Sum bitch, I'm home. How 'bout that?'

'Can you make it from here?' Declan asked him.

'I can hold my liquor. All six gallons of it.' Shifting, Remy caught Declan's face in his hand and kissed him hard on the mouth. 'I love you, *cher*. But if you'd been Abigail, I'd've slipped you some tongue.'

'Ugh,' was the best Declan could manage as Remy climbed out.

'You're the goddamnedest best friend I ever had, and that was the goddamnedest best bachelor's party in the history of bachelor's parties. I'm gonna go up, puke, and pass out now.'

'You do that. Wait till he gets in the door,' Declan told the driver, and watched Remy waver, split in two. Both of them stumbled inside the building.

'Okay, the rest is his business. You know where the old Manet Hall is?'

The driver eyed him in the rearview mirror. 'I guess I do.'

'I live there. Take me home, okay?'

'That's a long way out.' The driver shifted, turned, eyed Declan up and down. 'You got enough for the fare?'

'I got money. I got lotsa money.' Declan pawed through his pockets, came up with bills, littered the cab with them. 'I'm loaded.'

'You're telling me.' With a shake of his head, the driver pulled away from the curb. 'Must've been some party, buddy.'

'Tell me,' Declan muttered, then slid face first on the backseat.

The next thing he knew, clearly, a Dixieland band was blasting in his head. He was still facedown, but the beach of Waikiki had ended up in his mouth and his tongue had grown a fine fur coat.

Some sadist was hammering spikes into his shoulder.

'Holy Mary, Mother of God, pray for us sinners.'

'No point falling back on that now. Just roll over nice and slow, *cher*. Don't open your eyes yet.'

'I'm dying here. Call a priest.'

'Here now, Lena's got you.' Gently and with great amusement, she eased him over, supported his head. 'Just swallow this.'

He glugged, choked, felt something vile wash over the fur, through the sand and down his throat. In defense, he tried to push the glass away from his lips, and opened his eyes.

He'd go to his grave denying the sound that had come out of his mouth had in any way resembled a girlish scream.

Lena clucked her tongue. 'I told you not to open your eyes.'

'What eyes? What eyes? They've been burned to cinders.'

'Drink the rest.'

'Go away, go very far away, and take your poison with you.'

'That's no way to talk to someone who's come to tend you on your deathbed.'

He slid back down, dragged a pillow over his face. 'How'd you know I was dying?'

'Effie called.'

'When's Remy's funeral?'

'Fortunately, he's marrying a woman with a great deal of tolerance, understanding and humor. How many titty bars did y'all hit last night?'

'All of them. All the titty bars in all the land.'

'I suppose that explains why you have a pasty on your cheek.'

'I do not.' But when he groped under the pillow, he felt the tassel. 'Oh God. Have some mercy and just kill me.'

'Well, all right, honey.' She applied just enough pressure to the pillow to have him flapping his hands and shoving up.

His face was flushed, his bloodshot eyes just a little wild. 'That wasn't funny.'

'You had to see it from this side.' And she laughed. He still wore his clothes, the wrinkled, liquor-spotted shirt half in, half out of his jeans. Another pasty peeked out of the shirt pocket. This one was pink and silver. His eyes were narrowed to a pained squint.

'You're going to feel better in a bit – not good but better. You get a shower and some food, on top of that potion I poured into you, you'll get the feeling back in your extremities in two, maybe three hours.'

Someone had shaved the fur off his tongue, he discovered. He wasn't sure it was an improvement. 'What was in that stuff you gave me?'

'You don't want to know, but I laced it with four aspirin, so don't take any more for a while. I'm going to fix you a nice light omelette and some toast.'

'Why?'

'Because you look so pitiful.' She started to kiss him, then jerked back, waving a hand between them. 'Christ Jesus, do something about that breath, *cher*, before you kill someone with it.'

'Who asked you?'

'And make that a long shower. You smell like the barroom floor.' She pushed to her feet. 'How come nobody's around here today?'

'In anticipation of a hangover, I let it be known that anyone who came around this house before three in the afternoon would be executed without trial.'

She checked her watch. 'Looks like you got a few hours yet.'

'If I have to get out of this bed, I'm getting a gun. I'll feel bad about killing you, but I'll do it.'

'I'll be in the kitchen.' She cocked a brow. 'Bring your gun, *cher*, and we'll see if you remember how to use it.'

'Is that a euphemism?' he called after her, then immediately regretted raising his voice. Holding his head to keep it in place, he eased creakily out of bed.

She chuckled all the way downstairs. Laughed harder when she heard a door slam. Bet he's sorry he did that, she thought, then stopped, looked back when she heard another two slams.

Ah well … she supposed he couldn't threaten ghosts with a gun.

299

'Make all the racket you want,' she said as she headed back toward the kitchen. 'You don't worry me any.'

The library doors shook as she passed them. She ignored them. If a surly, smelly man didn't chase her off, a mean-tempered ghost wouldn't.

He'd looked so damn cute, she thought as she hunted up the coffee beans. All pale and male and cross. And with that silly pasty plastered on his cheek.

Men just lost half their IQ when they had a look at a naked woman. Put a pack of them together with women willing to strip to music, and they had the common sense of a clump of broccoli.

She ground the beans, set coffee to brew. She was mixing eggs in a bowl when it occurred to her that it was the first time in her life she'd made breakfast for a man she hadn't slept with the night before.

Wasn't that an odd thing?

Odder still that she was humming in the kitchen of an annoyed, smelly, hungover man who'd snapped at her. *Out of character, Lena. Just what's going on here?*

She'd been so intrigued by Effie's cheerful amusement over Remy's condition. And here she was, feeling the same thing over Declan's.

She peered out the window at the garden that had been wild and abandoned only months before. It bloomed now, beautifully, with new sprigs, fresh green spearing out.

She'd gone and done it after all. Gone and let him sneak into her, right through the locks and bolts.

She was in love with him. And oh God, she didn't want to be – as much for his sake as for her own.

He'd blown the dust off those young dreams she'd so rigidly put away. The ones colored with love and hope and trust. They were so shiny now that they were staring her in the face. So shiny they blinded her.

And terrified her.

Marriage. The man wanted marriage, and she didn't believe in making promises unless you'd shed blood to keep them.

Would she? Could she?

'I think I'd want to,' she said quietly. 'I think I'd want to, for him.'

As she spoke, a cupboard door flew open. A thick blue mug shot out and smashed at her feet.

She leaped back, heart hammering as shards rained over her ankles. Grimly, she stared down at the blood seeping out of tiny nicks.

'Seems I already have. You don't want that, do you?' Bowl still clutched in her hand, she spun a circle. 'You want anything but our being together. We'll see who wins in the end, won't we? We'll just see.'

Deliberately she reached down for one of the shards, then ran it over her thumb. As the blood welled, she held her hand up, let it drip. 'I'm not weak, as he was. If I take love, if I promise love, I'll keep it.'

The sound of chimes had her bolting straight up. It was Declan's tune. The first ringing notes of it. Fear and wonder closed her throat, had her bobbling the bowl.

'Goddamn it, answer the door, will you?' His voice blasted downstairs, full of bitter annoyance. 'Then murder whoever rang that idiot doorbell.'

Doorbell? She pushed her free hand through her hair. He'd installed a doorbell that played 'After the Ball.' Wasn't that just like him?

'You keep shouting at me,' she called as she marched down the hall, 'you're going to have worse than a hangover to deal with.'

'If you'd go away and let me die in peace, I wouldn't have to shout.'

301

'In about two shakes, I'm coming up there and wringing your neck. And after I wring your neck, I'm going to kick your ass.'

She wrenched open the door on the final threat, and found herself glaring at a very handsome couple. It took only one blink to clear the temper for her to see Declan's eyes looking curiously back at her out of the woman's face.

'I'm Colleen Fitzgerald.' The woman, tidy, blond and lovely, held out an elegant hand. 'And who are you? If that's my son's ass you're intending to kick, I'd like to know your name.'

'Mom?' Dripping from the shower, wearing nothing but ripped sweatpants, Declan rushed to the top of the stairs. 'Hey! Mom, Dad.' Despite the ravages of the hangover, he bolted down, threw one arm around each of them and squeezed. 'I thought you were flying down tomorrow.'

'Change of plans. Are you just getting up?' Colleen demanded. 'It's after one in the afternoon.'

'Bachelor party last night. Hard liquor, loose women.'

'Really?' Colleen said and eyed Lena.

'Oh, not this one. She came over to play Florence Nightingale. Colleen and Patrick Fitzgerald, Angelina Simone.'

'Good to meet you.' Patrick, long, lanky, with his dark hair gorgeously silvered at the temples, sent Lena a generous smile. His blue eyes were bright and bold as he held out a hand.

Then they narrowed in concern as he saw her thumb. 'You've hurt yourself.'

'It's nothing.'

'What'd you do? You're bleeding. Jesus, Lena.' Panicked, Declan grabbed her wrist, all but plucked her off her feet and rushed her toward the kitchen.

'It's just a scratch. Stop it, Declan. Your parents. You're embarrassing me,' she hissed.

'Shut up. Let me see how deep it is.'

Still in the doorway, Patrick turned to his wife. 'She's the one?'

'He certainly thinks so.' Colleen pursed her lips, stepped into the house. 'Let's just see about all this.'

'Hell of a looker.'

'I've got eyes, Patrick.' And she used them to take in the house as they followed Declan's hurried path.

It was more, a great deal more than she'd expected. Not that she doubted her son's taste. But she'd been led to believe the house was in serious, perhaps fatal, disrepair. And what she saw now were gracious rooms, charming details, glinting glass and wood.

And in the kitchen she saw her son, hovering over the hand of a very annoyed, very beautiful woman who looked perfectly capable of carrying out her earlier threat.

'I beg your pardon.' Lena elbowed Declan aside and smiled coolly at his parents. 'I dropped a cup, that's all. It's nice to meet both of you.'

Declan turned to root through cupboards. 'You need some antiseptic and a bandage.'

'Oh, stop fussing. You'd think I cut my hand off. And if you don't watch yourself you'll step on the shards and be worse off than I am. I'm sorry your welcome's so disrupted,' she said to his parents. 'I'm just going to sweep up this mess, then I'll be on my way.'

'Where are you going?' Declan demanded. 'You promised food.'

She wondered if he could hear her teeth grinding together. 'Pour what's in that bowl into a skillet, turn on the burner and you'll have food.' She yanked open the broom closet. 'Why aren't you getting your parents coffee or a cold drink after their long trip? They raised you better than that.'

'We certainly did,' Colleen agreed.

'Sorry. Seeing the woman I love bleeding all over the floor distracted me.'

'Declan.' Though her voice was low, Lena's warning was loud and clear.

'Coffee sounds great,' Patrick said cheerfully. 'We came here straight from the airport. Wanted to see this place – and you, too, Dec,' he added with a wink.

'Where's your luggage?'

'Had it sent to the hotel. Son, this place is enormous. A lot of space for one man.'

'Lena and I want four kids.'

She heaved the broken shards into the trash and rounded on him.

'Okay, three,' he amended without a hitch in his stride. 'But that's my final offer.'

'I've had enough of this.' She shoved the broom and dustpan into his hands. 'You clean up your own messes. I hope you enjoy your stay,' she said stiffly to Colleen and Patrick. 'I'm late for work.'

She strode out the back because it was closer, and fought off the towering urge to slam the door until the windows cracked.

'Isn't she beautiful?' Declan said with a huge grin. 'Isn't she perfect?'

'You annoyed and embarrassed her,' Colleen told him.

'Good. I tend to make more progress that way. Let me get the coffee, then I'll show you around.'

An hour later, Declan sat with his mother on the rear gallery while Patrick – who'd lost the debate – made sandwiches.

The worst of the hangover had receded. Declan imagined he had whatever mysterious potion Lena had given him to thank for it – and the pleasure of seeing her in the same room as his parents.

Jeez, he'd missed them, he thought. He'd had no idea how much he'd missed them until he'd seen them.

'So,' he said at length, 'are you going to tell me what you think?'

'Yes.' But she continued to sit and look out over his gardens. 'Warm, isn't it? Early in the year to be so warm, I'd think.'

'Actually, it's cooler today. You should've been here a couple days ago. You could've poached eggs out here.'

She heard the way he said it, with a kind of pride. 'You were never a big fan of the cold. Even when we went skiing, you'd prefer rattling around the lodge to charging down the slopes.'

'Skiing's something people invented so they can pretend snow's fun.'

'See if we invite you to Vermont this season.' But her hand moved over, touched his. 'The house is beautiful, Declan. Even what you haven't gotten to yet is beautiful, in its way. I liked to think your fiddling with tools and wood and so on was a nice little hobby. I preferred to think that. As long as you were a lawyer, it was probable you'd stay in Boston. You'd stay close. I dreaded seeing you go, so I made it hard on you. I'm not sorry. You're my baby,' she said, and touched him in the deepest chamber of his heart.

'I don't have to be in Boston to be close.'

She shook her head. 'You won't come swinging in the house unexpectedly. We won't run into you in restaurants or at parties or the theater. That's a wrench in me, one you'll understand when you have those three or four children.'

305

'I don't want you to be sad.'

'Well, of course I'm sad. Don't be a boob. I love you, don't I?'

'You keep saying so,' he said playfully.

She looked at him, gray eyes steady on gray eyes. 'Lucky for both of us, I love you enough to know when to let go. You found your place here. I won't deny I hoped you wouldn't, but since you have, I'm glad for you. Damn it.'

'Thanks.' He leaned over, kissed her.

'Now, as for this woman ...'

'Lena.'

'I know her name, Declan,' Colleen said dryly. 'As a potential mother-in-law, I'm entitled to refer to her as "this woman" until I get to know her a little better. As for this woman, she's nothing like what I'd imagined for you. Not when I imagined you climbing up the ranks in the law firm, buying a house close by and within easy access to the country club. Jessica would have suited my require-ments as daughter-in-law quite well in that scenario. A good, challenging tennis partner who plays a decent hand of bridge and has the skill to chair the right committees.'

'Maybe you should adopt Jessica.'

'Be quiet, Declan.' Colleen's voice was mild – and steel. Lena would have recognized the tone instantly. 'I'm not finished. Jessica, however well suited for me, was very obviously not suited for you. You weren't happy, and I'd begun to see, and to worry about that just before you broke it off. I tried to convince myself it was just pre-wedding jitters, but I knew better.'

'It wouldn't have hurt for you to clue me in on that one.'

'Maybe not, but I was annoyed with you.'

'Tell me.'

'Don't sass, young man, especially when I'm about to be sentimental. You were always a happy child. Bright, clever, a smart tongue, but I respect that. You had, I'd call it, a bounce in your heart. And you lost it. I see you've gotten that back today. I saw it in your eyes again when you looked at Lena.'

He took Colleen's hand, rubbed it against his cheek. 'You called her Lena.'

'Temporarily. I haven't made up my mind about her. And believe me, boy, she hasn't made hers up about your father and me, either. So, I'd advise you to stay out of it and let us get on with the job of doing so.'

She stretched out her legs. 'Patrick? Did you have to hunt down the pig for those ham sandwiches?'

Declan grinned, gave the hand he held a big, noisy kiss. 'I love you guys.'

'We love you, too.' She squeezed his fingers, hard, then let them go. 'God knows why.'

He dreamed of storms and pain. Of fear and joys.

Rain and wind lashed the windows, and the pain that whipped through him erupted in a sobbing scream.

Sweat and tears poured down his face – her face. Her face, her body. His pain.

The room was gold with gaslight and the snap and simmer of the fire in the grate. And as that storm raged outside, another spun through her. Through him.

Agony vised her belly with the next contraction. She was blind with it. Her cry against it was primal, and burned his throat with its passion.

Push, Abby! You have to push! You're almost there.

Tired, she was so tired, so weak. How could she live through such pain? But she grit her teeth. Almost mad. Everything she was, everything she had, focused on this one task, this one miracle.

Her child. Her child, Lucian's child, was fighting to come into the world. She bore down with all the strength she had left. Life depended on it.

There's the head! Et là! *Such hair! One more, Abby. One more,* chère.

She was laughing now. Better than screaming, even if the laugh was tinged with hysteria. She braced herself on her elbows, threw her head back as fresh, unspeakable pain rolled through her.

This one moment, this one act, was the greatest gift a woman could give. This gift, this child, would be held safe, would be cherished. Would be loved for all of her days.

And on the pain, with lightning flashing, on the roar of thunder, she pushed, pushed, pushed wailing life into the world.

A girl! You have a beautiful girl.

Pain was forgotten. The hours of sweat and blood and agony were nothing now in the brilliant flash of joy. Weeping from it, she held out her arms for the small wriggling baby who cried out in what sounded like triumph.

My rose. My beautiful Marie Rose. Tell Lucian. Oh, please bring Lucian to see our daughter.

They cleaned both mother and baby first, smiling at the mother's impatience and the child's irritable cries.

There were tears in Lucian's eyes when he came into the room. When he clasped her hand, his fingers trembled. When he looked at the child they'd created, his face filled with wonder.

She told him what she had vowed on the instant Marie Rose had been placed in her arms.

We'll keep her safe, Lucian. No matter what, we'll keep her safe and happy. She's ours. Promise me you'll love and care for her, always.

Of course. She's so beautiful, Abby. My beautiful girls. I love you.

Say the words. I need to hear you say the words.

Still holding Abigail's hand, Lucian laid a tender finger on his daughter's cheek. *I'll love and I'll care for her, always. I swear it.*

Chapter Nineteen

Patrick Fitzgerald took his wife's hand as they strolled through the Quarter. He knew their destination was Et Trois and their mission another look at Angelina Simone.

'You know, Colleen, this is very close to interference, and spying.'

'And your point is?'

He had to laugh. After nearly forty years of marriage, the woman could always make him laugh. He considered that, above all, a sign of a successful partnership.

'You realize she might not be there. Owning a bar doesn't mean you're in it all day, every day.'

'So, we'll get a look at her place of business, and have a drink. It's perfectly up front and respectable.'

'Yes, dear.'

He used that phrase, that tone, only when he was making fun of her. Colleen debated between giving him a good elbow shot in the ribs and laughing. Then did both.

The crowds, the noise, the *heat* and the somehow florid and decaying elegance of the city weren't things that appealed to her for more than a brief visit. She preferred the Old-World charm, and yes, the dignity, of Boston.

Certainly Boston had its seamier sides, but it wasn't so overt, so celebratory about it. Sex was meant to be fun and interesting – she wasn't a prude, for God's sake. But it was also meant to be private.

And still, the tragic wail of a tenor sax weeping on the air touched some chord in her.

If her son was determined to make his home here, she'd accept that. Maybe, with a bit more study and debate, she'd accept the woman.

'You'll have time and opportunity to grill her at the wedding tomorrow,' Patrick pointed out.

Colleen only sighed at the minds of men. God bless them, they were simple creatures. Guileless, really. The first step, obviously, was to observe the girl in her own milieu.

She considered the neighborhood, the positioning of the bar, the level of traffic. She decided Lena had chosen wisely, and had taste and sense enough to let the exterior of the bar blend smoothly into the other establishments.

She liked the gallery over it, the pots of flowers – bright colors against the soft creams. It demonstrated taste and style, an appreciation for atmosphere.

She'd pried the information out of Declan that Lena lived above the bar, and wondered now if she should wheedle a visit upstairs to check out the living quarters.

She stepped inside Et Trois, made a good, objective study.

It was clean, which met with her approval. It was crowded but not jammed, which met with her business sense. Too early for the rowdy night crowd, Colleen judged, too late for the lunch shift.

The music coming out of the speakers was Cajun, she

supposed, and she approved that as well. It was lively, but not so loud as to make simple conversation a chore.

A black man in a bright red shirt worked behind the bar. A good face, she decided, smooth hands. A young waitress – blond, perky, wearing jeans perhaps just a tad too tight – served one of the tables.

Colleen spotted what she decided were a number of tourists from their camera and shopping bags. Others she assumed were locals.

Whatever food had been or was being served put a hot, spicy scent over the air.

Lena stepped out of the kitchen. Their eyes met immediately and with instant acknowledgment. Colleen let her lips curve in a small, polite smile and walked to the bar with Patrick following.

'Afternoon, Mrs. Fitzgerald, Mr. Fitzgerald.' An equally small, equally polite smile curved Lena's lips. 'You've been taking in the Quarter?' she asked with a glance at the shopping bags Patrick carried.

'Colleen rarely passes a store without seeing something that needs to be bought.'

'That must be where Declan gets it. Can I show you a menu?'

'We've had lunch, thanks.' Colleen slid onto a stool. 'I'd love a martini, Stoli, very cold, dead dry, straight up, shaken. Three olives.'

'And for you, Mr. Fitzgerald?'

'Make it the same, and make it Patrick.' He took the stool beside his wife. 'You've got a nice place here. Live music?' he asked with a nod toward the stage area.

'Every night, nine o'clock.' As she began to mix the martinis, she sent him a genuine smile. 'You like to dance, you should come back. We'll get your feet moving. You enjoying your visit?'

'We're looking forward to the wedding,' Colleen commented. 'Remy's like family. And we're pleased to see Declan making such progress on the house.'

'He's happy there.'

'Yes.'

Lena took out the two martini glasses she'd chilled during the mixing. 'Be nicer for you if he'd be happy in Boston – and with the one he almost married.'

'Yes, it would, wouldn't it? But we can't choose other people's lives. Even our children's. And you certainly can't select the person they'll love. Are you in love with my son, Lena?'

Hands rock steady, Lena strained the martinis into the cold glasses. 'That's something I'll talk to him about, when I'm ready. These are on the house,' she added, sliding the olives in. 'I hope they suit your tastes.'

'Thank you.' Colleen picked up her glass, sipped. Raised an eyebrow. 'It's excellent. I've always felt mixing the perfect martini is a kind of art, and have been surprised and disappointed that often those who own a bar or club or restaurant make or serve imperfect martinis.'

'Why do anything if you don't set out to do it right?'

'Exactly. It's a matter of pride, isn't it? In self, in one's work, one's life. Flaws are acceptable, even necessary to make us human and humble. But to serve a guest or customer less than the best one is capable of, strikes me as arrogant or sloppy. Often both.'

'I don't see the point in doing anything halfway,' Lena said, and filled a bowl with fresh snack mix. 'If I can't make a martini, fine, then I step back until I learn how it's done. Otherwise I'd disappoint myself and the person who was counting on me.'

'A good policy.' Colleen sampled an olive. 'Without high standards, we tend to settle for less than what makes us happy and productive, and can shortchange the people who matter to us.'

'When someone matters to me – and I'm careful about who does – I want the best for them. They may settle for less. But I won't.'

When Patrick leaned over, peered closely at Colleen's martini, she frowned at him. 'What are you doing?'

'Trying to see what's in yours that isn't in mine.'

It made Lena laugh, had her shoulders relaxing. 'He's an awful lot like you, isn't he? Got his mama's eyes though. Sees right through you. Even when you don't want him to. He loves you both like crazy, and that says something to me. So I'm going to say something to you.'

She leaned a little closer. 'I come from plain stock. Strong, but plain. My mother, she's a dead loss, and more of an embarrassment to me than I care to speak of. But my grandfather was a fine and decent man. My grand-mama's as good as anybody, and better than most. I run this bar because I'm good at it – and I like it – and I don't waste my time on things I don't like.'

She swept her hair behind her ear, kept her gaze level on Colleen's. 'I'm selfish and I'm stubborn, and I don't see a damn thing wrong with that. I don't care about his money, or yours, so let's just set that aside. He's the best man I ever met in my life, and I'm not good enough for him. I say that knowing I'm good enough for damn near anybody, but he's different. Turns out under that affable exterior that man's even more stubborn than I am, and I haven't figured out what to do about that quite yet. When I do, he'll be the first to know. I expect he'll fill you in on that particular outcome.

'Now.' Unconsciously, Lena toyed with the key she wore around her neck. 'Would you like another drink?'

'We'll just nurse these for a while,' Colleen told her.

314

'Excuse me a minute. I see I have an order to fill.' She moved down the bar to where her waitress waited with an empty tray.

'Well?' Patrick asked. 'I believe she set you neatly in your place.'

'Yes.' Well satisfied, Colleen took another sip of her martini. 'She'll do.'

'I'm not nervous.' Pale, jittery, Remy stood in the library while Declan attached the boutonniere of lily of the valley to his friend's tuxedo lapel.

'Maybe if you say that another dozen times, you'll believe it. Hold still, damn, Remy.'

'I'm holding still.'

'Sure, except for the mild seizure you seem to be having, you're steady as a rock.'

'I want to marry Effie. Want to live my life with her. This is the day we've both been looking forward to for months.'

'That's right. Today,' Declan said in sober tones, 'is the first day of the rest of your life.'

'I feel a little sick.'

'It's too late to puke,' Declan said cheerfully. 'You're down to the final fifteen. Want me to call your dad back in?'

'No. No, he'll have his hands full with Mama. How many people did you say were out there?'

'Couple hundred last I looked, and more coming.'

'Jesus. Jesus. Why didn't we elope? How's a man supposed to stand up in front of hundreds of people and change his life forever?'

'I think the tradition started so the groom couldn't run away. They'd go after him like a lynch mob.'

'That sure does settle me down, *cher*. How about you find me a couple fingers of bourbon?'

Declan merely strolled over to a painted cabinet and took out a bottle. 'I figured you'd need a hit.' He pulled out a tin of Altoids as well. 'And these. Don't want to be breathing whiskey on the bride. She might be the one who runs.'

Declan started to pour, but when the door opened after a cursory knock and his mother marched in, he whipped bottle and glass behind his back.

'Don't you both look handsome! Declan, don't give him more than one shot of that whiskey you've got behind you, and make sure he chases it with mouthwash.'

'I got Altoids.'

'Fine.' Smiling, she walked over and fussed with Remy's tie. 'You're nervous because this is the most important day of your life. There'd be something wrong with you if you didn't have some shakes. I promise, they'll go away the minute you see Effie. She looks beautiful.'

Colleen framed Remy's face in her hands. 'I'm very proud of you.'

'How about me?' Declan demanded. 'I thought of the Altoids.'

'I'll get to you later. You're marrying the woman you love,' Colleen went on. 'You're surrounded by friends and family who love you both. It's a beautiful day, and your brother – the one of your heart – has seen to it that you have a beautiful setting. Now you take a shot of that bourbon, then take a deep breath. Then get your butt out there and get married.'

'Yes, ma'am. I purely love you, Miss Colleen.'

'I know it. I love you, too, but I'm not going to kiss you and smear my lipstick. One drink, Declan. This boy goes out there tipsy, I'm holding you responsible.'

Later, Declan would think his mother was right, as usual. When he stood beside Remy, and Effie, frothy in white, stepped out on the gallery, Declan felt the nerves drain out of his friend – his brother. He saw the wide, wide grin stretch over Remy's face, heard his soft: 'That's my girl.'

He found his own gaze traveling through the rows of people, meeting Lena's. *And you're mine*, he thought. *This time around we're going to make it work.*

So he stood in the spring garden, with the old white house rising over the green lawn, and watched his friends marry.

When they kissed, when they turned to be announced as husband and wife, cheers rang out, so much more liberating and celebratory than the applause Declan was more accustomed to.

He felt his own grin stretch, nearly as wide as Remy's.

The music started up almost immediately. Fiddles, washboards, accordions. When the photographer whittled down to just the bride and groom, Declan broke free and wove his way through the sea of people to Lena.

She wore red. Bright, poppy red that left her back bare but for an intriguing web of thin straps. Just above her heart, she'd pinned the enamel watch and gold wings Lucian had once given Abigail.

'I wondered if you'd ever wear it.'

'It's special,' she said, 'so I save it for special. It was a beautiful wedding, Declan. You did a fine job getting this place ready for it. You're a good friend.'

'I have lots of good qualities, which makes you a very lucky woman. I've missed you the last couple days.'

'We've both been busy.'

'Stay tonight.' He caught her hand, seeing denial and excuses in her eyes. 'Angelina, stay tonight.'

'Maybe. You've got a lot of people you should be talking to.'

'They're all talking to each other. Where's Miss Odette?'

Lena scowled. 'Your mother swept her off somewhere.'

'You want me to find them, cut Miss Odette loose?'

Pride stiffened her spine, her voice. 'My grandmama can hold her own against your mama any day of the week.'

'Oh yeah?' Amused, Declan narrowed his eyes in challenge. 'If they get physical, my money's on Colleen. She's got a wicked left. Why don't we get some champagne and go find them? See what round they're in.'

'If she hurts my grandmama's feelings—'

'She would never do that.' No longer amused, Declan gave her shoulders a little shake. 'What do you take her for, Lena? If she went off with Miss Odette, it's because she'd like to get to know her.'

'I suppose that's why she dragged your daddy into my place. So she could get to know me better.'

'They were in your place?'

'My bar, yeah.' Annoyed with herself for *being* annoyed, Lena reached out to take a flute from a waiter passing champagne. 'She came in to check the place out, and me with it. So, she got her an eyeful, and a damn good martini. And I set her straight.'

He experienced the jittery male panic at the image of the two most important females in his life squaring off. 'What the hell does that mean?'

'I said what I had to say, that's all. We understand each other fine now.'

'Why don't you bring me up to date so I can understand you fine, too?'

'This isn't the time or the place.'

'We're going to find the time and the place.'

Because she heard the temper in his voice, she shrugged. Then smiled and traced a finger down his cheek. 'Now don't get all riled up, *cher*. We got us a party here. You and me, we can fight anytime.'

'Okay, we'll schedule it in for a little later.' He caught her chin in his hand. 'I can't figure out who you're selling short, Lena. Me, my family or yourself. Let me know when you've got the answer.'

He bent, brushed his lips over hers. 'See you later.'

The reception moved into the ballroom, and still managed to spill onto the galleries, onto the lawn. For the first time in decades, the house filled with music and laughter. Racing children, crying babies, flirting couples and gossiping friends filled the great room, relaxed in the shade of white umbrellas at tables around the gardens or plopped down on the gallery.

Declan liked to imagine the house absorbing all that positive energy, even into the dark corners of the rooms he'd kept locked.

'Declan.' Effie laid a hand on his arm. 'May I have this dance?'

'Did somebody kill Remy?' He led her out on the floor. 'I figure that's the only way he'd let you more than a foot away from him.' He kissed her hand before taking her into his arms. 'Can't blame him. When you've got the most beautiful woman in the room, you keep her close.'

'Oh, Declan.' She laid her cheek on his. 'If I wasn't madly in love with my husband, I'd make such a play for you.'

'If you ever get tired of him, let me know.'

'I want to thank you for everything you did to give me this perfect day. I know my mama, my sister and I drove you a little crazy the last couple weeks.'

'Has it only been a couple weeks?' He laughed. 'It was worth every hour I hid in closets so none of you could find me.'

319

'I'm so happy. I'm so happy, and I love you. I love everybody today,' she said with a laugh. 'Everyone in the world, but today, next to Remy, I love you best of all so I want you to be happy.'

'I am.'

'Not enough.' She turned her lips to his ear. 'Declan, there's something in this house that's just not finished. I didn't think I believed in that sort of thing, but … I feel it. Whenever I'm here, I feel it. I feel it even today.'

He could feel the tremor move through her, rubbed his hand over her back to soothe it away. 'You shouldn't think about it today. You shouldn't worry today.'

'I'm worried for you. Something … it isn't finished. Part of it, somehow part of it's my fault.'

'Yours?' He eased her back now so he could see her face, then circled her toward one of the corners. 'What do you mean?'

'I wish I knew what I meant. I only know what I feel. Something I did, or didn't do for you. It doesn't make a bit of sense, but it's such a strong feeling. The feeling that I wasn't there for you when you needed me most. I guess I'm a little afraid something bad's going to happen again if it's not all made right. So, well, as silly as this sounds, I just want to tell you I'm sorry, so awfully sorry for letting you down however I did.'

'It's all right.' He touched his lips to her forehead. 'You couldn't know. Whatever it was, if it was, you couldn't know. And sweetheart, this isn't a day for looking back. It's all about tomorrow now.'

'You're right. Just … just be careful,' she said as Remy walked up and gave Declan a mock punch.

'That's my wife you're holding, *cher*. You go get your own girl.'

'Good idea.'

He hunted up Lena, found her in a clutch of people. The red of her dress was like a sleek tongue of flame over her dusky skin. He imagined his reaction to it, to her, transmitted clearly enough as he saw that knowing and essentially female look come into her eyes as he stepped toward her.

He turned slightly and held out a hand to her grand-mother. 'Miss Odette, would you dance with me?'

'Day hasn't come when I'll turn down a dance with a handsome man.'

'You look wonderful,' he told her when they took the floor.

'Weddings make me feel young. I had a nice talk with your mama.'

'Did you?'

'You're wondering,' she said with a chuckle. 'I'll tell you we got on just fine. And she seemed pleased when I told her I saw how you'd been raised up right the first time I met you. She paid me back the compliment by saying the same about my Lena. Then we chatted about things women often chat about at weddings, which would likely bore you — except to say we agreed what a handsome young man you are. And handsome young men should find more reason to wear tuxedos.'

'I could become a maître d'. But they get better tips when they have a snooty accent, and I'm not sure I could pull that part off.'

'Then I'll just have to wait until your own wedding to see you all slicked up again.'

'Yeah.' He looked over her head, but Lena had moved on. 'This one's working out pretty well anyway. I was a little panicked that the storm last night would screw things up.'

'Storm? *Cher*, we didn't have a storm last night.'

'Sure we did. A mean one. Don't tell me you slept through it.'

'I was up till midnight.' She watched his face now. 'Finishing the hem on this dress. Then I was up again 'round four when Rufus decided he needed to go outside. I saw lights on over here then. Wondered what you were doing up at that hour. Night was clear as a bell, Declan.'

'I ... I must've dreamed about a storm. Pre-wedding stress.' But he hadn't been up at four. Hadn't been up at all, as far as he knew, after midnight – when he'd walked through the house to turn off all the lights before going to bed.

Dreams, he thought. Wind and rain, the flash of lightning. The yellow flames of the fire in the grate. Pain, sweat, thirst. Blood.

Women's hands, women's voices – Effie's? – giving comfort, giving encouragement.

He remembered it now, clearly, and stopped dead in the middle of the dance.

He'd had a baby. He'd gone through childbirth.

Good God.

'*Cher*? Declan? You come on outside.' Gently, Odette guided him off the floor. 'You need some air.'

'Yeah. Southern ladies are big on swooning, right?'

'What's that?'

'Never mind.' He was mortified, he was awed, at what had happened to him inside his own dream. Inside, he supposed, his own memories.

'Go on back in,' he told her. 'I'm just going to take a walk, clear my head.'

'What did you remember?'

'A miracle,' he murmured. 'Remind me to buy my mother a really great present. I don't know how the hell you women get through it once. She did it four times.

322

Amazing,' he mumbled, and headed down the steps. 'Fucking amazing.'

He walked all the way around the house, then slipped back in for a tall glass of icy water. He used it to wash down three extra-strength aspirin in hopes of cutting back on the vicious headache that had come on the moment he'd remembered the dream.

He could hear the music spilling down the steps from the ballroom. He could feel the vibrations on the ceiling from where dozens of feet danced.

He had to get back up, perform his duties as best man and host. All he wanted to do was fall facedown on the bed, close his eyes, and slide into oblivion.

'Declan.' Lena came in through the gallery doors, then shut them behind her. 'What's the matter?'

'Nothing. Just a headache.'

'You've been gone nearly an hour. People are asking about you.'

'I'm coming up.' But he sat on the side of the bed. 'In a minute.'

She crossed to him. 'Is it bad?'

'I've had worse.'

'Why don't you just lie down a few minutes?'

'I'm not crawling into bed on my best friend's wedding day – unless you want to keep me company.'

'It's tempting. Seeing a man in a tux always makes me want to peel him out of it.'

'Maître d's must just love you.'

'There now, you made a stupid joke, so you must be feeling better.'

'Considering I gave birth less than twenty-four hours ago, I'd say I'm doing great.'

Lena pursed her lips. '*Cher*, just how much have you had to drink this evening?'

'Not nearly as much as I plan on having. You know how you had this theory that I was Abigail Manet? Well, I'm starting to think you're onto something seeing as I dreamed I was in that room down the hall, in the bed I've seen in there – that one that isn't there. I wasn't seeing Abigail on that bed, in the last stages of labor. I experienced it, and let me tell you, it ain't no walk on the beach. Any woman who doesn't go for the serious drugs is a lunatic. It beats anything they dreamed up for that entertaining era known as the Spanish Inquisition.'

'You dreamed you were Abigail, and you—'

'It wasn't like a dream, Lena, and I think I must've been in that room when I had the – flash or hallucination, or whatever we call it. I can remember the storm – the sound of it, and how scared I was, how focused I was on bringing that baby out.'

He paused, replayed his own words. 'Boy, that sounded weird.'

'Yes. Yes, it did.' She sat beside him.

'I heard the voices. Other women helping me. I can see their faces – especially the young one. The one close to my age – Abigail's age. I can feel the sweat running down my face, and the unbelievable fatigue. Then that sensation, that peak of it all when it was like coming to the point of being ripped open. Bearing down, then the relief, the numbness, the fuck-ing *wonder* of pushing life into the world. Then the flood of pride and love when they put that miracle in my arms.'

He looked down at his hands while Lena stared at him. 'I can see the baby, Lena, clear as life, I can see her. All red and wrinkled and pissed off. Dark blue eyes, dark hair. A rosebud mouth. Tiny, slender fingers, and I thought: There are ten, and she is perfect. My perfect Rose.'

He looked at Lena now. 'Marie Rose, your great-great-grandmother. Marie Rose,' he repeated, 'our daughter.'

Chapter Twenty

Their daughter. She couldn't dismiss it, and something deep inside her grieved. But she couldn't speak of it, wouldn't speak of it, not when her head and heart were so heavy.

Lena threw herself back into the crowds, the music, the laughter. This was *now*, she thought. Now was what counted.

She was alive, with the warm evening air on her skin, under the pure, white moonlight with the fragrance of the flowers and gardens rioting around her.

Roses and verbena, heliotrope, jasmine.

Lilies. Her favorite had been the lily. She kept them, always, in her room. First in the servants' quarters, then in their bedroom. Clipped in secret from the garden or the hothouse.

And for the nursery, there were roses. Tiny pink buds for their precious Marie Rose.

Frightened, she pushed those thoughts, those images, aside. Grabbing a partner, she flirted him into a dance.

She didn't want the past. It was dead and done. She didn't want the future. It was capricious and often cruel. It was the moment that was to be lived, enjoyed. Even controlled.

So when Declan's father took her hand, she smiled at him, brilliantly.

'This one here's a Cajun two-step. Can you handle it?'

'Let's find out.'

They swung among the circling couples with quick, stylish moves that had her laughing up at him. 'Why, Patrick, you're a natural. You sure you're a Yankee?'

'Blood and bone. Then again, you have to factor in the Irish. My mother was a hell of a step-dancer, and can still pull it off after a couple of pints.'

'How old's your mama?'

'Eighty-six.' He twirled her out and back. 'Fitzgeralds tend to be long-lived and vigorous. Something's upset you.'

She kept her cheerful expression in place. 'Now what could upset me at such a lovely time and place?'

'That's the puzzle. Why don't we get a glass of champagne, and you can tell me?'

He didn't give her a chance to refuse. Like father, like son, she thought as he kept her hand firmly in his. He drew her to the bar, ordered two flutes, then led her outside.

'A perfect night,' she said, and breathed it in. 'Look at those gardens. It's hard to believe what they were like just a few months back. Did Declan tell you about the Franks?'

'About the Franks, Tibald. About Effie and Miss Odette. About the ghosts, about you.'

'He bit off a lot here.' She sipped champagne, wandered to the baluster. Below, people were still dancing on the lawn. A group of women sat at one of the white tables under a white moon, some with babies sleeping on their shoulders, some with children drooping in their laps.

'He was bored in Boston.'

Intrigued, Lena looked away from the people, the charm of the fairy lights, and looked at Patrick. 'Bored?'

'Unhappy, restless, but in a large part bored. With his work, his fiancée, his life. The only thing that put any excitement in his face was the old house he was redoing. I worried he'd go along, end up married to the wrong woman, working in a field he disliked, living a life that only half satisfied him. I shouldn't have worried.'

He leaned back on the baluster and looked through the open doors into the ballroom. 'His mind, his heart, was never set on the path we – his mother and I – cleared for him. We didn't want to see that, so for a long time, we didn't.'

'You only wanted the best for him. People tend to think what's best for them is best for the people they love.'

'Yes, and Declan's nature is to do whatever he can to make those he loves happy. He loves you.'

When she said nothing, Patrick turned to her. 'You said he was stubborn. It's more than that. Once Declan sets his mind on a goal, on a vision, he's got a head like granite. He won't be turned away by obstacles or excuses or luke-warm protests. If you don't love him, Lena, if you don't want a life with him, hurt him. Hurt him quick and make it deep. Then walk away.'

'I don't want to hurt him. That's the whole point and problem.'

'He didn't think he was capable of loving anyone. He told me that after he broke it off with Jessica. He said he didn't have that kind of love inside him. Now he knows he does, and he's better for it. You've already made a difference in his life, an important one. Now you have to love him back, or leave him. To do anything in between would be cruel, and you're not cruel.'

She reached up, closed her fingers around the key on its chain, then dropped them – nervous now – to the wings on her breast. 'He's not what I planned for. He's not what I was looking for.'

He smiled then, kindly, and patted her hand. 'Life's full of surprises, isn't it? Some of them are a real kick in the ass.' Then he leaned down and kissed her cheek. 'I'll see you again,' he said, and left her alone.

The party rolled on a good two hours after the bride and groom were seen off in a shower of confetti – which Declan imagined he'd be finding in his lawn, his clothes, perhaps even his food for the next six months.

The music stayed hot, and the guests stayed happy. In the early hours of the morning, some walked to their cars. Others were carried, and not all of them were children.

Declan stood on the curve of his front steps and watched the last of them drive away. The sky in the east was paling, just a gentle lessening of the dark. Even as he stood, he saw a star go out.

Morning was waking.

'You must be tired,' Lena said from the gallery above him.

'No.' He continued to look at the sky. 'I should be, but I'm not.'

'It's going to take you a week to clean this place up.'

'Nope. The General and her troops are coming over tomorrow to deal with it. I'm ordered to keep out of the way, and that's one command I won't have any trouble obeying. I didn't think you'd stay.'

'Neither did I.'

He turned now, looked up at her. A kind of Romeo and Juliet pose, he thought, and hoped for a better ending. 'Why did you?'

'I'm not sure. I don't know what to do about you, Declan. I swear to God, I just don't know. Men've never been any trouble for me. Maybe I've been trouble for them,' she said with a faint smile. 'But you're the first who's given me any.'

He started up to her. 'None of them loved you.'

'No, none of them loved me. Wanted me. Desired me, but that's the easy part. You can be careless with wants. And I'll tell you the truth. Sometimes, most times, I enjoyed that carelessness. Not just the sex, but the dance. The game. Whatever you want to call that courtship that's no courtship at all. When the music stops, or the game's over, there might be some bumps and bruises, but nobody's really hurt.'

'But this isn't a game between the two of us.'

'I've already hurt you.'

'Bumps and bruises so far, Lena.' He stopped, face-to-face with her. 'Bumps and bruises.'

'When you look at me, what are you seeing? Someone, something else from before. You can't run the living on the dead.'

'I see you clear enough. But I see something else in both of us that shouldn't be ignored or forgotten. Maybe something that needs to be put right before we can move on.'

He reached in his pocket, pulled out Lucian's watch. 'I gave this to you once before, about a hundred years ago. It's time you had it back.'

Her fingers chilled at the idea of holding it. 'If this is true, don't you see it all ended in grief and death and tragedy? We can't change what was. Why risk bringing it on again?'

'Because we have to. Because we're stronger this time.' He opened her hand, put the watch into her palm, closed her fingers over it. 'Because if we don't set it right, it never really ends.'

'All right.' She slipped the watch into the pocket of the short jacket she'd put on. Then she unpinned the watch on her dress. 'I gave this to you once before. Take it back.'

When he took it, held it, the clock that had once stood inside the Hall began to bong.

'Midnight,' he said with perfect calm. 'It'll strike twelve times.' And he looked down at the face of the enameled watch he held. 'Midnight,' he repeated, showing it to her. 'Look at yours.'

Her fingers weren't so steady when she pulled it out. 'Jesus,' she breathed when she saw both hands straight up. 'Why?'

'We're going to find out. I have to go inside.' He looked up, toward the third floor. 'I have to go up to the nursery. The baby ...'

Even as he spoke, they heard the fretful cries.

'Let's just go. Declan, let's just get in the car and drive away from here.'

But he was already moving inside. 'The baby's crying. She's hungry. She needs me. Lucian's parents are sleeping. I always go upstairs early when he's not home. I hate sitting with them in the parlor after dinner. I can feel the way she dislikes me.'

His voice had changed, Lena realized as she followed him. There was a Cajun cadence to it. 'Declan.'

'Claudine will walk her, or change her, but my pretty Rosie needs her mama. I don't like having her up on the third floor,' he said as he hurried down the corridor. 'But Madame Josephine always gets her way. Not always,' he corrected, and there was a smile in his voice now. 'If she always did, I'd be alligator bait 'stead of married to Lucian. He'll be home tomorrow. I miss him so.'

As he started up the stairs, his gait slowed, and Lena heard the rapid pace of his breath. 'I have to go up.' It was his own voice now, with fear at the edges. 'I have to go in. I have to see.'

Gathering all her courage, Lena took his hand. 'We'll go in together.'

His hand shook. The cold that permeated into the air speared into the bone. Nausea rolled through his belly, rose up his throat. Clamping down against it, he shoved the door open.

He stumbled, and even as Lena tried to catch him, fell to his knees.

'He comes in. He's drunk. I don't want him coming up here, but he won't go away. Everyone says, they say how he looks just like Lucian, but they don't see his eyes. I have to make him go away, away from my baby. I wish Claudine hadn't gone off to meet Jasper. I don't like being alone up here with Julian. He scares me, but I don't want him to see it.'

His eyes were glazed, glassy smoke in a face that had gone pale as death. 'Declan, oh God, Declan, come back.' She squeezed his hand until she felt bone rub against bone.

'When he grabs at me, I get away.' His voice was breathless now. He still knelt, a rangy man with sun-streaked hair, wearing a tuxedo with the tie dangling loose. A man with a woman's memories, a woman's terror storming inside him.

'But I can't leave my baby. I get the poker from the fireplace. I'll kill him if I have to. I'll kill him if he touches me or my baby. Oh God, oh God, oh God.'

As her knees seemed to melt away, Lena sank to the floor beside him, tried to wrap her arms around him.

'He's stronger than me. I scream and I scream, but nobody comes to help me. He's drunk and he's crazy. He's crazy and he's drunk. He knocks me down, and he rips at my clothes. I can't get away. My baby's crying, but I can't get to her. I can't stop him.'

'Oh.' Shaking, Lena tried to hold him, rock him. 'No. No, no, no.'

'He rapes me.' Fire burned in the center of him. Pain, the pain, and the fear. Oh God, the fear. 'I call for help. I call for you, but you're not here.'

His voice tore with tears. 'You don't come. I need you.'

'Don't, don't, don't.' It was all she could say as she clung to him.

'He hurts me, but I fight him. I try to stop him, but he won't stop. I'm so scared, I'm so scared, but even then I know he's not doing this because he wants me. It's because he hates you.'

He turned his head, those storm-gray eyes drenched. 'He hates you. And because I'm yours, he has to break me. The way he broke your toys when you were children. I beg him to stop, but he won't. He tries to make me stop screaming, but I can't stop. I can't. His hands are around my throat.'

It doubled him over, that hideous pressure, that shocking loss of air. 'I can't breathe. I can't breathe. My baby's crying for me, and I can't breathe. He kills me. While my baby's crying in her crib. Our baby. While he's still inside me. He breaks me like a toy that belongs to his brother.'

He lifted his head, looked at her now. And when he spoke, his voice was so full of grief she wondered they both didn't die of it. 'You didn't come. I called, but you didn't come.'

'I'm sorry. I'm so sorry.'

'She came.' Declan got rockily to his feet. 'She came, and she saw what he had done to me. She looked down at me like I was a mess that had to be cleaned up before the neighbors came to call.'

His eyes were dry now, and narrowed at the slamming of doors on the second floor. 'Her house, her sons, and I was the bayou slut who'd trespassed. I watched her look down on me. It was like a dream, that watching. I saw her tell him to carry me out, down to the bedroom, while she cleaned up the blood, and the candle wax, and the broken crockery. He took my body out the gallery, but I watched her, watched her go over to my sweet baby, and I heard her mind wonder if it would be best just to smother the child. She considered it, and I believe if she'd tried, there was enough of me left that I could have struck her down like a lightning bolt.'

He walked back to the door. 'She thought I was weak, but she was *wrong*. They could kill me, but they couldn't end me.'

'Declan, that's enough.'

'No, not yet.' He walked down the steps, down the hall, opened the door to Abigail's bedroom. 'He laid me on the bed in here. And he wept. Not for me, but for himself. What would happen to him? His hand had defiled me, and killed me, but he thought only of himself. And does still. For he's in this house, he and Josephine. Walking and waiting in their little hell.'

He crossed over to the wall where the armoire had been, opened the door of it in his mind. 'They took some of my clothes. I had the gown in here for the ball. I was so proud of it I wanted to be beautiful for you. Make you proud of me. She dropped my watch, but didn't notice. She had Julian wrap me up, and they carried me out, with the suitcase full of my things. They got old bricks to weigh me down, and they carried me away.

'It was hard. Even though there was moonlight, even though it was cool, it was a hard walk carting all of that. Julian got sick, but she brooked no nonsense. They would say I ran off with another man. They would let the gossip spread that my baby was a bastard, fawned off on you as your own. She told Julian how it would be as they put the bricks over me, as they tied the cloak around me with rope, as they pushed me into the bayou.'

He looked back at her. 'You believed them.'

'No.' Lena was weeping now. For him, for Abigail, for herself, for Lucian. 'No.'

333

'Not at first. You feared for me. You searched for me. You wept for me. I tried to reach you, but you wouldn't let me in. You wouldn't let me in because some part of you already believed their lies. I *loved* you. With all my heart, my soul, my body. I died for you.'

'I couldn't stop what happened to you. I wasn't here to stop it.'

'No, you weren't here that night. And you were never really here again. Not for me, and not for our child. You broke your promise to me, the solemn vow you made to me in that bed the night she was born. More than death, that is what doomed us.'

'How did I break my promise?'

'You promised to love our child, to *care* for her always. I was always true to you, Lucian. You have to know.'

'I do know.' She closed her hand over the watch in her pocket and felt the weight, the grief, the sorrow.

'How could you leave her alone? How could you turn from her? You were all she had. You swore to me.'

'I don't know. I was weak. I wasn't as brave or as true as you. Maybe … I think maybe you were the making of me, and when you were gone, I had nothing to hold me straight.'

'You had Marie Rose.'

'Perhaps I loved you too much, and her not enough. Forgive me. Forgive me for what I did, for what I didn't do. I can't go back and change it.' She drew out the watch, held it face up in her palm. 'No matter how often time stops, it's too late. If I could, I would never leave you. I'd take you and the baby away. I'd do anything to stop what happened to you.'

'I loved you. And my heart *ached* every minute since they took me from you. Ached with grief, then with hope, and then with sorrow. You chose death, Lucian, rather than life. Still you choose loneliness rather than love. How can

I forgive, when you can't? Until you do, they've won, and the house that should've been ours still holds them. None of us will ever be free, until you choose.'

He turned, opened the gallery doors and walked outside.

The door slamming at her back made her jolt. It was, Lena thought, like a rude laugh aimed at someone else's misery. Ignoring it, she stepped outside, took a deep breath.

'Declan.'

He was leaning on the baluster, staring out at the first hints of dawn. 'Yeah. I'm trying to figure out if I need an exorcist, a psychiatrist, or if I should cash in and see about starring in a remake of *The Three Faces of Eve*.'

He rolled his shoulders, as if trying to shrug off an irritating weight. 'I think I'll settle for a Bloody Mary.'

Cautious, she stepped up behind him. 'I'll make us both one,' she began, and started to lay her hand on his back. He sidestepped, evading her touch, and left her standing there with her hand suspended.

'I don't need to be petted and stroked. Still a little raw here. Comes from getting raped and murdered, I guess.' Jamming his hands in his pockets, he strode down the steps.

She waited a moment, struggling for balance, then walked down to join him in the kitchen. 'Let me make them. I'm the professional.'

'I can make my own goddamn drink.'

It stung when he snatched the bottle of vodka out of her hand. Stung like a slap. 'All right then, make your own goddamn drink. While you're at it, you oughta think about living your own goddamn life.'

She spun away, and when he grabbed her arm, she lashed out with her own slap. When her hand cracked across his cheek, the clock began to strike again, and the doors to slam.

335

Cold settled gleefully into the bone.

'You ever been raped?'

She yanked her arm free. 'No.'

'Probably haven't been strangled to death, either?' Forgoing the niceties, he took a long drink straight from the bottle. 'Let me give you a clue. It tends to put you in a really foul mood.'

Temper drained out of her. 'Don't drink like that, *cher*. You'll only get sick.'

'I'm already sick. I need a shower.'

'Go on and take one. You'll feel better for it. I'm going to make some tea. Just let me do this,' she snapped out before he could argue. 'Maybe it'll settle us both down some.'

'Fine. Whatever.' He stomped up the stairs.

She sat for a moment, just sat because her legs were still shaking. Then she took the watch out of her pocket, studied the face. The second hand ticked around and around. But the time never went beyond midnight.

Putting it away again, she rose to brew the tea.

She carried it up, along with the tidy triangles of toast. The sickbed meal her grandmother had made for her in childhood. He was sitting on the side of the bed, wearing a tattered pair of sweatpants. His hair was still wet. His skin was reddened from vicious scrubbing. She set the tray beside him.

'Do you want me to go?'

'No.' When she poured a mug of tea, he took it, tried to warm his hands. Despite the blasting heat of the shower, he still felt chilled.

'I didn't just see it, or remember it. I felt it. The fear, the pain, the violation. The humiliation. And more – like that isn't bad enough – part of me was still me. That part, the big, tough guy part, was helpless, just helpless watching a terrified woman be raped and strangled. I can't explain it.'

'You don't have to. I felt some of it. Not as strong, not as clear as you, but … When you looked at me, when she was looking at me out of your eyes, I felt such grief, such regret. Such guilt. Drink your tea now, sweetheart.'

He lifted the mug obediently. 'It's good. Pretty sweet.'

'Sweet tea and toast. It's good for you.' She crawled onto the bed behind him, knelt and began to knead at his shoulders. 'She was stronger than he was. It's not his fault so much. He was raised weak. But he loved her, Declan. I know that without a doubt. Even without knowing the terrible thing that happened to her, he blamed himself. For not being with her, not giving her enough of himself.'

'He deserted the child.'

There was such finality in his voice. 'He did. Yes, he did,' Lena replied. 'And though it was wrong of him, wrong to take his own life and leave their baby an orphan, she had a better life because of it. She was surrounded by people who loved her, who valued the memory of her mother. She would never have had that life here, in the Hall.'

'She was entitled to it. He should have seen to it.'

She laid her cheek on the top of his head. 'You can't forgive him.'

'I can't understand him.'

'No, a man like you wouldn't understand a man like him. Maybe I do, maybe I understand a man who'd run off with a woman rather than stand up to his parents. One who'd bring her back into a house full of resentment and shadows instead of making them a home. One who'd fall apart enough to drown himself rather than live with the hurt and raise his own child with the love and compassion that had been denied him. He wanted to be more than he was. With her, he would have been.

'You shouldn't despise him, Declan. You should pity him.'

'Maybe. It's hard. I've still got a lot of her despair inside me.' Abigail's, he thought, and a good portion of his own.

'Can you rest?'

'I don't think so.'

'Why don't you try? I need to go change.' She slid off the bed, then lifted the tray and set it aside. 'Try to sleep awhile. I won't be long.'

He didn't try to stop her. It was probably best to be alone. He lay back, stared at the ceiling as the first birds began to sing.

Abigail had been broken, he thought. Body and heart.

He was feeling pretty much the same himself.

He must have dozed, for when he opened his eyes the sun was up. Still early, he decided, but the General and her troop of whirlwinds would be coming along shortly to storm through his house with mops and brooms and God knew.

Maybe the place needed to be cleaned up, shaken out. It was still his. He wasn't giving it up. Whatever had happened, whatever shared it with him, he wasn't giving it up.

And by Christ, he wasn't giving Lena up, either.

He sat up, scowling, and saw her sitting in the chair across the room. She wore jeans, a plain white T-shirt. There were three small bouquets lying in her lap.

'You up for a little drive?' she asked him.

'I guess.'

'Put a shirt on, and some shoes.'

'Where are we going?'

'I'll tell you on the way.'

She drove, and he kept the flowers in his lap now.

'I want to take flowers to her. To Marie Rose.' As her ancestor, Lena thought, as her father. 'I thought you might like to visit there, too.'

He said nothing.

338

'Grandmama told me,' Lena continued, 'how Marie Rose used to go to the cemetery once a year on her birthday. She'd bring him flowers. This morning, when I went over to change my clothes, she told me where we'd find his crypt, and we picked these from the marsh. I want to take flowers to Lucian, too.'

He picked one clutch up. 'Your symbol of pity?'

'If that's the best we can do.'

'And the others?'

'Marie Rose took them to her mother, once a year as well. A part of her must've known. She went to the river, every year on her birthday, and dropped flowers in the water. Grandmama told me where.'

She drove smoothly, a little fast, then slowed to turn into the cemetery. 'I know you're still angry with him, and with me. If you don't want to do this, you can wait in the car. I won't blame you.'

'Why are you doing it?'

'He's part of me. Through blood, and more. If I can find a way to accept who birthed me, if I can live with that, then I can find a way to accept this. To live with it.'

She stopped the car, took two of the bouquets. 'It's a little walk from here. It shouldn't take me long.'

'I'm coming with you.'

He got out, but didn't — as she'd grown used to — reach for her hand. They wound their way over the paths between the tombs, the ornate grilles, the marble angels and through shadows thrown by crosses.

She stopped at one of the raised tombs. There were many, simple and unadorned. Her grandfather rested here, and others who were parts and pieces of her. But today she had come only for one.

Her hands gripped tight on the flowers. Marie Rose, she read. Blood of my blood, heart of my heart.

'Grandmama, she told me Marie Rose was a happy woman, she had a good life. She was content with it. That might not be enough to make up for what was done, but if it had been done different ... Well, I don't see how I'd be standing here with you this morning.'

She started to lay the flowers, and Declan closed his hand over hers on the stems. They placed them on the grave – the baby, the girl, the old woman, together.

'He's a ways from here,' Lena managed. Her voice was thick, her vision blurry as she turned away.

They waited through the sunlight, through the shadows of the tombs, in silence.

The Manet crypt was a towering square, its porticoes carved, its doors thick and studded. Topping it was a fierce angel, holding a harp as a soldier might a shield.

'Cheerful,' Declan commented. 'I'd say none of them went gently into that good night.' He glanced around, saw the plain concrete box on a raised slab. The plaque read: LUCIAN EDUARD MANET. 1877–1900.

'He's out here?'

'He wasn't to be forgiven,' Lena explained. 'Not for his marriage, his child, his embarrassing death. They called it accidental drowning, though everyone knew it was suicide. But though Josephine wouldn't have him in the family crypt, she wanted him buried on consecrated ground. Otherwise, there would have been yet another scandal.'

Declan looked back at the crypt. 'Bitch.'

'He had no grandparents, as I did, to love him. To soften the blows. He had a twin brother who loathed him simply because he existed. He had money and position, education and privilege. But no love. Until Abigail. Then they took her from him.'

She laid the flowers for him. 'He did the best he could. It just wasn't enough.'

'You're stronger than he ever was. Smarter, more resilient.'

'I hope so. And I hope he rests soon. The flowers won't last long in this sun, but ... Well, you do what you can.'

She walked away without another word. Declan lingered a moment more, staring at the plaque, then the flowers. Then he went with his impulse, took a single flower out of the bouquet, and laid it on top of the tomb.

Lena put her sunglasses on because her eyes were tearing. 'That was kind.'

'Well, you do what you can.' This time, he took her hand.

They didn't speak on the drive back. Nor did Rufus or Odette come out of the house when Lena parked in front of it. He remained silent as she led the way through the marsh. Silent, as he remembered the way in the night, with the chill in the air, the flitting moonlight, the call of an owl. And the panting breaths of a killer and his accomplice.

'Do you want to go back? You're awfully pale.'

'No.' Sweat ran down his back despite the cold under his skin. 'I need to do this.'

'It's not much farther.'

There were marsh flowers springing up along the edges of the narrow, beaten path. He concentrated on them, on the color, the small beauty. But when she stopped on the bank, he was out of breath and dizzy.

'It was here. Right here.'

'I know. Marie Rose came here, to this spot. Her heart knew.' This time she handed him the bouquet and drew a single flower out.

Declan let the flowers fall into the river, watched the color, the small beauty, float on the brown water. 'Not everybody can put flowers on his own grave.'

'I'm sorry.' Tears slid down her cheeks. 'I'm so sorry.' She knelt, tossed the flower where it would drift alone. She groped for Declan's hand. 'I'm so sorry I hurt you.'

'Don't.' He drew her to her feet, into his arms. 'It's all right.'

'He didn't trust enough. I didn't. Too much grief and not enough faith. Then, now.'

'There's been enough grieving. Then, now.' He tipped up her face. And said what he'd realized was inside him – inside Abigail – at the moment they'd taken flowers to Marie Rose. 'I forgive you.'

'You're more forgiving than she was.'

'Maybe. Maybe that's why we keep going around. Gives us a chance to fix things we screwed up.'

'Or make the same mistakes again. I've got something else to give you. But not here. Back at the Hall. It's the right place to give it to you.'

'Okay.' He kissed her hand. 'We're okay.'

'I think we're getting there. I'd like to walk back, get my bearings.'

'Good idea.'

'There's something I'd like to ask you to do,' she said as they took the path again. 'I'd like to put up three markers, maybe near the pond. One for Lucian, one for Abby and one for Marie Rose. I think it's time they were together.'

'I think they are together now.' Or nearly, he thought. Very nearly, because there was a lightness in his heart he hadn't expected to feel again. 'But the markers would be a nice memory. We'll pick out a spot, put them in. Then we'll plant something there, together.'

She nodded. 'A willow maybe.'

'Like the one she liked so much.' He nodded. 'Sometimes you put things back the way they were, sometimes you change them. We'll do both. Then when our kids come along, we can have picnics near there, and tell them the story.' He waited a beat. 'You didn't tell me to shut up.'

'*Cher*, you just wear me out. Looks like your soldiers are here.'

He glanced over, wincing when he saw the cars. 'Won't this be fun? Look, let's sneak up the front stairs and lock ourselves in my bedroom. I feel like I could sleep for a week now.'

'The bedroom's fine, but I've only got an hour. Then I've got to go in to work.'

'I've got an hour in me,' he replied, then tapped a finger to his lips and crept up the stairs. 'Ever roll around naked in bed with a houseful of women scrubbing floors outside the room?'

'No, and that's not on the schedule for this morning.'

'Spoilsport.'

'Declan. No, leave the doors open. No, just hold on—'

'That's what I'm doing,' he said when he'd locked her in his arms. 'Holding on. And God, *God*, it feels good. I've missed you,' he murmured, and understood it was Abby as much as himself who held close.

A circle, nearly forged again, he thought. And this time, it wouldn't break.

She's losing, he realized. Josephine. It was all slipping out of her hands.

'I've got things to say to you.'

'I'm done with talking.' He laid his lips on hers in a soft, sumptuous kiss. 'Lie down with me, Lena. Just lie down with me. I've really missed holding you.'

'I need to do this standing up.' She eased away and stood in the spill of sunlight. 'I've done things my way up till now, and that's worked out just fine for me. You've complicated things, confused things, irritated me, and turned my life upside down with what was, what

343

is, what might be. I've never cared much for might be's, Declan.'

'How about will be's?'

'That's your hard head talking. I love that about you. I love so many things about you, I've lost count. So here I am stuck with some damn rich Yankee.'

Everything inside him swelled, then went bright as the sun. 'Angelina.'

'You just wait till I'm finished.' She sighed, paused until she was certain she could speak calmly. 'I've got a lot of friends who care about me, maybe even love me the way friends do. I had my grandpapa, who made me the light of his life. I've got Grandmama. But nobody ever loved me just like you do. And the hell of it is, I never loved anybody the way I love you. So.'

She lifted her arms, unclasped the chain around her neck. She held it out to him, the little key dangling. 'This is yours now, and has been for some time, I guess. You're the key, *cher*. You always were.'

He took it, then delighted her by clasping it around his own neck. 'I'm going to make you so happy.'

'You damn well better. We getting married or what?'

'You better believe it.' With a laugh, he scooped her off her feet, spun her around in circles. 'Do you feel it?'

'Feel what? My head's spinning.'

'The house is ours now. Only ours.' He set her on her feet. 'No more ghosts. No more lives but ours. And we're just beginning.'

She slid her arms around him, lifted her mouth to his. 'Welcome home.'

Still holding close, she drew out the pocket watch, turned it faceup. They watched time move on.